The King's Buccaneer

Raymond E. Feist was born and raised in Southern
California. He was educated at the University of
California, San Diego, where he graduated with
honours in Communication Arts. He is the author
of the bestselling and critically acclaimed Riftwar
Saga (*Magician*, *Silverthorn* and *A Darkness at
Sethanon*), *Prince of the Blood*, *Faerie Tale* and his
latest novel, *Shadow of a Dark Queen*, which
begins the long-awaited new series, The
Serpentwar Saga. He is also co-author (with Janny
Wurts) of *Daughter of the Empire*, *Servant of the
Empire* and *Mistress of the Empire*. Feist lives with
his wife, novelist Kathlyn Starbuck and daughter
Jessica Michele in Rancho Santa Fe, California.

Voyager

RAYMOND E. FEIST

The King's Buccaneer

HarperCollins*Publishers*

Voyager
An Imprint of HarperCollinsPublishers
77–85 Fulham Palace Road,
Hammersmith, London W6 8JB

This paperback edition 1996
3 5 7 9 8 6 4

Previously published in paperback by HarperCollins
Science Fiction & Fantasy 1993
Reprinted four times

First published in Great Britain by
HarperCollinsPublishers 1992

Copyright © Raymond Elias Feist 1992

The Author asserts the moral right to
be identified as the author of this work

ISBN 0 586 20322 2

Set in Times

Printed and bound in Great Britain by
Caledonian International Book Manufacturing Ltd, Glasgow

For Ethan and Barbara

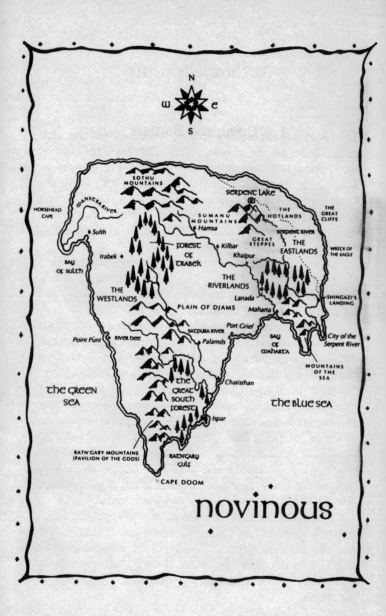

novinous

Acknowledgments

This work would not exist if it were not for the rich imaginations of the original 'Thursday Nighters' and of the 'Friday Nighters' who came after. Steve A., April, Jon, Anita, Rich, Ethan, Dave, Tim Lori, Jeff, Steve B., Conan, Bob, and the dozens of others who joined with us over the years gave Midkemia a quality of richness that no one person could author. Thanks for the wonderful world in which to play.

Thanks go to Janny Wurts for allowing me to learn from her as we worked together for nearly seven years. And to Don Maitz, for his vision, craft, and artistry, and for supporting Janny's choices.

Over the years I have worked with a variety of editors at Doubleday and Grafton, now HarperCollins. Special thanks to Janna Silverstein at Bantam Doubleday Dell for taking care of business and to Jane Johnson and Malcolm Edwards at HarperCollins for picking up where their predecessors left off, never missing a beat. Also to those I've named before at both publishers, some now gone on to other callings, but none forgotten. From sales to marketing to advertising and promotion to those who simply read the books and said nice things about it to their co-workers – to you all, thanks. Many of you worked above and beyond to make the work successful.

I would like to offer thanks to some people who never got mentioned before: Tres Anderson and his crew, Bob and Phylis Weinberg, and Rudy Clark and his people, who did more than sell books – they built enthusiasm and helped the work stand out from the crowd back at the start.

As always, thanks to Jonathan Matson and everyone at the Harold Matson Company for far more than good business advice.

Most of all, thanks to Kathlyn S. Starbuck, who took the time to make sure this one stayed on course. I couldn't have done it without her love, support, and wisdom.

RAYMOND E. FEIST
San Deigo, CA, February 1992

The King's Buccaneer

PROLOGUE
Meeting

Ghuda stretched.

Through the door behind him came a woman's voice: 'Get away from there!'

The former mercenary guard sat back in his chair on the porch of his inn, settling his feet upon the hitching rail. In the background the usual evening serenade was commencing. While rich travelers stayed at the large hostels in the city or at palatial inns along the silvery beaches, the Inn of the Dented Helm, owned by Ghuda Bulé, catered to a rougher clientele: wagon drivers, mercenaries, farmers bringing crops into the city, and rural soldiers.

'Do I have to summon the city guards!' cried the woman from inside the common room.

A large man, Ghuda had found enough hard work keeping up the inn that he hadn't run to fat and he still kept his weapons finely honed; more times than he cared to recall, he had been forced to toss one or another customer through the door.

Evenings, just before dining, were his favorite time of the day. Sitting in his chair, he could see the sun set over the bay of Elarial, the brilliant glare of the day dimming to a gentler blush that colored the white buildings soft oranges and golds. It was one of the few pleasures he managed to reserve for himself in an otherwise demanding life. A loud crash sounded from within the building, and Ghuda resisted the urge to investigate. His woman would let him know when he was needed to intervene.

'Get out of here! Take that fighting outside!'

Ghuda took out a dirk, one of the two he habitually

1

wore on his belt, and absently began to polish it. The sound of broken crockery echoed from within the inn. A girl's shriek followed quickly after, then the sounds of fists striking bodies joined in.

Ghuda looked at the sunset as he polished his blade. At almost sixty years old, his face was an aging map of leather – showing years of caravan guard duty, fighting, too much bad weather, bad food, and bad wine – dominated by an oft-broken nose. Most of his hair was gone on top, leaving him with a shoulder-length grey fringe that began halfway between crown and ears. Never one to be called handsome, he still had something about him, a calm, open directness, that caused people to trust and like him.

He let his gaze wander across the bay, silver and rose highlights from the sunset sparkling atop emerald waters, as seabirds squawked and dove for their supper. The heat of the day had gone, leaving a soft cool breeze off the bay, faint with the tang of sea salt, and for a moment he wondered if life could be better for one of his low station. Then he squinted against the glare of the sun as it touched the horizon, for out of the west came a figure purposefully marching down the road toward the little inn.

At first it was nothing more than a black speck against the glare of the setting sun, but soon it took on detail. Something about the figure set off an itch in the back of Ghuda's brain, and he fixed his gaze upon the stranger as he came clearly into view. A slender, bandy-legged man wearing a dusty and torn blue robe, tied above one shoulder, approached. He was an Isalani, a citizen of Isalan, one of the nations to the south within the Empire of Great Kesh. He carried an old black rucksack over one shoulder and used a long staff as a walking stick.

When the man was close enough for his features to be clearly identified, Ghuda said a silent prayer: 'Gods, not him.'

A wailing cry of anger came from within the building as Ghuda stood up. The man reached the porch and unshouldered his bag. A ring of fuzz surrounded an otherwise bald head; a face resembling a vulture looked solemn as he regarded Ghuda, then broke into a wide smile. His black eyes were narrow slits as he grinned at Ghuda. He opened the dusty old bag. In a familiar, gravelly tone he said, 'Want an orange?' He reached into the bag and withdrew two large oranges.

Ghuda caught the fruit that was tossed to him and said, 'Nakor, what in the Seven Lower Hells brings you here?'

Nakor the Isalani, occasional card sharp and con man, wizard in some sense of the word, and undoubted lunatic in Ghuda's estimation, was a onetime companion of the former mercenary. Nine years before, they had met and traveled with a young vagabond who'd convinced Ghuda – Nakor needed no persuading – to travel on a journey to the City of Kesh, a descent into the heart of murder, politics, and attempted treason. The vagabond had turned out to be Prince Borric, heir to the throne of the Kingdom of the Isles, and Ghuda had emerged from that encounter with enough gold to travel and find this inn, the previous owner's widow, and the most glorious sunsets he had ever seen. He wished never again to experience anything like that journey in this life. Now, with sinking heart, he knew that wish was likely to be a vain one.

The bandy-legged little man said, 'I came to get you.'

Ghuda sat back down in his chair as an ale cup came sailing through the door. Nakor nimbly dodged it and said, 'Some good fight you have there. Wagon drivers?'

Ghuda shook his head. 'No guests tonight. That's just my woman's seven kids tearing up the common room, as usual.'

Nakor dropped his rucksack and sat down upon the hitching rail and said, 'Well, give me something to eat, then we'll go.'

3

Returning to sharpening his dirk, Ghuda said, 'Go where?'

'Krondor.'

Ghuda shut his eyes a moment. The only person they both knew in Krondor was Prince Borric. 'This is not a perfect existence, by any measure, Nakor, but I'm contented to remain here. Now go away.'

The little man bit into his orange, pulled off a large piece of peel, and spat it out. He bit deeply into the orange and slurped loudly as he did. Wiping his mouth with the back of his wrist, he said, 'Contented with that?' He pointed into the darkened doorway, through which the wail of a child carried over the general shouts and breakage.

Ghuda said, 'Well, it's a hard life, sometimes, but rarely is anyone trying to kill me; I know where I'm sleeping every night, and I eat well and bathe regularly. My woman's affectionate, and the children – ' Another child's loud shriek was punctuated by the sound of an indignant infant's wailing cry. Looking at Nakor, Ghuda asked, 'I'm going to regret asking this, but why do we need to go to Krondor?'

'Got to see a man,' Nakor said as he sat back on the hitching rail, hooking one foot behind a post to keep his balance.

'One thing about you, Nakor, you never bore a man to death with unnecessary details. What man?'

'Don't know. But we'll find out when we get there.'

Ghuda signed. 'Last time I saw you, you were riding north out of the City of Kesh, heading for that island of magicians, Stardock. You were wearing a great cape and blue robe of magnificent weave, the horse was a black desert stallion worth a year's wages, and you had a purse full of the Empress's gold.

Nakor shrugged. 'The horse ate bad grass, got colic, and died.' He fingered the dirty, torn blue robe he wore.

'The great cape kept catching in things, so I threw it away. The robe is the one I still wear. The sleeves were too long, so I tore them off. The thing dragged on the ground and I kept tripping on the hem, so I cut it with my dagger.'

Ghuda regarded his former companion's ragged appearance and said, 'You could have afforded a tailor.'

'Too busy.' He glanced at the turquoise sky, shot through with pink and grey clouds, and said, 'I spent all the money and I got bored with Stardock. Decided to go to Krondor.'

Ghuda felt control leaving as he said, 'Last time I consulted a map, Stardock to Krondor by way of Elarial was considered the long way around.'

Nakor shrugged. 'I needed to find you. So I went back to Kesh. You said you might go to Jandowae, so there I went. Then they said you'd gone to Faráfra, so there I went. I then followed you to Draconi, Caralyan, then here.'

'You seem singularly determined to find me.'

Nakor leaned forward, and his voice changed; Ghuda had heard him take this tone before and knew that what he was saying was significant. 'Great things, Ghuda. Don't ask me why; I don't know. Just say that sometimes I see things.

'You need to come with me. We are going places few men of Kesh have ever gone. Now, get your sword and your pack and come with me. A caravan leaves for Durbin tomorrow. I have gotten you a job as a guard; they remember Ghuda Bulé. From Durbin we can find a ship to Krondor. We need to be there soon.'

Ghuda said, 'Why should I listen to you?'

Nakor grinned and his voice was again the half-mocking, half-mirthful sound that was the Isalani's hallmark. 'Because you're bored, true?'

Ghuda listened to his youngest stepchild wailing at

some outrage done by one of her six siblings and said, 'Well, it's not as if things around here were eventful . . .' Hearing another shriek, he added, 'or really peaceful.'

'Come. Tell the woman good-bye and let us go.'

Ghuda stood with a mixed feeling of resignation and anticipation. Turning to the smaller man, he said, 'Best go to the caravanserai and wait for me. I have to explain some things to my woman.'

Nakor said, 'You got married?'

Ghuda said, 'We never seemed to quite get around to it.'

Nakor grinned. 'Then give her some gold – if you have any left – and tell her you'll be back, then leave. She'll have another man in that chair and in her bed within the month.'

Ghuda stood by the door a moment, regarding the light from the vanished sun as it faded from sight and said, 'I will miss the sunsets, Nakor.'

The Isalani continued to grin as he jumped down from the hitching rail, picked up his bag, and shouldered it. 'There are sunsets above other oceans, Ghuda. Mighty sights and great wonders to behold.' Without another word, he turned toward the road down to the city of Elarial and started walking.

Ghuda Bulé entered the common room of the inn he had called home for nearly seven years and wondered if he would ever pass this way again.

1

Decision

The lookout pointed.

'Boat dead ahead!'

Amos Trask, Admiral of the Prince's fleet of the Kingdom Navy, shouted, 'What?'

The harbor pilot who stood beside the Admiral, guiding the Prince of Krondor's flagship, the *Royal Dragon*, toward the palace docks, shouted to his assistant at the bow, 'Wave them off!'

The assistant pilot, a sour-looking young man, shouted back, 'They fly the royal ensign!'

Amos Trask unceremoniously pushed past the pilot. Still a barrel-chested, bull-necked man at past sixty years of age, he hurried toward the bow with the sure step of a man who'd spent most of his life at sea. After sailing Prince Arutha's flagship in and out of Krondor for nearly twenty years, he could dock her blindfolded, but custom required the presence of the harbor pilot. Amos disliked turning over command of his ship to anyone, least of all an officious and not very personable member of the Royal Harbormaster's staff. Amos suspected that the second requirement for a position in that office was an objectionable personality. The first seemed to be marriage to one of the Harbormaster's numerous sisters or daughters.

Amos reached the bow and looked ahead. His dark eyes narrowed as he observed the scene unfolding below. As the ship glided toward the quay, a small sailing boat, no more than fifteen feet in length, attempted to dart into the opening ahead of it. Clumsily tied to the top of the mast was a pennant, a small version of the Prince of Krondor's naval ensign. Two young men frantically

7

worked the sails and tiller, one attempting to hold as strong a line to the dock as possible while the other furled a jib. Both laughed at the impromptu race.

'Nicholas!' shouted Amos, as the boy lowering the jib waved at him. 'You idiot! We're cutting your wind! Turn about!' The boy at the helm turned to look at Amos and threw him an impudent grin. 'I should have known,' said Amos to the assistant pilot. To the grinning boy, Amos shouted, 'Harry! You lunatic!' Glancing back, seeing the last of the sails reefed, Amos observed, 'We're coasting to the docks, we don't have room to turn if we wanted to, and we certainly can't stop.'

All ships coming into Krondor dropped anchor in the middle of the harbor, waiting for longboats to tow them to the docks. Amos was the only man with rank enough to intimidate the harbor pilot into allowing him to drop sail at the proper moment and coast into the docks. He took pride in always reaching the proper place for the land lines to be thrown out and in having never crashed the docks or required a tow. He had coasted into this slip a hundred times in twenty years, but never before with a pair of insane boys playing games in front of the ship. Looking forward at the small boat, which was now slowing even more rapidly, Amos said, 'Tell me, Lawrence, how does it feel to be the man on the bow when you drown the Prince of Krondor's youngest son?'

Color drained from the assistant pilot's face as he turned toward the small boat. In a high-pitched voice he began shrieking at the boys to get out of the way.

Turning his back on the scene below, Amos shook his head as he leaned back against the railing. He ran his hand over his nearly bald pate, the grey hair around it – once dark and curly – now tied back behind his head in a sailor's knot. After a moment attempting to ignore what they were doing, Amos gave in. He turned around, leaning forward and to the right so he could see past the bowsprit. Below, Nicholas was leaning into the oar, one leg braced firmly against the base of the mast, the oar firmly planted against the bow of the ship. He looked terrified. Amos could hear Nicholas shout, 'Harry! You'd better turn to port!'

Amos nodded in silent agreement, for if Harry pulled hard to port, the small sailboat would swing wide of the lumbering ship, getting banged around, perhaps swamped, but at least the boys would be alive. If they drifted suddenly to starboard, the boat would quickly be ground between the ship's hull and the approaching pilings of the dock.

Lawrence, the assistant pilot, said, 'The Prince is fending us off.'

'Ha!' Amos shook his head. 'Letting us push them into the dock, you mean.' Cupping his hands around his mouth, Amos shouted, 'Harry! Hard aport!'

The young squire only yelled a maniacal war whoop in answer as he struggled with the tiller, to keep the boat centered upon the ship's bow.

'Like balancing a ball on a sword point.' Amos sighed. He could tell by the speed of the ship and its location that it was time to ready the lines. He turned his back on the boys once more.

From below came the sounds of Harry whooping and yelling in exultation as the fast-moving ship pushed the small boat along. Lawrence said, 'The Prince is holding the boat in front. He's struggling, but he's doing it.'

Amos called, 'Ready bowlines! Ready stern lines!' Sailors near the bow and stern readied lines to throw to dockmen waiting below.

'Admiral!' said Lawrence in excited tones.

Amos closed his eyes. 'I don't want to hear it.'

'Admiral! They've lost control! They're veering to starboard!'

Amos said, 'I said I didn't want to hear it.' He turned

toward the assistant pilot, who stood with a panic-stricken expression on his face as the sounds of the small boat being crushed between the ship and the dock grated on their ears. The cracking of wood and tearing of planks were accompanied by shouts from the men on the dock.

The assistant pilot said, 'It wasn't my fault.'

An unfriendly smile split Amos's silver and grey beard as he said, 'I'll testify to that at your trial. Now order the lines, or you'll smash us against the wharf.' Seeing the remark didn't register on the shocked man, Amos shouted, 'Secure the bowlines!'

A second later the pilot called for the stern lines to be secured, and these were tossed to those waiting below. The ship had lost almost all its forward movement and, when the lines went taut, stopped altogether. Amos shouted, 'Secure all lines! Run out the gangplank!'

Turning toward the dock, he peered down into the churning water between the ship and the dock. Seeing bubbles amid the floating wood, line, and sail, he yelled to the dock gang, 'Lower a rope there to those two idiots swimming beneath the dock before they drown!'

By the time Amos was off the ship, the two wet youngsters had climbed up to the dock. Amos came to where they stood and regarded the soaked pair.

Nicholas, youngest son of the Prince of Krondor, stood with his weight shifted slightly to the right. His left boot had a raised heel to compensate for the deformed foot he'd possessed since birth. Otherwise Nicholas was a well-made, slender boy of seventeen. He resembled his father, having angular features and dark hair, but he lacked Prince Arutha's intensity, though he rivaled him in quickness. He had his mother's quiet nature and gentle manner, which somehow made his eyes look different from his father's, though they were the same dark brown. At the moment he looked thoroughly embarrassed.

His companion was another matter. Henry, known to

the court as Harry because his father, the Earl of Ludland, was also named Henry, grinned as if he hadn't been the butt of the joke. The same age as Nicholas, he was a half-head taller, had curly red hair and a ruddy face, and was considered handsome by most of the younger court ladies. He was a playful youngster who often let his adventure-some nature get the better of him, and from time to time his sense of fun took him beyond the limits of good judgment. Most of the time, Nicholas traveled beyond that border with him. Harry ran a hand through his wet hair and laughed.

'What's so funny?' asked Amos.

'Sorry about the boat, Admiral,' answered the Squire, 'but if you could have seen the assistant pilot's face . . .'

Amos frowned at the two youngsters, then couldn't hold in his own laughter. 'I did. It was a sight to behold.' He threw wide his arms and Nicholas gave him a rough hug.

'Glad you're back, Amos. Sorry you missed the Mid-summer's Feast.'

Pushing the Prince away with exaggerated distaste, Amos said, 'Bah! You're all wet. Now I'm going to have to go change before I meet with your father.'

The three began walking toward the wharf next to the palace. 'What news?' asked Nicholas.

'Things are quiet. Trading ships from the Far Coast, Kesh, and Queg, and the usual traffic from the Free Cities. It's been a peaceful year.'

Harry said, 'We were hoping for some rousing tales of adventure.' His tone was slightly mocking.

Amos playfully smacked him in the back of the head with the flat of his hand. 'I'll give you adventure, you maniac. What did you think you were doing?'

Harry rubbed at the back of his head and attempted an aggrieved expression. 'We had right-of-way.'

'Right-of-way!' said Amos, halting in disbelief. 'In the

open harbor, perhaps, with ample room to turn, but "right-of-way" doesn't halt a three-masted warship bearing down on you with no place to turn and no way to stop.' He shook his head as he resumed walking toward the palace. 'Right-of-way indeed.' Looking at Nicholas, he said, 'What were you doing out on the bay this time of day? I thought you had studies.'

'Prelate Graham is in conference with Father,' answered Nicholas. 'So we went fishing.'

'Catch anything?'

Harry grinned. 'The biggest fish you've ever seen, Admiral.'

'Now that it's back in the bay, it's the biggest, you mean,' answered Amos with a laugh.

Nicholas said, 'We didn't catch anything worth talking about.'

Amos said, 'Well, run along and change into something less damp. I'm going to refresh myself, then call upon your father.'

'Will you be at dinner?' asked the young Prince.

'I expect.'

'Good; Grandmother is in Krondor.'

Amos brightened at that news. 'Then I will most certainly be there.'

Nicholas gave Amos a crooked half-smile that was the image of his father's and said, 'I doubt anyone thinks it coincidence that she chose to visit Mother just in time to be here for your return.'

Amos only grinned. 'It's my boundless charm.' With a playful slap to the heads of both boys, he said, 'Now go! I must report to Duke Geoffrey, then I'm off to my quarters to change into something more fitting for dinner with . . . your father.' He winked at Nicholas and strode off, whistling a nameless tune.

Nicholas and Harry hurried along, stockings squishing in their boots, toward the Prince's quarters. Harry had a small room near Nicholas's, as he was officially Prince Nicholas's Squire.

The Prince's palace in Krondor rested hard against the bay, having in ancient times been the defensive bastion of the Kingdom on the Bitter Sea. The royal docks were separated from the rest of the harbor by an area of open shoreline that was contained within the walls of the palace. Nicholas and Harry cut across the open expanse of beach and approached the palace from the water.

The palace rose majestically atop a hill, outlined against the afternoon sky, a sprawling series of apartments and halls grafted around the original keep, which still served as the heart of the complex. Dwarfed by several other towers and spires added over the last few centuries, the old keep still commanded the eye, a brooding reminder of days gone by, when the world was a far more dangerous place.

Nicholas and Harry pushed open an old metal gate, which provided access to the harbor for those who worked in the kitchen. The pungency of the harbor, with its smells of fish, brine, and tar, gave way to more appetizing aromas as they neared the kitchen. The boys hurried down past the washhouse and the bakehouse, through a small vegetable garden, and down a low flight of stone stairs, moving among servants' huts.

They approached the servants' entrance to the royal family's private apartments, not wishing a chance encounter with any of Prince Arutha's staff or, more to the point, with the Prince himself.

Reaching the doors used by the serving staff closest to their own rooms, Nicholas opened it just as a pair of the palace serving girls approached from within carrying bundles of linens bound for the washhouse behind the palace. He stood aside, though his rank gave him precedence, out of respect for their heavy loads. Harry gave both the girls, only a few years older than himself, his version of a rakish grin. One giggled and the other fixed him with a look appropriate to finding a rodent in the larder.

As the young women hurried off, conscious of their impact on the two adolescent boys, Harry grinned and said, 'She wants me.'

Nicholas gave him a hard push that sent him stumbling through the door, saying, 'Just about as much as I want the belly flux. Keep dreaming.'

Hurrying up the stairs to the family's quarters, Harry said, 'No, she does. She hides it, but I can tell.'

Nicholas said, 'Harry the lady's man. Lock up your daughters, Krondor.'

After the bright afternoon sunlight, the hallway was positively gloomy. At the end of the hall, they turned up stairs that took them out of the servants' area to the apartments of the royal family. At the top of the stairs, they opened the door and peeked through. Seeing no one of rank, the two boys hurried to their respective doors, located halfway down the hall from the servants' door. Between this door and his own a mirror hung, and, catching his own reflection, Nicholas said, 'It's a good thing Father didn't see us.'

Nicholas entered his own quarters, a large pair of rooms, with enormous closets and a private garderobe, so he didn't have to leave the room to relieve himself. He quickly stripped off his wet clothing and dried himself. He turned and caught sight of himself in a large mirror, a luxury of immense value, as it was fashioned from silvered glass imported from Kesh. His body – that of a boy on the way to becoming a man – showed a broadening chest and shoulders; he had a man's growth of body hair, as well as a need to shave daily. But his face was still a boy's, lacking the set of features that only time can give.

As he finished drying, he looked at his left foot as he had every day of his life. A ball of flesh, with tiny protuberances that should have been toes, extended from the base of an otherwise well-formed left leg. The foot had been the object of medicine and magic since his birth, but had resisted all attempts at healing. No less sensitive to touch and sensation as the right foot, it nevertheless was difficult for Nicholas to command; the muscles were connected incorrectly to bones the wrong size to perform the tasks nature intended. Like most people with a lifetime affliction, Nicholas had compensated to the point of rarely being aware of it. He walked with only a slight limp. He was an excellent swordsman, perhaps the equal of his father, who was counted the best in the Western Realm. The Palace Swordmaster judged him as already a better swordsman than his two elder brothers were at his age. He could dance, as required by his office – son of the ruler of the Western Realm – but the one thing that he could not compensate for was a terrible feeling that he was somehow less than he should be.

Nicholas was a soft-spoken, reflective youngster who preferred the quiet solitude of his father's library to the more boisterous activities of most boys his age. He was an excellent swimmer, a fine horseman, and a fair archer in addition to being skilled at swordplay, but all his life he had felt deficient. A vague sense of failure, and a haunting guilt, seemed to fill him unexpectedly, and often he would find his mind seized by dark brooding. With company, he was often merry and enjoyed a joke as well as the next boy, but if left alone, Nicholas found his mind seized by worry. That had been one reason Harry had come to Krondor.

As he dressed, Nicholas shook his head in amusement. His companion for the last year, Squire Harry had provided an abrupt change to Nicholas's solitary ways, forever dragging the Prince off on some foolish enterprise or another. Life for Nicholas had become far more exciting since the arrival of the middle son of the Earl of Ludland.

Given his rank and two competitive brothers, Harry was combative and expected to be obeyed, barely observing the difference in rank between himself and Nicholas. Only a pointed order would remind Harry that Nicholas wasn't a younger brother to command. Given Harry's domineering ways, the Prince's court was probably the only place his father could have sent him to have his nature tempered before he became a regular tyrant.

Nicholas brushed out his wet, neck-length hair, cut in imitation of his father's. Alternately drying it with a towel, then brushing it, he got it to some semblance of respectability. He envied Harry his red curls, hugging his head. A quick toweling and a brush, then off he went.

Nicholas judged himself as presentable as he was likely to make himself under the circumstances, and left his room. He entered the hall to discover Harry already dressed and ready, attempting to delay another serving woman, this one several years his senior, as she was bound upon some errand or another.

Harry was dressed in the green and brown garb of a palace squire, which in theory made him part of the Royal Steward's staff, but within weeks of his arrival he had been singled out to be Nicholas's companion. Nicholas's two older brothers, Borric and Erland, had been sent to the King's court at Rillanon five years before, to prepare for the day Borric would inherit the crown of the Isles from his uncle. King Lyam's only son had drowned fifteen years earlier, and Arutha and the King had decided that should Arutha survive his older brother, Borric would rule. Nicholas's sister, Elena, was recently married to the eldest son of the Duke of Ran, leaving the palace fairly empty of companions of suitable rank for the young Prince before Harry was sent into service by his father.

Clearing his throat loudly, Nicholas commanded Harry's attention long enough for the serving woman to make her getaway. She gave the Prince a courteous bow coupled with a grateful smile as she hurried off.

Nicholas watched her flee and said, 'Harry, you've got to stop using your position to annoy the serving women.'

'She wasn't annoyed – ' began Harry.

'That wasn't an opinion,' said Nicholas sternly.

He rarely used his rank to command Harry about anything, but on those rare occasions he did, Harry knew better than to argue – especially when his tone sounded like Prince Arutha's, a sure sign that Nicholas wasn't joking. The Squire shrugged. 'Well, we have an hour to supper. What shall we do?'

'Spend the time working on our story, I should think.'

Harry said, 'What story?'

'To give to Papa to explain why my boat is now floating across half the harbor.'

Harry looked at Nicholas with a confident smile and said, 'I'll think of something.'

'You didn't see it?' said the Prince of Krondor as he regarded his youngest son and the Squire from Ludland. 'How could you miss the biggest warship in the Drondor-ian fleet when it was less than a hundred feet away!' Arutha, Prince of Krondor, brother to the King of the Isles, and second most powerful man in the Kingdom, regarded the two boys with a narrow, disapproving gaze they had both come to know well. A gaunt man, Arutha was a quiet, forceful leader who rarely showed his emotions, but to those close to him, old friends and family, the subtle changes in his mood were easy enough to read. And right now he wasn't amused.

Nicholas turned to his partner in crime. Whispering, he said, 'Good story, Harry,' in dry tones. 'You obviously spent a lot to time thinking about it.'

Arutha turned to his wife, his disapproval giving way to resignation. Princess Anita fixed her son with a scolding look that was mitigated by amusement. She was upset with the boys for acting foolishly, but Harry's blatantly artless pose of innocence was entertaining. Though she was past forty years of age, there was still a girlish quality about her laughter, which she fought hard to keep reined in. Her red hair was streaked with grey, and her freckled face was lined from years of service to her nation, but her eyes were clear and bright as she regarded her youngest child with affection.

The evening's meal was a casual one, with few court functionaries in attendance. Arutha preferred to keep his court informal when possible, quietly enduring pomp only when necessary. The long table in the family's apartment in the palace could comfortably hold a half-dozen more people than dined tonight. While the great hall of Krondor housed most of the Western Realm's battle trophies and banners of state, the family's dining hall was devoid of such reminders of wars, being decorated with portraits of past rulers and landscapes of unusual beauty.

Arutha sat at the head of the table, with Anita at his right hand. Geoffrey, the Duke of Krondor and Arutha's chief administrator, sat in his usual chair on Arutha's left. Geoffrey was a quiet, kind man, well liked by the staff, and an able administrator. He had served for ten years in the King's court before coming to Krondor eight years previously.

Next to him sat Prelate Graham, a bishop of the Order of Dala, Shield of the Weak, one of Arutha's current advisers. A gentle but firm teacher, the Prelate had ensured that Nicholas, like his brothers before him, would become a man of broad education, knowing as much about art and literature, music and drama, as he did about economics, history, and warcraft. He sat beside Nicholas and Harry, and showed by his expression that he did not find the excuse remotely amusing. While the boys had been excused his tutelage while he attended the Prince's council, he had expected them to be studying, not crashing their boat into warships in the harbor.

Opposite the boys sat Anita's mother and Amos Trask. The Admiral and Princess Alicia had enjoyed a playful relationship for years, which court gossip claimed was far more intimate than simply flirtation. Still a handsome woman of a like age to Amos's, Alicia positively glowed from his attention. Anita's resemblance to her mother was clear to see, although Alicia's once red hair was now grey and her features revealed life's passage. But when Amos told a quiet joke to make her blush, her sparkling eyes and embarrassed laughter made her seem girlish again.

Amos squeezed Alicia's hand while he whispered something to her, probably off-color, and the Dowager Princess laughed behind her napkin. Anita smiled at the sight, for she remembered how dreadfully her mother had missed her father after his death, and what a welcome addition to Arutha's court Amos had become after the Riftwar. Anita was always pleased to see her mother smile, and no one could make her laugh like Amos.

To the Admiral's left sat Arutha's military deputy, William, Knight-Marshal of Krondor, a cousin to the royal family. Cousin Willie, as everyone in the family called him, winked at the two boys. He had been serving in the palace for twenty years, and over that span of time had seen Nicholas's other brothers, Borric and Erland, discover every possible way to incur their father's anger. Nicholas was new to causing his father to lose his temper. William reached for a slice of bread and said, 'Brilliant strategy, Squire. No unnecessary details to remember.'

Nicholas attempted to look properly chastised, but failed. He quickly cut a piece of lamb and stuffed it in his mouth to keep from laughing. He glanced at Harry, who was hiding his amusement behind a cup of wine.

Arutha said, 'We'll have to think up a suitable punishment for you two. Something to impress the value of both

19

the boat and your own necks on you.'

Harry threw Nicholas a quick grin from behind the wine cup; both boys knew that they stood half a chance of Arutha's forgetting any serious punishment if the press of court business was heavy, as it often was.

The Prince's court was the second busiest in the Kingdom, and only by a little after the King's. Effectively a separate realm, the West was governed from Krondor, with only broad policy coming from King Lyam's court. In the course of one day, Arutha might have to see two dozen important nobles, merchants, and envoys, and read a half-dozen important documents, as well as approve every regional decision involving the Principality.

A boy in the purple and yellow livery of a palace page entered the room and came to the elbow of the Royal Master of Ceremony, Baron Jerome. He whispered to the baron, who in turn came to Arutha. 'Sire, two men are at the main entrance of the palace, asking to see you.'

Arutha knew that they would have to be something unusual for the guard sergeant to pass them along to the Royal Steward, and for the steward to disturb the Prince. 'Who are they?' asked Arutha.

'They claim to be friends of Prince Borric's.'

Arutha's eyebrows went up slightly. 'Friends of Borric's?' He glanced at his wife, then asked, 'Do they have names?'

The Master of Ceremony said, 'They gave the names Ghuda Bulé and Nakor the Isalani.' Jermone, an officious man to whom dignity and pomp were more essential than air and water, managed to convey a volume of disapproval as he added, 'They're Keshian, Sire.'

Arutha was still trying to piece together some semblance of understanding when Nicholas said, 'Father! Those are two who helped Borric when he was captured by slavers in Kesh! You remember him telling us about them.'

Arutha blinked and recollection came to him. 'Of course.' He told Jerome, 'Show them in at once.'

Jerome motioned for the page to carry word to the entrance of the palace, and Harry turned to Nicholas. 'Slave traders?'

Nicholas said, 'It's a long story, but my brother was an envoy to Kesh, about nine years ago. He was captured by raiders who didn't know he was from the royal house of the Isles. He escaped and made his way to the Empress's court and saved her life. These are two men who helped him along the way.'

Everyone was staring at the door expectantly when the page entered, followed by a pair of ragged and dirty men. The taller was a fighter by his dress: old, battered leather armor and a dented helm, a bastard-sword slung over his back, and two long dirks, one at each hip. His companion was a bandy-legged fellow, with a surprisingly childlike expression of delight at the new sights around him, and an appealing grin, although he could be described as nothing so much as homely.

They came to the head of the table and both bowed, the warrior stiffly and self-consciously, the shorter man in a haphazard, absent-minded fashion.

Arutha stood and said, 'Welcome.'

Nakor kept looking at every detail of the room, lost in thought, so after a long moment Ghuda said, 'Sorry to disturb you, Your Highness, but he' – he jerked a thumb at Nakor – 'insisted.' His speech was accented, and he spoke slowly.

Arutha said, 'That's all right.'

Nakor at last turned his attention to Arutha and studied him a moment before he said, 'Your son Borric doesn't look like you.'

Arutha's eyes widened in amazement at the direct statement and lack of an honorific, but he nodded. Then the Isalani regarded the Princess and he again grinned, a

21

wide slash of crooked teeth that made him look even more comical than before. He said, 'You are his mother, though. He looks like you. You are very pretty, Princess.'

Anita laughed, and glanced at her husband, then said, 'Thank you, sir.'

With a wave of his hand, he said, 'Call me Nakor. I was once Nakor the Blue Rider, but my horse died.' He glanced around the room, fixing his gaze on Nicholas. His face lost its grin as he studied the boy. He stared at Nicholas to the point of awkwardness, then grinned again. 'This one looks like you!'

Arutha was at a loss for words, but at last managed to say, 'May I ask what brings you here? You are welcome, for you did a great service to my son and the Kingdom, but . . . it's been nine years.'

Ghuda said, 'I wish I could tell you, Sire. I've been traveling with this lunatic for over a month, and the best I can get from him is that we need to come here and see you, then leave on another journey.' Nakor was off in his own world again, seemingly entranced by the glitter of the chandeliers and the dancing lights reflecting off the large glass window behind the Prince's chair. Ghuda endured another moment of painful silence, and said, 'I'm sorry, Highness. We never should have bothered you.'

Arutha could see the old fighter's obvious discomfort. 'No, it's I who am sorry.' Noticing the ragged, dirty attire, he added, 'Please. You must rest. I'll have rooms made ready, and you may bathe and get a good night's sleep. I'll have fresh clothing provided. Then, in the morning, maybe I can aid you in whatever mission you find yourself upon.'

Ghuda gave an awkward salute, not quite sure of the response; then Arutha said, 'Have you eaten?' Ghuda glanced at the heavily laden table and Arutha said, 'Sit down, over there.' He motioned for them to take the chairs next to Knight-Marshal William.

Nakor snapped out of his reverie at the mention of food and unceremoniously hurried to the indicated chair. He waited until the servants had his place set with food and wine, and fell to like a man starved.

Ghuda attempted to display as many manners as possible, but it was clear he was uncomfortable in the presence of royalty. Amos said something in a strange language, and the Isalani laughed. In the King's Tongue he said, 'Your accent is terrible. But the joke is funny.'

Amos laughed in turn. He said to the others, 'I thought I spoke the language of Isalan pretty well.' He shrugged. 'It's been near thirty years since I was last in Shing Lai; I guess I've lost the knack,' and turned his attention back to the Princess of Krondor's mother.

Arutha sat down. He became lost in his own thoughts. Something about the appearance of these two, the old tired fighter and the comic character his sons had told him of, brought him a feeling of discomfort, as if the room were suddenly colder. A premonition? He tried to shrug it off, but could not. He motioned for the servants to remove his plate, for he had lost his appetite.

After dinner, Arutha walked along the balcony that overlooked the harbor. Behind closed doors, servants bustled readying the rooms of the royal family's apartments. Amos Trask left the building and came to where Arutha stood staring out at the lights near the harbor.

'You asked to see me, Arutha?'

Arutha turned and said, 'Yes. I need your advice.'

'Ask.'

'What's wrong with Nicholas?'

Amos's expression showed he didn't understand the question. 'I don't take your meaning.'

'He's not like other boys his age.'

'The foot?'

'I don't think so. There's something in him . . .'

'That's cautious,' finished Amos.

'Yes. It's why I'm disinclined to really punish him and Harry for their prank today. It's one of the few times I've ever seen or heard of Nicholas taking a risk.'

Amos signed as he leaned upon the low wall. 'I haven't given this a lot of thought, Arutha. Nicky's a good enough lad – not full of pranks and troublemaking as his brothers were.'

'Borric and Erland were such a pair of rogues that I welcomed Nicholas's reserve. But now it's become indecision and overcautiousness. And that is dangerous in a ruler.'

Amos said, 'You and I have been through a lot, Arutha. I've known you – what, twenty-five years? You worry the most about those you love. Nicky's a good lad, and he'll be a good man.'

'I don't know,' came the surprising answer. 'I know he hasn't a mean or petty bone in him, but one can err on the side of caution as well as rashness, and Nicholas is *always* cautious. He's going to be important to us.'

'Another marriage?'

Arutha nodded. 'This goes no further than here, Amos. The Emperor Diiagái has let it be known that closer ties to the Kingdom are now a possibility. Borric's marriage to the Princess Yasmine was a step in that direction, but the desert people are a tributary race in Kesh. Diiagái thinks it time for a marriage to a Princess of the true blood.'

Amos shook his head. 'State marriages are nasty business.'

Arutha said, 'Kesh has always been the biggest threat to the Kingdom – except for the Riftwar – and we need to treat with her gently. If the Emperor of Kesh has a niece or cousin of the true blood he wishes to marry to the brother of the future King of the Isles, we had better be very secure in our borders before we say no.'

'Nicky's not the only candidate, is he?'

'No, there's Carline's two sons, but Nicholas might be the best – if I thought he was able.'

Amos was silent awhile. 'He's still young.'

Arutha nodded. 'Younger than his years. I blame myself – '

'You always do,' interrupted Amos, with a barking laugh.

' – for being too protective. The deformed foot . . . his gentle nature . . .'

Amos nodded and again fell silent. Then he said, 'So season him.'

Arutha said, 'How? Send him to the Border Lords as I did his brothers?'

'That's a little too much seasoning, I think,' said Amos, stroking his beard. 'No, I was thinking you might do well to send him to Martin's court for a while.'

Arutha said nothing, but from his expression Amos could tell the idea had struck home. 'Crydee,' said Arutha softly. 'That would be a different sort of home for him.'

'You and Lyam turned out well enough, and Martin'll see the boy stay safe without coddling him. Around here no one dares raise a hand or even their voice to the "crippled son of the Prince."' Arutha's eyes flashed at that term, but he said nothing. 'Send Martin instructions, and he won't let Nicky use his bad foot as an excuse for anything. Prince Marcus is about his and Harry's age, so if you send that troublemaker along, there'll be two companions of noble rank who are a little rougher than Nicky's been used to. He might be able to command them, but he won't cow them. The Far Coast is nothing like Highcastle or Ironpass, but it's not so civilized that Nicky can't be hardened a bit.'

Arutha said, 'I'll have to convince Anita.'

'She'll understand, Arutha,' said Amos with a chuckle.

25

'I don't think you'll have to do much. As much as she wants to protect the boy, she'll see the need.'

'*Boy*. Do you realize I was only three years older than Nicholas when I took command of my father's garrison?'

'I was there. I remember.' Putting his hand upon Arutha's shoulder, he said, 'But you were never young, Arutha.'

Arutha was forced to laugh at that. 'You're right. I was a serious sort.'

'Still are.'

Amos turned to leave, and Arutha said, 'Are you going to marry Anita's mother?'

Amos turned in surprise. Then he put his fists upon his hips and grinned. 'Now, who have you been talking to?'

Arutha said, 'Anita, and she's been talking to Alicia. The palace has been thick with gossip about you two for years now: the Admiral and the Dowager Princess. You've got the rank and the honors. If you need another title, I can arrange it with Lyam.'

Amos held up his hand. 'No, rank has nothing to do with it.' He lowered his voice. 'I've lived a dangerous life, Arutha. And every time I board a ship, there's no guarantee I'd be back. I can be a mean man, and no more than when I'm at sea. There was always the chance I'd get myself killed out there.'

'You thinking of retirement?'

Amos nodded. 'Since I was about twelve I've lived on ships, save that bit of scuffling around I did with you and Guy du Bas-Tyra during the Riftwar. If I'm to wed, I'll stay at home with my lady, thank you.'

'When?'

Amos said, 'I don't know. It's a difficult choice; you've seen some of what the sea can do.' Both remembered their first voyage together, as they braved the Straits of Darkness in the winter many years ago. Arutha had been changed by the journey, for not only had he faced death on the sea and survived, he had come to Krondor and met his beloved Anita. Amos continued, 'To leave the sea is difficult. Perhaps one last voyage.'

Arutha said, 'Martin's requested some aid in preparing the nw garrison at Barran, up the coast from Crydee. The *Royal Eagle* is in the harbor, ready to sail with enough weapons and stores to outfit two hundred men and horses for a year. Why don't you captain it? You can carry Nicholas to Crydee, continue up the coast to the new garrison, then visit with Martin and Briana awhile before you head back.'

Amos smiled. 'A last voyage, back to where my cursed luck began.'

'Cursed luck?' asked Arutha.

'To meet you, Arutha. Since we've met, you insist on ruining my fun every way you can.'

It was an old joke between them. 'You've done well enough for an unrepentant pirate.'

Amos shrugged. 'Well, I've done the best I could.'

Arutha said, 'Go pay court to your lady. I will join mine shortly.'

Amos clapped Arutha upon the back once, then turned and left. When he was gone, Arutha continued to watch the distant lights of the harbor, lost in thoughts and memories.

Arutha's reminiscences were interrupted by an unexpected presence at his side. He turned to find the odd little Isalani standing next to him, regarding the city below.

Nakor said, 'I needed to spend a moment with you.'

Arutha said, 'How did you get past the guards in the hall?'

Nakor shrugged. 'It was easy' was all he said. Then he stared out over the water, as if seeing something distant. 'You're sending your son on a voyage.'

Arutha turned sideways, eyes fixed upon the Isalani.

'What are you: seer, prophet, or wizard?'

Nakor shrugged. 'I'm a gambler.' He produced a deck of cards seemingly out of nowhere and said, 'That's how I get money most times.' He twisted his wrist and the deck vanished. 'But sometimes I see things.' He fell silent for a moment, then said, 'Years ago, when I met Borric, I felt drawn to him, so that when he befriended me, I stayed with him.'

He paused and, without asking leave, jumped atop the stones of the low wall, folding his legs under him. Looking down at the Prince, he said, 'Many things can't be explained, Prince. Why I know things and can do things – what I call my tricks. But I trust my gifts.

'I am here to keep your son alive.'

Arutha shook his head, a small motion of denial. 'Alive?'

'He moves toward danger.'

'What danger.'

Nakor shrugged. 'I don't know.'

Arutha said, 'What if I keep him here?'

'You cannot.' Nakor shook his head. 'No, that's wrong. You *must* not.'

'Why?'

Nakor sighed and his smile faded. 'A long time ago I met your friend James. He said things about you and your life and what he had done to gain your favor. He tells of a man who's seen things.'

Arutha's sigh echoed Nakor's. 'I've seen dead men rise and kill, and I've seen alien magic; I have known men born on other worlds. I've spoken to dragons and seen impossible visions become flesh.'

Nakor said, 'Then trust me. You've made a choice. Abide by it. But let me and Ghuda go with your son.'

'Why Ghuda?'

'To keep me alive,' said Nakor, and the grin returned.

'Borric said you were a wizard.'

28

Nakor shrugged. 'It serves my purpose at times to let others think such. Your friend Pug knew there was no magic.'

'You know Pug?'

'No. But he was famous before I met Borric. He has done many wondrous things. And for a time I lived at Stardock.'

Arutha's eyes narrowed. 'I've not seen him for a dozen years, and word came to us that he had removed to Sorcerer's Isle, wishing no contact with his old friends. I've honored that request.'

Nakor leaped from the wall. 'Time to ignore it. We will need to see him. Tell your captain we will have to stop there on our way west.'

'You know where I'm sending Nicholas?'

Nakor shook his head no. 'I only know that when I saw Ghuda again, after so many years, he was sitting watching the sunset. I knew then that we would eventually journey west, toward the sunset.' Nakor yawned. 'I'm going to bed now, Prince.'

Arutha only nodded as the strange little man let himself back into the hallway that led to the balcony. The Prince of Krondor stood silently for a long time, leaning against the wall as he pondered what had been said. Nakor's words echoed through his mind as he attempted to sort out the conversation.

One thing he knew, as he knew his own heartbeat: of all those whom he loved, Nicholas was the least able to care for himself should he travel in harm's way. It was many hours before Arutha at last went to his bed.

2
Voyage

The palace was in an uproar.

Arutha had spent a quiet morning with his wife, and by the time they were finished with breakfast, she had agreed that a year or two with Martin might be the right thing for Nicholas. She had lived at Crydee as Arutha's guest during the last year of the Riftwar and had come to think fondly of that modest town on the Far Coast. Rough by Krondorian standards though it might be, it was the place where she had come to know her beloved Arutha, with all his dark moods and worries as well as the lighter sides of his nature. She understood Arutha's concerns over Nicholas, and his fear that the boy could find himself in over his head with the fate of others in the balance; she also knew that Arutha would view such an occurrence as a failure on his part. She relented – though she would miss her youngest child – because she understood this was for Arutha as much as for Nicholas. Out of deference to her, Arutha had protected Nicholas from many of the harsher realities of the world he lived in. His telling argument was the simple statement that Nicholas stood third in line of succession to the crown, behind his brothers, and nothing so far in his life had prepared him for that awesome charge should ill chance unexpectedly bring the crown to him, as it had to his uncle Lyam.

Anita had also sensed something behind his words, more than simple anxiety over a youngster leaving home for the first time, but she could not tell what it was. But most of all, Anita understood that her husband ached to be able to take control, to provide guidance, protection, and support for Nicholas, and that to let him go was perhaps harder for Arutha than it was for her.

Within an hour of Arutha's telling Nicholas and Harry they were bound for Crydee with Amos, the thousand and one details of making ready for the voyage sent the household into a near state of panic. Yet with practice born of a thousand state occasions, the Royal Steward and his host of squires, pages, and servants rose to the occasion, and Arutha knew that when the ship left the following day, everything the Prince and his companion needed would be aboard.

The *Royal Eagle* lay ready to carry the arms and stores needed by the new garrison that Duke Martin was establishing. Amos was assuming command, and they would leave for Crydee on the early morning tide. The decision to leave so abruptly was made both because Arutha did not want time to second-guess his choice, and to take advantage of the favorable weather. The infamous Straits of Darkness would be navigable for the next few months, but fall would be upon Amos by the time he left for his return voyage. Once heavy weather set in, the straits between the Bitter Sea and the Endless Sea were too dangerous to attempt except in the most extreme need.

Amos walked down the long hall that led from the guest quarters. In the years he had lived in Krondor, he had never bothered to secure private lodgings outside the palace, as had most of the Prince's staff. He was the only member of the Prince's circle of advisers and commanders who was unmarried and did not require a place apart from court demands for a family. As he was at sea nearly three-quarters of the time, anyway, the days he stayed in the palace were few in any event.

But now he was wrestling with the notion of how his life would change after this voyage. He stood a moment, hesitating, then knocked upon the door. A servant quickly answered and, seeing the Admiral without, pulled the door wide. Amos entered and found Alicia sitting upon a divan before a wide glass doorway that gave upon her private balcony, opened to admit the morning breeze. She rose and smiled as he crossed to her.

He took her hand and kissed her cheek. While the servants knew well he had spent the night in this very apartment, they observed the pretense of not knowing in the name of court protocol. Amos had snuck out of the rooms before dawn and had returned to his own quarters. He had changed and journeyed to the harbor for a quick inspection of the *Royal Eagle*.

'Amos,' said the Dowager Princess. 'I didn't expect to see you until this evening.'

Amos was at a loss for words, which surprised Alicia. She had understood something was on his mind last night, for while he had been ardent, he had also been somewhat distracted. Several times he had appeared to be on the brink of saying something, only to switch into some inconsequential question or statement.

He glanced around, and when it was clear they were alone, he sat heavily beside her. Taking her hands in his own, he said, 'Alicia, my darling, I've given the matter some thought – '

'What matter?' she interrupted.

'Let me finish,' he said. 'If I don't get this out, I'm likely to lose my nerve, hoist sail, and leave.'

She tried not to smile, for he seemed very serious. But she had a good idea of what was next.

'I'm getting on in age – '

'You're still a youngster,' she said playfully.

'Dammit, woman, this is difficult enough without your trying to flatter me!' His tone was more exasperation than anger, so she was not offended. Her eyes betrayed a merry glint while she kept a straight face.

'I've done many things I'm not proud of, Alicia, and some I've confessed to you. Others I'd just as soon forget.' He paused, searching for words. 'So, if you're not

32

of a mind to, I'll understand and take no offense.'

'Mind to what, Amos?'

Amos almost blushed as he blurted, 'Marry.'

Alicia laughed and squeezed his hands tightly. She leaned forward and kissed him. 'Silly man. Whom else would I marry? It's you I'm in love with.'

Amos grinned. 'Well then, that's it, isn't it?' He threw his arms around her and held her close. 'You're not going to regret this, are you?'

'Amos, at my age I've had my share of regrets, I can assure you. I married Erland because he was the King's brother and my father was the Duke of Timons, not because I felt anything for him. I came to love my husband, for he was a kind and lovable man, but I was never *in* love with him. When he died, I assumed that love would be something I would watch in others younger than I. Then you showed up.' He sat back, and she gripped his chin in her hand, playfully shaking his head as she would a child's. Then her hand went to his cheek and she caressed it. 'No, I haven't enough time left for making poor choices. For all your rough edges, you've a quick mind and a generous heart, and whatever you did in the past is in the past. You've been the only grandfather my grandchildren have known – though they know better than to say it to your face – but that's how they feel. No, this is no mistake.' She leaned into his arms and again he held her tight. Amos sighed in contentment.

Alicia felt tears of happiness gather in her eyes, and she blinked them back. Amos had never been comfortable with open displays of emotion. Their relationship had been intimate for years now, but she had understood Amos's reticence in making a proposal, for she knew him a man not given to close attachments. That he cared for Arutha and his family was clear, yet there was always a part of Amos that was distant. She knew that he held back, and nothing she could do would force him to give

33

freely. Age had lent her a wisdom many younger women would not have understood. She had not wished to drive Amos off by asking him to choose between his love for her and his love for the sea.

Amos reluctantly released his hold on her. 'Well, much as I would love to stay awhile, I have been given a mission by your daughter's husband.'

'You're leaving again? But you only just got here.' There was genuine disappointment in her voice.

'Yes, true. But Nicholas is to go to Martin's court for a year or two of seasoning, and some stores must be taken to the new garrison at Barran on the northwest coast.' He looked into her green eyes and said, 'It's my last voyage, love. I'll not be gone long, and then you'll find how quickly you grow tired of having me underfoot all the time.'

She shook her head and smiled. 'Hardly. You'll find much to keep you busy on my estates. We'll have lands to tend, tenants to supervise, and I doubt Arutha will let you stay away from court more than a month at a time. He values your insights and opinions.'

They talked for a while, and then Amos said, 'We have much to do. I must ensure the ship is ready, and you and Anita will no doubt wish to get about the business of a wedding.'

They parted and Amos walked away from her apartment, feeling both elation and an unusual desire to keep sailing west once he droppped Nicholas off. He loved Alicia like no other woman he had met in this life, but the prospect of marriage was more than a little frightening to the old bachelor.

He almost knocked over Ghuda Bulé as he rounded a corner. The grey-haired mercenary backed away, bowing awkwardly. 'Excuse me, sir.'

Amos paused. Switching to the Keshian language, he said, 'No excuse needed . . .'

'Ghuda Bulé, sir.'

'Ghuda,' finished Amos. 'My mind was other places and I wasn't watching my way.'

Ghuda's eyes narrowed and he said, 'Forgive me, sir, but I think I know you.'

Amos rubbed his chin. 'I've been to Kesh a time or two.'

Ghuda smiled an ironic smile. 'I was a caravan guard, mostly; there's little of Kesh I haven't seen.'

Amos said, 'Well, it would have been a port, for I've never been farther inland in Kesh than I needed to be. Perhaps in Durbin.'

Ghuda shrugged. 'Perhaps.' He glanced around. 'My companion has vanished, as he does from time to time, so I thought I'd gawk a bit.' He shook his head. 'I was in the Empress's palace in the City of Kesh some years ago, when I traveled with your Prince's son.' He glanced at the high vaulted windows that looked out over the landward side of the city. 'Very different here, yet worth a look.'

Amos grinned. 'Well, get your fill of gawking, then. We leave at first light to catch the tide.'

Ghuda's eyes narrowed. '*We* leave?'

Amos's grin widened. 'I'm Admiral Trask. Arutha told me you two would be traveling with us.'

'Where are we going?' asked Ghuda.

'Ha!' barked Amos. 'Obviously that strange friend of yours hasn't told you. You and he are coming with us, to Crydee.'

Ghuda turned about slowly, talking to himself as much to Amos. 'Of course he didn't tell me. He never tells me anything.'

Amos clapped him on the back in a friendly manner. 'Well, I'm not sure why, but you're welcome. You'll have to share a cabin with the little man, but you seem used to his company. I'll see you in the courtyard before dawn tomorrow.'

'Of course we'll be there.' After Amos left, Ghuda shook his head. In a sour tone he muttered, 'Why are we going to Crydee, Ghuda? I haven't the vaguest idea, Ghuda. Shall we go find Nakor, Ghuda? Certainly Ghuda. Then shall we strangle him, Ghuda?' With a single nod of his head, he answered himself, 'With great delight, Ghuda.'

Nicholas hurried along the soldiers' marshaling yard, where an afternoon drill was under way. He was looking for Harry.

The young Squire was where Nicholas expected to find him, watching the team from Krondor getting ready for a football match with the visiting team from Ylith. The sport, played by Prince of Krondor rules – codified some twenty years earlier by Arutha – had become the national sport in the Western Realm, and now city champions challenged one another regularly. Years before, an enterprising merchant had erected a field and stands near the palace. Over the years he had improved it and expanded it, until it was now a stadium that could easily accommodate forty thousand spectators. It was expected to be full next Sixthday when the match was played. The visiting Ylithmen, the North Precinct Golds, were playing Krondor's champions, the Millers and Bakers Association Stonemen.

Nicholas arrived to see an attack drill, in which five Stonemen descended upon the goalkeeper and three defenders and, with three deft passes, scored a goal. Harry turned and said, 'I hate to miss the match.'

Nicholas said, 'Me too, but think of it: a sea voyage!'

Harry regarded his friend and saw an excitement in Nicholas he had never seen before. 'You really want to go, don't you?'

'Don't you?'

Harry shrugged. 'I don't know. Crydee sounds like a

pretty sleepy place. I wonder what the girls are like.' He grinned at the last and Nicholas grimaced in return. Nicholas was as shy of girls as Harry was shameless. Still, he enjoyed being around Harry when he flirted with the younger girls in the court and the servants' daughters, because he thought he might learn something – as long as the Squire wasn't bullying them, as he had the day before. At times Harry could be charming, but at other times he got too rough for Nicholas's taste.

Nicholas said, 'You may miss getting put in your place by the local girls, but I feel like I'm getting out of a cage.'

Harry's usual bantering manner vanished. 'It's not that bad?'

Turning away from the practice, Nicholas walked back toward the palace, Harry falling in at his side. 'I have always been the youngest, the weakest, the . . . cripple.'

Harry's eyebrows went up. 'Some cripple. I've got more bruises and cuts from sword practice with you than everyone else combined, and I don't think I've touched you more than twice in a year.'

Nicholas's crooked smile made him look like his father as he said, 'You've scored a point or two.'

Harry shrugged. 'See. I'm not bad, but you're exceptional. How could you be considered a cripple?'

'Do you have the Festival of Presentation in Ludland?'

Harry said, 'No, it's only for the royal family, right?'

Nicholas shook his head. 'No. It used to be that every noble child was presented to the people thirty days after birth, so that all could see the child was born without flaw.

'It fell out of practice in the Eastern Realm a long time ago, but it was practiced widely in the West. My brothers were presented, as was my sister – all the children of the royal family, until me.'

Harry nodded. 'All right, so your father didn't wish to show you off to the people. What about it?'

Nicholas shrugged. 'It's not what you are, sometimes; it's how people treat you. I've always been treated as if there was something wrong with me. It makes it hard.'

'And you think things will be different in Crydee?' said Harry as they left the precinct of the stadium and reached the gate to the palace.

Two guards saluted the Prince as he passed, and Nicholas said, 'I don't know my uncle Martin well, but I like him. I think I may have a different life in Crydee.'

Harry sighed as they entered the palace. 'I hope it's not too different,' he observed as a particularly pretty maid hurried past. He watched her until she vanished through a side door. 'There are so many possibilities here, Nicky.'

Nicholas shook his head in resignation.

The rowers pulled and the longboat backed away, as heavy lines ran out to the stern of the ship. Upon the docks Arutha, Anita, and a host of court functionaries stood, bidding Prince Nicholas good-bye. Anita had a glimmer in her eyes, yet she held back her tears. Nicholas was her baby, but she had seen three other children leave home before, and that kept her in balance. Still, she kept a tight hold on her husband's arm. Something in his manner made her uneasy.

Nicholas and Harry stood near the bow, waving to those upon the docks. Amos stood behind them, his eyes fixed upon his beloved Alicia. Nicholas looked from his grandmother to Amos and said, 'Well, should I begin to call you "Grandfather"?'

Amos gave Nicholas a baleful look. 'You do and you'll swim to Crydee. And when we clear the harbor, you'll call me "Captain". As I told your father over twenty years ago, Prince or not, upon a ship none is master save the captain. Here I'm high priest and king, and don't you forget it.'

Nicholas grinned at Harry, not quite ready to believe

that Amos could turn into some sort of raging tyrant once they were at sea.

The harbor crew continued to tow the large ship clear of the royal quay, then cast off. Amos shot a glance at the harbor pilot and shouted, 'Take the wheel, master pilot!' To the crew he shouted, 'Set all topsails! Make ready mainsails and topgallants!'

When the first three sails were deployed, the ship seemed to come to life. Nicholas and Harry felt the movement beneath their feet. The ship heeled slightly to the right as the pilot brought it about. Amos left the boys to their own devices and made his way to the stern.

Slowly the ship moved through the harbor, majestically passing dozens of lesser craft. Nicholas watched every detail as the crew sprang to answer the pilot's commands. Two smaller coastal cutters were entering the harbor mouth as they approached. Seeing the ensign of the royal house of Krondor atop the mainmast, they dipped their own Kingdom flag in salute. Nicholas waved to them.

Harry said, 'Not very dignified, Your Highness.'

Nicholas threw an elbow into Harry's ribs, laughing. 'Who cares?'

The ship turned into the wind near the harbor mouth, bringing it to a virtual halt. A small rowboat came alongside and the pilot and his assistant hurried down into it, turning command of the ship over to Amos.

Once the pilot's boat was clear, Amos turned to his first mate, a man named Rhodes, and shouted, 'Trim topsails. Set mainsails and topgallants!'

Nicholas involuntarily gripped the rail, for the ship seemed to leap forward as the wind filled the sails. In the brisk morning breeze the ship sped through the water. The sun began to burn through the early morning haze and the sky turned a vivid blue. Above, sea gulls flew after the ship, waiting for the day's garbage to be tossed over the side.

Nicholas pointed down at the bow wake, and Harry looked over to see dolphins racing the ship. Both boys laughed at the sight.

Amos watched the landmarks of the harbor fall away behind, then he consulted the position of the sun above the harbor. Turning to the first mate, he said, 'Due west, Mr Rhodes. We make for Sorcerer's Isle.'

For six days they tacked against the prevailing westerly winds, until the lookout called, 'Land ho!'

'Where away?' shouted Amos.

'Two points off the starboard bow, Captain! An island!'

Amos nodded. 'Look for the headlands, Mr Rhodes. There's a cove to the southwest that we can lie in. Pass word that we'll only be laying over for a day or so. No one is to leave the ship without permission.'

Rhodes, a laconic man, said, 'No one's going to wish to set foot on Sorcerer's Isle without a direct order, Captain.'

Amos nodded. He knew who lived there now, but old superstitions died hard. For years the abode of Macros the Black, the island was reputed to be the home of demons and other dark spirits. Pug, a magician related to Arutha by adoption whom Amos had met on a number of occasions, had come to live on this island almost nine years before, and for his own reasons made few welcome there. Without thought, Amos said, 'Pass the word to be alert.'

Looking around, Amos realized that there was no need. Every man on the ship had his eyes fixed upon the spot of land that was growing larger with every passing minute. Amos felt a little stirring of anticipation, for while he knew Pug had requested no visitors, he doubted he would attack a ship flying the Krondorian royal ensign.

Nakor and Ghuda had come up on deck, and the little man rushed to the bow, where Nicholas and Harry were already stationed. Nicholas grinned at the strange little man. He had taken a liking to Nakor, who had proved an entertaining companion on an otherwise dull voyage.

'Now you'll see some things,' said Nakor.

Ghuda said, 'Look, a castle.'

Upon a promontory, the outlines of a castle could be seen as they drew closer. As they neared, they began to discern details. It was built of black stones, and set upon a rocky finger of land that was separated from the rest of the island by a narrow fissure through which the surf pounded. Across the gap a drawbridge extended, but even with it down, there was little about the place that looked hospitable. A single window, high up in a tower, flashed an ominous blue light.

The ship swung to the south of the rocks that lined the cliff base below the castle, and soon they approached a small inlet. The boys, Ghuda, and Nakor heard Amos call out, 'Reef all sails! Drop anchor.'

Within minutes the ship had stopped, and Amos came forward. 'Well, who's going ashore besides these two?' he asked, indicating Nakor and Ghuda.

Nicholas said, 'I'm not sure what you're asking, Amos – er, Captain.'

Amos seemed to squint with one eye at the boy as he said, 'Well, then it seems your father was even less forthcoming with you than with me. All he said was I was to heave to at Sorcerer's Isle for a bit, so you could visit your cousin Pug. I thought you'd know all about this.'

Nicholas shrugged. 'I've not seen him since I was very young; I hardly know the man.'

Nakor said, 'You come.' He pointed at Harry. 'You too.' To Amos he said, 'You I don't know about. I think you come also, but I'm not sure. Ghuda comes with me.'

Amos stroked his beard. 'Arutha said to do as you asked, Nakor, so I'll tag along.'

'Good,' said the little man with a grin. 'Let's go. Pug is waiting.'

41

Harry said, 'He knows we're here?'

Ghuda shook his head. 'No, he's fast asleep and hasn't noticed this great ship approaching for the last half day.'

Harry had the decency to blush as Nicholas laughed. Amos turned to his crew, many of whom hung in the rigging, watching the flashing lights of the distant castle, and shouted, 'Lower a boat!'

The boat ground into the sand and two sailors jumped out and pulled it ashore. Nicholas and Harry climbed out and waded through the ankle-deep water as Nakor, Ghuda, and Amos followed.

Nakor immediately headed for a path that led up to a ridge overlooking the cove. Amos called, 'Where are you going?'

Nakor kept walking as he turned and said, 'That way,' pointing up to the top of the path.

Ghuda looked at the others, shrugged, and began to follow. The boys hesitated an instant, then also started walking up the path.

Amos shook his head and turned to the sailors. 'Return to the ship. Tell Mr Rhodes to keep a sharp eye out; we'll signal from here when we want the boat to pick us up.'

The two sailors saluted and pushed the boat back, while the two who were still sitting in it unshipped a pair of oars and started pulling against the breakers. The two at the bow leaped into the boat and soon there were four sailors pulling hard to get back to the relative safety of their ship.

Amos trudged after the other four to find them waiting at the top of the path. Another path diverted from the one that led to the castle, and Nakor started walking down that one.

Amos said, 'The castle's over that way, Keshian.'

'Isalani,' answered Nakor. 'Keshians are tall, dark people who run around without most of their clothing. And Pug is this way.'

42

Ghuda said, 'Best not to argue with him, Admiral,' as he followed. The others fell into step and followed Nakor down into a small defile, then upward to another ridge. From the top of the second ridge they could see down into a small vale. It was overgrown with brush and thick with ancient trees. The path seemed to vanish at the edge of the woods at the base of the hill.

Ghuda said, 'Where are you taking us?'

Nakor almost skipped as he walked, tapping his walking stick on the path. 'This way. It's not far.'

The boys hurried along, almost running, and soon were beside the Isalani. 'Nakor,' said Nicholas, 'how do you know Pug is here?'

Nakor shrugged. 'It's a trick.'

As they reached the edge of the forest, they encountered daunting-looking undergrowth and trees set so close together that passage seemed impossible. 'Where now?' asked Harry.

Nakor grinned. 'Look.' He pointed at the path with his staff. 'Look here. Don't look up.'

He started walking slowly, turning around so he was moving backward, dragging the point of his staff upon the ground. The boys followed after, keeping their eyes fixed upon the tip of the staff as it stirred dust in the pathway. They moved slowly, and after a moment Nicholas realized that they should now be stuck in heavy undergrowth but in fact the pathway was still clear. 'Don't look up,' said Nakor.

Gloom surrounded them, but they could clearly see the path where the staff touched it. Then suddenly there was light, and Nakor said, 'You can look now.'

Instead of a heavy forest, they stood before a large rambling estate, with a few well-tended fruit trees around the edges. On the other side of the estate, sheep grazed, and a half-dozen horses ambled across a large meadow. Nicholas looked back and saw Amos and Ghuda glancing

43

about as if lost. Nakor said, 'They were too slow. I'll go get them.'

From behind, a voice said, 'There's no need.'

Nicholas turned and saw a man in a black robe, slightly shorter than himself, looking at the three with a quizzical expression. The Prince's eyes widened, for the man could not possibly have been there a moment before. The man moved his hand, and suddenly Amos and Ghuda were staring with eyes wide. 'I've removed the illusion,' said the man.

Nakor said, 'I told you: it was a trick.'

The man looked over the two boys and Nakor, then studied Amos and Ghuda as they approached. After a moment his bearded face relaxed and years seem to fall away as he said, 'Captain Trask! I had no idea.'

Amos strode up to him and stuck out his hand. 'Pug, it's good to see you once more.' As they shook, Amos remarked, 'You look no different than you did after the Battle of Sethanon!'

There was some humor in Pug's voice as he said, 'I've been told that. Who are your companions?'

Amos motioned for Nicholas to step forward. 'I have the pleasure of presenting your cousin Prince Nicholas.'

Pug smiled warmly at the boy and said, 'Nicky, I haven't seen you since you were little more than a baby.'

Amos continued, 'This is Harry of Ludland, his Squire, and these two are Ghuda Bulé and – '

Before he could finish, Nakor said, 'I am Nakor, the Blue Rider.'

Unexpectedly, Pug laughed aloud. 'You! I have heard of you.' With genuine amusement he said, 'You are all welcome to Villa Beata.'

He motioned for them to follow as he led them toward the strangely designed home. A large central building, white, with a red-tile roof, was surrounded by a low white stone wall, which sheltered a garden of fruit trees and flowers. In the center of the garden, a fountain fashioned of marble in the form of three dolphins sent up a cheerful spray. Off in the distance, they could see outbuildings.

Stepping forward so he walked at Pug's side, Nicholas said, 'What is Villa Beata?'

'This place. In the language of those who built it, it means "blessed home", or so I was told. And so I have found.'

Amos turned to Nakor and asked him, 'How did you know not to go to the castle?'

The little man grinned and shrugged. 'It's what I would do.'

Pug said over his shoulder, 'If you had gone to the castle, you would have found it deserted, save for some lively traps in the tallest tower. I find it preserves my privacy to keep alive the legend of the Black Sorcerer. Wards I've set there would have alerted me to your trespass, so I would have come to see who called, but you've been saved a half day of wasted time.' Looking at Nakor, he said, 'We should talk before you leave.'

Nakor nodded vigorously. 'I like your house. It makes sense.'

Pug nodded in turn.

Reaching the gate through the low wall, he held open the gate for the others, letting them all pass through before he followed after. 'Be warned, not all my servants are human, and some may startle you. But none here will do you harm.'

As if illustrating this point, a tall creature appeared at the main entrance of the house. Ghuda's sword was half out of his scabbard before he remembered himself and put it away. The creature appeared to be a goblin, though taller than any Ghuda had ever seen. Goblins were usually smaller than men, but not by much. This creature's blue-green-tinged skin was smooth, and his eyes were huge and round, with black irises on yellow. He also possessed a finer cast of features than any goblin Ghuda had fought, though he did have the heavy brow ridge and comically large nose common to goblin kind. But his clothing was of fine weave and cut and he carried himself with an air that could only be called dignified. He smiled, showing long teeth that came close to being fangs. He executed a courtly bow and said, 'Master Pug, refreshments are ready.'

Pug said, 'This is Gathis, who acts as seneschal of my house. He will provide for your comforts.' Looking skyward, he said, 'I think our guests will dine and spend the night. Make rooms ready.' Turning to the five visitors, he said, 'We have ample room, and I think a relaxed evening would be appropriate.' He added to Nicholas, 'Highness, you do resemble your father at your age.'

Nicholas said, 'You knew my father when he was my age?'

The youthful-looking Pug nodded. 'Well. I shall tell you of it sometime.' To the entire party he said, 'Come. Refresh yourselves. I must see to some matters of urgency, but I will join you after you have rested.' So saying, he vanished through the door to the house, leaving them in the care of Gathis.

The odd-looking creature spoke with a sibilance due in the main to a large assortment of teeth, but his words were courtly. 'If you have any needs, gentlemen, please inform me and I shall endeavour to meet them at once. Please, come this way.'

He led them into a spacious entry hall, facing a large set of doors opening upon a very large central garden. To the right and left, corridors stretched away. He led them to the left, down to the first corner, then to the right. A portico extended from a door on their left, connecting another large building to the main one. Leading them to the next building, Gathis said, 'These are the guest quarters, gentlemen.'

Ghuda again almost had his sword out as a troll came ambling out through the doorway, carrying a large bundle of linens. The creature wore a simple tunic and trousers, but it was without a doubt a troll: humanlike in form, short, with tremendously broad shoulders and arms hanging nearly to the ground. The face was apelike, with large fangs protruding over the lower lip, and deep black eyes set back under a massive brow ridge. Without any fuss, the creature moved to the side and bowed slightly to the guests, letting them pass.

Gathis said, 'That is Solunk, who is the porter here. If you need fresh towels or hot water, pull the bell cord and he will answer. He cannot speak your Kingdom tongue, but he understands it enough to answer your requests. If you should have any needs he cannot understand, he will fetch me.' He showed them all to rooms in the building, and left each to himself.

Nicholas found himself in a well-appointed if not overly ornate room. A simple bed with thick comforter dominated one corner, beneath a large window looking out at the smaller buildings behind the great house. He glanced through and saw a man and another creature, similar to Gathis but not as large, carrying firewood into what appeared to be a cookhouse.

Nicholas turned to examine the other contents of the room, a simple writing desk with a chair, a large wardrobe, and a chest. Opening the chest, he saw fresh linens, while the wardrobe revealed a small array of clothing of varying cut, color, and weave, and several sizes, as if any number of guests might have left one or two items behind.

There was a knock at the door and Nicholas opened it to find Solunk, the troll, standing before the portal. He motioned to a large metal tub two men carried, and then to Nicholas. The boy understood and nodded, opening the door wide. The two men entered, and Nicholas couldn't help but stare. Both were dressed only in red

47

trousers, and their skin was black, but unlike the dark-skinned people of Krondor and Kesh, these men were not merely dark. They were black as if their bodies had been painted with lampblack or paint. They also showed no hair upon their heads and faces, and their eyes were a startling pale blue, with no visible white, against the sooty skin.

They set the tub down in the center of the room and left. The troll opened the wardrobe and without hesitation selected a pair of trousers and a tunic that appeared the proper size for Nicholas. He then rooted around in the chest, beneath the linens, and produced a pair of under-trousers and hose. The two men of unusual color returned with large buckets and filled the tub with hot water, leaving a towel, brush, and a bar of scented soap.

The troll made an inquiring noise and pantomimed scrubbing Nicholas's back. Nicholas said, 'No, thank you. I can manage.'

With a satisfied-sounding grunt, the troll motioned for the others to leave and followed them out, closing the door behind.

Nicholas shook his head in silent amazement, then stripped off his very dirty clothing and got in the tub. The water was hot, but not too hot, and he lowered himself gently into it. When he was sitting, he indulged himself in a long sigh and leaned back. He savored the luxury of the hot bath after a week in the close quarters aboard ship. From down the hall he could hear Harry singing to himself as he began to bathe and decided he should get on with scrubbing himself before the water cooled too much. Shortly he was covered with lather and softly humming a countermelody to Harry's more rambunctious vocalizing.

After a long, refreshing bath, Nicholas dressed and found the clothing laid out for him to fit almost as well as his own. He pulled on his boots and left the room. The hall was empty and he thought about disturbing the others; Harry still filled the air with his less than stunning voice.

He decided to wander a bit and explore. He entered the main house, passing through the main hallway, and turned through a doorway into the central garden. Like the one before the house, this garden was dominated by fruit trees and flowers, with small paths crossing from four central doors of the square, forming a cross. At the intersection of the two paths was set a fountain similar to the one before the house, and nearby was a small white stone bench. Pug sat there, speaking with a woman.

As he approached, Nicholas saw Pug look up and rise. 'Highness, I have the pleasure of presenting a friend, the Lady Ryana.' Turning to his companion, he said, 'Ryana, this is Prince Nicholas, son of Arutha of Krondor.'

The woman rose and curtsied with precision, startling green eyes fixed upon the boy. Her age was unguessable, being somewhere between the late teens and early thirties; her features were finely chiseled, 'aristocratic' being the only word that Nicholas could think of; in her presence he felt that he was the lowborn and she the noble. But beautiful as she was, there was something in her manner and movement that could only be called alien: her hair was not blond but truly gold and her skin was ivory, yet almost glinted in the sunlight. Nicholas hesitated a moment, then bowed correctly, saying, 'M'lady.'

Pug said, 'Ryana is the daughter of an old friend, come to study awhile with me.'

'Study?'

Pug nodded, indicating that Nicholas should sit where he had, while Pug sat upon the edge of the fountain. 'Many of those here are servants or friends, but some are also students of mine.'

Nicholas said, 'I thought you had built the academy at Stardock as a place of study.'

Pug smiled slightly, and there was a hint of irony in his

voice as he said, 'The academy is like most other human institutions, Nicholas, which means that as time passes, it will become more set in its ways, more concerned with "tradition", and less willing to grow. I've seen firsthand the results of such attitudes, and don't wish to see them repeated. But I have a limited influence at Stardock. It's been seven years since my last visit, and eight since I lived among the magicians there. I left soon after my wife died.' He looked at the sky, lost in thought. 'My old friends Kulgan and Meecham are gone as well. My children have grown and are married. No, there are few at Stardock I feel compelled to visit.'

He waved his hand in an encompassing gesture. 'Here I will take any who is worthy, and some are from other worlds. I doubt some you've already met would be welcome down there.'

Nicholas shook his head. 'I guess.' Attempting to be polite, he spoke to Ryana, 'M'lady, are you from one of those distant worlds?'

Her voice carried alien notes. 'No, I was born near here, Highness.'

Nicholas felt his skin crawl for reasons he could not put voice to. The woman was unusually beautiful by any standard, yet it was a beauty of another kind, something he could not be touched by. He smiled, for he could not think of another polite thing to say.

Pug seemed to sense his discomfort, so he said, 'What do I owe the pleasure of this visit to, Nicholas? I was rather pointed in my request to your father that I be left undisturbed here.'

Nicholas blushed. 'I really don't know, Pug. Father said Nakor insisted, and for some reason Father felt compelled to honor his request. I'm on my way to Martin's court at Crydee, to squire there for a while and . . . I guess get hardened on the frontier.'

Pug smiled, and again Nicholas felt calmed by the

smile. 'Well, it's rough compared to Krondor, but Crydee is hardly the frontier. The town is twice the size it was when I was a boy, I have been told. And the Jonril garrison is now a major town. There's a growing duchy out there. I think you'll like it.'

Nicholas smiled and said, 'I hope so,' without a great deal of conviction. He attempted to keep his expression even, but for the last couple of days he had been visited by an unexpected homesickness. The novelty of the journey had worn off, and now the tedious voyage, with nothing to do but sit in his cabin or pace the deck, was taking its toll.

'How are things at your father's court?' asked Pug.

Nicholas said, 'Quiet. And busy. The usual. No wars or plagues or other crisis, if that's what you mean.' Looking at Pug's face, he saw a questioning look. Nodding, Nicholas said, 'Your son is now Knight-Marshal of Krondor.'

Pug nodded, his expression thoughtful. 'William and I had a falling out over his choice to be a soldier. He has some strange and powerful gifts.'

Nicholas said, 'Father told me something about it, but I'm not sure I understand.'

Pug's smile returned. 'I'm not sure I do, either, Nicholas. For all my skills, being a father – at least with William – may have been a little beyond me. I insisted he study at Stardock and he would have none of it.' Pug shook his head and his expression turned rueful. 'I was very demanding, and he left without my leave. Arutha gave him a commission because of his being a cousin. I'm glad to see he's made something of himself.'

'You should go see him,' Nicholas said.

Pug smiled again. 'Perhaps.'

Nicholas said, 'I wanted to ask you something. Everyone calls William "Cousin Willie", and I've heard you also referred to as a cousin. But I know my grandfather

Borric had only three sons and no nephews . . . ?' He shrugged.

Pug said, 'I did your grandfather some service when I was part of his household. I was an orphan boy, and when he thought me lost, he added my name to the family archives in Rillanon. As I was not formally adopted as his son, the King couldn't refer to me as a brother, so "cousin" seemed appropriate. I don't speak of such things – no one here is concerned over matters of patents and titles – but I am considered a prince of one sort or another in the Kingdom.'

Nicholas grinned. 'Well, Highness, the other news is that your daughter has given birth to her third child.'

Pug's smile broadened. 'A boy?'

Nicholas said, 'At last. Uncle Jimmy loves his two girls, but he really wanted a son this time.'

Pug said, 'I've not seen them since their wedding. Perhaps I am overdue at Rillanon for a family visit, if only to see my grandchildren.' He looked at Nicholas with a friendly expression. 'I'll think about a visit to your father's court on the way, and perhaps a stubborn father and his equally stubborn son can find something to say to each other.'

Nakor and Ghuda appeared at the entrance to the garden, the fighter wearing a finely bordered shirt of silk and balloon trousers tucked into his battered old boots. His bastard-sword had been left in his room, but his dirks were prominently evident. The little gambler wore a short robe of bright orange, which looked garish to Nicholas, but which seemed to delight him. He hurried forward and bowed to Pug. 'Thank you for the fine robe.'

He caught sight of Ryana, and his eyes widened as his mouth opened in an O of amazement. He quickly spoke a few phrases in a language unknown to Nicholas. The woman's green eyes widened, and she regarded Pug with an expression that Nicholas could only call alarm. Something the little man said had frightened her badly.

Pug held up one finger to his lips in the gesture for silence, and Nakor glanced at Ghuda and Nicholas. With an embarrassed laugh, he said, 'Sorry.'

Nicholas looked at Ghuda, who said, 'I never ask.'

Pug said, 'Amos and Harry should be here soon. We can move to the dining room.'

The dining room turned out to be a large square room on the side of the central building farthest from the guest quarters. In the middle was a low, square table, with cushions on all sides. Pug spoke as Amos and Harry entered. 'I prefer eating in the Tsurani fashion; I hope you don't mind.'

Amos said, 'As long as it's food, I'll stand if I must.' Seeing Ryana, he halted, while Pug made introductions.

Harry couldn't tear his eyes from the woman, almost falling over a cushion as he came to Nicholas's side. Sitting next to the Prince, he whispered, 'Who is that?'

Nicholas spoke softly. 'A sorceress, or at least a student of Pug's. And don't whisper; it's impolite.'

Harry flushed and fell silent as the two odd black men entered, carrying platters of food. They quickly set plates before eveyone and left, returning a moment later with cups of wine.

As dinner was served, Pug said. 'I'm out of practice entertaining, so I apologize should you find anything lacking.'

Amos spoke on everyone's behalf. 'We gave no warning of our approach, so nothing you offered would be lacking.'

Pug said, 'You are kind, Admiral.'

Nicholas said, 'I thought Father had some means to contact you.'

Pug said, 'In an emergency only, Highness, and then only at great need. He has not needed to use the device I gave him. The Kingdom has been peaceful since I left.'

Conversation turned to gossip from court and other trivialities. Nakor was unusually silent, as was the Lady Ryana. Pug was a convivial host, able to draw the two boys into the conversation without making it obvious.

Both Nicholas and Harry had been drinking wine with dinner since they were old enough to sit at their parents' tables, but as with most noble children, theirs had been diluted with water. Tonight they were drinking a full-bodied Keshian red, and after two cups, both boys were in a celebratory mood, laughing loudly at two stories they had heard Amos tell many times before.

As Amos started telling his third tale of adventure and wonder, Pug said, 'If you will excuse me for a moment. Nakor, might I have a word in private with you?'

The little Isalani jumped to his feet and hurried toward the door Pug had indicated. They entered another of the many gardens on the property, and Pug said, 'I have been told that this visit was your idea?'

Nakor said, 'I never expected to meet . . .'

Pug said, 'How did you know?'

The Isalani shrugged. 'I don't know. I just know.'

Pug halted next to a low bench and said, 'Who are you?'

Nakor sat upon the bench, pulling his feet under him. 'A man. I know things. I do tricks.'

Pug studied him in silence for a long moment. Sitting upon the edge of a reflecting pool, he said at last, 'Ryana's people have come to trust me. She is the daughter of one I knew twenty years ago. They are among the last of their race, and most men think them legends.'

'I saw one once,' said the unabashed little man. 'I was traveling the road from Toowomba to Injune, in the mountains. At sunset I saw one off in the distance, resting upon the peak of a mountain, in the sunlight. I thought it odd that he should be sitting there alone, but then I considered he might think it odd that I was also there alone; so, it being a matter of perspective, I decided not to disturb his meditations. But I watched him for a few minutes. He was a thing of beauty, like your Lady Ryana.' He shook his head. 'Wonderful creatures. Some men count them gods, I have been told. I would like to talk to one.'

Pug said, 'Ryana is young, just having come to intelligence after years of living as a wild creature, in the fashion of her race; she is barely able to understand her own nature or her new power. It's better if we limit her contact with humans for a while.'

Nakor shrugged. 'If you say. I have seen her. That is enough, perhaps.'

Pug smiled. 'You are a rare man.'

Nakor shrugged again. 'I choose not to become upset about things I have no control over.'

'Why the visit, Nakor?'

The man's usually grinning visage took on a somber expression. 'Two reasons. I wished to meet you, for it was your words that brought me to Stardock.'

'My words?'

'Once you told a man named James that should he meet someone like me, he should say, "There is no magic."' Pug nodded. 'So when he said this thing to me, I went to Stardock, to find you. You were gone, but I stayed there awhile. I found many serious men who did not understand that magic is only tricks.'

Pug found himself grinning. 'I've heard you were a bit of a shock to Watum and Korsh.'

Nakor's grin returned to match Pug's. 'They are fussy men, who take their school much too seriously. I moved among the students and recruited many to my point of view. They call themselves the Blue Riders in my honor and are united to resist the insular notions of those two old ladies you left in charge.'

Pug laughed. 'The brothers Korsh and Watum were my

most apt students. I don't think they'd appreciate your calling them old ladies.'

Nakor said, 'They didn't. But they act like them. "Don't tell this; don't share that." They just don't understand that there is no magic.'

Pug sighed. 'When I looked at what ten years of work had brought forth at Stardock, I saw a repeat of the past, another Assembly of Great Ones, such as I knew upon the world of Kelewan: a band of men pledged to nothing but their own power and greatness, at the expense of others.'

Nakor nodded. 'They like being mysterious and pretending they're important.'

Pug laughed. 'Oh, had you visited me upon Kelewan, so many years past, you would have said worse about me.'

I've met some of your Great Ones,' answered Nakor. 'The rift gate still operates, and we still trade with the Empire. Tsurani goods come through and we send back metals. The Mistress of the Empire is a shrewd negotiator, and everyone stays happy on both sides. From time to time a Tsurani Great One visits. And some alien magicians from Chakahar. Did you not know?'

Pug shook his head and sighed. 'If cho-ja magicians from Chakahar are at Stardock, then the Assembly's control over the Empire has been ended.' His eyes misted over and he said, 'There are things I thought I would never see in my days, Nakor. The end of that tradition was foremost among them – much of what gave the Assembly its power was based on fear and lies: lies about magicians, lies about the Empire, and lies about those outside the Empire's borders.'

Nakor seemed to understand Pug's words. 'Lies can live a long time. But not forever. You should return and visit.'

Pug shook his head, not certain if the little man meant

Kelewan or Stardock. 'For nearly nine years I have put my past behind me. My children now look of an age with me, and soon will look older. I've seen my wife die, and my teachers. Old friends on two worlds have traveled into death's hall. I have no wish to watch my children grow old.' Pug stood and paced a bit. 'I do not know if I was wise, Nakor, only that I feared that more than anything.'

Nakor nodded. 'We are alike, in some ways.'

Pug turned and stared at the little man. 'In what ways?'

Nakor grinned. 'I have lived three times the normal span of a man. My birth was recorded in the census of Kesh in the time of the Emperor Sajanjaro, great-grand-father of the wife of Emperor Diiagái. I saw the Empress, his wife's mother, nine years ago. She was an old woman who had ruled for more than forty years. I remember when she was a baby, and I was then as you see me now.' Nakor sighed. 'I have never been a man to trust others, perhaps because of my trade.' He produced a deck of cards seemingly out of nowhere and fanned it with one hand; then, with a flick of his wrist, the cards vanished. 'But I understand what you say. No one I knew as a child lives today.'

Pug sat again on the fountain and asked, 'Why else have you come?'

Nakor said, 'I see things. I do not know how, but there are moments when I *know*. Nicholas is upon a voyage that will take him far beyond Crydee. And there is to be much danger in the boy's future.'

Pug was silent for a long time, thinking about what the small man had said. Finally he said, 'What must I do to help?'

Nakor shook his head. 'I am not a wise man by nature. I have been called a frivolous man – by Watum and Korsh, and by Ghuda most recently.' Pug smiled at that. 'I do not understand my abilities, sometimes.' He sighed. 'You are a man of great gifts and attainments, by all accounts. You live among creatures of wonder and do not think it strange. I saw the work you left behind at Stardock, and it is impressive. For me to advise you is presumptuous.'

'Presumptuous or not, advise.'

Nakor bit his lower lip as he thought. 'I think the boy is a nexus.' Waving his hand in a vague circle, he said, 'Dark forces move and they will be drawn to him. Nothing we do can change this; we must be ready to aid him.'

Pug was silent for a long time. At last he said, 'Nearly thirty years ago, Nicholas's father was such a nexus, for his death would have been a victory for dark forces.'

'The serpent people.'

Pug looked astonished at the remark.

Nakor shrugged. 'I heard of the Battle of Sethanon long after it was over. But there was one rumor that I found interesting, that the leader of those invading your Kingdom had a Pantathian mystic as an adviser.'

'You know of the Pantathians?'

'I have run across the serpent priests before,' Nakor said with a shrug. 'I assume that whatever your dark elves of the north may have thought, it was the Pantathians who were behind the entire mess, but beyond that I don't understand much of what occurred.'

Pug said, 'You would be even more surprising than you are if you had understood, Nakor.' He nodded. 'Very well. I shall help Nicholas.'

Nakor rose. 'We should go to bed. You would like us to leave tomorrow.'

Pug smiled. 'You I would like to stay. I think you could be a valuable addition to our community, but I understand what it is to be drawn to one's fate.'

Nakor's expression darkened, and he looked as serious as Pug had seen him since meeting him. 'Of this company, five shall cross the waters, with four more we have yet to meet.' His eyes grew unfocused as if seeing something distant. 'Nine shall depart, and some shall not return.'

Pug looked worried. 'Do you know who?'

Nakor said, 'I am one of the nine. No man may know his own fate.'

Pug said, 'You never met Macros the Black.'

Nakor grinned, and suddenly the mood was lighter again. 'I did once, but that is a long story.'

Pug stood. 'We must return to my guests. I would like to hear that tale sometime.'

'What of the boy?' asked Nakor.

Pug said, 'For the reasons I have just given you, I am not pleased with the prospect of becoming involved with any mortal, even if they are counted kin.' He shook his head as if irritated. 'But I cannot abandon those for whom I profess affection. I will help the boy when the time comes.'

Nakor said, 'Good. This is why I told his father we had to come here.'

Pug said, 'You are indeed an unusual man, Nakor the Blue Rider.'

Nakor laughed and nodded in agreement.

They came back into the dining hall and found Amos finishing another of his tall tales, to the delight of Ghuda and Nicholas. Ryana seemed perplexed, and Harry oblivious to it, as he was completely enraptured by her.

Pug called for coffee and a fortified wine, and the discussion turned again to mundane matters of common gossip in Krondor. After a short while, yawns gave evidence that the guests were ready to retire.

Pug bade his guests good night and gave his hand to the Lady Ryana, whom he escorted from the hall. Nicholas and his companions rose and made their way back to their own rooms. Nicholas discovered the bedding turned down and candles lit upon the night tables. Across the foot of the bed a nightshirt had been provided for his comfort.

Nicholas turned in and had just fallen asleep when a

hand shook him. He came awake with his heart pounding, to find Harry leaning over him. The boy was wearing a nightshirt similar to his own.

'What?' he asked groggily.

'You won't believe this. Come on!'

Nicholas jumped out of bed and followed Harry back to his own room at the far end of the hallway. Harry said, 'I was almost asleep when I heard a strange sound.'

He motioned for Nicholas to come to the window and said, 'Be quiet.'

Nicholas looked out Harry's window and saw the Lady Ryana standing in the distant meadow. Harry said, 'She was making these really strange noises, like chanting or singing, but not quite.' There was no mistaking the golden hair, almost aglow in the light from two of Midkemia's moons. Nicholas's mouth almost fell open. 'She's nude!'

Harry stared. 'She had clothes on a moment ago, honestly!' The lady was indeed without clothing and seemed in some sort of a trance. Harry whistled softly. 'What's she doing?'

Nicholas suppressed a shiver. Despite the astonishing beauty of the woman in the meadow, there was nothing remotely titillating or erotic about her appearance. He felt uneasy. Not only did he feel as if he was intruding, he felt a sense of danger.

Harry said, 'I've heard tales of witches mating with demons in the moonlight.'

Nicholas said, 'Look!'

A golden nimbus of light gathered around the woman and soon became blinding. The boys were forced to avert their eyes as the light grew in intensity. For long moments the night seemed broken by a beam of sunlight, then it started to fade. They looked again and the light had expanded to many times the size of the woman. As large as a house, then as large as Amos's ship, the envelope of light grew, and inside, something took shape. Then the light faded, and where the Lady Ryana had stood, now a mighty creature of legend spread wings a hundred yards across. Golden scales gleamed with silver highlights in the moons' light, and a long neck with silver crest extended, as the reptilian head looked skyward. Then with a leap, a snap of the giant wings, and a small blast of flame, the dragon lifted into the sky.

Harry gripped Nicholas hard enough to raise a bruise, but neither boy could move. When she had vanished into the sky, the boys turned to regard each other. Both had tears running down their faces, in mixed fear and awe. The great dragons were not real. There were smaller flying reptiles called dragons, but they were merely flying wyverns with no intelligence. None lived in the Western Realm, but rumor had them common in the western mountains of Kesh. But the golden dragons who could speak and work magic did not exist. They were creatures of myth, yet there, in the moonlight, the boys had seen a woman they had dined with transform herself into the most majestic creature to fly the skies of Midkemia.

Nicholas could not stop the tears, so moved was he by the sight. Harry at last gathered his wits and said, 'Should we wake Amos?'

Nicholas shook his head. 'Never tell anyone. Do you understand?'

Harry nodded, with no hint of his usual braggadocio, looking like nothing more than a scared little boy. 'I won't.'

Nicholas left his friend and returned to his own room. He entered and his heart almost seized up as he discovered Pug sitting upon his bed.

'Close the door.'

Nicholas complied and Pug said, 'Ryana could not long live on the meager food she could eat at supper and maintain her pretense. She will hunt for the next few hours.'

61

Nicholas's face was pale. For the first time in his life he felt far from home and the comfort of his father's protection and his mother's love. He knew Pug was considered a family member, but he was also a magician of mighty arts, and Nicholas had seen something not meant for him to see. 'I won't say anything,' he whispered.

Pug smiled. 'I know. Sit down.'

Nicholas sat down next to Pug on the bed, and Pug said, 'Give me your foot.'

Nicholas didn't have to ask which one and lifted his left leg so that Pug could examine the deformed foot. Pug studied it for several moments, then said, 'Years ago, your father asked me if I could mend your foot. Did he tell you?'

Nicholas shook his head. He still was frightened enough by what he had just witnessed that he didn't trust his voice not to break if he spoke.

Pug studied the boy. 'At the time I had heard of this deformity, and of the efforts to correct it.'

Nicholas whispered, 'Many tried.'

'I know.' Pug stood and walked to the window, looking out at the clear night brilliant with stars. Turning back toward Nicholas, he said, 'I told Arutha that I could not. That was not true.'

Nicholas asked, 'Why?'

Pug said, 'Because no matter how much your father loves you, Nicholas – and Arutha loves his children deeply, no matter how difficult it is for him to show it – no parent has the right to change a child's nature.'

Nicholas said, 'I'm not sure I understand.' The fear within was subsiding, and the boy asked, 'Why would healing me be wrong?'

Pug said, 'I don't know if I can make you understand yet, Nicholas.' He returned and sat next to the boy. 'We each of us have it within to make ourselves over, if we choose to do so. Most of us not only do not try, but don't even acknowledge that ability to ourselves.

'By any understanding of magic I possess, the healing used upon you when you were young should have worked. Something prevented those spells from being effective.'

Nicholas frowned. 'I don't understand. Are you saying I wasn't letting them heal me?'

Pug nodded. 'Something like that. But it's not quite so simple.'

Nicholas said, 'I would give anything to be normal.'

Pug stood. 'Would you?'

Nicholas was silent for a long moment, then said, 'I think I would.'

Pug smiled, his manner reassuring. 'Go to sleep, Nicholas.' He withdrew something from a large pocket in his robe and placed it upon the night table. 'This amulet is a gift. It is much like one I gave your father. Should you need me for anything, grip it tightly in your right hand while you wear it, and say my name three times. I will come.'

Nicholas picked up the amulet and saw it bore the symbol of the three dolphins he had seen in the fountains around the magician's estate. 'Why?'

Pug's smile broadened. 'Because I'm a cousin, and a friend. And in days to come, you may need both. And because I'm letting you and your friend keep a trust.'

'The Lady Ryana.'

'She is very young, and foolish to be seen so. In her race, the first stages of life are spent with little more thought than that of common animals. Every ten years the dragon hides in a cave to shed its skin, emerging a different color each time. Not a few perish during that time, for molting in the dark, they are helpless. Only those that live the longest span, surviving many human lifetimes, emerge with a golden skin and awareness. When intelligence at last comes, it is an unsettling thing. The sudden consciousness of self, and the sense of a larger universe, to a creature that is already old by human standards is a very great shock. In ancient times, others of her race would teach her.' Pug opened the door. 'There are few of the greater dragons left. Ryana's mother once aided me on a quest, so I help the child. It would not be wise to let men know that among them walk those who are not men.'

Nicholas said, 'Father has told me that over time there will be many things I shall learn that I cannot tell others about. I understand.'

Pug said nothing more as he closed the door. Nicholas lay back upon the bed, but sleep was a long time coming.

3

Crydee

The ship dropped anchor.

Crydee bustled with midday activity as the dock crew
made the *Royal Eagle* secure. Nicholas examined his new
home, drinking in the novelty of it. His bouts of homesickness had returned during the long voyage, only vanishing
while passing through the dangerous Straits of Darkness,
which had taken an eventful day and a half. Then northward past Tulan and Carse, and now to Crydee.

The town had grown in the last twenty years, with signs
of expansion everywhere. As they had sailed northward,
Amos had pointed out where a fishing viallage had grown
up south of the promontory he named Sailor's Grief. New
buildings were visible high upon a distant hillside to the
southeast as the ship entered the harbor. Nicholas
squinted against the bright sun reflected off the white
façades of the buildings. He saw two carriages and a pair
of wagons draw up and halt before a building bedecked
by a large royal standard, which proclaimed it the customs
house. Servants sitting atop the rear of the carriages
leaped from their stations and opened the doors. From
the first emerged a tall woman, followed by a taller man.
Nicholas recognized them as his aunt and uncle. A flurry
of activity followed as the other vehicles came to a halt.

Amos ordered the gangway run out. Nicholas and
Harry stood nearby waiting to disembark. Duke Martin,
Duchess Briana, and their court stood ready to welcome
the Royal Prince and his companions. Amos saw the
reception below and said, 'Well, we know at least one
pigeon made it from Ylith.'

For the twenty-eight years since the Riftwar, a relay of

messengers between Krondor and the Far Coast had been kept intact, including fast horses and carrier pigeons. With the sudden decision to sent Nicholas made only the day before he departed, word of his impending arrival reached Crydee just days before they came into sight of the harbor.

As the sailors made ready, Harry said, 'Who are those girls?'

Nicholas had noticed the two young girls who had accompanied the Duke and said, 'I expect one of them is my cousin Margaret. I don't know who the other one is.'

Harry grinned. 'I'll find out.'

When the gangway was out, Amos turned to Nicholas and formally said, 'Your Highness?' – indicating that Nicholas was expected to be the first one off the ship.

Harry stepped forward, to discover Amos's hand planted firmly on his chest. 'By rank, *Squire*,' he said pointedly.

Harry blushed and took a step back.

Nicholas descended to the quay and a tall man stepped forward. Martin, Duke of Crydee, smiled warmly as he bowed to his nephew. 'Your Highness, we are most pleased to welcome you to Crydee.' Martin resembled Arutha slightly, but was taller and heavier. His hair was nearly all grey, and his face was lined by sun and age, yet there was an air of strength about him that was clear for anyone to see. This was no sedentary noble who spent his days drinking wine and issuing orders to servants. This was a man who despite his age still spend nights sleeping on the ground under star-filled skies and who carried game home upon his back.

Nicholas smiled, a little embarrassed at the ceremony, and said, 'Uncle, I am pleased to be here.'

Amos was second off the ship, and said, 'Your Grace,' as he clapped Martin roughly on the shoulder.

All formality evaporated as Martin threw his arms around Amos. 'You old pirate,' he said, laughing. 'It's been too many years.' They slapped each other on the back and shook hands. Amos inclined his head toward Nicholas.

Martin returned his attention to the Prince. 'Your Highness. May I present my wife, the Duchess Briana.' Nicholas had not seen her since he was a toddler, and his memories of her were vague. It was like meeting her for the first time. A tall woman inclined her head toward Nicholas. Her hair, grey with a startling white streak at the left temple, flowed back from a high brow. There was nothing pretty about the Duchess, but she was a striking woman. Blue eyes set with lines from weather and age regarded the Prince from a face otherwise free of any mark of aging, though she was past fifty. She wore a very practical-looking outfit of leather vest over a silk shirt and trousers tucked into high boots. 'M'lady,' said Nicholas, taking her extended hand and squeezing it slightly in greeting. The grip he received was strong, and Nicholas knew the tales of his uncle's strange lady were mostly true. From the fallen city of Armengar – where women were soldiers alongside the men – Lady Briana could ride, hunt, and fight better than most men, from all reports. Looking at her, Nicholas didn't doubt it.

Martin continued the introductions. 'This is my son, Marcus.' Nicholas turned to his cousin and hesitated; there was something vaguely familiar about him. Brown eyes and brown hair: Nicholas judged he must resemble someone back in Krondor. The same height as Nicholas, Marcus wore his hair the same length as the Prince. But Marcus was almost two years senior to Nicholas and slightly heavier in build. Marcus gave Nicholas a stiff bow and stepped back.

Nicholas said, 'Cousin,' and nodded.

Amos came up to stand behind Nicholas and said to Martin, 'Remember when I first gleaned that you were Arutha's brother?'

Martin said, 'How could I forget? That was my first voyage, and you almost drowned us all.'

'Saved your worthless skin with my masterful sailing, you mean,' answered Amos. Waving a hand at Nicholas and Marcus, he said, 'But if the world ever needed proof of your parentage, there it stands revealed.' He stroked his chin. 'I think we'll have to paint one of them green so we can tell them apart.'

Nicholas looked at Amos in confusion, but Marcus's face was an unreadable mask. Amos said, 'The resemblance.'

Nicholas said, 'What resemblance?'

'To each other,' answered the admiral.

Nicholas turned to regard his cousin. 'Do you think . . . ?'

Marcus shook his head slightly. 'I don't see it . . . Highness.'

Amos laughed and said, 'You never will.'

Martin continued the introductions. 'Highness, this is my daughter, Margaret.'

One of the two young girls curtsied. Her hair was dark like her brother's, but she resembled her mother. Nature had given her a straight nose and high cheekbones, but with a less severe cast than Briana's. She wore her hair long to her shoulders, like her mother, without any adornment. Dark eyes glanced up at the Prince as he said, 'A pleasure, cousin.' She smiled at the greeting, and instantly she was lovely.

Nicholas's gaze drifted to the young woman at Margaret's side, and he felt his chest tighten. Cornflower-blue eyes that seemed the largest he had ever encountered regarded him. Suddenly he felt clumsy and unsure of himself. Margaret said, 'This is my companion, the Lady

Abigail, daughter of Baron Bellamy of Carse.' The slender girl curtsied and Nicholas was certain he had never seen anyone do it so gracefully. Unlike Margaret, Abigail had her blond hair gathered up in a silver circlet behind her head, where it cascaded in ringlets. Her skin was pale and clear and her features delicate. She smiled as she arose from her curtsy, and Nicholas couldn't help but smile back. After a moment the smile became a silly grin.

The sound of a throat clearing behind him brought Nicholas from his trance. He said, 'M'lady,' and his voice sounded strained in his own ears. Nicholas turned back toward Martin and said, 'This is Harry, my Squire,' as his companion came down the gangway, carrying Nicholas's and his own travel bags. The boy dropped them on the ground and bowed before the Duke of Crydee. Seeing the Princess and her companion, he grinned broadly.

Martin indicated that Nicholas should ride in the first carriage with himself and his lady. Harry began to walk after them, when Amos's hand again descended and gripped him by the shoulder. 'The first carriage is for the Prince, the Duke, and the Duchess. The second is for myself and the Duke's children.'

Harry said, 'But – '

Amos pointed to the wagons. 'You can make sure your Prince's luggage is in order as it's unloaded and packed on yon wagons. Then you can ride one of them when you're done.'

Nakor and Ghuda came down the gangplank and Harry said, 'What about them?'

Nakor grinned. 'We'll walk. It's not that far.' He pointed to the castle on the hill overlooking the harbor.

Ghuda said, 'I could use a little stretch.'

Harry sighed and took the two bags over to the first wagon. A drover said, 'Here, boy, what's this?'

Harry was in an ill temper and snapped, 'Prince of Krondor's baggage! I'm his *Squire*!'

The man made a lazy salute as he continued to lean against the wagon and said, 'Then where will you be wanting that lot, Squire?' He pointed.

Harry turned and saw the first load of luggage coming off the ship, as a pair of sailors carried one of Nicholas's heavy trunks down the gangway. It was followed by three more like it. As the creak of wood and the hum of ropes filled the air, a large cargo net from deep within the ship's hole rose majestically into view. Another dozen trunks and other assorted baggage was hauled over the side and lowered to the quay. Dock hands jumped to and began unfastening the net.

The drover said, 'And I suppose you know where that lot's to go, Squire?'

With a sign of resignation, Harry reached back into the wagon and pulled out the two bags that had been his and Nicholas's source of clothing and personal items for the weeks they had been aboard ship. Obviously, they would be among the last pieces to be loaded. Shaking his head, Harry said, 'And I'm supposed to supervise?'

With a knowing wink, the drover pushed himself away from the wagon. 'It'll go faster and be easier on us all, Squire, if you do your supervising from over there.' He pointed to a doorway a dozen yards off. 'Nice ale, good meat pies, and you can supervise through the window.'

Harry's mouth watered at the thought of meat pies after the ship's plain fare. But he said, 'No, I have my duty.'

The drover shook his head. 'Then do us both a favor, Squire, and supervise real quiet-like, if you catch my drift.'

Harry nodded and moved out of the way as the first pair of trunks were carried over to the wagon. He found himself a shady patch under the overhanging roof of the customs house and leaned against the wall. Glancing up the hill, he could see that Ghuda and Nakor were already leaving the dock area and walking up the broad street that ran through the town to the castle. They would most likely be in the castle a hour before Harry. Muttering to himself, Harry said, 'I thought this was going to be interesting.'

As the first carriage rolled into the castle courtyard, two rows of soldiers snapped to attention. Each wore the brown and gold tabard of Crydee and carried a shield with the golden sea gull of Crydee upon a brown field, and from each halberd a brown and golden pennant hung. Their armor shone in the sun. As a coachman opened the door and Nicholas stepped out, a short, bandy-legged man with grey hair and a leathery face shouted, 'Salute!' At once the soldiers snapped to attention. The halberds dipped, and after a moment the company of soldiers pulled them back. Martin and the others stepped out of the carriage, then the drivers urged the horses on to the carriage house in back.

Nicholas took a good long look at his new home. Castle Crydee was small in comparison to what he knew. There was an ancient keep, around which a single surrounding building had been erected, and later another hall had been added to the rear. Nicholas quickly calculated distances, and found with some disapproval that whoever had erected the outer wall had left a relatively narrow bailey. Should the wall ever be breached, there was little to keep an invader from reaching the central keep.

As if reading his mind, Martin said, 'My great-grandfather took this keep from the Keshian garrison stationed here, and built the wall around it.' With a half-smile that reminded Nicholas of his own father, he added, 'My grandfather built the two additional halls, leaving little further room for growth. Father planned on pushing the wall out to accommodate new growth . . . but he never

71

got around to it.' He put his hand upon Nicholas's shoulder. 'I never seem to find the time, either.'

A large black-skinned man, with a short black beard, walked slightly behind the short grey-haired man as the pair advanced between the lines of soldiers to come before Nicholas. They both bowed to the Prince.

Amos grinned at the short man. 'Swordmaster Charles!'

Martin said, 'Highness, my Swordmaster, Charles, and Horsemaster Faxon.'

Nicholas returned their salutes with an inclination of his head, and spoke a few words to Charles in a foreign language. The Swordmaster bowed and answered in the same language. Then in the King's Tongue he said, 'You speak excellent Tsurani, Highness.'

Nicholas blushed. 'Only a few words, really. But all in the court know of Uncle Martin's Tsurani Swordmaster.' To the dark-skinned man be said, 'And Horsemaster Faxon.'

Faxon said, 'Your Highness.'

Martin introduced other members of his household, and when the formalities were over, he took Nicholas by the arm. 'If your Highness will come with me.'

Martin and Nicholas mounted the steps to the castle, while Martin's children and Abigail followed, heading back to their own quarters.

Briana turned to Amos. 'We'll have a reception tonight, but in the meantime, we'll have someone show you to your quarters.'

Amos said, 'Just tell me which room, my lady. I lived here too many years to get lost.'

Briana smiled. 'Your old room is yours again, Amos.'

Amos glanced at the main gate to the castle, noting the pair of guards standing at their posts. 'You might tell those lads that in a few minutes a pair of very unlikely characters will heave into view. One's a short madman from Shing Lai named Nakor, and the other is a tall mercenary from Kesh, name of Ghuda Bulé. Let them in, as they're companions to Nicky.'

Briana's only reply was to raise an eyebrow. She turned to Swordmaster Charles and said, 'See to it, please.'

He saluted and hurried off to the gate to inform the guards.

Briana said, 'Who are these men, Amos?'

Forcing a light air, Amos said, 'As original a pair as you'd meet anywhere.'

Briana put her hand upon Amos's shoulder. They had served together in Armengar, her home, when Amos had aided in its defense against the armies of the Brotherhood of the Dark Path. 'I understand you well enough to know there's something else. What is it?'

Amos shook his head. 'Just . . . something Arutha told me before I left.' He glanced at the main door of the castle through which Martin and Nicholas had just passed. 'He said that should anything happen, listen to Nakor.'

Briana was silent a moment, thinking, then said, 'I have no doubt that "anything" means trouble.'

Amos forced a laugh. 'Well, I doubt he meant listen to the wizard if there was a surprise party!'

Briana answered with a smile. She gave Amos a hug and kissed his cheek. 'We've missed you, and your humor, Amos.'

Amos glanced around, remembering. 'I've seen too many men die on those walls and spent too many days defending them to have missed Crydee, Briana.' Then he kissed her cheek and squeezed her in a bear hug. 'But damn me if I haven't missed you and Martin.'

Arms around each other's waists, the tall Duchess and the large sea captain walked up the steps into Castle Crydee.

Martin indicated Nicholas should sit and moved behind a large desk. The Duke's office looked small compared to

Arutha's in Krondor, and Nicholas glanced around.

Behind Martin, on the wall, was the sea gull banner of Crydee. Above the bird's head were the faint outlines of a crown, where a piece of material had been removed. Nicholas knew that once his own grandfather had held this office, and had also been second in line to the crown Nicholas's uncle now wore. But Martin's line was prevented from inheritance by an illegitimate birth, and all marks of such succession had been removed from the family coat-of-arms.

Martin said, 'This office was your father's for a while, during the years of the Riftwar, Nicholas. Before that it was your grandfather's, and his father's and grandfather's before him.'

Nicholas noticed that beyond that one ducal banner, the walls were devoid of personal mementos or trophies; only a large map of the Duchy and another of the Kingdom graced the otherwise bare stone. Martin's desk was equally well ordered, with a solitary inkwell and quill, a bar of red wax for the ducal signet, and a candle. Two rolled parchments hinted at some unfinished business, but otherwise there was a sense of organization in this room, as if the present occupant was loath to leave at the end of the day with any task unfinished or unresolved. There was something familiar in that, Nicholas realized, as that drive for order was also a hallmark of his father. He returned his attention to his uncle, who was watching him closely. Nicholas flushed.

Martin smiled and said, 'You are with family, Nicholas, never forget that.'

Nicholas shrugged. 'I've heard Father tell of Crydee, and Amos has war stories that never end, but . . .' He glanced around once more. 'I guess I didn't know what to expect.'

Martin said, 'That's why you're here. Arutha wished you to know something of your heritage.

'We've a rough court, by Krondorian standards,' he continued. 'Close to primitive by the standards of Rillanon and the other eastern courts. But you'll find it comfortable enough in the ways that matter.'

Nicholas nodded. 'What exactly will I be doing?

Martin said, 'Arutha has left that up to me. I think for the time being I'm going to name you my Squire. You're a little old for the position, but that way you can stay close, and perhaps after a while I'll find better use for you. I'll assign your friend to Marcus.'

Nicholas was about to object when Martin said, 'Squires do not have squires, Nicholas.' Nicholas nodded.

'Tonight we'll have a formal reception, with a troupe of players who are in the town. Then tomorrow you'll begin your duties.'

'What will those be?'

'Housecarl Samuel will fill you in on some of your duties. Swordmaster Charles and Horsemaster Faxon will have others for you. You will do several things every day, mostly to make my time more efficient in governing the Duchy. You may have noticed new buildings above the south bluffs and beyond. Crydee is becoming quite the metropolis by Far Coast standards. There is much to be done. Now I'll have a servant show you to your rooms.'

'Thank you, Uncle Martin.' Nicholas rose as Martin came around the desk and opened the door, signaling for a servant to approach.

Martin said, 'Beginning tomorrow, Your Highness, you will address me as "Your Grace". You will be addressed as "Squire".'

Nicholas flushed, feeling embarrassed but not knowing why. He nodded and followed the servant to his quarters.

That night Nicholas sat between his uncle and his cousin Marcus. The food was hearty if plain, the wine was robust and flavorful, and the entertainment adequate. Nicholas spent the better part of the evening glancing past his aunt and uncle to where Abigail sat beside Margaret. The two girls seemed to have their heads together the better part of the meal, and several times Nicholas found himself blushing without quite knowing why. The few attempts he made at speaking with Marcus resulted in short answers and long silences. Nicholas was beginning to feel that somehow his cousin disliked him.

Amos, Nakor, and Ghuda Bulé were all at the far end of the table, beyond Nicholas's ability to speak to them. They were obviously having a good enough time swapping stories with Swordmaster Charles and Horsemaster Faxon.

Looking down the table, Nicholas saw Harry attempting to engage a quiet young man in conversation. The man seemed to speak quietly, as Harry was constantly leaning over to hear him. The man seemed not much older than the boys, perhaps in his late teens or early twenties. He had a shock of blond hair that hung to his shoulders, and had bangs that seemed to threaten his vision every moment, as he was constantly brushing them back with his hand. His eyes were blue, and Nicholas imagined that if he ever smiled, he'd be a likable-enough-looking chap.

'Cousin, who is that?'

Marcus looked to where Nicholas indicated. 'That's Anthony. He's a magician.'

'Really?' asked Nicholas, pleased that he had finally gotten more than one sentence from his cousin. 'What's he doing here?'

'My father asked your father to intercede with the masters of Stardock to send a magician to us a few years ago.' Marcus shrugged. 'Something to do with Grandfather, I think.' He put down the rib bone he had been gnawing, dipped his hands in the finger bowl, and wiped them on a linen napkin. 'Did your father ever talk about having a magician at court?'

Relieved that they were at last engaged in something like a conversation, Nicholas shrugged. 'A few stories. About Kulgan and Pug, I mean. I met Pug on this journey.'

Marcus kept his eyes upon the magician. 'Anthony is a good fellow, I'll warrant you that, friendly when you get to know him. But he keeps to himself a great deal, and those few times Father asks him for counsel, he tends towards the evasive. I fear the magicians at Stardock sent him here as something of a joke.'

'Really?'

Marcus fixed Nicholas with a sour look. 'You keep asking "really" as if I'm making this up.'

'Sorry,' said Nicholas, blushing a little. 'It's just a habit. What I mean is, why do you think the masters of Stardock would do that, send him here as a joke?'

'Because he's not a very good magician, from what I can tell of such things.'

Nicholas caught himself as he was about to say 'Really?' and instead changed it to, 'Interesting. I mean, you don't see a lot of magicians anywhere, but the few who've come to court don't do much by way of magic, at least not anywhere you can see them.'

Marcus shrugged. 'I guess he has his uses, but there's something about him that makes me cautious. He's got secrets.'

Nicholas laughed. Marcus turned to see if Nicholas was laughing at him. Nicholas said, 'I think that's part of the act, you know. Lurking in shadows and mysteries and the rest.'

Marcus shrugged again, allowing himself a faint smile. 'Perhaps. Anyway, he's Father's adviser, though he doesn't do much of that.'

Glad to be involved at last in something other than silence, Nicholas pursued the conversation. 'You know, I knew Horsemaster Faxon's father. I didn't know he'd bear such a resemblance to the old Duke.'

Marcus grunted a noncommittal sound. 'Gardan was an old man when he came back from Krondor. I never noticed.'

Feeling the conversation slipping away, Nicholas said, 'I was sorry to hear of his death last year.'

Marcus shrugged, his most expressive gesture, it seemed. 'He didn't do much but fish and tell stories. He was an old man. I liked him enough, but . . .' Again he shrugged. 'You get old, then you die. That's the way it works, isn't it?'

It was Nicholas's turn to shrug. 'I hadn't seen him for almost ten years. I guess he got older.' Realizing instantly that the remark was inane, he let the conversation lapse into silence for the rest of the meal.

At the finish of the meal, Martin rose and said, 'We welcome to our home our cousin Nicholas.' The gathered court and servants gave polite applause. 'Beginning tomorrow, he shall be acting as my Squire.' At this, Harry glanced at his friend with a questioning expression. Nicholas shrugged.

Martin said, 'And his companion, Harry of Ludland, will be Squire to my son.'

Harry made a face that said, Well, that answers that.

'Now,' said Martin. 'I bid you all good night.'

He extended his hand and Briana placed hers upon it, in ceremonial fashion, and he led her from the table. The ladies Margaret and Abigail followed, and then Marcus rose. Turning to Harry, he said, 'Well then, if you're to squire for me, I need you awake an hour before sunrise. Ask any servant where my quarters are and don't be late.' Turning to Nicholas, he said, 'Father will want you ready, too.'

Nicholas didn't care much for his cousin's tone, but he refused to be anything but polite. 'I'll be there.'

Marcus smiled and it was a shock, for it was the first time since meeting him that Nicholas had seen any expression other than a neutral frown. 'I expect you will.' Waving to the servants, he said, 'Show the Squires to their quarters.'

The boys fell in behind two servants, and as they passed by the magician, Harry said, 'See you around, Anthony.'

The magician muttered a reply. When they entered a long hallway, Harry said, 'That's the Duke's magician.'

'I know,' answered Nicholas. 'Marcus said he wasn't very good at his job.'

Harry indicated he had no opinion on that topic, but added, 'He seems a right enough fellow, if a little shy. Mumbles a bit.'

The servants led the two young men to doors next to one another. Nicholas opened the indicated one and entered what could only be considered a cell. It was barely ten feet in length and eight feet wide. A straw pallet lay on the floor and a small chest for personal belongings took up one corner of the room. A tiny table, a chair, and a rude lamp on the table were the only other features. Nicholas turned to the servant, who was walking away, and said, 'Where are my things?'

The servant said, 'In storage, Squire. His Grace said you won't need them until you're ready to leave, so he had them put down in the sub-basement. You'll find all you need in the chest.'

Harry clapped his friend upon the shoulder. 'Well, Squire Nicky, better turn in and get a good night's sleep. We're up early tomorrow.'

'Don't let me oversleep,' said Nicholas, with a sinking feeling in his stomach.

'What's it worth to you?'

Nicholas said, 'How about I don't knock you on your backside?'

Harry appeared to consider this for a moment, then said, 'Seems fair to me.' With a laugh he said, 'Don't worry. You'll get used to being a squire. Look at me; I've done right well being yours.'

He entered his own room, and Nicholas looked heavenward, as if to say, because you've never had to act like one. With a feeling of deep foreboding, he entered his cell, closed the door, and undressed. Blowing out the lamp, he made his way in the dark toward the pallet, and lying on the straw-packed sack, he pulled the single blanket up over him. The rest of the night was spent tossing and turning, with only a little rest and a deep sense of dread.

Nicholas was awake when the knock came. He fumbled his way in the dark and realized with a sinking feeling that he hadn't located any means to light the lamp before he had blown it out. He found the door handle in the dark and opened the door. Harry, who stood there, said, 'You planning on going like that?'

Feeling silly standing in only his undertrousers, Nicholas said, 'I forgot to locate the flint and steel.'

'They're on the table, behind the lamp, where they usually are. I'll light it; you get dressed.'

Nicholas opened the chest and found a simple tunic and trousers in brown and green, which he took to be the uniform of a Crydee squire, as Harry was garbed in like fashion. He put them on and found them a close enough fit. Pulling on his own boots, he said, 'What is this business of awaking before dawn.'

Harry put down the now burning lamp, closed the door, and said, 'Farmers, I guess.'

'Farmers?'

'You know. Country people. Always up before dawn, asleep with the chickens.'

Nicholas grunted a vague acknowledgment of the remark as he pulled on his boots. His left foot seemed slightly swollen, which made getting the specially made boot on that more difficult. 'Damn,' he said, 'must be damper here than at home.'

Harry said, 'You noticed! You mean the mold growing on the stones next to your bed didn't give you a hint?'

Nicholas swung a lazy backhand at Harry, which he avoided easily. 'Come on,' he said with a laugh, 'it wouldn't do to be late our first day.'

Nicholas and Harry found themselves alone in the hallway and suddenly Harry said, 'Where are the servants?'

'We're the servants, you dolt,' said Nicholas. 'I think I know where the family quarters are.'

By trial and error, the boys found their way through the castle to the family's wing. Modest quarters compared to what the Prince was used to at home, they were nevertheless considerably more comfortable than the cells the boys had inhabited the night before. A pair of servants were leaving two of the rooms, and Nicholas asked and was told that they were indeed Lord Martin and Lady Briana's quarters and young Master Marcus's.

Taking up their stations by the respective doors, the boys waited. After a few moments, Nicholas ventured a quiet knock. The door opened and Martin looked out and said, 'I'll be with you in a few minutes, Squire.'

Before Nicholas could answer, 'Yes, Your Grace,' the door was closed in his face.

Harry grinned and raised his hand to knock, but before his knuckles could strike wood, the door opened and Marcus stepped through. 'You're late,' he snapped. 'Come along.' He hurried down the hallway, and Harry almost had to leap to catch up with him.

A few minutes later, Martin emerged from his bed-chamber and moved down the hall without comment. Nicholas fell in behind him and followed along. Instead of heading for the main hall, as the boy expected, the Duke moved through the quiet keep to the main entrance, where stable hands were bringing out horses. Marcus and Harry could be seen riding out the gate as a servant thrust reins in Nicholas's direction.

Martin said, 'You can ride?'

Nicholas said, 'Of course . . . Your Grace,' he added quickly.

'Good. We've no shortage of green horses that need a firm hand out.'

As he climbed aboard, Nicholas instantly found himself in a contest with the horse. A quick half-halt jerk to the mouth and a hard seat brought the fractious animal under control. The gelding was young and probably had been cut late, given the stallion-like crest of his neck and his aggressive behavior. Nicholas also didn't care for the heavy saddle, which made contact with the animal difficult.

But Martin gave him no time for consideration of the finer points of horsemanship, having turned his animal and headed for the gate. Nicholas put heels to the sides of his mount and found he had to use a lot of leg to keep the horse moving forward. Then the explosion came: the animal bucked hard before trying to race through the courtyard. Nicholas automatically gripped with his legs, sinking down in the saddle and giving a quick and firm halt on the reins. He guided the horse into a circle, half-halting with the reins until the animal was calmed down to a nice posting trot. Then, when he was at the Duke's side, Nicholas slowed the animal down to a walk to match the Duke's mount.

'Did you sleep well, Squire?'

'Not really, Your Grace.'

'Aren't the quarters to your liking?' asked Martin.

Nicholas looked to see if he was being mocked, and saw only an impassive face regarding him.

'No, they're adequate,' he said, refusing to be baited into complaining. 'It's the newness of all this, I guess.'

'You'll get used to Crydee,' Martin said.

'Does Your Grace usually not eat in the morning?' asked Nicholas, his stomach already noticing the absence of breakfast.

Martin smiled, a slight upturn of his mouth, much like Nicholas's father's half-smiles, and said, 'Oh, we'll break fast, but there's always a couple of hours' work to do before we dine, Squire.'

Nicholas nodded.

They entered the town, and Nicholas saw that the streets were already busy. Shops might still have their windows shuttered and their doors locked, but workers were already on their way to the docks, the mills, and other places of work. Fishing boats could be seen heading out of the harbor in the grey light of dawn, the sun not yet above the distant mountains. Rich smells filled the air as bakers continued the work they had begun the night before, getting ready the day's wares.

A familiar voice cut the air as they reached the docks. 'Get those nets ready!' shouted Amos.

Nicholas saw that the Admiral was supervising the loading of some stores from the dockside. Marcus appeared around a corner, walking along beside a slow-moving wagon, Harry a step behind him. 'That's the last of it, Father,' Marcus called.

Martin didn't explain to Nicholas what was happening, but the Prince deduced that Martin was adding to the cargo bound to the new garrison up north. The Duke called, 'Amos, are you going to make the morning tide?'

'With minutes to spare,' roared back Amos, '*if* these

ham-fisted monkeys can get this cargo aboard in the next half hour!'

The dock workers seemed oblivious to the shouting, taking it as a matter of course, while they efficiently went about the business of loading the cargo nets. When they were full, the crew on the hoist raised up the cargo and swung it above the hold of the ship, lowering it down without missing a beat.

Amos came over to where Martin and Nicholas watched. 'The hard part's going to be unloading that mess. I figure the soldiers at the garrison can give us a hand, but it'll still take two or three weeks to get it all off the ship by longboat.'

'Are you going to have time for a visit on the way back?'

'Ample,' Amos replied with a grin. 'Even should I be gone a month, I can spend a few days here before we head back to Krondor. If the unloading goes quickly, I might give the men a week of rest before we brave the straits.'

'I'm sure they'll appreciate it,' said Martin.

As the net was quickly reloaded and the last of the cargo hauled away, Martin said to Nicholas, 'Ride back to the castle and tell Housecarl Samuel that we'll be up for our meal in a half hour.'

Nicholas started to turn, then said, 'Should I return here . . . Your Grace?'

Martin said, 'What do you think?'

Because he didn't know what to think, Nicholas's answer sounded awkward in his own ear. 'I'm not sure.'

Martin's tone was not scolding, but it wasn't warm, either. 'You're my squire. Your place is at my side until I tell you otherwise. Return as soon as you've done what I've told you.'

Feeling somehow inadequate for not having known that, Nicholas blushed furiously. 'At once, Your Grace.'

He set heels to the gelding and let the horse stretch out into a canter as he hurried away from the docks. Nearing the busy streets of the town he was forced to slow to a trot. Any horseman was likely to be a noble or a soldier, so most gave way as they heard Nicholas ride up behind or saw him coming. Still, he had to move cautiously. Slowing to a walk, he took in the sights around him. Shops were now opening and traders began setting their wares out in windows as costermongers displayed their produce upon their wagons, and more workers made their way to their places of employment. A couple of young women, not more than a year or two older than Nicholas, whispered to each other as he passed.

Crydee was strange to Nicholas. It was neither the rich quarters of Krondor nor the slums of the city; it was something else. The beggars one found haunting the merchants' quarters in Krondor were absent, as well as the thieves one didn't see, he suspected. He also doubted he'd find whores on the corner near the taverns in the evening, though he didn't doubt there were ample ladies of salable affections in the taverns near the docks. The heavy industry, the large mills, the dyers, the tanners, the wagonwrights, and the rest, were not evident. No doubt there were some dyers and tanners in Crydee, but the reek of their trade didn't reveal them the way it did down by the harbor in the Prince's city.

No, Crydee was a town – A big, bustling, growing town, but not a city, and as such it was a place both wondrous and fearful to Nicholas. His nervousness at being away from home was offset by his curiosity about this new place and the people in it.

Clearing the eastern edge of the town proper, he kicked his animal into another canter and hurried toward the castle. His desire to be efficient doing Martin's bidding was secondary to a more basic motivation: he was hungry.

4

Squire

Nicholas stumbled.

Harry said as he passed his friend, 'Hurry, or Samuel will have our ears!'

In the week since they had come to serve at Crydee, the boys had discovered their bane: Housecarl Samuel. The old steward, approaching eighty years of age, had been in the service of the ducal household of Crydee since Nicholas's grandfather's time. And he could still wield a stout switch.

The morning after Amos departed, Harry had stopped upon an errand to make the acquaintance of some local girls, and had returned overly late from his mission to find a tight-lipped Samuel waiting for him. When shown the switch, Harry had tried to joke his way past the punishment, for he hadn't been whipped since leaving his father's estates. When it was evident the old man wasn't jesting, Harry had shrugged off the punishment until he discovered that while Samuel was old, there was nothing feeble about his switch. Nicholas had tried to avoid the same punishment, but on the third day had managed to make hash of a series of tasks for the Duke. For a while he had faintly hoped that his rank would spare him the punishment, but all Samuel said was 'In my time I've switched your uncle the King, boy.'

The two Squires were racing across the courtyard to meet with their supervisor at first light. The Housecarl would inform them if there were any unusual duties to perform instead of reporting to their respective stations outside the Duke and Marcus's rooms. Usually, they were to remain available to Martin and his son should they need the boys, but sometimes the Duke thought of something for them to do after they had gone to bed; he would pass instructions through the Housecarl.

Reaching the hall that led to the old man's office, they found him opening the door as they hove into view. The rule was simple: if they weren't there by the time he was seated behind the large table he used as a work desk, they were late and would be punished.

Scrambling down the hall, the two boys were through the portal as the reed-thin old man sat down. Raising one nearly white eyebrow, he said, 'Cutting it a bit fine today, aren't we, boys?'

Harry tried to smile, but failed in the attempt. 'Anything special, sir?'

Samuel's eyes narrowed a moment as he thought; then he said, 'Harry, to the harbor and see if the mail packet from Carse came in during the night. It was due in yesterday, and if it still is not here, the Duke wants to know.' Harry didn't wait to see if Nicholas had anything special; when an order was given by the Housecarl, a lowly court page or squire didn't dare linger. Samuel continued, 'Nicholas, attend your master.'

Nicholas hurried back toward the Duke's quarters. Now that he was no longer dashing through the still-dark corridors, he suddenly felt very tired. He was not an early riser by nature. This business of being up before sunrise was taking its toll.

From the morning after the welcoming banquet, the alien quality of being in this frontier castle was slowly being replaced with a familiar routine: either being in a hurry or standing around waiting. And the hours were from before dawn to after the evening meal. The Prince had expected things to be somewhat different, but the impact of just how different things were was beginning to gnaw at Nicholas.

He reached Martin and Briana's chamber door and

waited. If the past week's experience was any predictor, the Duke and Duchess would both be awake and dressing and coming through that door in the next few minutes. Nicholas turned and leaned back against the wall. He gazed through a window that looked out over the court-yard and the town beyond the wall. The grey of morning was deep, and while Nicholas was becoming used to the landmarks of Crydee, there was still barely enough light to make out details. Within the hour the sun would rise, and the town would be bathed in morning brilliance – or still grey with overcast. The weather around here was very difficult to predict, Nicholas observed.

He yawned and wished he were back on his pallet. No, he corrected himself, he wished he were back in his own bed in Krondor. He had to admit that fatigue made the straw-stuffed mattress tolerable, but he would never think of it as comfortable. Nicholas still grappled with home-sickness, but only in rare moments like these when he had a few minutes to think about himself. The rest of the time he was too busy.

His uncle made Nicholas uncomfortable. Before he came to Crydee, his memories of Martin were of a large man with big, gentle hands who had carried him on his shoulders for a time when visiting Krondor. That had been nearly fourteen years ago. Martin had visited the Prince's court once since then, but Nicholas had been ill in bed at the time and had only had a five-minute visit from Martin. Now the warm, gentle memory of a large uncle was being replaced by the reality of a distant man.

Unlike Samuel, Martin never seemed to lose his temper or raise his voice. But he had a way of looking at the boys that made them wish they could crawl off into a hole and hide. If Nicholas or Harry failed in a task, he would say nothing, but turn away with unspoken disapproval in the air. It was for the boys to correct their errors.

Harry at least had Marcus, who was more than willing

to inform him how he was failing. Some of the staff had made it clear that part of Marcus's coolness toward the boys was due in part to the fact that until shortly before Nicholas's arrival he had squired for his father, so of course he was measuring everything they did by his own performance. Nicholas had once made the mistake of protesting that it wasn't fair to chide them for not knowing where something was when sent upon an errand, and Marcus had turned and cooly said, 'Then you need to find out where it is, don't you?'

The door opened and Nicholas came awake. Briana proceeded her husband from the sleeping room and smiled. 'Good morning, Squire.'

'My lady,' Nicholas said, bowing to her. His court manners always made her smile, and it had become something of a little game between them.

Martin closed the door as he came through and said, 'Nicholas, the Duchess and I ride alone this morning. Have our horses made ready.'

'Your Grace,' said Nicholas, and with that he was off down the hallway at a run. Samuel had informed Nicholas that when Briana and Martin went riding at dawn, it was usually a two- or three-hour trip, so the Squire knew they'd be stopping in the kitchen for some provisions. He decided a little initiative was called for and dashed for the kitchen.

Reaching the kitchen, he found the servants hard at work readying the meals for the nearly two hundred people who lived within the walls of Castle Crydee. Mastercook Megar, a solidly built old man, stood in the center of the kitchen supervising every aspect of his crew's labors. His old wife, Magya, hovered near the stove, her still-keen eyes fixed upon what cooked there. Nicholas slowed to a walk as he entered, saying, 'Mastercook, the Duke and his lady ride this morning.'

Megar gave Nicholas a friendly smile and a wave. The

kitchen had turned out to be the only place in the castle where Harry and Nicholas had found warm greetings, for the old cook and his wife seemed to have a fondness for boys. 'I know, Squire, I know.' He pointed to a saddle pack being filled with food. 'But it was a good thought,' he added with a grin. 'Now off to the stable with you!'

Friendly laughter followed Nicholas as he hurried from the kitchen, dashing outside toward the stable. Reaching the stabling area, he found it still quiet and knew that Rulf, the senior stableman, was still asleep. How the man had gained his rank was a mystery to Nicholas, although he had been told his father had held the position before him. As the boy hurried through the dark stable, the horses nickered in greeting and some stuck their heads through the stall doors, seeing if he might be arriving with something to eat.

At the far end of the breezeway, he almost ran into a still figure that had been hidden in the gloom. A dark face turned toward him and a soft voice said, 'Quiet, Squire.'

Horsemaster Faxon pointed through the door, and there upon his pallet lay the stout figure of Rulf, snoring loudly enough to rattle the heavens, thought Nicholas.

'Seems a pity to disturb such peace, doesn't it?'

Nicholas tried not to grin as he said, 'The Duke and Duchess ride this morning, Horsemaster.'

'Well, in that case . . .' said Faxon, as he picked up a water bucket, took one step across the small room, and emptied the contents upon the reclining figure. Rulf sat up with a gasp and uttered a cry of pure aggravation. 'Agh! What – '

'You oaf!' shouted Faxon, all friendliness vanishing from his manner. 'The day is half over and you're lying in your bed dreaming of town girls!'

Rulf sat up sputtering, and when he saw Nicholas, for a moment his eyes narrowed, as if the boy were the cause of his misery. Then he came fully awake and saw the

Horsemaster, and his manner changed. 'Sorry, Master Faxon.'

'Duke Martin and Lady Briana need their mounts! If the horses aren't tacked up and ready by the time my lord and lady are upon the front steps of the keep I'll have your ears upon the stable door!'

The heavyset man arose with a sour look, but said only, 'At once, Master Faxon.' Turning toward the loft, he shouted, 'Tom! Sam! You lazy boys! Get up! We have work to do and you didn't wake me as I told you to!'

Sleepy grunts from the loft answered, and a moment later, two young men scampered down the ladder from the hayloft. They were about a year apart in age, from their look, in their mid-twenties, and both bore an unmistakable resemblance to Rulf. He swore at them and sent them scrambling to get the indicated horses. Turning to Faxon, he said, 'They'll be ready in no time, Master Faxon.'

Nicholas turned to see Faxon regarding the three of them. 'One would never know it to look at them, Squire, but they're unusually good with the horses. Rulf's father was Horsemaster Algon's stableman when I was a boy.'

'Is that why you keep Rulf on?' asked Nicholas.

Faxon nodded. 'You'd probably never guess, but he was very brave when the Tsurani besieged the castle during the Riftwar. Many times he carried water to the soldiers – myself being one of them – right into the battle, armed with nothing more than two buckets.'

'Really?'

Faxon grinned. 'Really.'

Nicholas blushed. 'I've got to stop doing that.'

Faxon clapped him upon the shoulder. 'You'll get over it.' He looked out through the breezeway to where Rulf and his sons were tacking up the horses. 'And I feel sorry for Rulf since his wife died. She was the only gentle thing in his life. He and his sons have only one another and the stable. They have quarters over in the servants' wing, but they sleep here most of the time.'

Nicholas nodded. He realized at that moment he had always taken servants for granted, and there were those who had served him at Krondor of whom he knew nothing. He had just assumed, somehow, that they vanished into a servants' closet, keeping quietly out of sight until they were needed. Coming out of his reverie, he said, 'I'd best be back to the Duke.'

'The horses will be ready,' answered Faxon.

Nicholas hurried back to the kitchen and indeed found Martin and Briana there, inspecting the provisions. The Duke and his wife approved the selection of food. Briana motioned for a pair of servants to follow her out of the kitchen. Martin headed toward the armory. Without a word, Nicholas fell in behind him. When they reached the armory, a soldier on guard saluted and opened the door for Martin and Nicholas.

Inside, Martin waited while Nicholas quickly lit a lantern against the gloom of the always dark room. When the light flared, it was reflected from a thousand angles, dancing across polished metal. Racks of swords and spears, shields and helms, covered every wall. Nicholas hurried to another door and opened it for Martin, anticipating his need.

Martin stepped into the small room where his personal arms were stored, and selected a longbow that hung on one wall. He handed it to Nicholas while he himself filled a quiver with the long arrows called cloth yard shafts, because they were thirty-seven inches long, the measure a miller used to cut a yard of cloth. Nicholas had never seen a longbow's effects, as the soldiers at Krondor were all armed with crossbows or the small horse bow used by the cavalry, but he had heard tales of the weapon's fearful power: that a skilled bowman could punch a steel-headed shaft through nearly any armor.

Nicholas knew that his uncle had served as their grand-father's Huntmaster, back at a time when Martin's birth-right had been hidden from all but a few of the old Duke's most trusted advisers. Just before his death, Lord Borric had legitimized his eldest son, raising him from the ranks of the common to become in time Duke of Crydee, inheritor of his father's title. But before then Martin was still acknowledged as one of the finest bowmen in the Western Realm.

The Duke handed Nicholas the quiver of arrows. He inspected a row of blades upon a table, before choosing two large hunting knives and handing them to Nicholas. He then selected another bow, for Duchess Briana, which he also gave to Nicholas. A quiver of arrows for the shorter bow was his last choice, and they departed.

They reached the courtyard to find Lady Briana stand-ing next to a pair of horses. Nicholas didn't need to be told that this was not merely a morning ride but a hunting trip, and the Duke and his wife would probably be gone for the day or longer, if they decided to sleep in the forest.

Harry raced into view and between gasps for breath said, 'Your Grace. No word yet on the packet boat from Carse.'

Martin's expression darkened. 'Have Marcus pen a note for Lord Bellamy in Carse, asking if the boat turned back to Carse for some reason, then send it by pigeon.'

Harry bowed and started to run off, but Martin stopped him by saying, 'And, Squire . . .'

Harry stopped and turned. 'Your Grace?'

'Next time you're sent to the harbor on an errand, take a horse.'

Harry grinned sheepishly and bowed. 'Your Grace,' he said, and hurried off to do Martin's bidding.

Briana mounted without waiting for any unnecessary assistance and Nicholas handed her a bow, quiver, and knife. After Martin was mounted, Nicholas gave the remaining weapons to the Duke.

Martin said, 'We may be gone until tomorrow sunset, Squire.'

Nicholas said, 'Your Grace?'

'Today is Sixthday, if it's escaped your notice.' It had. 'You may have the afternoon to yourself. See to Master Samuel for any further instructions until we return.'

'Yes, Your Grace.'

As they rode out of the courtyard, Nicholas sighed. Sixthday: traditionally a half day of rest for the children of any castle or palace. Seventhday was a day of contemplation and worship, though Nicholas had noticed there were always plenty of servants to do his bidding back in Krondor on Seventhday. He and Harry had arrived on Seventhday the week before, so he had no idea what to expect with his first free time since coming off the ship.

The sound of boys shouting echoed across the side courtyard, near a small garden, which was called the Princess's Garden. It had been the province of Nicholas's aunt, the Princess Carline, when she had lived in Crydee, and the name had stuck.

A rough game of football was under way, with one of the soldiers acting as refereee. The teams were composed of the sons of the castle's servants, a few pages, and two of the younger squires. An area of the approved size had been chalked out in the dirt, with a battered goal net erected at each end. It might not match the emerald-green grass field of the professional stadium at Krondor, but it was a ball field.

Looking on were Margaret, Abigail, and Marcus, from a vantage point of seats on a low wall alongside the garden. Nakor and Ghuda were watching the game from the other side of the field, among a group of soldiers, and both waved at Nicholas. He waved back.

Nicholas had been running errands all morning for the Housecarl, and had finally stolen into the kitchen to eat a quick lunch that Magya had prepared for the Squires, and then had left to see what he could do with his time off. He was thinking about returning to his room for a nap when the sounds of the game distracted him.

Marcus nodded at him and the girls both smiled. He jumped up to sit on the wall, next to Margaret, and leaned forward to return Marcus's greeting. He then looked at Abigail, who smiled warmly and said, 'I've not seen you around much, Highness, save when you were running from one place to another.'

Looking at Abigail caused Nicholas's ears to burn. He said, 'The Duke keeps me busy, my lady,' and turned his attention to the game. What it lacked in skill it more than made up for in enthusiasm.

'You play football in Krondor, Squire?' asked Marcus, stressing the last words. As he spoke, he reached over and placed his hand upon Abigail's. The possessive gesture was not lost on Nicholas.

Feeling suddenly self-conscious, Nicholas said, 'We have professional teams in Krondor, sponsored by the guilds, merchants, and some nobles.'

'I mean do *you* play?'

Nicholas said, 'Not much.'

Marcus glanced at Nicholas's feet and nodded slightly. Marcus's gesture did not earn him Nicholas's thanks; Nicholas found himself irritated by his cousin's manner.

Margaret glanced from her brother to Nicholas, and her expression shifted slightly from neutral to dryly amused as Nicholas said, 'But when I had time, I was considered good.'

Marcus's eyes narrowed. 'Even with your foot.'

Nicholas felt his face flush and he was suddenly angry. 'Yes, even with my *foot*!'

Harry appeared, a bit of bread and cheese in his hand,

95

and Marcus only glanced at him for a moment. The Duke's son knew that Harry's time was now his own until the next morning. Harry gave the assembled group a general wave and said, 'How's the game?'

Nicholas jumped off the low wall and said, 'We're playing.'

Harry shook his head. 'I'm eating.'

With a smile, Marcus said, 'I'll keep the sides even.'

Harry grinned openly as he jumped backward to sit in the space Nicholas had just vacated, next to Lady Margaret. 'Give 'em hell, Nicky,' he said cheerfully.

Nicholas stripped off his tunic, feeling the warm sun and cool ocean breeze upon his skin. He hardly knew any of the boys on the field – just two of the pages – but he knew the game. Feeling irritated by Marcus's attitude, he needed to vent his anger.

A moment later, the ball went out of bounds. Marcus reached over and picked it up, saying, 'I'll throw it in.'

Nicholas ran out onto the field and glanced around. He waved over a kitchen boy and said, 'What's your name?'

The boy said, 'Robert, Highness.'

Nicholas frowned and shook his head. 'I'm the Duke's Squire. Who's our side?'

Robert quickly pointed out the seven boys that made up the rest of the informal team and Nicholas said, 'I'll guard Marcus.

Robert grinned and nodded. 'No one will dispute you that privilege, Squire.'

Suddenly Nicholas was moving, cutting off a boy who was hurrying forward to take the toss in from Marcus. By throwing his body almost out of bounds, he managed to kick the ball to a startled boy on his own team. After a brief hesitation, the fray was on.

Harry guffawed and said to the girls, 'Nicholas is as good at stealing inbounds as anyone I've seen.'

Margaret watched her cousin pick himself up off the hard ground and race to rejoin the game and said, 'That must hurt.'

'He's tough enough,' answered Harry. Glancing at the two girls beside him, he said, 'Any bets?'

The two girls looked at each other. 'Bets?'

'On who will win,' said Harry as Marcus deftly made a sliding tackle on the ball, knocking it loose for one of his teammates to intercept.

Abigail shook her head. 'I don't know who's better.'

Margaret gave an unladylike snort of contempt. 'Neither is "better", but those two will kill each other trying to find out.'

Abigail shook her head as Nicholas was slammed from behind by one of Marcus's teammates, out of view of the referee, so that no penalty was called. The boy threw a forearm at the back of Nicholas's head that had him seeing white lights for a moment. Marcus shook his head in sympathy as Nicholas pulled himself together and jumped to his feet. The boy who had leveled Nicholas was somewhere down the field. 'Got to keep your wits about you,' shouted Marcus. 'Not a lot of subtlety in this game.'

Shaking his head to clear it, Nicholas said, 'I've noticed.'

Then both boys were off toward the ball.

Harry said, 'Damn, they look alike out there, don't they?'

Abigail said, 'They could be brothers, certainly.'

In the middle of the fray, Marcus and Nicholas both angled for the ball, attempting to kick it out of the mess, each leaning into the other, elbows slamming into ribs.

Harry surveyed the two girls and said, 'About the bet?'

Margaret looked at Harry and her smile was wry. 'The stakes?'

'Easy,' said Harry, attempting an offhand manner. 'There's a festival in two weeks, I've been told. You'll need an escort.'

Margaret smiled and glanced at Abigail. 'Both of us?'

Harry guffawed. 'Why not? It'll drive them both crazy.'

Margaret laughed aloud. 'Some friend you are.'

Harry shrugged. 'I know Nicholas, and if I'm not mistaken, he and Marcus are only beginning a long and possibly colorful rivalry.' Looking directly at Abigail, he said, 'I think they're both smitten, my lady.' Abigail had the courtesy to blush, but her expression looked as if the observation was not news to her.

'And what are your ambitions, Squire?'

Margaret's frank question caught Harry off guard. 'Why, none, I think,' he said in confusion.

Margaret patted him in familiar fashion on the leg and Harry found he was now the one blushing. 'Whatever you say, Squire,' said the Duke's daughter.

Harry felt his body stir and warm at her hand on his thigh, and suddenly wanted to be anywhere but sitting next to her. He had never had a problem talking to the younger women of the Prince's staff in Krondor, either the serving women who were disadvantaged by their rank, or the daughters of the court nobles who were disadvantaged by their youth. But there was nothing of the shy, inexperienced girl in Margaret's manner. There was something positively worldly about this girl, who was almost the same age as Harry and Nicholas.

Abigail watched the game with obvious divided loyalties, but Margaret showed little interest. She glanced around and saw Anthony standing behind them in the garden and waved for him to join them.

The young magician came to where they sat and bowed awkwardly. Margaret smiled at him. 'Anthony, how are you?'

'Fine, my lady,' he said softly. 'I thought I'd get some air and sun and watch a bit of the game.'

'Sit there next to Abigail,' ordered Margaret with humor. 'She needs support. Two fools are shedding blood in her honor.'

Abigail blushed furiously, and her tone was cold. 'That isn't funny, Margaret.' They had never been particularly close; Margaret had spent most of her childhood playing with her brother and his rough friends. The few town girls – daughters of the richer merchants – who had been selected as her companions had been as appalled as Margaret's tutors when the Duke's daughter had shown indifference to the training reserved for young ladies of rank. Her mother had lived her early life as a warrior and had seen no benefit in much of what they attempted to teach Margaret, save reading and writing, and often spared her daughter punishment when she abandoned her needlework to go riding or hunting.

Abigail was just the most recent of a long line of companions for the Duke's rugged daughter, no better matched to Margaret than the others, save she got on her nerves less than most. Abigail usually had a good sense of humor, which was being sorely tested by her friend as, with a cheery air, Margaret said, 'I think it is.'

Harry smiled, glad the attention was off him for the moment. As the Duke's daughter watched the game, he studied her profile. At first glance, she was not a terribly pretty young woman, but there was something almost regal in the way she held herself, erect and proud: not the posturing of a vain court woman, but rather the same upright bearing her mother showed, that of a woman who had no doubt of her own ability or her place in the world. Suddenly Harry felt deeply inadequate.

The game moved up and down the field, and Harry observed that at some time in the last five minutes Nicholas had acquired a bloody nose. Scanning the field for Marcus, he noticed that the Duke's son was not too far from Nicholas, and that his left eye was puffing.

Harry caught Nakor's attention across the field, and the little man rolled his eyes heavenward and made a motion with his finger to his head indicating someone was crazy. Harry made a sign asking which one, and Ghuda, who had followed the exchange, motioned that both were. Harry laughed.

Margaret said, 'What?'

'They play rough here, don't they?'

Margaret laughed a very unladylike laugh, slightly more delicate than a honk, and said, 'Only when they think they have something to prove, Harry.'

Harry had never seen Nicholas play so aggressively. The boy had always used his head and his natural quickness in whatever sport he undertook, but he was hurling himself around the field with abandon, his play reaching previously unmatched heights of madness.

Marcus pushed himself away from Nicholas, and made a running interception of a pass, breaking toward the goal set up at the far end of the field. Nicholas was hot after him, and those looking on cheered loudly at the spectacle.

Margaret laughed and Abigail sat with her hands clenched in her lap, an expression of open concern on her face. Harry started to cheer, but the sound died in his throat. Nicholas was limping and Harry knew that he couldn't overtake Marcus. Nicholas strained and forced himself, but there was something wrong in the way he moved.

Harry jumped from the low wall, and Margaret asked, 'What?'

Ignoring her, he raced toward the far end of the field as Nicholas fell to the ground, ignored by the other players as Marcus deftly scored the winning goal. The referee shouted time and the match was over. As the winners gathered around Marcus, Harry reached Nicholas's side.

Kneeling next to his friend, he said, 'Nicholas! What is it?'

The Prince's face was contorted and drained of color, while tears ran down his face. He gripped his left leg and could barely speak as he gasped, 'Help me up.'

'No, damn it, you're hurt.'

Nicholas grabbed Harry's tunic and said, 'Help me to my feet.' His voice was an angry whisper, thick with pain. Harry gripped Nicholas's arm and helped him to his feet.

Marcus and the other boys approached, with Nakor and Ghuda crossing from the other side of the field. The Duke's son said, 'Are you all right?'

Nicholas forced a smile and said, 'I twisted my ankle that's all.' His voice was nearly unrecognizable to Harry, and the Squire looked at his friend to see his face was chalky. 'Harry will help me back to my room. I'll be all right.'

Before Marcus could say anything, Nakor fixed him with a narrow stare. 'You broke something?'

Nicholas said, 'No, I'm fine.'

Ghuda said, 'I've seen finer-looking corpses, son. Better let me help you back to your room.'

Before the old mercenary could move, Anthony took Nicholas's other arm, saying, 'I'll help him.'

The girls had come up beside Marcus, and Margaret regarded her cousin, all sarcasm forgotten. 'Are you all right?'

Nicholas forced a smile. 'Yes.'

Abigail stood silently beside the Duke's daughter, but her eyes showed her concern as Nicholas was helped away, supported on Harry's and Anthony's shoulders.

He hobbled between them until they rounded the perimeter of the garden, when he promptly fainted.

* * *

101

Nicholas revived as they reached his room. Anthony and Harry eased him down upon his pallet and Harry said, 'What happened to you?'

Nicholas said, 'Someone stomped on my bad foot and I felt something break.' His face was still drawn, and sweat streamed off it.

Anthony said, 'The boot will have to come off.'

Nicholas nodded and gritted his teeth as they removed the boot. His head swam from the pain but he remained conscious.

Anthony examined the deformed foot and said, 'I don't think there are bones broken, but something's dislocated. Look at this.' Nicholas levered himself up on his elbows and saw what Anthony was pointing at: a nasty-looking purple bruise that covered fully half of the top of the foot. Anthony pushed his thumb firmly into the bruise, and Nicholas exclaimed in pain. The magician kept pushing. An audible popping sound was accompanied by a grunt of surprise from Nicholas. Then he moved his foot, wiggling his vestigial toes. Anthony set the foot gently down and Nicholas fell back with a great sigh.

Anthony said, 'I'll send one of the servants down to the harbor for a bucket of salt water. Soak in it for a half hour, then keep the foot elevated and warm for the rest of the evening. You're going to be sore, but I think you'll be able to get around. I'll ask the Duke to excuse you from work tomorrow, and take things easy for a while. You're going to have a nasty limp for a few days, my friend.' The young magician stood up and said, 'I'll take a look in on you tomorrow, first thing.'

Harry said, 'Are you the Duke's healer, as well as adviser?'

Anthony nodded. 'Yes, as a matter of fact.'

Harry said, 'I thought healers were priests.'

Anthony smiled. 'Mostly, but some magicians are skilled at healing. I'll see you tomorrow, Nicholas.'

As the magician moved toward the door, Nicholas said, 'Anthony.'

The magician paused and looked down at Nicholas. 'Yes?'

'Thank you.'

For a moment Anthony paused, then he smiled, looking no older than either Nicholas or Harry. 'I understand.'

After he left, Harry turned to his friend and said, 'He understands what?' He pulled over the little stool and sat. From somewhere in his tunic he produced an apple, which he broke in half, giving a piece to Nicholas.

Lying back as he chewed on the apple, Nicholas said, 'He understands that Marcus and I are going to be knocking heads and thumping on each other for a while.'

'That wasn't a game out there, Nicky. That was war. You took more blows in one half today than I've seen you take in all last season, and that was thirteen matches. And I've never seen you throw as many elbows and shoulders either. You two weren't playing ball, you were trying to kill each other.'

Nicholas sighed. 'How did I get to this point?'

'You had the bad manners to want the same girl as Marcus, and while you're playing at Squire, he knows you're a Royal Prince of the Kingdom and he's only a Duke's son.'

'*Only* a Duke's son?'

Harry shook his head. 'You can be thick at times, my friend.' Waving his hand, he said, 'If Marcus came sailing into any city but Krondor or Rillanon, the local girls would be falling all over him for attention. Here on the Far Coast, he's the most eligible bachelor, related to the King and everything. But you, my bashful boy, are the most eligible lad north of the Empire of Kesh, now that your brothers are married, and you're the brother of our next King.

'The lovely Lady Abigail could be head over heels

103

about Marcus, but the moment you walk in, she's got to stop and take a long look.' With a shrug, he added, 'It's the sort of thing people do.'

At mention of Abigail, Nicholas sighed. 'Do you think she is?'

'Is what?'

'In love with Marcus.'

Harry shrugged. 'I don't know.' Then, with a grin, he said, 'But I can find out.'

Nicholas said, 'No, don't do anything. If you start poking around and asking questions, she'll find out.'

'Ha! You're afraid she'll find out you like her!' Harry laughed at Nicholas's discomfort. 'Don't worry about that, my friend. It's too late.'

Nicholas groaned. 'You think?'

Harry said, 'Certain of it. You look like you're going to faint every time you see her looking at you. How do you think Marcus knew? He's not amused.'

'He's a cool one,' said Nicholas, an observation that was half admiration, half dislike.

Harry nodded. 'You two are a lot alike, but he keeps things closer in than you do.'

Nicholas said, 'Well, everyone keeps saying we're alike, but I don't see it.'

Harry stood up. 'Well, soak the foot and wrap it, and have a good night. I'll bring you some food from the kitchen tonight.'

'Where are you going?'

'I'm heading back to the garden to find Abigail.'

'Not you too!' groaned Nicholas.

Harry waved his hand. 'Not a chance. I'm interested in Margaret.'

'Why?' said Nicholas as Harry paused by the door.

'Well, for one thing, Marcus is her brother, and while marriages between royal cousins aren't unheard of, in your case, I seriously doubt it. Besides, I think I love her.'

Nicholas's eyebrows shot up in skeptical surprise. 'Right.'

'No, I mean it. She gives me a stomach ache.' Saying no more, he left Nicholas alone.

Nicholas fell back, laughing, but soon his mirth fled, as he understood exactly what Harry was saying. Abigail gave him the most desperate twist in the stomach he had ever experienced.

5

Instruction

Nicholas winced.

He had been laid up all the previous day, and while his foot still hurt, he could move around. So before the sun rose, he was standing at his post outside the Duke's door, almost motionless.

Marcus's door opened and he emerged into the hall, motioning for Harry to follow. A moment later, Martin's door opened and Briana and Martin came through. The Duchess said, 'How is the foot, Nicholas?'

He managed a wry smile as he said, 'I'll live. It's a little tender, my lady, but I can get around.'

Martin said, 'Accidents happen. You're not going to be much use for running errands; go back to the Housecarl and see if he can find something you're suited for today.'

Nicholas said, 'Your Grace,' and limped off.

As he wandered through the halls toward the servants' wing, where Samuel had his office, he felt thoroughly disgusted with himself. The Sixthday game had been a debacle. As he had brooded over it all day, lying on his pallet, he realized he had looked like a fool.

Over the years, being the youngest son of the Prince of Krondor had forced Nicholas into many situations where he would rather have held back; there was no escaping public scrutiny when protocol dictated one be upon the balcony at a festival, or in attendance at court. But in most areas, Nicholas preferred to let others, like Harry, take the lead. In football, Nicholas had developed a justified reputation as a wicked defender, able to steal a ball and pass it off before the other side knew what had happened, but when it came to scoring, he always let others take the glory. Two days before had been the first time he had ever propelled himself to the fore, demanded the ball at every opportunity, and attempted to dominate by force of will alone. And every step of the way Marcus had shadowed him.

There had been scant satisfaction in realizing that he had been as effective at blocking Marcus's efforts as Marcus had been at blocking his; the game had been more or less a stalemate, save for the injury done his foot, which finally allowed Marcus to score.

As he gingerly moved down a flight of stairs, Nicholas was more sensitive to his birth defect than usual. Like most of those born with such a deformity, he had adapted to it and compensated for it without much thought. Being Arutha's son had saved him from much of the childhood taunting children of lower rank would have had to endure, but he had still experienced some of it, as well as more than his share of stares and whispers. But today was the first day he felt as if his foot was a true handicap. Had it not been for that, he was certain, he would have bested Marcus. He swore softly, being angry with everyone, himself most of all.

He reached Samuel's office door and said, 'Housecarl?'

Samuel motioned him to enter. Nicholas had been in the office only a half hour earlier and had been told there were no unusual duties. The Housecarl looked around as if seeking inspiration, then said, 'I have nothing that needs doing, Squire. Why don't you return to your room and rest that injured foot?'

Nicholas nodded and departed, not feeling very much like lying abed another day. He returned to his room and threw himself onto his straw mattress. Having slept most of the previous day, he felt little like resting, and the straw itched. Besides, he was hungry.

After a few minutes he heaved himself off his pallet and headed for the kitchen. By the time he reached it, the smell of food in the hallway had his mouth watering. Magya was busy supervising the kitchen staff, walking behind the cooks like a general overseeing her troops. She smiled at Nicholas and waved him over.

'Are you feeling better today, Squire?' asked the old woman. Tending toward the plump, she nevertheless moved about the kitchen quickly and efficiently, despite her age and weight.

'Yes, but not quite fit for duty, according to the Duke.'

She chuckled. 'But fit enough to be hungry?'

He smiled back. 'Something like that.'

Patting his shoulder, she said, 'I think we have something we can spare before the Duke and Duchess break fast.'

She pointed to a tray, which Nicholas picked up. She spooned out a thick porridge that was bubbling in a pot, sprinkled some cinnamon on it, put a large dollop of honey in the middle, and poured milk over it all. She placed the bowl on the tray, cut a slab of hot bread and a thick slice of ham, and motioned for Nicholas to carry it over to a small table in the corner.

Megar entered with two kitchen boys following behind, each carrying a basket of eggs. He waved the boys about their tasks and came over to sit at the table with his wife and Nicholas, who had taken to the old master cook, a large man with an open smile and kind manner, the first time they had met. 'Morning, Squire,' said Megar, a friendly smile on his open, lined face.

Nicholas said, 'Have you seen Ghuda and Nakor? I've not caught a glimpse of either since the game.'

Megar and Magya exchanged glances. 'Who?' asked Megar.

Nicholas described them. 'Those two,' said Magya. 'I've seen the short fellow talking to Anthony a few times in the last week. The big soldier went out with a patrol, for the fun of it, he said. Left yesterday morning.'

108

Nicholas sighed. They weren't real friends, but he knew them better than anyone in the castle save Harry. While the cook and his wife were nice enough, he didn't know them well and knew that they were only sparing a few moments out of courtesy, and that as soon as he was finished eating, they'd be about preparing the rest of the day's meals.

As Nicholas ate, they talked. They inquired how he was adjusting to life in Crydee, and then about this trip. At mention of Pug, they both smiled wistful, half-sad, half-pleased smiles. 'He was like our son,' said Megar. 'He was our fosterling, you know, so many years ago.'

Nicholas shook his head to show he hadn't known, and Megar started telling him a little of Pug, and of Megar and Magya's own son, Tomas, who had been Pug's closest friend. As the story of their lives unfolded – a mixture of reminiscence and spirited argument about who remembered what correctly – a picture formed in Nicholas's imagination.

He had heard tales of the Riftwar from Amos, and once in a while his father could be persuaded to reveal something of his own part in it, but Megar and Magya's simple retelling was by far the most compelling he had heard. The manner in which they related everything that occurred in their own references, how many buckets of water the kitchen staff carried to the walls, how many extra rations needed to be cooked, how they made do without this or that, when meals were cold because the cooking staff was tending the wounded – all wove a far more vivid picture in Nicholas's mind than even Amos's most colorful boasting.

Nicholas asked one or two questions, and suddenly a picture of Pug as a boy emerged. Nicholas smiled as Megar explained at great length how difficult it was for him as a child, being the smallest boy for his age in the keep, and how Tomas had become protective. By the time the stories were finished, Nicholas had eaten all that had been put before him. Magya's eyes were shining as she explained how Tomas had looked on the day he had become a man, at the Choosing – that ancient rite where all the boys are given over to the masters who would train them.

There was something familiar about the name Tomas, but Nicholas couldn't quite make it fit. He said, 'Where is your son now?'

Instantly he regretted asking, as a look of sorrow passed over both their faces. He thought the young man must have died in the war.

But to his surprise, Megar said, 'He lives with the elves.'

Suddenly Nicholas made the connection. 'Your son is the Elf Queen's consort!'

Magya nodded. With resignation she said, 'We don't see him much. We've had one visit since the child was born, and we get a message from time to time.'

'Child?'

'Our grandson,' answered Megar. 'Calis.'

Magya brightened. 'He's a good boy. He visits once or twice a year. He's more like his father than those elves he lives with,' she said with conviction. 'I often wish he'd come to live here at Crydee.'

The conversation died, and Nicholas excused himself and left through the door to the courtyard. He recollected what his uncle Laurie had told him about the last days of the Riftwar and what bits Amos had told him. Tomas wasn't human. At least, that was the impression Nicholas had been left with; he was something else, related to the elves, but different. Nicholas thought that if he had human parents, especially ones as warm and open as Megar and Magya, he must have been much like the other keep children. What could have changed him? wondered Nicholas.

Nicholas wandered over to the Princess's Garden, faintly hoping to find Abigail and Margaret there. Given the hour, they were probably in the hall, dining with Duke Martin, but Nicholas hoped anyway.

Instead of the young girls, Nicholas was astonished to find Nakor and Anthony, lying flat on their stomachs, staring at something under a stone bench.

'There. you see?' said Nakor.

'That one?' asked Anthony.

'Yes.'

They dusted themselves off as they rose. Nakor said, 'You must be sure it is the one with those tiny flecks of orange. If they are red, it is deadly. If it is any other color, it is useless.'

Anthony took notice of Nicholas and bowed slightly. 'Highness.'

Nicholas sat upon the bench they had just been peering under, taking the weight off his foot. 'Squire,' he corrected.

Nakor grinned his lopsided grin. 'For the present, Squire, but Prince always. Anthony knows this.'

Nicholas ignored the observation. 'What were you two doing?'

Anthony seemed embarrassed. 'Well, there's a small mushroom-like growth that you can find in dark, damp places – '

'Under the bench,' injected Nakor.

' – and Nakor was showing me how to identify it correctly.'

'For magic potions?' asked Nicholas.

'As a drug,' snapped Nakor. 'To induce sleep – if prepared correctly. Very handy when you have to cut an arrow out of a soldier, or remove a bad tooth.'

Nicholas indulged himself. 'I thought all you magicians have to do is wave your hand and put someone in a trance.'

111

Anthony shrugged, as if to say that he wasn't much of a magician, but Nakor said, 'See, that's what comes of letting children grow up uneducated.' He opened his bag and took out an orange. 'Want one?' he asked.

Nicholas nodded and Nakor tossed the fruit to him. He gave another to Anthony. Then he handed the bag to Nicholas. 'Look inside.'

Nicholas examined the large rucksack. He found it simple: black material, feeling like common felted wool. A leather drawstring had been sewn around the mouth of the bag, and a wooden frog and loop served as a clasp. The bag was empty. Handing it back, Nicholas said, 'There's nothing in it.'

Nakor reached in and withdrew a writhing snake. Anthony's eyes widened and Nicholas scooted backward on the bench, until he hit the wall behind. 'That's a viper!'

With a wave of his hand, Nakor said, 'This? It's just a stick.'

In his hand was a simple piece of wood, which he put back in the bag; then again he tossed the bag to Nicholas. Nicholas examined it closely and said, 'It's empty.' he handed the bag to Nakor. 'How did you do that?'

Nakor grinned again. 'It's easy if you know the trick.'

Anthony shook his head. 'He does some very impressive things, yet insists there is no magic.'

Nakor nodded. 'Maybe I'll explain it to you someday, magician. Pug knows.'

Nicholas glanced over his shoulder at the walls above the courtyard and said, 'I've been hearing a lot about Pug today, it seems.'

Anthony said, 'He is something of a legend here. At Stardock, too. He left before I joined the community there.'

Nicholas said, 'Well, you can't have been a member for long; he's only been gone from there about eight years.'

Anthony smiled. 'I'm afraid I'm a very junior magician. The masters felt – '

'Masters!' snorted Nakor. 'Those overblown fools Korsh and Watoom!' Shaking his head, he sat down next to Anthony. 'They were the reason I left Stardock.' He pointed to Anthony as he looked at Nicholas. 'This boy was quite gifted, but he is what those fools call a "lesser" magician. If I had stayed, I would have made him one of my Blue Riders!' Grinning at Anthony, he said, 'I sure made some trouble there, didn't I?'

Anthony laughed, and Nicholas saw him look as young as Harry and himself. 'That's the truth. The Blue Riders are the most popular faction at Stardock, and there are some very bitter fights – '

'Fights!' exclaimed Nicholas. 'Magicians fighting?'

Anthony said, 'Student brawls, really. There are some older apprentices, who call themselves the Hands of Korsh – though he doesn't care for that – who often start trouble in the taverns at Stardock. No one causes serious damage – the masters wouldn't allow that – but it can result in a cracked head now and again.' He sighed, remembering. 'I wasn't there long enough to become seriously involved with all that politics. I was having too much trouble with my studies. That's why they sent me here, at Duke Martin's request, because I'm not much of a magician.'

Nakor shook his head and made a face. 'If you're not much like them, that's a good thing.' He stood up. 'I'm going to the woods to look for some things. I'll see you at supper.' He pointed to Anthony. 'Put some salve on the boy's foot, so it'll be better tomorrow.'

Anthony said, 'I have some things that might help.'

Without further word, Nakor scampered from the garden, leaving the young magician and Squire alone.

Nicholas was the first to speak. 'I don't think I've ever known a stranger person.'

113

Anthony said, 'I've met a few strange ones at Stardock, but no one to rival Nakor.'

'Was he one of your teachers at Stardock, before he left?'

Anthony shook his head and sat in the spot Nakor had just vacated. 'Not really. I'm not sure what he was doing there, except causing trouble for Watoom and Korsh. The story is he showed up one day with a letter from Prince Borric and some claim that Pug told him to come to Stardock. He stayed about three or four years, and did some strange things, mostly converting a lot of students to the notion that everyone could learn magic – or what he calls "tricks" – and that magicians were not very bright for not being able to understand this.' Anthony sighed. 'I had problems of my own at the time, and didn't pay too much attention. I was a new student and saw Nakor only two or three times, around the island.'

Nicholas said, 'Is it true that they sent you because you weren't very good?'

Anthony said, 'I suspect as much. There were many more gifted students than I, and no small number of accomplished master magicians living at Stardock.'

Nicholas's face darkened. 'That's close to an insult, you know.'

Anthony's face flushed. 'I didn't.'

Nicholas said, 'I don't mean to belittle you, Anthony. You may be more talented than you think. At least, Nakor says you are,' he added quickly. Both knew it sounded a weak attempt to smooth over the remark. 'But the King's brother requested a magician, to fill a post once held by Pug's teacher. They should have sent one of their best.'

Anthony stood up. 'Perhaps.' His manner was stiff, caught between embarrassment and insult. He flushed a little as he said, 'Stardock doesn't feel it owes much allegiance to the Kingdom, I'm afraid. If Pug were still there, that might be one thing, him being a cousin to the King and all, but as it is today, Korsh and Watoom have a great deal of influence among the masters and they are from Kesh. They'd like to keep Stardock out of politics on both sides of the border, I think.'

Nicholas said, 'That might not be a bad idea, I guess, but it's still rude.'

Anthony said, 'If you come with me, I have some salves that may hasten your recuperation; at the least, they won't cause any problems even if they don't help.'

Nicholas followed the young magician. Glancing around the garden, he again regretted that the girls were nowhere in sight.

The weeks passed with surprising speed. Each day was full of duties from dawn to dusk, and Nicholas discovered that the hectic pace was to his liking. Being busy kept him from brooding, a trait inherited from his father. The strenuous routine of constantly being on the move, of having to pitch in with much of the physical labor, was hardening his youthful frame as well. Always fit from riding and sword practice, he was now gaining strength to go with his speed. After his first day hauling arms and armor out for cleaning and having to lug it all back into the armory, he thought he was going to die. Now he could carry twice the load and feel little strain.

The work seemed to agree with Harry, too, though he reveled in complaining whenever he had the chance. In the three weeks since coming to Crydee, both boys had found little time to spend with Margaret and Abigail, though Harry had found a bit more than Nicholas. He delighted in playing upon Nicholas's anxiety over the young lady-in-witing, sometimes teasing him to the point of anger. But most of their time was caught up in the seemingly endless routine of the court of Crydee. So far the only time Nicholas had found to pay court to Abigail was on Sixthday afternoons, and to his chagrin Marcus was always nearby.

The people of Castle Crydee took on individual identities to the boys from Krondor. The kitchen staff was friendly, the other servants respectful and distant. The younger serving girls viewed Harry with a mixture of amusement and wariness, while a few watched Nicholas with open admiration, attention he found somewhat disquieting. Swordmaster Charles was interesting but always formal in speech and manner. Faxon was open and friendly, and Nicholas found him a good listener. Nakor and Ghuda were rarely in evidence, always seeming to find something in town or the nearby woods to occupy their time. Slowly the alien quality that had overwhelmed Nicholas upon first arriving was wearing off, and while Crydee would never feel like home, it was becoming familiar. And Abigail occupied more of Nicholas's thoughts than any girl he had previously known. On those rare occasions he could find her without Marcus hovering by she was warm and attentive, and left him with conflicting feelings that he was making a total ass of himself and that she really cared for his company.

Nearly a month after the reception dinner, Nicholas and Harry dined with the Duke's court once again. Since they were members of the household, it was not an unexpected event, but it was the first time since they had come to Crydee that the boys had been free enough from duty to eat at the same time as everyone else. They sat at the foot of the table, removed enough from the Duke and his family that only faint snatches of conversation reached them. Not only was the household in attendance, but several important members of guilds and crafts from the town were seated at the Duke's table, while some visiting merchants and traders were seated around the hall.

Nicholas sat staring across the hall at Abigail, who seemed to be listening somewhat distractedly to something Marcus was telling her. She glanced at Nicholas with regularity and occasionally flushed and lowered her eyes when he caught her gaze.

Harry said, 'The girl likes you.'

Nicholas said, 'How do you know?'

Harry grinned as he sipped at a goblet of wine. 'She keeps looking over here at you.'

'Maybe she thinks I look funny,' Nicholas said with a note of fear.

Harry laughed. 'Given how much you and Marcus resemble each other, and that you're obviously the only two chaps she pays the least bit of attention to, I'd say she has a preference for a certain type.' Tapping his friend upon the shoulder, he said, 'She likes you, dummy.'

Dinner passed with the boys engaging in trivialities with the two young men who sat beside Nicholas. One was a gem dealer seeking to underwrite an expedition into a region of the Grey Tower mountains; he claimed there were gem deposits still untapped by dwarves or human miners. He was to be disappointed, Nicholas knew, for the Kingdom made no claims over the Grey Towers beyond the foothills; the gem dealer would have to treat with Dolgan, the King of the western dwarves, at village Caldara, a week's travel or more inland.

The other man was a traveler from Queg, a merchant in fine silks and rare perfumes, who had occupied most of the girls' afternoon showing them his wares, which was why Nicholas had not caught sight of them all day. Margaret was more given to hunting leather and simple tunics, like her mother, it seemed, though she wore the proper gowns and jewelry in court; but Abigail and most of the daughters of the town's richer merchants had purchased enough of the merchant's fineries to guarantee him a profitable trip before he visited Carse and Tulan on his way home.

The merchant was named Vasarius, and something

about him irritated Nicholas. Perhaps it was the way Nicholas had caught him staring at Margaret and Abigail, in a manner Nicholas could only consider covetous. When Nicholas caught him at it, he merely averted his eyes from the girls, or smiled at Nicholas as if he were but glancing around the room.

After dinner the merchants gathered before the Duke and his lady and a short period of socializing followed, before they were escorted out of the castle. Nicholas noticed that while the other merchants were attempting to get Martin's attention, Vasarius was chatting amiably with Charles and Faxon.

Nicholas was on the verge of saying something about this to Harry when Marcus approached. 'We're going hunting tomorrow,' he said. 'You two begin laying out everything we're going to need. Have a couple of servants go with you.'

Nicholas nodded, while Harry barely suppressed a groan. They hurried off and motioned for a couple of the servants to follow. Nicholas glanced over his shoulder and noticed Abigail watching his departure. She waved to him, wishing him a silent good night, and Nicholas turned to see Marcus looking at her with a sour expression. Smiling slightly, Nicholas felt better than he had since coming to Crydee.

It was late when Nicholas and Harry finished organizing the equipment for the hunt. They would be gone only two or three days, but there would be a half dozen in the party – Martin, Marcus, Nicholas, Harry, Ghuda, and Nakor – so a fair amount of equipment and provisions needed to be readied. After a minute of standing around in confusion, not knowing where to begin, the boys had allowed the experienced servants to take charge and had mostly observed, save when it came to choosing weapons. Both squires knew they were responsible for those choices, and by now both had a good idea of what Martin and Marcus would require. Like his father, Marcus was an excellent bowman and favored the longbow.

When everything was ready, Nicholas and Harry returned to the banquet hall. Nicholas left his friend and went up to the Duke. Martin finished his conversation with one of the local merchants and said, 'Yes, Squire?'

Nicholas said, 'All is ready for tomorrow, Your Grace.'

'Good. I have no further need for you this evening, Squire. We leave at first light.'

Nicholas bowed and departed, leaving Martin to his guests. Harry was likewise on his own, from all appearances, as he hurried across the hall to Nicholas. 'Where are you going?'

'I thought I'd turn in. It's an early start tomorrow.'

'Lady Margaret mentioned that she'd be taking a stroll through the Princess's Garden.'

'Well, there you go,' said Nicholas. 'Now's your chance.'

Harry grinned. 'Abigail went with her.'

Nicholas grinned in return. 'What are we waiting for?'

With a signal lack of decorum, the boys hurried out of the Duke's great hall just a stride short of a full run.

As the boys leaped the three steps to the Princess's Garden, Margaret and Abigail exchanged glances and smiles. Margaret's was confident and amused; Abigail's was shy and pleased.

Both boys came to an abrupt halt and bowed with a fair amount of courtly dignity. Grinning self-consciously, Nicholas said, 'Good evening, ladies.'

'Good evening, Squire,' replied Margaret.

Abigail spoke softly. 'Good evening, Highness.'

The two boys fell in, Nicholas next to Abigail and Harry next to Margaret. The boys were silent for a moment, then both started to speak at the same time.

The girls laughed and the boys had the good grace to look embarrassed. Again there was a silent moment, then Harry and Nicholas began to speak again.

Margaret said, 'I know you two can't seem to live a moment apart, but why don't you come over here with me, Squire Harry.'

Harry glanced at Nicholas and his expression was a mix of surprise, pleasure, and panic as Margaret took him firmly by the hand and led him off toward a small bench beside the blooming roses.

Nicholas and Abigail walked slowly to the far end of the small garden to another bench, where they sat. Softly Abigail said, 'You seem to be adjusting to living with us, Highness.'

Nicholas said, 'It's "Squire" here, my lady.' He flushed a little and said, 'I . . . think I like it. Some of it.' He stared at her, amazed at how delicate her features were, almost doll-like. Her skin was clear and smooth and without the usual blemishes girls her age endured. He was certain he had never seen eyes as big or blue, almost luminous in the faint light of the torches upon the wall. Her hair was gathered back, encircled with a silver ring, then fell to her shoulders in a cascade of golden silk. He glanced down and said, 'Some things I find a great deal more appealing here than others.'

She flushed a little, but smiled, then said, 'Is His Grace overworking you? I hardly ever see you in the castle. We've spoken little more than a dozen words in weeks.'

Nicholas said, 'I have a lot to do, but in truth I find it more interesting than going to lessons, or attending my father's court and being a fixture at the parades, presentations, and receptions that go on all the time in Krondor.'

'I would have thought that a wonderful life,' she said. Her tone was disappointed. 'I can't imagine anything more thrilling than being presented in your father's court, or the King's court.' Her eyes were wide and her expression earnest as she spoke. 'The great lords and beautiful ladies, the ambassadors from distant lands – it all sounds so wonderful.' She positively glowed to Nicholas's eyes as she said this.

Trying not to sound too blasé, Nicholas said, 'It's often colorful.' In fact, he found the entire demands of court pomp an unrelenting bore. But he was sure Abigail didn't wish to hear that, and at this particular moment causing her any sort of disappointment was the last thing he wished. She looked at him with eyes so wide he felt he could fall into them; he forced himself to inhale, as somewhere in the last moments he had forgotten to breathe. 'Perhaps someday you can visit Krondor or Rillanon.'

Her expression turned from wondering to resigned. 'I'm the daughter of a Far Coast Baron. If my father has his way, I'll be pledged to marry Marcus soon; I'll be an old woman with children before I have a chance to visit Krondor, and I'll never see Rillanon.'

Nicholas didn't know what to say; all he knew was that a tightening in his throat and stomach seemed to reach painful proportions when she spoke of marrying Marcus. At last he said, 'You won't have to.'

'Have to what?' she asked, a faint smile upon her lips.

'Marry Marcus if you don't want to,' he said awkwardly. 'It's not as if your father can command you to.'

'He can make it very hard for me to say no,' she said, lowering her eyes and looking at him from beneath lashes that were impossibly long.

Feeling as if his hands were slabs of wood, he reached out and took her hands in his own. Holding them awkwardly in one hand and patting them with the other, he said, 'I could . . .'

Softy, her eyes fixed upon his own, she said, 'What, Nicky?'

Feeling as if he were choking upon the words, he said, 'I could ask my father – '

Abigail said, 'Nicky, you're wonderful!' She reached out and put her hand behind his neck, pulling his face to hers.

Nicholas suddenly found himself being kissed. He had never known a kiss could be so soft, sensual, and pleasant. Her lips rested perfectly upon his, and her breath was as sweet as roses. His head swam as he began to return the kiss. He felt his body warming as he drew her to him, feeling her softness beneath his hands. She moved in such a way it seemed she melted into him, fitting perfectly within the circle of his arms.

Abruptly she pulled away. 'Marcus!' she whispered and before Nicholas could gather his wits she was gone. He blinked in confusion, feeling as if someone had poured icy water over his head. A moment later, Marcus came into view, entering the garden from the rearmost steps, the ones by the football field. Nicholas had been so caught up in the kiss he had not heard his cousin approach.

When Marcus saw Nicholas sitting upon the bench, his expression darkened. 'Squire,' he said coldly.

'Marcus,' answered Nicholas, feeling thoroughly irritated.

'I don't suppose the Lady Abigail is here.'

Nicholas discovered that he didn't like the way in which Marcus was looking at him, and even more to the point, he disliked hearing him mention her name. 'She's not here.'

Marcus glanced around. 'But unless you've taken to wearing her cologne, she was here moments ago.' With narrowed gaze he said, 'Where is she?'

Nicholas stood. 'Over there, I think.'

Marcus moved away, and Nicholas had almost to jump to catch up with him. They both crossed to the other side of the Princess's Garden, where they found Harry sitting on the bench. The Squire from Ludland was flushing furiously.

Standing, he nodded to Marcus and Nicholas.

Marcus said, 'I suppose you were entertaining my sister.'

Harry's flush deepened to a blush of heroic proportion. 'I'm not sure,' he said. Looking off toward the castle – in the direction the girls had obviously gone – he added, 'She is a most remarkable girl.'

Marcus stepped away and turned to face them both. 'I hoped you two would figure things out for yourselves, but obviously you haven't. Well, here's how it's going to be.' Pointing at Harry, he said, 'My sister can take care of herself, but she's slated for bigger things than a meaningless romance with the son of a petty Earl.'

Harry's face burned scarlet, and his eyes flashed anger, but he kept his silence.

Looking at Nicholas, Marcus said, 'And you, *cousin* . . . Abigail doesn't need any fancy court boy sweeping her off her feet, then leaving her behind when he goes home. Is that clear?'

Nicholas stepped forward, 'What I do, Marcus, when your father doesn't have duties for me, is *my* business. And who Abigail chooses to spend her time with is *her* business.'

Appearing to be on the verge of coming to blows, the two cousins were separated by Harry, stepping between them. 'It won't do anyone any good if you two start brawling,' he said, his anger making his voice hard and scolding. Looking as if he would welcome any excuse to brawl himself, he turned a challenging gaze at Marcus. 'The Duke would be displeased, wouldn't he?'

Marcus and Nicholas both looked at Harry in momentary surprise, then locked gazes. Marcus said, 'We leave at first light, *Squire*. See that everything is ready.' He turned and marched away, his back as straight as a poll arm.

Nicholas said, 'He is going to cause trouble.'

'You're the one who's already caused trouble,' answered Harry.

'She doesn't love him,' said Nicholas.

'Oh, she told you this?' asked Harry.

'Not in so many words, but – '

'Tell me on the way to our rooms. We've got to be ready for tomorrow.'

As they walked, Nicholas said, 'She doesn't want to stay here with Marcus, that's certain.'

Harry nodded. 'So you think you'll take her back to Krondor?'

'Why not?' said Nicholas with an edge of anger in his tone.

'You know why,' answered Harry. 'Because you're going to marry some Princess from the court of Roldem, or a Duke's daughter, or a Princess of Kesh.'

With anger in his voice, and the memory of Abigail's kiss still fresh in his thoughts, he said, 'What if I don't want to?'

Sighing, Harry said, 'What if your King commands you to?'

Nicholas's jaws tightened, but he said nothing. He ached with frustration, the frustration of the interrupted embrace and the frustration of wanting to plant his fist in Marcus's face. At last he asked, 'What did Margaret do that got you so flustered?'

Harry blushed again. 'She's . . . amazing.' He drew a deep breath and blew it out theatrically. 'She started by asking me how the men in Krondor kiss, then asked me to show her. One thing led to another.' He stopped as if catching his wind. With red cheeks, he said, 'She got very bold, and . . .' He paused, then blurted, 'Nicholas, she asked me if I'd ever been *with* a woman!'

'She didn't!' exclaimed Nicky, half laughing, half groaning.

'She did! Then . . .'

'What?'

'Then she asked me *what it was like*!'

'She didn't!'

'Will you stop saying that. She did.'

'So what did you say?'

'I told her what it was like.'

'And?'

'She laughed at me! Then she said, 'When you know what you're talking about, Squire, come let me know. I'm curious.' Then she went back to kissing me, and moving around against me so I thought I was going to burst! Then Abigail came running over and said Marcus was coming, and they hurried off.'

'Amazing,' observed Nicholas, his anger and frustration vanishing before his astonishment at his unusual cousin Margaret.

'She's that,' Harry said.

'You still think you're in love?' Nicholas asked jokingly.

'My stomach hurts worse than ever, but . . .'

'What?'

'Your cousin Margaret is really scary.'

Nicholas laughed and bade Harry good night. As he returned to his own quarters, he lapsed into a memory of soft lips, warm perfume, and the most incredible eyes he had ever beheld. His body warmed at the memory. And his stomach hurt like mad.

6

Raid

Martin signaled.

The party halted as he turned and said, 'All of you wait here a bit. There's something ahead.'

The two boys were glad of the halt. They were footsore and tired. They had left the boundary of Crydee town at dawn. Martin had been teaching the two city boys something of wood lore, so they were moving on foot the entire way. Their destination was another day's walk away, the banks of the river Crydee. They waited with Nakor and Ghuda while Martin and Marcus moved into the woods, vanishing silently. 'How do they do that?' asked Nicholas.

Huntmaster Garret said, 'Your uncle was raised by the elves as much as by the monks at Silban's Abbey who found him, and he's taught Marcus and myself everything we know.' Nicholas had met the Duke's Huntmaster Garret for the first time the night before.

Nakor waved absently at the woodlands and said, 'We're being watched.'

Ghuda, his hand resting absently on his sword, said, 'For about half an hour.'

Neither sounded concerned. Nicholas glanced around, while Harry said, 'I don't see anything.'

'You have to know where to look,' said a voice from their left.

A young man emerged from the woodlands, his movements as stealthy as Martin's and Marcus's. 'And it's been closer to an hour,' he added. He was dressed in leather tunic and trousers dyed deep green. His hair was blond, but rather than the pale straw color of Anthony's, it was nearly sun-golden. It hung to shoulder-length, but was cut at the sides, revealing lobeless but otherwise normal ears. His eyes were blue, but almost too pale, and his movement hinted at tremendous power, despite his slight frame.

Then with a grin that made him look years younger he said, 'This is a game with Martin and us.'

'Us?' asked Nicholas.

The boy signaled and another three figures emerged from the woodlands, and Nicholas said, 'Elves!'

The young human said, 'I am Calis.'

The three elves stood silently nearby, then one turned suddenly as Martin and the others appeared. With a half-smile, Marcus said, 'You didn't think we were fooled by that false trail, did you?'

Martin made what looked to be slight gestures to the elves, who nodded slightly, or raised an eyebrow. Garret whispered to Nicholas and the others, 'They have a subtle speech with few words when they want.'

Then Martin spoke aloud. 'This is Nicholas, son of my brother, Arutha, and his companions, Harry of Ludland, Nakor the Isalani, and Ghuda Bulé from Kesh.'

Calis bowed and said, 'Greetings. Are you bound for Elvandar?'

Martin shook his head. 'No. Garret returned to the castle yesterday, carrying news that you were south of the river, so I thought it a good excuse to have you meet my nephew while we hunted. Perhaps in the future I'll bring Nicholas to your court.'

'And me,' said Nakor.

Calis smiled and scratched his temple, his hand brushing back his long hair. Nicholas was surprised that Calis looked and sounded entirely human.

Martin frowned slightly, but Nakor said, 'I have never talked to a Spellweaver before and would like to.'

Calis and Martin exchanged glances, but it was Nakor

who continued to speak. 'Yes, I know about your Spell-weavers, and no, I am not a magician.'

The three stood seemingly motionless for a moment, then Calis grinned. 'How do you know so much?'

Nakor shrugged and said, 'I pay attention when other people are babbling. You can learn a lot when you shut up.' Reaching into his ever present bag, he said, 'Want an orange?'

Producing four pieces of fruit, he tossed them to Calis and the elves. Calis bit into the fruit and tore away a bit of peel, then sucked the juice. 'I haven't had an orange since the last time I visited Crydee.'

The other elves sampled the fruit and nodded their appreciation to Nakor. Harry said, 'I wish I could figure out how you can fit so many oranges into that bag.'

Nakor began to speak, but Nicholas interrupted: 'I know. It's a trick.'

Nakor laughed. 'Maybe someday I'll show you.'

Martin said, 'Why has your Queen sent you south of river Crydee?'

'We're growing lax in our patrols, Lord Martin. Things have been peaceful too long on our borders.'

'Trouble?' said Martin, instantly alert.

Calis shrugged. 'Not to talk about. A moredhel band crossed the river to the east of our borders a few months ago, heading south at great speed, but they did not trespass upon our lands, so we left them in peace.' Nicholas knew of the elves' dark cousins, called the Brotherhood of the Dark Path by humans. Their last rising had been broken at the Battle of Sethanon. 'Tathar and the other Spellweavers speak of vague echoes of dark powers, but they can sense nothing that threatens us directly. So we mount more active patrols and venture farther from home than we have for years.'

'Anything else?'

Calis said, 'One report of a strange sighting near your

new fortress up at Barran, near the river Sodina. Someone beached a long boat in the mouth of the river one night a few weeks ago. We found marks in the mud and tracks of men coming and going.'

Martin's face reflected his consideration as he was silent for a moment. 'No smuggler would be willing to come that close to a garrison; besides, there's no one to trade with that far to the north.'

Marcus said, 'Scouts?'

'For whom?' asked Nicholas.

Martin said, 'We've no neighbors to the north, save goblins and moredhel. And they've been quiet since Sethanon.'

'Not too quiet,' said Calis. 'We've had a few skirmishes along the northern borders of Elvandar.'

Marcus said, 'Are they preparing to invade again?'

Calis said, 'There's no pattern to it. Father rode out and thinks it's nothing more than migrations due to failed crops or clan wars. He sent word to the dwarves at Stone Mountain that they may have unwelcome neighbors soon.'

Suddenly Nicholas made the connection: this was Megar and Magya's grandson! His father was Tomas, the legendary warrior from the Riftwar.

Martin nodded. 'We'll send word to Dolgan that they may be returning to the Grey Towers as well. It's been more than thirty years since the great migration; the moredhel may be returning to their abandoned homelands.'

'Thirty years is not very long as elvenkind counts time,' observed Garret.

Marcus said, 'To have the Dark Brothers in the Grey Towers and the Green Heart again would mean serious trouble.'

'We send word to the commander at Jonril as well,' said Martin. 'If the Dark Brothers establish villages in the

Green Heart, every caravan and mule train from Carse to Crydee is at risk.'

Marcus glanced around. 'We should make camp, Father. The light is failing.'

Martin said, 'Calis, will you join us?'

Calis glanced at the sky, noticing the fading light, then at his companions, who seemed to Nicholas to remain motionless, but after a moment he said, 'We'd be pleased to share the fire with you.'

Turning to Nicholas and Harry, Martin said, 'Better start gathering firewood, Squires. We make camp.'

Harry and Nicholas glanced at each other, but both knew it was futile to ask where one finds firewood. They moved away from the clearing and began looking about. Many fallen branches and some dead trees were in sight. As Nicholas started to pick out a deadfall, a hand touched him upon the shoulder. Nearly jumping straight up, he turned to find Marcus behind him, holding out a hatchet. 'This might be easier than trying to chew through the branches,' he said. He handed another to Harry.

Feeling foolish, Nicholas watched his cousin return to the others. He said, 'Sometimes I could really learn to hate him.'

Harry began chopping at the deadfall. 'He doesn't seem overly fond of you, either.'

'I have half a mind to take Abigail and return to Krondor with Amos.'

Harry laughed. 'Oh, what I'd give to be a fly on the wall when you explain *that* to your father.'

Nicholas fell silent as he continued to hack away at the wood. When a full armload was ready, they gathered it up and returned to the clearing. Martin had already begun a fire with twigs and some moss, and fed the branches into the flames. 'Good, this is a fine start. Bring us three times that, and we'll have wood for the night.'

130

With a barely hidden groan, the dirty and sweating Squires returned to the deadfall and resumed hacking.

The sentry leaned out of the tower. Something was moving across the water into the harbor mouth. His station at the top of Longpoint lighthouse was the most vital post in the Duchy, as Crydee was more vulnerable from the sea than from any other quarter, a lesson hard learned during the Riftwar. The Tsurani had burned half the village with fewer than thirty men.

Then he saw: six low shapes gliding across the water. Each shallow boat was rowed by a dozen men, with another dozen standing in the middle, armed and ready.

The soldier had orders to toss a pot of special powder on the fire that would turn the flames bright red; then he was to strike a gong. Reivers were entering the harbor! As he turned, a line snapped out, weighted at one end, and before he could take another step, his neck was broken.

The assassin had concealed himself beneath the window of the tower, crouching low upon a support beam, barely two inches of which protruded beyond the stone. He quickly pulled himself into the window and removed the metal hooks he had used to climb the wall by embedding their points in the mortar between the stones. He hurried down the winding stairs, killing two more guards along the way. Three men served each night in the tower, with another three in a small guard shack at the base. As he reached the shack, the assassin saw three bodies slumped over a table, while a pair of black-clad forms moved away. He quickly overtook them, and the three killers hurried along the causeway of land called Longpoint that led from the town to the lighthouse. One of the black-garbed killers glanced toward the harbor. Another dozen pinnaces followed the first six, and the raid would soon begin in earnest. Still no alarm sounded, and all was proceeding as planned.

Longpoint broadened, with a low dock on one side and shops and storage buildings on the other. Silent ships rested alongside the quay, with half-alert sentries dozing upon their quarterdecks. A door opened as the three assassins passed, and the last patron of a dockside inn stumbled out. He was dead before he took two steps, as was the innkeeper who had shown him the door. One of the three killers glanced through the door, and the innkeeper's wife died from an expertly thrown knife before she realized it was a stranger in the doorway instead of her husband.

They would fire the docks and destroy the ships at anchor, but not yet. It would alert the castle, and if the raid was to succeed, the garrison must not be roused until after the keep gates were opened.

The three killers reached the main docks. They passed one last ship in its berth and saw movement at the bow. One assassin drew back a throwing knife, ready to kill any who might give alarm too soon, but a familiar black-clad figure waved once, and climbed over the rail, shinnying down the bowline to join his three companions. The guards on that ship were now all dead. They continued south along the docks, to where they found the small boats pulling in. Two other black-garbed men waited. They kept their distance from the armed men who now silently climbed up from the shallow boats tied off below. This was a murderous crew, men of no loyalty and one goal: killing and booty. The six men in black felt no kinship with these brigands.

But even these hardened men stepped away in dread to clear a path for the hooded and robed figure who climbed up from the last boat. He motioned toward the castle, and the six dark assassins sped up the road toward the keep. Their task was to climb the walls and open the gates. All other considerations were to wait for the breach of the final defense of Crydee.

The robed man beckoned and a small group stepped away from the main force. This band he had picked to be the first through the gate. They were the men he judged most likely to keep their wits and follow orders during the first frenzied moments of combat. But to drive home their instructions, he said, 'Remember, your orders. If any man breaks my commands, I will personally cut out his liver and eat it before life fades from his eyes.' He smiled, and even the hardest of these men felt a chill, for the man's teeth had been filed to points, the mark of a Skashakan cannibal. The leader threw back his hood, revealing a head devoid of hair. His massive brow was close to a deformity, as was his protruding jaw. Each earlobe had been pierced and stretched until long loops of flesh hung to his shoulders, with gold fetishes tied to the loops. A golden ring decorated his nose, and his fair skin was covered in purple tattoos, which made his blue eyes even more startling and terrifying.

The captain glanced back into the harbor, where the third wave of pinnaces should be approaching, another three hundred men. Silence was less a problem for the third wave, as he fully expected the alarm to sound before the third band of raiders reached the docks.

Another man approached and said, 'Captain, everyone is in place.'

To the group nearest to him he said, 'Go, the gates will be open when you reach them. Hold or die.'

To the man who had approached he said, 'Does everyone understand the orders?'

The man nodded. 'Yes. They can kill the old men and old women, and any children too young to survive the journey, but everyone who is young and healthy is to be captured, not killed.'

'And the girls?'

'The men don't like it, Captain. A little rape is part of the caper. Some say it's the best part,' he added with a smirk.

The captain's hand shot out and gripped the man's shirt. Pulling him close enough so his sick-sweet breath filled the man's nostrils, he spoke in tones of low menace. 'Vasarius, you have your orders.' He pushed the man roughly away and pointed to where a half-dozen men stood silently observing. Cross-gartered sandals too light for these cooler climates were all the protection afforded their feet, and except for the black leather harnesses that formed an H on back and chest, and leather masks covering their faces, they wore no clothing save black leather kilts. They stood motionless in the cool night air, ignoring whatever discomfort the other men might have felt. They were slavers from the guild in Durbin, and their reputations were enough to cow even as hard a crew as Captain Render's band of cut-throats.

Render said, 'Well enough I know who put that complaint in the men's minds. You're too hungry for the feel of young girls' flesh to make a good slaver, Quegan, so mark this: if one of these maidens is violated, I will kill the offending man and take your head for good measure. With your share of the gold you can buy yourself a dozen young girls once you reach Kesh. Now see to your men!' He shoved the Quegan pirate away and turned to the remaining reivers, who stood ready to attack.

He held his hand aloft, signaling the men on the docks to be quiet. They waited for the sound of battle to reach them. Long moments passed, then suddenly an alarm sounded from the keep. The pirate captain signaled and the assembled throng of cut-throats roared as one and sped into the town. Within minutes, flames were lighting the night, as torches were put to strategic buildings.

Captain Render howled a delighted laugh, knowing that the once peaceful town of Crydee was dissolving into chaos. He was in his element, and like the master of ceremonies at a grand palace gala, he delighted in every aspect of the event unfolding as planned. Pulling his own sword from its scabbard, he turned and raced after his charging men, intent on getting his fair share of the murder.

Briana's eyes opened. Something was wrong. A child of Armengar, a city of constant warfare, she had learned to sleep in armor with a sword in her hand before reaching womanhood. Past sixty years of age, she still moved out of her bed with the fluid grace of a woman half her age. Without thought, she drew her sword from the scabbard that hung from the wall peg closest to her dressing table. Clad only in a thin nightshirt, her grey hair tumbling around her shoulders, she moved toward the door of her suite.

A scream echoed down the hall and Briana hurried toward the door. It opened as she reached for it, and she leaped back, her sword coming up. Before her stood a stranger, holding a sword leveled in her direction. A rough voice shouted from down the corridor and the distant sounds of fighting came from somewhere else in the keep. The figure in the door showed no features, as another stood behind him holding a torch, rendering the first man in silhouette. Briana brought her sword up, shifted her stance, and waited.

The shadowy figure stepped forward: a short man with close-cropped blond hair, his blue eyes half-mad under heavy brows as he grinned at her. 'Just a grandmother with a sword,' he complained, his voice almost a whine. 'Too old to sell. I'll kill her.' He lashed out with his sword. The Duchess parried easily, slipping her blade around his and running up inside his guard to catch him under the arm in a swift killing blow.

'She's killed Little Harold!' cried the man holding the

torch. Three men rushed forward past the torchbearer, fanning out. Briana stepped back, keeping her eyes on the centermost, while remaining aware of the other two. She knew the center opponent was likely to feign attack, while the true attack would come from one or both of the men on the flanks. Her only hope was that these men were not practiced in fighting in a coordinated fashion and would inconvenience one another.

As she anticipated, the center swordsman leaped forward and then back. The man on her left, her weakest side, was moving toward her, his massive cutlass held high for a slashing bow. Briana ducked under his blade, impaling him on her sword point. As the man's legs went rubbery, she gripped his free hand with her own. Swinging him to her right, she propelled him into the path of the attacker on the right.

The center attacker was the next to die, as he fully expected her to be occupied by his companions and did not anticipate her attack. Briana's sword lashed out, taking him in the throat, and he stumbled back, unable to make a sound as blood fountained from the gaping wound under his chin. The last man died as he tried to free himself from the body of his companion, a slashing blow to the back of his exposed neck killing him instantly.

Briana reached down and freed a long dagger from the belt of the last man to die, as she knew she would have no time to don armor or find a shield. The raider who stood before the door holding the torch was watching down the hall, expecting the other three to have finished the lone woman in her chamber. He died before he had time to turn and see if the murder was done.

The dying man fell atop his torch, extinguishing it. Briana turned in shock as the hallway remained lighted. Angry red and yellow light illuminated the corridor, and she saw that the far end of the hall was ablaze. A scream caused Briana to turn from the flames and run as fast as she could toward her daughter's rooms.

Bare feet slapped on flagstones as the Duchess of Crydee raced to the far end of the hall. There Abigail crouched in a doorway, her nightgown half torn from her shoulders. Her eyes were wide with fear and she screamed again. At her feet lay a dead raider, and at her side Margaret crouched, a long dagger held ready to defend herself. A wounded man eyed her warily, and Margaret never acknowledged her mother's approach, so as not to give the man warning. He died a second later as Briana struck him from behind.

Margaret grabbed the fallen man's sword and felt its balance. Abigail rose, and Margaret thrust the dagger at her, hilt first.

Abigail looked down at the bloody weapon and reached to take it, then clutched at falling fabric as the nightdress slipped down off her shoulder.

'Damn it, Abigail, worry about your modesty later! If you live long enough.'

Abigail took the dagger, and the torn nightgown fell to her waist. She covered her breasts with her left arm and awkwardly gripped the bloody hilt. Then she grabbed the fabric of her gown and tried to cover herself.

Briana pointed down the hallway, saying, 'For them to be here, they've already killed our soldiers on the lower floors. If we can hold at the tower until the rest of the garrison fights its way from the barracks to the keep, we may survive.'

The three women headed toward the far door, to the southern tower of the keep. But before they were halfway to the door, a half-dozen men came into view. Briana halted and motioned for her daughter and Abigail to move back toward their quarters, as she stood ready to defend them.

Margaret took one step and halted as more men came into view behind them. She spun, back to back with her mother, and said, 'We can't.'

Briana glanced behind her, then said, 'Try to hold as long as you can.'

Margaret pushed Abigail to her left, saying, 'They will try to come at me from my weak side.' When Abigail looked confused, she said, 'My left side! Don't worry about your right. Stab at anything that moves on your left.'

The frightened girl awkwardly held the blade out, her knuckles white from holding it so tight. Her left arm pressed hard across her chest, holding up the top of her tattered nightdress. The men at both ends of the hall approached warily. They stopped out of sword range and waited.

Then those facing Margaret and Abigail moved aside, to let three large men in black masks come to the fore. The leader of the three looked at the women a long moment and said, 'Kill the old one, but do not harm the two young ones.'

With unexpected speed, one of the three men lashed out underhand with a heavy black whip. The slaver's strap snaked toward Margaret's sword arm. She instinctively twisted her wrist in a downward parry, but this was not a blade she attempted to block. The cord turned over in a serpentine and suddenly snapped around her arm, the stinging impact bringing a gasp from her. Rough leather closed down on her forearm as the large slaver pulled hard on the whip. Margaret was a strong young woman, but she was pulled off balance, yelling as she fell.

Briana spun around to see what was wrong with her daughter, and found Abigail staring, eyes wide with terror, as Margaret was dragged along the floor by the big slaver. Briana leaped forward, blade slashing down, trying to sever the whip.

Margaret rolled on her back, yelling to Abigail, 'Cut it!'

Then she saw Briana's eyes widen. Behind her stood a raider, and Margaret knew he had seized the moment to strike from behind. 'Abby! Cut the cord!' screamed Margaret, but her companion could only huddle in fear, pressing her back to the wall.

'Mother!' screamed Margaret as Briana fell to her knees. Another man stepped up behind the first and grabbed the Duchess by her hair, pulling her head back for a killing blow. Briana reversed her sword and thrust backward hard. The man holding her hair screamed in agony, doubling over as blood fountained through his fingers while he clutched at his groin.

The man who had struck Briana first didn't hesitate. He drew back his sword and plunged it hard once again into her back. Rough hands grabbed Margaret's arm and twisted it cruelly, forcing her to release the sword. 'Mother!' she screamed again as Briana's eyes went vacant and she fell foward onto the stone floor.

The third slaver rushed forward and grabbed Abigail by the hair, yanking her roughly up, forcing her to stand on tiptoe. She screamed in terror and the dagger fell from her hand as she reached upward to relieve the pain of being pulled up by her tresses, and her gown fell to her waist.

The men howled and laughed in delight at the sight of her bare breasts. One started to move toward her, stepping over the still body of the Duchess, and the first slaver shouted, 'Touch her and die!'

Two men hauled Margaret, kicking and clawing, up off the floor and quickly tied the girl's wrists, then hobbled her feet so she couldn't kick out. The slaver who had used his whip on her slid a wooden rod through the cords around her wrists and ordered the two men to hold her up. Margaret, like Abigail, had to stand on tiptoe, which gave her little opportunity to resist. The leader of slavers reached out and ripped the bodice of Margaret's gown. She spat at him, but he ignored the spittle upon his black mask. Gripping the waistband, he tore away the remaining cloth and she stood naked before him. With a practiced eye, he inspected her. He touched her small breasts, and ran his hand down her flat stomach. 'Turn her,' he commanded. The two men turned Margaret to face away from the slaver. The slaver ran his hand down her back; there was nothing intimate in the touch. He inspected her the way a horse trader inspected a potential purchase. He fondled her buttocks and ran his hand down long legs that were well muscled from riding and running. With a satisfied grunt, he said, 'This one isn't pretty, but she is steel under that velvet skin. There's a market for strong girls who can fight. Some buyers like them mean and rough. Or she may earn her life fighting in the arena.'

He then looked back at Abigail. He motioned and another slaver tore away all her gown. The men laughed appreciatively at the sight of the rest of her body, and several complained openly about not being able to take her right there.

The slaver's eyes lingered over Abigail's full young form, and he said, 'That one is unusually beautiful. She will fetch twenty-five thousand golden ecus, perhaps as high as fifty if she's a virgin.' Some of the men laughed and others whistled at the amount; it was more wealth than they could imagine. 'Wrap them both so there are no marks on their skin. If I see so much as a scratch that wasn't here this moment, I'll know they were not cared for and I will kill the man who marks them.'

The two other slavers produced soft shapeless robes that were fashioned so they could be tied over the shoulders and around the neck, so the captives could be covered without their arms and legs being freed. Abigail wept openly and Margaret continued to struggle as rough hands lingered while they covered the girls. One of the men still fondled Abigail even after the robe was properly tied.

'Enough!' shouted the slaver. 'You'll be getting ideas before long, and then I shall have to kill you!' Pointing at the men who had blocked the way to the tower, he said, 'Finish your search.'

The man on the floor moaned in pain, and the slaver glanced back at him as Abigail had her hands tied to a pole above her head. 'Nothing can be done. Kill him.'

One of his companions said, 'Sorry, Tall John. We'll use your share of the gold to hoist a drink in your name,' and cut the man's throat expertly. As life fled from the dying man's eyes, the one who killed him wiped his blade on the dead man's tunic and said in a friendly way, 'See you in hell someday.'

A man ran from the far end of the hallway, shouting, 'The fire's spreading!'

'We leave!' commanded the slaver. He led the band and their two captives away. Tied to a pole, the ends carried upon the shoulder of a man in front of and one behind her, and with her feet hobbled, Margaret still refused to come along meekly. She gripped the pole and kicked with both feet at the man behind her, sending him to the floor. She lost her footing and found herself sitting upon the flagstone staring backward. The lead slaver shouted, 'Carry her if you must.' Quickly her feet were tied to the pole, and she was hanging like a trophy animal. As she was picked up, she could see back into the hall. Through eyes filled with tears of rage and sorrow she saw her mother lying facedown on cold stones, her blood pooling around her.

A grunt of irritation woke Nicholas, and then he was aware of a questioning voice. 'What?'

The boy rose, and in the dim moonlight he saw Nakor

standing over Martin, shaking his shoulder. 'We must leave. Now!'

Marcus and the others were also waking and Nicholas reached over and gave Harry a shake. Harry's eyes opened instantly and he said, 'Huh?' in a cross tone.

Martin said, 'What is it?'

Nakor turned his back, gazing to the southeast. 'Something bad. There.' He pointed.

In the night sky a faint glow could be seen.

'What is it?' asked Harry.

Martin was on his feet, quickly gathering his belongings. 'Fire' was all he said.

Calis spoke quickly to the three elves. One nodded and all three hurried off into the early morning darkness. Calis turned to Martin. 'I'll come with you. This may have something to do with those odd sightings.'

Martin only nodded, and Nicholas was suddenly aware that he was almost ready to travel, as was Marcus. Poking Harry, Nicholas said, 'We're going to be left behind if we don't jump!'

The two Squires quickly gathered up their belongings, and by the time they were ready to move, Martin and Marcus had already left the clearing, Calis at their side. Garret said, 'I'll make sure you get back safely, but Lord Martin couldn't wait.'

Nicholas understood; there had been a grim focus of purpose in Martin's reaction to the light in the sky. For a fire to be that large, to illuminate the heavens enough to be seen a half day's march away, would mean terrible destruction, either to the woodlands near the town, or to the town itself.

Ghuda and Nakor waited for the boys, then the five remaining members of the hunting party headed off. Garret said, 'Keep in a single line behind me, all of you. I'll stay on the trail, but there are still many places to hurt yourself in the dark if you're not careful. If I go too fast for any of you to keep up, call out.'

'Want a light?' asked Nakor.

'No,' answered Garret. 'A torch or lantern won't light far enough to help and would make it harder to see ahead into the woods.'

'No, I mean a good light!' said the little man. He opened his bag and pulled out a ball that he tossed into the air. Rather than come down, the ball spun and began to glow, first faintly, then with increasing brilliance. As it grew brighter, it rose until it hung fifteen feet above their heads, illuminating the woodland trail for a hundred yards ahead and behind.

Garret glanced at the blue-white object, shook his head, and said, 'Let's go.'

He set off at a fast trot, not quite a run, and the others kept pace. They hurried through the woodlands, illuminated to stark contrast and absolute black shadows by the alien glow. Nicholas expected they would overtake Martin and the others quickly, but they never did.

The journey became a series of seemingly unconnected images of a brilliantly lit pathway leading into the blackness, with occasional obstacles, a deadfall to climb over, a small stream to be leaped, or a rock outcropping to be skirted. Still tired from the previous day's march and interrupted sleep, Nicholas fought back the urge to ask for a halt. His nerves jangled with fatigue and tension; Martin's and Marcus's faces had been grim masks, expressions he had never seen before, and he felt his stomach knotting in dread anticipation.

The minutes ground away to hours, and at some point Nicholas became aware that Nakor's light was gone, and the entire woodland was illuminated by the grey dawn. This close to the coast, the light from the east was diffused by ocean-born mists carried inland through the valleys and dells surrounding Crydee. Nicholas knew that the haze would burn off around midmorning if the day did not remain overcast.

Later, Garret called a halt and Nicholas leaned against a tree. He was drenched in perspiration, and his left foot throbbed from exertion and changes in the weather. Absently, he said, 'There's a storm coming.'

Garret nodded. 'My joints ache. I think you're right, Squire.'

As they caught their breath in a small clearing, the haze burned away and Harry said, 'Look!'

To the southwest, a giant plume of black smoke rose into the sky, a terrible sign of destruction. The old mercenary said, 'At least half the town, from the look of it.'

Without comment, Garret resumed his trot and the others fell in behind.

It was nearing midday when Nicholas crested a hill with the others, putting them in sight of the keep and the town below. As they drew near, the size of the column of smoke appeared to grow. When they gazed down on Crydee, their worst fears were confirmed.

The castle stood a gutted, fire-blackened shell of stone, with smoke still pouring from the central keep. What had been the peaceful seaside town was a charred landscape of smoking timbers interspersed with fires still out of control. Only in the distant hills to the south could a few untouched buildings be seen.

'They've destroyed the entire town,' whispered Harry, his voice hoarse from exertion and the bitter smoke that stung eyes and lungs.

Garret forgot the others as he ran toward the town. They moved at half his speed, Harry and Nicholas almost in shock from the sight of the destruction ahead.

Nakor shook his head and muttered to himself, and

Ghuda searched all quarters for signs of troubles. It was a full five minutes before Nicholas noticed that the Keshian had his sword out and ready. As an afterthought, Nicholas drew his hunting knife. He didn't know what else to do, but having a weapon in his hand made him feel somehow more prepared to deal with whatever they might find.

At the edge of the town, on a road between what had once been modest houses belonging to workers and their families, Nicholas and the others found the bitter stench of blackened wood almost too strong to endure. With eyes tearing, they hurried along, until they reached one of the smaller market squares leading to the main square at the center of town. Here they stopped, for more than a score of bodies littered the ground.

Harry took a moment to absorb the sight of the blackened and hacked bodies, then turned away and vomited. Nicholas swallowed hard to keep his own stomach from rebeling, and Harry looked as if he might faint. Ghuda reached out and steadied the young Squire with a firm grip on his arm, while Nakor said, 'Barbaric.'

'Who did this?' whispered Nicholas.

Ghuda let go of Harry's arm and examined the bodies. He moved among them, inspecting how they lay, and then looked at the surrounding buildings. Finally he said, 'These were some cruel bastards.' He pointed to where the houses stood. 'They fired those buildings and waited out here. Those that ran out first were hacked to bits, and those that stayed inside finally ran out when the fire became too hot to endure.' He wiped perspiration from his face. 'Or were roasted alive.'

Nicholas found tears in his eyes. He didn't know if it was from the smoke or the terror. 'Who were they?'

Glancing around, Ghuda said, 'They weren't regular soldiers.' Looking at those bodies nearby and others down the street, he said at last, 'I don't know.'

'Where were our soldiers?' asked Harry in disbelief.

Ghuda said, 'I don't know that, either.'

They began moving among the corpses toward the town market and the castle entrance. A sick, sweet smell assaulted Nicholas's senses, and suddenly he knew he was smelling burnt flesh. Unable to retain control over himself, he turned and lost the contents of his stomach as Harry had a moment before.

Harry still stumbled along, half in a daze, as if his mind couldn't accept what lay around him. Ghuda said firmly, 'Come along. We're going to be needed.'

Shaking his head to keep from blacking out, Nicholas turned and followed the mercenary. Along every step of the way they encountered devastation. Nicholas was struck by the occasional odd item that somehow survived intact. A blue clay bowl lay in the middle of the road, and without knowing why, he stepped over it, leaving it untouched. A child's doll fashioned of rags and straw sat upright against a portion of intact brick wall, as if silently observing the insanity.

Nicholas looked at Harry and saw his ashen face was streaked with tears, cutting white trails down his sooty cheeks. Glancing at Ghuda and Nakor, he saw that their faces also were now grey from the haze of smoke that hung in the air. Nicholas examined his own hands and saw that they were covered in fine dark soot, and he touched his own cheek; his fingers came away wet and he almost quit moving, so overwhelmed was he by helplessness.

As they neared the castle, it got worse. Most of the townspeople had fled for the expected safety of the Duke's keep, only to be cut down near their failed sanctuary. Three men lay on the ground where two streets met, their bodies riddled with arrows.

Nicholas and Harry saw their first signs of life as they passed through the remains of the town's main market. A small child sat in stunned silence next to the body of his mother. His eyes were round with mute terror and his face was caked with dried blood.

Nakor scooped up the child, who seemed not to notice. 'Scalp wound.' He clucked at the boy, who reacted by gripping Nakor's ragged blue robe with both hands. 'Not bad. Looks worse. Probably saved his life: they thought he was already dead.' The child, who could not have been more than four, kept his eyes fixed upon Nakor, who at last placed his free hand upon the child's face a moment. When he removed it, the child's eyes closed and he slumped against the Isalani's chest. 'He'll sleep. It's better for him. He's too young for such horror.'

Harry choked out, 'We're all too young for this, Nakor.'

Carrying the still child, the little man continued toward the keep. Sounds alerted them to other survivors, some weeping loudly, others groaning.

Reaching the main gate of the keep, Nicholas and the others halted. In a scene from the lower depths of hell, the central keep was a blackened skeleton of stone, lit from within by still-furious flames. In the central courtyard before it, the wounded lay wherever there was space, while the few remaining survivors able to move attempted to provide what comfort they could.

Nicholas and Harry picked their way through the tableau of injured and dying humanity and caught sight of Martin, Marcus and Calis. Martin knelt above a figure who lay upon the ground.

Hurrying to where they were gathered, Nicholas found Swordmaster Charles lying upon the ground, his nightshirt stiff with his dried blood. The former Tsurani soldier's face was drenched in perspiration and almost devoid of color from pain and injury. Nicholas didn't have to be told he was dying. The lifeless twist of his legs below the nightshirt and the still-crimson stain in the center of his shirt told the young man that the Swordmaster of Crydee had taken a killing wound to the stomach.

Martin's face was a stone mask, yet his eyes betrayed his pain. He leaned over Charles and said, 'What else?'

Charles swallowed and in a ragged whisper said, 'Some of the raiders . . . were Tsurani.'

Marcus said, 'Renegades from LaMut?'

'No, not soldiers from the war. Brimanu Tong.' He coughed, then gasped. 'Assassins. Hired murderers. They . . . are without honor . . .' His eyes closed a moment and then he opened them again. 'This was . . . not honorable . . . combat. This was . . . slaughter.' He groaned and his eyes closed and his breathing became shallow.

Anthony came into view, limping, his left arm in a sling. In his right hand he carried a water bucket. Harry hurried over and took the bucket from him. The magician knelt painfully next to Charles and examined him. After a moment he looked at Martin and shook his head. 'He will not awaken.'

Martin stood slowly, his eyes not leaving his Swordmaster. Then he said, 'Faxon?'

Anthony said, 'Died in the stable with some of the soldiers; they were trying to hold the stable while Rulf and his sons got the horses out. They died as well, fighting with blacksmith's hammers and pitchforks.'

'Samuel?'

'I haven't seen him.' Anthony looked around and for a moment Nicholas thought he was about to break down, but the young magician swallowed hard and continued. 'I was asleep. I heard sounds of fighting. I couldn't tell if they came from in the keep or outside. I hurried to the window and looked out.' He glanced around at the carnage. 'Then someone broke into my room and threw something at me . . . an axe, I think.' He frowned as he tried to remember. 'I fell out the window. I landed on . . . someone.' He seemed almost embarrassed as he added, 'He was dead. I didn't break anything, but I was senseless for a time. I remember reviving and feeling this terrible heat. I dragged myself away from it. I don't remember much after that.'

Nicholas said, 'Marcus, your family?'

His cousin said in flat tones, 'My mother is still in there.' He pointed to the raging fire that had been the family keep the day before.

Grief was quickly followed by anger, then alarm. 'Margaret! Abigail?'

Anthony said, 'Someone said the girls were carried off. Some of the young men, too, I think.' He closed his eyes as if suddenly pained, then added, 'From the town, as well; girls and boys were dragged away.'

A nearby soldier, leaning on a broken spear, said, 'I saw them leading some of the captives away, Your Grace.' He indicated the wall and said, 'I was on duty there. I heard someone in the courtyard and looked, then was struck from behind. When I revived, I was hanging halfway out of one of the crenels – someone tried to throw me off the wall, I guess. I got cut some, but I pulled myself back.' He said, 'There were a couple of dead men nearby, and the castle was already in flames. I looked out at the town and I saw men herding boys and girls toward the harbor.'

Ghuda said, 'Did you see who they were?'

'It was lit up like day; more than half the town was fired by then. There were maybe four or six of them; big men, they wore these harnesses, kilts, and masks of black leather and they all had whips.'

Ghuda said, 'Durbin Slavers' Guild.'

Martin said, 'We'll sort this out later, but now we've injured to look after.'

Nicholas and Harry nodded and moved off, and in minutes they were hurrying with buckets of water. As the day dragged on, they helped aid those who could move to shelter in the eleven buildings that had escaped damage at the south end of town. Others were carried to the fishing village a mile farther down the coast.

Slowly the shocked and shattered population of Crydee that remained began the torturous task of reviving. More people died and they were carried to a pyre that was being erected in the town marketplace.

Nicholas helped a soldier with a bandaged head lift another corpse atop the mass of dead, piled on some wood that had been dragged in from the forest, and noticed that somehow it had become night. Another soldier stood nearby with a torch and said, 'That's the last of it. We'll probably find more of them tomorrow, but it's time to quit.'

Nicholas nodded mutely and stumbled away as the torch was applied to the wood. As the flames rose up to consume the dead, he plodded to the far end of Crydee, to the welcoming lights and the sound of voices. He thought the reservoir of anguish had dried, but as he dragged himself through the burned-out remains of a once thriving town he found himself choking back tears. His mind had rejected the grotesque images, the partially burned bodies that had to be carried to the pyre, the children that had been hacked to death, dogs and cats with arrows in them for no reason. The bitter comment that one soldier had made that the raiders had saved them from a lot of work, for half the population had been cremated already, hit Nicholas as he stood alone in the middle of an empty patch of earth, a small market square. He leaned forward, hands on his knees, and began to shiver, though the night was only cool. Trembling to the point where his teeth began to chatter, the boy sucked in a bitter lungful of smoky air and gave a low, angry groan. Forcing his right foot ahead, he pulled himself erect and commanded his body to move forward. He had a feeling that if he stopped again before reaching the place where

Martin and the others waited, he might never move again.

He plodded along until he reached the largest building still standing. It was to have been a new inn once construction was finished. The walls rose up into the darkness, and the first floor – covering only half of the common room – had been raised, but the roof was still missing, so part of the commons was exposed to the sky. A score of townspeople huddled under the first-floor overhang, while Martin and his companions ate quietly under the stars, around a small fire pot that burned brightly. Some of the fishing folk had provided a hot fish stew and bread from their meager resources.

Nicholas stumbled over to where Harry sat at Marcus's side, and shook his head when offered a bowl of stew. He had no stomach and thought he'd never get the smell of smoke out of his nose.

Garret was saying, 'A dozen trackers and foresters have reported in so far, Your Grace. The rest should be in by dawn tomorrow.'

Martin said, 'Send them out again. I want as much game caught and brought in as they can manage in the next week. We have almost no food, and in less than two days we'll have a great many hungry people. The fishermen can catch only so much with most of the boats gone.'

Garret nodded. 'Some of the soldiers could help in the hunt.'

Martin shook his head. 'I have fewer than twenty able men left in the garrison.'

Marcus said, 'We had over a thousand men-at-arms here, Father.'

Martin nodded. 'Most died in the barracks. The raiders killed nearly everyone on the wall, opened the gate, barred the barracks doors at both ends, and fired the roof. Then they threw earthen jars of naphtha through the windows. It was an inferno inside before most of the soldiers were awake. A few managed to get out the windows, and they were cut down by bowmen. Others in the keep were killed in the room-to-room fighting. We've another hundred walking wounded, and when a few of those are mended we can spare some to hunt. Fall is fast upon us, and the game is moving south. We'll need to depend on Carse and Tulan to get through the winter.' Martin chewed a mouthful of bread and said, 'Another hundred or so lie near death. I don't know how many will survive. Anthony said those most badly burned will surely die, so by the first snowfall we may have a hundred and fifty men-at-arms left.'

Marcus said, 'There are the two hundred men at Barran.'

Martin nodded. 'I may call them back. But let's see what Bellamy can send us before then.'

Harry handed Nicholas a torn chunk of bread, thick with butter and honey, and without thought Nicholas began eating it. Suddenly he was ravenous, and he motioned to the woman passing out the stew that he would take a bowl after all.

Nicholas said nothing as he ate, listening to the grim surmises as to what happened the night before. During the day someone had mentioned that the Duchess had killed as many as a half-dozen raiders before she was at last overwhelmed, cut down trying to rescue her daughter and the other young girls. A wounded soldier had seen her lying dead before Margaret's room as he had escaped the fire in the keep. The flames had been too hot and he had been too injured to bring the Duchess out of the conflagration.

Nicholas waited for mention of the girls' fate, but Martin and the others spoke only of immediate concerns. As people came to report and left again, a picture of the destruction formed in Nicholas's mind. Of a prosperous town with nearly ten thousand citizens, fewer than two thousand lived, and many of those would not survive another week because of their injuries. Of a thousand soldiers, one man in five might live to serve the Kingdom again. Every building from Longpoint Lighthouse to the south end of the old town was destroyed, and half the new buildings were gone. No business survived intact. Of the assorted Craftmasters, only one blacksmith, two carpenters, and a miller lived. A half-dozen journeymen and a score of apprentices would be able to help rebuild. Most of those who had survived were fishermen and farmers. They would be pressed into service where needed, but for the foreseeable future, Crydee was reduced to a rude village, a primitive enclave on the Far Coast of the Kingdom.

Nicholas heard Martin saying, 'And we'll have to ask Bellamy and Tolburt down in Tulan to send us craftsmen. We need to start rebuilding the castle at once.'

Nicholas couldn't stand it any longer. Softly he asked, 'What about the girls?'

All talk halted, and every eye in the circle turned to look at him. With ill-hidden bitterness, Marcus said, 'What do you propose we do?'

Nicholas could say nothing.

Marcus said, 'They burned every ship in the harbor. They burned most of the boats. Shall we take a fishing skiff and row to Durbin?'

Nicholas shook his head. 'Send word – '

'To your father?' asked Marcus bitterly. 'He's halfway across the Kingdom! Is there a carrier pigeon alive? Is there a horse fit to ride to Carse? No!' His pain and anger at his loss were turned on the only target available, Nicholas.

Martin put a restraining hand on his son's shoulder, and Marcus fell silent. 'We'll talk about this tomorrow.'

Nicholas didn't ask permission to leave, he just stood and moved away from the warmth of the small fire. He found a relatively sheltered place beneath the stairs leading up to the first floor and huddled there. After a few minutes, he was struck by the need to be home, with his own mother and father and his sister and brothers, his teachers, and those who had always protected and loved him. For the first time in years he felt like a very small boy again, afraid of those boys who taunted him and mocked him when his protectors were absent. Feeling sick and ashamed, Nicholas turned his face to the wall and wept.

7

Choices

The storm struck.

Nicholas was awakened by wetness on his face. His sleep had been deep and dreamless; he awoke stiff and still exhausted. There had been a brief moment of disorientation as he had come awake, then all too quickly he knew exactly where he was and what had happened.

Despair struck him as rain came pounding through the opening above the common room. Those who slept along the wall or under the stars quickly moved in with those huddled under the first-floor overhang. The wet chill was accompanied by a deeper, more profound chill as the memories of the previous day's horrors returned.

Nicholas saw that it was growing light, despite the rain, and knew it must be past sunrise. Harry picked his way carefully among those who tried to keep dry, his hair already matted to his head. 'Come on, we have work to do.'

Nicholas nodded and awkwardly stood up. His foot hurt and he limped as he forced himself to walk into the downpour. Within seconds he was soaked to the skin. The only relief in the storm was that the burning stink of the night before was diminished.

Reaching the open door of the inn, the boys walked outside to where Martin stood. His only concession to the rain was an oilskin cover that protected his longbow and another on his quiver of arrows. 'We need to find as much useful wood as we can, Squire,' he said to Nicholas.

Nicholas nodded and turned to where three men huddled under a small overhang, offering only the illusion of protection against the weather. 'You three,' Nicholas shouted over the tattoo of the rain, 'are you injured?'

The three men shook their heads, and one said, 'But we're wet, Squire.'

Nicholas waved for them to join him. 'You're not going to get any wetter for working. I need you.'

One of the men glanced at Martin, who nodded once, and the three men got to their feet and followed after Nicholas.

For the rest of the day they picked their way through the wreckage of Crydee, finding a timber here, a few planks of wood there, carrying the manageable items back to the inn. The location of the larger pieces was noted for future use.

By midday the storm had lessened. Nicholas and his three companions – a farmer whose house on the far edge of town had been burned, and two brothers who had worked in the mill – had managed to find a half-dozen barrels of nails, some undamaged carpentry tools, and enough wood to erect a dozen rude shelters. The carpenter who had survived the raid had inspected the tools and announced that should lumber be found and cut, he could finish the roof on the inn within a week with the help of three able men. Martin said they would see if enough cutting equipment had survived to fell trees.

One fact presented itself to Nicholas through this day: the ancient tradition of having each boy in the keep practice a variety of crafts before finally being selected at the Choosing for his trade was proving a boon. While these men were not carpenters or masons, they did know the fundamentals of those trades, and showed amazing retention of the things learned while boys.

By nightfall, Nicholas was again exhausted and starving. Food was going to be a problem soon, but for the second night the fishing village provided enough for all to eat. A soldier, limping as he used a rude crutch, entered the inn as Nicholas was eating and reported to Martin that a half-dozen horses had been found near the river. Martin seemed pleased at the prospect of being able to mount a small patrol and send word to Baron Bellamy by fast rider. A fishing boat had been dispatched toward Carse that afternoon, but it would take many days to get down the coast.

Harry came over to sit by his friend, and he dug into the bowl of hot stew. Between spoonfuls, he said, 'I never knew fish stew could taste so good.'

Nicholas said, 'You're hungry.'

Bitterly, Harry said, 'No, really?'

Nicholas said, 'I'm in no mood for this either, but don't take your nasty temper out on me, Harry, and I won't take mine out on you.'

Harry nodded and said, 'Sorry.'

Nicholas stared off into space for a moment. He said, 'Do you think we'll ever see them again?'

Harry sighed. He didn't have to ask whom Nicholas meant. 'I heard Martin and Marcus earlier today. They say if Bellamy can get word to Krondor fast enough, our fleet can blockade Durbin before the raiders return there. They think your father can force the Governor of Durbin to turn over all the captives.'

Nicholas sighed. 'I wish Amos was back. He knows about this sort of thing. He was a Durbin captain once.'

Harry said, 'I wish he was here, too. A lot of this doesn't make any sense. Why would they kill so many and burn down everything?'

Glancing around the miserable company in the inn, Nicholas was forced to agree. Then something struck him. 'Where's Calis? I haven't seen him since Charles died.'

'He went back to Elvandar,' answered Harry. 'He had to tell his mother what happened, he said.'

Alarm struck Nicholas. 'Gods. What about his grandparents?' Nicholas hadn't seen Magya or Megar among the survivors.

'I think I saw Megar down at the other end of the fishing village earlier today. It looked like him. He was supervising the cooking of this food for everyone.'

Nicholas had his first laugh since they had left to go hunting. 'That had to be him.'

Robin, a page who had worked for Housecarl Samuel, picked his way through the crowded room and sat next to the two Squires. The three boys compared notes on what they saw during the day, and the picture was as bleak as they had feared. The entire castle staff except for Megar and Magya, another cook and a scullery boy, two other Squires, and a handful of pages and servants had been killed during the raid or died from wounds shortly after. During the night and morning, another dozen soldiers had died from wounds, and many of the townspeople were sick or injured.

After the meal, Nicholas, Harry, and Robin went to where Martin spoke with Anthony and Marcus. Seeing the boys arrive, Martin said, 'Have you eaten?'

The three nodded, and Martin said, 'Good. The rain has ended the fires, so at first light head up to the castle and help me see what can be salvaged. Now get some sleep.'

Nicholas and Harry looked around the room for some clear space in which to sleep and saw a small opening near the far wall. The three boys picked their way over sleeping townspeople and crowded their way into the mass. Nicholas found himself sleeping between Harry and an old fisherman who snored loudly. Rather than minding the noise, he was comforted by the closeness and the warmth.

Days passed, and life began again in Crydee. The carpenter and his helpers finished putting the roof on the inn, and that became the Duke's headquarters, though Martin refused to sleep in any of the rooms on the first floor, giving them over to the injured and sick most in need of shelter and warmth. Another hundred or so townspeople and soldiers had died from wounds or sickness, despite all of Anthony's and Nakor's skills. Somehow word of the tragedy had reached the distant Abbey of Silban on the edge of Elvandar, and a half-dozen monks of that order had arrived to lend aid.

Harry had become the unofficial innkeeper, as the man who was building the new inn had died in the raid. He passed out what food there was, settled arguments, and kept an orderly establishment. Despite his irreverent attitude before the raid, Harry displayed an unexpected gift for negotiation and mediation. Given how short-tempered and emotionally battered everyone in Crydee was, Nicholas was impressed by his skills. Harry had the knack of bringing out the reasonable in people who were in no mood to act rationally. Nicholas made a mental note that someday, when they had returned home to a world less mad than this, Harry would make a valuable administrator in the Prince's court.

Nicholas had accompanied Martin and Marcus to the keep, finding nothing left intact. Between the naphtha used to start the fires and the combustibles in the keep, the flames had become so hot they scoured everything in their path. The fire had reached such intense heat that many of the century-old stones had cracked or exploded, and even the metal holders in the torch sconces on the walls had melted.

Wending their way through the blackened halls, they had found the top floor burned clean of anything recognizable. Martin and Marcus had both lingered for a long time near the door to Margaret's room, looking down at the scorched and cracked flagstones, and the fragments of melted hinges where doors had hung. Those who had died left no remains, as the intense flames had even reduced

159

their bones to black ash. A few puddles of metal, now hardened to the stone, showed where weapons had been dropped and left behind.

Down in the lowest basement, a few usable stores survived: some cloth, cloaks, and blankets that reeked of smoke, and several trunks of old clothing, as well as old boots, belts, and dresses.

Harry discovered battle stores; Martin inspected the food. He observed that it must have been there since the Riftwar. The jerked beef was now blackened and hard as ancient leather; the hard bread crumbled like dried clay. But three barrels were of more recent vintage, and were sealed with paper and wax. When one was opened, it contained still-edible dried apples. And to everyone's amusement, a half-dozen casks of fine Keshian brandy were uncovered as well. All were marked to be carried to the town, under Nicholas's supervision.

As they left the castle, Nicholas was silent; he had waited for some remark by Martin or Marcus about the Duchess's death, but neither husband nor son said a word.

The day dragged by and slowly the town began to heal itself. A second, then a third building was repaired, and as the injured returned to health, they joined in the hard work, speeding the recovery.

Later in the week, Calis returned, with a dozen elves carrying game. Three deer were dressed out and carried on poles, while quail and rabbits were carried in bunches tied at the feet. The hungry people of Crydee thanked the elves and set to cooking everything offered.

Calis spent an hour with his grandparents, then joined Martin's group for supper. Nicholas and Harry ate venison steaks as the young elfling said, 'My mother and father were very disturbed by this raid, and I have more bad news. Your fortress at Barran was hit as well.'

Martin's eyes widened. 'Amos?'

Calis nodded. 'His ship as well, though he fought off those who tried to burn it. He's made repairs and should be here in a day or two.'

Martin said, 'This makes less sense as we uncover more information. Why would slavers strike a garrison of soldiers?'

'My father thinks it may be to prevent you from following after,' ventured Calis.

Marcus shook his head. 'Why would we spend weeks chasing those slavers to Durbin when we can get word to Krondor with Bellamy's pigeons and cut them off?'

Calis's gaze narrowed in an expression of concern as he said, 'Has any word from Carse reached you yet?'

Martin put down the rib he had been eating and said, 'Gods! The packet boat from Carse. It never did arrive.'

Marcus said, 'If Bellamy's been raided . . .'

Martin rose and looked around the room. Seeing a familiar face, he called one of the garrison's soldiers to him. 'At first light I want a pair of riders off to Carse. If they should encounter any men of Carse bringing news of a raid down there, have them continue down to Bellamy, change horses, and then on to see Tolburt at Tulan. I want full reports on what has happened as soon as possible.' The soldier saluted and left. The remaining horses were staked out in a picket outside the inn, and there had been enough odds and ends of tack found to outfit a pair of riders.

Martin sat again. Ghuda and Nakor entered the inn and came to where Martin sat brooding. The little man said, 'I think most of those who live now will recover.'

Marcus said, 'At last a little good news.'

Martin motioned for them to sit and eat, and after a while said, 'I have a very bad feeling that we've only seen the start of something far more significant than a raid.'

Ghuda said, 'I've seen Durbin slavers' handiwork

before, my lord, and this is nothing like it. This was butchery.' He shook his head. 'For sport, if you can believe it.'

Martin closed his eyes a moment, as if he had a headache, then opened them and said, 'I haven't felt this uneasy since the Riftwar.'

Marcus said, 'Do you think the Tsurani are again turning their eyes toward us?'

Martin shook his head. 'No. The Mistress of the Empire has too firm a hand on things for that. She's proven a shrewd trading partner since her son became Emperor, but a fair one. A few unlicensed merchants, slipping through the rift somehow to trade for metals, I might accept that. But this' – his hand described an arc indicating the entire town – 'makes little sense if it was Tsurani renegades.'

'But Charles said some of the raiders were Tsurani, Father,' Marcus pointed out.

'What did he call them?' asked Ghuda. 'Tong?'

Nakor said, 'Brimanu Tong. That means "Golden Storm Brotherhood."'

Martin said, 'You speak Tsurani?'

Nakor nodded. 'Enough. Those were assassins. Tsurani Nighthawks if you prefer: guild killers who are paid for death. The Mistress of the Empire destroyed the most powerful Tong, the Hamoi, fifteen years ago, but there are others.'

Martin shook his head and pinched the bridge of his nose. 'What does it all mean?'

It means you've got serious trouble, my friend,' said a familiar voice from the door of the inn.

Everyone turned and saw the bulky outline in the doorway as he stepped forward.

'Amos!' said Martin. 'You're here sooner than I thought.'

'I piled on every inch of canvas I could and worked the

162

men to dropping,' said Trask as he moved across the common room, removing a canvas foul-weather coat. He tossed it on the floor and sat next to Martin.

'What happened at Barran?' asked the Duke.

Amos removed his wool cap, stuffed it in his pocket, and took a mug of hot tea offered him by Harry. Where Harry had found the tea no one knew, but in the cool of the evening, everyone welcomed its pungent comfort. 'We were hit seven nights back, which means the night before you were, I think.' Martin nodded. 'Ever since my run-in with the Tsurani during the war, I've kept an extra watch up during the night when I'm at anchor. Good thing, because most of the watch died before the alarm was raised. One of my men got us up in time, though, and we killed all the bastards who tried to burn my ship.' He sighed. 'The garrison wasn't as lucky. We'd just finished unloading most of the arms and stores – one more day would have seen us done. Your Knight-Lieutenant, Edwin, halted work on the stockade to help get the ship unloaded, so the gate wasn't finished. The raiders were inside killing men in the barracks before the alarm was sounded. Still, we bled the bastards before they fired the fort.'

'The fort burned?' asked Marcus.

'To the ground,' Amos confirmed.

'The garrison?' asked Martin.

'I had no choice. I brought them back with me.'

Martin nodded. 'How many survived?'

Amos sighed. 'A little fewer than a hundred, I'm sorry to say. Edwin's getting them off the ship now. He'll give you a full report when he gets here.'

'We managed to get some goods out of the wreckage, and there was the little that hadn't been unloaded, but most of the weapons and stores were destroyed. There was no fortress, and winter's heading our way, so it seemed prudent to abandon the entire project until next spring.' Amos ran his hand over his face. 'From the looks of Crydee, you need every able hand you can find down here, anyway.'

Martin said, 'That's the truth.' He filled Amos in on what they knew about the raid, and as he recounted facts, Amos's face clouded over.

When he reached a description of the raiders' boats, provided by one of the fishermen, Amos said, 'This makes no sense!'

Marcus said, 'You're not the first one to say that, Amos.'

Amos said, 'No, not just the raid. Anyway, go on.'

Martin continued his recounting of the raid, gleaned from reports gathered from eyewitnesses since the Duke returned. It took another half hour to finish the narrative.

Amos stood and attempted to pace around the crowded floor of the inn, his hand rubbing his bearded chin as he thought. At last he said, 'From what you've told me, there must have been closer to a thousand men involved in just this part of the caper.'

'Caper?' asked Harry.

'Job, undertaking, endeavor,' supplied Nakor with a grin. 'Criminal idiom.'

'Oh,' said the Squire.

'So?' asked Marcus.

Amos turned to look at him. 'That would mean at least six, probably eight Durbin captains working together. That's not happened since I left.'

'Really?' said Martin dryly. Amos's distant past was known to him; he was once the most feared raider on the Bitter Sea, Captain Trenchard, the Dagger of the Sea. As the years had passed, Amos's personal history had changed as he told it, so that by now he was fond of saying that he had been a privateer, working for the Governor of Durbin.

'Yes, really!' said Amos. 'The Captains of the Coast

are a fractious lot and don't cooperate in much of anything. The only reason they're allowed to remain in the city is that they keep Queg at bay, and that's fine with Kesh, for the Empire doesn't wish to pay money to provision a fleet there.' Looking at Martin, he said, 'And as your brother's Admiral, I'm a lot more comfortable with a dozen argumentative pirate captains I can personally bully in Durbin than an Imperial Keshian squadron. Politics, my dear Martin, can make almost anything respectable.'

'So they put aside their usual differences and banded together for one haul?' said Ghuda.

Amos shook his head. 'Not likely. A raid on Carse and Crydee? And the new fortification up at Barran as well? I'll bet there's not one deepwater ship left in Tulan, either.' He struck his hand on the bar, which he leaned against. 'What I would give for a brandy,' he muttered.

Harry said, 'Well, I was saving this for Anthony and Nakor to use with the sick,' as he reached under the bar and produced a small bottle of Keshian brandy. He poured a cup and Amos lifted it.

Smacking his lips, Amos said, 'Heaven will remember you for this, boy.' Returning to Martin's circle, he knelt. 'Look, this wasn't any raid out of Durbin.'

'The slavers – ' protested Marcus.

Amos held up his hand. 'I don't care. It's a false trail, son. Slavers will slip up on a village and hit it, stealing healthy children and fit men and women. They don't go burning everything in sight. They don't conduct wholesale warfare, and they don't go kidnapping the nieces of Kings. Tends to bring too much trouble down upon them.' He rubbed his chin. 'If I knew who was in on this, which of the captains . . .'

'One of the soldiers says the leader was a tall, fair-skinned man with tattoos all over his face.'

'With teeth filed to points and blue eyes?' asked Amos.

Nicholas nodded.

Amos's eyes widened and he whispered. 'Render. I thought he was dead.'

Martin leaned forward. 'Who is this Render?'

Amos spoke softly, a note of astonishment in his tone. 'A foul son of a demon. He was lost in the western archipelagoes when he was a seaman. He and the rest of his crew were captured by Skashakan Islanders. Render somehow gained their trust and they adopted him into their tribe. He was the only one of his crew to survive. He's covered from head to toe with clan tattoos and his teeth were filed to points in the ritual that made him one of the clan. To be initiated, he had to eat one of his shipmates. The Skashakan Islanders are cannibals.'

Amos sat. 'I first met him in Margrave's Port. He was first mate on Captain Mercy's ship.'

'Mercy?' asked Nicholas with a disbelieving laugh.

'Most of the Captains of the Coast are known by false names,' said Amos. 'I was Trenchard, and Trevor Hull was White-eye; Gilbert de Gracie was Captain Mercy; he'd once been an initiate in the Temple of Dala the Merciful. He obviously didn't have the calling, but the name stuck.' Amos turned away, a small frown on his face.

Martin said, 'What is it, Amos?'

'Render knew the slave trade, for that was one of Mercy's pastimes, but he was never a Durbin captain, Martin. He wasn't even a captain when I knew him; last I heard, he was part of John Avery's crew, and Avery betrayed Durbin to a Quegan raiding fleet. Render's a dead man if he ever sets foot in Durbin again.'

One of the soldiers nearby said, 'Begging your pardon, Admiral, but did you say Quegan?'

Martin turned to the soldier. 'What is it?'

'My lord, I didn't recall until this moment, but there was one other man who looked familiar, though I barely noticed in all the chaos. Remember that Quegan trader who visited a few nights before you left to hunt? He was with some of the raiders.'

'Vasarius,' said Nicholas. 'I didn't like the way he kept looking at Abigail and Margaret.'

'And he asked the Swordmaster and Horsemaster a lot of questions about the castle and how we were garrisoned,' said the soldier.

'Friendly like, but probably measuring the defenses.'

Amos said, 'This grows more complicated by the moment. Durbin raiders wouldn't pull this sort of caper. It's declaring war. Their reputation is partially due to picking their prey carefully, and avoiding those capable of retaliation. The only reason for a raid of this scale would be to keep anyone from following, because it's obvious that's the only thing they fear.'

Martin looked confused. 'What do you mean?'

'Your people reported Durbin guild slavers among the raiding party. What if they weren't real? What if the raiders wanted you to think they were heading for Durbin? They should know you have means to send messages faster than they could return to the Bitter Sea. You could get riders over the mountains and to the Free Cities and have a fast ship take you to Krondor and have the fleet at sea ambush off the Durbin coast by the time they could get down the coast and through the Straits of Darkness this time of the year. No, they're not heading for Durbin, and they don't want us following after them.'

Nicholas said, 'How could we follow? I mean, there's no trail on the sea.'

Amos grinned. 'Because I know where they're going first, Nicky.'

Martin sat up straight at this. 'Where are they taking my daughter, Amos?'

'Freeport. Render's a Sunset Islands man – at least, that's the last I heard of him – and from what you've told me about those boats that they used, that's about as far as they can travel.'

'I don't understand,' said Marcus. 'What about the boats?'

To Martin, Amos said, 'Remember when I said it didn't make sense?'

Martin nodded.

Amos said, 'I was speaking of the boats. They were pinnaces. They're small, narrow craft with a single mast that can be taken down. No large ship could have come close enough to Crydee to unload such a force and not have been spotted by your lookouts on Longpoint and down at Sailor's Grief. From what you've said, nearly a thousand men struck here, and we had another two hundred on our necks up at Barran. The only place those sorts of boats could have come from without the scum manning them starving to death in transit is the Sunset Islands.'

Marcus said, 'But the Sunset Islands pirates have been quiet for years.'

Amos nodded. 'Someone's stirred them up. That's the other thing that bothers me.'

'What?' said Martin.

'If every black heart who lived in the Sunset Islands since I was a boy came ashore, and they brought their grannies and their grannies' cats with them, they couldn't mount a force of more than five hundred. We're talking more than twice that, including some trained Tsurani assassins and maybe some genuine Durbin slavers and a Quegan renegade.'

Martin nodded. 'So where did all those raiders come from, and who sent them?'

'Could this Render be behind it?' asked Nicholas.

Amos shook his head. 'Not unless he's changed more than I think he has in the last thirty years. No, this caper was put together by someone with bigger ideas than

Render's. And it cost money, too. Getting those Tsurani assassins through the rift from Kelewan . . . someone was bribed, probably people on both sides. And the Durbin slavers demand guarantees. If every pretty girl and boy taken was sold at the top of the market, they'd probably not break even on what it cost to underwrite this venture.'

Martin said, 'We need to leave.'

Amos nodded. 'It will take a few days to ready the ship.'

'Where are we going?' asked Nicholas.

Amos said, 'The Sunset Islands. That's where we'll pick up their trail, Nicholas.'

Later that night, Martin asked Harry and Nicholas to come outside with Marcus and Amos. When they were clear of casual listeners, Martin said, 'Nicholas, I've decided that you and Harry will stay here in Crydee. Knight-Lieutenant Edwin will need help, and when a ship gets here from Tulan or Krondor, you can return to your father's court.'

Martin turned away as if that was the end of it, but Nicholas said, 'No.'

Martin said, 'I wasn't asking you for agreement, Squire.'

Nicholas paused a long moment, holding his uncle's gaze, then took a deep breath and said, 'Highness, or Prince Nicholas, Lord Martin.'

Marcus snorted and said, 'You'll go where Father sends you – '

Nicholas didn't shout, but his tone was cold and angry as he said, 'I will go where I please, Master Marcus.'

Marcus stepped forward as if about to strike Nicholas, when Amos said, 'Stop this!' Marcus halted and Amos said, 'Nicky, what are you thinking of?'

Nicholas looked from face to face, then, fixing his gaze on Martin, said, 'Uncle, you swore an oath, and so did I.

When I was given my office on my fourteenth birthday, I vowed to protect and defend the Kingdom. How could I claim to have upheld that vow if I ran home now?'

Martin said nothing, but Amos said, 'Nicholas, your father sent you here to learn something about the differences between the frontier and the royal court, not to go chasing slavers across the ocean.'

Nicholas said, 'My father sent me out here to learn to be a Prince of the Kingdom, Admiral. I am as much a Prince of the Blood Royal as Borric and Erland, and I am bound as much as they are to see to the safety and well-being of our subjects. At my age, Borric and Erland had already been fighting a year on the frontier with Lord Highcastle.' Looking at Martin, he said, 'I wasn't asking your permission to go with you, my lord Duke. I was giving you a command.'

Marcus's mouth opened and he was about to speak, but Martin's hand upon his shoulder restrained him. Softly he asked, 'Are you certain, Nicholas?'

Nicholas looked at Harry. The once fun-loving boy from Ludland was dirty from days of working in the sooty town, and his eyes were dark with fatigue circles, but he nodded once.

'I am certin, Uncle,' said Nicholas.

Martin gripped Marcus by the shoulder and quietly said, 'We are bound by our oath . . .' Then he added, 'Your Highness.'

Marcus's eyes narrowed, but he said nothing as he turned to follow his father. Amos waited until they were gone, then snapped, 'I thought I'd raised you to be smarter than this, Nicky.'

Nicholas said, 'Margaret and Abigail are out there somewhere, Amos, and if there is any way to find them, I will.'

Amos shook his head. Glancing around the destroyed town in the moonlight, he sighed in resignation. 'I love you like my own grandson, Nicky, but given a choice, I'd rather have a little magic than a wet-behind-the-ears Prince giving orders on this voyage.'

Nicholas said, 'Pug!'

Amos said, 'What about him?'

Reaching inside his tunic, the boy said, 'He gave me this in case we needed him.'

Amos said, 'Well, I can't think things could be much more needy than they are now.'

Nicholas gripped the talisman in his right and repeated Pug's name three times. The little metal amulet warmed in Nicholas's hand, but that was the only sign magic was being employed.

A moment later, Nakor came out of the inn. 'What are you doing?' he asked.

'You felt that?' asked Harry.

'Felt what?'

'The magic.'

'Bah. There is no magic,' he said with a dismissive wave. 'I saw Martin and Marcus come into the inn, and they did not look happy.'

Amos said, 'The correct military term is "pulling rank". Our young Prince here has decided he's going with us, no matter what his uncle or I say.'

'He's supposed to,' said Nakor.

'What?' asked Harry.

The Isalani shrugged. 'I don't know why, but without Nicholas, whatever waits for us out there will prevail.'

'He is the son of the Lord of the West,' said a voice from behind.

They all turned to see Pug step out of shadows. He was dressed in a dark brown robe with a hood, which he pulled back to reveal a face etched with concern. 'I was going to ask why you've summoned me.' He glanced around the charred landscape. 'But I think that's obvious.'

* * *

Pug and Martin spoke for a long time, out of earshot of the others. Amos had called Martin back out of the inn at Pug's request. Now he and the others who had witnessed Pug's arrival waited to see what would happen next.

Harry said, 'Do you think he can wish them back here?'

Nakor said, 'He is a very powerful man. But I don't think wishes have much to do with it. We shall see.'

Pug and Martin returned to where the others were standing and Pug said, 'I am going to attempt to locate Margaret and her friend.' He glanced around. 'I need some space around me. Please stay here.'

He moved away from the inn toward a large open area in front of it that had been earmarked as a new market-place. Now it was merely a weed-covered lot, with a large rock protruding from the middle. Pug stepped up on the rock and held his hands up over his head.

A faint sensation, like a distant humming, struck Nicholas and he glanced at Harry, who nodded that he also felt it. After a long minute, Anthony came from inside the inn and joined the others. Softly the young magician said, 'Is that Pug?'

Nakor nodded. 'He's looking for the girls. It's a very good trick if he can do it.'

The sense of vibration increased, until Nicholas felt as if something were crawling over his skin. He resisted the urge to scratch.

Anthony said, 'What's that?'

Nicholas squinted toward where the magician pointed and he saw a faint red light in the distance, about a handspan above Pug's head. It seemed to be growing brighter.

After a moment Nakor shouted, 'Get down!'

When Anthony hesitated, Nakor pulled on his sleeve, forcing him down, and then he was likewise yanking on Nicholas's arm. 'Get on the ground! Cover your eyes! Don't look! *Now!*'

They did as he asked, and Nicholas looked up to see the red light approaching at terrifying speed.

Nicholas felt Nakor's hand upon his head, forcing his face into the soil. 'Don't look! Cover your face!'

Suddenly, in the darkness, Nicholas felt heat. A searing sensation struck his head and shoulders, as if he lay before a suddenly opened furnace or oven. The impact of the heat sucked the breath from his lungs. He almost opened his eyes, save for Nakor repeating his warning.

Then the heat passed. 'Look!' Nakor shouted.

Pug stood transfixed, surrounded by a sizzling nimbus of red energies, white sparkles of lightning seeming to explode along the surface as tiny flecks of silver danced inside. Nakor was on his feet and running toward him.

The others were only a few steps behind. When Nakor was an arm's length from Pug he halted and held out his arms in warning for the others not to get too close.

Pug was immobilized inside the red energies, a statue with his arms upraised. Nakor walked completely around the strange envelope of red light and shook his head.

Amos said, 'What is this?'

Anthony said, 'Very powerful magic, Admiral.'

Nakor made a dismissive gesture with his hand. 'Ha! There is no magic. *This* is a very loud warning: stay away!' He nodded, and said, 'And more.'

Martin said, 'What else?'

'You have more trouble than we thought.' He started walking back toward the inn.

'Are you going to leave him there?' asked Harry.

'What do you want me to do?' said Nakor. 'There's nothing I can do for Pug that he's not already doing for himself. He'll be fine. It's just going to take some time for him to get out of that trap.'

'Shouldn't we wait?' said Nicholas.

'You can if you want,' answered Nakor. 'But I'm cold

173

and I want something to eat. I'm sure Pug will come inside when he's done.'

'Done with what?' asked Amos, following after.

'Whatever it is he's doing in there. It wouldn't take him so long to get free if that's all he wanted to do. He's doing something else, I'm certain.' With that, the little man reached the door to the inn and opened it. The others followed behind, save Anthony, who elected to wait nearby and observe.

Pug moved through shadow. He had extended his senses to the southwest, toward those islands Amos had claimed would be the most likely place for Margaret and her companions to be held. He had found the islands quickly, for there was a large town, and the energies of the people there were like a bonfire on an otherwise deserted beach.

Then an alarm had sounded. Some warning sense told him he was under attack. He put up his mental defenses as the red energies struck. The defenses were more than equal to the task. Pug did not resist the attack, beyond protecting himself. He could have destroyed the imprisoning magic, but to do so would have clearly warned the caster that he was free. He chose to investigate instead.

As with all such sendings, there was a trail of magic from source to target. Pug examined the feel of it, the direction from whence it came, and how it was constructed, then he created his shadow.

It was not really a shadow, but that was how Pug envisioned it, how he conceived the entity. The shadow was a construct of magic, a non-real creature that existed only as a conduit for Pug's consciousness. He suspected his intuition had him think of shadow, for he would hide this creature in those dark and formless places along the track of magic, where the caster of the hostile spell would be unlikely to notice such a being.

Once the shadow was formed, he sent it creeping up

the trail of magic, hiding in non-places, blending into dark voids along the trail. The search would take time, but he would be more likely to discover the source and identity of this attack.

Pug began his search.

It was near dawn when Pug suddenly stepped free of the light. Anthony dozed nearby, a cloak pulled tightly around his shoulders and over his head. He quickly came fully awake as he saw Pug stagger away from the light. The cocoon remained in place, the white sparkles flashing across the red; inside, a shadow, resembling Pug as he had stood there moments before, remained.

Anthony rose and gripped Pug by the arm. 'Are you all right?'

Shutting his eyes a moment, he said, 'Just tired.' He took a deep breath and opened his eyes. Inspecting the red energies that still stood like a ruby obelisk, he asked, 'Where are the others?'

'Inside,' said Anthony.

Pug nodded, touching the red light with a finger as he studied the shadow form of himself. 'This will do for a while,' he said. He turned and began walking toward the inn.

As Anthony fell in beside him, Pug asked, 'Do I know you?' Anthony introduced himself and Pug said, 'So then you're my replacement?'

Anthony blushed. 'No one can replace you, master.'

'Call me Pug,' said Pug. 'If time permits, remind me to tell you what a miserable failure I was when I lived here in Crydee.' Anthony could only smile weakly, his expression showing he didn't believe it. 'I'm serious,' Pug said. 'I was a terrible magician at first.'

Pug opened the door and Martin was instantly awake. Marcus and the others roused quickly with a shake or word. Harry got up stretching and yawning and said, 'I think I still have coffee. I'll see.' He moved sleepily toward the bar.

Pug squatted next to Martin and said, 'I think Amos's surmise is correct. The raid was a mask for something else.'

'What was that red light out there?' asked Martin.

'A very clever trap.'

Nakor nodded. 'A warning, no?'

Pug said, 'Yes, that as well.'

Martin said, 'Margaret and the others?'

'They are where Amos suspects,' observed Pug. 'I can't say exactly, because I was attacked just as I located them. I can only say that it's a large room, and dark. Perhaps a warehouse. I had a sense of their mood. They are all terribly frightened and there's a strong sense of despair.' Then Pug smiled. 'Though your daughter has a great deal of anger, too.'

Martin couldn't hide his relief. 'I had feared . . .'

Pug nodded. 'At least last night she was well.'

'Who tried to trap you?' asked Nakor.

'I don't know.' Pug looked thoughtful. 'The attack didn't come from where the girls are. It came from someplace a great deal farther away, and it was fashioned by someone of no mean skill and power. It was sent in response to my looking for the captives.'

Nakor sighed. 'So whoever sent it is telling you to mind your own business.'

Pug nodded. 'My shadow construct outside will collapse soon. I plan on being far from here when it does, so when they attack again, I will not draw their wrath on anyone else. I can defend myself, but I'm not sure how many of you I can protect if they broaden or intensify their assaults.'

Nakor chewed his lip. 'So we shall have to go without you.'

Martin narrowed his eyes. 'I don't follow.'

'The warning,' said Nakor. 'Pug is being circumspect. He doesn't want to upset you further.' Looking at the bearded magician, he said, 'You'd better tell him.'

'Tell me what?' asked Martin.

Pug shook his head as Harry approached with a tray of mugs filled with hot coffee. He passed them out, and after a sip, Pug said, 'I don't know how our colorful friend here could know, but there was a warning attached to this attack: if I try to follow the prisoners, if I use magic to aid their escape, if anything should reveal pursuit from the Kingdom, the girls and boys will be killed, one at a time until those who follow withdraw. They are not merely captives; they are also hostages.'

Amos blew out his cheeks as he exhaled slowly. 'Which means that if they see a sail on the horizon and a Kingdom flag, they'll start cutting throats.'

Pug said, 'Exactly.'

'How did you know?' Harry asked Nakor.

The Isalani shrugged. 'I didn't. I assumed. It was logical they would know Pug was kin to the Duke and might come after his daughter. Threatening to kill the prisoners is a logical choice.'

Anthony said, 'But who cast the spell?'

Pug said, 'It is alien. I've never seen its like.' Looking at Martin, he added, 'If anything proves Amos is correct that this is no mere raid for slaves, that spell does.'

Nakor nodded, and his usually bright face turned glum. 'These slavers have very powerful allies, Lord Martin.'

The room fell silent.

Then Amos's face slowly brightened as a truly impressive grin manifested itself in the grey and black of his beard. 'I have it,' he said with obvious glee.

'What?' asked Martin.

'I know how we can sail into Freeport and not have the prisoners harmed.'

'How?' asked Pug.

Now grinning like a boy who had just found a new toy, Amos said, 'Gentlemen, as of today, you're all buccaneers.'

Workers furiously crawled over the *Royal Eagle*. Following Amos's instructions, they were doing everything he could imagine to change the appearance of the ship. Amos worried that some of those who had escaped the attack on the ship up at Barran might remember her, and if she was recognized before reaching the safe haven of Freeport, the enterprise might end in disaster.

A pair of carpenter's apprentices were altering the figurehead, changing the eagle to a hawk. Amos had yelled at them for hours until they were ready to quit, but at last he judged the bird different enough to serve. He then ordered the white and gold figurehead painted an ominous black, with red eyes. The name *Royal Eagle* had been scraped off the bow and stern, and a painter was trying to hide all signs of the removal.

Yards were relocated wherever possible, and spars were shifted. A false rail was added amidships; it wouldn't stand close inspection, but Amos was not planning on having visitors aboard. From the dockside, it looked like part of the original structure, as did a pair of ballista platforms that had been located in the bow and were now placed one on each side of the ship. Archers' platforms had been removed from the masts, as only Kingdom warships used them. In their place, rope and canvas slings – where crossbowmen could sit and fire down upon enemy crews – were hung between the masts. The bowsprit was hoisted and reblocked, so a man could now stand in the bow under it.

Another band of workers were hard at work 'dirtying her up', as Amos called it. Loath to see the beauty and discipline of the Royal Kingdom Navy put aside, many of the sailors had to be bullied into scratching off paint, allowing the sea air to turn metal to rust, and generally making the ship look as if only minimal effort had been put into keeping her seaworthy. Amos had no doubt that from any reasonable distance the ship looked very different from the way it had before the overhaul.

Martin, Pug, and Nicholas stood at the top of the wharf, the only place they could watch without interfering. There was still a great deal of debris and litter along the quay from the damage done by the raiders. Amos waved as he approached.

'How goes it?' asked Martin.

Amos said, 'She's starting to look like a rough bitch instead of the fine lady she is.' He turned and inspected the work, rubbing his chin as he studied her. 'I could really disguise her if I had another week, but considering that those raiders who saw her were around at night . . . this should do.'

'It had better,' said Martin.

'When do we leave?' asked Nicholas.

Amos shook his head. 'I know you've decided to come along, Nicky, but I wish you would change your mind.'

'Why?' he challenged.

Amos sighed. 'You know I love you like a grandson, boy, but you've got to think like a Prince and not a lovesick child.' He held up his hand before Nicholas could speak. 'Spare me. I saw the way you looked at the Lady Abigail the first night you were here. Normally, I'd wish you well and tell you to get the girl bedded as fast as you can, but now it's serious stakes, Nicky.' He put his hand upon the boy's shoulder. 'Have you looked in the mirror lately?'

Nicholas said, 'Why?'

'Because you're the image of your father. He's not exactly an obscure fellow, you know. He's been Prince in

179

Krondor for nearly thirty years, and more than one of those cutthroats out in the Sunsets will have clapped eyes on him.'

Nicholas frowned. 'I can alter my appearance. I'll let my beard grow . . .'

Amos looked pained as he softly said, 'Look down, Nicky.'

Nicholas looked down and suddenly knew what Amos meant. The misshapen boot, with the foot it compensated for, was a banner heralding his identity. Amos almost whispered as he said, 'That foot is nearly as famous as your father, Nicholas. It's no secret Arutha's youngest son is his sire's get, save for the deformed left foot.'

Nicholas felt his ears and cheeks burn. He said, 'I can – '

Martin put his hand upon Nicholas's other shoulder. 'You can't hide it, Nicholas.'

The boy pulled away from the contact. He looked first at Amos, then at Martin, then at last at Pug. Something in the magician's expression caught Nicholas's attention. 'What?' he demanded.

Pug looked from face to face, then looked Nicholas in the eyes. Firmly he said, 'I can help.'

There was a pregnant pause, and Nicholas said, 'What else?'

Pug said, 'I can help, but only if you have more courage than I think you do.'

Nicholas bristled. 'Show me what to do!' he demanded.

Pug said, 'We will need privacy.' He put his hand on Nicholas's shoulder, pulling him away from the others. To Martin he said, 'I am going to take him to the castle. I'm going to need help. Will you ask Nakor and Anthony to join us there?' Martin nodded and Pug firmly led Nicholas away.

The Prince followed the magician silently, until they were almost back at the burned-out castle. Nicholas had a chance to consider his rash demands and the fact that his deformed foot had often been a trigger for unreasonable displays of temper.

At the gate, Pug turned and said, 'We'll wait for the others.'

Nicholas was silent for a while, then let out a long breath as his anger faded. After another silent minute, Pug said, 'How do you feel?'

Nicholas said, 'The truth?'

Pug nodded. Nicholas looked away at the distant harbor, where little remained that resembled the lovely town he had seen his first evening in Crydee. 'I'm scared.'

'Of what?' asked Pug.

'Of failure. Of coming along and causing better men than me to fail. Of getting the girls killed. Of . . . many things.'

Pug nodded. 'What do you fear the most?'

Nicholas thought a long moment. 'Of not being as good as I should be.'

Pug said, 'Then you stand a chance, Nicholas.'

Nothing more was said until Anthony and Nakor approached, walking steadily up the hill. When they reached the gate, Anthony said, 'Duke Martin said you asked us to join you.'

Pug nodded. 'Nicholas is going to try something, and he'll need our help.'

Nakor nodded, but Anthony said, 'I don't understand.'

Nicholas said, 'Pug's going to fix my foot.'

Pug said, 'No.'

Nicholas said, 'But I thought – '

Pug held up his hand. 'No one else can fix your foot, Nicholas.'

Nakor added, 'Except you.'

Pug nodded. 'All we can do is help. If you really want us to.'

Nicholas said, 'I don't understand.'

181

Pug said, 'Come along, and we'll explain.'

They entered the burned-out entry hall and moved down the hall to the northern tower, then climbed the charred stone stairs. At the first doorway, Pug said, 'This was once my room, and my master Fulgan lived above me.'

Anthony said, 'This is my room . . . or was until last week. I took it rather than the one above because of the odd chimney' – he pointed to a hole in the wall where metal had run down the wall – 'there. Kept the room warm.'

Pug nodded. 'I had it built.' He glanced around the room, and for a moment Nicholas, Nakor, and Anthony could see the memories were returning to him. At last Pug said, 'Then it's doubly fitting.' He motioned for Nicholas to enter and said, 'Sit by the window. Take off your boots.'

Nicholas sat on the blackened floor and removed his boots. Pug sat opposite him, ignoring the soot that clung to his robe and hands; Nakor and Anthony stood on either side. Pug spoke. 'Nicholas, you must understand something about your own nature, something you share with most people.'

'What?'

Pug said, 'Most of us move through life with little chance to learn much about ourselves. We know some things we like and some things we dislike, we have a few ideas about what makes us happy, and we die in ignorance regarding anything profound within ourselves.'

Nicholas nodded.

Pug continued. 'There are reasons things happen like your foot being deformed at birth, reasons that are often impossible to understand. There are a lot of theories, especially when you speak with the priests of the various temples, but no one knows for certain.'

Nakor said, 'It may be your foot is a lesson for you in this lifetime, Nicholas.'

Pug nodded. 'So many believe.'

Nicholas said, 'What can I learn from a deformed foot?'

Pug said, 'Many things: limits, overcoming adversity, humility, pride.'

Nakor added, 'Or nothing.'

Pug said, 'I know your father tried to have your foot cured when you were a small child. Do you remember?'

Nicholas shook his head. 'A little, but not much. Only that it hurt.'

Pug put his hand upon Nicholas's. 'I thought so.' His brown eyes made contact with Nicholas's and his voice became soothing. 'You must know that you are the only one with the power to heal what is flawed within you. Do you understand fear?'

Nicholas felt his eyes growing heavy and he said, 'I don't know . . . Fear?'

'Fear holds us and binds us and keeps us from growing, Nicholas.' Pug's voice took on an insistent quality. 'It kills a small piece of us each day. It holds us to what we know and keeps us from what's possible, and it is our worst enemy. Fear doesn't announce itself; it's disguised, and it's subtle. It's choosing the safe course; most of us feel we have "rational" reasons to avoid taking risks.' He smiled reassuringly. 'The brave man is not the one without fear but the one who does what he must despite being afraid. To succeed, you must be willing to risk total failure; you must learn this.'

Nicholas smiled. 'Father once said something like that.' His words were becoming slurred, as if he were drunk or half-asleep.

'Nicholas, had you wished to be healed as a child, the priests and magicians and healers would have made your foot well. But something in you held on to your fear;

something in you loves your fear and binds it to you as a mother or lover. You must confront that fear and banish it; you must embrace it and let it devour you. Only then will you know your fear; only then can you heal yourself. Are you willing to try?'

Nicholas found he couldn't speak, so he nodded as his eyes grew too heavy to keep open. He let them close.

From a distance, Pug said, 'Sleep. And dream.'

Nicholas floated in a dark, warm place. He knew he was safe. Then a voice came into his mind.

Nicholas?

Yes?

Are you ready?

A sense of puzzlement. *Ready?*

Ready to know the truth.

A stab of panic and the dark place was no longer warm. After a time he said, *Yes*.

Blinding light seared him and he floated in a room. Below him he saw a little boy sobbing in the arms of a redheaded woman, and her lips moved. He couldn't hear her, but he knew what she said; he had heard it before. She said that as long as she was there, nothing would ever hurt him.

A flash of anger struck him. She lied! Many times he had been hurt. The image faded and suddenly there was the boy again, this time a few years older, walking awkwardly down the long hall that led to his room. Two pages walked by, and when he had passed, they whispered. He knew they were speaking about him, mocking his deformity. He ran to his room, tears flowing down his cheeks. He slammed his door behind him and vowed he would never leave his room again. He was consumed with anger, rage, and pain, and he cried alone until a page came to tell him that his father was coming.

Pulling himself off his bed, he washed his face in the

basin on the nightstand. By the time the door opened again, the boy had composed himself; he knew his father didn't like to see the boy cry. Arutha beckoned for the boy to come along for some function in the great hall, and the boy complied. An affair of state demanded his attendance, and he forgot his vow never to leave the room. But it was a vow he had made hundreds of times and would make hundreds of times again, since he was only six years old.

The image faded and he stood before two tall young men, with hair the same color as his mother's. They mocked him, teasing, pretending they couldn't see him or calling him "monkey", and he fled from them, again stabbed by chilling pain.

Other pictures presented themselves: a sister too consumed with the business of being a young princess to have time for a younger brother. Parents whose time was dictated by politics and protocol, who couldn't always be there for a shy and frightened child. Servants who were dutiful, but who felt no affection for the youngest son of their liege lord.

Over the years many images had etched themselves in Nicholas's mind, and as he returned to the present, he heard Pug's voice. 'Are you ready to face your pain?'

Panic struck Nicholas. He mumbled, half-asleep, as he said, 'I thought . . . that's what I was . . . doing.'

Pug's voice was soft and reassuring. 'No. You were remembering. Your pain is with you now. You must root it out and face it.'

Nicholas felt a tremble run through him. 'Must I?'

'Yes,' answered a voice, and he fell deeper into the dark emptiness.

A voice came to him. It was soft and warm and familiar. He tried to open his eyes, but couldn't, then suddenly he could see. A young woman with golden hair moved toward him, through a vaguely defined hallway. Her gown was translucent, hinting at a ripe fullness beneath the thin cloth. Her features resolved as she reached out to him, and he said, *Abigail?*

She laughed, and he felt the sound rather than heard it. *I'm whoever you wish me to be.* The sensual feel of her voice sent a thrill through him. Then he felt like crying, for something about the young woman was terrifying as well as seductive.

Suddenly his mother stood before him, but as he had known her when he was very little. Soft white arms reached down to pick him up, and she cradled the little boy to her bosom, murmuring reassuring sounds in his ear. He felt her warm breath on his neck and he felt safe.

A warning note sounded, and he pushed away. *I'm no child!* he shouted, and under his hand a firm breast filled his palm. Soft blue eyes stared into his and ripe lips parted. He shoved Abigail away and shouted. *What are you?*

Suddenly he was alone in the darkness, a chill running through his body. No answer was forthcoming, but he knew there was another presence in the murk. He tried to see, but there was nothing in the gloom, yet he knew he was not alone.

By force of will he steered himself and his voice rang in his own ears: *What are you?*

From a great distance away, he heard Pug's voice. 'It's your fear, Nicholas. It's your reason for holding to it. See it as it really is.'

Nicholas felt a constriction in his chest and felt afraid. 'No,' he whispered.

Suddenly something was close to him; that distant presence was now a hovering menace. Something was coming that could harm him; something was approaching that was able to rip away his defenses and destroy him!

A gathering darkness surrounded him, pressing in and confining him. He pulled one way, then another, but as he struggled, the pressing in on all sides restricted his movement, until he was rendered immobile.

A suffocating sensation visited him and he gasped, but no air filled his lungs. A sensation of helplessness overwhelmed him and he choked on it. A scream died in his throat and a soft sob came out as tears ran down his face.

Nicholas, said the warm and reassuring voice. Soft hands reached for him and he saw the beautiful features of his mother . . . no, Abigail, approaching. *Just reach for me*, said the soft voice.

Then Pug's voice came to him. 'What is it really, Nicholas?'

The women before him vanished, and he was alone in the room in the tower. Behind him the day was gone and the night was upon him, cold and indifferent. He was alone.

He stood and paced around the room, but he couldn't find the door. Looking out the window, he saw that Crydee was no more. Not even the ashes of the town remained, nor did the rest of the castle; only this single tower stood. Below was a blasted plain of rock and sand, lifeless and without hope. The sea was black, oily waves rolling listlessly to crash with indifference on rocks so sterile that even moss did not grow on them.

'What do you see?' came the distant voice.

Nicholas struggled to speak, and at last he found his voice. 'Failure.'

'Failure?'

'Complete and utter failure. Nothing survives.'

'Then go there!' commanded Pug's distant voice.

Immediately he was out on the blasted plain, and the mournful sound of the lifeless waves rang in the still air. 'Where do I go?' he asked the dead sky.

'Where do you wish to go?' asked Pug.

Suddenly he knew. Pointing across the bay toward the west, he said, 'There! I want to go there!'

'What's stopping you?' asked Pug.

Nicholas looked around and said, 'This, I think.'

At once Pug stood beside him. 'What is your fear, Nicholas?'

Nicholas looked around and said, 'This. Utter failure.'

Pug nodded. 'Tell me of failure.'

Nicholas breathed deeply and said, 'My father . . .' He found his eyes tearing and his voice tightening. 'He loves me, I know.' Letting his pain wash through him, Nicholas said, 'But he doesn't accept me.'

Pug nodded. 'And?'

'And my mother, she is afraid for me.'

'And?' asked Pug.

Nicholas looked out across the blackened sea. 'She scares me.'

'How?'

'She makes me think I can't . . .' He fell silent.

'Can't?'

'Can't . . . do what I need to do.'

'What do you need to do?'

Nicholas cried openly. 'I don't know.' Then suddenly something he had been told by Housecarl Samuel struck him, and his tears turned to laughter. 'That's it! I need to find out what I need to do!'

Pug smiled and suddenly a weight left Nicholas. He looked at Pug and repeated, 'I need to discover what it is I need to do.'

Pug motioned for the young man to follow him. 'Why do you fear failure so much, Nicholas?'

Nicholas said, 'Because my father hates it more than anything else, I think.'

Pug said, 'We haven't much time. Things move apace and I must leave soon. Will you trust me to teach you something?'

Nicholas said, 'I guess so, Pug.'

Suddenly Nicholas stood upon a ledge, high above the

188

sea. Below, rocks beckoned and waves slammed against the cliff face. A dizziness struck him and his knees buckled, and Pug's voice said, 'Step forward.'

'Will you catch me?' he asked and his voice sounded very young to his ears.

'Step forward, Nicholas.'

Nicholas did, and suddenly he was falling. He screamed.

The rocks raced to embrace him and he knew he would die. Numbing pain struck him and he groaned as he lay on the unyielding rocks, the waves washing over him.

Gasping as he spit out bitter water, he said weakly, 'I'm alive.'

Pug was on the rocks before him, extending his hand. 'Yes, you are.'

Nicholas gripped it and suddenly he was back upon the ledge. 'Step forward,' Pug said.

'No!' said Nicholas. 'Do you think I'm crazy?'

'Step forward!' commanded Pug.

Hesitating, Nicholas closed his eyes, and stepped forward. Closing his eyes didn't help, as he sped through the air to slam against the rocks once again. Stunned a moment, he was astonished to discover himself still conscious. Pug was again kneeling before him. 'Are you ready?'

'What?' he asked groggily.

'You have to do it again.'

Sobbing, he asked, 'Why?'

'You have to learn something.'

Nicholas gripped Pug's hand and suddenly he was on the ledge. 'Step forward,' Pug said softly.

Nicholas stepped forward, but his foot was fused into the rock of the ledge. An emptiness hit his stomach as he lurched into the void, but his left foot held him firmly to the ledge.

Wrenching pain visited his leg as he hung there, upside

down and backward. Pug suddenly appeared before him. 'Hurts, doesn't it?'

'What's happening?' Nicholas asked.

'This is your pain, Nicholas.' Pug pointed to the foot in the rock. 'This is your mother love and your mistress. This is your excuse. Because of it, you can't fail.'

Nicholas said bitterly, 'I fail all the time.'

Pug's smile was unforgiving. 'But you have a reason for failing, don't you?'

Nicholas felt a cold stab to his stomach as he said, 'What do you mean?'

'You fail not because you're lacking but because you're the lame child.' Pug floated in the air before Nicholas. 'You have two choices, Prince of the Kingdom. You can hang here until you grow old, knowing that there are all manner of great things you might do: save innocents, find the woman of your dreams, protect your subjects . . . if only you didn't have a lame foot. Or you can cut yourself free from your excuse.'

Nicholas tried to pull himself upright but couldn't gain any leverage.

Pug pointed an accusing finger. 'You've hit the rocks! You know what it is.'

'It hurts!' cried Nicholas.

'Of course it hurts,' chided Pug, 'but you get over it. It's only pain. You're not dead, and you can try again. You can't succeed unless you're willing to risk failure.' Pointing at the place where ankle was fused to rock, Pug said, 'This is an excuse. We all have them if we wish. You have gifts that advantage you far more than this trivial deformity handicaps you!'

A powerful certainty struck Nicholas. 'What must I do?'

Pug stood. 'You know.' And he was gone.

Nicholas reached up and gripped his left leg. The blood

pounded in his head and he felt the muscles of his left leg tearing as he pulled upward. Forcing himself to bend forward, he scraped his fingers on the rock, gaining inches as he cried in agony and frustration.

Suddenly he was sitting on the ledge, his foot still fused to the rock. At his side a knife hung, where none had been a moment before.

He understood. He took the knife and hesitated a moment, then slashed at his own ankle. Pain shot up his leg and his foot burned. Gasping at the pain, he forced himself to cut. The ankle cut like thick bread, not like bone and sinew, but the pain shot through him like lightning flashes.

As he cut through the last fiber of his own flesh, Nicholas found himself standing. He held the knife to the throat of his own mother. Blinking, he pulled back. The figure of Anita, Princess of Krondor, said, 'Nicholas! Why do you hurt me? I love you.'

Then Abigail stood before him, wearing a diaphanous gown. With hooded eyes and sensuous lips, she said, 'Nicholas. Why do you hurt me? I love you.'

Terror struck the young man, and he stood rooted a moment, then he shouted, 'You are not Abigail! Or my mother! You are an evil thing that binds me!'

A sad expression crossed the vision's face and she said, 'But I love you.' Nicholas shouted incoherently and lashed out. The knife cut through the woman, turning her to shadow and vapor.

Pain exploded behind Nicholas's eyes and he screamed. Something precious was torn from within his chest and he felt a terrible sense of loss. Then suddenly a weight left him and, with giddy relief, he passed into darkness.

Nicholas opened his eyes, and Nakor and Anthony helped him sit up. He rested his back against the cold black stones of the tower wall. It was gloomy as the sun set. 'How long have I been here?' he asked. His voice was raw and his throat scratchy.

Anthony said, 'A day and a half.' He held out a waterskin, and Nicholas found he was parched.

He drank deeply and said, 'My throat is sore.'

'You were shouting and screaming a long time, Nicholas,' said Anthony. 'You've endured a terrible struggle.'

Nicholas nodded and his head spun. 'I'm dizzy,' he said.

Nakor handed him an orange and said, 'You're hungry.'

Nicholas tore a section of peel away and bit deep into the fruit, letting the sweet juice run down his chin, and chewed the soft pulp. He swallowed and said, 'I feel as if I lost something.'

Anthony nodded and Nakor said, 'Men love their fears. That is why they hold on to them so tightly. You've learned something very young, Prince, something that even older men rarely understand. You've learned that fear isn't a terrible-looking thing but something lovely and seductive.'

Nicholas nodded and finished the orange. Nakor handed him another. As he tore the peel off that one, he said, 'I killed my mother, or Abigail – or something that looked like them.'

Nakor said, 'It was neither. You killed your fear.'

Nicholas closed his eyes. 'I feel like crying and laughing at the same time.'

Nakor laughed. 'You just need food and sleep.'

Sighing, Nicholas said, 'Pug?'

Nakor said, 'His shadow construct collapsed and the red thing vanished. Pug said bad things were going to come after him soon, and he didn't want to be around people. He took your talisman and gave it to Anthony.'

Nicholas reached up and found the thong and dolphin charm missing. Anthony reached into the neck of his robe and showed Nicholas he now wore it.

'I don't know why, but he said I must keep it for a while, but not to use it again unless there was no other choice.'

Nakor nodded. 'Then he said good-bye and went away.'

In the gloom, Nicholas peered down his left leg. Something alien rose up from his left ankle. He experimented and found he could wiggle his toes. Tears welled up in his eyes as he said, 'Gods!' He looked at the healthy, well-formed foot that matched its mate for the first time in his life.

Anthony said, 'The transformation was difficult. I don't know what Pug did, but you and he were in a trance for many hours. I watched the bones and flesh stretching and moving as it healed. It was astonishing. But the pain must have been extreme, for you cried and screamed yourself hoarse.'

Nakor stood up. He extended his hand downward. Nicholas took it, and the little man proved surprisingly strong as he helped Nicholas stand upright. Testing his weight upon his newly healed foot, Nicholas found his balance felt alien. 'I'll have to get used to this.'

Nakor looked down at the well-formed foot on Nicholas's left leg and shook his head. 'You had to do it the hard way, didn't you?'

Nicholas threw his arms around the little man's neck and laughed. He laughed so hard his ribs hurt. After a while he pushed himself away. With tears running down his face he said, 'Yes. I did.'

Martin looked up as Anthony, Nakor, and Nicholas walked toward him. Nicholas picked his way gingerly over the rocks and grimaced as if stepping on something painful.

Martin was about to say something to the soldier beside him when he noticed that Nicholas was barefoot. More significantly, both of Nicholas's feet were normal!

The Duke of Crydee walked away from the soldier and hurried up to his nephew. He looked deep into Nicholas's eyes, and tried to understand what he saw there. At last he said, 'What can I do?'

Nicholas grinned and said, 'I could use a new pair of boots.'

8

Accident

Nicholas lunged.

Marcus leaped back, parrying his blow, then disengaged and riposted. Nicholas easily countered and forced him to retreat another step.

Nicholas stepped back himself. 'Enough.' The young men were breathing hard and drenched with perspiration. Each had let his beard grow, and now both looked remarkably sinister.

Harry walked out of the inn to where the cousins had been practicing and said, 'What do you think?'

Even Marcus's usual stoic demeanor cracked as he regarded the flamboyant figure. Harry wore purple breeches tucked into large, cuffed boots, and a yellow sash around his waist. His shirt was green, with faded golden brocade up the front and at the cuffs of ballooning sleeves; over that he wore a vest of maroon leather, tied in front by a single cord and wooden frog, and upon his head a long stocking cap of red and white tipped off to the right at a jaunty angle.

'You look a fright,' said Nicholas.

'What are you made up to be?' asked Marcus.

'A buccaneer!' said Harry. 'Amos said they tend to dress colorfully.'

'Well, you are that,' admitted Nicholas.

Nakor appeared, eating an orange. He looked at Harry and started to laugh. Harry had let his beard grow as well, but it was coming in thin and patchy.

'What is a buccaneer, anyway?' asked Harry.

'Bas-tyran word, very old,' said Nakor. 'Originally, *boucanier*; means fellows who light fires on beaches to

195

lure ships ashore, wreckers, thieves, pirates.'

'So many words for the same thing,' said Harry, 'reiver, corsair, pirate . . .'

'Many languages,' said Nakor. 'This Kingdom is like Kesh, built upon conquest. In ancient times, men of Darkmoor and men of Rillanon couldn't speak to each other.' He nodded and winked, delighting in sharing trivia.

Marcus said, 'I hope Amos doesn't insist we all dress that way.' Turning to Nicholas, he said, 'Another?'

Nicholas shook his head. 'No. My leg hurts and I'm tired.'

Suddenly Marcus was advancing, with a wicked slash toward Nicholas's head. 'What happens when you find someone coming at you when you're tired?' Nicholas barely blocked the cut, which would have caused serious damage had it gotten through. Marcus pressed the attack and Nicholas fell back.

'People try to kill you at the most inconvenient times,' shouted Marcus, executing a combination of high and low attacks.

The two cousins were using sabers, a weapon foreign to both. With the rapier, no one in Crydee was Nicholas's equal, but with the bulkier weapon, slashing attacks were far more important, and Marcus was quick and strong.

Nicholas grunted in exertion as he blocked a stabbing attack to the groin, then with a shout he attacked. A flurry of vicious attacks high and low moved Marcus back, and finally Nicholas caught him in a binding move and ripped the hilt from Marcus's fingers. Leaning back against a newly rebuilt low brick wall, Marcus found Nicholas standing before him, the point of his sword touching Marcus's throat. Marcus back away, and fell over the low wall, landing on his rump. Nicholas leaned forward, keeping the point of the sabre at Marcus's throat.

Harry took a tentative step forward and halted. Nicholas's eyes were wide and his anger was clearly showing. He said coldly, 'Your point was well taken, *cousin*.' For a long second he said nothing, then stepped back, lowering his blade. With a wry laugh he said, 'Very well taken.' He offered his hand and helped Marcus to his feet.

Another voice said, 'You would do well to know, Marcus, that irritating a better swordsman than yourself is a good way to end up dead.'

The three young men and Nakor turned to see Amos leaving the inn. The Admiral had abandoned his muted dark blue uniform and now wore a pair of heavy black boots, with wide bands of tooled red leather around the tops. His loose breeches and short jacket were a faded blue, the jacket trimmed with dull silver brocade at the cuffs and lapels. He wore a once-white shirt, now yellowed, with limp silk ruffles down the front. Upon his head rested a black three-cornered hat trimmed in gold, topped with a bedraggled yellow plume. A cutlass of impressive weight hung from the baldric across his shoulder. He had oiled his hair and beard so that his face was surrounded with ringlets.

Removing his hat, Amos ran his hand across the top of his bald head and said, 'Stick to your longbow, Marcus. Your father never had the knack for the sword your uncle Arutha has, and Nicky is a better swordsman than all of you.' He turned to Nicholas. 'How's the foot?'

Nicholas grimaced. 'Still hurts.'

Nakor said, 'It's "phantom pain"; it only hurts in his head.'

Nicholas limped a little as he came to sit next to Marcus, who had retreated into a sullen pose.

'Phantom pain?' said Amos. 'That hardly makes sense.'

'Well, it hurts like the real thing,' admitted Nicholas. 'Nakor claims it will stop hurting when I finally understand the lessons I began in the tower the other night.'

'This is true,' agreed the little man. 'When he truly understands, there will be no more pain.'

'Well, you'd better learn it in a hurry. We leave on the morning tide.'

Marcus nodded and said, 'I have some things to do before we leave.'

After he had departed, Amos said, 'You two really don't like each other, do you?'

Nicholas looked down at the ground, but it was Harry who spoke. 'They won't much until Abigail makes a choice between them.'

Bitterly Nicholas said, 'If she can. I'll get my things together.' He departed.

Amos turned to Harry. 'Why do I have a feeling that if they don't find a reason to make peace, sooner or later one is going to kill the other?'

Harry said, 'Chilling, though, isn't it?' He leaned against the still-standing section of wall and commented. 'They're too much alike; neither will give an inch.' He looked at the door of the inn. 'Most of the time I've known Nicholas he's been easygoing, Admiral. You've known him longer, but I think I know him better.' Amos nodded agreement to that. 'Something in Marcus just turns an otherwise agreeable lad into a serious pain in the backside.'

Nakor laughed.

'Marcus is acting like a pig-headed lout, too,' said Amos. Slapping Harry on the back, he added, 'And you'd better start calling me "Captain", Harry, not "Admiral". I'm Trenchard the Pirate once more.' With a menacing grin, he pulled out his belt knife and began testing the edge with his thumb. 'I'm years older and a step slower, but what the years have taken away I more than make up for by being mean.' Suddenly he had the knife pointed at Harry's nose. 'Any disagreement?'

Harry yelped as he jumped back a step. 'No sir! Captain! Sir!'

Amos laughed. 'In my former trade, the captain was the meanest bastard in the crew. That's how you got elected. You scared the crew into voting for you.'

Harry grinned and inquired. 'Is that how you got to be a captain so young?'

Amos nodded. 'That and killing a swine of a second mate when I was still a cabin boy.' He leaned against the wall and put his dagger back into his belt. 'I was twelve years old when I first went to sea. On my second voyage the second mate – man named Barnes – thought he'd beat me for something I didn't do. So I killed him. The captain had a drumhead trial – '

'Drumhead?' asked Harry.

'Right then and there before the crew. Not a lot of legal niceties. You plead your case and the crew decides. Turned out most of the men hated Barnes, and I made it clear I was being beaten for something that wasn't my fault. The guilty man came forward and told the captain that I hadn't done whatever it was I was accused of . . .' Amos's eyes grew distant. 'Funny, isn't it? I don't remember what it was I was accused of. Anyway, the guilty man was flogged though the captain went easy on him because he'd been honest to save my life. I was made third mate. By the time I'd been on that ship four years, I was first mate.

'I was a captain by the time I was twenty years old, Harry. I had raided most every port in the Bitter Sea save Krondor and Durbin by the time I was twenty-six. At twenty-nine I went straight.' He laughed. 'And on my first honest voyage the Tsurani burned my ship and left me high and dry here in Crydee. That was over thirty years ago. So here I am, past sixty and once again a pirate!' He laughed again. 'Hell of a circle, isn't it?'

Harry shook his head in open amazement. 'Quite a history.'

Amos looked up at the burned-out hulk that had once been Castle Crydee. A pair of masons had arrived from Carse the day before and were now beginning preliminary inspection of the grounds for reconstruction. Martin was there with them, giving them instructions so that work could begin as soon as the snows retreated, whether or not he had returned. 'When I first came to that keep, I found some astonishing people.' He looked down, thoughtfully. 'They changed my life. I owe them a great deal. I used to chide Arutha for taking all the fun out of life, and truth to tell, he can be a sour sort.' Gazing at the inn once again, Amos observed. 'But he's a wonderful man, in many ways, and my first choice for a mate should I be sailing into stormy waters. I love him like a son, but *being* his son is no easy task. Borric and Erland had many gifts, not the least of which was being very different from their father, but Nicholas . . .'

Harry nodded. 'He's just like him.'

Amos sighed. 'I've never admitted this to anyone, but Nicky's always been my favorite. He's a gentle lad, and while he has many of his father's strengths, he has his mother's tender ways.' Amos pushed himself off the wall. 'I pray I can return him to his family undamaged. I don't relish the notion of explaining to his grandmother why I let anything ill happen to him.'

Harry said, 'I pray you feel the same about me and telling my father, Captain.'

Amos gave Harry an evil grin. 'I'm not marrying your father, Squire. You're on your own.'

Harry laughed, but it wasn't entirely convincing. Then a shout sounded from up the hill as one of the masons from Carse came running down the hill, almost out of control. He shouted something and Amos looked at Harry.

Harry said, 'I can't understand . . .'

Then the man shouted again, and Amos said, 'Oh, gods, no!'

'What?' said Harry.

Nakor said, 'There's been an accident.' He began running toward the castle.

Suddenly Harry understood. Only three people were up at the castle: two masons and the Duke. Harry said, 'I'll get Marcus and Nicholas.' He rushed off to the inn.

Before he ran to the castle, Amos called after Harry, 'And find Anthony! We're going to need a healer!'

By the time they all reached the castle, one of the monks from Silban's Abbey was tending Martin. He lay unconscious on a clear patch of ground, his face drawn and pale as the monk inspected his injuries.

Marcus shouted, 'What's happened?' as he rushed up to his father's side.

The senior mason said, 'A section of the parapet gave way and His Grace fell. I told him it was dangerous up there.' His manner showed he was more interested in avoiding blame than in anything else.

Marcus looked at the monk. 'Is it bad?'

The monk nodded, and Anthony and Nakor knelt beside Martin. They whispered, and after a moment Anthony said, 'We need to carry him down to the inn.'

Nicholas asked, 'Should we make some kind of stretcher?'

Anthony said, 'We don't have time!'

Harry, Nicholas, and Marcus lifted Martin, and slowly they moved down the hillside, picking their way along the most forgiving path.

At the inn, they moved Martin into one of the smaller rooms on the second floor. Anthony motioned for the others to step outside, and he and Nakor closed the door.

The others hovered by the door of Martin's room for a

few moments; then Amos said, 'No use waiting here. We have a hundred things to do before tomorrow.'

Marcus said, 'Tomorrow? You can't be serious.'

Amos paused and looked back at Martin's son. 'Of course I'm serious. We leave on the morning tide tomorrow.'

Marcus took an angry step forward. 'Father will be in no condition to travel by tomorrow.'

Amos said, 'Your father will be in no condition to travel until spring, Marcus. We can't wait for him.'

Marcus began to protest and Nicholas said, 'Wait a minute.' He asked Amos, 'How do you know?'

Amos said, 'In my years, Nicky, I've seen men fall from the yards and hit hard decks.' Looking at Nicholas's cousin, he said, 'Marcus, Martin is closer to seventy years of age than sixty, though you'd never know it to look at him. Younger men than he have died as a result of such injuries. No one's going to lie to you and say your father isn't in danger. But so are your sister and the other captives. Our waiting here won't make your father any safer, but it will certainly place your sister in more peril each day we wait. We leave tomorrow.'

Amos turned and left the three young men standing in the hallway in silence. At last Nicholas said, 'I'm sorry, Marcus.'

Marcus glanced at Nicholas; then without saying anything else he hurried down the stairs.

Calis entered the inn, ducking out of the sudden rain. He shook his head as he removed his hooded cloak and hung it on a peg near the door. The inn was still crowded, but not as packed as the last time the elfling had been in Crydee, for several new shelters had been raised.

Seeing Nicholas and Harry sitting at a distant table, he moved quickly to sit with them. 'I have messages for your uncle, Prince Nicholas.'

Nicholas told him of the accident. Calis listened impassively, then said, 'This is ill news.'

Anthony appeared on the stairway and, seeing Nicholas, hurried down to the table. 'His Grace has regained consciousness; where is Marcus?'

Harry jumped up. 'I'll find him.'

Anthony nodded to Calis, who said, 'I have messages for the Duke.'

Anthony said, 'You can have a few minutes.'

Nicholas rose as well, and the magician said, 'Only one at a time.'

The Elf Queen's son followed Anthony up the stairs, and in a few minutes Marcus and Harry entered the inn. Nicholas came up to his cousin as Marcus said, 'Father's awake?'

Nicholas nodded. 'Calis brought a message from the Elf Queen and is with him now. You can go up as soon as he comes out.'

Calis appered at the top of the stairs and Marcus started up. The elfling put a restraining hand upon his chest and said, 'His Grace wants a word with Nicholas.'

Marcus's eyes flashed, but he said nothing as Nicholas hurried up the stairs past him. He entered the room and found Martin propped up by a down comforter, a heavy blanket pulled up to his chest.

Anthony, Nakor, and the monk who tended him hovered nearby. Nicholas said, 'Uncle?'

Martin extended his hand and Nicholas took it, squeezing it briefly. Martin's voice sounded shockingly weak as he said, 'I need to speak with you, Nicholas. Alone.'

Nicholas glanced at the others. Anthony said, 'We'll be outside.'

Martin closed his eyes and lay back, perspiration beading upon his brow. After he heard the door close, he said, 'Calis brought me this.'

He held out a ring to Nicholas, which the Prince took

and examined. It was made of silver-black metal, and it sparkled coldly. There was something repellent about its design, two serpents intertwined, each holding the other's tail in its mouth. He started to hand it back to Martin, who said, 'No, you keep it.'

Nicholas put it in a small pouch he wore at his belt. Martin asked, 'How much has your father told you of Sethanon?'

Nicholas was surprised at the question. 'Some,' he replied. 'He doesn't speak of it often, and when he does, he tends to be modest about his part. Amos has told me a great deal, though.'

Martin smiled weakly. 'No doubt. But there are many things concerning that battle Amos doesn't know.' He motioned for the young man to sit upon the side of the bed. As he did, Martin said, 'I may be dying.'

Nicholas started to object, but Martin said, 'We don't have time for meaningless protestations, Nicholas. Too much is at stake. I may be dying, or I may live; that's as the gods will it – though without Briana . . .' For the first time, Nicholas saw the pain of Martin's loss. Then his uncle's face hardened. 'You must know certain things and I have little breath to tell you.'

Nicholas nodded, and Martin rested a moment before he went on, 'In ancient times, our world was ruled by a powerful race.' Nicholas blinked in surprise. Martin continued. 'They were known to themselves as Valheru. Our legends call them the Dragon Lords . . .'

Marcus fumed. 'Why did he ask to see Nicholas?'

Harry shrugged. 'I know as little as you.' Harry studied the young man he had been Squire to for the last months. He still didn't know Marcus well, but he knew him well enough to know that there was rage bottled up, barely kept in check. First the rivalry for the affections of Abigail, then the death of his mother and abduction of his sister, then Nicholas's refusal to play at Duke's Squire anymore and asserting himself as Prince of the Kingdom – all had combined to keep Marcus at the verge of boiling over for a week.

Nicholas appeared at the stairs and motioned for Anthony, Nakor, and the monk. They reentered the room as Marcus took the stairs two steps at a time. Nicholas said, 'He wants to see you.'

Marcus passed him without a word and Nicholas continued down the stairs. Harry saw the thoughtful expression of his friend and said, 'What is it?'

'I need some air,' Nicholas answered.

Harry fell in beside his friend as they left the inn, and, misreading Nicholas's expression, he asked, 'The Duke . . .?'

Nicholas said, 'His leg is broken above the knee and below, and Anthony says there's some bleeding inside.'

'Is he going to . . .' Harry had almost said 'die', but caught himself and said, '. . . be all right?'

Nicholas said, 'I don't know. He's older than I thought, but he's still pretty tough.' Nicholas continued to walk, heading in the general direction of the ocean.

Harry said, 'There's something else, isn't there?'

Nicholas nodded.

'What?'

'I can't tell you.'

Harry said, 'Nicky, I thought we were friends.'

Nicholas stopped and regarded his companion. 'We are, Harry. But there are things that only the royal family may know.'

There was something about his tone that stopped Harry in his tracks. He hesitated, then fell in beside Nicholas again. 'It's serious?'

Nicholas nodded. 'I can tell you this much: there are forces out there working to destroy us and everything – I mean *everything* – we love. And they may be the hand

205

behind what's happened here.'

From out of the dark a voice said, 'Indeed.'

Both Harry and Nicholas turned, and Nicholas had his sword half out of his scabbard before he recognized Galis. The son of the Elf Queen stepped out of the shadows and said, 'I think I had much the same talk with my father that you did with your uncle, Prince Nicholas.'

Nicholas said, 'You know of the serpents?'

Calis said, 'One of our scouting parties encountered a band of moredhel near the border with Stone Mountain and there was a fight. That serpent ring was found on the body of a moredhel. It may be something from the days of the Great Rising, when the false Murmandamus marched against Sethanon. If so, there is nothing to fear.'

Nicholas nodded. 'But if it's not . . .'

'Then trouble stirs again.'

Nicholas said, 'What do Tomas and your mother propose to do?'

Calis shrugged. 'Nothing presently. Reacting to shadows is not our way. But because there may be some risk hidden in the gloom, I will travel with you.'

Nicholas smiled. 'Why you?'

Calis smiled in return. 'I am human as well as of the elvenkind. My looks will not betray me as they would anyone else from Elvandar.' He glanced around at the wreckage of Crydee. 'I would see what sort of men can do this thing.' He looked again at Harry and Nicholas. 'And I would learn more of my human heritage.' He shouldered his bow. 'I think I shall spend this evening with my grandparents. I see them rarely as it is, and we may be gone a long time as they count such things.' Saying no more, he left.

Harry waited a moment before he said, 'What's this about a ring?'

Nicholas removed the ring and held it out for Harry's inspection. In the twilight it seemed to have a glow of its own. 'That's an ill-aspected piece of jewelry,' commented Harry with a grimace.

'It may be more,' said Nicholas. He put it back in his belt pouch and said, 'Come along. We have a dozen things to do before we leave.'

The ship cleared the harbor and Amos called for all sails. The day had dawned clear and warm, an auspicious start, Nicholas hoped. He stood on top of the forecastle, watching a nimble sailor scamper along the forechannel, adjusting the shrouds on the masthead. Nicholas looked down at the foaming water coursing past. Dolphins jumped off the bow wake, seeming at play.

'A good omen,' said the sailor who clambered down from the rail. He landed lightly upon bare feet and hurried to his next task.

Nicholas considered the appearance of the crew and contrasted it with what he remembered from his journey to Crydee. Then each sailor had worn some variation of the uniform of the Kingdom fleet: blue trousers, blue-and-white-striped shirt, and a blue wool cap. Now they wore the most outlandish collection of castoffs and borrowed finery he had seen. Filthy trousers and tunics had been gladly exchanged by the fisherfolk of the village for the sturdy and warm naval issue. From out of the old trunks in the basement of the castle had come silk jackets and trousers, shirts of fine linen, hats of various fashion, some with plumes and others with tassels. From the fashion and cuts, the clothing had belonged to Lord Borric, Nicholas's grandfather, and King Lyam and Nicholas's father, when they had been boys at Crydee. A dozen gowns that must have belonged to Princess Carline or her mother, Lady Catherine, had also been put to good use, for Amos had made it clear that outrageous finery was one of the hallmarks of the Brotherhood of Corsairs, as he called them. So now common Kingdom sailors were wearing tunics owned by a young man thirty years ago who was now King of the Isles, and sewn upon the cuffs and collar were brocades and laces once adorning the gowns of the present Duchess of Salador, the King's sister.

Nicholas had to smile. He had elected to dress in some of his father's old clothing; the fit and cut betrayed them as Arutha's without doubt. He wore a pair of black, calf-high riding boots with a high flare of leather protecting the knee. Plain black trousers, full enough for easy movement, were topped with a plain white shirt, with loose collar and puffed sleeves. A black leather vest over that provided some protection against a sword's point. His only concession to the more flamboyant choices of the crew was a red sash around his waist. Over his right shoulder hung a baldric of tooled black leather, a series of vines intertwining in the design. From this hung a saber, not the weapon Nicholas would have chosen, but one far more common than the rapier, widely known as the weapons favored by the Prince of Krondor and his sons. At his belt hung a long dagger.

Nicholas left his head uncovered. His long hair had been pulled back into a tail, tied with a red ribbon, and his beard now approached ten days' growth.

Harry still wore his fanciful riot of colors, but at Amos's insistence he had let them become dirty and start to fade in the sun. He complained of the discomfort, but Amos insisted that while colorful, buccaneers were usually a filthy lot.

Marcus came up on deck and Harry laughed. The Duke's son was turned out in almost identical fashion to Nicholas, save that his belt sash was blue and he wore his hair loose about his shoulders, with a blue wool cap upon his head. At his side he wore a cutlass, the weapon of choice for boarding a ship during battle, when fighting was in close. 'If you two don't look like brothers – ' But

Harry fell silent as he received twin glares from the cousins.

Nicholas said, 'How was your father?'

Marcus said, 'He said very little to me. He smiled and wished me well, then fell into a deep sleep.' Putting his hands on the rail, he gripped it tightly. 'I stayed at his side all night . . . but he still was asleep when I left this morning.'

Nicholas said, 'He's a strong man for his age.'

Marcus only nodded. After a long silence, he turned to face Nicholas. 'Let's be clear on something. I don't trust you. I don't care what you've done since you've come to Crydee; once the situation turns bloody, I think you'll quit. You don't have the stomach for what we're going to have to do soon.'

Nicholas felt his color rise with the accusation, but he kept calm. 'I don't care if you trust me or not, Marcus, as long as you obey me.' He turned his back and began to walk away.

Marcus shouted after him, 'I'll not be named oath breaker, Nicholas, but if you cause any harm to my sister or Abigail . . .' He let the threat go unfinished.

Harry hurried down the companionway to overtake Nicholas. 'This has got to stop,' he said.

Nicholas said, 'What?'

'This rivalry with Marcus. It's going to get someone killed if you're not careful.'

Nicholas moved aside as a pair of sailors pulled a heavy rope past them, repositioning a yard. Amos shouted instructions from the quarterdeck. Nicholas said, 'Until Marcus chooses to stop hating me, or at least distrusting me, there's nothing I can do.'

Harry said, 'Look, he's really not such a bad fellow. I've spent enough time around him to know. He's a lot like your father in some ways.' Nicholas's eyes narrowed at that remark. 'No, I mean it; your father's a pretty hard man, but he's fair. Marcus just lost any reason to be fair to you, that's all. Do something to give him the chance to do what's right, and he'll do it.'

'What do you suggest?'

'I don't know, but somewhere you've got to find a way to let him know that you're not his enemy.' Hiking his thumb over his shoulder toward the west, he added, 'The real enemy's out there.'

Thinking on the incredible things his uncle had told him the night before. Nicholas could only nod. 'I think I may have a way, then.'

Harry said, 'Well I'm going to go talk to Marcus and try to make him see reason. If you think of something to help, do it, because we're all going to need each other out there before this is through, I'm certain.'

Nicholas grinned. 'When did you get so smart, Harry of Ludland?'

Harry returned the grin. 'When things stopped being fun.'

Nicholas nodded. 'I'm going to talk to Amos. Have Marcus come to his cabin in a few minutes, will you?'

Harry nodded and ran forward while Nicholas worked his way back to the quarterdeck. Reaching Amos's side, he said, 'We need to talk.'

Amos glanced at Nicholas's face and saw the seriousness of his expression. 'Privately?'

'In your cabin is best, Amos.'

Amos turned to his first mate. 'You have command, Mr Rhodes.'

'Aye, Captain!' shouted the mate.

'Keep her on course. I'll be in my cabin.'

They made their way to the captain's cabin. In the companionway, they glanced through an open door to the cabin Marcus shared with Nakor, Calis, Ghuda, and Anthony. Those four lay on their bunks, content to rest after the long night's preparation and in anticipation of more hectic days to come. Nicholas waved to them as he and Amos passed by.

Amos opened the door to his own cabin and, once inside, said, 'What is it, Nicky?'

'We need to wait for Marcus.'

A few minutes later a knock sounded and Nicholas opened the door. 'What is it?' asked Marcus as he stepped into the room.

Nicholas said, 'Sit down.'

Marcus glanced at Amos, and the captain nodded.

Nicholas said, 'I know about Sethanon.' He looked at Amos.

Amos said, 'I've told you about it, Nicky. What do you mean?'

'I mean Uncle Martin told me everything.'

Amos nodded. 'There are things about that battle that your father and uncles know that even those of us who were there are ignorant of. I've kept from asking questions. If they judge it important enough not to speak of . . .' He let the thought go unfinished.

Nicholas spoke to Marcus. 'What has your father told you?'

Marcus looked at Nicholas with a sour expression. 'I know of the Great Rising of the moredhel. I know of the battle, the aid from Kesh and from the Tsurani.'

Nicholas took a deep breath. 'There is a secret, known only to the King and his brothers. My brother Borric knows, because he will be King next. My brother Erland knows, because he will be Prince of Krondor after my father. Now I know.'

Marcus's eyes narrowed. 'What secret would my father tell you that he would hold back from me?'

Nicholas withdrew the ring from his belt pouch and handed it to Marcus, who examined it and passed it along to Amos. Amos said, 'Those damned snakes.'

211

Marcus said, 'What is it?'

Nicholas said, 'I'm swearing you both to secrecy. What I say now to you both must stay in this cabin. Do you agree?'

Marcus nodded, as did Amos. Nicholas said, 'What few people know is that the Great Rising, when the false moredhel prophet Murmandamus invaded the Kingdom, was the handiwork of others.'

'Others?' asked Marcus.

'The Pantathian serpent priests,' said Amos.

Marcus looked confused. 'I've never heard of them.'

'Few have,' said Nicholas. 'Murmandamus was a false prophet in more ways than one. Not only wasn't he the long-dead leader returned to lead his people against us, he wasn't even a true dark elf. He was a serpent priest who had somehow been magically transformed to resemble the legendary leader. The moredhel were duped and never knew of the deception.'

Marcus said, 'I see. But why is this so secret? I should think it would help us along our northern borders if the moredhel knew they were led by an impostor.'

Nicholas said, 'Because there is much more at risk. Within the city of Sethanon is an artifact. It is a great stone fashioned by an ancient race known as the Valheru.'

Marcus's eyes widened at this, and Amos nodded as if he saw pieces in a puzzle falling into place. Marcus said, 'The Dragon Lords?'

Marcus glanced at Amos, who sat in open amazement. Nicholas continued. 'The Pantathians are some sort of race of lizard men, so your father says, Marcus. They worship one of the ancient Valheru as a goddess, and they wish to seize the Lifestone to use its vast power to bring her back to this world.'

Amos said, 'But Sethanon was abandoned. Rumor has it a curse was laid upon the city. None dwell there. Is this precious thing left unguarded for a reason?'

'Martin said there was a guardian, a great dragon who is also an oracle. He wouldn't say more save to tell me to go there someday. After we return from this journey, I will ask my father for leave to visit the oracle.'

Marcus said, 'Why didn't my father tell me this himself?'

Nicholas said, 'Your father was sworn to an oath by Lyam. Only the King, my father, your father, and Pug knew of the existence of this stone and the guardian.'

'Macros knew,' said Amos. 'I'm certain.'

'Macros the Black vanished after the battle,' answered Calis as he opened the door.

Amos roared. 'Do you not knock!'

The Elf Prince shrugged. 'My hearing is sharper than others, and these cabin walls are not as thick as you would like.' He leaned against the door. 'And my father also knows of the dragon who guards the stone, as she was once a friend to him, and he has told me of the battle at Sethanon. But why do you break your oath, Nicholas?'

Nicholas said, 'Because Marcus is my blood and of the royal family, even if his father has renounced all claim to the throne for his line. And Amos is to wed my grandmother, so he will be family as well. But more important, because I trust them and because should anything happen to me, others *must* understand the stakes here. More seems to be at risk than the lives of those taken, no matter how much we love them. There may be a time when it seems prudent to quit the chase, and if I am not here, I want you to know why you can never give up.' Nicholas paused as if weighing his words. To Marcus he said, 'Your father is not the type of man who is given to overstating anything, but I can scarcely believe what he said last. This thing, the Lifestone, is somehow linked with every living creature upon Midkemia. Should the Pantathians seize it, they will attempt to free their mistress, she whom they count a goddess, but in so doing they will be destroying

213

every living creature on this world. *Everything*, he said to me, from the mightiest dragons down to the smallest insect. Our entire world will be reduced to an otherwise lifeless place, with only the returned spirits of the Dragon Lords walking the land.'

Marcus's eyes widened, and he glanced at Calis. The half-elf said, 'So my father also has warned me. He, too, is not given to overstating things. It must be so.'

Marcus's voice was almost a whisper. 'Why would these Pantathians do such an evil thing? They will die as well?'

Nicholas said, 'They are a death cult. They worship a Valheru who gave them shape and intelligence, for, before, they were merely serpents.' He shook his head in disbelief at what he heard himself saying. 'I wish I had known of this before Pug left. There are questions I would ask. In any event, they think she will rise to rule all and they will rise at her side, as demigods, and all who went before, all who died, will rise as well, as their servants.

'Even if they know the truth, death holds no fear for them. They would welcome the destruction of the world to recall their "goddess". Now you can see why we must continue on, even if some of us perish in the cause?'

The last was said to Marcus, who nodded. 'I understand.'

Calis said, 'Then you wisely know when blind obedience is foolish.' He smiled.

'Do you see that there can be no contention between us?'

Marcus stood and said, 'Yes.' He extended his hand. They shook, and suddenly Nicholas was looking at the same crooked smile his father showed, as he added, 'But when this is over, and Abigail is safely home in Crydee, look to guard yourself, Prince of the Kingdom.'

The challenge was half in jest, half-serious, and Nicholas took it in the spirit it was made. 'When she's safely home, with your sister and the others.'

214

They shook again, and Nicholas and Marcus left the cabin. Calis glanced at Amos, who was smiling faintly. 'What do you find so amusing, Captain?'

Amos sighed. 'Just watching a couple of boys becoming men, my friend. The fate of the world perhaps hangs upon what we do, yet they still find time to contest over a pretty girl.' Then his expression turned dark as he roared. 'And if you ever dare enter my cabin again without leave, I'll have your ears nailed to my door as a trophy! Understand?'

Calis smiled and said, 'Understood, Captain.'

Alone in his cabin, Amos Trask thought back to the dark days of the Riftwar and the Great Rising that followed hard after it. Many people he had known died, aboard his ship *Sidonie*, during the siege of Crydee, then later when the *Royal Swallow* was burned by goblins and he and Cuy du Bas-Tyra were captured. Then came the years at Armengar and the constant warfare between Briana's people and the dark elves in the northlands, ending at the battle of Sethanon.

Sighing at the memories, Amos Trask addressed a small prayer to Ruthia, the Goddess of Luck, followed by the injunction, 'Don't let it happen again, you fickle witch.' Thinking of Briana made him sad, and he hoped Martin would pull through.

Then, impatient at memories and morbid thoughts, he pushed himself out of his chair and left the cabin. He had a ship to captain.

9

Freeport

The girl wept.

Margaret said, 'Will you please shut up?' Her tone wasn't threatening or commanding; just a request for respite from the almost constant wailing and crying of one or another of the town girls and boys.

Duke Martin's daughter had fought the entire way as she had been carried like a trophy animal to the boat waiting in the harbor. The image of her mother lying face down on the floor of her family's castle with flames brightening the far hallway was etched into her memory and had fueled her with manic fury.

The days that followed were no less a nightmare for being a blur. The captives had ranged in age from seven or eight years of age to a few in their late twenties. Most were between twelve and twenty-two, young, strong and certain to fetch a good price at the slave docks of Durbin.

Margaret had no doubt that these murderers would find a royal fleet waiting to intercept them somewhere between the Straits of Darkness and Durbin. Her father was sure to get word to her uncle, Prince Arutha, and she would be saved along with all the other captives. So she turned her mind to protecting those around her until help arrived.

The first night had been the worst. They had all been packed together in the holds of two large ships, lying just over the horizon from Crydee. A few of the smaller boats were sailed away, but the majority were sunk out in deep water, their crews crowding the decks of the larger ships for the trip to their destination. Margaret had been around enough ships to guess they couldn't be traveling far, for there wouldn't be anywhere near enough provisions for both crews and captives.

Abigail alternated between fitful dozing as her mind retreated from the horrors witnessed and fearful speculation about their eventual fate. Occasionally she would show a spark of alertness, but all too quickly the oppression of their surroundings came crushing in upon her, reducing her to tears and, finally, silence.

After the first day, some semblance of order had been established, as the prisoners made the most of their cramped quarters. There was no privacy, and everyone was forced to crawl to a corner of the hold to add to the growing pile of human waste accumulating in the bilge below. The stench had become a mute thing in the background of Margaret's awareness, unpleasant but only that, as had the constant background noise of the wood hull groaning, people crying or cursing, and soft conversation. What caused her concern was the prisoners who had developed stomach illness or chills and fever. They were not doing well in the confines of the hold, and she attempted to make their lot more comfortable. She ordered those in the hold to move around so that the ill might have some shred of comfort. Between her rank and her natural confidence, she was obeyed without question.

One of the older girls from the town muttered. 'They're the lucky ones. They're going to die soon. The rest of us are doomed to be drudges or whores for what's left of our lives. We might as well get used to the idea: no help's coming.'

Margaret turned and struck the woman hard across the face. With narrowed eyes she stood over the now cowering woman. 'If I ever hear that drivel from anyone again, I'll tear her tongue from her head.'

Another voice, a man's, said, 'Lady, I know you mean well, but we saw the raid! All our soldiers are dead. Where could help be coming from?'

'My father,' she said with certainty. 'He'll return from his hunting trip and send word at once to Krondor, and my uncle the Prince will have the entire Krondorian war fleet waiting for us before we reach Durbin.' Then her tone turned softer and she pleaded, 'We need to endure. Nothing more. Just survive and, if we can, help each another to survive.'

The woman who had voiced her doubts said, 'Sorry, milady.'

Margaret said nothing but patted the woman's arm in a conciliatory fashion. Sitting back down in the cramped space allotted her, Margaret saw Abigail staring at her.

'Do you really think they'll find us?' Abigail whispered, a faint flickering of hope starting to show in her eyes.

Margaret only nodded, but silently she said to herself, 'I hope so.'

A scraping sound caused Margaret to come awake. During the day, light entered through the latticework hatch cover, the only source of air in the otherwise fetid hold. At night, faint moonlight cast a pale glow across part of the hold, while the rest remained in inky darkness. Margaret heard the scrape again and saw a sliver of moonlight above. She saw a rope drop and a figure shinny down it. One of the raiders landed between two sleeping prisoners, a dagger between his teeth.

He went to a young girl nearby and clamped his hand over her mouth. Her eyes widened in shock and she attempted to move away, but was held in place by the bodies on either side of her and the man's weight on her. He whispered, 'I've a knife, dearie. One sound and you're dead, got it?' The terrified girl stared at him with wide eyes, luminous in the faint light. He put the point of the dagger to her stomach and said, 'Either I stick you with this or with something more friendly. All the same to me.'

The girl, barely more than a child, could not react for

her terror. Margaret stood, keeping her balance as the ship rose and fell through the swells. Margaret whispered, 'Leave her alone. She doesn't understand what men like.'

The man turned, pointing the dagger in Margaret's direction. All the captives wore the same garment: a simple piece of cloth with a hole to stick the head through, tied around the waist. Margaret untied the thong around her waist, and pulled off the garment, leaving herself nude. The man hesitated, obviously able to see her movement in the faint light. Smiling at the would-be rapist, she stepped forward into the moonlight, so he could better see her, and said, 'She's a child. She'll just lie there. Come to me and I'll show you how to ride the pretty pony.'

Not a beautiful girl, Margaret was still attractive, and years of riding, hunting, and an unusually rigorous life had left her with a firm, fit body, which she displayed to good effect as she stood erect and proud. In the faint light, she looked clearly inviting, with her shoulders thrown back and a welcoming smile.

The man grinned, revealing teeth blackened with decay as he released the girl he had been threatening. 'Good,' he said. 'They'd kill me for messing with a virgin, but it's clear you've been down this path afore, darlin'.' He came to her, holding the knife outward, and said, 'Now, be quiet and old Ned'll give you as good as he gets, and we'll both have some fun. Then I'll climb up and my friend can come down here and do you.'

Margaret smiled and reached out to touch his cheek tenderly. Then she suddenly gripped the wrist of his knife hand, and with her other she reached down and grabbed him hard between the legs. Ned howled in pain. While bigger than the girl, he was not much stronger and couldn't free himself from her painful grasp.

The prisoners began shouting. Quickly a pair of guards and a slaver came down the rope from above. The guards pulled away the would-be rapist. The slaver took one look at the nude girl and at Ned, and said, 'Take him up on deck. And seize the one who let him open the hatch cover. Bind them, cut them deep on the arms and legs so they bleed, then throw them to the sharks. I will have it known that no one may disobey our orders and go unpunished.'

Another rope was lowered and the two guards were hoisted up by those on deck, each of them holding firmly to the sobbing Ned.

The slaver turned to Margaret and asked. 'Did he harm you?'

'No.'

'Did he take you?'

'No,' she answered.

'Then cover yourself.' The slaver turned as one of the ropes was lowered again. Shortly the captives were alone once more. Margaret found her eyes fixed on the faint sliver of monlight as the slaver crawled through it. The lattice hatch scraped loudly, then slammed home with a note of finality that underscored their helplessness.

The ship dropped anchor a week after the raid and voices from above shouted for the captives to get ready to leave. The hatch was moved aside and a rope ladder was lowered. The week of cramped quarters and scant food and water had taken its toll; as Margaret assisted the wobbly-legged prisoners up the ladder, she began to notice those who had died during the night. Each morning a pair of slavers had come down into the hold and carried those who had died to a point beneath the hatch where a rope with a loop in it hung. They fixed the rope under the arms of the dead, and they were hauled upward. One of the men had mentioned that there were always sharks following the ship, and now she understood why.

Margaret was kneeling beside two townspeople, a man and a woman, who were too weak to climb the rope. A rough hand fell on her shoulder and a voice said, 'Are you ill?'

With no attempt to hide her contempt for these men she said, 'No, swine, but these are.'

The slaver who held her shoulder propelled her toward the ladder. 'Up on deck. We'll care for these.'

As she climbed the ladder, she saw a second slaver kneel beside the woman and, with a swift move, wrap a cord around her throat. He twisted once, crushing the woman's windpipe. She twitched and convulsed, then died.

Margaret looked upward, refusing to watch the man die. The blue sky above was blinding after the week in the darkness, so her tears were not remarkable to those already on deck.

Abby kept close to Margaret as they were moved slowly toward the rail. A dozen longboats, with masts folded down the middle, waited with four rowers each. The prisoners crawled down nets hung over the side, and when twenty were in each boat, they were rowed to shore.

Margaret climbed down the ladder, her arms and legs shaking with the effort. As she reached the boat, a hand ran up her leg as a sailor assisted her into the boat. She kicked out and the man ducked easily away with a rude laugh. She glanced over to see Abigail shrinking away from another who fondled her breast through her robe. From the deck a warning shout came: 'Leave those girls alone, Striker.'

With a laugh, the man waved back. 'We won't damage the merchandise, Captain. Just having some harmless fun.'

Under his breath, the man muttered, 'Damn Peter Dread's eyes, but this is the last I'll sail with him. Ripe beauties to gladden the heart of a Durbin whoremonger, and not so much as a tweak on the rump or it's over the side to the sharks.'

Another man said, 'Shut yer gob; it's more gold than you'll see in your life. You'll have enough to spend on whores until you can't walk and then some. It's worth it to behave.'

They were rowed to the beach and saw that those before them had been herded toward a rude building on an otherwise deserted island. Margaret and Abigail were among the last inside, and as the large doors closed behind them, they surveyed their new habitation. There was nothing inside besides miserable dejected people: only a dirt floor to sit on, and what light there was entered through the cracks between the log walls. One quick survey and Margaret saw that many of those inside were sick. Knowing full well the fate of the injured or ill, she said, 'Listen!'

Her voice cut through the low murmuring and sobs, and those nearby looked her way. 'I am Margaret, daughter of the Duke.' Glancing around again, she said, 'Some of you are ill. Those who are not must help them. Carry them to that wall there.' She pointed to the wall farthest from the door. A few started to move hesitantly. 'Do it!'

Those who were barely able to walk were helped to the far wall, then Margaret moved to the wall. She moved along it, and Abigail said, 'What are you doing?'

'Looking to see if the land slopes.'

'Why?'

'We need a privy trench, so we don't end up sleeping in filth. It will keep more of us alive.' She reached the far wall and began moving along it. Then she said, 'Here,' pointing at a depression under the bottom log, where light could be seen. 'Dig here.'

'Milady,' said a man sitting next to the base of the wall, 'we have no tools with which to dig.'

Falling to her knees, Margaret dug into the loose, sandy soil with her bare hands. Watching her a moment, the man turned and started scooping out handfuls of dirt. Soon a dozen more had joined in.

Seeing the work under way, Margaret returned to the door and started shouting, 'Guard!'

From the other side a rough male voice answered, 'What?'

'We need water.'

'You'll get it when the captains order it.'

'Valuable property is dying. Tell your captains that.'

'I'm tellin' them nothing,' came the answer.

'Then I'm telling the first officer who enters that you tried to rape one of the girls.'

'Ha!'

'And a dozen others will bear witness.'

There was a long silence, then the large latch was opened and the door parted a crack. A waterskin was handed through, and the guard said, 'You'll get more when they bring it. This'll have to do until then.'

Without thanks, Margaret took the waterskin and headed over to the sick prisoners.

For the next ten days they endured the confinement, packed close together, with no care for their comfort provided. Other prisoners joined them, and from their accounts, Margaret learned that Carse and Tulan had also been raided. By all reports, Tulan's garrison on the island in the mouth of the river had successfully resisted, but Castle Carse had endured much the same fate as Crydee, though the town had fared better. Abigail fell into a deep depression when no one from Carse could tell her if her father lived. Margaret felt returning pain at the memory of her mother's death, but put it aside as she concentrated on caring for others. All the prisoners were now filthy and wretched. At least a dozen had died and been carried away. The slit trench helped keep illness from spreading, though the stench and flies were difficult to endure. Margaret tore strips from the hem of her simple gown to bind wounds that wouldn't heal, leaving the garment a ragged mess at her knees.

On the eleventh day, everything changed.

The six Durbin slavers entered, accompanied by a dozen guards, men in black whose faces were hidden, and who carried an impressive array of arms. The slavers moved to the center of the large building, ready to begin the daily examination of the slaves.

Suddenly the twelve black-clad men took their bows and shot the slavers. Many of the captives screamed and pushed themselves against the wall, fearful that the murder would continue, while others sat in wide-eyed horror.

Another company of men entered the building, and one shouted, 'Prisoners outside!'

Those nearest the door hurried outside, and Margaret helped some of those who were ill but could still walk. Blinking against the bright light, she took in the scene before her. There stood a band of men unlike any Margaret had seen in her life. They wore turbans similar to those worn by the Jal-Pur desert men, but much larger. The turbans were white and all had gems of astonishing size and color set above their foreheads. Silk robes showed these were men of rank and prosperity. They spoke Keshian, but with an accent unlike anything Margaret had heard, and frequently used words she had never read when studying the language. Behind them were armed men, but instead of the ragged pirates who had guarded the prisoners on the first leg of the journey, these were soldiers, dressed alike to a man: black tunic and trousers and a red cloth tied around their heads bandanna-style. Each carried a curved sword and a round shield, black, with a golden serpent painted upon it.

They inspected the prisoners, dividing them into those who were fit and those who were not. A dozen were too sick to travel, and after the entire company of captives was examined, they were led back into the building. Soon screaming from inside, quickly cut off, showed their fate.

The remaining prisoners were led to the water and told to strip and bathe. The seawater provided scant comfort, but Margaret was glad to wash away the filth. As she was washing, she saw the ship.

Abigail squatted in the shallow water, trying to ignore the remarks of the nearby guards. Even dirty, her hair matted with filth, she was clearly a beauty. Margaret spoke low. 'Have you seen a ship like that before?'

Coming out of her dark introspection, Abigail let her eyes focus on the ship. At last she said, 'No. Never.'

Twice the size of any Kingdom ship, it rode easily on the ground swells off the shore. It was a black ship, with high foredeck and afterdeck, and four high masts. 'It looks like a Quegan galley, but there are no rowing banks. It's gigantic.'

Dozens of boats were rowing toward the beach, and Margaret realized that all the remaining prisoners were to be taken to that ship. A dozen longboats on the beach were already beginning to load the first prisoners coming out of the sea.

It took almost an entire day, but at sundown the black ship hoisted anchor and the journey began.

Deep within the hold of the ship, Margaret and the other women were moved to the port side of the ship, on the lowest of three decks. Individual pallets were provided for each prisoners, with room for them to move around. They were placed one at the head of each pallet and told to remove their robes. Glad to be rid of the filthy rag, Margaret quickly obeyed. Abigail hesitated, and when she let her robe fall to the deck, she quickly tried to cover herself.

'Abby,' said Margaret in a scolding tone, 'if you fear for your modesty, that gives these animals another weapon to use against you.'

Abigail's eyes were wide with fright as she said, 'I'm not strong like you, Margaret. I'm sorry.'

'You're stronger than you think. Keep your chin up!'

Abigail nearly jumped when a man with a writing tablet came up to her. 'Your name,' he asked.

'Abigail,' she answered softly.

'Who are your people?' said the man, his voice oddly pitched and his accent tantalizingly familiar to Margaret.

'I'm the daughter of Baron Bellamy of Carse.' The man looked at her, then said, 'Go stand over there.'

Awkwardly, the nude girl moved with her arms clutched around her to a place at the far end of the hold. The man repeated the question to Margaret, and, not seeing any clear benefit in lying, she told them her true name. Like Abigail, she was sent to the far end of the hold. She watched as the interview continued. Each captive was inspected, closely, by a pair of men who made marks on their tablets as they examined each. They poked and prodded like physicians, and the prisoners were forced to endure the inspection in silence. When the men were done, they handed each captive a fresh robe. Crewmen followed and began locking chains around the prisoners' ankles, binding them to the foot of their pallets, and long enough so they could move around a little, but in no way escape the hold.

Then they came to Margaret and Abigail and said, 'You come.'

The girls climbed a ladder to the next deck and walked along a narrow companionway. Even Margaret tried to cover her nudity as they passed more than a dozen leering men. Entering a large cabin, the man who guided them said, 'Find something that fits.' An array of fine clothing lay around the room. The girls quickly found clothing that fitted and dressed, glad to be covered again. Simple gowns, they were nevertheless a vast improvement over the smocks the girls had been forced to wear since being captured.

Then the man led them to a large cabin at the stern of the ship. There two men waited. They stood respectfully when the girls entered and motioned for the girls to sit on a divan. 'Ladies,' said one in that strange accent, 'we are pleased to find those of your rank among your company. May we offer you some wine?'

Margaret stared at the small table covered with fruits and cheese, bread and meats, with a chilled pewter flagon of wine. Despite her hunger, she said, 'What do you want?'

With a smile that held no friendliness, the man said, 'Information, milady. And you will give it to us.'

The lookout shouted, 'Land ho!'

Amos looked up, shielding his eyes against the setting sun. 'Where away?' he called.

'Two points off the port bow!' came the reply.

Amos hurried down the companionway to the main deck and crossed to the forecastle. He climbed the companionway to come to the bow, where Nicholas and the others watched. They had slowly been gathering there since noon, as Amos had said he expected to see the first of the Sunset Islands before too long.

'It's been more than thirty years,' mused Amos. 'No wonder I was off.'

Nicholas smiled. 'Two points is off?'

Amos waved his hand in a dismissive gesture. 'It should lie dead ahead. Now I have to swing wide to the south, to compensate.'

'Is this a problem?'

'No, but it offends my sense of elegance.' He called up to the lookout. 'Do you see a single peak?'

'Aye, Captain,' came the reply. 'A twisted mountain with a peak like a broken blade.'

'Good,' said Amos. Calling back to the helm, he shouted, 'Five points to port, Mr Rhodes!'

'Aye, Captain,' came the reply.

Harry said, 'Captain, exactly who lives here?'

Amos sighed, as memories came flooding back to him. 'Originally, there was a pitiful Keshian garrison, a bunch of dog soldiers with Imperial officers and a couple of small ships. When Kesh pulled out of the province of Bosania – Crydee and the Free Cities of Yabon – they evidently forgot about the little garrison.

'Years went by, and no one knows if the soldiers revolted and killed their officers or if the officers led them, but about the time Nicholas's great-grandfather was attempting to conquer Bosania, this happy little band of cut-throats started raiding. They usually hit trading ships out of Keshian Elarial and the Far Coast, heading to or from Queg, the Kingdom, and Kesh.'

Marcus said, 'They've raided Tulan from time to time.'

Harry said, 'Why hasn't the King or the Emperor of Kesh gotten rid of them?'

'Ha!' laughed Amos. 'Do you think they've not tried?' He rubbed his chin. '*Look* at that island ahead.' He pointed to the peak. 'Past that are another dozen large islands and a hundred tiny ones. This area is part of a long series of islands that stretches to the far west, ending in a great archipelago.' Harry looked blank. 'A vast chain of islands, more than a thousand of them, a month's sailing from here. Some are huge, perhaps a hundred miles across. No one knows who lives on most of them. Others, like Skashakan, are too well-known. That's where our friend Render was shipwrecked.

'There are perhaps five hundred islands spread out between here and the archipelago, some no more than sandbars, and only one harbor deep enough for a ship like this: Freeport.

'If a single Kingdom warship sails into view, it finds a very hot reception at Freeport. Remember those pinnaces they used to raid Crydee? They draw no more than five feet of water; so if we bring a fleet, by the time we pull into Freeport, everyone's packed up and left. We can burn the town to the ground – both Kesh and the Kingdom have done so at different times – and they build it all right back up after we leave.

'No, the Freeport pirates are like cockroaches: you can kill them by the score, but you can't get rid of them.'

Turning away, he shouted to the first mate, 'Assemble the crew, Mr Rhodes!'

As Amos made his way to the quarterdeck, the first mate shouted, 'All hands on deck!'

The order was passed, and quickly the crew gathered on the main deck, Nicholas and his companions listening from the foredeck. Amos surveyed the crew. 'Men, you're all known to me, save for you soldiers from Crydee who agreed to come along, and you were handpicked by the Duke. I trust you all. If I had doubts, you would not be here.

'From this moment, you are men of the Kingdom no longer. You are pirates, fresh in from Margrave's Port. If you've never been there, ask those who have; it's a small enough town and not much to see. If you can't remember the description, keep your mouth shut when we reach Freeport.'

He glanced from face to face. 'Soon you're going to be facing men who've killed your fellow sailors and soldiers, your friends and families. You will want to strangle the bastards, but you can't. Freeport is governed by laws as strict as those in Krondor, but it's a far rougher justice. The Sheriff of Freeport is the law in the town, and the only appeal from his rule is to the Council of Captains, and that's rare. Disputes are settled by the blade, and brawling is not permitted. So if you meet the bastard who killed your brother, smile at him and know that sooner or later his day will come.

'We are not here for revenge. We are here to find Duke Martin's daughter, and the other boys and girls who were stolen from Crydee. We're here to find your children, or the children of your friends.

'If any man here thinks he cannot keep his temper, then do not go ashore. For I swear I will hang the man who starts a brawl, and if we fail in rescuing the children, he'll burn in hell, too.'

His warning was unnecessary, for these men were determined to rescue every prisoner or die in the attempt. Amos smiled. 'Good. Now, the first bastard among you who calls me Admiral will be whipped fore-to-aft, clear?'

With laughter among the men, one called out, 'Aye, Captain!'

With a broad grin Amos said, 'I'm Captain Trenchard! The Dagger of the Sea! I've sailed the Straits of Darkness on Midwinter's Day! My ship's the *Raptor* and I've taken her into the Seven Lower Hells, drunk ale with Kahooli, and sailed home again!' The men laughed and cheered at the boast. 'My mother was a sea dragon, my father was lightning, and I dance a sailor's jig on my victim's skulls! I fought with the war god, and kissed death herself. Men tremble at my shadow and women swoon at my name, and no one lives who can call me liar! I'm Trenchard, the Dagger of the Sea!'

The men laughed and cheered and applauded. Amos said, 'Now, break out the Black Ensign, and every man to his place. We're being watched this very minute.' He pointed to the distant peak.

'Day watch below!' shouted Rhodes. 'Night watch aloft!'

One of the men went below and returned with a large black banner that had been sewn to Amos's specifications in Crydee. They ran it up the stern mast, where it flapped in the breeze.

Nicholas looked at the flag, a skull of white on a black field, and behind the skull a long dagger pointing downward at an angle, with a ruby drop suspended from the tip. Nicholas looked at Harry, Calis, and Marcus and found them staring at the standard. Nakor grinned, while both Anthony and Ghuda remained impassive.

Harry said, 'What's odd is that . . . he wasn't acting, was he?'

Nicholas shook his head. 'I think Amos would say he had a rough childhood.'

Ghuda said, 'I thought I knew him back at the palace.'

Nicholas said, 'Yes?'

Ghuda said, 'I was in Li Meth once when he raided. Saw him from the other side of the barricade.' Ghuda shook his head. 'Old memories.' He glanced over his shoulder at the approaching island, which the ship would pass to the left. 'I saw a glint up there a while back.' He indicated the peak.

'Lookout,' said Marcus.

'No doubt,' said Ghuda.

'I wonder what sort of reception we'll get in Freeport?'

'We'll soon know,' answered Nakor with his usual sunny demeanor.

They reached the harbor mouth as the sun began to set. Amos had reefed all sails save the topgallants, and the *Raptor* moved majestically into Freeport. The harbor was a wide oval of coral-bound beaches, with a steeply rising mountain close behind, which towered like a giant blackstone hand, cupping the harbor against a sky turned orange and purple, with black, grey, and silver clouds, as it hid the setting sun. Ringing the harbor were buildings, rudely built, with thatch roofs. Lanterns and torches burned at every quarter, as Freeport began its night activities.

Ghuda said, 'I've heard of places like this island.'

Nicholas said, 'What do you mean?'

Ghuda said, 'See how that peak rises in an almost perfect circle around the harbor?'

Nicholas said, 'Yes?'

'This used to be the heart of a volcano.'

Nakor nodded. 'Very big volcano.' He seemed delighted by that fact. 'Almost a half-mile across inside!'

Lights began to spring up on the mountainside, and Nicholas watched with fascination as it became a glittering panorama. A warm breeze greeted them as the ship moved slowly into the center of the harbor. Seven other ships of varying size, from two almost the equal of the *Raptor* to two very small trading ships, swayed at anchor on the gentle swell of the harbor. Reaching the best position he could, Amos ordered the last sails reefed and called for the anchor to be dropped. A gentle breeze blew across the harbor, carrying the faint scent of spices and perfume to tantalize the senses. Distant voices echoed from farther inland, but the harbor was almost silent.

Marcus said, 'For so many lights, it's very quiet.'

Ghuda said, 'I think they're waiting to see if we're under false colors.'

When the ship was anchored, Amos called for a long-boat to be lowered, and the crew hustled to obey. He barked insults and threats, and Nicholas was surprised at the harshness of his remarks until he realized that Amos was putting on a performance for the benefit of anyone onshore who was listening.

Ghuda said, 'A word to you both.' Marcus and Nicholas both turned and the mercenary said, 'I've traveled a fair bit and seen many places like this; we're strangers and will not be trusted. There will be no benefit of the doubt.

You'd better agree on names for yourselves, for there is no dispute you're related.'

Nicholas and Marcus exchanged looks, and finally Nicholas said, 'I hold title to the estates near the village of Esterbrook. I've visited several times.'

Ghuda nodded. 'Marc and Nick of Esterbrook it is. Who was your father?' he demanded suddenly.

With a wry smile, Marcus said, 'Mother didn't know.'

Ghuda laughed and slapped him playfully on the back. 'You'll do, Marc.'

'Who was your mother?' he asked Nicholas.

'Meg of Esterbrook,' said Nicholas. 'She's a serving woman at the only inn there, run by a man named Will, and she's still a handsome woman who can't say no to a man.'

Ghuda laughed again. 'Well said.'

Making their way to the main deck, they joined Amos, who was putting on a first-rate display of his knowledge of invectives and insults. A couple of soldiers were playing along, swearing colorfully for the benefit of any onlookers on the docks.

As they sat in the longboat, Amos said, 'You boys have your stories set?'

Nicholas said, 'Marc is my elder brother. We come from Esterbrook. We don't know our fathers.'

Marcus said, 'Nick is a little slow, but we put up with him for Mother's sake.'

Nicholas gave his ersatz brother a frown and said, 'This is only our second voyage. We signed on with you in . . .' He hesitated, then added, 'Margrave's Port.'

Pointing at Ghuda and Nakor, Amos said, 'You two are who you are.' Then he rubbed his chin. Looking at Anthony, who appeared very uncomfortable in trousers and tunic, with a large floppy hat on his head, Amos mused. 'What are we to claim you are?'

'Your healer?' suggested Anthony.

Amos nodded. 'Are there things you need?'

Anthony was grim as he said, 'There are any number of herbs, roots, and other goods that I can use to heal wounds. I can do a convincing job of shopping in the town.'

'Good,' said Amos. To Calis he said, 'Playing a hunter from Yabon should offer little difficulty.'

The elfling nodded. 'I speak the Yabon tongue should there be a need.'

Amos grinned. 'Now, should anyone ask, all you know is that I'm Trenchard, and I've recently returned to the Bitter Sea. I may have sailed for Kesh or the Kingdom before that, but no one is certain. You know better than to ask.'

They all nodded and fell silent as two sailors rowed them toward the dock. After a few minutes they reached a low landing, where a half-dozen boats were secured. No one was in sight as they tied up and came ashore, walking up the stone steps to the top of the wharf.

Suddenly a voice called out, 'Halt! Identify yourself!'

Peering into the gloom, Amos bellowed, 'Who wants to know?'

A single figure emerged from between two buildings. He was a bald-headed man with a sharp beak of a nose, slender but broad-shouldered. His face was set in an expression of amusement, and he spoke in a deep and pleasant voice. 'I wish to know.' He waved vaguely around him. 'And a few friends, as well.' A dozen armed men moved to surround the party.

Amos whispered, 'Stand easy,' as crossbows were leveled.

The bald man walked purposefully to stand before Amos and said, 'You fly a well-known banner, friend, though it's one not seen in these waters for over thirty years.'

234

Suddenly Amos exploded in laughter. 'Patrick of Duncastle! They haven't hung you yet?' Then he slammed his fist into the man's face and the fellow flew backward through the air to land on the hard stones of the wharf. Amos stepped forward and pointed an accusing finger. 'And where are those twenty golden royals you owe me!'

Grinning as he rubbed his jaw, the man said, 'Why, hello, Amos. I thought you were dead.'

Amos pushed past two of Patrick's men, who had their weapons trained on him, and extended his hand. Pulling the man to his feet, Amos threw his arms around him and bellowed loudly as he squeezed him hard.

Putting the man down, he said, 'What are you doing in Freeport? I heard you were running weapons to renegades in the Trollhome Mountains?'

Throwing his arm around Amos's shoulders, Patrick said, 'Gods, that was a long time ago, nearly ten years now. I'm Sheriff of Freeport, these days.'

'Sheriff? I thought that evil little Rodezian bastard – what was his name? – Francisco Galatos was Sheriff.'

'That was thirty years ago. He's dead, and two since him. I've been Sheriff for five years now.' Lowering his voice, he said, 'Where have you been these years? Last I heard, you were running weapons from Queg to the Far Coast.'

Amos shook his head. 'Speaking of years past, it's a long story, better told over a mug of ale or wine.'

Patrick stopped. 'Amos, things have changed since you were last here.'

'How?' asked Amos.

'Come with me.' He motioned for his men to escort Amos's companions and they all walked from the dock area to a small street that paralleled the waterfront. As they moved along the street, local citizens peered curiously from windows and doorways. A few colorfully painted women called out invitations, contingent on their not being hung first. These remarks were universally met with appreciative laughter.

Amos said, 'These hovels don't seem to have changed much, Patrick. They're still the same flytraps they always were.'

Patrick said, 'Just wait.'

They reached the top of a broad boulevard and turned the corner. Patrick of Duncastle pointed down the street. 'Here we are,' he said.

Amos halted and took in the sight. For as far as the eye could see, the street was lined with two- and three-story buildings, painted and clearly well tended. From the throng that hurried to and fro along the way, it was obvious Freeport was a busy community. In the distance, they could see the roadway wind up the mountainside.

Amos said, 'I don't believe it, Patrick.'

Duncastle rubbed his chin absently, on the spot Amos had struck it. 'Believe it, Amos. We've grown since you were last here. We're not a small village with a tavern and a whorehouse but a city.' Turning to walk down the street, he motioned for the others to follow. 'We're not quite as law-abiding as those in the Kingdom, but we're no more corrupt than most of the cities in Kesh, and probably less than Durbin. I've got fifty men-at-arms working for me, and we're well paid to keep order in Freeport.' Gesturing to buildings on either side, he said, 'Many of the merchants here do business in the Kingdom, Queg, and Kesh.'

'Without benefit of customs, I expect,' said Amos with a barking laugh.

Patrick smiled. 'Usually. Others, however, are on the square with the customs houses in Kesh and Isles – they stand to lose too much by having their cargoes confiscated when they get to their destinations. And it doesn't require much to claim that a cargo originated somewhere else –

we like to keep Freeport's part in these transactions quiet. As a result, we do tremendous business in trans-shipping.' Pointing to one of the many buildings still doing business, he said, 'You're looking at the largest independent spice trader north of the city of Kesh itself.'

Amos laughed. 'Independent. I like that. As the spice trade in Kesh is an Imperial monopoly, he can't very well operate legally inside the Empire.'

Patrick smiled and nodded. 'But he has his sources inside the Empire, and I suspect he has contacts even inside the Imperial Court. He deals with traders from lands we've never heard of, Amos. From the Tsurani world. From Brijana on the far side of Kesh. From places I can't even pronounce, across seas I didn't know existed until recently.' He resumed walking and the others followed.

They passed building after building, still busy despite the hour. 'Some of these men you know, Amos,' said Patrick. 'Like us, pirates in their younger days, now they find that shrewd commerce turns a better profit at less risk.'

Nicholas saw a city little different than others he had visited, save that the citizenry seemed more raucous and fractious. A pair of men were arguing loudly, but a pair of the Sheriff's men silenced their dispute with a curt instruction to move along. The son of the Prince of Krondor could see that by any standard, Freeport was a prosperous town.

Amos said, 'So this is why you've turned into such a suspicious bastard in your old age, Patrick.'

He nodded. 'I have to be. The days when we could run into the hills and wait for a raiding fleet from Krondor or Elarial to grow bored and leave are long over. We have too much to lose now.'

Amos fixed his old friend with a baleful eye. 'So that's why we were met with a dozen bashers?'

Patrick nodded. 'And if you can't convince the Council of Captains you're what you say you are, it's also why we'll have to take your ship.'

In a menacing, low tone, Amos said, 'Over my dead body.'

Suddenly a dozen crossbows were again leveled at Amos and his companions. With a regretful expression, Patrick of Duncastle said, 'If need be, Amos. If need be.'

The Captains of the Sunset Islands met in a house at the far end of the boulevard. Along the way, Nicholas and the others were treated to a scene of changing exotica. A babble of tongues filled the night air, and a profusion of colorful costumes and fashions tantalized the eye at every turn. Gambling halls and brothels stood side by side with traders and brokers. And in every doorway, signs in a dozen tongues proclaimed the services offered.

Vendors pushed wagons or carried trays, heaped with every imaginable ware from silks and jewelry to baked sweets and candy. Nicholas glanced around so often he felt overwhelmed by the sights; Freeport looked larger and certainly far busier than Crydee.

Amos said, 'How has this come to be, and we've never heard of it in the Kingdom Sea?'

'That counts against you, Amos,' answered Patrick. 'The customs of every nation move along two paths, the square and the dodgy. And everyone who practices trading on the sly soon hears of where the best fence is, where the cargoes that are ill gotten can be unloaded. You can't have been sailing under that infamous flag of yours recently and not heard that Freeport was now the world's clearinghouse for booty. And even honest traders are hearing of us, because of our lack of customs and tariff.'

Amos fell silent as they continued down the street. 'As I said, Patrick: it's a long story.' At the far end stood a building with a large sign that proclaimed itself 'Governor's House'. It was a modest building, with a wide porch and two windows, one on either side. Shutters were thrown wide and Nicholas could hear loud voices issuing from within.

Amos and his company were marched up the stairs into the building. Whatever walls once existed inside had been removed, so that one large room occupied the entire lower floor. A stairway along the back wall led to the second story. From above, a chandelier of wood with a dozen candles provided light.

A long table had been placed before the stairs, and seven men sat there. Amos removed his large hat, out of respect, and the others with him followed his example. But that appeared the full measure of his deference as he strode up to stand before the centermost captain and bellowed, 'Just what in the Seven Lower Hells gives you the right to greet a brother captain with armed men, William Swallow?'

The grey-haired captain at the center of the table said, 'As meek as ever, I see.'

A younger man, with his hair in dark ringlets that hung to his shoulders, and a finely trimmed moustache, said, 'Who is this buffoon, Swallow?'

'Buffoon!' shouted Amos, turning to face the young man. 'As I live and breathe, Morgan! Heard your father had drunk himself to death and you'd taken command of his ship.' Fixing the man with a baleful eye, he said, 'Boy, before you'd left your mother's teat, I was burning Keshian cutters and sinking Quegan galleys. I sacked Port Natal and drove Lord Barry's fleet back to Krondor like a pack of whipped dogs! I'm Trenchard, the Dagger of the Sea, and I'll kill the first man who says I'm not!'

Morgan said mildly, 'I thought you were dead, Amos.'

Amos pulled a dagger from out of his coat and, before

anyone could react, flipped it and pinned the sleeve of the young captain's coat to the table. 'I'm better now,' he snarled.

Nicholas nudged Marcus, and the older cousin looked where Nicholas indicated. At the far end of the table sat a fair-skinned man covered in blue tattoos. He wore a golden ring in his nose, and his blue eyes were dramatic in his pale face.

Patrick of Duncastle said formally, 'Captain, this is Amos, Captain Trenchard, and I know him.'

Captain Swallow said, 'We heard you were sailing for the Kingdom, Amos.'

Amos shrugged. 'For a while. Before that I was involved in a caper in the north. I've done a lot of things. Sailed for Kesh and against them, sailed for the Kingdom and against them, too. As has every man in this room.'

'I say you be Kingdom spies,' said one of the captains at the far end of the table.

Amos turned and, mocking the man's speech, said, 'And I say you still be an idiot, Peter Dread. How you ever made captain is a mystery; did Captain Mercy die, or did you and Render over there "retire" him?'

The man began to stand and Patrick said, 'No brawling!'

The man with the tattoos said, 'My men tell me you sailed in under the black banner, but your ship's a Kingdom warship.'

Facing him, Amos said, 'It was a Kingdom warship, Render, until I stole it.' Fixing him with a harsh look, he glanced back at Dread, then returned his gaze to Render. 'The quality of leadership around here has gone to hell, it seems. Dread and Render captains?' He shook his head. 'What became of your captain John Avery, Render? Did you eat him?'

Render gripped the edge of the table and looked as if he would spit, but he kept silent. Almost hissing at Amos, he said, 'The *Bantamina* sank off Taroom ten years past, Trenchard. That's when I became a captain!'

Patrick said, 'We can stand around and insult each other all night, Amos, but it will not aid your cause.'

Amos looked around the room. 'I was a captain in the Brotherhood before any of you, save William Swallow. Who denies me my right of free passage? Freeport has always been an open harbor for any captain with the sand to sail here. Or do you now have tax collectors? Are you turning *civilized*, damn you?'

Patrick replied, 'Things are not the same as they once were, Amos. We have much to lose here should anyone come snooping.'

Amos said, 'I'll give you my oath.'

'What's your business in Freeport?' asked a young captain who had been silent so far.

Amos regarded the man, a short, barrel-chested fellow with a red beard and shoulder-length curly red hair. Letting his smile broaden, he said, 'You must be James Scarlet.'

The man nodded. 'I was chased from Questor's View to the lee side of Queg by a ship that looked like yours, Trenchard.'

Amos grinned. 'Two years ago, last spring. I would have caught you, too, if you hadn't run in close to shore and those Quegan galleys hadn't come out to see what we were playing at.'

Slapping the table, Scarlet roared, 'You were sailing for the King!'

Amos roared back, 'I just said I was! Are you deaf or merely stupid? I was being paid bounty for every one of you motherless rogues I could catch, and a pardon for my past crimes, and in my place, no man here would have thought twice about doing exactly the same!' Leaning on the table so he was eye to eye with Scarlet, Amos spoke softly. 'Especially when the alternative is the gibbet.'

'We have a problem,' said Patrick. 'You're known to many of us, Amos, but you've not been seen in these parts for more years than I can recall, save when you were sailing for the King. You say you've turned pirate again, but what surety can we have that you're not going to sell us out to the highest bidder?'

'The same you have from any of these motherless cutthroats.' shouted Amos, indicating the other captains.

'We have stakes here,' said Scarlet. 'This is the sweetest enterprise in the history of the islands, and the take is steady. We'd be fools to poison this well.'

Amos snorted. 'What do you require?' he asked Patrick.

'You have to stay here awhile, Amos.'

'How long?'

'Long enough to make sure a raiding fleet isn't lying in wait somewhere over the horizon,' said Scarlet.

'Or some proof you'll not sail back to Krondor and bring back a fleet,' added Swallow.

Patrick of Duncastle said, 'In any event, Amos, it'll be no more than a few months, a year at the most.' He smiled as if it were only a minor inconvenience.

'You're daft,' said Amos. 'I came here for a reason and I have pressing matters to pursue.'

'He's a spy,' repeated Dread.

'What is this pressing matter? asked Patrick.

Amos pointed an accusing finger at Render. 'I'm here to kill that man.'

Render leaped to his feet, a sword in his hand. Patrick shouted, 'Enough!' Turning to Amos, he said, 'What is your grievance with Render?'

'A month ago he led an army of murderers, including Durbin slavers, into Crydee. He burned the whole damn town to the ground and killed nearly everyone there.'

Render snorted in derision. 'I was sailing off the

Keshian coast a month ago, Trenchard. I haven't been in Crydee since I was a cabin boy. What's worth stealing there?'

Patrick said, 'He denies the raid. And even if he had raided Crydee, why should this cause an issue between you?'

'Because I had five years of plunder secreted away in a warehouse on the docks and I was on my way to move it out when he stole it!'

'There was no plunder!' shouted Render.

Eyes turned to regard him as Amos grinned an evil smile. 'If he hadn't raided Crydee, how would he know that?'

Render said, 'He's lying about me and the raid, so he must be lying about the plunder.'

Patrick glanced from captain to captain and they all nodded. Patrick said, 'It is the law of Freeport. No captain may raise his hand against another – else crews would be warring. You can settle this once you're clear of the harbor, but if either of you starts a fight, his ship will be confiscated and he'll be thrown into the hole.'

Nicholas had watched Render throughout the exchange. Softly he said, 'He's lying.'

Marcus turned to say something, but before he could, Patrick of Duncastle said, 'What did you say?'

Nicholas said, 'I said he was lying. I had friends in Crydee. He's a murderous dog who slaughters women and children. If Captain Trenchard can't take it, then *I* mean to have his life.'

Patrick said, 'Render claims he was off the Keshian coast last month. It must have been someone else.'

Nicholas shook his head. 'Two pirate cannibals with blue eyes? No, it was him.'

Turning to Amos, Patrick said, 'Captain Trenchard, you and your crew are on probation. You have the freedom of the town, but if you or any of your men start

243

trouble, we'll seize your ship and sell your crew to Queg as galley slaves. You control your men here. You may return to the council any time you wish, and if you've convinced four of the seven captains sitting that your story is true, you'll be readmitted to the company of captains.'

Amos said nothing, nodded once, then turned and left. The others fell in with him. As they walked down the steps, he whispered to Nicholas. 'That was good.'

Ghuda said, 'Yes now he's certain to try to kill you.'

Nicholas said, 'That's exactly what I expect.'

Reaching the street, Amos said, 'The captains think we're going to be here another month, but I mean to be out of here the moment we locate the prisoners.' To Harry he said, 'Back to the boat and pass the word that all but the station keeping watch have leave to come ashore. Tell them to behave themselves and to keep their wits about them. I want every man listening for rumors. Look for us at that inn with the red dolphin sign we passed on the way here.' Harry ran off. Amos said to Anthony, 'Start your shopping.' Anthony left. With a nod of his head, Amos indicated that Ghuda should follow behind the magician at a discreet distance. When they were gone, the captain said, 'Now let's go find that inn and see if we can keep Nick alive.'

The Red Dolphin Inn was modest and clean, and relatively quiet, given its usual clientele. Amos had taken a private room in the back and Nakor sat by the door, keeping it cracked open so he could see who approached. Amos said, 'It's obvious we can't take the time to convince the captains one at a time. With Render as one, that means we have to change the minds of four out of six.' He drummed his fingers on the table. 'I think another of them was involved, too.'

'Why?' asked Marcus.

Amos said, 'Too many things still don't fit. You saw the

ships in the harbor?' Marcus nodded. 'Someone's had to bring a lot of mercenaries from somewhere, then ship them out in those raiding flotillas that hit the Far Coast. That's a lot of planning and a lot of men. I think there were at least two deep-water ships, maybe three, and that means at *least* one other captain besides Render.'

Nicholas said, 'Then we've got to work fast.'

Amos said, 'We've got maybe a week before someone in the crew makes a mistake and we're fighting our way out of here.'

Nicholas sat beside him at the table, while Marcus stood behind Amos. Nicholas said, 'If the captives are still here, we need to find them before they're moved again.'

Amos shook his head. 'There's almost no chance they're still here.'

'Why do you say that?' asked Marcus.

Nakor turned and said, 'Because Captain Render was lying to everyone. He says there was no raid. Yet he brought the captives here, Pug says. Too many lies.'

Amos nodded. 'Which means that whoever backed Render's raid probably took the captives away quickly.' He took off his hat and wiped his brow. 'I forgot how muggy these islands get.' He sighed. 'Now that I see how big Freeport has become, I can understand how Render could have mounted his raid and hid it from the other captains.'

Motioning with his hands, Amos continued, 'There are a dozen islands within a half day's sail of here that could be used as a base. He could sail out of the harbor at sundown, claiming he was bound to raid the coast of Kesh. Then he sails to where his other raiders are waiting, picks them up, loads the pinnaces into the holds of the two ships, sails to just beyond the horizon from Crydee, unloads the pinnaces, and begins his assault on the Far Coast.'

245

'Why would they strike from these waters, Amos?' asked Marcus. 'If they didn't want the other pirates to know about it, why even start here?'

Amos said, 'There are bound to be strangers moving through Freeport all the time. And where better to make the bargain for this sort of crime? But the question is, where can he hide several hundred captives?'

Nakor's face clouded over as he remembered. 'Pug said something about a big building. A big, dark building.'

Amos said, 'I think we need to start spreading out.' Looking at Marcus, he said, 'How good a sailor are you?'

Marcus said, 'I can handle a small boat well enough not to drown myself.'

'Good. Find one tomorrow and buy it. If anyone asks you what you're doing, tell them you're going to explore the nearby islands because Trenchard is thinking of building a house. Some of the captains have their own little kingdoms around here. Take Harry with you, and see he doesn't drown himself.

'Render may have too much to lose to start trouble because Nicholas and I have threatened him, and we've been enjoined from going after him.' Grinning, Amos patted Nicholas's hand. 'You, my lucky boy, have the unenviable task of irritating Render into doing something stupid. We'll set a watch on him, and you're going to have to be after him constantly. I want you to be so close to him he'll think you're his shadow.'

Nicholas nodded.

Amos uncorked a large jug of ale and said, 'Now, who's for a drink?'

10

Discoveries

A gull squawked.

Marcus, Calis, and Harry walked to the harbor as the sun rose above the horizon. For the half-elven youth, who looked no older than Harry despite being thirty years old, Freeport was an alien bounty of sights and sounds. He had remained quiet, content to let his companions do whatever talking was necessary, but he watched and listened and seemed fascinated by the variety of humanity living on the island. Harry had confided to Nicholas the night before that it was entirely possible to forget the elfling even existed until he chose to move or speak, so adept he was at being silent and still.

Harry was about to ask him a question when a slight form hurried from behind an overturned boat and fell into step beside them. Calis had his knife out and ready before the others could turn. Harry almost jumped from fright at the sudden appearance. 'Gods! What do you want?'

A voice whispered, 'More to the point: what is it you three want?'

The slight figure was clad in a shapeless tunic and trousers; dirty toes protruded from under the too-long pants. The thin arms that extended from ragged sleeves were as dirty as the feet, and the face was only marginally cleaner. A narrow chin and small mouth were dominated by high cheekbones and enormous blue eyes. Ragged longish red-brown hair flew about in all directions.

'Go away, boy,' said Marcus impatiently.

'Boy!' said the beggar. With a vicious kick to Marcus's

shin, the girl danced back. 'For that you'll pay double for your information.'

Marcus winced at the blow and Harry stood in mute astonishment. Calis calmly said, 'Then, go away, girl.'

They resumed their walk, but the girl came hurrying to walk backward beside Marcus. 'I know lots of things. Ask anyone in Freeport and they'll tell you, "Want to know something? Ask Brisa!"'

Harry said, 'And you're Brisa?'

'Of course.'

Marcus and Calis said nothing, but Harry said, 'Our captain is looking for an island to build a house on.'

Brisa stopped walking backward and stood directly in Marcus's path. 'Right,' she said derisively.

Marcus was forced to stop as the others passed to her right. He looked down at her and said, 'Yes, that's right.'

She grinned, and Marcus was startled to notice she had dimples. Showing his irritation, he repeated, 'Yes, that's right,' and tried to step around her.

She moved with him, cutting him off.

'I have no time for these silly games,' he said, and tried to move the other way.

She stepped back a half-step and caught her heel on a coil of rope. Falling backward, she landed hard on her bottom. Marcus smiled and Harry laughed, while Calis remained impassive. Brisa made a disgusted noise as Marcus walked past her, and shouted, 'Fine! When you're tired of sailing in circles, come see me!'

Marcus turned back toward her and, in an atypical display of amusement, saluted her. Even Calis smiled, while Harry continued to laugh.

Late that night, Harry, Calis, and Marcus climbed up a ladder where their sailboat was tied and found Brisa sitting on a bale of cloth, eating an apple. 'Tired?' she asked.

They glanced at one another and moved past her, but she jumped down and was at their side, walking with her hands behind her back. Like a child at play, she sang, 'I know what you're looking for.'

Marcus said, 'We told you – '

'No you're not,' she said in a singsong voice.

'Not what?'

'Looking for an island for your captain.' She took a last bite from her apple and threw the core over her shoulder into the sea. Gulls squawked and dove for it.

'Then what are we looking for?' asked Harry, impatient from a day spent sailing through a half-dozen deserted islands.

Brisa crossed her arms and said, 'What's it worth to you to find what you're looking for?'

Marcus shook his head. 'We have no time for clever games, girl.'

The three began to walk faster, Brisa said, 'I know where the Durbin slavers went.'

They stopped. They exchanged glances and turned around. Calis walked back to where the girl waited and firmly grabbed her arm. Marcus said, 'What do you know?'

'Ow!' she cried, trying to twist away, but Calis held fast. 'Let me go or I'm not saying anything!' she demanded.

Marcus put his hand upon Calis's arm. 'Let her go.'

Calis did so, and the girl stepped away. Rubbing her sore arm, she pouted. 'Didn't your mother tell you there are better ways to get a girl's attention?' Turning an angry eye upon Marcus, she said, 'You're not half-bad-looking for a scruffy brigand, though you'd look better without the beard, I think. I was going to be nice, but now my price has gone up.'

Harry said, 'Look, what do you know and what do you want?'

'I know that a month ago some strange men came through town; a lot of them. Many more gathered in the nearby islands, doing their best to avoid being seen by those who live here in Freeport. They spoke Keshian, mostly, but with a strange accent, one I've not heard before. Others came to town and bought supplies. Not all at once, but enough that I got curious. Nothing happens around here out of the ordinary that I don't notice. So I decided to snoop around.' She smiled. 'I'm good at finding things out.'

Harry couldn't help smiling. 'I expect you are.'

'Now, do we have a deal?' she demanded.

'What's your price?' asked Marcus.

'Fifty golden royals.'

Marcus said, 'I don't carry that kind of gold around.'

Harry said, 'What about this?'

He held out a ring, a faceted ruby set in a gold band.

'Where did you get that?' asked Marcus.

Harry shook his head slightly, 'I forget.' To the girl he said, 'It's worth twice what you ask.'

The girl said, 'Very well. I followed one group, marked their course, and sailed a boat out after sunset. I found where they mustered. There was the biggest ship i'd ever seen, anchored off the point. It was black and looked like a Quegan galley, with high fore- and aftercastles, large mainsails, and a hell of a lot of beam. It rode high, so I figure it was empty, but men were moving back and forth to that island constantly. They couldn't sail the big ship in, so they had to spend days moving men and supplies by small boat. From what they had on the beach, it looked like they were heading out for a long trip, maybe down to the far end of Kesh. They also had patrols out, and I had to get out of there.

'A few weeks later there were some boats moving through the islands, but staying away from Freeport.' With a bright grin, she said, 'I got curious and went back to the island, and saw that most of the men were being ferried to the big ship. But a dozen smaller boats deposited a lot of captives on the island. There was six Durbin slavers in charge.'

'How do you know that's what we're interested in?' asked Harry, hanging on to the ring.

'You're on a Kingdom ship and all the captives spoke the King's Tongue. Some famous captain shows up after thirty years – it's all too coincidental for me. Your captain's the real thing, but the rest of you are too damn clean and polite; you're Kingdom Navy. You've come looking for those captives, right?'

Harry flipped the ring in the air and Brisa caught it. 'Where did they take the captives?' Harry asked.

'Two islands to the west, on the lee side,' she said. She was off and running, and called over her shoulder, 'And when you get back, I can tell you more.'

Harry shouted, 'How will we find you?'

'Just ask for Brisa anywhere!' came the answer as the girl vanished between two buildings.

That night, several of the *Raptor's* crew had spotted the tattooed captain in the town, and had passed word. Nicholas and Ghuda put in an unexpected appearance at an inn Render favored.

They took seats near enough to hear normal conversation, and Render and his men instantly fell silent. After a moment, Nicholas said, 'It's just a matter of time, isn't it?' He spoke loudly enough to be heard by everyone in the room.

Ghuda said, 'Sooner or later.' He had no idea what Nicholas was talking about, but he played along.

'One of these days a ship's going to come in from the Far Coast, carrying word of the raids; no commerce and no plunder for years to come. Then every merchant in the city will be mobbing Governor's House to have the culprit's head on a pole.' Glancing at Render, who glared back, Nicholas clearly said, 'And I'll be pleased to hand it to them.'

Render whispered furiously to two of the men who sat there, then rose and departed. The two men kept their eyes on Nicholas and Ghuda as if daring them to follow their captain.

Nicholas sat back and waited.

Anthony, Nakor, and Amos left at first light the next day with Marcus to investigate the island. In three hours they reached it. The island was similar to dozens in the area, formed ages ago in volcanic upheaval. Eroded by wind and water, covered in brush and tough grasses carried over the water by seabirds, it was an inhospitable place of a high cliff with no beaches on the lee-side. After an hour spent circling the island, they came to a shallow inlet on the windward side. A huge building squatted near the high-water line on the beach, sheltered by high rocks that hid it from the view of anyone approaching from any direction except directly into the inlet. There was no sign of anyone on the island.

They beached their sailboat and looked around. Amos said, 'A lot of boats have been in and out of there recently.' He pointed to marks on the sand above the high-tide line. A wide path of footprints led to the building. 'Good wind or rain and we'd not see those. They've been made within the last few days.'

They walked up to the crudely fashioned building. They pushed open large doors and went inside. The stench of recent human waste and something even more foul filled the place. A cloud of flies rose high into the air, and on the ground they saw what they had been feasting upon.

Amos swore. He quickly counted and said, 'There are more than a dozen of them.' Littered across the floor were corpses.

Choking back his bile, Marcus forced himself to examine the closest body. A boy lay close enough to the door so that the light made it easy to examine him. Marcus said, 'He died in pain.'

Amos shook his head. 'I've seen that look before.'

Nakor looked at another. 'They've been dead maybe three, four days. Skin is all puffy and the flies have blown maggots.'

Amos glanced around the room and said, 'It's no picnic in here, Marcus. If you want to wait outside . . .'

Marcus knew Amos was trying to spare him the possibility that his sister or Abigail might be among the dead. 'No,' he said shortly.

They picked their way through the grisly scene, and at the center of the room, Amos found something that made him swear. 'Bannath's boils!' he said, invoking the god of thieves and pirates.

Six men in the guild dress of Durbin slavers lay on the floor, their bodies riddled with arrows. Amos forced himself to kneel and examine one of the men. He removed the black mask and saw a guild tattoo upon the corpse's face. 'These are true Durbin slavers,' he whispered in awe. 'Who would face the wrath of their guild?'

But he knew who would: the same merciless enemy that had seized control of the Assassins' Guild in Krondor, subverting it to their own ends, and who had perpetrated the greatest fraud in the history of Midkemia in raising the standard of the legendary Murmandamus to cause the nations of the north – the dark elves, or moredhel, and goblins – to invade the Kingdom. Only they would kill six masters of the Durbin Slavers' Guild, and Amos knew why. No living man knew where the Pantathian serpent priests lived, only that they dwelt in some distant land across the sea.

Anthony paced around inside, his face impassive despite the carnage. The dead prisoners had been too weak to continue on and had had their throats cut.

Nakor said, 'There is only one girl, see, over here.'

They hurried to look and Anthony said, 'This is Willa. She served in the kitchen.

Nakor pointed to another corpse, a man who had died with his pants down around his ankles. 'This was a bad man. He tried to take this sick girl before he killed her,' he said as if he could read the past, 'and someone else killed him for trying.' The little man shook his head. Glancing around the large room, he said, 'To herd children in here as if they were cattle is cruel; to leave them here for days with the dead and dying is inhuman.'

Amos said softly, 'No one said those behind this were human, Isalani.'

Anthony kept pacing around the building as if looking for something. As Amos was about to order their departure, Anthony found a few scraps of clothing, torn from a tunic or dress. He picked them up and inspected them. Suddenly his eyes widened as he held one that had been used as a bandage, from the blood upon it, and he said, 'Margaret!'

Amos said, 'How do you know?'

The magician said, 'I just know. She wore this.'

Marcus examined it. 'Is she hurt? Look at the blood.'

Anthony shook his head. 'I think . . . she used this as a bandage on someone else.'

'How do you know?' asked her brother.

'I . . . just know,' he repeated.

Amos glanced around. 'This raid was planned well in advance and every contingency planned for. Most of the raiders may have come from Kesh or somewhere else, but there must have been at least a hundred people from Freeport in on it.' Leaving the building and returning to the boat, he said, 'The problem's going to be finding one who was involved, and who will talk. Whoever ran this caper probably paid well, and' – he pointed to the half-naked man who'd had his throat cut – ' we saw how quickly they dispense punishment. Few will be willing to betray these masters.' To Marcus he said, 'You've got to find that girl again and see what else she knows.'

They were silent all the way back to Freeport harbor.

They returned to the Red Dolphin at sundown. Reaching the room in the back, Amos found Harry waiting for them. 'What's happened?' Amos asked.

'Render almost challenged Nick today,' said Harry with a grin. 'He decided to sup at noon at a different tavern. One of our men spotted him, so Nick showed up and sat nearby. So he left, and we found him at a third tavern, so Nick showed up there. Render started yelling at him. He's not doing well. Our people have started a lot of gossip about the raids, and the townspeople are starting to wonder if something has gone on; enough people around here knew something was up for the last few months that more and more they're inclined to believe us and doubt Render.' Harry shook his head. 'Given the right circumstances, say if we have a particular hot Sixthday night and someone were to start buying lots of drinks for those inclined to listen to how Render ruined everyone's business for the next five years, I can imagine they'd riot and haul Render out and hang him without benefit of proof.' Harry's gleeful expression turned more serious. 'I think Render's had about enough of us. Word on the street is he'll be sailing tomorrow or the day after to raid along the Keshian shore and he's looking for extra crewmen.'

Amos scratched his chin. 'Extra crewmen? Then he'll come after Nicholas tonight if he's a mind to.' Amos considered, 'There's a couple of ways Render can play this: the smart way would be to sail out late tonight and never return to Freeport. But Render's never been known for being especially smart; clever and cunning, yes, but not smart.'

Amos thought a long moment, then went on, 'He'll probably try to take my ship on the way out, if I know that cannibal – that's why he needs the extra men.' Almost to himself he said, 'He'll kill Nick, put the blame on me, demand I be hung, and get the best warship in the islands all in one night.'

Marcus said, 'So what do we do?'

Amos said, 'Why, we let him try.' He told Harry, 'Go find Ghuda, Nick, and as many of the men as you can and have them come by here.'

Harry was off. Amos said to Anthony, 'Start looking for those who might know something about that building where the captives were held; they might have brought their own carpenters from wherever they hail from, but they probably didn't lug all the lumber along. And don't get yourself into trouble.'

Anthony and Marcus left, and Amos said, 'I wonder how the magician knew that cloth was Margaret's?'

Nakor grinned. 'He's a magician. Besides, he's in love with her.'

Amos said, 'Really? I took him for something of a bloodless sort.'

Nakor shook his head. 'He's shy. But he loves her. It's why he can find her at the right time.'

Amos narrowed his gaze. 'You being mysterious again, Isalani?'

Nakor shrugged. 'I'm going to take a nap. It will get very noisy around here later.' He tipped back his chair until he leaned against the wall, and closed his eyes. A moment later he was snoring softly.

Amos glanced at the sleeping little man and said, 'How does he do that?'

* * *

The ship groaned and Margaret said, 'Listen!'

Abigail looked over with faint interest. 'What is it?'

Margaret said, 'We've changed course. Don't you feel the difference in the way the ship is handling?'

'No. So what?' asked Abigail in flat tones. Even with the larger accommodation, a cabin of their own because of their rank, and good food, the girl couldn't shake her dark moods. She still wept uncontrollably at times.

Margaret said, 'We were on a southerly heading, and I expected we should turn toward the east, to run the Straits of Darkness. But we're turning to starboard' – Abigail looked blank – 'to the right! We're heading southwest!'

Abigail shook her head in confusion. Then a spark of interest fanned in her eyes. 'What's that mean?'

Feeling fear without any leavening of hope, Margaret whispered, 'We're not going to Kesh.'

The whores laughed loudly as men shouted across the room in greeting or friendly insult. Nicholas drained his seventh or eighth glass of wine. Across the room, Render sat with five of his men, whispering. Nicholas and the pirate captain had been glaring across the room at each other for almost an hour, and Ghuda and Harry had urged Nicholas loudly to stop drinking. He'd ignored them. An hour earlier he had begun to utter threats against Render. At first they had been barely heard by those not standing next to him, but for the last five minutes, everyone close by could clearly hear him.

Suddenly Nicholas lurched to his feet and staggered across the room toward Render's table. Ghuda and Harry were slow to react and reached him only as three of the five men with Render stood, their hands on their sword hilts.

'I'm going to cut your heart out, you murderous swine!' shouted Nicholas, and the room fell silent. 'Before the gods, I swear you'll pay for what you did.'

Render glared at the young man as Ghuda and Harry pulled him back. One of Render's companions shouted, 'Take that drunk away before we put him out of his misery.'

Ghuda said evenly, 'You could try. It might prove amusing.' His calm expression and the array of weapons clearly displayed upon his person prevented further threats.

Render stood and pointed an accusing finger. 'Everyone has heard. This man has threatened me repeatedly. If any trouble begins, it's his doing and Captain Trenchard is responsible! I vow before everyone here that I will only raise my hand in self-defense!'

Nicholas began to struggle, trying to get at Render, but Ghuda and Harry restrained him. They half dragged, half carried Nicholas out of the tavern. Aiding their friend down the boulevard, they reached the Red Dolphin and went inside. Carrying Nicholas up the stairs, they entered the room at the far end of the hall.

Inside, Nicholas pulled himself upright and Harry said, 'How are you?'

'I've never drunk so much water so fast. Where's the night pot?'

Harry pointed to the pot, and Nicholas relieved himself. 'Do you think we can trust the barman?'

'No,' said Ghuda, 'but I paid him sufficient gold and threatened him enough that he'll say nothing for a day or two.'

Nicholas said, 'Now we wait.'

Near dawn, a band of men crept into the common room of the Red Dolphin. A bar boy slept under a table and he came instantly awake. It was his job to guard the commons and alert the innkeeper should guests arrive at odd hours or beggars or thieves enter.

Seeing men with ready swords, the boy pulled himself back under the table and huddled against the wall. He was not about to raise an alarm with this many armed cut-throats nearby.

As the intruders reached the far door, every door in the hallway swung open and more armed men leaped out. The sound of steel against steel rang through the halls and the fight was on in earnest.

Nicholas and Ghuda held the door at the far end of the hall, and two of the attackers made halfhearted attempts to move toward them, but the presence of armed men in the doorways between deterred them. Then a shout from the far end of the hall, at the top of the stairs, cut through the sounds of fighting. 'Halt! In the name of the Sheriff, stop fighting!'

The men trapped in the hallway turned, and several attempted to fight their way down the stairs. They were quickly overwhelmed by a dozen men wielding billy clubs and swords, who killed two of them and overpowered the rest. Those still in the hallway drew into a cluster, and from the center a voice called, 'We will not resist!'

Nicholas smiled at Ghuda. 'That's Render,' he said with grim satisfaction.

Amos and Harry emerged from one door, with William Swallow one step behind. Anthony, Marcus, and Nakor came out of another room. They followed Render's men down the stairs to where more than a dozen of Patrick Duncastle's men waited to take them all into custody.

Amos approached the boy under the table and gave him gold coin. 'You did well. Tell your master that I thank him for the use of the inn.'

The boy left, and Amos pushed Render into the large room at the back of the commons. Four of the captains of Freeport sat at the table and looked at Render as he knelt before them.

William Swallow followed Amos into the room. 'It's

259

true, as Amos said, Render and his men came up with murderous intent.'

Taking his place at the table, Swallow said, 'You know the law, Render. Your ship is forfeit and you're consigned to the hole.'

'No!' shouted Render. 'I was tricked.'

Amos said, 'Before you drag this garbage out of here, there are some things I need to ask him. You may be interested in his answers.'

Swallow looked at the other captains, all who were in port save Captain Dread, and they nodded. Amos said, 'Who paid you to raid the Far Coast?'

Render spat at Amos, who responded by striking him in the face with a gloved fist. Render struck the floor hard and lay there with blood running down his chin. Kneeling next to him, Amos said, 'I haven't the time to be gentle with you, Render, and am even less possessed of the inclination. If we toss you into the street and let it be known that you've destroyed the commerce along the Far Coast for the next five years, that you've worked on behalf of Durbin slavers, and cut the other captains and their crews out of the booty, how long do you think it would take for the citizens of Freeport to tear you apart?'

Render's eyes grew wide, but he said nothing. Amos said, 'Think of the whores who'll see no gold now that shipping from Crydee, Carse, and Tulan has stopped. Think of the men of Freeport who will have no ships to prey upon. Think of the honest merchants who will have no markets closer than Elarial or the Free Cities.'

Swallow said, 'Amos, we've heard the rumors; is it really true?'

Amos said, 'It's true, William. This bastard led more than a thousand men against the Far Coast last month and burned Castle Crydee to the ground. The fortress at Barran was destroyed, and Carse and Tulan were raided

– we don't know how badly, but we assume the worst. You'll have little trading and no raiding in the Duchy for years to come.'

William Swallow stood, his face white with anger. 'You fool!' he shouted at Render. 'You'll bring the Kingdom's war fleet down on us! And for what?'

Render was silent, but Amos took him by one long earlobe, and twisted the fetish there. As the man squealed in pain, Amos said, 'For either more gold than he could honestly steal in a lifetime – you'd best send men to inspect the hold of his ship – or . . .'

Amos grabbed the pouch at Render's belt and looked inside. A snake ring fell upon the floor among coins and gems. Holding it up, Amos showed it to William Swallow. 'Have you seen its like?'

Swallow looked at it and passed it to the other captains. All said they'd not seen it before. Nicholas asked, 'Is he a hired servant or a willing pawn?'

Amos grabbed Render's arm and pulled him to his feet. 'He doesn't have the courage of conviction to be a religious fanatic. He's a bought servant.'

Swallow said, 'Amos, we thank you for the warning. We must prepare for the Kingdom's revenge.' Pointing his finger at Render, he said, 'You will be hung at dawn! And every man in your crew will be sold!'

Amos said, 'Do what you will with the men, but I need Render.'

'For what?'

'To find those whose bidding he does.'

Swallow said, 'We can't let him go, Amos. If we do, what's the Captain's Covenant worth?'

Amos shrugged. 'It's worth what it always was: little. It's a truce bought by fear, and it's always balanced against greed. There was never enough profit for a captain to break the covenant, until someone showed up with more gold than Render's got sense.' He glanced around the room. 'And speaking of those who have no sense, where's Peter Dread?'

Swallow said, 'He was told to be here.'

Amos sighed. 'Send word to find him. I suspect there were two idiots involved in that raid. Was Dread around during the raid last month?'

'We thought he was looking for prey in the Bitter Sea,' answered Morgan.

'Find him before he warns his masters that you're on to them,' insisted Amos. 'I'll make you a bargain.'

'What bargain?' said Swallow.

'If you let me find out what I need to know from Render, I'll promise that no reprisal fleet reaches Freeport.'

Swallow's eyes narrowed. 'How can you do that?'

Amos said, 'Because I'm the King's Admiral of the Western Realm.'

The five captains exchanged glances. 'So,' said Scarlet, 'you were more than trading your services for pardon when you were chasing me off the Quegan coast.'

Amos nodded. 'Let me give you the full of it, and then you decide. We have no time for, nor any interest in, putting a stop to your enterprise here. We're after the daughter of Duke Martin and others taken from Crydee. Someone put Render and Dread on this caper and sent along a thousand raiders, including Tsurani assassins and Durbin slavers.' He told them what he knew of the raid and finished by saying, 'So we have more urgent matters than putting an end to your livelihood.'

Swallow said, 'What's to keep us from holding you here as hostages, Amos?'

'Because the only way we can keep Arutha from sending his fleet to burn your city to the ground is by getting his niece back in one piece and returning her to the Kingdom, you idiot!' Amos bellowed. 'Do I have to paint you a picture?'

Nicholas said, 'And we can make it worth your while.'

Swallow said, 'How?'

Nicholas said, 'Commerce was never one of my better subjects, but I do know that you've gained wealth because what you provide is needed.' He looked at the five captains. 'For a year, no reprisals will come against Freeport. Then a Kingdom ship will come here. Any who remain will be granted full pardon for past crimes, so long as they swear fealty to the Kingdom and do not transgress the law. Any who choose otherwise are free to leave with guaranteed safe passage and start somewhere else in the meantime.'

'What's in it for us?' challenged Scarlet.

'Peace of mind, for one thing,' said Marcus.

Ghuda said, 'And protection from Kesh and Queg should they start thinking you'd look good on the map as part of their realm.'

Swallow said, 'Kesh, Queg, the Kingdom, it make little difference. Governors and tax agents, and laws and the like. It'll be the death of our way of life.'

Nicholas said, 'Partly. No more raiding.'

Amos grinned. 'We're both getting a little on in years to be chasing merchant ships like they were maidens at the Midsummer's festival and we were cocky lads, William.'

Swallow nodded. 'True, but what's the reason to stay, Amos? If we become another Kingdom port . . .'

Nicholas said, 'What if Freeport continued to operate without duties? What if a trader could come here and deliver cargo legally without needing to pay tariff or tax to the Kingdom?'

Swallow said, 'Some would continue to come here, even though it's the long way around from Queg to

Krondor, for certain cargoes with high profits.'

Amos said, 'The King will never sit still for that, Nick.'

Nicolas said, 'I think he will. The danger of Freeport has been shown too clearly in the last few weeks. It's worth some lost revenue to keep things quiet out there. If Kesh can let the captains of Durbin come and go as they please, why not the Kingdom and Freeport?'

'Why not?' agreed Amos.

Swallow said, 'Can you get the King to agree, Amos?'

'Probably not, William. But his nephew probably can,' he answered, placing his hand on Nicholas's shoulder.

'Nephew?' said Scarlet.

Amos said, 'This stays within this room, by your oath, and you'll decide how to tell the populace what's been agreed to here. But this boy is Nicholas, son of the Prince of Krondor, and cousin to Margaret, the girl who was taken.'

Marcus said, 'And I'm her brother, Marcus. My father is the Duke of Crydee.' Thinking of his father caused Marcus's eyes to narrow slightly, but he remained otherwise calm.

Swallow said, 'Do we have any choice?'

'You're not entitled to any,' admitted Amos, 'but we'll give you one anyway. You've a year to ponder things.'

Nicholas said, 'Give me paper and quill and I'll pen a note to my father or whoever sails this way next spring against our not returning. By this time next year, you'll have had to decide, one way or the other.'

Swallow agreed.

Nicholas said, 'Patrick?'

The Sheriff said, 'Ah . . . Highness?'

Nicholas said, 'Things will remain as they have been, but should the captains convince the citizens to agree to our terms at any time in the next year, you will act as the King's High Sheriff of Freeport. If you're agreed?'

Patrick nodded and stepped back.

Nicholas said, 'You five captains will be given letters of marque, as the King's western squadron of the Krondorian fleet. It will look more convincing when my father shows up here next spring if you're flying Kingdom colors from your mastheads. You can decide who ranks among you.'

Amos turned to Render. 'Now you're going to tell us what we need to know, you murderous cur. The only question is, do we get the information the easy way or the hard way?'

Render spat at Amos. 'I demand my rights as a captain under the covenant! We're not part of the bloody Kingdom yet, Trenchard! You've no writ over me, and I can demand personal justice.

Amos faced the other captains. 'Are you going to – '

Swallow interrupted. 'We must, Amos. We dare not break the covenant until the people have accepted the King's laws. To do otherwise . . .'

'You said we could question Render in exchange for the Kingdom's keeping hands off!' bellowed Amos.

'We gave blood oath to the Captains' Covenant!' Morgan shouted in return, as the others voiced loud agreement. 'If we have *any* claim to honor this side of hell, it's our oath!'

William Swallow said, 'You were of the Brotherhood long enough to know that, Amos. Killer, thief, or blasphemer, we'll make you one of us, but be named oath breaker, and no man will sail with you again.'

Looking at the prisoner, Morgan said, 'I'd gladly hand this traitor's heart to you myself, Trenchard, but our word is our bond. If we break it, we're no better than he is.'

Amos nodded. 'Very well, Render,' he said, removing his hat and jacket, 'if you wish captain's privilege . . .'

'No!' said Render. 'Not you, Trenchard. Him!' He pointed at Nicholas.

Swallow said, 'It was the lad who was his accuser, and the covenant forbids captains from fighting one another.'

Nicholas said, 'What is this?'

Amos stepped close and said, 'As a captain, Render has the right to defend himself by personal combat. You're the one who must kill him.'

Nicholas looked startled and whispered, 'I've never killed anyone, Amos.'

Glancing at Render, who had removed his jacket and shirt, revealing the purple tattoos all over his chest and back, Amos said, 'Well, I can't imagine anyone you'd have to work less hard to hate, boy. That's the man who was responsible for your aunt Briana's murder and who kidnapped your cousin and that little girl you're so fond of.'

Nicholas's expression showed he was unconvinced. 'I don't know if I can . . . just kill him.'

Amos said, 'You're not going to be given a choice, son. If you refuse, he walks away a free man.'

'They can't – '

'They can and they will. This is not the Kingdom, and your rank means nothing.' Lowering his voice and putting his hands on Nicholas's shoulders, he said, 'Now, he's certainly going to try to kill you if you give him the chance, so don't. If he wins, he walks out of here with the right of passage and no pursuit. That's captains' law. So you must kill him.'

'What about the girls? We won't know – '

Amos said, 'These lads' – he indicated the captains – 'are less concerned with the prisoners than they are with their own necks. Give them half a chance to reconsider, and they may decide holding you hostage against your father showing up with my fleet isn't such a poor notion after all. Worry about getting information after you've managed to stay alive, Nicholas.' There was genuine

266

concern in his voice and expression. 'Now you *must* do this thing.'

Nicholas nodded, removing his baldric and coat. The common room was quickly stripped of tables and chairs. Captain Scarlet drew a large circle on the floor in chalk. Swallow positioned a man with a crossbow on the stairs and said, 'It's simple justice. Both of you walk into the circle; one walks out. If a man tries to flee the circle, he'll be judged guilty and shot.'

The two combatants stepped into the circle, barely more than twenty feet across. Harry whispered to Nicholas, 'It's just like the fencing corridor at the palace. Keep your mind on the blade.'

Nicholas nodded. Part of their training had been to duel along a narrow hall, where one could neither advance quickly nor move too far to one side or another without risking injury. Footwork would play little part in this duel; bladework, everything.

Render took a heavy saber and held it upright, then cocked it back behind his head. Nicholas extended his own saber, knowing that his opponent could bring the blade slashing around instantly either to block an attack or to remove his head. Swallow said, 'May Banath, god of thieves and pirates, give strength to him who is in the right in the cause.'

Nicholas stood ready, when suddenly he felt a stabbing pain in his left foot. Then Render's sword was hissing through the air and Nicholas barely had time to bring his own blade up to block. He took the blow and felt the shock all the way up his arm. That was when Nicholas knew that this was no drill at home, nor practice with a civilized opponent; this was someone trying to kill him.

Fear exploded in Nicholas's heart, a clutching deep dread and near panic, but hours of training each day over years saved him. Reflexes worked where his mind wouldn't, and he successfully blocked each blow. In less than a minute, Render had launched no fewer than ten attacks, each countered by the Prince. His foot stabbed him each time he put weight on it, and each stab hurt worse than the one before.

Nicholas found his own perspiration sour in his nose, as terror drove him to survive. But still he had not ventured any counterattack of his own. Harry called encouragement, but the others were chillingly silent.

On and on Render pressed forward, and each time Nicholas met him with a stout defense. His foot hurt enough that he wished to scream, to fall to the floor and roll up in a ball, holding it until the fire and throbbing stopped, but to do so was to die.

Render slashed at Nicholas, and he forced himself to block and return a strike, which sent the tattooed sea captain stumbling back at the unexpected response. Nicholas didn't follow through, as pain stabbed up his leg, causing his left knee to tremble.

Nicholas stepped back, looking Render in the eyes, and he forced himself to breathe slowly. 'It's going to hurt,' he warned himself softly, 'but you'll live. It's only pain, and you can ignore pain.'

Render advanced, wary now that he'd seen the young man's speed. Nicholas waited, without moving, his eyes following the captain as he advanced. Nicholas maintained a balanced stance, weight evenly distributed on both feet, though his left burned in agony. Then Render was moving, a combination of blows, high, low, and high again, forcing the younger man to move back in lock step with him. Nicholas took each blow and focused all his concentration on the other man's sword. The stink of fear in his nose, the pain in his foot, the surroundings – all of it was put aside as he lost himself in the rhythm of the attack.

Then Render overextended his high attack and Nicholas snapped a blow that caught the pirate upon the shoulder, cutting him deeply. Blood flowed over the purple tattoos and white skin, but Render barely acknowledged the injury.

Nicholas stepped forward and then back. As he moved away from Render, he lost his concentration, and suddenly pain shot upward from his foot, causing him to gasp. He wavered and Render pressed the attack, sensing the younger man was somehow distracted.

A slashing cut to the neck was barely blocked and Nicholas received a terrible glancing blow to the elbow. Almost blind from the pain, he countered and found his blade slamming into Render's ribs. The other man gasped in pain and pulled back, and Nicholas felt his own fingers starting to go numb. He transferred his saber to his left hand, and blinked to clear his vision.

Render stood gripping his ribs, and suddenly Nicholas could hear Amos's voice shouting, 'He's open, lad! Kill him!'

Nicholas held the blade awkwardly in his left hand, and Render's vision seemed to clear. Despite the blood running down from his shoulder and from the wound in his side, he smiled. Nicholas tried to advance and again pain stabbed his left foot, which was now the lead. He retreated and Render leaped.

Nicholas braced for the attack, swept Render's blade to the side, and riposted, the point of his weapon taking the tattooed man in the pit of the stomach. Render's eyes widened in disbelief as blood came gushing from his mouth and nose.

For a moment his eyes looked into Nicholas's, and instead of hatred or fear, there was a questioning look, as if he was asking the Prince, 'Why?' Then he collapsed.

The men gathered around Nicholas and Amos said, 'What happened to you?'

Nicholas took a long moment to understand the question and his leg began to tremble. Suddenly it collapsed beneath him, and as he fell, Harry and Marcus grabbed him. Softly he said, 'My foot . . .'

He was carried to a nearby chair and sat down. He let Harry pull his left boot off, and when he saw his foot, he winced. It was discolored, purple and black. 'Gods,' said Harry. 'It looks like a horse stepped on it.'

'What's wrong?' asked Amos.

Nakor shook his head and said nothing.

After a moment the pain faded, and, before their eyes, the discoloration began to fade as well.

Nicholas's vision cleared and at last he said, 'What did you say, Amos?'

'I said, what's wrong?'

Nicholas said, 'Oh, my arm?' He looked at his arm and saw no blood. Pulling up the sleeve, he saw an angry red welt on the elbow, quickly darkening, but no sign of a cut or break.

Harry said, 'I've seen you practice for hours left-handed; why did you have so much trouble?'

Nicholas said, 'I don't know. My foot . . .'

Amos and the others from Crydee looked down and saw nothing wrong with either of Nicholas's feet. 'It's changed!' exclaimed Ghuda.

Nicholas shook his head. His foot now looked normal. 'It hurt. A sharp pain when I stepped on it, It got worse as the fight wore on.'

'Does it hurt now?' asked Nakor.

Nicholas stepped upon it and said, 'Only a little . . . It's stopped hurting.'

Nakor nodded again but didn't say anything.

Amos turned to the other captains and said, 'Well, there's your justice for you.' To Marcus and Harry he said, 'Take some of our boys and accompany the Sheriff,' and to Patrick, 'If you don't mind?'

'I don't,' said Patrick.

Amos said to Marcus, 'After you've rounded up Render's crew, tell them that I'll buy the freedom of any man who can tell us who took the girls from that island and where they were bound. Question them one at a time, because every one of those motherless dogs will lie to you.'

Marcus nodded and he and Harry left.

Amos turned to find Nicholas staring down at the lifeless body of Render. The boy's face was ashen and he looked as if he might be sick. Clapping his hand upon Nicholas's shoulder, Amos said, 'Don't worry, son. You'll get used to it.'

Nicholas's eyes began to tear and he said, 'I hope not.' Ignoring the stares of those around him, he picked up his jacket and slowly walked to the stairs and up them, toward his room.

Nicholas slept late the next day. The capture of Render's crew had proved easier than expected. All of the men were aboard his ship, *Lady of Darkness*, waiting for orders to row over to the *Raptor* and take her. A few threats from the surrounding dozen longboats, and the promise to burn the boat to the water line if they didn't give up their arms, was all it took. Amos had observed they were a less resolute lot than Kingdom sailors, because they sailed for booty. But it had been only five hours to dawn when they were done, and Nicholas was exhausted from the duel and the capture.

The sound of footsteps hurrying up the stairs greeted him as he opened the door. Harry stood at the top of the stairs, breathless.

'What is it?' Nicholas asked his friend.

'You'd better come.' He hurried back down the stairs and Nicholas followed.

Down in the large private room Amos was using as headquarters, they found him in conference with William

Swallow and Patrick Duncastle.

Amos looked up and said, 'They're dead.'

'Who?' asked Nicholas, fearful he was about to hear Margaret's and Abigail's names.

'Render's crew. They're all dead.'

Nicholas's eyes narrowed as he attempted to take in the news. 'All of them?'

'Yes,' said Patrick, his face a mask of barely controlled rage. 'And a half dozen of my men as well. Someone poisoned the drinking water at the jail and killed everyone last night. I've lost five guards and a cook.'

'No one lived?'

'It was a nasty piece of business. Someone salted the food, so they all wanted water. We're not a cruel bunch, so we gave them water. The jailers ate the same as the prisoners, and they're all dead.'

'There's more,' said Amos.

Swallow said, 'A dozen men have turned up dead here and there in the city.'

'Probaby men who went on the raid,' said Amos.

'If we could find Peter Dread and his crew, I'd bet we'd find them at the bottom of the sea. And I think we'd find those six Tsurani assassins down there with them, as well. Someone's covering tracks.'

Nicholas said, 'They're *all* dead?'

Amos nodded. 'It's easy enough to do if you've got religious fanatics willing to die. Poisoning a ship's water is far easier than a jail's. And I'll warrant we'll find another couple of dozen corpses around the town before nightfall. Not that I begrudge that fate to any of the dogs who raided the Far Coast, but I'd like to squeeze one or two for information.'

Patrick said, 'I'll put the word on the street that anyone who went raiding with Render and Dread has a better chance to stay alive if they come forward.'

'Don't think it'll do any good,' said Amos, standing up.

He scratched his head. 'You've got a jail full of dead men to call that promise a lie.'

'Dammit, Amos,' said Patrick, 'I'll make sure no one we don't know gets near anyone who gives himself up.'

Amos shook his head. 'And you claim I've been too long away from the dodgy path, Patrick. What would you do if you'd been on the raid? Same thing I would. You'd head for the hills and live off fruit and seabirds' eggs as long as you could until you thought whatever wants you dead has left the island.'

Swallow's eyes narrowed. 'Whatever?' His voice lowered. 'Don't you mean whoever, Amos?'

Amos said, 'You don't want to know, William.' Looking at Marcus and Harry, he said, 'You know what to do?'

Marcus nodded. 'We've got to find that girl.'

Marcus came awake with a sense he was not alone. Ghuda motioned for silence as he reached for his sword. Then a voice said, 'I told you all you needed to do was ask around and I'd find you.'

Brisa was sitting on the foot of Marcus's bed, and he suddenly felt self-conscious. He quickly reached for his tunic and trousers. 'What do you know of where the captives were taken?'

Brisa studied Marcus as he struggled to dress while he sat in bed. With a cocked smile she said, 'You've a nice body there, my glowering lad. What was your name again?'

'Marcus,' he answered brusquely.

With a grin she said, 'You're cute when you're upset, did you know?'

Marcus sat motionless for an instant, then he finished dressing under the covers. Ignoring her banter, he pushed back the covers and pulled on his boots. 'What did you find out?'

'The price?'

'What do you want?' he asked sourly.

Feigning a pout, Brisa said, 'I thought you liked me.'

His patience at an end, Marcus reached out suddenly
and gripped the girl's thin arm. 'I don't even – '

He found a dagger at his throat. He let go and the girl
said, 'That's better. I don't like being grabbed like that.
If you'd given me half a chance, I'd probably have shown
you how I like to be grabbed, but now that you've spoiled
my mood, it's going to take gold.'

Then Brisa's arm was seized in a vicelike grip and
Ghuda was pulling the point away from Marcus's throat.
'Enough of the games, girl,' said the old mercenary. 'And
don't try pulling that other dagger from your boot. I'll
snap your arm before you can.' He waited a moment,
then released her.

With a scowl, the girl said, 'Very well. A thousand
golden royals and I'll give you what you want.'

Marcus said, 'What makes you think we'd pay that?'

She gave him a black look as she said, 'Because you
will.'

Marcus hesitated, then said, 'Wait here.'

He left, to return a few minutes later with Nicholas and
Amos behind. 'This girl claims to know what happened
when the prisoners were taken from the island. She
demands a thousand golden royals to tell us.'

Amos quickly nodded. 'You'll have it. Now, where are
they?'

'The gold first.'

Amos fumed, but said, 'Very well.' To the others he
said, 'Let's go.'

'Where?' asked Nicholas.

'To the ship.' He nodded and Ghuda again held the girl
in a firm grip.

'Hey!' she complained.

'I don't carry a thousand gold royals on my person, girl.

They're in my cabin. And I won't harm you; you have my word on that. But if you're lying, we'll pitch you over the side and you can swim home.'

Grumbling but not struggling, Brisa came along. Amos quickly roused the others of his crew in the inn and they all made their way to the docks. The majority of the crew were already aboard the *Raptor* and the rest came aboard with Amos.

He moved to where his first mate, Rhodes, waited, and spoke quietly with him for a minute. Then he led the girl and Nicholas to his cabin. Marcus and the others waited on deck.

Reaching the cabin, Amos entered and motioned for the girl to sit, and for Nicholas to stand before the door, blocking it. 'Now, girl,' he said, 'where are the captives?'

Brisa said, 'My gold.'

Amos went to a desk, behind which was a trap in the floor. He opened the trap and pulled a bag out of it. The sound of metal clinking came from the bag. He placed the heavy bag upon the desk and untied a leather thong. Drawing forth a handful of gold and showing them to the girl, he said, 'There is the gold. Now tell us what you know.'

'Give me the gold,' demanded the girl.

'You'll have it when you tell us where the captives are.'

Brisa hesitated, and for a moment Nicholas thought she was going to force an impasse, but at last she said, 'All right. When I told your friend that I had followed some cut-throats to where they held your friends captive, I didn't tell him everything.'

She paused, and Amos said, 'Go on.'

'There was a ship anchored in deep water, far off the island. I've never see its like, and I've seen a lot of ships in Freeport in my day.' She described the ship to Amos. 'More than a score of boats were ferrying people from the island to the ship. I didn't get too close, but I know they were taking everyone off that island.'

'Where did they go?'

'I didn't stay around long enough to see that, but they had only one clear channel out of there, so they had to sail south until they were a couple of days away from here. That ship drew more water than this, so you'll know what I'm talking about.'

Amos nodded. 'If it draws that much, the ship probably sailed a week south to be clear of the reefs between the islands.'

Nicholas said, 'So you didn't see where it went. Why should we pay you the gold?'

'Because two days ago a Keshian trader came in from Taroom. She'd been blown west a week by a squall and had turned northeast to come back to Freeport. A sailor off that ship told me that he was on lookout a couple of days before they reached Freeport and saw the biggest ship he'd ever seen, black like the night, sailing into the sunset.'

'Sunset!' said Amos. 'That's to the southwest this time of year.'

'But Kesh lies to the east,' commented Nicholas.

'And the islands run due west of here,' added Brisa.

'There's nothing out there,' said Nicholas. 'That's the Endless Sea.'

Amos said, 'Your father once showed me some charts . . .'

Nicholas said, 'From Macros the Black! Those charts that show other continents!'

Amos was silent a moment, then nodded. 'Open the door.'

Nicholas obeyed. Standing there was the first mate. Amos said, 'Mr Rhodes, send word ashore I want the crew back as soon as possible. We catch the evening tide.'

'Aye, Captain,' he replied.

The girl came out of her seat. 'My gold!' she demanded.

'You'll get it,' answered Amos, 'when we get back.'

'Get back!' she spat like an angry cat. 'Who said I'd be willing to travel with you to the ends of the world?'

Amos returned a grin as evil as Nicholas had ever seen it. 'I did, girl. And if I find you're sending us after phantoms, your swim home will be a lot longer than across the harbor.'

The girl was up with her dagger out, but Nicholas was ready, and his sword knocked the blade from her hand. 'Behave yourself,' he said with the sword leveled at her for emphasis. 'No one here will hurt you if you don't cause trouble. But these people we seek are important to us, and if you're lying it'll go hard. Better tell the truth now.'

The girl looked like a cornered rat and her eyes darted to every quarter, looking for an escape route. Seeing none, at last she said, 'I'm not lying. The sailor had too many details about the ship right. It's the same one. He was six hours south of Headers Reef, to the west of Three Fingers Island. Do you know it?'

Amos nodded. 'I know it.'

'Take a bearing a hour before sunset, with the sun about five points to the starboard and you'll be on a dead line with the black ship.'

Amos nodded. 'If your information is right, you'll get your gold and more. Now I'll have blankets put by for you in the rope locker. Stay away from my men, and if you cause trouble, I'll lock you in the chain locker, which is far less comfortable. Understood?'

The girl nodded sullenly. With a defiant toss of her chin, she said, 'May I go now?'

Amos stood. 'Yes. And, Nicholas . . .'

'Yes?'

'Stay close to her until we're too far from land for her

to swim home. If she makes a break for the rail, hit her over the head.'

Nicholas smiled ruefully, and said, 'I'll be happy to.'

The girl threw him a dark and angry glare as she left the cabin, a half-step ahead of him.

11

Pursuit

Margaret shuddered.

Abigail asked, 'What is it?'

'That . . . odd sensation, again.' Margaret closed her eyes.

'What else? Tell me,' demanded Abigail. For a month, once or twice a day, Margaret had been visited by a strange feeling. Sometimes she likened it to a chill; other times it was a tingling sensation over her entire body. It wasn't painful or threatening but alien.

'It's closer,' said Margaret.

'What's closer?'

'Whatever's making me feel this way.' Margaret rose and crossed to the large window. They had been given a cabin in the aft of the ship, above the rudder house. It was not large, being one or two below the captain's cabin, but it had the benefit of something larger than the tiny porthole in their first cabin. There was a divan at the foot of the two beds, their heads under the window, a small table between them. Meals were served by silent men who refused to engage in even the most meaningless banter. Twice a day they were taken up on deck, weather permitting, and allowed to take the sun and stretch their legs.

The weather was changing, growing warmer. Margaret found this odd, given they were approaching early winter, but the crew seemed to think nothing of the balmy days. And the days were growing longer. Margaret had pondered these oddities aloud, but Abigail had been totally uninterested.

Margaret climbed up on her bed and pushed open the

small window. She could stick her head out and look down at the large rudder as the water swirled behind. The ability to keep the air in the cabin fresh was welcome after the days spent below in the hold of the smaller ships. She often wondered how the less fortunate prisoners were doing, for despite their having their own small bunks, there was no fresh air and little light in the slaver's decks.

The door opened and a familiar face appeared. Arjuna Svadjian bowed in his strange fashion, both hands pressed together, the steeple of his fingers before his face. 'I trust you are well,' he said, in what the girls now knew was a formal greeting.

Margaret and Abigail had been visited each day by this man, and each day he had engaged them in what seemed pointless conversation. There was nothing menacing about his behavior or appearance; he was of medium height, he wore his beard closely trimmed, and his clothing was of expensive weave but plain cut. He looked the part of a prosperous businessman, and could even have passed for a trader from a distant port of Kesh, had he been traveling in the Kingdom.

At first the conversation was a welcome diversion from the sameness of each minute. The cabin might be more comfortable than the previous accommodation, but it was still a cell. Then the girls went through a period of being difficult, giving him meaningless answers to his questions, or purposely contradicting themselves. He seemed equally indifferent to either tack, merely absorbing whatever they said.

Every once in a while he was accompanied by another man, one they had met the first day called Saji, who said little. He would occasionally pause to write something down on a tablet of parchment he carried, but otherwise he just observed.

'Today I would ask you to tell me more of your uncle, this Prince Arutha,' said Arjuna.

'Why, so you can better prepare to make war on him?'

The man showed neither irritation at the accusation nor amusement, saying, 'To conduct a war across so vast a sea is difficult.' He provided no further comment on her question, but said. 'Do you know Prince Arutha well?'

'Not well,' she answered.

He was not a man to show the girls any emotion, but something about the way he moved forward slightly gave Margaret the feeling he was pleased at that answer.

'You have met him, though?'

'When I was a small child,' answered Margaret.

To Abigail he said, 'What of you? Have you met this Prince Arutha?'

Abigail shook her head. 'My father has never taken me to court.'

Arjuna whispered something to Saji in an alien language, and the small man made a note on his tablet.

The interview wore on. The questions were seemingly unrelated to those asked at previous interviews. After most of the morning was past, the girls were bored, tired, and frustrated, but Arjuna never seemed to tire during these interviews. At midday, a small meal was provided the girls, but he did not eat, merely slowing the interview so that they could consume the simple meal of biscuits, dried meat, dried fruit, and a cup of wine. They had learned early to eat all the food brought them, for Abigail had refused to touch her meal one day. Two of the silent men had entered and one had held her in place while the other had force-fed her. All Arjuna had said was 'You must keep up your strength and be well.'

After the meal, he excused himself, and they heard him enter the cabin next door. Margaret hurried to the bulkhead that separated the cabins and tried to listen, as she did each time he entered that cabin. There was a mysterious passenger whom Arjuna consulted with from time to time, but no one else ever entered the cabin. Margaret had once boldly asked who was in there, but Arjuna had ignored the question and countered with one of his own.

A low murmur of voices could barely be made out, but no words were intelligible. Then suddenly Margaret was again visited by that strange tingling sensation, this time stronger than ever. At the same moment, a voice was raised in alarm in the next cabin, and the sound of feet moving toward its rear came through the bulkhead.

Margaret glanced out the small window to the left, and there she saw a hooded figure half leaning out of the window. The figure extended an arm, pointing behind the ship, and exclaimed, *'She-cha! Ja-nisht souk Svadjian!'*

Margaret pulled back inside the cabin, her face ashen and her eyes wide.

Seeing her expression, Abigail whispered, 'What is it?'

Margaret reached over and took Abigail's hand. Gripping it tightly, she said, 'I saw our neighbor. He . . . it stuck its hand out. It was covered with green scales.'

Abigail's eyes widened and her eyes brimmed with tears. Margaret warned, 'If you begin crying again, I'll slap you so hard you'll really have something to cry about.'

Voice trembling, Abigail said, 'I'm frightened, Margaret.'

'And you think I'm not?' asked the other girl. 'We can't let them know we know.'

Abigail said, 'I'll try.'

'There's something else.'

'What?'

'We're being followed.'

Abigail's eyes widened again and she looked hopeful for the first time since they had been captured. 'How do you know? Who is it?'

Margaret said, 'That thing in the next compartment felt

282

whatever it is I've been feeling lately, and he complained that someone was overtaking us.'

'You heard that?'

'I heard the tone, and it wasn't pleased. And there's something in that sensation I've been feeling that finally makes sense to me.'

'What?'

'I know who's following us.'

'Who?'

'Anthony.'

Abigail said, 'Anthony?' in a disappointed tone.

'He's not alone, I promise you,' said Margaret. 'It must be some magic of his that I'm feeling.' Her expression turned reflective. 'I wonder why I can feel it and you can't.'

Abigail shrugged. 'Who understands magic?'

'Do you think you could squeeze through that window?'

Abigail glanced at it and said, 'I might if I wasn't wearing this gown.'

'Then we'll take our gowns off,' said Margaret.

Abigail said, 'What are you thinking?'

'The second I see a ship behind us, I plan on getting off this one. Are you a good swimmer?'

Abigail shook her head and looked afraid to answer.

'Can you swim at all?' asked Margaret incredulously.

Abigail said, 'I can paddle some if the water's not too difficult.'

Margaret said, 'Lives by the sea her entire life and she can padde some.' Looking hard at her friend, she said, 'You'll paddle, and I'll keep you out of trouble if I must. If a ship's coming after us, we won't be in the water that long.'

'What if they don't see us?'

'Worry about that at the time' was Margaret's answer.

Then Margaret again felt the strange tingle and she said, 'They're coming.'

* * *

283

Anthony pointed, and Amos sighted along his arm and said, 'Two points to port, Mr Rhodes.'

Nicholas, Harry, and Marcus watched the magician for a minute, then Harry said, 'I don't know how he can be certain. Everyone at Crydee said he wasn't a very good magician.'

Nicholas said, 'He may not be a good magician, but Nakor says he just knows where' – he was about to say 'Margaret', but knowing of Harry's infatuation with her, he changed it to – 'the girls are. Nakor's pretty certain Anthony's on the right track. And Pug said to follow Nakor's advice.' Amos had Anthony use his magic three times a day, at sunrise, noon, and sunset, to correct his course.

Nakor was up at the bow of the ship, talking to Calis. Ghuda was off by himself, a short distance away from the little Isalani, lost in his own thoughts.

Harry glanced around the horizon. 'How anybody can know anything about where they are on this endless expanse of water is beyond me,' he said.

Nicholas was forced to agree. Save for some white clouds to the north of them, the sky was empty, as was the ocean. There was nothing to break up the constantly moving surface of the water. For the first three weeks of the journey, they had seen islands here and there, all part of the Sunset Islands chain, and it broke up the monotony of the journey.

Once the excitement of being in relatively close pursuit had worn off, the ship had fallen into a routine. The tension remained, for Marcus paced the deck, when weather permitted, like a caged animal, and when the weather was inclement, he sat brooding. Nicholas and Harry lent a hand wherever possible, trying to relieve the boredom, and were becoming fair deep-water sailors in the process. The constant work and meager food had given Nicholas and Harry a rangy, lean appearance, and the time spent aloft or on deck had turned Nicholas a deep tan. Harry's fair skin had burned badly until Anthony had soothed it with salve, and now he was as brown as if he had lived all his life upon the beach. Nicholas had shaved his beard, while Marcus had let his grow, so while there was still a resemblance, it wasn't as obvious.

The others had fallen into their own routine. Nakor and Anthony spent much of the time discussing magic, or 'tricks', as Nakor insisted on calling it, and Ghuda seemed content to keep his own company, though from time to time he could be seen in deep conversation with Calis.

The progress of the ship matched the deepening of concern in all aboard the vessel, for Amos had ordered rations cut. He had felt they were reasonably provisioned when they had set out, but not knowing if land was only moments beyond the horizon or still weeks off, he felt it better to stretch them out. And with the hunger that came with the rationing came the realization that they were truly sailing into unknown waters.

For the last month they had sailed out of sight of any land, their final contact with the Sunset Islands being a pitiful little series of sandbars and coral outcroppings that could hardly be called islands. Once they had fallen behind, there was nothing but the sea.

Nicholas knew that there was another land across the water. He had accepted it as a fact, because that's what his father had told him. But here he stood on the decks of a ship, sailing into what was commonly called the Endless Sea, to a land where no man of the Kingdom had ever ventured, and no matter how he tried, he could not leave aside the little nagging doubt, a small voice that said, 'Perhaps the sailors are right; perhaps the map is a hoax.'

Only two things kept the sailors calm and going about their business as usual: their training in the Kingdom

Navy and Amos's firm command. They might not believe the magician could tell where the black ship was on the water ahead of them, but they could believe that if any man could sail them across the Endless Sea and back it was Admiral Trask.

Nicholas glanced up at the top of the main mast, where a lookout was stationed, against hope that they might catch sight of the ship they followed. Amos speculated from the girl's description that the ship was a galleon, a design used occasionally in Queg in days past, sometimes with rowing banks, sometimes without. If so, he judged it a far slower ship than his own, and that despite its ten or more days' lead time, he might even overtake it before it reached its far port.

Nicholas hoped so, for as he grew bored and restless aboard the *Raptor*, he found his mind drifting more and more to fanciful reunion with Abigail. The sour memory of killing Render continued to intrude on him from time to time, and no matter how he tried, the feel of the saber in his hand as it drove hard into Render's stomach still clung to him. Even when he practiced with the sword with Marcus, Harry, or Ghuda, dueling across a pitching deck, he anticipated that sudden difference, that oddly soft feeling of a sharp blade cutting flesh as opposed to ringing off an opponent's blade. And thinking of the blood and death made him feel ill.

He had talked about it with Harry and Ghuda, and neither could help him cope with the feeling of somehow being dirty. No matter how much Nicholas tried to justify killing Render, no matter how much he told himself that this had been the man who had killed his aunt, destroyed hundreds of lives, and reduced a thriving town to a burned-out collection of ruins, he couldn't bring himself to feel that he had acted correctly.

Nicholas knew better than to bring up the subject with Marcus, for how could he express regret over killing one of the men who had murdered Marcus's mother and kidnapped his sister?

And Nicholas had spoken with no one about his deepest fear: that if need be, he couldn't bring himself to kill again.

Brisa came up on deck and Nicholas was forced to smile. The girl was like no one he had ever encountered before, and she amused him. In one fashion, she reminded him a little of 'Uncle James', one of the King's advisers in Rillanon, and a former companion of his father. Now he was a Baron of the King's court, and he and his wife and children visited Krondor on a regular basis. There was something wild and daring in him just below the surface, and Nicholas had heard tales that when he was a boy, James had been a thief in Krondor. There was that same wildness in Brisa, though it wasn't hidden very deep below the surface. And it came out with alarming regularity when she was around Marcus.

Nicholas and Harry exchanged glances, and Nicholas found Harry grinning as the girl started straight for them, her eyes fixed on Marcus. For reasons none of them could fathom, she had taken a clear liking to the often dour son of the Duke. At least, she delighted in teasing him at every opportunity, and often Nicholas couldn't be sure if her provocative invitations were teasing. She could become quite scandalous at times. She was at home with the sailors, for while she was female, and several held to the odd superstition regarding women on ships, she could swear with the best of them, climb the rigging like a monkey, and tell the foulest jokes of anyone on the ship. Where Amos had worried that some of the younger sailors might try to take advantage of her presence on the ship, causing conflicts among the crew, his worry had been baseless. The slender girl with the ragged hair and large eyes had managed to turn almost the entire ship's company into surrogate big brothers, any of whom would be happy to thrash any other member of the crew who grew abusive of their Brisa. And they all seemed to take equal delight in watching her make Marcus blush.

Coming to where Marcus stood, a resigned expression on his face, she said, 'Hello, handsome. Want to go below and learn a few things?'

Marcus shook his head, his color rising, as he said, 'No. But I do need to go below. I've not had my midday meal yet.' She took a step after him as he turned, adding, 'Alone!' He left the girl who feigned a pout, and Harry and Nicholas grinned as he went below.

Harry said, 'Why must you tease him so?'

Shrugging, the girl said, 'Oh, it gives me something to do. It's pretty boring around here otherwise. Besides, there's something about him that appeals to me. I think it's his total lack of a sense of humor. It's a challenge.'

Nicholas considered himself fortunate that she had singled out Marcus instead of himself. He found himself sympathizing with his cousin: the street girl from Freeport was a force of nature. He studied her and found himself conceding that she was pretty in a boyish, incomplicated fashion. A few days after the voyage began, he decided her ragged clothing and dirty appearance had been more a product of guile than of carelessness; being a pretty girl in a town like Freeport was dangerous enough, but without a protector, it was an open invitation to rape and bondage. With shapeless clothing several sizes too large, and dirt on every exposed inch of skin, she looked far less inviting and often could pass as a boy.

Putting her hands behind her back, she whistled a nameless tune as she sauntered down to the companion-way. Nicholas laughed.

'What's so funny?' asked Harry, already knowing the answer.

'Just considering how fast we'll find Marcus back up here on deck.'

288

'One of these days she may be surprised.'

Nicholas said, 'I doubt much catches our street girl by surprise.'

'Wonder what she'd look like in some proper clothing,' said Harry.

Nicholas said, 'I was just thinking the same thing myself. She's rather pretty under all that ragged hair and has lovely eyes.'

Harry said, 'Forgetting Abigail already, are we?'

Nicholas's mood instantly turned dark. 'No,' he said coldly.

'Sorry. I was making a joke.'

'It was a bad one,' said Nicholas.

Harry sighed. 'I'm sorry.' Then his mood lightened. 'I was thinking how she'd look in one of those gowns Margaret and Abigail wore to that last reception, the ones that had all that lace down the front.'

Nicholas couldn't help but grin. 'You mean the low-cut ones that my mother thinks are so scandalous.'

Harry grinned in return. 'Well, Brisa has that long, slender neck, and her arms are really graceful.'

'Looks like I'm not the only one who's forgetting whom we're looking for,' chided Nicholas.

Harry sighed. 'Guess you're right. Perhaps it's the boredom. But except for Brisa, I haven't paid attention to a girl, pretty or otherwise, since the last night we spoke with Margaret and Abigail. There may have been a few around since then, but I was a little too busy to notice.'

Nicholas nodded.

'One thing,' said Harry.

'What?'

'I wonder why she picked Marcus and not me?'

Nicholas glanced at his friend and saw that the question was only half-joking.

The lookout cried, 'Captain! I see men in the water!'

Amos shouted back, 'Where away?'

289

'Three points off the starboard bow!'

Amos hurried to the bow, and by the time he had gotten there, Nicholas, Harry, and half the crew were behind him. In the water, small figures could be seen floating. Amos nearly spat. 'Slavers,' he said with murderous fury, barely controlled. 'Those that die are thrown to the sharks.'

'One of them is alive!' shouted the lookout.

Amos turned and shouted, 'I want a boat lowered. Make ready to pick up the survivor! Put her into the wind, Mr Rhodes!'

The ship was turned to slow her movement while a boat was lowered. The men started rowing toward the floating bodies and the one survivor, when the lookout shouted, 'Sharks!'

Amos looked to where he pointed and saw a fin cutting the water. 'Brown tip; he's a man-eater.'

'There's another,' said Harry, pointing a little farther off.

Nicholas asked, 'Can your men get to the survivor first?'

'No,' said Amos. 'If the sharks grab one of the dead men first, maybe there's a chance. Sharks are funny that way. They can swim around you for hours or come straight in and take you the minute you hit the water. There's no telling.' He shook his head.

Calis said, 'Maybe I can distract them.' He unlimbered his bow and drew out a long shaft, fitting it to the bowstring. He drew back and sighted on the shark closest to the ship, then let fly. The steel-tipped arrow sped through the air and struck the shark just below the fin, causing a noticeable fountain of blood.

Instantly three of the other sharks veered away from the floating corpses and sole survivor and made a straight course for the thrashing shark.

Amos said, 'Lucky shot. Shark hide's tough. That's like

punching an arrowhead through armor.'

Without boasting, Calis unstrung his bow. 'Luck had nothing to do with it.'

The men in the longboat got the survivor into the boat and began rowing back to the ship. Amos called, 'Ready a sling!'

By the time the boat reached the side of the *Raptor*, a sling and two ropes were ready. A couple of the crew climbed halfway down to aid the injured man as he was hauled up on deck.

By the time he was aboard, Anthony had reached him. He examined the man's color, rolled back an eyelid, and put his ear on the man's chest. Nodding once, the healer said, 'Get him below.'

Amos motioned for two men to pick up the man and take him to the crew's quarters, and turned toward the helm. 'Get her back on course, Mr Rhodes!'

'Aye, Captain,' came the answer.

Amos scratched his beard. 'If one of them is still alive . . .'

Nicholas said, 'Then we're not too far behind!'

Amos nodded. 'Two days at most.' He calculated quickly, then said, 'Unless I miss my guess, we'll catch sight of them by sundown tomorrow.' There was a gleeful look in his eye, and Nicholas didn't need to ask what was on his mind. When Amos overtook the men behind the sack of Crydee, there'd be murder to pay.

Nicholas, Marcus and the others waited on deck as the sun sank in the west. Amos had gone below with Nakor and Anthony, to see to the man they had fished from the sea. They had been down for most of the day and still no word was forthcoming.

At last Amos appeared on deck and motioned for Nicholas and his cousin. They left the others, who were gathered on the foredeck, and joined Amos on the main deck. 'He's still alive, but barely,' said the Admiral.

'Who is he?' asked Marcus.

'He says his name is Hawkins and he was apprentice to a wheelwright in Carse.'

'Then he *was* from the black ship!'' said Nicholas.

Amos nodded. 'He also said that he had been in the water two days before we'd found him. They throw those who are dead and those too ill to recover overboard at sunrise, along with the garbage. He clung to a bit of a broken crate that was tossed, which is how he survived. He has a hacking cough, and Anthony figures that's why he was tossed overboard. It's a miracle he's still alive.'

Nicholas said, 'What about the girls?'

'Rumors. They were taken away from the other prisoners the first night the ship put out, so he knows they were on board then, but he hasn't seen them since. He says that someone claims a sailor mentioned they're kept in better quarters because of their rank, but he doesn't know.'

Marcus said, 'Will we overtake them before they reach their home port, Admiral?'

Amos nodded. 'Unless we're closer to land than I think, we will.' As the sun sank beneath the horizon, he said, 'The color of the water's different here, it's deep.' Glancing upward, he added, 'But I have no idea where we really are; the stars are in places I've never seen before. Some old familiar ones have fallen below the northern horizon over the last month, and there are ones new to me visible in the southern sky. I judge we've still got a way to go before we reach our friend's port, if I remember that map.'

'That makes it a long journey,' observed Marcus.

'Nearly four months from Krondor to the northern shore of that landmass on the map, I'm guessing. We've been more than two months from Freeport, and I think we're still two weeks from landfall,' said Amos. He shook his head. 'Assuming Anthony is right about their course.' Glancing at the deck as if he could see the sick man from Carse through the planks, he said, 'And our near-dead friend down there shows that Anthony knows at least that much magic.'

'Will we have trouble getting back?' asked Nicholas.

Amos shook his head. 'I can retrace our course, allowing for the winds. Every night I record my best guess as to heading and speed, and I've been doing this long enough that my best guess is fairly reliable. The stars may have changed, but I've marked the new ones, and where the more familiar ones rise each night. It may take a bit of work, but we'll hit somewhere between Keshian Elarial and Crydee when we get back.'

He returned to the quarterdeck and left the cousins alone with their thoughts.

Anthony came on deck, looking drawn and exhausted. Nakor came out behind him. Nicholas asked, 'How is he?'

'Not good,' said Anthony. With bitterness he said, 'The slavers knew their trade. Even if he recovers, he's never going to be a hearty man, certainly not someone who can be sold on the slave block.'

Nicholas said, 'When will we know if he's going to make it?'

Anthony exchanged glances with Nakor, then said, 'If he lives through the night, he stands a fair chance.'

Nakor shrugged. 'It's up to him, I think.'

Nicholas said, 'I don't understand.'

Nakor grinned. 'I know. When you do, your foot won't hurt any more.'

The short man took Anthony by the elbow and led him away to the other side of the ship where they could be alone. Nicholas glanced at Harry, who shrugged and said,

'Let's practice.' Pulling out his saber, he said, 'If we're going to overtake that ship soon, I want to be as sharp as this blade.'

Nicholas nodded and they marked off a portion of the main deck and began exchanging blows.

Nakor looked at the young men at practice a moment, then said, 'You did well, magician.'

Anthony ran his hand over his face, clearly fatigued by his efforts. 'Thank you. But I'm not sure what you were doing in there.'

Nakor shrugged. 'Some tricks. Sometimes it is not the body that needs healing. If you practice, you can see other things inside the person. I was talking to his spirit.'

Anthony frowned. 'Now you sound like a priest talking.'

Nakor shook his head vigorously. 'No, they mean soul.' The little man looked at a loss for words for a moment, then said, 'Close your eyes.'

Anthony did so.

'Now, where is the sun?'

Anthony pointed over toward the bow of the ship.

'Ah,' said Nakor in a tone of disgust. 'I mean, where do you feel it?'

'On my face.'

'This is hopeless,' Nakor said, his disgust even more apparent. 'Magicians. They mess your minds up at Stardock, fill your brain with nonsense.'

Anthony was usually amused by the strange man, but now he was too tired. 'What nonsense?'

Nakor screwed up his face as if in concentration and said, 'If you're a blind man, can you tell where the sun is?'

'I don't know,' answered Anthony.

The ship shuddered as Amos ordered a slight course change because of a wind shift, and Nakor said, 'A blind man can feel the warmth of the sun on his face and "look" at it.'

Anthony said, 'All right. I'll accept that.'

'Very generous of you,' snapped Nakor. 'Close your eyes again.' Anthony did so. 'Can you feel the sun?'

Anthony turned to face the bow of the ship and said, 'Yes. There's more warmth there.'

'Good, now we're getting somewhere.' With a grin, Nakor asked. 'How can you feel the sun?'

Anthony said, 'Well . . .' He looked surprised. 'I don't know. You just can.'

'But it's up there.' Nakor pointed to where the sun hung in the late afternoon sky.

'It gives heat,' responded Anthony.,

'Ah,' said Nakor with a grin. 'Can you feel the air?'

Anthony said, 'No . . . I mean, I can feel the wind.'

'You can't see the air, but you can feel it?'

'Sometimes.'

Nakor grinned. 'If there are things you know are there that you can't see, then might there not also be things you don't know are there that you can't see?'

Anthony looked befuddled. 'I suppose.'

Nakor leaned against the rail, and adjusted the rucksack he always had with him. Opening the bag, he took out an orange. 'Want one?'

Anthony found he did, and asked, 'How do you do that?'

'What?'

'Always have oranges in there. We've been at sea nearly four months since leaving Crydee and you've never bought any that I'm aware of.'

Nakor grinned. 'It's a – '

'I know, a trick, but how do you do it?'

Nakor said, 'You'd call it magic.'

Anthony shook his head. 'But you don't.'

'There is no magic,' Nakor insisted. 'Look, it's as I said: there are things you can't see but are there.' He made an arch in the air with his hand. 'You do this, you feel the air.' Then he rubbed his thumb and forefinger together. 'But you do this, you can't feel it.'

Looking out over the ocean, he said, 'The universe is made up of very strange stuff, Anthony. I don't know what this stuff is, but it's like heat from the sun and wind. Sometimes you can feel it, and even move it.'

Anthony was now intrigued. 'Go on.'

Nakor said, 'When I was a boy, I could do tricks. I knew how to do things that amused the people in my village. I was to have been a farmer like my father and brothers, but one summer a traveling magician came through our village, selling curatives and spells. He wasn't a very good magician, but I was fascinated by the tricks he could do. The night he came, I left my father's house and went to him and showed him some of my tricks, and he asked if I wished to be his apprentice. So I followed him, and never again saw my family.

'For years I stayed with him, until I discovered that my tricks were better than his and I could do more, so I set off to find my own fate.' Sticking his thumb into the orange, he pulled away a section of peel. He bit into the orange and paused as he chewed. Then he said, 'Years later, I had discarded all pretense of magic, for I learned I could do things without the chanting and the powders in the fire, without the marks in the dirt, or the other trappings. I just did them.'

'How?'

'I don't know.' He grinned. 'See, I think Pug is a very smart man, not because he's so powerful, but because he knows how much he doesn't know yet. He understands that he's passed beyond his training.' Nakor fixed one squinting eye on Anthony. 'I think you also could move past your training should you but come to understand one thing.'

'What?'

'There is no magic. There is only this stuff that makes up the universe, and magic is what less enlightened people call it when they manipulate this stuff.'

'You keep calling it 'stuff'. Do you have a name for this magical element?'

'No.' Nakor laughed. 'I have always thought of it as stuff, and it's not magical.' He held his thumb and forefinger as close together without touching as he could, while he took another bite out of the orange in his other hand. Talking around the mouthful of fruit, he said, 'I imagine this tiny space. Now imagine it half again as small. Then halve it again, and then again. Can you imagine it that small?'

'I don't think so,' admitted Anthony.

'It's a wise man who knows his limits,' said Nakor, his grin widening. 'But even so, imagine this space, and imagine you are in it, and imagine that it's huge, the size of the biggest room, and make your fingers so.' He held out his hand again. 'Then begin once more, and do it all again. In that last space, it would be so very small, there is where you would find stuff.'

'That is small,' admitted Anthony.

'If one could but look, that is where you would see it.'

'How did you discover this stuff?'

'As a small boy I just could do things, my tricks. I was a mischievous child, and I would spill a bucket of water, or put a sleeping cat on the roof of a hut. My father, who was an important man in our village, sent to the city of Shing Lai for a priest of the order of Dav-lu, whom you in the Kingdom call Banath, for he is known in the province where I grew up as the Prankster, and my father was certain we were being troubled by an impish spirit or demon. I set a hot brand to the priest's backside and was found out. The priest told my father to beat me, which he did, and then I was admonished to behave, which I did most of the time.'

Taking another bite of orange, he said, 'Anyway, all my life I have found that I could do things, what I call tricks, because I knew how to manipulate this stuff.'

Anthony shook his head. 'Can you teach others?'

'It is what I was trying to tell people at Stardock when I was there: anyone can learn.'

Anthony shook his head. 'I think I would fail should you try to teach me.'

'I'm already teaching you.' Nakor laughed. 'It is that stuff that I was talking to in the sick man below. There is energy in everything, this stuff I can manipulate.' Opening his sack, he said, 'Reach in and get another orange.'

Anthony reached into the bag and said, 'There's nothing there!'

Nakor said, 'It's a trick. Close your eyes.' Anthony complied. 'Can you feel a seam at the bottom, at the side away from me?'

'No.'

'Try harder. It is very faint, very difficult to feel. Try concentrating on the tip of your longest finger, just hooking the nail under the fabric. Can you feel it there?'

Anthony concentrated, then said, 'I think I feel something.'

'Gently pull back that fabric, moving it toward me.'

Anthony said, 'I think I'm losing it . . . I have it.'

'Once you've moved that fabric out of the way, reach below and you'll feel an orange.'

Anthony reached and felt the fruit. He pulled it out and opened his eyes. 'So it is a trick.'

Nakor took the rucksack off his shoulder and handed it to Anthony. 'Look inside.'

Anthony thoroughly examined the heavy felted wool

bag, and at last said, 'I can't see the false bottom.' Wadding up the fabric, he said, 'And I can't feel any false compartment.'

'There is none,' said Nakor with a laugh. 'You moved aside a layer of stuff and found a small passage through to another place.'

'Where?'

'A warehouse in Ashunta where I once labored awhile. It belongs to a fruit merchant, and when you reach through, your hand is right above a big container the merchant keeps filled with oranges.'

Anthony laughed. 'That's how you do it. It's a rift!'

Nakor shrugged. 'I think. I don't know. It doesn't act like a rift, from what little I know of them. It's more like a crack in the stuff.'

'But why a fruit merchant? Why not a treasury?'

'Because that's what I was thinking of when I first tried the trick and I haven't been able to move it since.'

'You lack discipline,' observed Anthony.

'Perhaps, but your spellcasting is nothing more than getting your mind oriented so you can manipulate stuff. You just didn't know *that's* what you were doing. I think Pug found out. He's not bound by your Greater Path and Lesser Path and this path and that path nonsense. He knows that you just reach out and take a hold on the stuff and move it around.'

Anthony laughed again. 'Doesn't the merchant miss those oranges?'

'It's a very big bin, and I only take a few each day. And the merchant only has workers in there once or twice a week. My one difficulty is when I hide things on top of his bin, so that the bag appears empty if searched. Once I put some gold coins in the bin. There was a very happy worker at that fruit warehouse the next day, I think.'

Anthony was about to speak when a shout came down from the lookout upon the main mast: 'Ship ahoy!'

Amos called up from the quarterdeck, 'Where away?'

'Dead ahead, Captain.'

Amos hurried to the bow, where he found the others already peering ahead. 'There!' said Calis, pointing.

Nicholas squinted against the setting sun, and there upon the horizon was a tiny speck of black. 'Is that them?' he asked.

Amos said, 'Unless friend Anthony is deluding us with his magic, it is.'

'When will we overtake them?' asked Harry.

Amos rubbed his chin. 'Hard to guess. Let's see how much distance we make up tonight, and I'll have a better guess.' Turning to the stern, he called out, 'I'll have an extra watch aloft and another in the bow tonight, Mr Rhodes. Keep a weather eye out for lights.'

'Aye, Captain,' came the answer.

'Now we wait,' said Amos to those nearby.

12

Disaster

The lookout pointed.

'Ship ahoy!'

'Where away?' demanded Amos.

'Dead ahead, Captain!'

Amos stood in the bow with the others as the sun rose grudgingly behind them. A heavy mist obscured the western horizon, but a few minutes after the lookout identified the black ship, Calis said, 'I see it.'

Amos spoke low. 'You've got younger eyes than I, elf.'

Calis said nothing, but he ventured a slight smile at being called an elf. Then he pointed. 'There!'

In the blue-grey morning a single dot could be seen, a black speck that was recognized as a ship and sails only by those who had spent years on the sea. 'Damn,' swore Amos. 'We're not gaining that much.'

'How long?' asked Marcus.

Amos turned away, moving toward the ladder to the main deck. 'At this rate, we'll need a week to overhaul her.' He glanced above. 'Three points starboard, Mr Rhodes!' he shouted, as much out of frustration as a need to be heard. 'Trim the sails! I want her as tight into the wind as you can get her on that line!'

'Aye, Captain,' came the response, and without being told, sailors leaped up and climbed the ratlines into the rigging to trim the sails aloft, while those on deck hauled on sheets to move large booms and yards.

Nicholas overtook Amos on the main deck. 'I thought we were faster, Amos.'

'We are,' he answered, climbing the ladder to the

quarterdeck. 'But we're a different kind of ship. She's going to run fastest almost full to the wind. We're faster off that line, running a tighter reach, but on the same line as she is, well, we're faster, but not by much.'

'What about taking off on a broad reach, then coming about and cutting her off?'

Amos smiled. 'This isn't a boat race in the harbor, Nicky. There's a lot of ocean out there, and by the time we'd come back to where we expect her to be, her captain could have changed course and be miles away. No, it's stern chase all the way.'

'And a stern chase is a long chase,' Nicholas said, repeating an old seaman's axiom.

Amos laughed. 'Where did you hear that?'

Nicholas grinned. 'You only say it every time you tell that story about helping Mother and Father escape Krondor, when Jocko Radburn tried to overhaul you.'

Amos returned the grin. 'Damn me! You paid attention to those stories.' Throwing an arm around Nicholas and giving him a playful punch to the stomach with his free hand, Amos said, 'You're now my favorite grandchild-to-be.' Pushing him away, he said, 'Now get off my quarterdeck and don't come up here again without asking permission, *Your Highness*.'

'Aye, Captain,' said Nicholas with a laugh. He left the quarterdeck, glad for the momentary respite from the tension.

He returned to the bow and found everyone still there, eyes fixed on the black speck before them. Calis and Marcus were both as still as statues, while Harry hummed a nameless tune. Brisa kept one hand on Marcus's shoulder, and he didn't seem to notice. Ghuda had his sword out and was polishing it with a cloth he always carried. Nakor and Anthony simply watched.

Nicholas studied Anthony's face. The magician's

expression was focused, as if he was trying to see something in the distance.

Margaret shivered. Abigail stood up from her seat on the divan and crossed to sit next to her friend on one of the beds. She said, 'Are they . . .'

Margaret nodded. 'Anthony,' she whispered. Her eyes grew shining with tears.

Abigail reached out and took her hand. 'What is it?'

Fighting back tears, Margaret said, 'I don't know, but it's a feeling . . .' She shook her head and smiled. 'I can't describe it. It's just the way Anthony reached out to me, that's all.'

Abigail's expression showed she didn't understand. She rose and went over to the window, peering out across the ocean. 'They're back there somewhere.'

Margaret came and stood next to her. 'Yes.' Then her eyes narrowed. 'There!' she said, trying to rein in her excitement. 'That small black speck!'

Abigail looked for a long time before she whispered, 'I see it. It's them!'

The girls stood watching, silently willing the pursuing ship to move faster. For an hour they stood there, trying to see more detail, a sail or a banner, until they heard the approach of footsteps outside. Margaret closed the window, and they were sitting when the door opened and Arjuna entered, Saji following. 'Good day, ladies,' Arjuna said coolly.

He sat upon the divan, while Saji remained standing. Arjuna said, 'Now, Lady Margaret, what do you know of the city of Sethanon?'

For three days they kept vigil on the ship ahead. Each morning Nicholas and the others would hurry to the bow to see how much distance they had made up. Now they could clearly see the outline of sails and hull. It was a huge ship and moved through the ocean like a stately queen, but for those on the *Raptor*, there was nothing lovely in it.

Near midmorning, the lookout called, 'She's changing course, Captain!'

Amos asked, 'On what quarter?'

'She's moving to port!'

Amos said, 'Bring her a bit to port, Mr Rhodes.'

Nicholas shouted from the bow, 'What's she doing?'

Amos shook his head, indicating he didn't know. Then he called to the lookout, 'Keep a sharp eye out for reefs!' Turning to his first mate, he said, 'Extra lookouts aloft and in the bow, Mr Rhodes.'

Within minutes, sailors were stationed in the bow and on the yards, peering down at the water, looking for changes in color that would indicate reefs. Amos said, 'See if we can get back on her line, Mr Rhodes. If she's moving through shoals, I want her to show us the way.'

'Water's changing color, Captain!' shouted a man in the bow.

Amos hurried to the bow and hung out far enough for Nicholas to feel compelled to hold his belt. 'It's getting shallow,' said Amos as he pulled himself back on deck, 'but it's not that shallow.'

The others had gathered nearby and he said, 'I think we're about to come into sight of land. Islands, or perhaps that continent on the map.' He called to the lookout, 'Keep your eyes on the stern of that ship. If she trims sails or changes course, sing out!'

'Aye, Captain.'

Amos motioned for Nicholas and his companions to gather around him. 'Ghuda here has the most experience as a soldier, so I advise you all to stay close to him.' Looking at Nicholas, Marcus, and Harry, he said, 'Don't get excited and try to win this thing by yourself. That's one hell of a big ship, and she could be carrying as many as a hundred armed men besides her normal crew.' Looking over his shoulder at the crew busy on deck, he added, 'My lads are as tough as they are good, so they'll take care of themselves.' He glanced at the distant ship. 'This sort of thing can change unexpectedly. If they are forced to a different reach before the wind, we might suddenly be on top of them, so the fight could start at any moment. Good luck.'

He turned and left; Nicholas faced Ghuda. The old mercenary said, 'I've served marine duty before.' He stared over Harry's shoulder at the distant ship as he said, 'She's a large bitch, riding higher in the water than we are. That's bad. We can either swing down out of the rigging or climb ropes on grappling hooks. Swinging's faster. But those that swing over are going to have to hold the rail so the others can climb up without getting their heads split. Stay close and watch each other's backs, because there's no line of battle. The man behind you might be one of them.' To Nakor and Anthony he said, 'Probably best if you two stay here for a while, then come after to tend the wounded.'

Nakor said, 'I have a trick or two that might help.'

'No doubt,' said Anthony dryly, but he nodded agreement to Ghuda's suggestion.

Ghuda now addressed Calis and Marcus. 'You two can help the most by getting into the rigging and using your bows. Pick your targets, because if that ship is carrying guards, they'll surely have crossbowmen in the rigging.'

Calis said, 'Our longbows can reach much farther than any cross-bow.'

Marcus nodded. 'If they have crossbowmen, they'll all be dead before we've closed.'

Ghuda said to them all, 'I know it will be difficult, but try to rest as much as you can now. When the battle starts, you're going to have to be as sharp as you can be, and a tired soldier is one who makes mistakes.' So saying, he hunkered down next to the bulkhead, wrapped his coat around himself, and proceeded to doze off.

Harry and Nicholas moved away from the mercenary and Harry said, 'How can he do that?'

Marcus nodded with approval. 'He's done this before, so there's little mystery or surprise in store for him.'

'Maybe,' answered Harry, 'but I don't think I could ever just drop off to sleep like that.'

Nicholas said, 'I saw you do it at Crydee.'

Harry was forced to nod agreement. Mentioning the exhausted state they had endured – seemingly without end – while working to help those left alive after the raid put them all in a somber mood. Even Brisa, standing quietly off to one side, was without a joke or comment.

Nicholas looked at the distant ship and wondered what they would find once they got aboard. He put away unpleasant thoughts and returned to his cabin, to attempt some rest.

Margaret opened the window. She caught movement out of the corner of her eye and pulled back before the occupant of the next cabin could see her. She held up a finger, warning Abigail to silence, and listened.

The voice she heard was Arjuna's and it spoke the same language the lizard creature spoke, alternating guttural and hissing sounds. It was answered by the creature, who obviously wasn't pleased by the tone of his voice, if Margaret could judge something that alien.

Abigail came and looked out the window. The pursuing ship could be clearly seen now, and even with her small knowledge of such things, she could see it was a Kingdom ship. Whispering, she said, 'When shall we try to escape?'

Margaret shook her head and reached out to close the window. Whispering in return, she said, 'I think they may be close enough early in the morning. We'll try then if they keep coming at the same rate. That'll put them less than a mile behind us and we can swim to meet them easily.'

Abigail didn't look convinced, but she nodded.

The door opened and Arjuna entered. 'Ladies,' he said, bowing in his strange fashion, now familiar to them both. 'No doubt you have noticed we are being pursued by a ship. While it may not fly the King's banner, we think it from your homeland. Were we certain it was your King's navy behind us, we would throw a prisoner over the side as a warning.' He seemed to regret the lack of certainty. 'But as it may be a pirate from Freeport, we must resort to other measures. I wish to assure you that while rescue seems a possibility, it is not. But against your attempting some foolishness, I'm afraid we must take measures.' He motioned and two crewmen entered the cabin. Pushing past the girls, they removed hammers from their belts and drove large nails into the window frame.

'Once we are free of those who follow, we will allow you to open the window again.' The sailors left the cabin and Arjuna closed the door, leaving the girls alone.

Abigail said, 'What do we do?'

Margaret inspected the nails and attempted to pull one free with her fingers. She tried to get a hold on the large nailheads, but couldn't. In exasperation she swore, and then, glancing around the room, she moved to inspect the small table. It was heavy, so it wouldn't slide around in rough seas, but it was attached to the deck by nothing more than pegs through holes in the base of the legs. Margaret knelt on her bed and motioned for Abigail to pick up the other side and, experimentally, the girls lifted. With reluctance the table rose, and Margaret said, 'Put it down.'

Once the table was back in place, Margaret said, 'I think we throw the table into the window.'

'Will it work?'

307

Margaret inspected the window. 'If we take off these gowns first, then smash the window with the table, we should break out enough of the glass and wood to crawl through . . . We may get some cuts and bruises, but we should be able to manage it before they can get in to stop us.'

Abigail didn't look convinced, but she nodded.

'Now we wait until morning.'

Margaret sat and brooded, trying to ignore the memory of the fin cutting the water behind the ship.

Calis stood on the port forechannel, hand gripping a line to the bowsprit, staring ahead. The sun was still below the horizon behind, and before him the night was giving way to murk. His eyes were keenest of all and he had been in the bow when Nicholas rose, seeking signs of the black ship.

Nicholas said, 'Are they still ahead?'

'They're still there,' answered the elfling. 'They doused all lights at midnight, and changed course to shake us, but Anthony has been giving the captain corrections each hour.'

Nicholas peered ahead but could see nothing. Minutes dragged past and Nicholas turned to find Marcus beside him. Harry stood off to one side next to Brisa, who hugged herself against the morning chill. Abruptly she leaned against Harry, who put his arm around her, an expression of surprise and pleasure on his face.

The weather had been growing progressively hotter as they passed southward. Amos had judged that they had passed below the equator and were now sailing into late spring. He had heard of the backward seasons in the distant states of the Keshian Confederacy, but had never been that far south before.

As the sun brightened the eastern sky, Calis pointed. 'There!'

Nicholas peered and then he could see the ship, black against dark grey, now clearly seen for what she was, a huge thing with high aftercastle, and a rear lateen spanker sail. The ship had all sails out, and heeled over against the wind.

Amos came to the bow and observed a minute. 'She's a wallowing bucket, isn't she?'

Marcus said, 'How soon?'

Amos judged the distance and speed and said, 'We'll be on her before noon.'

'Land ho!' cried the lookout aloft.

'Where away?' asked Amos.

'Dead ahead.'

As they all stared ahead, the dark gloom behind the ship began to resolve itself. The morning mists burned off as the sun brightened the day, and visibility increased by the minute. As if a veil was lifted, the air cleared, and those on the bow of the ship could see what the lookout had discerned a minute earlier. Amos swore. 'Gods! Look at that.'

A gigantic escarpment rose above a rocky beach. Easily a hundred feet high at the lowest point, possibly three times that at its highest, it reared before them like a distant wall. It shone pink and orange in the sunlight of dawn, yellow at the crest.

Amos turned and shouted, 'Lookouts aloft! We're shoaling!' Instantly a half-dozen sailors scrambled aloft and began looking for signs of sandbars and other shallow-water hazards.

Amos said, 'Look!' and pointed to rocks to the right of the ship, only a hundred feet off. The faint sound of breakers carried over the water. 'Damn. We could have run up on a sandbar a dozen times last night. Ruthia must love us.'

Nicholas said, 'Are they trying to wreck us?'

'Maybe,' answered Amos. 'But they draw far more

water than we do, so there must be a safe channel here.' He closed his eyes and said, 'I'm trying to remember that damn map your father showed me. If my old mind hasn't failed me, we're looking at the continent of Novindus, and that's the northeast coastline.' Moving his hands as he spoke, he said, 'Somewhere to the south of us, a week's sailing or so, I think, there's a peninsula, then once around it, it's northward to some city.'

Nicholas had vague recollections of that map as well, but remembered fewer details than Amos.

'She's turning, Captain,' said Calis.

Anthony had been silent since sighting the ship, but now he said, 'And there's something – '

A crack of energy exploded above them. A lookout screamed and fell from the yards, to land in the water beside the ship. To Nicholas there was a feeling of being a conduit for lightning, having a nameless power run from his head and down his body into his feet and through them to the ship. Brisa's high pitched scream could be heard above the shouts of terror from the men, and when Nicholas looked around he saw Ghuda with his sword drawn and even the taciturn Calis looking for a nameless enemy.

Then the feeling of energy changed, and Nicholas felt his skin and hair tingle. He saw blue lightning, with a crackling discharge, dancing across the yards and saw his companions' hair standing on end, spread about like fans around their heads.

Then silence.

Amos blinked and said, 'What . . .'

The ship began to rock slowly from side to side. 'Damn me!' said Amos, hurrying to the side of the ship. Glancing over the rail, he said, 'We're becalmed.'

'But how can we be?' demanded Nicholas. 'Look!'

Amos looked at the black ship, which was moving

slowly away, sails full and heeling to port as she proceeded at top speed. 'I don't understand.'

'Magic,' said Anthony.

'A trick,' grumbled Nakor. 'They sucked the wind out of the air around us. Very nasty trick.'

Amos felt as if his eyes betrayed him. Around his ship for fifty yards in all directions the water was quiet, while beyond that the fresh breeze whipped whitecaps on the water. Amos struck the rail in frustration. 'We were almost upon them.' Taking a breath, he called, 'I'll have a longboat lowered, Mr Rhodes! Make ready a towline.'

'You're going to tow us out of this magic?' asked Marcus.

'I've been becalmed before' was all Amos said. 'Sometimes it's all you can do.'

Nicholas turned and looked at the others. Ghuda said, 'Better get some rest.'

But Nicholas stayed where he was, watching the fleeing black ship as it grew slowly smaller and smaller.

'They've stopped,' said Margaret.

'What?' asked Abigail.

'They're falling behind.'

Abigail looked through the small panes of glass and said, 'Oh, gods, no!' Her eyes began to brim with tears, but she forced back her urge to cry. 'What will we do?'

'We go now!' said Margaret as she hurried to unfasten her gown. Pulling at the laces up the front, she was about to let it fall from her shoulders when the door opened and Arjuna stepped into the cabin.

'Ladies, I advise keeping your clothes on. Seeing you naked would distract my men.'

He signed and two large, black-clad sailors entered. Arjuna said, 'They will watch you awhile, until even one as rash as you, Lady Margaret, wouldn't risk swimming through such a distance of shark-infested water. Then they will remove the nails and you can once again have fresh air in this cabin.'

He smiled, turned, and left. Abigail sat down and looked at her friend. Margaret gave her a nod and smile, for she knew the girl was forcing herself to bear up and not give in to the urge to break down in tears. Slowly Margaret relaced the bodice of her gown, staring out the window at the rapidly diminishing ship.

Brisa let out a groan of aggravation. 'Who called it *becalmed!*' Glancing at her companions, she said, 'The noise is making me crazy!'

Nicholas shared a sympathetic glance with Harry. They understood how the girl felt. Within minutes of the magic that stole their wind, they all became aware of the thousand sounds they'd never noticed before. In a brisk wind, the sound of the bow cutting the water, the hum of ropes, and the noise of men going about their business were the only noticeable sounds.

Now the ropes hung loosely from the spars and canvas limply from the yards. The ship rocked lazily with the rise and fall of ground swells. The hull groaned as planks and timbers shifted and flexed. A hundred blocks and pulleys swung on loose ropes, cracking into masts or each other, setting up a clatter that was constant. Planks creaked, hinges squealed, and always there was the distant sound of the surf upon the shore.

The rowers had pulled the ship nearly five miles, with no relief. Nakor had decided the spell was moving with the ship and was at a loss as to how to counter it. 'It's a very good trick,' was all he would say on the matter.

For the rest of the day they had watched in frustration as the black ship sailed off. Amos had ordered the crews in the longboat relieved, and the ship was now drifting on the current as those in the boat rowed back to the ship to turn it over to their replacements. He swore and paced the quarterdeck, then left to join Nicholas and the others on the bow. 'Is there anything you can do?' he asked Nakor.

The little man shrugged and said, 'Maybe, if I think about it long enough. Maybe not. It's hard to say.'

Anthony said, 'There's a spell I've studied, but never used: a weather control incantation. But it may not work.

Amos fixed him with a baleful eye. 'And what else?'

'It's dangerous.'

Nakor said, 'Doing tricks you don't know how to do is always dangerous.'

Amos scratched his beard. 'What's your guess about this spell we're trapped in?'

Anthony said, 'It's the same sort of magic – '

'Trick,' interrupted Nakor.

' – that I'm proposing to try. If we do nothing, it will linger for at least another day, perhaps longer. If the magician who cast it is especially gifted or learned, it could last as long as a week.'

Amos swore, then said, 'What other choice do we have?'

Nicholas said, 'If we can get to that ship before they dock or not long after, we stand some hope of finding the prisoners. But if they reach port more than a few days ahead of us, it might be impossible to find them.'

Amos didn't look pleased, but he nodded agreement. He said to Anthony, 'Do you need anything special?'

Anthony said, 'Just all the luck you can muster.'

Amos shouted, 'I want all hands on deck, Mr Rhodes.'

When the crew was mustered, Amos addressed them from the foredeck. 'Men, we're going to try to break this spell that becalms us. We have no notion of the consequences, so I want every man at his station ready to jump to any task needing to be done.' He said nothing more, and Mr Rhodes gave the order for the men to rig for foul weather.

Some of the sailors paused a moment to say a silent prayer to this or that deity, but all of them were standing by when Amos nodded to Anthony.

Anthony said, 'Nakor, if you can give me any help, now is the time.'

Nakor shrugged and said, 'I don't know this trick, so I wouldn't know if you were doing it right or not. Better just do it and trust the gods are not too angry with us today.'

Anthony closed his eyes and said, 'In my mind I see the matrix, and in the matrix is held the power. The lock to the matrix is my will, and in the matrix my will becomes the power.' He repeated the chant and his voice grew softer, until Nicholas and the others could no longer hear him. His lips continued to move and he swayed rhythmically.

A faint gust touched Nicholas upon the cheek and he glanced at the others. Marcus and Brisa both looked at the mast above them. Nicholas also looked up and saw canvas beginning to stir.

With what sounded like a sigh of relief, the wind freshened, and the ship began to turn as the wind filled her sails.

'Trim your sails, Mr Rhodes, and set a course after the black ship!'

The lookout reported that he could still make out the faint form of the large ship on the horizon to the south, and gave a position. Amos bellowed, 'All lookouts aloft! Keep a sharp eye for reefs!'

Anthony continued to chant and Nicholas glanced at Nakor. The little man shrugged. 'I said I don't know this trick.'

The wind picked up in strength, and Amos shouted,

'Keep a watch for weather, Mr Rhodes!'

Nicholas glanced behind them and shouted, 'Look!'

To the northeast, a large roiling mass of dark clouds was forming in an otherwise blue sky. As if someone poured them from a bowl, the clouds spilled down and spread out behind the ship, forming a line of dark fury in the air.

A drop of wetness struck Nicholas's cheek and he saw rain begin to fall from the clouds, blown toward them by the rising wind. Amos ordered the sails trimmed for a storm and men scrambled about in the rigging, reefing the larger sails, trimming others.

Men hurried below and returned and began rigging storm lines across the deck, while others handed out oiled-canvas coats. Moment by moment, the sky darkened as the black clouds spread from above, and through the entire process, Anthony stood motionless, his eyes closed, his lips moving.

Nicholas shouted over the rising wind, 'Nakor! Should we stop him?'

'How?' said the little man. 'I don't know what he's doing.'

Ghuda said, 'Sometimes the direct approach is best.' He gripped Anthony by the shoulder and shouted his name. The magician failed to respond. Ghuda shook harder and still was unable to get through to the blond mage, who now stood drenched to the skin. 'If the storm's not distracting him, my shouting won't.'

'Do something else!' demanded Brisa, who now looked thoroughly terrified. The wind was doubling in fury and large waves were picking up the *Raptor* as easily as a child moves a toy, and the lurch of the deck as it seemed to fall out from under her feet was more than she could endure. 'Do anything!'

Sailors aloft hurried frantically to reef sails, for they were carrying too much canvas for a wind that blew stronger with each second. Spars and yards groaned in protest at the strain as winds began to howl through the rigging.

Nicholas joined Ghuda and shook Anthony, calling his name. A cry from the stern caused them all to turn, and Amos's voice cut the fury of the wind like a knife. 'Banath, preserve us!'

A wave larger than any before was building off to the northeast. 'Hard aport, Mr Rhodes. Put her into the wind!' To those nearby he shouted, 'Grab something and hold fast! If that wave hits us broadside, we're going to lose a mast or worse.'

Nicholas gripped the rail nearby and watched in terrified fascination as the water rose up higher and higher as it bore down upon them. Like a black wall, the water advanced while the crew fought to turn the ship bow-first to face it.

When the ship was not quite turned, the water struck. The ship seemed to try to climb the water, its bow lifting high into the air as it heeled far over to starboard. Brisa screamed as she hung desperately to a rope that had come free of a davit. Marcus reached out and grabbed her around the waist, pulling her to him as he clung to a deck line.

The ship kept trying to climb the water, and Nicholas watched in amazement as it seemed the world tilted. He nearly lay on his back, or so it felt, as the ship climbed still higher up the wave, then suddenly everything pitched forward.

Men screamed as they were thrown from the rigging, while others cursed as they clung to anything nearby for their lives. Now Nicholas saw the ship heading downward into the trough, at as steep an angle as they had climbed, and knew that magic was changing the laws of the sea: this wave was nearly as steep behind the crest as before. Then he saw water swamp the bow of the ship.

Down into the water the ship plunged, and Nicholas knew in that moment they were doomed. He closed his eyes as water washed over him, hitting him like a solid wall, threatening to tear his arms out of his shoulders as he clung to the rail, and then he felt himself get suddenly heavy as the deck lifted up under him.

He lost his footing and fell, but still he clung to the rail as he thrashed about underwater, then abruptly he was again in the open air. Water streamed away in all directions as the bow of the ship burst upward out of the brine.

Gasping for air, Nicholas blinked salt water out of his eyes and looked around. Everyone was still in sight, clinging to some part of the ship. Ghuda stood like a rock against the tide, clutching Anthony around the waist with one arm, and clinging to a line with the other hand. The ship continued to roll to starboard, then when it almost seemed about to lie over on its side, it rocked back to port, and they all clung desperately to stay aboard. Then it righted itself and for a moment seemed to be on an even keel.

'Look!' shouted a nearby sailor.

Nicholas turned to see another wave, larger than the last, bearing down on them. As the bow began to lift again, he shouted to Ghuda, 'Do something!'

Ghuda nodded and let go of Anthony. Before the magician could move a foot away, the big mercenary struck him hard across the jaw with his clenched fist. Anthony slumped unconscious to the deck.

Instantly the sky was again clear, but to Nicholas's horror the wall of water bore down upon them still as the *Raptor's* bow rose to meet it. 'Hang on' was all he could shout as the ship once more began its impossible climb.

Shouts and screams filled the air as men were thrown once more from their stations, and loud crashes echoed through the now still air as gear lashed to the deck broke loose and smashed against the mast or quarterdeck.

Higher and higher the ship climbed, and this time Nicholas felt even more terrified, for he could see clearly, with no rain blinding him. Only spray from the advancing mountain of water filled the air as the ship struggled to keep afloat. Nicholas was vaguely aware of Brisa screaming and Harry cursing, and he realized he had lost sight of Calis during the last wave.

Then, as it seemed the ship would tumble over on its back like an overturned turtle, they crested the wave. Down the other side they raced, and Nicholas's voice joined others in voicing incoherent terror. The absence of magic had robbed the sea of its fey driving force, and instead of another rising wave behind, the sea was at its normal level. Against any reasonable expectation, the water was collapsing back to its former calm state, rather than carrying through its fearful onslaught, so rather than their having survived the worst of the giant wave, its dissipation was adding impetus to the ship's downward plunge. Nicholas could see the sandbars and reefs through the ocean below, as if staring through green glass. He knew with certainty they would not survive this plunge, for there was not enough water ahead to cushion the ship's bow.

The floor of the ocean rushed upward and Nicholas felt the water strike him like a blow from the hand of a giant. He felt the ship drop away beneath his feet as the water claimed him, then felt the grinding crash of wood against rock. The ship cried out as it died, a screaming tearing of wood and iron, joined by the terrified cries of its crew.

Then Nicholas was pulled under the white foam. Holding his breath as well as he could, he felt himself being dragged deep into the water. Blind from the water in his face, Nicholas was dragged downward by a force he had never experienced. He was cast into a world of sounds and vibrations, tossed around so violently that direction was confused. He kicked as hard as he could against the

318

undertow as the mass of the ship created a vacuum around it, sucking down everything nearby.

Then suddenly he felt his feet strike wood, as if he had landed hard on the floor of his room. Hot pain stabbed through his left foot, and he gasped. Suddenly his mouth and nose filled with water. Nicholas felt his lungs burn as seawater choked him. He flailed about, water churning around him, hurling him to his knees upon the deck and forcing itself deeper into his lungs. In a shocking moment of clarity, he knew he was going to die. A detached sense of peace settled over Nicholas, and he could feel the pounding blood in his own temples and chest as a distant thing, and the burning in his lungs a faint echo of the pain he had endured a moment earlier.

Then suddenly he was moving upward at amazing speed, as if a giant hand had lifted him. The ship had bounced off the sea floor and rose back up on the air trapped inside its hull. It shot upward, clearing the less than fifty feet of water between the floor of the ocean and the surface.

The ship broke through the surface, and Nicholas was tossed into the air. He gasped, spitting salt water from his lungs, his arms flailing as if he were trying to fly. Then the ship dipped back into the waves and he struck the surface of the water. As the ship righted itself beneath him, Nicholas half crawled, half swam to the rail, where he clung for his life. Like a wounded animal, the *Raptor* heeled over to port, water filling its hold and throwing it out of trim.

Nicholas spat and coughed, and gasped a painfully deep breath, then coughed again, retching out the last of the water. He blew salt water out of his nose, wiped his face with one hand, and looked around. All three masts had been shattered, the foremast snapped above the main yard, and the others below. The deck was littered with debris, bodies, and seaweed. It took almost a minute for the confusion to sort itself out.

Marcus and Calis both clung to what was left of a line from the forechannel, and Brisa gripped Marcus around the waist with both arms. Ghuda still held Anthony tightly with one arm while the other was wrapped around a capstan. Blood ran down his face from a messy-looking scalp wound. Nakor was enmeshed in what remained of one of the foremast ratlines, and he was shouting for someone to cut him loose.

Then Nicholas realized who was missing. 'Harry!' he shouted. Suddenly his stomach constricted and he vomited seawater.

The ship groaned and rolled and Amos pulled himself out from under a broken spar. Heaving himself to his feet, he glanced around at the damage. He came to give Nicholas a hand up and said, 'What a mess.' Turning to the stern of the ship, he shouted, 'Mr Rhodes!'

No answer came. Amos set about examining his ship and quickly came back to Nicholas. 'Gather everyone on the main deck, and salvage whatever you can. Get as many water casks and skins into the longboats as possible, and whatever food you can find. We're sinking.'

'Is there anything we can do?' asked Nicholas.

Amos shook his head and turned away. Nicholas went to where Calis was cutting Nakor loose from the tangle of ropes that confined him and said, 'Everyone to the main deck. We're abandoning ship.'

Word quickly passed and Marcus and Nicholas hurried to their cabins, where water could already be seen coming up through the planks of the deck. They grabbed whatever they could from the jumble and hurried up above. Calis had retrieved his bow and arrows, both protected by oilskin, but Marcus's bow was lost. Knowing that they were about to be cast adrift on a hostile shore, Nicholas forced his way past a tangle of debris and bodies and entered Amos's cabin. He opened the small trap and removed the pouch of gold Amos had shown him when Brisa had been brought aboard. He began to hurry out, then remembered something and sloshed through the rising water to Amos's desk. He pulled it open and found a red-leather-covered logbook, which he picked up. Putting the gold in his tunic and the log under his arm, he entered the companionway and saw water swirling. The ship was going down fast.

Hurrying up the ladder to the main deck, Nicholas felt another stab of pain in his foot and almost dropped the log. He made it to the deck in time to see a few surviving sailors leaping off the railing into the water. Amos stood on the deck and motioned him over.

Reaching Amos, Nicholas gave him the logbook. 'I've got the gold from your cabin, too. We're probably going to need it.'

'Bless you, boy, for keeping your wits about you.' He hugged the book to his chest. 'With this, we can get home someday.'

Nicholas climbed over the rail and found a longboat waiting only five feet below. Glancing upward, he said, 'Amos?'

'I'm coming, Nicky.' He took one last look around the deck. 'I'm coming.'

They climbed down into the longboat, and Ghuda and a sailor pulled hard to put as much distance as possible between the longboat and the dying ship.

When they were less than a quarter mile away, the *Raptor* formerly the *Royal Eagle*, pride of the Krondorian fleet, rolled over into the water.

Bitterly Amos said, 'Damn, I hate losing ships.'

Nicholas didn't know why, but he found the remark terribly funny, and try as he might, he couldn't keep himself from laughing. He tried to hold it in, but in a few moments he was nearly convulsed in mirth. Amos bristled, but Brisa and Ghuda both joined in, and even

Marcus couldn't help himself. Nakor never seemed to need an excuse to laugh, so he made no attempt to hide his mirth. After another minute, only the unconscious figure of Anthony and a bristling Amos Trask were not laughing.

'What's so damned funny?' demanded Amos.

Ghuda said, 'How many ships have you lost?' His face was covered in sticky blood, but otherwise he looked all right.

Amos said, 'Three,' then suddenly his face split into a grin and he found himself infected as those in the longboat nearly collapsed at the answer.

From outside the boat a hoarse voice said, 'If you're not enjoying youself too much up there, can someone give me a hand?'

Nicholas glanced over the gunwales of the boat and saw a familiar figure clinging to a broken spar in the water. 'Harry!' he shouted, and leaned over to help his friend into the already crowded boat.

'I'd thought you drowned,' said Nicholas.

With a wince from a bruise somewhere on his person, Harry said, 'I see it caused you a great deal of grief.'

Nicholas's expression turned somber. 'We were just a little giddy after escaping,' he said.

Harry nodded. 'I got tossed overboard. I saw the bow bounce off the bottom and thought you had all been killed.'

Amos said, 'I'm surprised more of us aren't. Look.' He pointed and they turned to see another pair of longboats drawing toward them. When they were within shouting distance, Amos shouted, 'Is Mr Rhodes with you?'

A sailor answered, 'I saw a spar take his head off, Captain. No doubt but he's dead.'

'How many are you?'

'Twenty-seven in this boat and nineteen in the next, sir.'

'Provisions?'

'None, sir in this boat.'

From the second longboat, a sailor called out, 'We have a barrel of pork and another of dried apples, Captain.'

Glancing around, Amos said, 'Well, we need to make for shore. It'll be dark in a few hours, and I don't wish to drift along aimlessly.' Signaling for the boats to take up positions, he said, 'Follow us in.'

Ghuda and a sailor began to row, and Amos said, 'Calis, keep an eye out for rocks ahead. Look to the breakers and see if there's water spilling in two directions, for there'll be rocks beneath the surface if you do.'

They rowed toward the massive cliffs and Nicholas said, 'I wonder what's up there?'

Calis said, 'Perhaps woods or brushland, or plains. Somewhere I can hunt.'

'Or maybe there's a town up there,' ventured Harry, still looking like a drowned rat.

Brisa said, 'Someplace I could get a clean shirt.'

'And something to eat,' ventured Nakor, with a halfhearted grin.

They picked their way among some rocks to reach a place where the water rushed through, and followed this small current into the roll of combers. Cresting a wave, they let it push them along toward the beach.

Suddenly Calis shouted, 'Rocks! Turn to the right!' As Ghuda, sitting on the left, began to frantically back water with his oar, a ripping sound rang out and the boat stopped as if they had hit a wall. Calis and Marcus were pitched over the bow and Brisa screamed.

A spire of rock no more than an inch high protruded from the bow of the longboat, but water was rushing in around it. 'We're holed,' yelled Amos. 'Grab what you can and get out and swim!'

He turned and shouted to the other boats. 'We've struck rocks! Keep clear!'

The sailor in the bow of the second boat waved in reply to show he understood and they steered to the left of Amos's boat, giving it a wide berth.

Nicholas grabbed a pair of waterskins and went over the side. He swam easily to where he could stand, then waded ashore. Everyone else made it in good order as the other boats attempted to land.

The second boat slid sideways along an underwater shelf of rock, and sailors cursed as they were also forced to abandon their boat. The third boat was warned off in time and made it to the beach without taking damage.

Amos gave orders for some of his sailors to swim out and see if they could pull the second boat off the rock shelf. 'The waves will break it up on the rocks if we can't.'

More than a dozen men, all exhausted, waded into the surf and swam to the second boat. They pushed and pulled, trying to move the massive longboat off the shelf, but could not.

Finally Amos signaled for them to return. When they were back on the beach, the sailor who had spoken to Amos from the bow of that boat said, 'She's taken water, Captain, and she's sitting as firm on that shelf as a vulture on a dead dog.'

'Damn.' Amos turned and inspected their present location. The shadows from the massive cliffs rearing above them had already extended into the water, and he could feel a chill. 'See if you can find the makings of a good-sized fire,' he said to Nicholas, Marcus, Calis, and Brisa in general. 'It's going to be cold soon and we've not one blanket among us.' He quickly summed up: forty-nine soldiers and sailors, and Nicholas and his companions, fifty-eight survivors in all – out of a company of more than two hundred. He made a quick prayer to Killian, the goddess of sailors, asking for her mercy on the lost men.

With a sigh of resignation, he said to his crew, 'Fan out and see if anything useful's being washed ashore.' Glancing around, he said, 'We've still got a couple of hours' light, so let's see where we are.'

The men obeyed and most fanned out along the beach, some moving to the northwest, others to the southeast along the rocks. A few too injured to move simply sank to the sand, silent in their wet misery.

Amos watched them leave and said to Nakor and Ghuda, who still held the unconscious Anthony, 'Wake him if you can, but help look around. I have a feeling we're going to need every advantage we can wring out if we're going to survive.'

Ghuda put the unconscious magician down and shook him, but he didn't move. After a moment Ghuda rose and left him, joining the others who were looking for anything that might wash ashore. Nakor turned to Amos and said, 'Sorry about your ship.'

Amos nodded. 'As am I.'

Nakor reached into his rucksack and jerked his hand out as if he had been stung. 'Oh, that's bad,' he said.

'What is?' asked Amos.

'There's a merchant in Ashunta who is going to be very upset when he discovers his fruit has been ruined by seawater.' Shaking his head sadly, the bandy-legged man moved away from the captain, and began to search among the rocks.

Alone, Amos turned to where his ship lay on her side in the water, sinking slowly behind the breakers. Feeling a sadness beyond any he could express, he kept his eyes upon her as she slid below the waves.

13

Ascent

The fire smoldered.

Brisa hugged herself in a vain attempt to stay warm beside the dying embers. Others huddled around two other little fires or walked up and down the beach trying to stay warm. The previous day they had explored up and down the coast. At every turn in the shoreline they found nothing but beach and rock, and a seemingly endless wall of stone to their backs. What little wood they had found was now gone, and while the days were searing hot, the nights were bitter. Enough wreckage had washed ashore so a rude lean-to had been fashioned from sails and broken spars, but the wood that had drifted ashore from the ship was too wet to do more than smolder on the fire. The salt pork had been ruined, but the dried apples were edible. There was a fair supply of water and enough salvage to permit a few of the sailors to fish off the rocks. Some fish were trapped in tide pools, but without a pot to cook them in, they were poor fare. Seabirds were absent in any numbers, and the few that flew overhead did not appear to be nesting anywhere close.

Anthony had regained consciousness the next morning, without much memory after his attempt to cancel the spell that had trapped them. He was shocked and shaken to discover the ship gone, and had seemed to come out of his own panic only when it was obvious his skills as a healer were needed.

The second morning was dawning and Amos came to Nicholas. 'We're dying,' he said flatly. 'If there's a less hospitable stretch of coast in the world, I've not seen it.'

'What do you want to do?' asked Nicholas.

'One longboat isn't going to carry fifty-eight of us. We have two choices. Either we select a crew to attempt to row south, past this escarpment, to whatever passes for civilization around here, coming back with help for the rest of us, or we all try to climb the cliff face. Or we do both.'

Nicholas said, 'No. We stay together.'

Amos seemed on the verge of arguing, but then shook his head. 'You're right. One thing is certain: we can't stay. We'll starve.'

Nicholas said, 'We'd better start looking for a way up.'

Amos nodded. 'I'm the oldest man here, and I don't relish the climb, but it's the cliffs or nothing.'

Nicholas sighed. 'I've never done much climbing. My foot . . .' He turned to Calis and Marcus. 'Would either of you know a path up these cliffs if you saw one?'

Marcus frowned, but Calis nodded and stood up. 'Which way?'

'You go that way,' said Nicholas, pointing to the northward. Turning to Marcus, he said, 'And you go the other way. Travel no more than half a day. When the sun is overhead, return here.'

They nodded and set off, moving purposely but not fast enough to deplete energy they couldn't restore. Hunger was on everyone's mind, and Nicholas knew that without fresh food soon, they would all begin dying. At least a dozen sailors were hurt or ill from the effects of the shipwreck, either from water in their lungs or from internal injuries. Nakor and Anthony worked hard to make them comfortable, but there was little they could do without Anthony's bag of curatives. Nicholas sympathized with them; he felt aches and bruises worse than any he'd had before and knew that the least abused among them felt as battered as he did. He was surprised there weren't more serious injuries, but he grimly admitted that anyone who was badly hurt during the shipwreck hadn't survived.

While Calis and Marcus were gone, they took inventory of what little they had scavenged from the wreckage washing up on the beach. They had only a few weapons among them: Nicholas and Ghuda each had their swords, Calis had his bow, and they possessed a collection of daggers and knives. There was one sack of hard biscuits that had survived in a small barrel that washed ashore, to supplement the dried apples. There were ropes strewn up and down the beach, so Nicholas set the men to gathering them up, and separating the lines that they could use to climb the cliffs from rope too far gone to be reliable.

Nicholas was distressed to discover that the inventory took less than an hour for the entire company. Trying to ignore his own hunger, he sat down before the now dead fire and waited.

Brisa came and sat next to him, and looked at Nakor and Harry, both of whom were trying to conserve their depleted energy by sleeping .

She turned to Nicholas. 'Can I ask you something?'

He nodded. 'What?'

Marcus . . .' She began, then fell silent.

'What about him?'

'You know him well –' she started again.

Nicholas cut her off. 'I hardly know him at all.'

'I thought you were brothers,' she said.

Nicholas said, 'I thought you knew.'

'Knew what?' she asked.

'Who Marcus is.'

'He's some Duke's son, or so Harry told me. I didn't know if I should believe him.'

Nicholas nodded. 'He's not my brother,' he said. 'He's my cousin.'

'But you said you hardly know him,' she said.

'I don't. I met him for the first time a few weeks before I met you. I don't live on the Far Coast.'

'Where do you live?'

'In Krondor,' he answered.

She nodded. 'I was hoping you could tell me about him.'

Nicholas felt sorry for the girl, since he realized that her teasing preoccupation with Marcus now masked a deeper emotion. 'I don't know what to tell you. Most of us are from Krondor. Maybe one of the soldiers . . .'

She shrugged. 'It's all right. We're probably not going to get out of here, anyway.'

Nicholas said, 'Don't say that.' His tone was sharp and commanding.

She looked at him with eyes wide and Harry sat up, half-asleep, and said, 'What?'

He realized he had spoken loudly. 'I mean, don't say it, even if you think it. Despair is a plague. If we give up here, we're going to die. There's no choice but to move ahead.'

Brisa lay back, beside the snoring Nakor, and said, 'I know.'

Nicholas glanced up and down the beach, realizing it was too soon for either Marcus or Calis to return. All they could do was wait.

Near sundown, Calis came into view, and a few minutes later, Marcus approached from the other direction. Calis said, 'There's nothing that looks remotely like a trail or even a difficult climb.'

Marcus said, 'Nothing to the south, either.'

Nicholas said, 'Then we either climb here or more farther to the south.'

'Why south?' demanded an exhausted Marcus. 'I just said there was nothing there.'

'Because south is where we are heading anyway. If

329

we're going to face an arbitrary choice, we may as well move toward our eventual goal.'

Amos nodded. 'If we're going to do something, that's as sound a plan as any I can suggest. Let's get some sleep and start at first light.'

Nicholas said, 'Good. Eat what we can't carry so we'll have as much strength as possible.'

Nakor and Anthony approached in the failing light, carrying some wood. 'We left these up on the rocks to dry,' said the little man.

Anthony said, 'If you can get a flame started, they should burn.'

Calis gathered together the remnants of the previous night's fire, small pieces of wood that hadn't completely burned, and hacked away at the char, creating a small pile of splinters and kindling. He took his belt knife and a flint he kept there and struck sparks. Soon he had a small flame, which he carefully fed with larger pieces of wood until he had a substantial fire going. Then the wood carried by Anthony and Nakor was carefully placed atop the flames, and soon a good-size blaze held the cold night at bay.

The sailors gathered around and Anthony took a brand and started a second fire a short distance off, so that more could feel the warmth. He and Nakor moved the sicker men closer to the heat, and they settled in for the long night.

Nakor sat beside Nicholas. No one was in the mood to talk; most either tried to rest or ate what they could of hard biscuits, dried apples, and half-cooked fish. Without preamble, Nakor said, 'Water is a problem.'

Nicholas said, 'Why?'

Nakor said, 'We've not seen any source of fresh water nearby. We have the skins we salvaged from the ship, but not enough of them, and we can't haul casks very far.'

Amos said, 'Certainly we can't haul them up the cliffs.'

Nicholas sighed. 'What do you suggest?'

Nakor shrugged. 'Have everyone drink as much as they can before we start off. That will help. If we find a place to climb close to where Marcus stopped, we can send some men back to refill the skins. If we're a long way down the coast, we make do with what we have.'

'What about food?' asked Nicholas.

'There won't be much by tomorrow,' answered Anthony as he sat down near the fire, weariness etched on his features. 'A man died a few minutes ago.'

Amos swore. Calling a pair of sailors to him, he said, 'Get some canvas. We can't sew him into a shroud, but you can wrap him in sail and tie rope around it. Then tomorrow we'll carry him out to the rocks and bury him at sea, or as close as we can get.'

The two men nodded and left to do as they were bid. Amos sounded old as he said, 'There will be others.'

No one spoke after that.

For the next day and a half they trudged down the coast. Nicholas called for a halt regularly, for the lack of food, scant water, and heat were taking their toll. Late in the second day, Marcus said, 'This is where I stopped my search before.'

Nicholas felt a sense of despair. It had taken almost two days to get those sick and injured down the beach as far as Marcus had traveled in a half day by himself. Nicholas forced aside his dark mood and said, 'You and Calis scout ahead.' Silently he added a prayer that they quickly find a way up.

Marcus and the half-elf both turned and jogged away from the resting sailors. Amos motioned for Nicholas to walk ahead with him, and when they were out of earshot of the others he said, 'We're going to have to start up the cliff tomorrow, no matter what.'

Nicholas said, 'We're going to start dying soon.'

Amos said, 'We're dying already. In two or three days, even if we find a clean ascent, half the men won't have the strength to make the climb.' He flexed his hand as if it was stiff, and he said, 'I might be one of them.' Glancing around, he said, 'My hand is throbbing. There's a weather front heading this way.'

'Storm?'

Amos nodded. 'Usually. Sometimes just a break in the weather.'

Glancing at the darkening eastern sky, Nicholas said, 'It's going to be dark in a couple of hours. Let's call it a day and rest. We'll need it.'

Amos nodded and they returned to the others. Amos ordered the meager stores passed out among the men while Nicholas went to where Harry was sitting, massaging his aching feet, with Brisa beside him. The girl had her knees drawn up under her chin and was hugging her legs, as if cold already.

'How are you doing?' Nicholas asked.

Harry said, 'My feet hurt and I'm hungry.' Then he grinned. 'Makes me something unique around here, doesn't it?'

Nicholas couldn't help but smile. Harry was the last person who would lose his good spirits, he knew. 'I want you to bring up the rear tomorrow,' said Nicholas. 'We're going to have to attempt the cliffs and I need someone at the rear who can make sure no one falters or loses heart.'

Harry nodded. 'I'll do what I can.'

Turning to the girl, Nicholas asked, 'How are you?'

Sourly she said, 'My feet hurt and I'm hungry.'

Nicholas laughed. 'You two are a pair.' He rose and moved over to talk to some of the other men.

Brisa watched him depart, staring after him a long minute, then said, 'He really tries, doesn't he?'

Harry said, 'I guess. It's in the blood, I think. Born to service and obligations of the nobility and that.'

332

'You?' she said, half-mocking.

'I'm not a prince. I'm a second son of a minor noble, which means I have fewer prosects than your average ale merchant, unless I can hook my fortune to one of the mighty.'

Brisa said, 'Him?' – indicating Nicholas with a thrust of her chin. Her tone was disbelieving.

'Don't scoff,' said Harry. 'Nicky's a lot more than you'd think. He's going to be a very important and powerful man someday. Brother to the King, you know.'

'Right,' said Brisa, her tone clearly disbelieving.

'I'm not joking,' said Harry. 'He's Prince Arutha's youngest son. Truly. And Marcus is the son of the Duke of Crydee.'

'Scruffy-looking bunch for nobles, if you ask me.'

'Well, believe what you want. But he will be an important man someday.'

Brisa snorted. 'Assuming we live that long.'

Harry had nothing to say to that.

Brisa leaned in to Harry. 'Don't get any ideas. I'm just trying to stay warm.'

Feigning hurt, Harry said, 'Oh, I'm a substitute for Marcus, is that it?'

Brisa sighed. 'No, I just feel the need and you're safe.'

'Now I really am hurt,' said Harry. 'Safe?'

Brisa kissed him chastely upon the cheek. 'You have charms, Squire, in a clumsy, boyish way. Don't take it too hard. You'll grow out of it.'

She snuggled down into the crook of his arm, and he enjoyed the feeling. But he still felt stung. 'Clumsy?'

Calis and Marcus did not return that night.

At sunrise, Nicholas had them up and moving. An hour later, Marcus came into view, waving his hand above his head. Nicholas hurried to meet him and said, 'What did you find?'

'Calis marks a spot about a half-mile from here. We think it's a way up.'

Dropping his voice so that those approaching behind couldn't overhear, Nicholas said, 'We must try today. Many of the men aren't going to make it as is. We can't wait any longer.'

Marcus looked at the ragged band of seamen and nodded once.

It took them some time to reach Calis, as the sick and injured could not easily make it across the sand. Nicholas hurried across the deep sand to where the elfling waited. Calis indicated a ledge about ten feet above them. He made a stirrup with his hands, and Nicholas stepped in. With a boost, Nicholas climbed up on the rise to discover a large outcropping of rock, with a small cave leading off into the cliffs. Marcus boosted Calis up, and then Calis dropped his hand for Marcus to leap and grab. When all three were on the ledge, Nicholas said, 'The cave?'

'No,' said Marcus. It's shallow and goes nowhere. It'll provide protection for those who stay behind.'

Nicholas said, 'No one stays behind. Anyone we leave will die.'

Marcus's voice grew harsh, but it was with frustration, not anger, as he said, 'Nicholas, some of the men can barely walk with help. They're not going to be able to climb that!' He pointed upward and Nicholas's eyes followed.

Near the entrance to the cave, two faces of stone met in a V. Along one face a narrow path rose, following along until it switched back. From where Nicholas stood he couldn't see what became of the ledge after that. 'Have you been up there?'

Calis said, 'I have. It moves halfway up the face of the cliffs, then stops, but about six feet above the end of the ledge a stone chimney rises. From what I could see, it can be climbed to the top of the cliffs.'

'How?' asked Nicholas.

'It's the hardest part. But if two or three of us can work our way up there, bare-handed, we have enough rope to lower down a line from the cliffs to the top of the ledge and pull up those who need help.'

Then Marcus said, 'But the seriously injured and ill won't be able to make it – whoever's coming up that chute will need to work hard. We can't dead-haul ten or fifteen men more than three hundred feet up. Those makeshift ropes won't take it.'

Nicholas felt a sense of helplessness flowing over him, and angrily shoved it aside. 'We'll do what we can. The first thing is to get everyone up here.'

The stones on which they stood were growing hot with the midday sun, so the Prince instructed everyone who could to shelter in the cave. He took Amos aside and said, 'As soon as the sun is off the cliff face, I'm going up with Calis and Marcus.'

'Why you?' Amos demanded.

'Because unless I'm completely off, we're the three most fit here.'

'But you've never tried anything remotely like this before?' said Amos.

'Look, sooner or later everyone's going to have to try, or rot on this beach. If I'm going to fall and get splattered on the rocks, I'd just as soon do it discharging my duty as having someone try to haul me up on a rope.'

Amos swore. 'You're getting more like your father every day. Very well, but once that rope's secured, I want Ghuda up there.'

'Why?'

'Because we certainly don't need his sword down here, but who knows what's up there!' he said impatiently.

'Very well. But you're coming after him.'

'After my men,' insisted Amos.

Nicholas put his hand on Amos's shoulder. 'Some of

them aren't coming. You know that.'

Amos turned away, looking over the ocean. 'I'm their captain. I must be last to come up.'

Nicholas was about to argue, but something warned him off. 'Very well, but you are coming.'

Amos nodded and went away. Nicholas returned to the cave mouth and sat, waiting for the sun to move off the rocks.

Nakor came to sit beside Nicholas. The Prince was watching the shadow that had crept about an inch or so from the face of the rocks. 'You go soon?' asked the little man.

Nicholas nodded. 'A few more minutes, to get the sun off all the rocks. They're still pretty hot to the touch.'

'How do you feel?'

Nicholas shrugged. 'Hungry, tired, and not a little worried.'

'Worried?'

Nicholas stood and motioned for Nakor to move outside with him. Making a show of looking at the angle of the sun, he lowered his voice and said, 'There are a half-dozen men who can't make it up those cliffs, Nakor, maybe more.'

Nakor sighed. 'Everyone dies. We know that. Yet the death of one close to us is always troubling, even if it's someone whom we've said no more than a few words to in a few minutes.'

Nicholas turned his back to the cave, looking down at the beach and the ocean beyond. An afternoon breeze had risen and blew his shoulder-length hair behind him. 'I've seen a lot of death recently. I don't know if I can get used to it.'

Nakor grinned. 'That's good. One can be philosophical in the ease of a comfortable room, with a glass of fine wine in the hand, a log upon the fire, but in the heat of the moment, when lives are at risk, one doesn't think. One acts.'

Nicholas nodded. 'I think I understand.'

Nakor put his hand upon Nicholas's arm. 'Do you know why some men will die today?'

'No,' Nicholas answered bitterly. 'I wish I did.'

'It is because some spirits love life while others grow fatigued.'

'I don't understand.'

Nakor moved his hand in an all-encompassing circle. 'Life is stuff.'

'Stuff?'

'The stuff everything is made out of.' He looked out at the ocean. 'You see all that, water, clouds, you feel the wind. But there's stuff you can't see too. Stuff that fools like Anthony insist is magic. All of that, from your boots to the stars in the heavens, it's all made of the same thing.'

'This "stuff", as you call it?'

Nakor grinned. 'If I could imagine a more elegant name, I would call it something else. But whatever this basic stuff is, it is something you can't see; it's like glue – it holds everything together. And one of the ways it manifests itself is what we call life.' He looked Nicholas in the eyes. 'You have gone through much in a short time and you are not the boy who left Krondor so recently.

'But you are not yet the man you will be. So understand this: sometimes death comes unexpectedly, and those it takes to Lims-Kragma's halls go unwillingly. That is fate. But when the spirit has a choice, as these men here have, then you must accept that choice.'

'I'm still not clear about your meaning,' said Nicholas. His expression showed he was trying to understand.

Motioning with his head back toward the cave mouth, Nakor said, 'Some of these men's spirits are ready to die. It is their time to move on. Do you see?'

Nicholas said, 'I think so. That's why a man with injuries more severe will make it while another will die?'

'Yes. You must not feel responsible for this thing. It is a choice each man makes, though he may not know he does. It is beyond the realm of princes and priests. It's between a man's spirit and fate.'

Nicholas said, 'I think I understand. When the ship went under the water the second time, I was choking on seawater. I couldn't breathe and was being pulled farther and farther down, and I thought it was my time to die.'

'How did you feel?'

'Terribly afraid, but then at the last, before I was cast upward into the air, I felt a strange calmness.'

Nakor nodded. 'It is a lesson. But it wasn't your time. For some of these men, it is time. You must accept that.'

'But I don't have to like it.' ——

Nakor grinned. 'That is why you may be a good ruler someday. But for the moment, you need to climb that cliff, don't you?'

Nicholas smiled, and it was an expression of relief and fatigue. 'Yes. I must lead now, or I never will.'

Nakor said, 'Have you thought of the amulet?'

Nicholas nodded. 'Pug said to give it to Anthony, and he's to use it only against the greatest need.' He stared into the cave, as if he could see Anthony back at the rear, tending the injured and wounded. 'I trust he'll know what is the greatest need. For now, I think anything we may survive without aid doesn't meet that description.'

'You must go.'

Nicholas looked upward and saw that the sun was now fully hidden from the face of the cliffs. He nodded and crossed to the cave mouth. 'Marcus, Calis. It's time.'

Calis nimbly jumped up and gathered a long coil of rope, and tied it firmly into a large loop. Then he slipped one arm and his head through the coil. Marcus and Nicholas did the same. When all three were at the top, they'd tie the three coils together and lower the rope down, providing an easier way upward. Harry came to Nicholas and said, 'I wish you'd let me go instead.'

Nicholas grinned. 'You?' Putting his hand on his friend's shoulder, he said, 'I thank you, but I'm not the one whose hands grow clammy standing on the rampart of the castle, remember? You never did care for heights.'

'I know, but if one of us is going to fall – '

'No one is going to fall.'

Nicholas walked past his friend, into the cave mouth. To the sailors gathered he said, 'We should be at the top before sundown. We'll lower the rope and you can start climbing.' To Amos he said, 'You judge the order of the climb and who is to help those less able. If we can, I want every man up there by nightfall.'

Amos nodded, but they both knew it was an impossible request. One of the sailors hobbled forward, his leg swollen from a broken ankle. The man's face was ashen with pain, but he gamely said, 'I'll make sure as many make the climb as can, Highness.'

Nicholas nodded and moved toward the cave. Glancing over his shoulder, he saw Amos hand the man his own dagger and he quickly turned away. He knew why the man had asked for the weapon. Hunger and thirst were not clean ways to die.

Nicholas climbed up on the narrow trail and moved to the base of the chimney, where Calis and Marcus waited. Harry followed after. Calis said, 'I will go first, since I am the most experienced. Marcus, you come next, Nicholas, watch clearly where we place our hands and feet. Something that looks solid may not be; there are cracks in the stone behind which water gathers. If it freezes, it weakens the rocks. Test each hand- and foothold before trusting it with your full weight. If you become fatigued or get into trouble, say something. We are not in a hurry.'

Nicholas nodded, relieved the elfling had taken charge.

This was not a time to dwell upon rank. He turned to Harry and said, 'When we drop the rope, call for the others to begin climbing.' He put his hand on Harry's shoulder and whispered. 'And make sure Amos comes before you. If you have to hit him over the head with a rock and we have to haul him up the cliff, don't let him stay behind with the wounded.'

Harry nodded.

Calis placed his hands on a small outcropping of stone and pulled himself upward, bracing his legs on either side of the chimney. Reaching out to the opposite side of the fissure, he found another handhold and moved upward. Marcus and Nicholas both watched closely, and when Calis was ten feet up the chimney, Marcus began his ascent.

Nicholas watched his cousin, and when he had enough height, the Prince reached up and placed his hands where the others had. He felt sudden panic, as there wasn't much to grip. For an instant he hesitated, then he pulled himself upward, putting his feet where he had seen the others place theirs. A dull ache struck his left foot and he swore softly, 'Not now, damn it!'

Marcus looked down. 'What is it?'

'Nothing,' answered Nicholas. He turned his mind away from his balky foot and stared up, surprised at how deep the gloom in the chimney was against the bright sky. Willing himself to see Calis and Marcus, he watched how they moved. He reached across the chimney and put his hand upon the opposite face and pulled himself upward.

Like three insects climbing a wall, they inched their way up the rocks.

Time blurred. For Nicholas it became a series of pauses, watching those ahead, then moving up a little at a time. Three times Calis called down warnings of possible weak purchase along the way, and once his foot slipped, sending small rocks cascading down upon Marcus and Nicholas.

Several times Nicholas halted to catch his breath, but he found that most of the time moving was no more demanding on his arms and legs than hanging motionless. He was tired, but he simply focused his mind on the task of putting one hand higher than the other, of moving a foot, securing it, and pushing himself up a little bit higher.

Once he looked down and was surprised to discover that they had come only a third of the way up the cliff from the path. He decided to avoid that, as the disappointment that struck him was accompanied by a stab of pain in his left foot.

Despite his being in the shadows, the heat caused sweat to run down his face, blinding him momentarily when he looked up. He wiped his eyes upon his shoulder several times, and cursed the need.

Time passed as he struggled to keep up with Calis and Marcus. Each passing hour brought them closer to the top, but when he had begun to feel optimistic he heard Calis say, 'We have a problem.'

Nicholas looked up, but couldn't clearly see the elfling past his cousin. 'What?' he called.

'The chimney widens here.'

'What do we do?' asked Nicholas.

'This is tricky. When you get here, you'll see that the left side tapers up and away. It looks like you only need to extend out a little to reach it, but it's dangerous. Better to back down a little, swing both feet to that side, and propel yourself up with your back on the right side, feet on the left. Do you understand?'

Nicholas said, 'I think so, I'll watch Marcus.'

Marcus remained motionless for what seemed a long time, and Nicholas felt his arms and legs starting to knot as he held the same position without moving. He felt a stab of panic as his left hand began to slip upon the face of the rock, then he gripped harder. Breathing deeply, to become calm, he told himself, 'Don't let your concentration lapse.'

Time dragged on, and Nicholas felt small cramps and aches and knew that he had never been so tired before, when suddenly Macus said, 'Calis has cleared the wide spot.'

Nicholas watched as his cousin climbed another ten feet or so, then swung his right leg and planted it firmly on the left face, his back against the right. Bracing himself with one leg, he'd lift the other, then use his hands against the rocks to raise his body to the new height. The progress was slow, but to Nicholas it didn't look too difficult. A small voice warned, *Don't take anything for granted*.

When he reached the point where Marcus had turned, he suddenly felt a hot stab in his left foot. 'Damn,' he said softly as he attempted to put his weight upon it. His left leg trembled and he had to shut his eyes to concentrate on keeping pressure on the foot. His every instinct was to pull back, but he willed himself to continue. Then his right foot was firm against the opposite wall and he withdrew pressure from his left. Taking a deep breath, he glanced up.

Marcus was now shifting back to his original position, when suddenly his left foot slipped. He cried out as he scrambled to find a grip, and suddenly he was hanging by his hands from a tiny ridge of stone, his feet scrambling for purchase on the smooth rock face.

Nicholas felt a stab of panic through his stomach and shouted, 'Hang on!' He forced his aching legs and knotted back to obey as he muscled his way up the chimney.

Marcus shouted, 'Get back! If . . . I fall . . . I'll hit you.' From the gasps between each word, Nicholas could tell that he was struggling heroically just to keep his handholds.

Nicholas ignored the warning and forced himself to a

reckless pace. He blinked against dirt and gravel that rained down upon him as he moved closer to Marcus. He could see nothing of Calis.

Reaching a point below Marcus's dangling feet, he shouted. 'Hold still a moment!'

Marcus hung there silently, while Nicholas shimmied up below him. Gently he put one hand upon Marcus's boot and said, 'Don't kick me, or we'll both fall.' He resisted the almost instinctive urge to grip the boot before his face.

Wedging himself as firmly into place as he could, Nicholas put his hand under Marcus's right foot. 'Push down slowly!' he shouted.

Marcus put his weight upon his cousin's hand. Nicholas grimaced at the effort, feeling his shoulders burn from the effort as the skin beneath his tunic was scraped by the stone. His legs trembled and his left foot burned as if on fire, but he held firm as Marcus pushed down.

Nicholas found himself taking shallow, rapid breaths and forced himself to breathe deeply. Tears ran down his face from the pain in his back and legs, but he held himself as taut as a bowstring, as rigid as an iron rod, for he knew that to relent in his concentration for an instant would cost both Marcus and himself their lives.

Then suddenly the weight was gone and Marcus was again moving upward. Nicholas wished to the gods he could relax, but he knew he was in the most perilous position he had been so far in the climb. He needed to lower himself down slightly, then start upward again.

With burning shoulders and legs, Nicholas felt himself slide down a few inches, and suddenly he knew he was wedged in. 'Ah . . . Calis!' he called.

'What?' came the question from above.

'I've got a small problem.'

'What?' asked Marcus, looking down.

'I've let my feet get above my shoulders. I can't lower my feet, and I can't get enough push to get my shoulders higher.'

'Don't move,' shouted the elfling. 'I'm almost at the top!'

Nicholas knew that once Calis was up there he could lower the rope and pull him up. All he had to do was hold tight.

Seconds slowed and passed before Nicholas's mind's eye like a parade of snails upon the garden path. He forced himself to look at the unforgiving rock face opposite him, for he knew that if he looked down he might fall.

He felt panic start to rise, and his left foot now throbbed as badly as when it had been injured back at Crydee. He wanted to flex his calf to remove some of the discomfort, but couldn't without slipping. He closed his eyes and turned his mind to Abigail.

He remembered sitting in the garden with her, that last night, and he remembered the swell of her bosom against the gown she wore, the ringlets of her hair, golden with highlights from the torches on the wall. She smelled of summer blossoms and spice, and her eyes had been enormous pools of blue. He relived the moment of their first kiss and could feel her full lips upon his. He had to get to the top of the cliff, he told himself. If he ever hoped to see Abigail again, he must not let himself fall.

Suddenly he felt something slap him in the face as a voice shouted, 'Tie it around your waist!'

Nicholas opened his eyes to see a rope before him and he reached for it with his left hand. He pulled; more line was fed out to him, and he snaked it around his waist. Pushing his shoulders hard against the rocks, ignoring the pain of torn skin and burning muscles, he reached below and found the rope with his right hand. He pulled it up and around and awkwardly tied it about his middle. 'I don't know if it will hold.'

'It's not far. Just grip tight with both hands.'

He gripped the rope with his right hand and shouted, 'Ready?'

'Ready,' came the answer.

He let go with his left hand, grabbing the rope as his feet lost purchase on the opposite wall. Suddenly he was hanging from the rope, twisting as he felt it slip around his waist. He swung into the rocks, bruising his face. The rope seemed to hold, and he shouted, 'Pull!'

Faster than he had thought possible, he rose, scraping every exposed inch of skin on unyielding rock. Then he was at the rim of the cliff, and saw two large brown eyes staring down at him.

The goat gave a surprised bleat and scampered away as Nicholas was dragged up and over the edge of the cliff. He let himself be pulled away from the brink, rolled over on his back, and stared at the blue sky. Then he tried to sit up. Every muscle in his stomach and back clenched in spasm and he cried out in pain.

'Don't move,' cautioned Marcus. 'Just lie there and rest.'

Nicholas turned his head and saw Calis standing a short distance away, putting down the rope. 'He pulled me up by himself?'

Marcus nodded. 'He's a lot stronger than I thought.

Calis said, 'I have unusual parents.' Without further comment, he took Marcus's rope and tied it to the end of his own with a strong knot. He ran it out and re-coiled it until he had inspected each foot for possible frays and damage. Judging it suitable for the task, he said, 'I need the other.'

Marcus helped Nicholas sit up, and while every muscle in his body was agony, he could move. He let Marcus pull the rope off his shoulder, and looked around. They were in a small glade with tough grass growing below odd-looking trees, with bark that grew upward in points like a ring of blades, from the base to the top, some twenty feet or more above their heads. There large broad green leaves grew like giant fans, providing shade. A murmur of water nearby announced the presence of a small spring, and near the edge he saw a small band of goats, including the one who had greeted his arrival.

Calis went to the edge and shouted down, 'Can you hear me?'

A faint response indicated they could, though Nicholas couldn't understand the words. He motioned for Marcus to help him to his feet, and when he was standing he said, 'I'm glad that's behind us.'

Marcus smiled, the first open expression other than hostility Nicholas had ever seen in him. 'I'm glad you were behind me,' he said, extending his hand.

Nicholas shook it. 'I'd say it was my pleasure, but I'd be lying.' He stretched his shoulders and commented, 'I don't think there's an inch of me that doesn't hurt.'

Marcus nodded. 'I know.'

'How high did we climb?'

Marcus said, 'Less than three hundred feet, I judge.'

'I thought it was a couple of miles.'

'I know the feeling,' said Marcus.

Calis stood with his feet planted in the ground and said, 'I could use some help.'

Marcus said to Nicholas, 'You rest,' and went to hold the rope with Calis.

After less than five minutes, Brisa's head appeared above the edge of the rim, and she clambered over. She rose and dusted herself off and smiled at Marcus. 'I've done a lot of climbing in my day. Made sense for me to come up first. Ghuda's next.'

Nicholas hobbled up to stand behind Marcus, and he

346

took a grip on the rope. Even though there were now three others beside him, the little effort he could expend to assist them caused his shoulders and legs to cramp. But he was determined to help, and after a few minutes, Ghuda appeared.

The large mercenary pulled himself over the edge and stood up at once. he looked at Calis and said, 'I'll spell you.' He took the elfling's place at the head of the rope and planted his feet. 'If we had another hundred feet of rope, we could wrap it around that date palm.'

'Is that what it is?' said Nicholas, grunting with exertion.

'Yes. I'll show you how to climb one if you'd like. Should be dates up there we can eat. It may be fall at home, but it's spring here.'

'I don't think I'll be wishing to climb anymore today,' Nicholas answered as a sailor climbed over the edge of the cliff. As the sailor got to his feet, Calis said, 'Lend a hand.'

Saying nothing, the sailor came to where Nicholas was and took his place on the rope. Nicholas stumbled to the edge of the pool and knelt, his entire body protesting. He drank deeply. He pulled himself upright and took a deep breath, then looked up. Suddenly the sky turned above him and he fell into a black pit.

Nicholas regained consciousness in the dark. He saw Harry's face above him, illuminated by firelight. 'How long?' he asked.

'You passed out a couple of hours ago. Ghuda said to just let you rest.'

Nicholas sat up and found he was still light-headed and bruised from head to toe, but he didn't have the horrible cramps that had seized him after letting go of the rope.

'Harry helped him to his feet. Nicholas looked around and saw that a fire had been built in the center of the clearing. Men sat around eating quietly. 'Is everyone up here?' asked Nicholas.

Amos came and said, 'All who are going to come.'

Nicholas counted and found only forty-six in the clearing. 'Another eleven?'

'Six were too ill to climb,' said Amos bitterly. 'And the rope parted as the other five were climbing. Night was coming, and they panicked and didn't wait long enough to let the men before them get up the rope. It could hold three, but not five.'

Harry said, 'Calis and Ghusa lowered the rope as far as they could and I climbed up with the broken part and fastened it with a good knot and I climbed up. I was the last that came.'

Nicholas said, 'Perhaps we can lower some food.'

Ghuda said, 'Come with me.'

Nicholas glanced at Amos, who nodded. Calis approached and the three walked through a small screen of tough grass, and then into another opening. Nicholas halted.

Before them the grass stretched out a few dozen paces, then, beyond that, sand. Under the moonlight, sand stretched away as far as the eye could see. Calis said, 'The men below are dead. 'You must accept that. We will need all the food and water we can carry.'

'How far?' asked Nicholas.

'I don't know,' answered Ghuda. I saw it just after the sun set, before it got really dark, but my guess is a three- or four-day crossing. We can hope to find another oasis out there.'

'There's something else,' said Ghuda.

'What?' asked Nicholas.

It was Ghuda who answered. 'Those goats. Someone left them here. There was a glyph tattooed into the ear of the older ones. The young ones did not have it.' He stroked his grey beard. 'I've traveled the Jal-Pur. If the desert men leave animals at the oasis, it's because a particular tribe claims that water. Other tribes leave them alone. It can cause blood feud to take another tribe's water without its permission.'

Nicholas said, 'You think someone is coming here?'

'Sooner or later,' said the mercenary. 'I don't know if there are smugglers using the cliffs or if these are just wanderers who don't like strangers, or why they'd have a herd out here at the edge of the world, but I can promise they'll not look happily on our having butchered their entire herd. They won't leave them here long untended, as goats would strip this oasis of every plant in less than a year. That little herd was someone's food reserve, and they won't be thrilled by our eating their stores.'

'And we've two swords, a bow and quiver of arrows, and two dozen daggers and knives among forty-six of us,' pointed out Calis.

'Not much of an army,' agreed Nicholas. 'How are our food and water?'

'We have enough dates, goat meat, and water to last five days if we're careful,' said Ghuda.

Recalling some desert lore he had heard as a child, Nicholas said, 'Should we move at night?'

Ghuda said, 'Given our health, that's best. I'll show everyone the proper way to rest during the day, and we'll move at night.'

Nicholas nodded. 'Then we'll spend tonight and tomorrow regaining our strength. We'll start at sundown tomorrow.'

14

Bandits

The winds came.

Nicholas lay on the ground dozing, a stick held in the crook of his arm, propping up a makeshift shelter above him. Ghuda had insisted that everyone try to find a way to shade himself during the day, using whatever was handy, to keep an airspace between the material and the skin. The had all donated whatever clothing they possessed beyond tunics and trousers. All vests, great cloaks, sail scraps – anything used to protect them from the bitter cold of night, even food sacks – had been cannibalized to make head coverings. They had even taken the clothing from those who had died the first night in the desert. As he tried to rest during the second day of unrelenting heat, Nicholas understood why Ghuda had been so insistent that the protection of the living was far more important than any concern for the dignity of the dead. They all had to have shade for their heads and protection for their feet. The sands were hotter than Nicholas had imagined possible.

The desert was nothing like what Nicholas had expected. Like most citizens of the Kingdom, he knew of the Jal-Pur Desert at the northern frontier of the Empire of Great Kesh, but he had never seen it. He had imagined an endless expanse of shifting sand.

Instead, this desert was mostly broken rocks and salt flats, with enough sand wastes in between to make Nicholas thankful it wasn't all sand. Whenever they came to the sand there was an audible groan from at least half the party. The travel was slowed by more than half as fatigued legs had to push terrain that slipped away underfoot and provided nothing to push against as they tried to step.

The wind rubbed his nerves raw; it was a dry thing, sucking moisture from the body even if cold. And there was always a grit in it, a sand so fine that no amount of cover could keep it out of eyes, mouths, or noses. As much as his parched mouth made Nicholas dream of water, he longed to wash his face, his hair, and his clothing. The constant friction of the fine grit had rubbed raw spots on arms and legs, as well as making food crunch between the teeth.

They had moved out two nights before and made slow but steady progress. Ghuda had taken it upon himself to circulate through the party, ensuring that no one broke the order of march, drank before it was permitted, or stopped walking. They all knew that any who fell would be left behind. There simply wasn't enough strength among them for any to carry anyone else.

Nights in the desert were as bitter cold as they had been on the beach, and moving kept everyone warm, but exposure was taking its toll. Then when the sun rose, the heat came in waves.

Nicholas remembered the day before. At first the sky had brightened, and when the sun topped the plateau, it seared. As soon as the sun had cleared the cliffs, Ghuda had ordered the halt. He then squatted and took out one of the sticks – a long twig cut from a plant in the oasis – and showed how to sit upright with the stick holding his cloak above his head, fashioning a tent. He then hurried to supervise everyone else's attempts.

When sundown had come the night before, Ghuda had ordered everyone to their feet, telling them to scan the horizon for any sign of water, either birds in flight or changes in the heat pattern. There were none, and they discovered that three more men had died. Now they were forty-three. Nicholas knew that when they rose for their third night's trek, it was likely more men would not get up. He felt a dull ache of frustration at not being able to do more for them.

Nicholas dozed, unable to sleep. When he at last fell into a deeper sleep for a moment, the movement of the stick jerked him awake. A few had tried to dig holes or use rocks for the sticks, but they were resting upon hardpan, and it was as unyielding as stone. Ghuda had promised that while they would feel tired, they would get enough rest during the day to continue on at night. At this point, Nicholas doubted it. When he peered out at the desert surface, waves of heat rose in shimmers that distorted the horizon.

Nicholas let his mind wander as he tried to sleep. The desert made him remember his brother Borric's tale of being carried as a prisoner through the Jal-Pur, but nothing he had told Nicholas compared with this. Since leaving the oasis behind, there was no sign of life upon the plateau. Nicholas thought about his brothers, and how they had changed during their journey to the Empress's court in the City of Kesh. They had blundered into a convoluted attempt to destroy the Empress's family by pulling the Empire into war with the Kingdom. Borric had been captured by slavers and had escaped and during his travels had met Ghuda and Nakor. There had been another, a boy named Suli-Abul, who had been killed attempting to aid Borric. The experience had made Borric much more considerate of the little brother he had once teased unmercifully. Nicholas felt a stab of nostalgia and came fully awake. He suddenly felt very young again, and wished deeply he could be back at home once more, a little boy in the bosom of his family, defended from the harsh realities of the world by a warm and gentle mother and strong, protective father.

Nicholas closed his eyes again and tried to will sleep to come. His memories drifted and soon he was thinking of Abigail, but in this dream he couldn't quite make out her face. He knew she was beautiful, but details shifted in his memory and suddenly she resembled a serving girl in Krondor or a girl glimpsed in the village of Crydee.

A voice cut through his half-dream. 'It's time.'

Shaking himself awake, Nicholas unbent from his cramped position and stood, pulling the loose cape around his shoulders. He carried the stick in the left hand. Without being told, he started peering at the horizon, toward the sunset, seeking any sign of birds heading for water. The others looked to different quarters, but no one shouted any news of birds.

Nicholas glanced around them and saw that two more figures still lay upon the ground. Swallowing bitter certainty, he went to examine the two and for a moment felt a stab of fear when he saw one of them was Harry. He knelt next to his friend and was almost overcome with relief when he heard a faint snore. Shaking him awake, he said, 'It's time.'

Harry came slowly awake, blinking eyes swollen with heat and lack of water. 'Huh?'

'It's time to move.'

Harry came reluctantly to his feet, and Nicholas said, 'I don't know how you can manage to truly sleep.'

'You get tired enough, you sleep,' said Harry thickly.

Ghuda came and said, 'One more dead.'

Now they were forty-two. Others quickly stripped the body and passed out the clothing to those who needed additional protection from the sun. Ghuda handed a waterskin to Nicholas, who shook his head no.

'Drink,' commanded the mercenary. 'It's murder to drink more than your share, but it's suicide not to drink when it's time. I've seen men refuse their ration and be dead two hours later before they had a chance to ask.'

Nicholas took the skin, and the moment water touched his lips, warm and sour as it was, he started drinking. 'Two mouthfuls only,' cautioned Ghuda.

Nicholas obeyed and passed the skin to Harry, who also drank his allotment and passed the skin along. Nicholas was glad the men were Royal Kingdom Navy, for their discipline kept a desperate situation from becoming hopeless. He knew each of them longed to gulp as much water as possible, but each followed orders and limited their intake to two swallows.

Nicholas glanced at Amos, who stood motionless, watching three of his men push rocks over the dead man. Nicholas knew he had seen many of his crewmen dead over the years, but he was doubly troubled by the death of these men, who had left Krondor expecting a simple voyage to the Far Coast, then home to their Admiral's wedding.

Nicholas wondered how his grandmother was enduring Amos's absence. He knew that word of the raids had reached Krondor by now, and most likely his father would be leading a fleet of relief ships to the Far Coast, ready to run the Straits of Darknes even as the weather of late fall and early winter closed them down. Aid would be coming over the North Pass through the Grey Towers mountains, from Yabon, as well.

Nicholas then wondered how his uncle Martin was doing. Was he still alive? Thinking of Martin, he turned to look at Marcus. Marcus had changed his attitude toward Nicholas profoundly since the climb up the cliffs, and while no one would ever accuse his cousin of being a demonstrative man, Nicholas could feel the difference in him when they spoke. They might never be friends, but they were no longer rivals. Both knew that whoever Abigail chose, they were agreed to honor her choice.

Ghuda signaled and they set off. They moved south, for the same reason they had traveled south along the beach; with no clearly superior choice, they picked the route that would lead most directly to their ultimate destination.

Within an hour of sunset, the air turned cold. Those walking along began gathering their assortment of shirts, tunics, and cloaks around them.

They tried to keep their rest breaks to a minimum, but they couldn't move continuously throughout the night. One fact Amos had gleaned from the position of the stars and the rising and setting of the sun was that indeed the seasons were backward here, and the days were lengthening, as spring approached summer – which meant the days would be getting hotter. Nicholas judged that at the present rate they must find shelter and water in two more days or they would all die.

They trudged on through the night.

Now they were thirty-four.

Nicholas knew that this night's march would be their last unless they found water. They were moving at roughly half the speed they walked the first night. Ghuda estimated they had come less than ten miles the previous night, and they would be lucky if they could match that tonight.

Ghuda rose from his tiny tent of shirts and cloaks, and said, 'It's time.'

They scanned the horizon and suddenly one of the sailors shouted, 'Water!'

Ghuda glanced at the direction the man pointed and Nicholas followed his gaze. There, in the west, a faint blue shimmering on the horizon beckoned. Nicholas said, 'Ghuda?'

The old mercenary shook his head. 'It could be a mirage.'

'Mirage?' asked Harry.

Nakor said, 'Hot air does funny things. Sometimes it acts like a mirror in the sky, showing you the blue of the sky on the ground. Looks like water.'

Ghuda didn't move, as he stood rubbing his chin. He

looked at Nicholas and his expression showed he did not want to make the decision. If it was a mirage, they were all dead. If it was water and they ignored it, they were dead.

Nicholas said, 'Keep looking until the sun's down.'

It was Calis who saw them. 'Birds.' The sun was just vanishing below the western horizon when he spoke.

'Where?' said Nicholas.

'There, to the southwest.'

Nicholas stared and saw nothing. All the remaining sailors peered to where the elfling pointed, but no one confirmed his sighting.

'Your eyes must be magic,' said Amos, his voice gravelly from lack of water.

Calis said nothing but started walking toward his sighting of birds.

An hour later, they reached the edge of the desert. In the darkness it was hard to see, but they all felt it underfoot. Suddenly there was a springy feeling instead of the harsh, unyielding sand or rock. Brisa fell to her knees and said, 'I've never smelled anything so sweet.' Her voice was a croak of dryness.

Nicholas bent and plucked a long blade of tough, dry grass and rubbed it between thumb and finger. If there was ever water in it, it was now a memory. He said, 'Calis?'

The elfling said, 'That way,' pointing to the southwest.

Leaving the desert and entering the grasslands added a spark to the party. They moved a little faster and with more purpose. But Nicholas knew they were still only hours from death.

The terrain rose slightly and the sandy soil underfoot soon changed to hard dirt. As night deepened, Calis said, 'Over there!'

He took off at a weak half-trot and Nicholas and the

others attempted to follow his lead. At a staggering, lurching run, Nicholas forced his fatigued legs up the small rise and then he saw it in the moonlight. A spring! He half ran, half stumbled down the little hillock to the depression. A few birds nesting in reeds squawked and took flight as Calis plunged facedown into water.

Nicholas was there a moment later and did the same. He took a long drink and was about to take another, when Ghuda's large hand gripped his collar and pulled him back. 'Drink slowly, or you'll just vomit it all back up,' he warned.

He repeated the warning to the others, who barely seemed to hear. Nicholas let the warm water run down his face. It was muddy and had an aroma and taste he thought it best not to dwell on, with the nesting of birds so close by, but it was water.

He rose unsteadily to his feet and inspected this second oasis. The water hole was screened on three sides by palm trees, while to the east the desert continued. Nicholas moved among the men with Amos and Ghuda, ensuring they didn't drink too much too fast. After the first gulping swallows, most seemed content to follow orders, while a few had to be physically pulled away from the edge of the pond.

Calis said, 'I'll scout around.'

Nicholas nodded and motioned for Marcus to accompany him. Seeing Marcus unarmed, Nicholas pulled a large knife from his belt and handed it to him. Marcus nodded thanks and followed after Calis, saying nothing of the unspoken warning: there might be others nearby, now that they were free of the desert, and those others might be hostile. They moved off to the southwest.

Some of the men had recovered enough of their strength for Amos to organize a foraging party and post some sentries. A couple of the fitter sailors climbed trees to bring down dates. Nicholas signaled for Harry to accompany him. He left the oasis, heading toward the northwest, and when they had traveled a hundred yards, they saw that the desert was changing.

'Look,' said Harry.

Nicholas studied where he was pointing, and nodded. Odd-looking plants stood in clumps all over the landscape, and in the distance some sort of alien trees rose up, rough and without leaves. But they didn't look dead. Nicholas said, 'Perhaps they're dormant in the heat.'

'Maybe,' agreed Harry, who knew less about plants than Nicholas. 'Margaret would know.'

Nicholas was surprised by the remark. 'How?'

'Last time we were in the garden, she told me she's spent a lot of time in the forest with her father, brother and . . . mother.'

Nicholas nodded. 'I'm scared, Harry.'

'Who isn't? We're a long way from anything familiar and I don't know how we're going to find the girls, let alone get them home once we do.'

Nicholas shook his head. 'Not that. Anthony will lead us to the girls, I'm certain.'

'You think?' asked Harry.

Nicholas thought it best not to mention Anthony's feeling for Margaret, not because he considered Harry a serious rival for the girl's affection, but because he wanted to spare his friend any distress, and most of all, because he was simply too tired to deal with it. He just said, 'I think so.'

Harry said, 'How about getting home?'

Nicholas surprised Harry with a grin. 'With the most famous pirate in the Bitter Sea with us, you can ask that? Why, we steal a ship.'

Harry grinned, but it was a weak one. 'If you say so.'

'No, what has me scared is that somehow I'm going to cause us to fail.'

Harry said, 'Look, I'm a good-for-nothing, or so my

father's told me often enough, but I wasn't totally asleep on those rare occasions when he forced me to help him run the barony. And I've seen enough of your father's court to know that a lot of what makes one man a ruler and another not is simply a willingness to be wrong.'

Now it was Nicholas's turn to say, 'You think?'

'Yes. I think a lot of it is just saying "Here's what we are going to do, even if it's wrong," and then doing it.'

'Well,' agreed Nicholas, 'Father always did say that you can't be right unless you're willing to risk being wrong.'

A shout from the water hole caused them both to turn and hurry back. Marcus and Calis had returned, and Marcus said, 'You'd better come and see this.'

Nicholas, Harry, Amos, and Ghuda followed Calis and Marcus out of the oasis and across a gentle depression to a rise. When they reached the crest, they moved down into a small gully, then up to an even higher ridge.

Once they had topped it, Nicholas could see that they were at the southwest corner of a plateau, or tableland, and that the terrain fell away rapidly, turning greener as it receded from the plateau. The desert extended off to the northwest a great deal farther than Nicholas's eye could follow and at last he said, 'South was the right choice.'

Calis said, 'Certainly. Had we moved westward, we surely would have died.'

Marcus said, 'There's more. Look.' He pointed, and in the distance Nicholas made out a faint haze in the air.

'What is it?'

'A river,' said Calis. 'Given the distance, a large one, I'd say.'

'How far?' asked Amos.

'A few days' travel, maybe more.'

Nicholas said, 'We rest for the remainder of the day and all day tomorrow, then we leave at dawn the day after.'

They turned away from the vista and Nicholas put all thoughts of failure behind as they returned to the oasis.

Thirty-four survivors of the wreck of the *Raptor* moved purposefully down the incline, heading for the distant river. They had been on the march two days, and after the desert's terrible heat, the trees' shade made the still-hot weather seem clement to them. There was ample water, as whatever source fed the spring on the top of the plateau also emptied into a rill they had discovered flowing south out of a fissure in the rocks. Calis advised following it, as it likely ran down to the river, and if not, at least they would have water for part of their journey.

Near noon, they paused to rest and Calis moved out to scout ahead. Nicholas was coming more and more to stand in awe of the half-elf's strength and stamina. While everyone else showed the ravages of the wreck and the subsequent journey, Calis looked much the same as he had the day they had met, save for a little dirt and a torn tunic.

Calis returned almost at once, saying, 'Nicholas, you'd better see this.'

Nicholas gestured to Marcus and Harry to come as well, and the four of them hurried down a small vale the water ran through, reaching an incline of rocks. Calis motioned for them to follow him as he climbed, topping a ridge about a dozen feet above their heads.

Nicholas did so, and when he was standing next to Calis, they could clearly see the river, now a thin blue ribbon cutting through green grasslands.

'How far?' asked Nicholas.

'One, two more days.'

Nicholas grinned and said, 'We're going to make it.'

Marcus smiled faintly, as if not convinced, but Harry returned the grin.

Returning to the others, Nicholas said, 'We're moving

in the right direction.' That simple statement seemed to pick up the spirits of the entire company, even Brisa, who had fallen into an atypical silence since crossing the desert. Nicholas almost wished she'd return to her rude teasing of Marcus, so he'd know she was back to her old self, but while the girl wasn't sullen, she was distant and spoke only to answer direct questions.

Calis returned to his scouting and the others waited, resting during the hottest hours of the day, while he found the easiest way down to the grasslands below.

After more than an hour had passed, Nicholas started to feel alarmed, for Calis was unusually reliable when it came to being where he said he would be when he said he would be there. Nicholas was about to send Marcus after him when the half-elf returned, bearing a creature across his shoulders. It resembled a small deer, but had two twisting horns that swept upward and back from the head.

Ghuda grunted. 'Some sort of antelope, though I've not seen that kind in Kesh.'

Calis threw it down and said, 'There's a herd down near the ridge of the grasslands. I took this one and dressed it out. We'll have ample to eat if that band doesn't wander too far.'

A fire was quickly built and the creature was cooked, and Nicholas could swear he had never had meat this savory and filling.

They were less than a day from the river when Nicholas saw the smoke west of them. Calis and Marcus saw it at the same instant and Nicholas signaled a halt. He motioned to Ghuda to take Harry and circle from a more easterly quarter, while Marcus and one of the sailors were to approach from the western side. He indicated that Calis should come with him and headed straight toward the smoke. They were now traveling through high grass, sometimes reaching to their chests, and the going was slow. There was always water nearby, and Calis's prediction of ample hunting in the area had proven true. While their fare wasn't rich, it was enough to return the entire company to a semblance of health. Nicholas wondered how he looked. Everyone else was filthy, ragged, and gaunt, but most sprains, bruises, and cuts had healed.

Reaching a small rise, Nicholas looked down on a scene of destruction. Six wagons were drawn up in a circle, near the river, and two of them were burning. Another two were on their sides. A dozen horses lay dead in their traces, and there were bodies scattered around. From the gaps in the circle of wagons, it was obvious others had left the scene of battle.

Nicholas said, 'I'm going straight in. You move around the edge of the clearing and see if anyone's still around.'

Calis nodded and Nicholas moved down the hill as the elfling vanished into the high grass. Nicholas reached the first wagon and glanced around. The raid had happened no more than three or four hours earlier, from the state of the still-burning wagons. The others had burned out, leaving charred skeletons.

The wagons were high-sided, with large iron frames that held canvas, forming a roof and covering the sides. The canvas could be raised to admit air and light, and to make unloading easier, or lowered to protect cargo. The wagons were commodious, ample for large cargo or many passengers. The rear of the wagons was solid wood, hinged at the bottom so that, let down, the rear served as a loading ramp, with a smaller, man-sized door in the middle permitting access when the ramp was up. The overturned traces were set up for four horses each.

Nicholas turned over one of the bodies and saw a man of average height, slightly darker in skin than himself, but not as swarthy as most Keshians. He could have been a citizen of the Kingdom from his look. He had a ragged wound in his chest, obviously a sword blow, that had killed him quickly.

It took only a few minutes to realize that nearly everything of value had been taken. Nicholas found a sword under one of the dead horses and pulled it free. It was a broadsword, again like those common to the Kingdom.

Marcus appeared with the sailor, and Nicholas handed him the sword. 'We're too late.'

Marcus said, 'Or luckier than we have any right to be.' He pointed to the far side of the circle and Nicholas looked. 'There's twenty, thirty dead men there.' He indicated the bodies scattered outside the wagons and said, 'A big company hit this caravan – big enough to have chopped us without a second thought, I'd guess.'

Nicholas nodded. 'Maybe you're right. We have no idea who these people are or who raided them.'

Ghuda and Harry appeared from the east and began examining bodies over there. Nicholas moved toward them and said, 'Ghuda? What do you think?'

The old mercenary scratched his face. 'Traders and hired guards.' He glanced around and said, 'They were hit first from over here,' indicating the tall grasses Nicholas had left. 'That was a feint, and then the main party hit from the river side.' He pointed at the mass of bodies on that side. 'Most of the fighting was there. It was fast and over quickly. These' – the dead outside the wagons – 'are either attackers or those who tried to run.'

To the sailor, Nicholas said, 'Go back and get the others, and bring them here.' The sailor saluted and ran off.

'Bandits?' asked Marcus.

Ghuda shook his head. 'I don't think so. This was pretty well laid out. Soldiers, I'd say.'

Nicholas said, 'I don't see any uniforms.'

'Soldiers don't always wear uniforms,' observed Ghuda.

Just then Calis appeared, a slight figure before him. It was a small man, obviously terrified, who threw himself down upon the ground before Nicholas and the others and began speaking at a furious rate. 'Who is this?' asked Nicholas.

Calis shrugged. 'A survivor, I think.'

'Can anyone understand that chatter?' asked Nicholas.

Ghuda said, 'Listen to what he's saying.'

Nicholas listened and suddenly realized the man was speaking heavily accented Keshian, or a language so close to Keshian that there was little difference. The difficulty in understanding him stemmed more from the accent and his nearly frantic pleas for them to spare his life than from its being a foreign tongue.

Marcus said, 'Not unlike Natalese, really.' The language of Natal was an offshoot of Keshain, as Natal had once been a province of the Empire.

'Get up,' said Nicholas in Keshian. He was not comfortable in the language, but he had studied it.

The man understood well enough to obey, '*Sah, Encosi.*'

Nicholas glanced at Ghuda who said, 'Sounded like "yes, Encosi," to me.' When Nicholas showed he didn't understand, Ghuda said, 'Encosi is a title, meaning "master", or "boss", or "lord". Used in the area of the Girdle of Kesh when you don't know what someone's official rank is.'

'Who are you?' Nicholas asked the little man.

'I am being Tuka; wagon driver, Encosi.'

'Who did this?' asked Nicholas.

The man shrugged. 'I am not knowing which company, Encosi.' The way he shifted his gaze from face to face, it was clear he wasn't entirely convinced those he spoke with might not be responsible.

'Company?' asked Harry.

'They flew no banner, and wore no' – he used a word Nicholas didn't catch – 'Encosi,' said Tuka to Harry.

Ghuda said, 'I think he said they wore no badges.'

The man who had named himself Tuka shook his head vigorously. 'Yes, a non-lawful company, no doubt, Encosi. Brigands, most certainly.'

Something about the way he spoke confused Nicholas. He motioned for Ghuda to step away and said, 'He doesn't believe that. Why is he lying?'

Ghuda glanced over Nicholas's shoulder. 'I have no idea. We don't know what the politics around here is like, and it may be we've wandered into some sort of fracas between two lords or two business organizations or who knows what. It could also be that he does know who the raiders are, but playing stupid will keep him alive.'

Nicholas shrugged and turned toward the man. 'Are you the only survivor?'

The man looked around as if trying to decide which answer would best serve him. The expression was not lost on Ghuda, who drew out a hunting knife and stepped before the man. 'Don't lie, you scum!'

The man fell to his knees and started to beg for his life, imploring them to spare him because of his three wives and uncountable children. Nicholas glanced at Marcus, who nodded slightly to let Ghuda continue. The big mercenary made an almost comic show of menacing the little man, but whatever humor was in it was lost on Tuka. He crawled upon the ground and wept copiously, screaming that he was innocent of any duplicity and calling on at least a half-dozen gods unknown to Nicholas to protect him from harm.

At last Nicholas waved Ghuda away and said, 'I won't let him harm you, if you tell us the truth. We have nothing to do with those who burned these wagons. Now, who are you, where were you headed, and who raided you?'

The little man glanced around the circle of faces, and after another short spurt of imploring heaven for aid and comfort, he said, 'Encosi, mercy upon me. I am being Taka, a servant of Andres Rusolavi, a trader of majestic accomplishments. My master holds patents from six cities and is considered friend by the Jeshandi.' Nicholas hadn't a clue who or what the Jeshandi were, but motioned for the little man to continue his narrative.

'We were bound home from the Spring Meeting, carrying cargo of great wealth, when we were struck this morning by a band of riders who forced us to circle. My master was served by Jawan's Company, who fought well, and we were protected against this trivial raid, but then we were assaulted from the river, by men in boats, who overcame us. All of my master's servants and Jawan's Company were put to the sword, and my master's four remaining wagons were taken away.' The man looked terrified as he said, 'I was upon that wagon' – he pointed to one of the two overturned wagons – 'and when it upended, I was thrown into the grass there.' He pointed to a point near where Calis had found him. 'I am not being a very brave man. I hid.' He said the last as if ashamed to admit his cowardice.

Nicholas said, 'Do we believe him?'

Ghuda asked him to step aside and said, 'I don't think he's lying. He expects we know who these Jeshandi are and who this Jawan was, or he would have said who they were. But he didn't expect us to know his master, so that's why he told us what an important man he is.' Ghuda turned to the man and said, 'Are you of Rusolavi's house?'

The man nodded furiously. 'As was my father. We are his free servants!'

Ghuda said, 'I think we'd best keep who we are to ourselves for a while.'

Nicholas nodded. 'You circulate and tell everyone to

watch what they say around this fellow, while I ask him some more questions.'

Nicholas motioned for the little man to accompany him over to the wagons, and made a stab at finding out what this valuable cargo was. The others appeared soon after and Ghuda warned them all about keeping their identity secret.

At one point, after Nicholas had some sense of what the caravan was carrying, Tuka asked, 'Encosi, which company is this?'

Nicholas glanced at the ragged band of sailors and soldiers who had survived the trip from Crydee, and said, 'It's my company.'

The man's eyes widened. 'May I have the honor of your name, Encosi?'

Nicholas,' said the Prince, and he almost added, 'of Krondor,' but caught himself.

The man's expression turned to one of puzzlement, but he said, 'Of course, mighty one. Your reputation precedes you. Your deeds are legendary, and every other captain shakes with fear or trembles in envy at your name.'

Nicholas didn't know what to make of the flattery, but as he told the little man to follow him, he said, 'We're not from around here.'

'By your accent and manner of dress, I am gleaning that fact, Encosi. But your fame spreads throughout the land.'

'Speaking of which,' said Nicholas, 'what land is this?'

Tuka looked confused at the question, and it wasn't a function of language. Nicholas judged the context wrong, and said, 'How far are we from your destination?'

The little man brightened and said, 'We are but four days from the rendezvous at Shingazi's Landing. There my master intended to load our cargo upon barges and take them downriver.'

'Where?' asked Nicholas as they reached the others.

At this Tuka looked even more confused. 'Where? Why, the City of the Serpent River. Where else would one go in the Eastlands, Encosi? There is no other place to go.'

Nicholas glanced at his companions, who waited.

Margaret craned her neck, attempting to see around the large rudder. 'It's a seaport,' she said.

'How interesting,' said Abigail sarcastically. She had alternated between bitter humor and black despair since they left the pursuing ship behind. 'We were going to reach one sooner or later.'

'One thing you learn in the wilderness, Abby, is that you're a fool to follow a trail without marking your way.'

'Whatever that means,' said Abby.

Margaret turned around and sat down on one of the beds. 'It means that when we escape, we don't want to find we haven't a clue to how to get back.'

'Back where!' said Abby, her bitter anger now directed at Margaret.

Margaret gripped her friend by the arms. Keeping her voice low, she said, 'I know you're upset. I felt just as distressed when we lost Anthony and the others. But they're coming. They may only be a day or two behind. When we get free of these murderers, we'll need to backtrack along this route, for that's where help will be.'

'If we get free,' said Abby.

'Not if – when!' insisted Margaret.

Abby's eyes teared and she let go of her anger. 'I'm so frightened,' she said as Margaret took her in her arms.

Soothing her friend's terrors, Margaret said, 'I know. I'm frightened, too. But we've got to do whatever we need to, no matter how scared we are. There's just no other way.'

Abby said, 'I'll do what you ask.'

'Good,' said Margaret. 'Always stay close to me, and if

I see any opportunity to escape, I mean to take it. Just follow me.'

Abigail said nothing.

The door to the cabin opened unexpectedly. Two black-clad sailors entered, taking up guard positions on either side of the door. Instead of Arjuna Svadjian, a woman entered. Her hair was nearly black, which, coupled with fair skin and blue eyes, gave her an exotic appearance. She wore a robe which, once inside the cabin, she threw back across her shoulders, showing she wore little beneath; her breasts were covered by a light halter, while around her waist she wore but a simple short silken skirt. The scant garments were finely fashioned and well made, and she wore a ransom in jewels.

Margaret knew this was no tavern dancer or even a rich courtesan, for there was something terrifying in this woman's eyes. She spoke easily, in the King's Tongue. 'You are the Duke's daughter?'

Margaret said, 'Yes, I am. Who are you?'

The woman ignored the question. 'You are then the daughter of the Baron of Carse?' she said to Abigail.

Abigail only nodded.

The woman said, 'You will be taken from here, and whatever is asked of you, do it. You must know that you may live well, live poorly, or watch some of your countrymen die incredibly painful, lingering deaths – I can assure you we have the means to make it seem an eternity. It is your choice. I urge you to choose well.' In an offhanded manner she added, 'The pain of your countrymen is of no consequence, but you nobles of the Kingdom have a strong sense of being caretakers to these cattle. I hope this proves sufficient motivation for your cooperation.'

She motioned with her hand, and from outside the cabin two more guards entered, dragging a young girl with them. Without taking her eyes from Margaret, the woman said, 'Do you know this girl?' Margaret recognized her: she was one of the kitchen staff from the castle, named Meggy. Margaret nodded.

'Good,' said the woman. 'She is not very well, so killing her will only lose us one mouth to feed.' She waited a moment, then said, 'Kill her.'

'No!' screamed Margaret as one of the two guards quickly drew a dagger, gripped Meggy by the hair, and pulled her head back. With a swift stroke of the blade, he easily slashed her throat. So quick was the act that the girl had only a moment to emit a strangled cry and then her eyes glazed over and she collapsed to her knees, as blood fountained from her neck.

'You didn't have to do this!' accused Margaret, while Abigail stood mute, eyes wide in horror.

'A demonstration,' said the woman. 'You have special value to me, and I will not risk harming you as long as I have other options. But I will not hesitate to take the youngest child from your home and slowly cook him over coals before your eyes to get your cooperation. Am I making things clear to you?'

Margaret swallowed hot anger, leaving the taste of raw bile in her mouth. Her eyes were moist with tears of rage, but she forced her voice to calmness as she said, 'Yes. Very clear.'

'Good,' said the woman. Turning, she drew her robe about her and left. The guards who had dragged the girl in picked up her lifeless body and carried it out. The other two guards closed the door, leaving the cabin as it had been before, save for the spreading crimson pool on the deck.

When everyone had gathered at the site of the ambush, Nicholas had the area searched. They discovered three swords in the tall grass, as well as a handful of daggers. A barrel of hard bread and dried beef was found and quickly passed among the men.

Tuka observed the ragged band and said, 'Oh, Encosi, it would seem your company has fallen upon hard times.'

Nicholas observed the little man and judged him a shrewd customer. 'You could say that,' he answered. 'As you have, it seems.'

The little man visibly sagged at that. 'So true, mighty Captain. My master will be sore vexed to have lost so valuable a caravan. His standing in the Dhiznasi Bruku will diminish, and I shall be the one held accountable, no doubt.'

Nicholas didn't know what a Dhiznasi Bruku was, but he was darkly amused by the little man's last remark. 'Why should your master, obviously a man of perspicacity, hold you, a lowly wagon driver, responsible?'

Tuka shrugged. 'Who else is there being alive to blame?'

Ghuda laughed. 'No matter how far you travel, some things never change.'

'This is so,' said Nakor, who had come up behind the Prince. 'So it would be likely that this intelligent man might also be thankful for the recovery of his property.'

A feral light arose in Tuka's eyes. 'Would so mighty a captain accept a commission from one being so lowly as myself?'

Ghuda imperceptibly shook his head no, and Nicholas said, 'I would not, but I would accept one from your master should you be empowered to act upon his behalf.'

'Ayee,' said Tuka with a genuine note of frustration. 'You make sport of poor Tuka, Encosi. You know that I cannot. I may endure shame and punishment from the Bruku, perhaps being cast out and fated never to know honest work again, but I cannot be binding my master to any contracts, oh no.'

Nicholas rubbed his chin, at a loss for what to say next. Ghuda, however, said, 'Well, I suppose we could go after

371

these brigands and simply take from them what they took from your master.'

Now Tuka looked thoroughly stricken. 'Oh, mighty Captain, should you do that, I shall be again cast upon the river of hopelessness. No, some bargain must be possible.'

Amos, who had been standing silently nearby, finally said, 'Well, laws of salvage are pretty much the same everywhere.'

Nicholas turned and said, 'On the sea, perhaps, but in – where we're from, we hang those who receive stolen goods, remember?'

Amos sighed. 'The niceties of civilized law; I'd forgotten,' he said dryly.

Nicholas said, 'Tell you what: we'll see what we can do after we've scouted out these bandits, and if we can recover anything, we'll take the usual fees.'

Something like hope appeared in Tuka's expression. 'How many warriors in your service, Encosi?'

'Thirty-three besides myself,' sad Nicholas.

Tuka pointed to Brisa. 'Including the girl?' he asked, instantly seizing upon any chance to bargain.

A dagger suddenly appeared between Tuka's feet, vibrating in the earth from the force of the throw. Brisa smiled with as nasty an expression as she could muster. 'Including the girl,' she said.

'Women warriors,' said Tuka, with a forced smile. 'I am being a progressive man. Thirty-three warriors and you, Encosi. From here to Shingazi's Landing, with a bonus for fighting, you would be entitled to sixty-six Khaipur cerlanders, and – '

Not waiting for the man to finish, Ghuda grabbed him and pulled him around roughly. Seizing his tunic, he half lifted the little man and said, 'You seek to cheat us!'

'No, master of kindness, I was merely beginning my accounts!' He looked about to faint. 'I mean sixty-six cerlanders, each day, with food and drink, and a bonus to the captain when we reach Shingazi's Landing!'

Nicholas shook his head. 'When we reach the City of the Serpent River, and your master, you mean.'

Turning pale, Tuka looked as if he might offer another option, but Ghuda hiked him up so that his toes dangled an inch above the ground. 'Eeep!' the little man said as he rose into the air. 'If that is the Encosi's pleasure, then I'm sure my master will be obliged.'

Ghuda set him down and Nicholas said, 'Oh, your master is obliged, if he wants to see his cargo back.'

Tuka looked as if he were dancing on hot coals as he shifted his weight back and forth from foot to foot; at last he said, 'Done!'

Ghuda said, 'I'll take Calis.'

Nicholas nodded. He said to Marcus, 'Supervise one more sweep through the surrounding grass and see if there's anything useful we've missed.' Turning to Tuka, he asked, 'Is there any place between here and Shingazi's Landing where those men on the wagons could have offloaded what they've stolen to the boats?'

'No, Encosi. They were small boats, in any event. If they have large riverboats, they will be at Shingazi's Landing.'

'Then that's where we're bound,' said Nicholas.

Nicholas consulted with Amos, and quickly they evaluated their forces. The company now possessed one bow, five swords, and enough knives and daggers to arm the others. Of those men who survived the wreck, all were seasoned soldiers, or sailors with some experience in a fight.

Nicholas discussed a variety of plans with Amos, but mostly to keep his own nervousness under control, as he knew little of warfare save from his lessons. Theory he had more of than any man present, he was sure, but in battle he was the least experienced. Marcus had fought goblins with his father, and even Harry had ridden out with his father to chase off bandits before coming to Krondor.

Calis returned near midafternoon. He leaned on his bow and said, 'Ghuda watches. There was a supply of wine or ale – '

'Fine spirits,' supplied Tuka.

'Well, those with the wagons are determined to drink most of it before joining their fellows at the landing. They've pulled off the road and are working on a heroic drunk.' Motioning for Nicholas to move off out of Tuka's hearing, he said, 'There's more. They have prisoners.'

'Prisoners?'

'Women.'

Nicholas thought for a long moment, then slowly, with great drama, drew his sword. He advanced upon Tuka, who turned pale as the rough-looking young man bore down upon him. 'Encosi?' he croaked.

Putting the point of his sword to the little man's throat, Nicholas said, 'Tell me of the women.'

Tuka fell to his knees, crying, 'Spare me, master, for I am being a fool to lie to so august a captain as yourself. I am telling you all if you will but grant me leave to breathe until Lady Kal takes my life.'

'Speak,' demanded Nicholas, trying his best to look threatening.

He must have been convincing, for Tuka told everything in a flood of words. The women were a noble's daughter, the Ranjana by title, though Nicholas didn't have any idea what that meant, and her four maids. She, from the city of Kilbar, was bound to someone called the Overlord, ruler of the City of the Serpent River. She was to be his wife. Tuka's master, Andres Rusolavi, was being paid a large sum to broker the arranged marriage and provide safe transport for the girl from the city of Khaipur to the City of the Serpent River.

Tuka swore that he believed the bandits to be men sent to cause friction between the Overlord and the Dhiznasi Bruku – which Nicholas guessed to be a trading consortium or association – and drive a wedge between them.

'Who would wish to do so?' asked Ghuda.

Tuka looked confused. 'Surely you are not being from so distant a place that you do not know the Overlord is being a man of multitudinous enemies? Most certainly it is being the work of the Raj of Maharta, he being the ruler with whom the Overlord is presently at war.'

Nicholas said, 'We are from a very distant city.'

'My master, and his associates, seek to bring favor upon their lot by sending gifts to the Overlord along with his newest wife.'

Ghuda said dryly, 'And they're probably sending gifts to this Raj, as well.'

Tuka grinned. 'My master is known as a man to consider all options, Sab.'

Sab was a term Nicholas did recognize, and he knew it meant 'master'. Nicholas said, 'So, if we rescue this girl and her companions, we stand to gain from both your master and this Overlord.'

Tuka said, 'My master, most certainly, Encosi, but the Overlord . . . ?' He shrugged. 'He has many wives already.'

Calis said, 'Attacking will be little problem.'

'But keeping the girls alive will be,' said Amos.

Hunkering down in the dirt, Nicholas said, 'How are they deployed?'

Calis drew with a dagger in the dirt. 'Four wagons, and they're pretty confident they're not going to find trouble, because they've made no laager. They've only pulled off to the roadside.' He made four long lines in the soil, representing the wagons. 'The girls were in the second wagon.'

'How many men?'

'Four per wagon, all well armed.'

'How close can we get?'

'There's a lot of tall grass away from the riverside. I think five or six of us could get within a dozen paces of the wagons.'

Nicholas thought. 'How many can you kill from that distance?'

Calis said, 'All of them, if I had enough shafts. I could probably bring down three or four before they were aware of what was going on. More if they're drunk enough.'

Nicholas said, 'I'm going to circle through the grass with Marcus and a few of the men. I'll come in from this end while Ghuda will lead another ten or so from this side. The rest will attack along the length of the wagons, and I want you to give the order to attack, Calis. We'll come when we hear shouts.'

Calis thought a moment, then said, 'You want me to kill those closest to the women?'

Nicholas said, 'No telling what they'll try to do: kill them or use them as hostages. We can overwhelm sixteen of them, but we can't ensure the women will be safe. That's your job.'

Calis nodded. 'I'll keep the bandits away long enough for you to reach them.'

'Good.'

Nicholas instructed the men who were selected to attack the bandits. He turned to Anthony and Nakor. 'Stay here with those who aren't strong enough to fight, and follow after things get quiet. We may need your skills.'

Anthony said, 'I've found a couple of things here that I can use on wounds.'

Nakor nodded. 'I'll wait.'

A half-dozen others were told to wait behind, including Brisa, who seemed not in the least anxious to join the attack.

It took them until amost sundown to reach the point where Ghuda waited. He lay on a rise overlooking the last wagon in the train. When Nicholas came up beside him, he said, 'They're pretty drunk already; I think there was a fight a while back over the women. Look.'

Nicholas looked where he indicated, and saw a body lying under one wagon. 'They're not gentle about settling disputes, are they?'

'Indeed,' said Ghuda. 'What's the plan?'

'I'm taking a bunch around to the far end,' said Nicholas. 'Calis will keep the bandits off the girls while we hit them from three sides.'

Ghuda said, 'Basic, but I can't think of anything better.'

Nicholas signaled for those not staying with Ghuda to follow him and Calis. Calis took the lead and moved along the back side of a ridge that parelleled the road. When he was opposite the second wagon, he motioned for Nicholas to lead his company to the far end.

Nicholas ran along half-crouched, and when he was at his designated position, he motioned the men to be ready. Everything depended on speed and surprise. If the bandits got organized, fifteen well-armed men fighting in concert would be more than a match for Nicholas's band.

Suddenly a shout erupted from the men with Calis, and Nicholas was up and running. He didn't look to see if the others were behind; he assumed they were.

A blur of images greeted him. A man stood up, holding a small cask from which he poured amber liquid down his gullet, and he turned to see Nicholas running at him; he stood blinking in confusion as the attackers came at him, letting the liquor pour down his chin. He finally dropped the cask and pulled his sword, but someone threw a dagger, catching him in the shoulder.

Nicholas dashed past him and killed a man who was turning to see what the noise was. Then another swordsman stood opposite him, and the duel was on.

377

Nicholas was vaguely aware of the fighting around him, but kept his concentration on the man facing him. He was middle-aged, a veteran, and his attack was basic and direct. Nicholas took only a minute to discern the pattern of his attack and kill him.

Suddenly the fighting was over. Nicholas looked around and realized that his own men had struck a disorganized and drunken band, and that most of the bandits had been killed before they knew they were under attack.

Nicholas saw one of the sailors from Amos's ship. Grabbing the man, he said, 'Gather up every weapon you can find, and anything else that might be useful. Make sure no one dumps the bodies in the river.'

He went to the second wagon, where five women, all about his own age, were cowering in terror. Two of them had their clothing torn, and their faces were bruised. Thinking of nothing else to say, Nicholas asked, 'Are you all right?'

One of the women, wearing fine silk robes, said, 'We're not hurt.' Her wide brown eyes and trembling voice indicated she wasn't certain if they had been saved or simply had traded in one band of captors for another. Nicholas paused a moment when he was struck by her strikingly beauty.

Shaking himself out of staring at her, Nicholas said, 'You're safe now.'

He looked around and found Ghuda. The old mercenary was inspecting the camp. When Nicholas reached him, he said, 'These were not trained soldiers, Nicholas.'

Nicholas looked around and was forced to agree. 'They've picked one of the least defensible places on the road to camp, and they had no sentries.'

Ghuda scratched his beard. 'Either they thought there was no one around . . .'

'Or they expected reinforcements,' said Nakor, appearing at Nicholas's side.

Nicholas said, 'We'd better get organized and get moving as soon as possible.'

'Too late,' said the little man, pointing to the ridge where Ghuda and his company had waited before the charge.

Upon the ridge a line of horsemen watched impassively.

15

Discovery

Nicholas signaled.

Quickly men ran to places of defense behind the wagons, while others stripped the dead bandits of their swords and bows. Marcus appeared at Nicholas's side carrying a short bow. 'Not to my liking,' Marcus observed, testing the bow's draw, 'but it'll do.'

Tuka said, 'Jeshandi!' as he pointed to the dozen men on horseback.

Nicholas said, 'Are they friends?'

The little man looked clearly worried at the question. 'There is being a bond of peace upon the Spring Meeting, where all may come and trade. But the meeting ended and we are on their side of the river.'

'Their side of the river?' asked Harry, holding a well-used short sword.

Tuka nodded. 'From Shingazi's Landing to the north, then westward to where the Serpent River comes near to meeting the Vedra, and from the river to the desert, the grasslands are the home to the Jeshandi. None may pass without their leave. At times their hospitality knows no ending, but at other times they can be little better than brigands. That one who is in front with the red tassels upon the bridle is a Hetman, that being a very important personage.'

Nicholas said, 'Well, we can wait as long as they can.'

Then another dozen men each appeared on the northern and southern edges of the ridge. Nicholas said, 'Maybe we can't wait.'

He climbed up on the wagon and held his sword high, so they might clearly see it. Then he made a show of putting it in the scabbard at his side. Nicholas leaped down from the wagon and said, 'Ghuda, come with me. Marcus, you and Calis be ready to give us cover if we need to get back here in a hurry.'

Ghuda joined Nicholas and the two of them walked to a point halfway between the wagons and the ridge. Two riders left the others and slowly picked their way down the ridge.

As they neared, Nicholas studied them. Each rider carried a bow and quiver, as well as an assortment of swords and knives. They wore long dark cloaks over tunics and trousers, and on their heads they wore conical hats of indigo or red, some with cloth neck coverings. Their faces were protected against the dust by cloths that left only their eyes exposed.

When they reached Nicholas and Ghuda, they reined in. Nicholas touched his hand to his forehead, his heart, and his stomach in the fashion of the desert men of the Jal-Pur and spoke their formal greeting. 'Peace be upon you.'

Speaking in the variant of Keshian that seemed the common language in this land, one of the riders said, 'Your accent is terrible.' Jumping from his horse, he added, 'But you have manners.' He waved his hand. 'And peace be upon you as well.' Then he stepped closer and Nicholas saw a pair of vivid blue eyes above the indigo face covering. Pointing to the wagons, he said, 'What passes here?'

Nicholas told of the raid and their retaking of the wagons. When he was finished he said, 'We are leaving the lands of the Jeshandi and mean you no disrespect. This caravan was on its way from the Spring Meeting.' He hoped that he was convincing in his claim that whatever peace bond was in effect at the meeting carried force until those at the meeting had quit Jeshandi territory.

The rider who spoke removed his face covering, and

Nicholas saw a young face, dominated by high cheekbones and piercing eyes. Something familiar confronted Nicholas and he suddenly understood.

Turning to the wagons, he said, 'Calis! You'd better come here.'

As the elfling leaped down from the wagon, Ghuda said, 'What?'

'Look at his face,' said Nicholas.

The rider said, 'Do you take offense at my face?' His manner was tense and he seemed ready to settle the issue at a moment's notice.

'No, just that we did not expect to meet one of your kind here, under these circumstances.'

The rider's tone grew clearly belligerent as he leaned forward, stared Nicholas in the eyes, and said, 'And what do you mean, "one of your kind"?'

Calis reached them in time to hear the last exchange and he spoke. 'He meant he did not expect to meet one of the edhel here.'

The rider looked puzzled and said, 'Whatever that word means, I will be addressed by my name and title.'

Calis hid his surprise poorly. 'Your name and title?'

'I am Mikola, Hetman of the Zakosha Riders of the Jeshandi.'

Nicholas bowed again, distracting the Hetman from Calis's confusion. 'I am Nicholas, captain of this company and enemy to no man who would be my friend.'

'Well spoken,' said Mikola with a broad smile. 'But I care nothing for the concerns of city men.' He pointed an accusing finger at Nicholas and the smile vanished. 'What concerns me is who is going to pay me for my goats!'

Nicholas said, 'Your goats?'

'Certainly. Did you not see the tattoo in the ears of the mature goats? Did you not recognize my mark? Don't tell me you didn't notice as you slaughtered and ate them. And what were you doing so near the edge of the world?'

Not waiting for Nicholas to answer, he said, 'We shall camp here and discuss many things. But most of all, we shall discuss your payment for our goats.'

He remounted his horse and rode up the rise, shouting orders to his companions.

Ghuda said, 'What was that all about?'

Nicholas said, 'He is an elf.'

Ghuda said, 'I didn't notice anything, and his ears were hidden. Besides, I've never met one before Calis.'

Calis nodded. 'You may not have met any of my mother's people, but it is so. He is of the edhel, and more, he doesn't know what the word means.' Calis stared after the rider, obvious concern on his face.

After nightfall they were hosted in the tent of Mikola. Calis remained silent through most of the evening. The leader of the Jeshandi might be upset about his goats, but his sense of hospitality was clearly demonstrated by the feast his people provided to the survivors of the wreck of the *Raptor*.

Tuka came with Nicholas, Harry, Ghuda, Nakor, Marcus, Amos, and Anthony to the Hetman's tent, which he called a yurt. It was a large circular creation of felted goat's hair and sheep's wool stretched over a wooden lattice, and Mikola's could comfortably seat two dozen people. The interior was hung with standards and pennants of different colors and fashion, red cloth with gold icons, animal hides with beaded work around the edges. The air was heavy with the smell of spices, for an incense burner provided fragrant relief from the more pungent odor of horses and human sweat. It was clear to Nicholas that these people didn't often have access to water for bathing.

Brisa was told, to her irritation, that women were not permitted in the Hetman's yurt, save for wives, and then only for his pleasure. She did not make a scene, but her muttering gave clear indication of what she thought. Nicholas noticed Marcus's smile when he overheard the girl's foul language; Nicholas was certain his cousin was feeling the same way he was about the girl: glad to see her old spirit returning.

After they had eaten a particularly fine meal, accompanied by some robust wine, Nicholas said, 'Mikola, your bounty is without measure.'

Mikola smiled slightly, and said, 'The Laws of Hospitality are inviolate. Now, tell me a thing: I have an ear for accents, and have never heard your like. Where are your people from?'

Nicholas told them of their journey, and Mikola seemed unfazed by their claim to have come across the great sea. 'There are many tales of such journeys in ancient times.' Looking directly into Nicholas's eyes, he said, 'Which god do you worship?'

Sensing something strained in his tone, Nicholas trod lightly. 'We revere many gods among our company – '

Nakor interrupted, 'But above all is Al-maral.'

The Hetman nodded. 'You are outlanders, so your worship is your own concern, and so long as you take hospitality with the Jeshandi your safety is guaranteed. But know that once you depart these lands, should you ever return you will swear to worship the One True God, of whom all others are but a facet, or forfeit your lives.'

Nicholas nodded and glanced at Nakor. Calis said, 'What do you know of those ancient tales, Hetman?'

'We were once of that land from which you come,' said Mikola. 'Or so the Book tells us, and in it only the true words of God are written, so it must be so.' Looking at Calis, he said, 'There is something else you wish to know?'

Calis nodded. 'You are kin to my people.'

The Hetman's eyes widened slightly as he said, 'You are of the long-lived?'

Calis brushed back his hair, showing his slightly upturned ear. 'Al-maral be praised,' said Mikola. In turn, he brushed back his long blond hair and revealed the expected pointed ear. 'Yet yours is different. How is this so?'

Calis spoke slowly. 'My mother is of your kind. She is Queen of our people, in Elvandar.'

If Calis expected a reaction to this, there was none forthcoming. Mikola said, 'Tell me more.'

'My father is human, though gifted of special magic.'

'In truth, he must be,' said the Hetman, 'for in the longest memory of our tribe no union of the long-lived and short has produced offspring.' He clapped once and a servingman brought a bowl of water. He washed his hands as he said, 'For this reason, such a union is forbidden among the Jeshandi.'

'Such unions are not forbidden among my people,' said Calis, 'but they are rare and almost always unhappy.'

Mikola said, 'Are you short-lived or long?'

With a wry smile, Calis answered, 'That remains to be seen.'

'In the Book,' said Mikola, 'it is written that the long-lived were wanderers in this land when the faithful came from across the sea. Bitter was the struggle between us until those of the long-lived heard the word of God and embraced the faith; Al-maral is ever merciful. Since then we have lived as one.'

Calis said, 'That explains much.'

'The Book explains everything,' said the Hetman with certainty.

Nicholas looked at Calis, who indicated that he was finished. Nicholas said, 'Mikola, we cannot begin to thank you for your hospitality.'

'No thanks are required; it is the giver who should be grateful, for it is written that only in giving may one come to learn generosity.' Picking his teeth with a long sliver of wood, he said, 'Now, how do you propose to pay for my goats?'

A round of haggling commenced, and Nicholas knew he was at a disadvantage, because the sale had been made; they were only arguing price. As the night wore on, the quality of the animals continued to rise while Nicholas could do little beyond arguing they were stringy, tough, and lacking flavor. In the end he paid at least three times their worth. If Mikola was curious about the mark of the Kingdom on the gold coins Nicholas gave him, he hid it; he was pleased with the quality and weight of the coins, and that was enough.

Then Nicholas bargained for weapons and stores, and by the time they were done, his entire company was outfitted, he was tired, and it was late. He bid the Hetman good night and returned with his companions to the wagons.

On the way, Nicholas said, 'Calis, what were you saying about the passage from the Book explaining a lot?'

Calis shrugged. 'I have always been taught that the edhel, the elves, were one race, with one Queen, my mother, and one home, Elvandar. Before that we were servants of the Valheru. After the Chaos Wars, we split into three distinct groups: the eledhel, my mother's people; the moredhel, whom you call the Brotherhood of the Dark Path; and the glamredhel, or mad ones.' Looking over his shoulder a moment, he said, 'Now I see that there are those of our kin who never knew of our home in Elvandar. Our lore speaks only of those who live on the same continent as your Kingdom. We know nothing of these people.'

'And they know nothing of yours,' said Nakor.

'What was that about Al-maral?' asked Nicholas.

Nakor shook his head. 'Bad things. Religious wars, the worse kind. Centuries ago, there was a great schism in the

Church of Ishap, between those who believed that he was the One God Above All, and those who believed he was "Al-maral", or all gods, each of the lesser gods being but one of his different facets. As such things tend to do, the schism also masked a power struggle within the temples of Ishap, and at last the followers of Al-maral were declared heretics and hunted down. Legend has it that those in Great Kesh fled into the desert and died, but some few departed by ship, sailing into the Endless Sea.'

Ghuda said, 'That would explain why they all speak Keshian.'

'More like Keshian that was spoken a few hundred years ago,' said Harry.

Tuka said, 'Encosi comes from across the great sea?'

Nicholas said, 'I told you we came from a distant city.'

Something in Tuka's eyes betrayed his thinking as he said, 'So then it must be a matter of great importance that brings such a company across the great sea, yes?'

Nicholas said, 'A matter for me to discuss with your master.' Seeing the little man's dreams of wealth dry up, he added, 'To your credit, along with the return of the Ranjana to the Overlord.'

Tuka said, 'My master will at his most generous judge my accomplishments barely sufficient to offset my failures in protecting his caravan.'

'Take us to your master, and we'll make it worth your while.'

Once again the man's expression changed. 'Oh, thank you, most generous Encosi.'

'We have some learning to do about the way things are done here, so in exchange for our generosity, you will tutor us in the customs of this land.'

'Most assuredly, Encosi.'

Reaching the wagons, they discovered Brisa being guarded by two of the sailors. 'What's happened?' asked Nicholas.

One of the sailors said in the King's Tongue, 'She was about to strangle that girl in the wagon when we pulled her off, Highness.'

Nicholas said, 'Don't call me that anymore. I'm the captain of this company, and speak Keshian or Natalese.'

The sailor switched to the Natalese dialect and said, 'I don't know what caused it, but I found this one trying to murder the girl with all the jewelry.'

'Jewelry?' said Nicholas.

'The one the others call the Ranjana.'

Kneeling down, Nicholas said, 'Brisa, what happened?'

'No one calls me that name – '

Putting up his hand to silence her, Nicholas said, 'Start at the beginning.'

'I was minding my own business when that snot-nosed child called me over and asked me to get her this box that was in the first wagon.' Narrowing her eyes, she gazed at the second wagon. 'So, I figure why not? I got it, and she opens it and starts putting on all this jewelry. Then she orders me to draw water so she may bathe. I told her to draw it herself, and then she called me – '

Nicholas stopped her again. 'So you tried to kill her?'

'Only a little. I would have stopped before she was completely dead.'

Nicholas stood. 'I think I'll go visit our guest.'

He went to the second wagon and saw that it had been completely covered by having the canvas sides lowered. At the rear, Nicholas paused to knock on the door.

A voice from within asked who was there, and he answered, 'Nicholas . . . Captain Nicholas.'

The door opened and a young girl's face appeared. She said in very imperious tones, 'My mistress is distressed over the attack of the whore. She will see you tomorrow. Don't kill the whore until my mistress is awake to watch.'

The door closed and Nicholas stood there blinking. He resisted the urge to open the door and enter, judging everyone would benefit from a good night's sleep. Besides, he really didn't know what he would say.

He returned to the campfire where Brisa sat and said, 'I'll straighten this out in the morning.'

'She called – '

'I know what she called you,' interrupted Nicholas. 'I'll sort it out in the morning. Now get some sleep.'

Nicholas had Tuka, Amos, Marcus, Ghuda, and Nakor join him by the fire. Nicholas said, 'Tuka, we can make you, if not a wealthy man, at least a prosperous one. If you seek to mislead us, thinking somehow to gain advantage later, my friend here' – he indicated Ghuda – 'will be pleased to wring your neck. Now, tell us of this nation.'

The word seemed lost on Tuka. 'Nation, Encosi?'

'This land. Who rules?'

'On this side of the river, the Jeshandi claim all these lands as theirs.'

'On the other side of the river?'

'No one, Encosi. We are too far from the City of the Serpent River for the Overlord's soldiers to reach, so he has no claim. And the other cities are on the other side of the mountains. Those who live here are their own masters.'

They talked on into the night, discovering what to Nicholas and the others were strange and alien things about this land they found themselves in. There were no kingdoms or empires or any large political entities close enough that Tuka even understood the term. This was a land of city-states and independent rulers, each claiming whatever lands they were able to subjugate by force of arms. In the Eastlands, the realm dominated by the City of the Serpent River, power resided with a loose confederation of clans, tribal people related to the Jeshandi. Now they were dominated by this Overlord, a man who had come to power twenty years earlier, and who kept his position by pitting one clan against another.

As the talks wore on, Nicholas realized that to travel from any point in this land to another required the services of a mercenary army, hence Tuka's belief that Nicholas was a 'mighty captain', and his thirty-three companions a mercenary band.

When the little man had told them as much as they could absorb after so many fatiguing days and so large a meal, Nicholas ordered everyone to turn in. Nicholas asked Amos to select a few men to stand guard, though there seemed little need with the Jeshandi camped so close. He still wanted a soldier by the Ranjana's wagon.

After sleeping on the ground for more than two weeks, the bedroll he had purchased from Mikola felt like the softest feather bed he had ever known. Nicholas lay down and, for the first time since the wreck, fell into a deep, relaxed sleep.

Nicholas jerked awake as a scream rent the air. Coming to his feet with his sword in hand, he blinked like an owl startled by light as he attempted to get his bearings. A couple of the sailors were also standing with their weapons drawn. Then another scream caused them to turn toward the second wagon. Nicholas put away his weapon, for the scream was clearly one of outrage, not pain or fear.

Nicholas approached the end of the wagon and found one of the soldiers from Crydee there. He shrugged apologetically and said, 'Sorry, Captain, but she wanted to see you and I wouldn't wake you, so she started shrieking.'

Nicholas nodded and motioned for the man to step aside. Nicholas knocked on the wooden door and waited for a moment; a face appeared. The same girl who had greeted him last night said, 'You're late!'

Nicholas said, 'Tell your mistress I'm here.'

'She will see you presently.'

Nicholas was feeling grumpy from having been awakened from a sound sleep and from not having had anything to eat. He said, 'She will see me now!' as he pushed past her. He stooped as he entered the low wagon.

Inside he discovered the wagon had been converted into a bedchamber, with bedrolls at the far end wide enough and long enough so the five women who traveled together could sleep in comfort. In the end where he stood, both sides of the wagon were piled high with small trunks, which he suspected carried their personal belongings. A tent flap on the left side of the wagon, away from the campfire, was opened, letting in the sun so the Ranjana could primp before her mirror.

Nicholas got his first good look at the young woman in good light. He was impressed. His first impression had been one of a pretty girl; now he realized she was easily as beautiful as Abby, though she was like night to Abby's day. Where Abby was blond with fair skin, the Ranjana was dark, with black hair and skin the color of lightly creamed coffee. She had enormous brown eyes with impossibly long lashes, and she had a full mouth, which was at the moment set in a particularly unattractive line. She hurriedly closed her red silk blouse, which had revealed a black breast band designed to heighten the curve of her bosom. Nicholas flushed slightly at the exposed skin. Her expression robbed him of that momentary awareness as she turned her wrath on him.

'You dare enter without my leave!' she demanded.

'I dare,' he replied. 'You may be someone of importance where you hail from, Ranjana, but here I rule. Never forget that.' Bending one knee, so he could look the sitting girl in the eyes, he said, 'Now, what is this nonsense about your expecting me to come to you at your whim?'

Anger flashing in her eyes, she said, 'No more nonsense

391

than your expecting me to come at yours. I am the Ranjana! Of course you will come when I call you, peasant!'

Nicholas flushed. He had never been addressed in this fashion in his life and he didn't like it. He was tempted to explain to her that his father was a Prince and he was brother to a man who would be King, but decided simply to put it in more basic terms. 'Lady, you are our guest, and it would take very little to turn you to a prisoner. I don't know what fate those from whom we rescued you had in mind for you, but I can guess.' Inspecting the other four girls closely, he said, 'The five of you would bring us enough wealth on the slave block to live on for several lifetimes.' Pointing an accusing finger at her, he added, 'Though we would certainly lose some profit for your foul temper.' He rose. 'So don't tempt me!'

He turned away, and she said, 'I haven't dismissed you!'

Reaching the door, he turned and said, 'When you learn some manners and some gratitude for those who saved you from cut-throats, we'll talk. Until then you can stay in this wagon!'

He left the wagon and closed the door behind, saying to the guard, 'Don't let them leave for a while.'

The soldier saluted and Nicholas returned to his bedroll. He rolled it up and motioned to Marcus and Amos to follow him. A short distance from the others, he said, 'Only the three of us, and Calis, know what's really at stake here, so we can't lose sight of that. But this situation we find ourselves in has possibilities.'

'How?' asked Amos.

'We can take this loud and rude child to her future husband and put ourselves in good stead with him, and arrive in the city with a plausible story: we're another mercenary company and we just happened by at the right time.'

Marcus called Tuka over to where they stood. When the little man joined them, Marcus asked, 'What can we expect when we reach this City of the Serpent River?'

'Encosi?'

'He means, does the Overlord keep a watch at the gate, or shall we have to inform any official of our presence in the city?' said Nicholas.

Tuka smiled. 'You shall be wanting to hire a crier to announce to all your great deeds, so that you may be offered rich commissions, Encosi. As far as the Overlord is concerned, what occurs in the city is of little consequence, so long as his peace is not being too disturbed.'

Ghuda said, 'I've visited some places like that. Treat it like an armed camp and you'll do well.'

Amos said, 'We've got one small problem before we need to worry too much about the city.'

Nicholas nodded. 'Shingazi's Landing.'

Marcus said, 'You think those bandits in the boats will be waiting there?'

'We have to assume so, otherwise it could be a short trip.' He asked Amos, 'Did everyone get armed?'

'Not as well as I would have liked. We have a half-dozen short bows, and every man has something that looks like a sword. No shields, and the ones the Jeshandi use are made out of hide, anyway. No armor. As mercenary companies go, we're a pretty poor one.'

Nicholas said, 'We do have one advantage.'

'That being?' asked Harry.

'They don't know we're coming.'

An hour after Nicholas had left the Ranjana's presence, one of the handmaidens had tried to leave the wagon and was prevented from doing so by the guard. That set up a howling exchange between the guard and two of the girls and forced Nicholas to return. At the end of his patience, he simply used a strong hand and pushed the girls back

393

inside, closing the door, then ordered it barred.

As he left, he noticed Brisa looking on with an expression that could only be called insufferably well pleased. With the coming fight on his mind, Nicholas was in no mood for smugness. 'Give me half an excuse, and I'll toss you in there with them.'

Brisa pulled her dagger and made a show of testing the edge with her thumb. 'Oh, please, brave Captain. Please.'

Nicholas waved her away in disgust. A shout went up from the Jeshandi camp, and suddenly there was a flurry of movement.

Amos came to Nicholas and said, 'They're striking their camp.'

Nicholas nodded. 'We'd better be on our way, as well. Tuka says that if we roll all day and an hour into the night, we can arrive at this landing at sunset the next day.'

Amos stroked his chin. 'Talk it over with Ghuda, but I think it might be wise if we pulled up a little short and showed up at dawn the day following.'

Nicholas considered. It was a truism of battle that had been drilled into him by his teachers that men were at their worst at dawn. Either still asleep or fatigued from long, boring, quiet guard duty, they were at their least alert just before sunrise. 'I'll talk to Ghuda.'

A few minutes after the order was given to move, every Jeshandi tent had been taken down and the community was moving out. Nicholas was impressed. Before his own little caravan was ready, they had completely vanished from sight.

The heat along the river was more moderate than upon the plateau, but not by much. And what was gained in slightly cooler temperatures was more than offset by biting flies. Nicholas rode on the second wagon, the Ranjana's, next to Ghuda, who turned out to be an experienced hand with horses in harness. As the four wagons were moved out, Nicholas could hear the Ranjana's complaints echoing from within his wagon. The girl seemed oblivious to the fact that mere hours before, sixteen bandits had held them prisoner, and one had died because he had wanted to indulge himself in the pleasure of their bodies.

After a few minutes, Nicholas was startled by a touch on his shoulder. He almost jumped off the wagon, but he maintained enough composure to turn and discover a face looking out of a tent flap in the front of the wagon. One of the handmaidens said, 'My mistress complains of the heat.'

'Good,' said Nicholas. Something about the girl irritated him more than anyone he had known since his older sister, who had been a serious plague for a small boy. But even Elena had turned into a reasonable human being once Nicholas had stopped playing little-brother tricks on her.

A moment later the complaint was repeated. Nicholas turned and saw a different girl at the window. 'If your mistress had the manners to personally come and ask me nicely to take down the canvas walls, I might consider it.'

There was a flurry of voices from within and the first maid reappeared. 'My mistress requests most modestly that the walls of the wagon be raised to admit some air.'

Deciding not to push the issue, Nicholas turned and climbed down from the wagon. As they were moving slowly enough to permit those not in the wagons to walk alongside, it was not difficult for him to walk along and untie the cords binding the canvas sides. He then pulled the cords that raised the canvas and tied them off.

A particularly pretty maid leaned out. 'My mistress thanks the brave captain.'

Nicholas thew a half-aggravated glance over his shoulder and saw the Ranjana staring off to the side of the road, ignoring him. He decided the maid had presumed to be polite on the Ranjana's behalf.

The day passed without incident, and Nicholas took stock of their situation, conferring with Ghuda on various options. At one point the old fighter said, 'There's one thing about those boys that troubles me.'

'What?' asked Nicholas.

Ghuda flicked the reins and said, 'They weren't what they seemed to be. When we buried them I got a good look, and they weren't soldiers.'

'Bandits?'

'No.' Ghuda looked concerned. 'If this Tuka is telling us true, the raid was conducted in pretty decent fashion, nothing fancy, but effective. The company set to guard this wagon train was good, according to Tuka. But those fifteen we hit were as green a bunch as I've seen in the field. Decent swordsmen, who could fight as individuals, I think, but there was nothing like order among them.' He shook his head. 'Half of them . . . their hands were soft, and despite their clothing, they weren't poor bandits. More like rich boys in costume.'

Nicholas shook his head. 'What do you think?'

'I think someone expected these wagons to be found, maybe by the Jeshandi.' Ghuda scratched his chin. 'I think we're only seeing a little bit of what there is to see.'

Nicholas said, 'So you think there may be no one waiting at Shingazi's Landing to meet those men.'

'Or someone who's there to ensure that if they do show up, they don't go any farther.'

Nicholas nodded. He climbed down from the wagon and ran to the first wagon, to where Tuka sat next to Marcus. 'Tuka,' Nicholas called.

The little man looked down. 'Yes, Encosi.'

'Is there anyplace between here and Shingazi's Landing that you would judge a likely spot for an ambush?'

Tuka thought, then said, 'Yes, Encosi. There is being a wonderful place a half-day before us, where a small band might be causing great difficulty for an army.'

'Wonderful,' said Nicholas. He said to Marcus, 'Pull up.' Waving to the other wagons behind, he ran to the third, where Calis rode next to Harry. To the half-elf he said, 'Tuka says there's a perfect place for an ambush a half-day ahead, and Ghuda thinks that's likely.'

Calis nodded and jumped down without a word, setting off at a half-run. Moving to the fourth wagon, where Amos and Brisa rode, he informed them of the reason for the unexpected stop.

Amos leaped down and said, 'Well, Ghuda knows his craft, I'll warrant.'

Nakor and Anthony had been riding in the rear of the last wagon, with the men who still needed attention. They came up and Nakor said, 'Ghuda knows enough to lead his own company, should he have the ambition.'

Glancing around, he said, 'Anthony. This is as good a place as any.'

Nicholas said, 'For what?'

Anthony said, 'To see if I can locate the prisoners again. I haven't tried since the shipwreck.'

Nicholas nodded and Anthony closed his eyes. After a long minute, he said, 'It's faint, but there.' He pointed to the south.

Nicholas said, 'Well, that's where we're going.'

Calis lay on the ground. He pointed. 'There.'

Nicholas squinted against the setting sun. They lay in the tall grass to the west of a large inn, surrounded by a low wall. What Nicholas strove to see was a company of men who were keeping to themselves in the far corner of the yard. After counting, he said, 'There are twelve, I think.'

Ghuda said, 'There are a lot more inside, from the sound of it.'

What they could hear were clearly celebratory, shouts and laughter, music and the playful noises of men and women enjoying themselves. Nicholas crawled backward down the hillside. They were close enough for him to take no chance of being seen, even with night rapidly approaching.

As the others followed, they hurried back toward the waiting wagons, camped a mile down the road. Ghuda had already suggested to Nicholas that they make cold camp, in case someone at the inn was alert enough to notice light in the distance. The Ranjana had let it be known that she didn't care much for the notion, and was even more irritated at being ignored by Nicholas.

When they were a bit down the road, Ghuda said, 'It's that dozen or so hanging out by themselves in the court who make me nervous.'

'Why?' asked Nicholas.

'Those are professionals, if I know my trade. They were the ones who led that raid, who coordinated its timing, and the others are . . . I don't know who they are. But while they're in the inn getting drunk and getting into fights over the whores, the professionals are outside having a meeting about something.'

'Betrayal?' asked Nicholas.

Ghuda shrugged, the gesture clear in the falling light. 'It's on my mind. Those who were left to bring in the wagons were certainly abandoned to their fate. If their mission is to mess up Tuka's master's alliance with this Overlord, why didn't they just kill the girl? Or why not take her to the slave auctions? Or hold her for ransom? Why not put her on the boats? And why would they leave all those jewels she's wearing? For bandits, they're pretty indifferent to plunder.' Ghuda scratched his chin. 'There are a lot of questions here, and I don't have any answers.'

Nicholas said little as they made their way back to the campsite. As they approached, a voice cut through the darkness. 'Good evening, Captain.'

Nicholas waved at the sentry, who had hidden himself

behind a low scrub bush, and smiled slightly at the title. It had taken a while to get everyone into the habit of calling him Captain, but now they all did, including Amos, who seemed to like the irony of it.

Reaching the center of the wagons, which had been drawn up into a defensive square, they found Marcus and the others eating a cold meal. Kneeling next to his cousin, Nicholas said, 'Most of them are getting a snootful in the inn.'

Marcus said, 'When do we hit them?'

'Just before dawn,' answered Nicholas.

Brisa, who was sitting next to Marcus, observed, 'You said most of them.'

Nicholas said, 'There are about a dozen that look like they know what they're doing, and they may be a problem.'

'How big a problem?' asked Marcus.

Ghuda said, 'They look like seasoned veterans.' He glanced around at the faces of the sailors and soldiers who were close by and said, 'We've a good number of hard men with us, too, but we're poorly armed and some of us aren't back to full strength yet.'

Nicholas nodded. 'But we do have surprise on our side.'

'I hope you're right,' said Ghuda.

Harry asked, 'How are we going in?'

Nicholas took out his dagger and said, 'The inn sits beside the landing, with one side right up against the river.'

Tuka said, 'Encosi, there is a trapdoor below the storage room, that Shingazi put in to make it easier to bring in ale and food from the river.'

'You've been there before?'

'Many times,' said the little man.

Ghuda said, 'I'd say from the look of the place that the owner doesn't expect much trouble.'

Tuka said, 'No, Sab. The Jeshandi ceded the land to

his father years ago, and traders and travelers are putting in there most regularly. Shingazi has many friends and no enemies, as he is being a fair trader and innkeeper. It would be most difficult for any company bringing trouble to Shingazi's Landing. It would be making them many enemies.'

Nicholas said, 'So if we hit these bandits there, we're going to be making things difficult for ourselves?'

'Sorry I am to be saying this, Encosi, but that is true.'

Nicholas said, 'If we don't show up, someone's going to come looking for us. Those who were left with these wagons may have been lazy and sloppy, but they couldn't take more than another half-day to reach the landing, so by late tomorrow, someone's going to come looking.'

'And there goes our surprise,' said Calis.

Nicholas said, 'Marcus and Calis, each of you take five men and all the bows. I want Calis's group to circle around and come back up the river toward us. Marcus you'll be coming down along the river. The rest of us will trail down the road, and leave it this side of the last ridge before we see the inn. We'll circle around and come over that ridge opposite the main gate.' He thought for a minute, then said, 'If they're drunk enough, maybe we can slip in and disarm them.'

'If that dozen who were outside are all asleep,' said Ghuda.

'No, if they leave only three or four sentries.'

'That low wall gives no defense, Nicholas, but it provides a little cover,' said Ghuda.

Nakor said, 'I have a trick.'

All eyes turned to where the little man sat next to Anthony. Nakor put his hand on Anthony's wrist. 'He'll help me.'

'I will?'

Nakor had taken to carrying his rucksack again and he reached in and said, 'Ha! The merchant has repaired his

400

storage room!' Pulling out his plunder, he held it up for all to see. 'Anyone want an apple?'

Nicholas laughed. 'Sure.' Taking a bite, he said, 'What's the trick?'

Nakor said, 'I'll swim down the river, climb up through the trapdoor that Tuka said is there, and light a bunch of wet grass. It'll make a lot of smoke, and when it's really burning, I'll start shouting "fire"!'

Nicholas laughed. 'I thought you meant magic.'

Nakor made a face. Nicholas half expected him to say, 'There is no magic,' but instead he said, 'How do you think I'm going to get in unseen, if the trapdoor is bolted, and start the fire?'

Nicholas said, 'Ghuda?'

'If we take out guards outside, there's only the one door and a couple of big windows . . . maybe.'

Nicholas said, 'Let's try it.'

Brisa said, 'I may be a little stupid, but why are we attacking this place?' From the sound of her question, it was clear that she didn't like the idea. 'Why don't we just circle around it?'

'Because that's where the boats are,' said Harry.

'Boats?'

'Which we'll take downriver to the City of the Serpent River,' said Nicholas. Looking at Tuka, he said, 'How long to the city by wagon?'

'Almost impossible,' said the little man. 'The trails south of the landing are for hunters and horsemen. There is no more road. Even if a road was being there, such a journey would be taking months. My master is expecting myself and the other wagoners to return to Kilbar with the empty wagons, after the cargo and the Ranjana were put on the boats. By the river it is taking only weeks.'

'So,' said Nicholas. 'They've got the boats and we need them, and we don't want to turn every mercenary band in this land against us, so we want to do this without

401

damaging the inn. Having a confused, hung-over band of men scrambling to get out of a burning building in the middle of the night sounds like the best plan to me.'

They discussed the details of the plan for an hour, then ate cold food. Nicholas was suggesting to everyone that they turn in and rest as much as they could when one of the sentries came hurrying into the camp. 'Captain!' he said.

'What?' asked Nicholas, seeing the alarm on the man's face.

'The inn at Shingazi's Landing is burning.'

Nicholas looked to the south and there a red-yellow glow could be seen just above the horizon.

They reached the crest above the inn as the fire reached its height. Nicholas and the twenty fittest soldiers and sailors had run the mile and a half to this point, while the rest remained behind guarding the wagons.

From their position on the hill, they could see that the entire building was engulfed in flames. And in the light of the fire, they could clearly see the bodies scattered around the courtyard.

Ghuda counted. 'Seems like someone had the same idea as we did, but used a real fire instead of smoke. I count thirty or more bodies in that courtyard. Those poor bastards came out the door and windows and were cut down as they did.' He considered. 'It's the same tactic they used in Crydee.'

Nicholas felt his back hairs stand up. 'You're right.'

They walked down the hillside, seeing details of the carnage as they neared the inn. They stepped over the low wall and picked their way through the litter of bodies and debris. Tuka knelt to inspect the dead. After a minute, he said, 'Encosi! These are clansmen!'

He pointed to one man who wore a silver lion's head

on a leather thong around his neck. He moved quickly from body to body and said, 'This man is being a Bear clansman, and this over here is from the Wolf's clan. This is an alliance, all who must have turned against the Overlord.'

Ghuda walked to the farthest corner of the yard, as close as he could get to the heat coming off the building and said, 'Nicholas, over here!'

Nicholas, with Calis, Amos, and two of the soldiers, hurried to where Ghuda stood. There he pointed at a pile of bodies, some of which were smoking in the heat from the fire. 'There are those mercenaries I told you about.'

'Damn,' said Amos. 'When you spin a tale of betrayal, you really know what you're talking about.' He glanced around. 'Someone's gone to a lot of trouble to get everyone involved in this caper very upset.'

Nicholas knelt down and tried to see something. Amos followed his gaze and said, 'Gods preserve us!'

'What is it?' asked Marcus.

'That helm, there, on the man beneath those two other dead men.'

Marcus looked. 'The red one?'

'Yes, that's the one.'

'What about it?' asked Marcus.

'I've seen its like, though when I last saw it, it was black.'

Nicholas said, 'Father's spoken of its like. A full metal helm, covering the face, dragon crest, with two wings downswept to cover both sides, and all the rest.'

'Did he tell you who wore them?' asked Amos.

'Yes,' said Nicholas. 'He did. Murmandamus's Black Slayers.'

Tuka said, 'That's the helm of the Red Slayers.'

Nicholas said, 'And what do you know of them?'

The little man made an elaborate gesture, a ward

403

against evil. 'They are very bad men. They are a brotherhood of warriors and they serve the Overlord of the City of the Serpent River.'

Nicholas glanced at Calis, Amos, and Marcus. While he seemed to be addressing everyone, he was speaking only to them. 'We're heading in the right direction,' he said.

16

River

A man coughed.

Nicholas and the others turned toward the sound and moved quickly. Two men lay dazed against the outside of the wall, and Ghuda helped two of the soldiers pull them farther away from the fire.

One had a cut to the head that bled copiously, and the other had taken a crossbow bolt in the shoulder.

The man with the bolt in his shoulder was unconscious, but the man with the scalp wound was starting to move. 'Give me some water,' said Ghuda.

One of the soldiers passed over a waterskin and Ghuda cleaned off the man's face. Amos said, 'Gods! If that isn't the ugliest man I've ever seen . . .'

Spitting water, the man blinked his eyes and shook his head. 'Ooh,' he said, putting his hand to his temple. 'That was a mistake.' He opened his eyes again and looked from face to face. Looking at Amos, he said, 'You're not exactly my idea of beautiful, either.'

The man had a brow ridge that looked like nothing so much as an extrusion of granite. It was covered in dark hair, an eyebrow that formed a single line above the man's eyes. They were dark pits, sunken deep below the ridge, and separated by a glob of a nose, one that might have once held a shape, but had been broken so many times since that there was no hint of its original design left. A ragged beard covered most of the jaw, but it was clear it jutted out in a pugnacious fashion, and the man's lips were odd-looking, as if they had been struck so many times the swelling was permanent. What skin they saw above the beard had pock marks and scars and was blotched and mottled in the firelight. He was, Nicholas thought, as Amos said: the ugliest man he had ever seen.

His unconscious companion, on the other hand, was as handsome as the other was not. Dark hair, a neatly trimmed moustache, and a fine profile were evident in the firelight.

Ghuda gave the ugly man a hand to rise to his feet and asked, 'What happened?'

The man put his hand to his head. 'All sorts of murderous treachery.' Glancing around the group, he said, 'And I don't think that's much of a surprise to you, judging how you're armed.'

Nicholas, seeing that all his soldiers were still holding their weapons at the ready, gestured to them to put up their weapons.

'Who are you?' asked Marcus.

The man said, 'I'm Prajichetas, and this is my friend Vajasiah. Call us Praji and Vaja.'

Ghuda said, 'Were you part of this band of mercenaries?'

He said, 'Not so you'd notice. We were looking for passage up river, heading for the wars – '

'Wars?' asked Nicholas.

'Who's this?' asked Praji of Ghuda.

'He's the captain.'

'Him? Looks like a boy – '

Nicholas said, 'Talk to me.'

'He's the captain,' said Harry.

Praji said to Ghuda, 'I'll believe he's your son, or your pet, or your – '

Nicholas had his sword point at the man's throat. 'I'm the captain,' he said softly.

Praji looked him up and down, then carefully moved the point aside with his hand. 'Anyway, Captain,' he said to Nicholas, 'we were heading upriver to the wars – '

'What wars?' interrupted Amos.

The man turned quickly to look at Amos and put his hand to his head. Closing his eyes, he said, 'That was a bad idea. Anyone here have a drink?'

Nicholas said, 'Sorry, but we do have water.'

'That'll have to do,' said Praji. He took the offered waterskin and drank deeply. Anthony came over and examined his friend, opening up his tunic. 'This isn't bad,' he judged. 'He's wearing a mail shirt under this tunic. It took most of the blow.' He managed to pull the crossbow bolt out of the man's shoulder and staunched the blood flow with a rag from a pouch he had prepared against the consequences of the raid. 'He'll live.'

'Good,' said Praji. 'We've been through too much for the bastard to die without me.'

'You were speaking of wars,' said Marcus.

Fixing him with a squinting eye, he said, 'Was I?'

'You were heading upriver,' supplied Amos.

'And we were looking for passage to a village called Nadosa, between Lanada and Khaipur, on the Vedra. We hooked a ride with a wool trader who dropped us off a few miles south of here, and we hiked in here. We were going to journey up to the western headwaters of the river – there are always wagon caravans heading from there to Khaipur – anyway, we found this merry band of cutthroats and clan boys, and when the drinks started flowing, we joined in. Someone was buying for the house, and I'm not one to pass up free ale.'

'So you're not with this group?' asked Nicholas.

'If we had been,' he said, 'we'd be over there.' He pointed to the bodies that were now smoking near the burning wall of the inn.

'What happened?' asked Nicholas.

The man sighed. 'We was sitting around and drinking with a bunch of foolish children, and some regular mother-murderers, and the bloke who's been buying all the ale comes over and whispers that there's some work for us and we should join the other professional soldiers outside the inn. We didn't like the way it sounded, so we came out, but we headed a little away from the others, keeping the bulk of them between us and the guy who called us out.

'Suddenly there's shouting and crossbow bolts are flying everywhere. Vaja and I jumped over the wall and landed hard. I saw him get hit and suddenly everything went dark.' He frowned and reached inside his tunic. Feeling around, he found what he had been looking for and pulled out a pouch. 'Good,' he said as he loosened the drawstring. He took out a tiny roll of parchment, less than three inches wide, and a finely pointed piece of wood. He licked the end of the wood, which Nicholas noticed had been blackened, and unrolled the little parchment. Looking down a line of scrawls, he poised the writing tool over the parchment and said, 'Is Overlord one word or two?'

Though the most of the dead were already half burned, there wasn't enough wood close by for a pyre, so Nicholas ordered them buried. By the time they had finished and brought the wagons up, it was midday. The man called Vaja regained consciousness an hour after they found him, and he corroborated Praji's story.

Leaving the two wounded men to rest, Nicholas took Calis, Marcus, and Harry on a quick search of the area. Whoever had killed the mercenaries and clansmen had left it completely.

When they returned, Nakor greeted them with the news that most of the lower storage room Tuka had told them about had survived the fire. Nicholas led a group of men through the smoking char of the inn and found the trapdoor. While it was blackened, it was intact. The Prince lowered himself down into the room and was followed by Tuka, Ghuda, Nakor, and Marcus.

Harry handed down burning torches to Marcus, then

joined them. Nicholas turned and almost fell over the body of a man. He was unburned, but his face was contorted into a mask of pain. Tuka looked at him and said, 'Shingazi. He must have tried to hide down here when the fire came.'

Nakor examined him and said, 'He died from smoke, I think. Not pleasant.'

'There's a pleasant way to die?' asked Harry.

Nakor grinned. 'Several. There's a drug that will kill you, but in the last few minutes of life, you'll experience ecstasy beyond imagining, and then a particularly beautiful woman – '

'Enough,' said Nicholas. 'See what you can find down here that might be useful.'

They searched and suddenly Marcus said, 'Look at this!'

Nicholas crossed to the section of the cellar where his cousin waited and there they found an armory. 'Looks like our host was ready to outfit an army.'

Nicholas saw stacks of chain mail, unmarked shields, swords of all description, crossbows, bows of various sizes, arrows, bolts, and knives. Nicholas said, 'Get some men down here and start passing these up.'

Ghuda broke open a barrel and reached in. Pulling out some dried meat, he tasted it. 'A little smoky, but not bad.'

Nicholas turned around and said, 'Let's get it all up so we can see what we've got.'

He returned to the trapdoor and Harry gave him a boost up. Leaving the burned-out inn, he heard shouts coming from the wagons. Glancing heavenward, he swore. The voice belonged to the Ranjana.

Reaching the wagons, Nicholas saw the young noblewoman standing before Amos, hands on her hips in a defiant pose, as she shrieked like a wounded cat. 'What do you mean, no boats! I am supposed to be in the City of the Serpent River within two weeks' time – '

Nicholas said, 'What's this?'

A guard stood nearby, nursing an impressive set of scratch marks on his cheek, and said, 'I tried to keep her in the wagon, High – er, Captain, but she overheard someone say the inn was destroyed – '

'And came to see for myself what situation you fools have taken me into,' she finished.

'What we've done,' Nicholas said, his patience nearing an end, 'was save your life, and your virginity, and your wealth, and put up with your nonsense . . . *Now get back to your wagon!*' The last was a loud shout of anger.

The girl turned defiantly and strode off, managing to keep her chin up the entire way without tripping. As she reached the back of the second wagon, she turned and said, 'When the Overlord hears what I've had to endure at the hands of a dirty, rude, and barbarous mercenary, you'll wish you had been born a slave!'

Nicholas watched her and then turned to Amos. 'Dirty?'

Amos grinned. 'You're no nosegay, Nicky. None of us are.'

Nicholas looked at the company and realized they all looked filthy and villainous. He ran his hand over his chin and realized that the beard he had shaved on the *Raptor* was now a ragged stubble.

Looking around, he said, 'Well then, I guess we'll take some baths.'

Amos grinned. 'If you say so, Captain.'

Groaning in disgust, he pushed past Amos and shouted at those men carrying goods out of the inn, 'Find out if there's any soap down there.'

A supply of clothing had been found in the basement along with the other goods, and most of their ragged, filthy clothing had been replaced. It was an odd assortment of items, from men's plain trousers and tunics, to a few items of fashion, richly appointed. Ghuda and Tuka both surmised the more expensive items were things either left behind or used as security against room and board by those short of funds. From the look of things, Shingazi had been a soft touch or in love with odd fashions.

Nicholas ordered the discovered clothing washed to rid it of the reek of smoke, and then for the men to bathe before changing. In the late afternoon heat, the clothing quickly dried on lines tied between the wagons. By sundown, all the men had bathed, and those who were inclined had shaved or trimmed their beards.

One thing that pleased Marcus was the discovery that another longbow was counted among the many weapons. By the time the men were cleaned and ready, Amos and Harry approached carrying a charred ironbound wooden chest. 'Look what we found,' said Amos.

They opened it: it was filled with small pouches. Nicholas opened one to discover gems. Others contained jewelry, silver, and gold. 'We're rich,' said Harry in awe.

Nicholas took one of the bags of gold and carried it over to where Praji and Vaja rested in the shade of a wagon. Both men had eaten and were now dozing. Praji stood as Nicholas approached and Nicholas tossed him the bag. 'For you.'

Praji listened to the sound of coins as he hefted the bag and said, 'What for?'

'I could use two men who knew their way around the City of the Serpent River.' He pointed to the bag. 'You keep that, for your trouble and to help you on your way, whatever you decide, but we're a new mercenary company and we have no one but that little wagon driver who knows his way around down there. And we can always use a couple of men smart enough to avoid getting murdered when everyone else around them couldn't.'

411

Praji glanced down toward his friend, who was half-asleep and said, 'Well, we're not fit for traveling on foot as is; Vaja will be all right by the time we reach the city by wagon. But one question . . .'

'What?'

'Are you for the Overlord or against him?'

The expression on the man's face showed it was an important question, and Nicholas said, 'Neither; we have other matters of importance. But from the presence of that Red Slayer's helm back there I suspect we may find ourselves on the other side of the battle lines once they're drawn.'

Praji rubbed his bearded chin as he said, 'Well, we'll ride along with you, and by the time we reach the city we'll have a better take on one another. We're not inclined to sign compacts until we've seen more of you. Fair?'

'Fair,' agreed Nicholas.

Then Praji grinned, which was a scary sight, and said, 'Now that the Overlord's on my list, I can't very well help anyone who's with him, you see?'

'List?' asked Harry.

'I've got this list, see, and when someone does me dirt, I put his name on it if I can't sort him out on the spot. I'm not saying I'll be able to settle accounts with everyone on it, but I never forget.'

Harry was about to comment when Calis appeared suddenly, jogging into camp from the south. He had been scouting all day, and when he reached Nicholas, he said, 'We've got company.'

'Where?' asked Nicholas.

'Four, five miles down the river. A company of riders, twenty-two by my count. They're armed to the teeth and know how to set out sentries. Regular soldiers wearing black tunics and carrying a banner, a black flag with a golden serpent on it. It looks like they're breaking camp and getting ready to ride at sundown.'

Praji had been leaning against the wagon. 'Those are the Overlord's. Damn far from the city for regulars.'

Nicholas signed for Ghuda and the others to join him, and when he had shared Calis's intelligence, asked the mercenary, 'What do you think?'

Ghuda shrugged. 'I've seen enough bloody double-crosses in my life, and half of them in the last two days; I expect they're up here to find the wagons, kill the "guilty", rescue the princess, and ride home in triumph.'

Praji said, 'Are you saying all this was a setup of some kind?'

Nicholas said, 'If I told you the wagons had been attacked by clansmen, what would you say?'

There was a brightness in the man's eyes that spoke of a quick wit. 'I'd say the clans were trying to cause major trouble for the Overlord's treaty with the northern trading alliances. Which would surprise no one. What would surprise everyone would be that they'd be so dumb about doing it publicly, especially leaving witnesses.'

'And what would you say if someone told you all the clansmen were found killed?'

'That's tricky,' answered Praji. 'Depends on who killed them. If it's the Overlord, they – ' He interrupted himself. 'If it could be made to look like there was some sort of falling out, it would drive the clans apart.'

Ghuda said, 'How secure is the Overlord?'

Praji shrugged. 'There's been talk of rebellion for twenty years. He's still there.'

Nicholas said, 'Well, we've walked into a fight that's not ours, but those on either side won't care about that, so we'd better get ready to fight.' Glancing around, he said, 'If those soldiers are another part of this plot, they're going to expect sixteen clansmen with those wagons, so I want sixteen men on the wagons. Drive them back over the ridge.' He pointed to Calis. 'I want you to head south

413

again, and when you see the riders approach, I want you to shoot a shaft into the courtyard as a warning; can you do it without hitting anyone there?'

Calis gave him a look that said he needn't have asked. Nicholas pointed to where he wanted him stationed, and then turned to Ghuda. 'I want you to stay here with me, with some men lying in the courtyard. Those soldiers will expect to see corpses spread around, so we won't disappoint them. When they reach the wagons, we'll be behind them.' Ghuda nodded. 'Amos, you're in charge of the wagons. Once you're over the ridge, build some campfires down the ridge so the riders will see the light in the sky, but not the fires. And built them so that the riders will be looking into them as they crest the ridge. I want them outlined against the flames when we come up behind them.' Amos saluted with a smile and motioned for the wagons to be hitched up.

Nicholas said, 'Harry, you take the girls down by the river, in the tall grass, and keep them out of sight and quiet.'

Brisa said, 'What about me?'

Nicholas said, 'Go with Harry. If the Ranjana makes a sound, you can go back to killing her.'

Brisa grinned. 'Thanks.'

Soldiers and sailors jumped into action and Nicholas said to Praji, 'If you're going to help, better move your friend out of harm's way. He doesn't look like he's ready to fight.'

Praji said, 'He's not, but I am. I'll put him in one of the wagons, and ride with your ugly friend there.'

Amos looked over his shoulder and feigned an injured look. 'Ugly?'

Those stores that had been carried out into the courtyard were quickly hidden out of sight as the wagons were driven off. By the time the sun was lowering beyond the horizon, Nicholas had everyone in place.

He chose to lead those in the courtyard himself, and lay waiting for the signal. As time passed, he found that his left foot was throbbing a little. He was irritated by it more than pained, and he pushed it from his thinking as he reviewed his plan of attack, looking for any flaws.

He became so lost in his thinking that he was startled when a single arrow landed in the center of the courtyard with a thunk. Instantly he was alert. The sound of riders could be heard, and he gripped his sword tightly.

The sound of horses' hooves upon the ground grew louder, and then the company of soldiers was riding into the clearing south of the inn. A man swore. 'Where are those damned wagons?'

'I don't know, Captain. They should have been here by now,' said another voice.

A third said, 'Look, Captain, there's a glow in the sky; there are fires on the other side of that ridge.'

'Those lazy bastards couldn't travel the extra quarter-mile!' said the voice that Nicholas knew belonged to the man the second speaker had addressed as 'Captain'. 'Well, we'll do what we came for.' He heard weapons being drawn, and then a half-grunt, half-yell as someone drove his horse forward.

Nicholas waited only a moment for them to leave the inn behind, and he was on his feet. Softly he said, 'Now!'

His men were up and running, and those with bows took up position in the road. As he hoped, when the riders crested the hill, they were clearly visible against the glow of the campfires.

'Now!' shouted Nicholas, and the bowmen let loose with a flight of arrows. Amos's men did the same from the other side, and before they knew what happened, half the horsemen were falling from their saddles.

Those without bows shouted and charged, and the horsemen, who had been confident of finding sixteen probably drunken and inexperienced men at the wagons, were now

415

being attacked by thirty battle-trained soldiers and sailors.

One rider attempted to charge back down the hillside, and he was taken from his saddle by a long arrow. Nicholas glanced behind and saw Calis hurrying up, notching another arrow.

Then the captain on the ridge ordered a charge and the remaining nine horsemen rode for their lives.

Two more were taken from their mounts by bowfire, but the others rode low over the necks of their animals. 'Shoot the horses!' shouted Nicholas. 'Don't let anyone escape.'

The sound of steel against steel told Nicholas that some of the men who had fallen were not dead, and had come to their feet ready to fight. The first rider bore down upon those in front of Nicholas, and he got ready to take the charge in turn. Practicing against a horseman who knew the intended target was his Prince's son was one thing. This was quite another, and Nicholas knew it.

Nervous sweat ran down his back, and he felt the grip on his sword grow clammy. He flexed his knees, and as the charging horseman closed, he held his sword high, in a cavalry pose.

To stand before a charging horse and rider with only a broadsword was foolish, Nicholas knew. Had he a bastard-sword such as Ghuda carried or even a heavy falchion, he could risk taking the horse's legs out from under him while avoiding the rider's attack. But with a broadsword, he had to attempt to get the horse to shy or change course, while protecting himself from both animal and rider.

As the rider bore down on him, the horse screamed and its front legs collapsed. The rider was thrown forward; like a trained acrobat, he attempted to take the fall on his shoulder and roll. Someone in the gloom had shot the horse or struck it with a blade.

The rider landed heavily, and let out a painful-sounding

grunt, but he scrambled to his feet. Nicholas charged. As the man lurched upward, Nicholas drove his shoulders into him. The man cried out in pain and Nicholas surmised he had broken something in the fall. Lashing out with his sword, Nicholas took the man in the arm and the soldier's sword fell from limp fingers. He scrambled backward and turned to flee. Two of Nicholas's men ran up and grabbed the soldier, driving him to the ground, where they quickly had his hands tied. Nicholas had ordered prisoners if possible.

He glanced around and saw the fight was over.

Nicholas ordered a campfire built and then checked on his own men. The surprise was so effective that not one of them suffered worse than a shallow cut on the arm, and that man looked embarrassed at being the only one. The rest suffered only bruises, muscle pulls, or sprains.

Nakor inspected the wounds of the two prisoners and reported to Nicholas, 'The captain may live, though his arm wound is deep, and he has broken ribs, but the other man will certainly not. It's a wound to the stomach, and the man ate before the attack, he told me. He's an experienced soldier and asked for a quick death.'

Nicholas shuddered and saw that Ghuda nodded. 'Belly wound's a bad way to die.'

'Is there anything you can do?' asked Nicholas of Anthony.

'If I had all my usual herbs and other curatives, perhaps, but even then it would be tricky. A healing priest might save him with prayers and magic, but out here, with what I have, no. There's nothing I can do.'

Amos took Nicholas by the elbow and took him out of earshot of the others. Lowering his voice, he said, 'Nicky, I've not said a word to you since you've taken command, because by most standards you've chosen to do the right thing, and what mistakes you've made were not the sort

417

even an experienced leader could have avoided. But now you've got to understand some of the harder choices of your rank.'

'You mean I have to let Ghuda kill that prisoner?'

'No, I mean you're going to have to kill them both.'

'Crowe,' said Nicholas with resignation.

'What?' asked Amos.

'It's a story my father told me, of the ride north during the time the Brotherhood of the Dark Path invaded the Kingdom, before he found you and Guy du Bas-Tyra in Armengar. They were being tracked by a party of Black Slayers.' He closed his eyes. 'A man named Morgan Crowe, a renegade, spied them out, and Father had to order him killed.' He shook his head. 'He said that of all the men whom he had to pronounce punishment on, that was the hardest.' Looking into Amos's eyes, he said, 'I don't even have the pretense of right by law here, Amos. This isn't the Kingdom, and this man isn't trying to kill me because of anything more than an order given him by his master. He's not a traitor to my King the way Crowe was.'

Amos said, 'I understand, but out here there's no law, save what we make for ourselves. You're a captain of a company on a sea of grass, and you must act as if these were pirates boarding your ship for plunder. You've got to order them dead after you get as much information out of them as you can.'

Nicholas looked hard into the eyes of the man who would be, gods willing, his step-grandfather. At last he took a deep breath and nodded firmly.

Returning to the circle around the fire, he nodded once to Ghuda, who slipped away. 'Bring the captain here,' he ordered.

Two men brought the injured captain, who moaned as he was eased to a sitting position at Nicholas's feet. Nicholas said, 'What's your name?'

'Dubas Nebu,' he said, 'Captain of the Second Company of His Radiance's Own.'

Praji had ambled over and said, 'Damn, it's the Overlord's private guards.'

Nicholas said, 'Meaning?'

Praji scratched his face and said, 'Either the Overlord's in on all this or he's got a traitor high up in his own government.'

Praji reached down and tore open the man's tunic, which brought forth a scream of pain. 'Get this animal away from me!' cried the captain.

Praji found something about his neck and pulled it free. 'Look at this,' he said, handing it to Nicholas. He examined the talisman, as Praji added, 'Clan symbol.' Then his tone turned puzzled. 'Though I've never seen its like before.'

Nicholas said, 'I have.' The token was of two snakes, in a pattern identical to that of his own ring.

Amos started to say something, but Nicholas cut him off. 'Everyone, leave me alone with this man.'

Amos again started to speak, then stopped himself and nodded. He signaled for the others to follow him, and when Nicholas was alone with the wounded man, he knelt opposite him. 'You fool,' he whispered in his best conspiratorial tone, 'what were your orders?'

Captain Dubas's eyes were bright with his injury, and his face was drenched in perspiration, but he didn't seem unclear as he said, 'I have no idea what you're talking about, renegade.'

Nicholas reached into his belt pouch, pulled out the ring that Calis had brought to them from Elvandar, and showed it to the man. 'I don't wear this save when I need to identify myself!' Nicholas said. 'Now, what fool ordered you here? We were to kill the clansmen and bring the Ranjana to the city.'

Dubas said, 'But . . . Dahakon told me that . . . there

419

was to be no other company.'

Nicholas pulled his dagger and put it against the man's chest. 'I should kill you now, but someone higher up has made a mess of this.'

'Who are you?' asked the captain.

'What were your orders?'

Pain made Dubas's face pale and he said, 'I was to take those who came with the wagons. The Red Slayers are already on their way back with the boats . . . I don't understand . . .'

'What about the prisoners?' asked Nicholas.

'There were to be no prisoners,' said Dubas. 'I was to kill the girls and bring their bodies in with me.'

'No, the other prisoners. From the ship?'

Dubas said, 'The ship . . . ?' Suddenly understanding registered. 'You know of the ship!' Before Nicholas could react, the captain lunged forward, throwing himself atop Nicholas. He cried out in a weak croak as Nicholas's blade was driven into his chest by the force of his own weight.

Seeing the struggle from a few yards away, Amos and the others hurried back. 'What happened?' asked Amos as he pulled the dead man off Nicholas.

'He killed himself,' said Nicholas bitterly. 'I was being clever and overplayed my hand.'

'Did you learn anything?' asked Harry, helping his friend to his feet.

'I did get a name.'

'What name?' asked Praji.

'Dahakon.'

'Oh, that's just wonderful,' said Praji. 'You've a grand assortment of enemies, Captain.'

'Who is Dahakon?' asked Marcus.

'He's the Overlord's Grand Adviser, and the meanest son of a bitch in the Eastlands, the Riverlands, hell, the whole damned world.'

Nicholas said, 'And from what I can see, he's a traitor.'

'Can't be,' said Praji.

'Why not?' asked Harry.

'Because he's the man who's kept the Overlord in power since he took control of the city, twenty years back. He's the man that's truly feared in the city.'

'Why?' asked Marcus.

'He's a magician.'

Nicholas said, 'That's special around here?'

'Ha!' said Praji. 'Obviously you're from one hell of a long way off.' In serious tones he added, 'Captain, there's only one magician in the Eastlands. That's Dahakon. Used to be a few here and there, but it's death for any magician to be found in the city. And it's not a pretty death, from what the rumors say: he eats them.'

Nicholas glanced at Nakor and Anthony and shook his head slightly. Praji continued. 'It's said that he's the man who created the Red Slayers, and they do his bidding, not the Overlord's. He talks to the dead and has a soul drinker for a lover. She's the one who keeps him alive; he's supposed to be hundreds of years old.'

Nakor made a sign. 'Very bad. Necromancy is the worst practice there is.'

Anthony nodded, and Nicholas could tell he was shaken. Pointedly he said, 'We've no magicians among us, so we needn't worry.'

'That's good,' said Praji. 'No, Dahakon can't be the traitor; he could remove the Overlord any time he wished.'

Nicholas sighed. 'Well, we'll never figure out who's behind this plotting standing here. How's the best way to get down to the city?'

Praji said, 'Boats. But with this place in ruins, you'll never get a river caravan to put in; they'll figure we're the murderers who've done the job, and if the Jeshandi wander this way anytime soon, you'll have some fast talking to do while they roast you upside down over a fire; back when they granted this land to Shingazi's father, they put this little inn under their protection.'

He glanced around, as if speaking the nomads' name might make them appear. 'Best we be moving south, down the river road. There's a village five days from here, and boats put in there from time to time. If we don't find a boat ride along the way, we can be in the city in a month or two.'

Nicholas said nothing. A month would be far too late.

Abigail screamed. 'Get away from me!' She kicked out and the thing pulled away.

Margaret said, 'I don't think it's going to harm you.'

'I don't care,' said Abigail angrily. 'They're disgusting.'

The creatures she referred to were human-shaped, but rather than having skin, they were covered in green scales. A broad brow ridge dominated the forehead, and large black reptilian eyes stared out of an expressionless face. The teeth were odd, not as sharp as a reptile's, yet not as regular as most humans'. If they had gender, there were no external indications of sex; the chest was flat and without nipples and the crotch appeared smooth. Margaret didn't know what the creatures were, but she knew they were somehow related to the one that had occupied the cabin next to their own on the black ship.

The girls had been taken from the ship in a large boat, rowed to the docks by a crew of men in black tunics and trousers, wearing red head coverings. Rather than being taken to a slave pen, as Margaret had expected, the girls had been loaded aboard a caravan of wagons and taken out of the city, to a large estate surrounded by high walls. There they had been taken to the rooms they occupied now, and Arjuna Svadjian resumed the questioning. Margaret was now convinced there was a pattern to his seemingly random questions, but she couldn't quite make it out. She knew much of what he asked was to mask the design of his interrogation, which his manner and choices of topics made it difficult to guess at. They never saw the mysterious woman who had ordered the murder of the girl to demonstrate that their countrymen's lives depended upon the girls' cooperation. Once Margaret asked Arjuna about her, but he ignored her and posed another question.

Asking Aigail to help discover what his purpose was had helped the girl come out of her last round of despair. Now she was angry, and she seemed ready to help Margaret in her next attempt to escape; Margaret had again stated her intention to get away as soon as possible.

Their routine became predictable. They were allowed their privacy, save when Arjuna came to question them. At breakfast, the noon meal, and supper they were served by attendants who refused to speak. In the afternoon, they were permitted to spend a few hours in a garden under a gauzy awning that cut the harsh glare of the sun.

Then things had changed. That morning, instead of Arjuna coming to question them, the two creatures had been admitted to the room. Abigail had fled to the farthest corner, while Margaret had stood ready to defend herself with a chair. The two creatures had hunkered down and watched for a while, each studying one of the girls.

Abigail had returned at last to sit on her bed, and for another hour one of the creatures had sat staring at her. Then it had tried to touch her.

Margaret said, 'Have you ever heard of anything like these?'

'No,' said Abigail. 'They're some sort of demon.'

Margaret studied the one who stared at her. 'I don't think so. There's nothing that seems magical about them. But their skin looks like the hand I saw when I looked out the window on the ship that one time.'

The door opened and the servants brought in the morning meal. The girls didn't feel much like eating, but they knew that if they didn't, they would be force-fed. As they ate, the interest of the two creatures seemed to increase and they tried to get closer. Abigail drove off hers by throwing a plate at it, while Margaret simply ignored the other.

After the meal, Arjuna entered, and before he could speak, Margaret shouted, 'What are these creatures?'

In his always calm tone, he said, 'These? They are harmless. Companions for you.'

'Well, I don't want them here!' insisted Abigail. 'Take them away.'

All Arjuna would say was 'They will do you no injury. They will remain.' He pulled up a chair and said, 'Now, what do you know of the legend of Sarth?'

Margaret looked at the creature who stared at her, and for a moment there was something in its dead eyes that glimmered with intelligence. She felt a shiver down her back and turned away.

The boats moved lazily down the river. Nicholas sat on the foredeck of the first, a lumbering thing of high gunwales, a half-barge, with a mast that lay folded along its length, as they used the currents of the Serpent River to carry them toward their destination. Two long oars beat halfheartedly against the current, keeping them moving faster than the water just enough so the tiller would do some good. They'd been aboard the boats for a week now, and would reach the City of the Serpent River soon.

Nicholas reviewed their situation. Between what they had salvaged from Shingazi's Landing and the treasure, Nicholas's Company, as they were now calling themselves, was well outfitted and relatively wealthy. They had

424

moved downriver to the village that Praji had spoken of, and rested there.

At first the villagers had fled in terror, believing them to be bandits, but Nicholas had waited calmly with the wagons for a day until one of the braver men had ventured out of the nearby woods to speak with him. It took only a few kind words and a gold piece to convince the man they weren't going to steal everything in sight, which they could have done while the villagers were hiding.

The villagers had turned out and feted the company for more than a week, and Nicholas's injured recovered. He had hated to lose the time, but Nicholas had agreed that everyone needed rest before they attempted to move south by wagon. And the village was the most logical place to hail any passing river traffic. During this time, Praji's companion, Vaja, had recovered sufficiently to join in conversations with the others. Nicholas discovered him to be a vain man, proud of his handsome profile and curly locks. The younger women of the village reinforced his high opinion of himself, lavishing attention on the handsome fighter, bringing him water, fresh fruit, and honeyed bread during the day and, Nicholas suspected, more intimate proof at night. Nicholas had also discovered that Vaja's noble-sounding speech was an affectation, and that, on balance, he wasn't a very intelligent man. Praji seemed to be the brains of the pair, but he was content to let others think the more charismatic Vaja was.

While the men had convalesced, Nicholas had undergone a quick course of instruction from Ghuda on the deployment of men at the company level. If Praji and Vaja stayed with them, they would number thirty-five soldiers and Brisa. The sailors had grumbled about the drills, but the soldiers had mocked them unmercifully until they had become practiced enough to hold their own in the mock drills and cambat. Each man was put through endless sword and bow practice, until all were able to use the weapons, even if with only marginal skill. From what Praji and Tuka said, thirty-five was a small number for a company of any repute – some of the larger numbered as many as six hundred – but it was sufficient for them to be believable mercenaries.

At the end of the week, a river caravan hove into sight and Praji had run up a white banner, the sign for a parley. The first boat came close enough to shore for Nicholas and the caravan captain to negotiate, and after nearly ten minutes of shouting across the water, Nicholas had to have someone swim out and give the man gold.

Nicholas elected to send Harry, while Marcus, Calis, and the other bowmen were ready to provide either punishment or retreating cover should either prove necessary. But as soon as the captain of the boats saw the gold, the other boats swung into shore. It had taken nearly two hours to board everyone.

In the distance, Nicholas could see a dark smudge on the horizon, and he asked Praji, 'What is that?'

'Smoke, from the City of the Serpent River. We'll be there before nightfall.'

They had spent the entire journey considering their options and now they had a plan. At least, Nicholas hoped it was a plan, for he couldn't admit to the others he had the feeling that he was leading them into disaster. The only thing that kept him going was the thought of Abigail and Margaret coming to harm, and the certainty that behind all the mysterious betrayals of the last two weeks stood the Pantathian serpent priests.

17

City

Nicholas tensed.

The Serpent River had been cutting through marshlands for an hour, and now they were crossing a huge lake. The boat crew began rowing in earnest once they were in the lake, as the currents were diffusing into the large body of water. The tillerman leaned hard against his pole and the boat turned, toward the river emptying from the lake on the east side. Nicholas sat up straighter to get a better look at the distant city. Turning to Praji, he asked, 'Where are wę?'

'Lake of the Kings,' answered Praji.

'Why is it called that?' asked Nicholas.

Praji lay back against a bale of cargo while Vaja slept nearby; they were hardly ever apart, it seemed to Nicholas. 'This city started a long time ago as a meetin' place for the southern tribes of the Eastlands. Over the years the city built up and now you can't hardly tell the city men are kin to the Jeshandi and the other plains tribes.' Praji started cleaning his nails with the point of his dagger. 'Each tribe had a King, see, and each year it was a different tribe's turn to preside over the annual meetin'. That sort of turned into each year the city got a different King hell-bent on getting even for whatever the other Kings did to his tribe for the thirteen years before – fourteen big tribes, you see?

'Anyway, the folks who lived in the city got pretty tired of it after a couple of hundred years and there was a big revolt, and when it was over, all fourteen Kings and quite a number of their kinfolk was dumped into this here lake. That's why it's the Lake of the Kings.'

'What happened then?' asked Nicholas, as Marcus and Harry came to sit and listen. They were now about halfway across the lake and could see another river emptying out of it, a river that seemed to wind around to the east side of the city.

'Well, for a while they tried getting along without rulers, but after a few major fires and some riots where hundreds died, they decided that was a stupid idea, and they decided their clan chiefs could have this council. As there was members of the same clan in more than one tribe, that seemed fair, and nobody got too upset, and things was pretty good, as I hear it, for a few hundred years.'

'Then the Overlord showed up?' said Harry.

'Well, he was around for a while, I guess,' said Praji. He scratched his chin. 'I've heard a few stories here and there about who he was, but nobody knows for sure. It doesn't pay to ask questions in too many places.'

'Secret police?' asked Nicholas.

'Called the Black Rose, if you can swallow that. Run by somebody known only as "the Controller", and nobody knows who he is. Some folks figure it's what keeps Dahakon in check; others think Dahakon is the Controller. Nobody I know knows, that's a fact.'

Praji put up his knife. 'Here's what I do know about the Overlord. His name is Valgasha, which isn't a Jeshandi name, nor from anyplace I've ever been. He's a tall man, 'cause I seen him once on a parade day at the End of Summer Festival. Big as your friend Ghuda, I'd say. Looks about thirty, but I hear he looks like he did the day he took control, and with those stories about his magician, who knows. Has a pet eagle he hunts like a falcon. Folks say that it's a magic bird.'

Nicholas asked, 'How much longer to the city?'

Praji said, 'Not too much longer.' He pointed to a distant stand of trees on the far shore. 'Lake empties over there, into the river that leads around the city.'

Praji fell silent awhile, then said, 'When we get there, we'd best find you someplace to put up; a company's got to have a place potential employers can find it.' He said, 'You got any objection to simple living?'

Nicholas said, 'No. Why?'

'Well,' answered Praji, 'you've got more gold than sense, from what I can see, and a small company living too high is a beacon for trouble. Wouldn't do to put up at the priciest hostel in the city and have a couple of hundred fighters come visiting the second or third night. But if you live too plain, then folks will think you're broke or cheap.' He thought about it a minute, then said, 'I think I know the place. Just off the bazaar. Modest, not too dirty, and the hostler won't rob you blind.'

Nicholas smiled. 'I assume it's someplace we might be able to hear a thing or two?'

'You can assume all you like,' said Praji with his broken-toothed grin, 'but the trick isn't hearing stuff, it's sifting out the truth from the rumors from the lies.' He yawned. 'In twenty years on the road, I'll tell you I've never seen anyplace quite like the City of the Serpent River. Now, you take Maharta, for one. Clean city, brisk trading town, lot of civic pride. They call it the Queen City of the River, and yet a man can get murdered for a copper coin there as easily as anywhere else.' Praji continued his speculations on the strengths and weaknesses of different cities he had visited, while Nicholas watched the approaching city begin to take form in the distance. Where only a vague shadowy greyness had been visible on the horizon, now towers and walls began to be visible.

There were marshes all around the lake, and low rush beds, making it difficult to see where water ended and land began. Somewhere beyond the edge of the lake, a series of low earthen mounds rose, all barren except for a few tough-looking plants. To the right, the western side of the lake, the ground rose away from the marshes. Some broken masonry proclaimed that once someone had built there, but the area was completely deserted. Above it stood a small cliff face, perhaps fifty feet high, and on that Nicholas could see some activity, though it was too distant to make out what it was.

'Farms,' said Praji, as if reading Nicholas's mind. 'You'll see lots of small ones in close to the city, for protection. A few burned-out ones on the far side of the river. It's tough land to defend, and the Overlord's soldiers won't stir unless someone's attacking the walls or he's in the mood.' He spit over the side.

After a while they entered the eastern river and picked up speed as the currents increased. As they skirted the edge of the city, they saw a burned-out farmhouse on the east bank. 'I see what you mean,' said Nicholas.

'Wasn't raiders did that,' said Praji. He pointed to a hill a half-mile away upon which a large estate house rose, surrounded by a high wall. 'That's the estate of Dahakon. When he's not in the Overlord's palace, that's where you'll find him, though why anyone would want to is beyond me.' He made a good-luck sign. 'He decided the farm was too close to his estates and ordered it burned by the Red Slayers.'

After they passed under a bridge that led to the magician's estate, they entered an area of huts and houseboats clustered along both sides of the river. These were poor people by the look of things, fishermen, workers in the city who couldn't afford to live there, and some farmers with terraces of land behind their huts. Small boats darted here and there, running errands and carrying foodstuffs. From several of the boats, children waved and laughed as the river caravan passed, and Nicholas waved back.

The farther downriver they moved, the more boats

430

crowded around them. Near the landing, Nicholas saw that some of the riverside buildings were old, built up to two and even three stories high. From the balconies of several, women in varying states of dress sat, displaying themselves and calling out their names to the rivermen.

'Whores,' said Praji indifferently.

Nicholas blushed as one called out to him and suggested something he hadn't realized was possible. Praji saw him turning red and laughed. 'Captain,' he said dryly.

The eastern bank fell away as the river's mouth broadened, and they entered an estuary. Holding tightly to the right-hand shore, they followed it around until they encountered the first of a large series of docks and quays. A small boat cut across their bow, heading for a ship anchored out in deeper water, and the helmsman of Nicholas's boat cursed the man at the tiller of the smaller craft as they barely missed colliding.

Nicholas followed the craft and then his eyes settled on something in the harbor. 'Marcus,' he called.

Marcus moved forward. 'What?'

'Tell Amos to look over there.' He pointed.

Marcus looked, then nodded and went back to the stern of the boat. He shouted to the second boat, where Amos sat. 'Nicholas says to look over there.'

Amos shouted back. 'Tell him I already saw it. It's the same one.'

Marcus returned and said, 'Amos says it's the same one.'

Nicholas nodded. 'I thought so.'

Riding high at anchor, her hold empty, the black ship sat like a beacon for them. Nicholas turned to Marcus. 'We did make the right choice.'

Marcus put his hand on Nicholas's shoulder and said nothing.

* * *

They left the boats and made their way through the crowded dockside, down a broad street that led to a huge open-air bazaar. Praji and Vaja led the party through the press in the market, telling them to stay close lest they get lost.

Nicholas's senses were dazzled by the exotic display of costumes and wares. The people were as diverse as those in Krondor or the north of Kesh. Men and women of all colors, from fair-skinned and blond to dark as night, thronged the market, shouting the value of their wares and haggling over price. The dress of the locals was diverse enough that the outlandish dress of Nicholas's crew did not attract notice. Garish colors were common, so even Harry's choices of colors drew no attention.

Praji turned the company south at a large intersection of two open malls and down through another quarter of the bazaar. Soon they left the market and passed through a narrow street, to another, where they found themselves before the hostel. Praji entered with Nicholas and shouted, 'Keeler!'

A stout man, with a scar running down his left cheek, appeared from a back room. 'Praji!' he said, picking up a meat cleaver. Slamming it down into the wood of the bar for emphasis, he said, 'I thought I'd seen the last of your miserable face a month back.'

Praji shrugged. 'Got a better offer.' He indicated Nicholas with a bob of his head. 'This is my new captain.'

Keeler squinted at Nicholas through beady blue eyes, then scratched his stubbly chin. 'Very well. What do you need . . . Captain?'

'Quarters for forty of us.'

'I've room for fifty,' he said. 'Six private rooms that will hold up to four each and a common sleeping room for twenty-six. You can squeeze a few more in if you're friendly,' he added with a smile.

'We'll take them all,' answered Nicholas. 'I'm seeking

new recruits.' They had agreed that this story would give them a few days to sit and apparently do nothing. Mercenary companies did not tarry long between assignments, and to linger in the city beyond a few days would begin to attract suspicion. Nicholas and Keeler agreed on a price, and Nicholas gave the hostler a small pouch of gold as security against the bill.

Nicholas signaled to Harry, who stood at the door; Harry passed word and the company entered. The Ranjana threw Nicholas a black look as she came in with her maids and inspected the hostel common room. Nicholas had not shared with her the details of why the Overlord's soldiers had come to Shingazi's Landing. The girl had expected to be taken straight to the Overlord's palace and was outraged that she was being required to continue another day in Nicholas's company. Putting her under Brisa's watchful eye proved the proper solution; the Freeport street girl informed the Ranjana that if she caused a fuss, Brisa would be happy to cut her tongue out.

Once they were in their quarters, Nicholas inspected the hostel. They had use of the common room, its courtyards – which Nicholas judged would be sufficient for the men's drilling – the stable, which was currently empty, save for a shaggy donkey who viewed the approach of strangers with beatific indifference, and the common room. It was traditional for the company occupying a hostel to decide if the common room would be open to outsiders or not. That was the first topic of conversation for his first meeting with those he decided would act as staff: Marcus, Ghuda, and Amos, as well as Praji. Nicholas had concocted a story about their being from a very distant city on the other side of the continent, which Praji seemed to accept at face value; the lands between the city-states were so chaotic that men seldom traveled more than a few hundred miles from the place of their birth, and even widely traveled soldiers for hire such as Praji had journeyed only as far away as the city of Lanada, home of a Priest-King who was the current cause of regional unrest, for he was involved in a three-way war with the Raj of Maharta and the Overlord of the City of the Serpent River.

Nicholas sat with his lieutenants in the common room, while Harry oversaw getting the men into their rooms and stowing their gear. Nicholas said, 'Praji, what's the best choice? Keep the commons open or close it?'

Praji said, 'If you close it, with you not being well known, that'll make people curious. If you open it, you can figure that within an hour of sunset this place will be crawling with whores, thieves, pickpockets, beggars, and a bunch of spies for different clans, guilds, factions, and other companies.'

Nicholas said, 'Amos, what do you think?'

Amos shrugged. 'It's been my experience in places like this that you can either go out and look for information or wait and let it come to you.'

Nicholas nodded. 'Let's open up the commons, but I want it made clear that any man who drinks too much and says the wrong thing is going to answer to me.' He tried to sound menacing, but felt foolish. Still, no one at the table smiled at the remark.

Looking at Praji, Nicholas asked, 'Why would other companies come snooping around?'

Praji says, 'Maybe you've a contract they can poach. If you're onto something big, then maybe they can cut a better deal with your contract holder; maybe they're going out on a job that needs a bigger company and they're looking for another small company or two to join forces with.' Praji fixed Nicholas with a steady gaze. 'You don't need to tell me what you're here for, as long as we're getting paid and you don't get us hung for something I didn't have anything to do with, but for a company of mercenaries you're looking pretty raw.' He hiked a thumb toward Ghuda. 'He looks like he knows his way around, but the others' – he glanced over his shoulder to where a pair of sailors from Amos's ship were entering the commons – 'they're somethin' else. From the way they jump to when they get orders, and keep to themselves and never get into serious arguments or fights, regular army is my guess.'

Nicholas said, 'You're no fool.'

'Never said I was. I just let people guess what they will, and usually it's to my advantage.' Gesturing to where the bulk of the men were making ready their quarters, he added, 'Those boys are probably good soldiers, but as mercenaries they don't look convincing. Now, Ghuda's a convincing mercenary.'

Praji looked Nicholas in the eyes. 'There are three types of captains: the first are mean bastards who'll scare their men into doing what they tell them to; the second are the kind that make their men rich; the third are the kind that men follow anywhere, because their captain keeps them alive. You don't look convincing being the first; sorry, but you couldn't scare my old granny. You're not throwing gold around and wearing jewels on your fingers, so no one will think you're making your men rich – so you better work on convincing anyone who asks that you're the third kind.'

Nicholas said, 'I've studied tactics and strategy all my life, Praji, and I've led men into combat.' He didn't add that his experience began only a few days before meeting Praji.

Standing up, Praji said, 'You talk a good fight. When you want to tell me what's going on, I'll tell you if Vaja and I want in. Until then I'm going to get some sleep.'

After he was gone, Nicholas said, 'Can we trust him?'

Ghuda said, 'Well, he's not the type to swear undying loyalty to the crown, but he'll fight for whoever holds his bond, or,' he added with a grin, 'against whoever ends up on his "list". I think he's what he seems to be.'

Marcus said, 'What next?'

'We need to find out where the prisoners were taken. With that many prisoners being offloaded here, someone had to see where they've gone. We just need to be careful in how we ask.'

Amos said, 'I think I should nose around down at the docks.'

'Take Marcus with you, and start looking for a ship to steal.'

Amos grinned. 'We're pirates again?'

Nicholas returnd the smile. 'As soon as we find out where Margaret, Abigail, and the others are, we're buccaneers.'

Amos and Marcus left, and Nicholas said, 'Ghuda, can you make the men look more like mercenaries?'

Ghuda stood up as Harry and Brisa walked into the commons. As they approached the table, Ghuda said, 'I'll talk to all of them in twos and threes and give them some idea of what to expect and how to act.'

'Thanks,' said Nicholas as he left.

Harry and Brisa sat down and he said, 'All right, what do we do now?'

Nicholas said, 'Well, first thing, I've got to figure out what to do with the Ranjana.'

Brisa said, 'Sell her to someone.' From her cheerful smile, Nicholas was almost sure she was joking.

Harry said, 'Why not hang on to her for a while and see if we need to get into the palace?'

'I don't understand,' said Nicholas.

'Look,' said Harry, 'it's hard for me to imagine that a ship like that could come sailing into this harbor with a couple of hundred captives and not involve some official notice. Maybe this Overlord's in on this thing himself.' He shrugged. 'If he is, what better way to get in to see him than to bring him his wife-to-be?'

'But he tried to kill her,' Nicholas pointed out.

Brisa said, 'That was out there.' She waved in the general direction of the north. 'He can't very well kill her in the palace and blame it on the clans, can he?'

Harry nodded. 'The palace is the safest place for her in the city.' He leaned forward. 'Look, hang on to her for a couple of days, and if we don't need to go to the palace, you can pack her off back to her father on the next river caravan heading north. If you do need to get in, she's your entrance.'

'Seems pretty indifferent to the girl,' said Nicholas.

Brisa snorted. 'Girl? That bitch has a hide tough as a turtle's shell. Never mind the big eyes and pouty mouth, Nicky, she'd cut your heart out and smile while doing it. She may look like someone's spoiled darling, but there's a toughness in her you surely can see, given you hardly look at her above the neck.'

Nicholas's eyes narrowed. 'Wait a minute!'

Brisa waved the objection away. 'She's a beauty, I know, but she's not what she seems.'

Harry nodded. 'I've talked to her and there's something . . . cold about her.'

Nicholas decided to ignore Brisa's accusation. 'Well, I won't decide anything today. Why don't you start snooping around. Brisa, you know your way around streets like these, and Harry, you can scrounge a bit.' He took some gold out of his purse and pushed it across the table toward him. 'Buy anything you think we might need – and take Anthony with you to replenish his supplies.' He looked around. 'Speaking of which, where is he, and where is Nakor?'

Harry said, 'I saw Anthony in one of the back rooms looking over Vaja's wound. I haven't seen Nakor since we got here.'

Nicholas waved them off and sat alone with his own

437

thoughts for a while. Calis appeared and sat down unbidden, saying, 'You look troubled.'

Glancing around the room, Nicholas said, 'Let's go for a stroll.'

They rose and left the common room, entering the short street that led directly to the bazaar.

The bazaar was a giant square, divided by an open roadway running north and south, and by another running east and west. At the intersection a large plaza had been built, and on the steps of that plaza an assortment of beggars, fortune-tellers, and entertainers clustered. The road leading from Keeler's hostel entered the bazaar from the south. There were a half-dozen roads entering from all sides, save the east, which fronted on a wall that marked the outer boundary of the Overlord's palace.

Entering the press of humanity that thronged the bazaar, they passed by stalls erected for the day and listened to the calls to examine pottery, jewelry, sweets, cloth, and every other imaginable commodity. Calis said nothing as Nicholas made a pretense of examining some of the weapons that were being offered by a one-legged man. As they pushed past a fruit seller's cart, Nicholas said, 'I'm feeling . . . out of place.'

Calis nodded. 'I understand.'

'Do you?' asked Nicholas, looking at the half-elf.

'I'm a little older than your older brothers, yet I look your age,' said Calis. 'Yet, to my people, I'm little more than a child.' He glanced around the bazaar. 'All this is alien to me. I've visited Crydee many times in my life, and save for when your uncle Martin and Garret or the occasional ranger from Natal visited Elvandar, I've never spoken to a human for more than one or two evenings at a time.

'Yes, I know what it is to feel out of place.' Then he gave Nicholas a rare smile and said, 'But that's not what you're talking about, is it?'

Nicholas shook his head. 'No. I feel like an impostor pretending to be Captain to a company of mercenaries.'

Calis shrugged. 'You shouldn't. At least, I don't think you should. The others have accepted your leadership and so far you've done nothing to show their judgment is wrong.'

He paused as they moved aside to let a wagon full of slaves drive past. Nicholas scanned the faces of those in the wagon on the off chance he might recognize someone. The slaves kept their eyes down and their expressions placid, as if they knew their lives were forever under the control of others.

Nicholas watched after the wagon a moment, then said, 'Thank you. I guess that if I play the part well enough, it's of little consequence how I feel about it.'

Calis smiled slightly. 'You're a great deal like your uncle Martin; he ponders things. It's ironic, but you're probably more like him in many regards than Marcus.'

Nicholas smiled slightly. 'That would be ironic.'

They spent a half hour wandering through the bazaar, dazzled by the astonishing assortment of merchandise offered, until they found themselves near the plaza at the center. There they were assailed by beggars asking for gifts in exchange for blessings, and curses followed after them when they turned a deaf ear. Fortune-tellers offered to read their future in cards, bones, or smoke, and they, too, were ignored.

As they circled the plaza, they came to another quarter of the bazaar that was drawing a large crowd. They worked their way through the crowd to find a large platform erected halfway between the plaza and the wall of the Overlord's palace. The crowd spread out to about a dozen yards from the wall, then left a clearing. Glancing up, Nicholas saw cages hanging from the wall. In the cages were bodies, a pair of skeletons, and one man who moved feebly. Calis followed his gaze and said, 'Death by exposure is the local choice, I see.'

'And a clear message to everyone in the city: don't cause trouble,' said Nicholas. He turned his back and looked at those upon the platform.

An auctioneer was offering slaves for inspection. Nicholas glanced from face to face, half hoping, half fearing to see someone he recognized from Crydee, but after a few minutes he decided these wretched were natives of the city. A few young girls brought spirited bidding, as did one particularly strong-looking man of middle years, but the rest of the slaves were either too old or too young to be of profit.

Disgusted with the entire proceedings, Nicholas said, 'Come along. Let's return to the hostel.'

They made their way back to the north side of the bazaar, and half-way to the hostel, they saw people clearing the way for an advancing company of men. A boy beat a drum at the van, while behind him marched a man carrying a pole. Upon the top of the pole two ropes descended to the ends of a rod, from which hung a banner, a long piece of grey cloth on which a red hawk stooping over its prey was sewn. Nicholas and Calis stepped aside to allow them to pass and watched as two hundred armed men strode by. As they moved away, Nicholas turned to a man following after them and said, 'Who was that?'

'Captain Haji's Redhawks.' The man looked at Nicholas as if he was crazy to have asked, and hurried along.

Nicholas said, 'I guess Tuka wasn't exaggerating about the need to announce ourselves.'

'Perhaps,' said Calis, 'when we know what it is we wish to have known about us.'

'Good point.'

They returned to the hostel and found that Marcus and Amos had returned. Nicholas sat at the table with them, while Calis went to his room. 'That was quick,' said

Nicholas. 'Did you find a ship?'

Amos lowered his voice, so Keeler, who was tending bar, couldn't overhear. 'There are any number of ships that will do, now we know how long the voyage takes, but there are two Kingdom ships in the harbor.'

'What?' said Nicholas.

Marcus said, 'And one of them is the *Raptor*.'

Nicholas stood on the end of the quay and stared in open-mouthed amazement.

Amos said, 'Close it, or you'll start to catch flies.'

'How is this possible?'

Amos said, 'Look closely. She's not really how we turned her out. There are some slight differences. And I'd never rig her quite that loose, even at anchor. Sudden wind, and you'll lose a spar. And some of the shrouds and sheets are not right. She's a copy of the *Royal Eagle*, and someone's tried to turn her into the *Raptor*.' He then pointed to the other ship, slightly smaller, but otherwise the twin of the first. 'That's either an exact copy of the *Royal Gull*, or the real one.'

'I thought the real one sank off the Keshian coast in a storm two years ago,' said Nicholas.

'That's what I thought, but maybe not.'

Nicholas nodded. 'That still doesn't answer the big question.'

Amos said, 'Yes. Why are they here?'

The three of them said nothing more as they walked back to the hostel.

Back there, Nicholas asked several of the men if they had seen Nakor. All of them answered no; the little man had vanished shortly after the company had arrived.

Nicholas decided to return to the room he had secured for himself, to rest awhile and ponder the mystery of those two ships in the harbor. As he passed the door to the Ranjana's quarters, a shriek caused him to halt.

As he reached for the door, it opened and a frightened maid said, 'Master. Please.'

Nicholas entered the room to find the other three maids all cowering in the corner while the Ranjana picked up a brush from the table she used as a vanity and threw it at them. 'I will not stay here a minute longer!' she shouted.

Nicholas said, 'Lady – '

Before another word could come out of his mouth, he was ducking a wicked-looking hair comb, three tines of gold, but sharp enough to cause harm. He stepped forward and grabbed the girl by one wrist, which proved a tactical mistake, as he then felt her other hand hard across his face. Grabbing the free hand, he shouted, 'Stop this, lady!'

She began kicking him in the shins, and he shoved her away with enough force to cause her to sit hard on the floor. Pointing his finger at her, he said, 'That will be enough!'

She was up and at him again, and he pushed her back hard on the floor. The second time she hit the hardwood, her eyes widened in astonishment. 'You *dare* lay hands upon me!'

'I'll do more than that if you don't tell me what this ruckus is about,' said Nicholas, his voice harsh.

'I demand to be taken at once to the palace,' said the Ranjana. 'I spoke to one of your men, and he had the temerity to tell me to wait until you'd returned.' She stood up. 'I want him hung. Now, take me to the palace.'

'There's a problem with that,' said Nicholas.

'Problem!' shrieked the girl. She formed claws with her fingernails and came at Nicholas. He grabbed her wrists again and said, 'Will you stop!' The girl continued to struggle, clearly intent on removing his eyes from his head. At last he pushed her back even harder than before, so that when she hit the floor she slid backward until she struck the wall.

Before she could move, he advanced to stand over her. '*Don't get up!*' he warned. 'Just sit there and listen, or I will have you tied up!'

She sat, but her expression was defiant. 'Why won't you take me to the palace?'

Nicholas sighed. 'I was hoping to avoid this, but I guess you must know. I'm not taking you to the palace because it appears that the man responsible for the attack upon you was the Overlord himself.'

'That's impossible. I am to wed the Overlord on the next Summer's End Night.'

Nicholas saw that the fight had gone out of her, and leaned over to offer his hand. She slapped it away and stood up without help. As he watched her stand with a dancer's grace, Nicholas was forced to admit that Brisa wasn't entirely wrong. Given her choice of fashion, skimpy tops and light skirts, leaving her midriff bare, her body was displayed to good advantage, and it was an exceptionally nice body. But her mood was as ugly as the rest of her was lovely. 'You're lying,' she said. 'You want to hold me for ransom.'

Nicholas sighed. 'If that were true, I'd simply lock the door and put a guard outside your window. No, if we discover that the Overlord is the man who tried to have you killed, we'll arrange for you to travel back to your father – '

'No,' interrupted the Ranjana. There was genuine panic in her voice.

'No?'

'No. My father would kill me.'

Nicholas said, 'Why would he do that?'

'My father the Raj has thirty-nine wives. I am the youngest daughter of his seventeenth wife.' She lowered her eyes and said, 'My only value to him is to be married to an ally. If I return, he will be enraged and order me beheaded. I would be of no further value, for to send me to another ally for marriage after offering me to the Overlord would be an insult.'

'Well, maybe the Overlord didn't have anything to do with the attack, and if not, we'll get you to the palace.'

Nicholas was confused by all this, for the girl suddenly looked vulnerable and afraid, and his feelings were churning unexpectedly. Feeling irritation at this sudden attack of concern, he said, 'I'll do what I can.' He turned and quickly left the room. Finding himself in the hall with no idea what he had been doing before he had entered the girl's room, he returned to the common room to wait for Harry and Brisa.

By two hours after sundown the common room was crowded with both Nicholas's company and strangers. He had selected a table for himself and his companions nearest the hall leading to the sleeping rooms. Harry, Anthony, and Brisa still hadn't returned, and no one had caught sight of Nakor since before they had reached the hostel. Nicholas was beginning to worry.

Twice mercenaries had approached to ask if there was room for new recruits in Nicholas's company. He was noncommittal and said it depended on a possible contract and they should come back in a few days.

The food provided was filling and hot, if not especially tasty, and the wine was above average, which suited everyone in the company; it was a great improvement over the beans and bread they had eaten every night on the boats, along with a cold piece of salted pork. As they were eating, Harry, Anthony, and Brisa at last returned.

They sat down and Nicholas said, 'What kept you so long?'

Harry smiled. 'It's a big city.'

'Did you have to see all of it in one day?' asked Amos with a grin.

Harry said, 'We didn't see a tenth, but we did find out some interesting things, or more to the point, Anthony and Brisa did.'

Anthony said, 'I've found a man selling magic charms down by the docks. He's a fraud, of course, and his trinkets are useless, but he did let loose with some gossip about the Overlord and his Grand Adviser.'

Nicholas leaned forward as Anthony's voice dropped. 'Praji wasn't joking about the ban on magic. One of the things the trinket seller told me is there's a ward on the city that alerts this Dahakon if anyone uses magic within the walls of the city. At least, that's the rumor. He claimed a special property of the trinkets was their ability to work without alerting the Adviser.' Anthony shook his head. 'Anyone want this?' he said, taking a strange-looking fetish out of his pocket. It was a man with a giant penis. 'It's supposed to make one irresistible to women.' He blushed as Brisa laughed, her hand over her mouth.

'Anthony, I must have you,' she said jokingly.

Nicholas wasn't amused. 'Put that away. What that means is you can't use your powers to find the girls.'

'Girls?' said Harry.

'The prisoners,' said Anthony. His blush continued. 'I have been able to locate Margaret and Abigail,' he said.

Nicholas knew he was stretching the truth a bit because of Harry's interest in Margaret, but thought that was a pretty trivial consideration now. He said, 'What else did you find out?'

Brisa said, 'There's something like an organization of thieves around. You're from Krondor, so you've heard of the Mockers.'

Nicholas nodded.

Brisa said, 'It's something like that, but I have a feeling from what we've seen that it's a lot less efficient and probably less powerful.'

'Why?' asked Nicholas.

'I've never seen so many armed men in a square mile in my life, not even in Freeport, and half of them belong to one clan or another or to the Overlord.'

Harry said, 'She's right, Nicky. There are soldiers everywhere, and everyone has a bodyguard or guards on his house or mercenaries. It's like Ghuda said, it's an armed camp here.'

Nicholas considered. Krondor had its number of private guards and mercenaries working for merchants and nobles, but most citizens went unarmed in all but the Poor Quarter or the docks at night, for the city watch and the Prince's garrison kept the peace and kept the Mockers somewhat under control. Also, he had learned from his father that the guild of thieves liked things orderly, for any martial law crimped their business severely.

Nicholas asked, 'Did you find out anything in the slave market?'

'Not enough to talk about,' said Harry. 'It was difficult. If you weren't buying, you were looked on with suspicion. One thing, the wall behind the slave market is marked off by a white line a dozen yards away from it. Did you see that?'

Nicholas said, 'Calis and I wandered over that way, but I didn't notice it.'

Harry said, 'It's a deadline.'

Nicholas nodded. He knew that meant there were archers on the walls or soldiers in the market with orders to kill anyone who crossed the line. 'The Overlord doesn't want anyone freeing the condemned,' said Nicholas.

'Or he doesn't want unexpected visitors,' offered Brisa.

Amos said, 'If you ran this city of cut-throats, would you?'

Nicholas said, 'If I ran it, it would run differently.'

Amos laughed. 'You're not the first to think that before taking the job. Ask your father sometime about the deals he made with the Mockers early on in his reign.'

Nicholas asked Brisa, 'Do you think you can make contact with the local thieves?'

'It might take a couple of days,' she answered. 'There's a hunted-dog look about half the people here.' She lowered her voice even more. 'My guess is you've got a half-dozen informants and spies in this room already. There's not a lot of trust in this city.'

Nicholas said, 'Well, eat, drink, be merry . . .' He let the old saying go without finishing it.

Margaret awoke with a start, her heart pounding. Something caused her to turn slowly toward the other bed. A figure loomed over her in the darkness of the room. Blinking, she strained to make out the figure in the gloom.

When she sat up, her sudden movement startled the figure, which pulled back. She reached for a shuttered lamp, which was kept burning low at night, and opened the shutter. Sitting on the floor next to the bed was one of the two lizard creatures. It shielded its dark eyes against the light and scuttled backward, making soft sounds.

Margaret froze, her mouth open as she drew in a gasp of fear. The creature had spoken a word, softly. It had said, 'No.' But what terrified Margaret was the sound: it was nothing alien or inhuman. The voice had belonged to a human woman. The voice sounded like her own.

18

Secrets

Nicholas looked up.

Coming across the room was the wagon driver, Tuka, and a florid-faced, puffing man of imposing girth, dressed in a riot of colors: a yellow overtunic, a plaid shirt, red trousers, a green sash, and a purple hat in the fashion of the area, with a wide brim rolled up on either side to hug the crown.

Ghuda asked, 'Harry, did someone steal your clothes last night?'

Harry yawned, not being quite awake after having drunk an unusual amount of ale for him. 'Looks like it,' said the Squire from Ludland. 'Mine were in better taste, though.'

Ghuda and Amos refrained from comment, watching the strange pair as they approached.

'Encosi,' said Tuka, 'with humility I am presenting Anward Nogosh Pata, my master's representative in the city.'

Without leave, the man sat at the only remaining chair at Nicholas's table and whispered, 'Is it true?'

'Is what true?' responded Harry.

Nicholas waved away Harry's question and said, 'Yes. We have the girl.'

The man blew out his cheeks as he exhaled and drummed his fingers upon the table. 'I've known Tuka for years, and while he's no more reliable than any other driver, he's not intelligent enough to fabricate such a wicked tale of betrayal and murder by himself.' Leaning across the table, he lowered his voice even more. 'What do you mean to do? Ransom? Reward?'

Nicholas frowned. 'What would you have me do?' he asked.

The man resumed his finger-drumming on the table. 'I'm uncertain. If my master falls prey to some plot to create friction between the clans – many of whom have strong ties to important trading houses here and in other cities – few of those clansmen may be inclined to remember that my master was merely a dupe in some larger plot.' He made a wide gesture with his hands while he shrugged. 'And truth to tell, my master would be less than pleased to be named a dupe – for all his more excellent qualities, he is not without his vanity – and the effect such an appellation would have upon his trade could not be considered salubrious.'

Nicholas said, 'There are matters of concern to my men and me that might have some impact upon this matter.'

'You propose?' asked Anward.

'To do nothing for a few days,' answered Nicholas. 'We've surmised that if the Overlord's hand is in this series of attacks and murder, the girl's life is worthless in the palace, but if she's the prize in a game we don't understand, that may be the safest place in the world for her. Let me ask you something: what would your master's reaction be to sending her back?'

'He would not be pleased, but that displeasure would be for the failure of the undertaking, and if the undertaking was doomed from the outset because of duplicity, he would be disinclined to place blame needlessly.'

'Would the girl's father punish her?'

'Her father has many daughters, it's true, but he values all of them. No, he wouldn't harm her. Why do you ask?'

Thinking quickly, Nicholas said, 'Just making sure I understand all the stakes of the game.'

'What of the precious gifts that accompanied the Ranjana?'

'They are all safe,' said Nicholas.

449

'I shall send a wagon and guards to recover my master's wares.'

Nicholas held up his hand. 'I would prefer it if you would wait a little. I don't think anyone who saw us arrive suspected we had anything to do with all the murder upriver, but you can never be sure. If we are being watched, I don't want to advertise that we found any treasure or the Ranjana. Let them think the girls with us were our camp followers.' When Anward looked at him suspiciously, Nicholas said, 'You have my word; when the Ranjana leaves here, she takes all her gold and jewels with her.'

The factor rose, saying, 'I will employ caution, but I shall set about seeking information about who is truly responsible for this misery. You will be here awhile?'

'A few days.'

Bowing in respect: 'I bid you good day, Captain.'

When Tuka didn't follow him, Ghuda said, 'You got the heave-ho?'

The little wagon driver shrugged. 'It was so, Sab. I am discharged from service for failing to protect my master's cargo, but for having returned with the news of the Ranjana's presence here in the city I am not being beaten or killed.'

Marcus said, 'I take it work is hard to come by around here?'

Amos said, 'It must be, for workers to put up with such treatment.'

'Very hard, Sab,' answered Tuka. He looked genuinely downcast as he added, 'I may have to turn to thievery to eat.'

Nicholas couldn't help but smile at the little man's comic pose. 'I don't think you have the knack for it.' Tuka nodded in agreement. Nicholas went on, 'Tell you what. You've done us some good service, so why don't you work for us while we're in the city. We'll make sure you don't starve.'

Tuka's face lit up. 'Encosi has need of a wagon driver?'

'Not so you'd notice,' said Nicholas. 'But I do need someone who knows his way around this land, and we don't know a lot of people here. What did they pay you?'

'A Serpent River copper pastoli a week and my food, and permission to sleep under the wagon.'

Nicholas frowned. 'I'm not familiar with local currency.' He dug a few coins out of his pouch, one of those taken from Shingazi's Landing. Laying them on the table, he asked, 'Which is the pastoli?'

Tuka's eyes widened at the coins. 'This one, Encosi.' He pointed to the smallest copper coin in the bunch.

'What of the others?' asked Ghuda.

If Tuka thought it strange that mercenaries didn't understand the worth of the local coins, he said nothing. 'This is the stolesti,' he said, pointing to a larger copper piece. 'It is being worth ten pastolis.' He went through the others, the twenty-stolesti silver kathanri, and the golden drakmasti, or, simply, a drak. The rest were coins from other cities, and Tuka explained that so much alien currency was in use it was common to pay by type of coin and weight as much as by official value; most merchants had their own touchstones and no money changers as such existed. Nicholas tossed him a stolesti and said, 'Go buy yourself something to eat and a clean tunic.'

The little man bowed furiously and said, 'Encosi is most generous.' He hurried out of the common room.

Marcus said, 'I thought the poor in the Kingdom didn't have much, but that's poor.'

Ghuda said, 'They pay wagon drivers about a tenth of what they make in Kesh.'

Nicholas frowned. 'Trade was never a strong subject of mine, but my guess is that all the fighting and disruption

451

of trade means few jobs, and a great deal of pressure to make profit.' He shrugged. 'Cheap labor.'

Ghuda nodded.

Amos said, 'Which means one good thing.'

'What?' asked Nicholas.

'Bribes will go further here,' he said with a grin. 'And it means we're not simply well off with Shingazi's treasure, we're rich, very rich.'

Nicholas said, 'That's good, but it doesn't get us any closer to finding the prisoners.'

'That's true,' said Amos.

Nicholas said, 'Where are Harry and Brisa? They should have been back by now.' He had sent them back into the bazaar to see if Brisa could make contact with the local thieves and beggars. 'And where the hell is Nakor?'

Ghuda shrugged. 'Nakor? He'll show up. He always does.'

Nakor entered the palace. A few minutes earlier, he had spotted a band of monks heading there just as he was wondering how he might get inside. Taking note of their attire, yellow and orange robes, cut short at knee and elbow, with a black sash across the shoulder, he quickly improvised. He fell in step behind the last monk, turning his rucksack around so that it looked as if he carried a bundle, with a black sash over his shoulder, and instantly he was another monk from the order of Agni – which he knew was the local name for Prandur, the fire god – and walked boldly into the palace past a pair of Red Slayers at the doors.

He glanced out of the corner of his eye at one as he passed, and compared him to Amos's description of Murmandamus's Black Slayers during the Riftwar. Amos, the only member of the company who had seen one, had told Nicholas and the others about them after finding the helm at Shingazi's Landing. These Red Slayers were motionless, covered from neck to boots in red chain mail. Their helms entirely covered their heads, with two narrow eyes slits. Atop the crest a dragon crouched, his wings descending to form the sides of the helm. The dragon's eyes were either onyx or sapphires, Nakor couldn't be certain, and he wasn't about to take a closer look. Each guard wore a red tabard with a black circle in the center, in which a golden serpent with a red eye formed an S.

The entrance to the palace was a long passage through what Nakor assumed was a massive outer wall. Then they were under open sky and crossing an ancient bailey, to enter the central palace proper. They climbed some steps to a broad entranceway, between high columns that held an out-thrusting third story aloft. Atop that was a low battlement with defensive arrow slits. Nakor noticed that the attempt at some sort of classical style hadn't completely abandoned the concerns of defense. On the whole, he judged the Overlord's abode a particularly ugly place.

They marched into the great hall, where others were already assembled. Conventional soldiers lined the hall, dressed in black with the same serpent design on their tabards, as a dozen orders of clerics had gathered ahead of the Fire Monks. A hundred or so wealthy-looking men, some traders by their fashion, and the others important captains of mercenary companies, milled around the formal assembly of monks and priests.

Nakor fell a step behind the last monk of Agni as they took up their position to one side of the giant courtyard. They lined up so that Nakor was even with two guards standing before giant columns of carved marble. He glanced to the right and left, then took a step backward, putting himself behind the two guards. He turned and smiled in a friendly fashion to a merchant who was watching him, then gestured for the man to take his place, as if he might get a better view. The man smiled his thanks and stepped forward to occupy Nakor's former spot. Nakor ducked into the shadow of a column to observe the ceremony.

Across the room, a number of men and women entered between large curtains to the rear of a high dais; the last was an impressive figure, clearly six inches over six feet tall. He was heavily muscled but not fat, looking more on the lean side if anything. His face was long and would have been handsome if there had not been something cruel in the eyes and the set of the mouth, evident even from Nakor's distant vantage point. There was no doubt this was the Overlord. He wore a simple purple toga, cut short at the knees, which displayed his powerful physique to good effect. He raised a gloved hand and whistled. An answering shriek sounded from high above in the vault of the hall and the flap of wings accompanied the descent of an eagle. Nakor looked at the black bird, a young golden eagle. Though young, the bird was big enough that only the strongest man could hold it long upon his wrist. Yet the Overlord bore the creature with ease.

Entering next were two women, both dressed in provocative fashion. One was blond, wearing a halter top of silk embroidered with gold thread and rubies. Her only other clothing was a sheer white skirt that hung from the hipbone, gathered up to reveal one long leg as she walked, and held in place by a giant ruby and gold pin. Her hair was pulled behind her head with a gold clasp and fell to her shoulders. She had pale skin and, Nakor assumed, blue eyes, but he couldn't tell at this distance. She was by any standard a strikingly beautiful woman, if too young for Nakor's taste. She moved close to the tall man's side, but kept a pace behind.

The other was equally beautiful, though older. Her hair was black, but her skin was almost as fair as the first's. She wore a short red vest, partially open in front, showing an ample glimpse of a high bosom. Her skirt was cut in similar fashion to the other woman's, but black. Her

jewelry was no less ornate, sapphires and gold, though
her skirt clasp was set with a single emerald. She joined a
black-robed man who pushed back the robe's hood,
revealing his face. He had a bald head and wore a gold
ring through his nose. She took the man's arm.

A herald called, 'Gather and attend, O holy men and
women. Our gracious Overlord requires your counsel, for
a feast is needed. He takes a wife, the Ranjana of Kilbar,
and would have ceremony and celebration during the next
End of Spring Festival.'

The expression of the young blonde showed she was
not in the least pleased at this announcement, but she
kept her place quietly behind the Overlord.

The herald called, 'The Lady Clovis.'

All eyes shifted to the dark-haired woman as she spoke.
'My lord Dahakon asks that you all bless this union and
prepare those ceremonnies that you deem appropriate for
such a state occasion.' The man whom Nakor took to be
Dahakon stood motionless and silent.

Very interesting, thought Nakor.

The Warlord began to speak, and Nakor listened carefully. He moved slowly behind the row of columns that
supported a gallery above the hall and followed it down
to the corner. There he ducked deeper into the darkness
and slowly made his way toward the dais, to get a better
look.

Harry and Brisa entered the inn. They made their way
through the crowded room and Harry indicated to Nicholas that he should join them in one of the back rooms.
Nicholas motioned for the others at his table to remain,
and followed them into the hall.

They entered Nicholas's room and Brisa whispered.
'We've found where the prisoners have been taken.'

'Where?' asked Nicholas softly.

Harry said, 'That estate we saw across the river.'

'Are you sure?'

Harry grinned. 'Brisa took the better part of the day and half the evening, but we finally found one of the Ragged Brotherhood – '

'Who?'

'Thieves,' said Brisa. 'That's what they're known as. Not much to speak of, mostly beggars and a few pickpockets. All the really good thieves work alone or are hunted down by the Overlord's men and killed.'

Nicholas said, 'Harry, go get Calis and Marcus.'

Harry left, and while he was gone, Nicholas asked, 'Anything else of interest?'

Brisa shrugged. 'I don't know much about cities. I've lived all my life in Freeport, and that's nothing to judge by, but if there's a more miserable pesthole on the planet than this place, including Durbin, I've never heard of it.'

She frowned, and Nicholas asked, 'What?'

'Just . . . something one of the beggars said. While I was getting on his good side, convincing him I wasn't one of the Overlord's "Black Roses", he said he only thieved where it was permitted.'

'Permitted?'

'Later I asked another thief what he meant, and was told that there's sort of an unofficial set of rules about where you can get away with thieving and where you're likely to find yourself in the cage.' She shivered. 'Nasty way to go. You hang there getting frozen at night, roasted during the day, can't quite sit or stand, seeing everyone down in the square going about their business and always feeling like somehow it's not real.'

'You sound as if you've thought a lot about this,' said Nicholas.

'Show me a thief who hasn't thought about getting caught, and I'll show you a stupid thief.' She made a face. 'Truth to tell, we're all stupid. We think about getting caught, but none of us ever think *we'll* get caught.'

Nicholas smiled slightly. 'That's pretty self-critical.'

Brisa shrugged. 'I've been around Harry too much lately.' She grinned. 'He's trying to reform me.'

Just then the door opened and Harry, Calis, and Marcus entered. Nicholas told Calis and Marcus what he had been told, then said, 'Wait until late tonight, and see if you can get across the river without being seen. I don't know how close you can get to that place unobserved –'

Calis said, 'I can get very close.'

' – but see if you can obtain any idea where our people are being held.'

Calis said, 'If I go alone, I can do it much better.'

Nicholas raised an eyebrow. Then he remembered the game in the forest, and glanced at Marcus.

'He probably can,' said Marcus. He looked at Calis, who was regarding him with a sardonic smile. 'Oh, very well. He can.'

Nicholas paused, then said, 'Go with him halfway. I want someone close enough to give him some help if he's coming away from that place in a hurry.'

Calis smiled. 'Thank you for the concern. I hope it won't be warranted.' He told Marcus, 'We should leave now and take our time reaching that burned-out farmhouse. I can scout from there.'

They left. Nicholas turned to see Harry standing with his arm around Brisa's waist in a familiar fashion. 'Oh?' he said, eyebrows rising.

Harry said, 'Oh, what?' He noticed he had his arm around the girl and said, 'Oh!' as he disengaged himself.

With a wry smile, Brisa said, 'Nothing to get excited about, Nicholas. I'm just contributing to Harry's education.'

She sauntered out of the room, closing the door behind her, leaving Harry blushing and Nicholas looking at his friend. 'I wonder about you,' said Nicholas.

Harry's blush deepened. 'Well, we've been spending a

lot of time together, and she's really very pretty if you look past all those terrible clothes and dirt she wears.'

Nicholas put up his hands. 'You don't have to explain.' He glanced at the door, as if he could see through it. 'I find that lately Abigail is hard to remember.' He shook his head. 'Funny, isn't it?'

Harry shrugged. 'I don't think so. We haven't seen Abigail or Margaret for months and . . .' He shrugged again.

'And Brisa in your bed is a little more real than Margaret in your dreams?' supplied Nicholas.

'Something like that.' Then he looked as if he was growing angry. 'But it's more than that. She's a decent girl, Nicky. If you or I had it as rough as she's had it when we were children, we wouldn't have half her worth. And I know I can get her to stop being a thief.' Nicholas again put up his hands. Harry said, 'Besides, Anthony's in love with Margaret, really in love with her.'

'You figured it out?'

Harry grinned. 'Took me a while, but I finally figured out it was one of the two girls he was focusing on when he did that spell. Then I remembered that he was pretty relaxed when he was around Abigail, but Margaret made him fidget like crazy.'

'Where is Anthony?'

'He went looking for Nakor,' said Harry.

Nicholas made an aggravated sound. 'And where is Nakor? It's been two days now.'

Harry had no answer.

'I wish they'd stop that,' said Abigail.

Margaret nodded. 'I know. It's unnerving.'

The two creatures sat nearby, mimicking the girls' movements as they ate dinner. If Margaret cut her meat with a knife, one of the creatures imitated the motion on an imagined plate and table.

The two creatures stayed a comfortable distance from the girls during the day, never coming closer than arm's reach. But they constantly studied the two girls and now they were doing these irritating mimicries.

Margaret pushed aside the empty plate and said, 'I don't know why I'm eating so much; we don't do anything. Yet I don't seem to be putting on weight.'

Abigail said, 'I know. I don't want to, but I'm not going to be held down and force-fed again.' She dutifully chewed a mouthful of food and swallowed, then said, 'And have you ever seen them eat anything?'

'No,' said Margaret. 'I thought maybe they were fed after we slept.'

Abigail said, 'And I've not seen them . . . you know.'

Margaret smiled a wry smile. 'Use the chamber pot,' she said.

Abigail nodded. 'I don't think they sleep, either.'

Margaret remembered the one time she had found the creature hovering over her bed and she said, 'I think you're right.'

Margaret stood and turned, and saw the creature she now thought of as hers do likewise. She heard Abigail gasp.

Turning, Margaret saw that the creature's body had changed slightly. She was taller, Margaret's height, and her hips and chest had broadened, while her waist had narrowed.

Margaret whispered, 'What is going on?'

Nicholas looked up as the door to the hostel crashed open. Three armed men barged in, and before any of the soldiers in the common room could react, a half-dozen bowmen followed.

A large grey-haired man entered after the bowmen, who covered everyone in the room. 'Who commands here?' he demanded.

Nicholas stood up and said, 'I do.'

The old man walked over to Nicholas and looked down his nose at him. He shook his head. 'I commend your bravery to your captain, boy, but you do him no honor hiding him from me.'

Nicholas said, 'Step outside, grandfather, and I will be pleased to show you that I am, indeed, captain of this company.'

The burly old man said, 'Grandfather? Why, you puppy – '

Nicholas had his sword out and the point to the man's throat so fast the bowmen didn't have a chance to pull back and release. 'If you think your men can kill me before I can drive the point home, you can order them to shoot.'

The old man held up his hand, warning the bowmen to hold fire. 'If you are the captain of this company, we've a matter to settle. We may both be dead in moments, so don't lie to me. It does no man honor to go to the House of Lady Kal with a falsehood on his lips.'

Nicholas's men had been moving around the room slowly, getting ready for the fight. Amos roared, 'Anyone do anything particularly stupid and most of us will be dead before any of us have an idea what the bloody hell is going on!'

The old man glanced down. 'Are you sure he's not the captain?'

Nicholas said, 'He's the captain of my ship.'

The old man asked, 'A ship? You have a ship?'

Nicholas ignored the question. 'Now, care to tell me why you come barging in here threatening my men and demanding to see me?'

Slowly the old man put the palm of his gloved hand against the blade of Nicholas's sword and gently pushed it aside. 'I came to see if you're the men who killed my sons.'

Nicholas looked the man over; he was tall, at least his uncle Martin's height, and as broad in the shoulders. He wore his hair pulled back and tied off in a warrior's tail that fell to his shoulders. From the scars on his face and arms, Nicholas judged the hairstyle was not a vanity. The sword at his side was old but well kept. 'Grandfather, I haven't killed so many men that I wouldn't remember one. Who were your sons, and why would you think I was the man who caused their death?'

The old man said, 'I am Vaslaw Nacoyen, Chieftain of the Lion Clan. My sons were named Pytur and Anatol. I think you know of their death because one of my men saw you enter the city. With you was a girl I think comes from the City of Kilbar.'

Nicholas glanced at Ghuda and Amos, then put up his sword. 'This is not a good place to talk,' he said, indicating the room full of men neither of his company nor with Vaslaw.

'We can speak outside,' said the old man.

Nicholas signaled to Amos and Ghuda to accompany him. The two men rose, and as they reached the door, Nicholas said, 'Would you ensure no one leaves until we return?'

Vaslaw instructed his bowmen to keep everyone away from the door, and stepped outside. A dozen horsemen waited outside, and behind them another dozen fighters on foot. Nicholas said, 'It looks as if you came prepared for any answer.'

The old man grunted, his breath condensing in the night air. He motioned for Nicholas and the others to follow and they moved to the center of the armed company. 'No one who is not of my blood can overhear us. Do you know something of my sons?'

Nicholas said, 'If they were involved in a very foolish raid up at Shingazi's Landing, yes, I do know of them.'

'They are dead?'

461

'If they were with that raiding party, they are certainly dead.'

'Did you kill them?'

Nicholas carefully framed his answer. 'I don't think so. We killed some clansmen who took a wagon caravan, but we found only bear and wolf talismans.' He purposely neglected to mention the snake. 'The others were green mercenaries who didn't even think to put out a guard.' Nicholas told of the entire encounter, from finding Tuka and the burned wagons to the discovery of the dead clansmen and mercenaries.

The old man said, 'You just happened by?'

Nicholas refused to divulge his origin, so he said, 'We just happened by.'

Vaslaw didn't seem satisfied. 'Why should I believe you?'

'Because you don't have a reason not to,' Nicholas said. 'What motive would I have to attack that wagon train?'

'Gold,' the man said quickly.

Nicholas sighed. Being the son of the Prince of Krondor didn't acquaint one with a proper sense of greed, he realized. 'Let's say that gold is far down my list of things to covet. I have other concerns.'

Amos said, 'Look, you heard him say I was captain of his ship. His father has a fleet.'

'Who is your father?' asked Vaslaw.

Ghuda said, 'He rules a distant city. This is the third son.'

The old man nodded. 'Ah, proving your manhood in war. I understand that motive.'

'Something like that,' said Nicholas. 'Besides, a far more important question is to ask yourself who profits by the death of your sons.'

The old man said, 'No one. That's the damnable part of it all. The raid was an ill-conceived plot to irritate the Overlord dreamed up by my sons and some hotheads from the other clans. Killing all those young men profits no one, not even the Overlord. All it achieves is distrust between all the clans and the Overlord, and a general lessening of trust in a city that knows precious little of it already.'

Nicholas said, 'Well, there's a lot about this that doesn't make any sense. What if I told you that twice the raiders left behind enough gold to ransom a city? And what if I told you that one of the dead we found was clutching a Red Slayer helm?'

'Impossible,' said the old man.

'Why?' asked Nicholas.

'Because no Red Slayer has ever left the city without the Overlord. They are his most personal bodyguards.'

Nicholas weighed what to say next. There was something very basic about this old man, something that spoke of simpler times when these people lived much as the Jeshandi did, roaming the plains of grass, living in yurts, riding after the grazing herds. The clansmen might be city men for generations, but they honored their heritage. They were rulers and warriors, still a people whose word was considered their bond. 'What if I told you that another detachment of soldiers came to finish off anyone who managed to escape and to kill the Ranjana, and that these were from the Overlord's personal guards, His Radiance's Own?'

'What proof do you have?'

'I killed a man named Dubas Nebu.'

'I know that swine. Captain of the Second Company. Why did you kill him?'

Nicholas explained in detail what they found at Shingazi's, leaving out only the part about the serpent talisman. When he was finished, the old man said, 'You've given me and the other clan leaders something to ponder. Someone is attempting to set us all against one another, and against the Overlord.'

463

'Who would benefit from such chaos?' asked Amos.

Vaslaw said, 'That is one thing I must discuss in council with the other clan leaders. We have many rivalries and feuds among the families of the various clans – that is tradition – but this sort of disaster could set us back a dozen years in our alliance with the Overlord.'

'You have an alliance with the Overlord?' asked Nicholas.

'We do,' said the old man. 'I can't explain our history to you standing out here in the cold. Come to my house in the Western Quarter of the city tomorrow night and dine with me – bring your companions if you fear for your safety. I can tell you more then.'

He signaled, and a horse was led over. Despite his years he easily swung into the saddle, while another fighter opened the door and signaled for the bowmen to leave the hostel. Vaslaw said, 'I shall send a guide for you tomorrow. Until then.' He turned and led his company away. Amos, Ghuda, and Nicholas watched the Lion clansmen leave, and then re-entered the commons.

Returning to the table, they sat, and Harry said, 'What was that all about?'

'A dinner invitation,' said Nicholas. Amos and Ghuda broke out laughing.

Calis signaled to Marcus to wait. They had been in the burned-out farmhouse for nearly an hour, and both had remained silent, against any possibility of sentries or patrols. Crossing the river had proved more difficult than they had expected, as a squad of guardsmen stood watch on the bridge. They had made their way stealthily to the docks, where they appropriated a small boat. They rowed across the river and left the boat concealed in the bushes.

Calis signaled two, and Marcus nodded. If he wasn't back in two hours, Marcus was to assume he had been captured or somehow prevented from leaving. Marcus would return with the information for Nicholas.

Calis left at a quick trot, dodging across the open road that ran past the farmhouse into a stand of trees. Between the boles, he ran quickly, feeling certain of his ability to hide should the need arise. The woods were familiar, though he had never trodden the paths between these trunks before. His eyes peered into gloom where no human could see and saw clearly the outlines of brush and branches – his nature was such that he needed almost no light to see. Only absolute darkness rendered him sightless.

Reaching the edge of the woods, Calis paused. He listened, his senses extending as far as possible. Animals scuttled nearby, rabbits or ground squirrels. Calis sent forth a thought of reassurance, and the rustling sound quietened.

Calis was unique among mortals on Midkemia. His mother was an elf, but his father was a human with many of the powers of the legendary Valheru, whom men called the Dragon Lords. It was his father's magic that had made his birth possible, and his father's magic that had given to his son abilties that could only be called magical. Calis smiled slightly, considering what Nakor would say to that. He had overheard much of Nakor's discussions with Anthony on the ship – Nakor would say there is no magic and that the universe is all composed of stuff. Calis knew that Nakor was closer to the truth than he understood, and wondered if he should take Nakor to Elvandar to visit with the Spellweavers should they all manage somehow to return home.

Calis sprinted from the woods across the road that ran along the boundary of the estate, little more than a blur in the moonlight unless someone was staring directly at him. He moved with unnatural silence, even for one elven-born and taught. When he halted behind a solitary oak that stood near the wall, his breathing was still slow and normal and there was no sign of the exertion that burst of speed had taken save for a slight sheen of dampness on his brow.

Calis inspected the wall and waited. He had inhuman patience and stayed in one place, unmoving, for more than a half hour. There was no sign of movement atop the crenellated wall. Ducking under a low-hanging branch, Calis hurried to the base of the wall. It loomed fifteen feet high and had little purchase for climbing. Calis had carried his bow in his hand; he now slung it over his back and bent deep at the knees. With all his power he jumped straight up and with both hands grabbed the top of the wall.

Silently he pulled himself up high enough to peek over the wall. The parapet was empty. He pulled himself up and over the outer edge, and crouched down on the rampart in the shadow of the chest-high merlon, so as not to become silhouetted against the night sky – even a few blocked stars might catch the notice of an alert guard, and the city's distant light was directly behind him.

Studying the grounds below, he saw why there was no guard atop the wall. The estate was immense, with pathways leading between gardens and outbuildings. The central house was more than a quarter-mile away and had its own protective wall.

It was not in Calis's nature to curse fate or demand anything of the gods. The search of these grounds would take many nights unless he was lucky. He also knew he had less than an hour left to explore before he needed to return to Marcus. Not that he worried about getting back across the river without the boat – he could swim the strong currents of the river as easily as he jumped to the top of the wall – but he was concerned about Marcus's safety. Close to the same age as elves count such things, he was the only friend Calis had in many respects. Like

Martin, Marcus had accepted Calis without reservation, while even his closest friends in Elvandar kept some distance. Calis felt no rancor or sadness – it was simply the elvish way. His father also had few friends in any real sense, but his father had the love of a wife and the respect granted a proven Warleader. Calis knew his fate was eventually to leave Elvandar, which had been one of the things prompting him to accompany Marcus on this voyage.

Calis marked the path through the garden below him, and saw how it meandered through several landscaped terraces before reaching the main compound. He jumped down lightly from the parapet and followed the path, listening for any sounds of anything approaching as he explored.

Margaret awoke, pulling herself upward through a murky cloud of disorientation. Her head ached with a strange thudding, and her mouth felt dry. Once, when first allowed to drink wine at her father's table, she had felt this way, but she had not had any spirits with her meals.

The light was grey, as dawn was still not quite upon them. Forcing herself to sit up, she pulled a deep breath of air into her lungs and was aware of a strange spicy odor, not unpleasant or offputting, but alien.

In the gloom of the bedroom, she saw Abigail's still form on the other bed, her breathing evident by the rise and fall of her breasts under the thin blanket. Abigail's face was contorted, as if she was having a bad dream.

Then Margaret remembered: it had been a dream that had awakened her. She had seen herself being held motionless by creatures . . . she couldn't remember them.

Then she saw movement as one of the two strange creatures stirred. It made a brushing motion with one hand, and Margaret felt a dull surprise, as if strong emotions were being damped by whatever was giving her the headache. The creature appeared to be brushing back its hair

Margaret got out of the bed, forcing weak and unwilling legs to move. Heavily she plodded across the room to where the two creatures sat, their heads close together as if whispering. Margaret felt a distant stab of alarm. The creatures had changed. As grey light began to come in through the window, illuminating the room in tones of grey and black, she could see that the creatures' skin was somehow smoother and lighter, and atop their heads hair was now sprouting. Margaret took a step back, her hand going to her mouth. One of the creatures had hair that matched Abigail's blond locks, while the other's was exactly the same shade as her own.

Marcus drew back his bow, though he was certain that it was Calis who approached. Few other men, perhaps only Marcus's father and some among the Rangers of Natal, would have sensed his approach in the early morning gloom.

'Put away your bow,' Calis whispered.

Marcus was up and moving without being told. They were cutting it very fine if they were to get back across the river without being noticed. Once they were safely within the flow of river traffic they'd be just another boat, but anyone seen putting out from this side of the river this close to the Grand Adviser's estate would be suspect.

Once in the boat, Marcus began rowing. He said, 'Did you find anything?'

'Little useful. One oddity: there seemed to be no guards and few servants.'

For an estate that size?' said Marcus.

Calis shrugged. 'My experience with human estates is limited.' With a wry grin showing in the predawn light, he added, 'This is the first I've seen.'

Marcus said, 'From the size of those walls and how far they stretch, I thought it would be a town within.'

'It's not. Many gardens, empty buildings, and odd signs.'

'Signs?'

'Footprints like none I've seen before; smaller than a man's but shaped somewhat manlike. Scratchmarks before the toes.'

Marcus didn't need to be told that meant claws. 'Serpent men?'

'I won't know until I see one,' said Calis.

'You're going back?'

'I must. There are many places I must explore if we are to find the captives and discover what is being undertaken there.' He smiled to reassure his friend. 'I shall be careful, and methodical. I will explore the entire outer estate before I explore the inner. And I will explore that before I venture into the great house.'

Marcus didn't feel reassured, but he knew Calis was fast and strong, calm and quick-witted. 'How long?' he asked, meaning to finish the search.

'Three, maybe four more nights. Less if I find them before I go into the great house.'

Marcus sighed and said nothing as he rowed back toward the docks on the other side of the river.

19

Explorations

A guide appeared.

Marcus had selected Amos and Ghuda to accompany him, while Harry and Brisa were out scouting the city for more clues to the prisoners' fate. Calis's report had troubled Nicholas; the absence of guards and servants was simply one more thing that made no sense. There were too many mysteries in all of this for the Prince's liking. The only positive possibility was the track that *might* have been that of a Pantathian serpent priest, in which Nicholas found little comfort. He also wasn't pleased at Calis's plan to return, but he couldn't think of a good reason to say no.

Anthony would remain at the inn with Praji, Vaja, and the other men, to listen and see what local gossip they could uncover. Praji and Vaja had elected to stay in exchange for a stiff payment from Nicholas, since he had still not told the local mercenaries all the facts of this journey, but just enough to satisfy them, apparently. Praji was certain at least a half-dozen agents of other companies, the mysterious Black Rose, and other clans were in the commons asking discreet questions.

Nicholas and his two companions left the hostel. The journey on foot took the better part of an hour, which gave Nicholas a good chance to examine further the City of the Serpent River.

The bazaar and the merchants' quarters that surrounded it, as well as the docks, were something of a common ground, where men of all clans and alliances passed freely; peace was maintained by a garrison of the Overlord's personal guards. Those black-clad soldiers walked in pairs everywhere, and occasionally a patrol of a dozen could be seen moving briskly through the crowd.

But once they left the commercial center of the city, it was clear they were entering something close to a war zone. Barricades had been erected at the ends of streets, forcing wagons and horsemen to make slow turns to get past them, so charges couldn't be easily mounted. Men traveled in numbers. Women were never seen without armed escort. Many times passersby moved to the other side of the street rather than trust Nicholas and his friends to be harmless.

Nicholas had noticed that all who passed wore badges of one sort or another. The majority were the heads of animals, and these he understood were the clan badges of which both Tuka and Praji had spoken. The others wore mercenary badges, showing to which company they owed allegiance. Nicholas had thought about having badges made for his men, but hoped they'd be gone from the city on their way home before that step was necessary. He already felt they had been here too long.

When they had neared their host's house, the hereditary home of the Lion Clan, Nicholas saw another example of just what sort of life those who lived in this city endured: it was an armed camp, and there were sentries for blocks before the house could be seen. The house was of three stories, with an observation turret atop the third floor. Archer platforms were manned and the outer wall was seven feet high. They entered the gate and Amos said, 'A bailey!'

The clear area between the outer and inner wall stretched away and around the corners of the estate. An inner wall rose twelve feet high, and the distance between the two walls was thirty feet. The guide said, 'Two hundred years ago the Rat Clan and their allies forced their way into the house itself. The Clan Chieftain at the time was exiled in shame; his successor built the two walls so that this might never happen again.'

Vaslaw Nacoyen met them at the entrance, with a dozen of his clan warriors in attendance. Nicholas was thankful they had met the Jeshandi before, as he now could see the relationship between these two peoples. The city-dwelling clansmen might wear robes of fine silk and bathe in perfumed waters, but they were still related in their dress and weapons. The men atop the roof carried the short horse bow; not one crossbow or longbow was in evidence. The men wore the same warrior's topknot that Mikola had worn in his yurt, and most of them wore long, droopy moustaches or closely trimmed beards.

Vaslaw led them into a large room that looked as much like a council chamber as a dining hall. A long table stretched across it, set for dining, with servants waiting. Vaslaw motioned for Nicholas and his guests to sit. The old man made introductions to his one surviving son, Hatonis, and two daughters. Yngya, the elder, looked to be near the end of pregnancy, and she stood clutching the hand of a man Nicholas took to be her husband. The younger girl, Tashi, about fifteen years or so, blushed and kept her eyes lowered. Then Vaslaw introduced Regin, Yngya's husband.

When they were all seated, servants began bringing an assortment of foods, small portions on numerous plates, and Nicholas asumed they were to sample a little of everything. A variety of wines were poured into goblets at the right hand of each diner, to be sampled with different dishes.

As they dined, Nicholas waited for his host to begin discussions. The old man was silent throughout the first portion of dinner. Then Regin asked, 'You've traveled far, Captain?'

Nicholas nodded. 'Very far. I am among the first of my people to visit this city, I suspect.'

'Are you from the Westlands?' asked Yngya.

The continent of Novindus was roughly divided into thirds. The Eastlands, where they had landed, was comprised of the Hotlands, as the desert was called, and the Great Steppes, the home of the Jeshandi, as well as the City of the Serpent River. The Riverlands comprised the heart of the continent, being the most heavily populated portion of Novindus. The Vedra River ran southeast from the Sothu Mountains through this rich farm belt. To the west of the river was the Plain of Djams, a relatively inhospitable grassland populated by nomads, more primitive than the Jeshandi. Beyond was a gigantic range of mountains, the Ratn'gary – the Pavilion of the Gods – which ran north from the sea to the mighty Forest of Irabek, which lay between the Ratn'gary and the Sothu mountains. It was beyond this north–south barrier of mountains and forest that the Westlands lay. The average residents of the Eastlands knew little about the Westlands and those who lived there. Even less was known of the Island Kingdom of Pa'jkamaka, which lay five hundred miles beyond. Only a handful of bold traders had ever visited those distant cities.

Ghuda asked, 'When is your baby due?' freeing Nicholas from having to answer.

'Soon,' Yngya said with a smile.

As the first-course dishes were being cleared away, Nicholas said, 'Vaslaw, you spoke last night of my need to understand some history.'

The old man nodded as he sucked out the last bit of a clam and put the shell on the plate so the servant could remove it. 'Yes,' he said. 'Do you know much about the city's history?'

Nicholas told him what he had learned so far, and the old man nodded. 'For centuries, after we disposed of the Kings, the council of chieftains ruled well and the city was peaceful. Many old feuds were resolved, and we had many marriages between the clans, so that as time passed,

473

we were forming a single people.' He paused to collect his thoughts. 'We are a very traditional people. In our own tongue, we are called *Pashandi*, which means "Righteous People".'

'You are kin to the Jeshandi,' observed Amos.

'That means "Free People". But we are, simply, *Shandi*, "the People". Old ways die hard for us. It is still important to be a hunter and warrior before all else. I am a trader of no small accomplishment, with ships and river caravans leaving and arriving year round. I've traded to the Westlands twice in my life, and once even reached the Kingdom of Pa'jkamaka, and to every city on the Vedra, but my wealth is of no importance in the council of my clan; it is my good eye and skill with a bow, my stalking and riding, my strength with a sword that earned me the right to rule.'

His son looked on with pride, as did his daughters and son-in-law. 'But being first with a sword or bow or on horse does not mean a man is a wise ruler,' said Vaslaw. 'Many chieftains over the years did foolish things for reasons of pride and honor, and many times their clans suffered. The council had final rule in the city, but only a chieftain could rule those within his clan.' He shook his head. 'Then almost thirty years ago bad things began to happen.'

'Bad things?' asked Nicholas.

'Rivalries became feuds, and blood was spilled and open warfare erupted between clans. There are fourteen clans of the Pashandi, Nicholas. At the height of the fighting, six clans – Bear, Wolf, Raven, Lion, Tiger, and Dog – were locked in a struggle with five others – Jackal, Horse, Bull, Rat, and Eagle. The Elk, Buffalo, and Badger attempted to remain outside the struggle, but they were being drawn in.

'At the height of the fighting, a mercenary captain

474

called Valgasha and his company seized the council building. He declared he was speaking for the non-clan people of the city and declared the bazaar and docks under his protection. He killed every clansman that came armed into those areas. He almost united the clans against him, but before we could mount our offensive, he sent couriers begging for truce. We met with him and he convinced myself and the other chieftains to end the fighting; he took the title Overlord. He's acted as arbiter and peacemaker with the clans since then, though there have been many issues left unresolved over the years and the feuds continue.'

Nicholas said, 'I was under the assumption he was the absolute ruler of the city.'

'He is, but at that time he seemed a more reasonable alternative to constant fighting. As peace returned to the city, his hold increased. First he turned his mercenary company into a city watch, patrolling the bazaar and docks, then the merchants' quarter. Next he created a standing army, elevating his oldest and most loyal soldiers to his private guard, "His Radiance's Own", and he expanded the old Kings' palace and took it for his own. Then Dahakon appeared.' Vaslaw almost spat the name. 'That black-hearted, murderous swine has been responsible for the city's becoming a principality with Valgasha as Prince. He created the Red Slayers, who are fanatics who need to be hacked to pieces, for they will not stop fighting once they are set loose.'

'When did all this happen?' asked Amos.

'Twenty-seven years ago the trouble started; twenty-four years ago the Overlord became absolute.'

Nicholas glanced at Amos, who nodded. Nicholas said, 'What about this raid we blundered across?'

Vaslaw nodded to his son-in-law. Regin said, 'Some of the younger warriors seek to undermine the Overlord's domination by sabotaging his treaty with a trading consortium to the north, and they acted without permission from their chieftains.'

The old man sighed. 'It was a foolish thing, no matter how bravely they acted. Such a setback is little more than an irritation to Valgasha.'

Nicholas said, 'I think we have common cause. As I said, I think the Overlord or someone high in his court was responsible for the death of your sons.' Nicholas retold the story he had told the night before, about the attack, the presence of the Red Slayer helm and the arrival of the Overlord's personal soldiers, but with more detail.

It was Hatonis who asked the first question. 'One thing: what were you doing there?'

Nicholas glanced at Ghuda, who shrugged, and Amos, who indicated Nicholas should speak on. Nicholas said, 'I need your oath that what I tell you does not leave this room.'

Vaslaw nodded. Nicholas said, 'I am the son of the Prince of Krondor.'

Hatonis said, 'Father said your father ruled some city. I've never heard of Krondor. Is it in the Westlands, as my sister asked?'

'No,' answered Nicholas. He then spent the next hour telling them of the Kingdom of the Isles and the Empire of Great Kesh, of their journey across the water and the raids.

By the time he had finished, the meal was over and they lingered over brandies and sweetened coffee. Vaslaw said, 'I will not call a guest in my home a liar, Nicholas, but I can scarcely credit your tale. I can imagine lands such as you describe, barely, as a storyteller's device – far-reaching kingdoms and armies in the tens of thousands. But in real life? That I find impossible to believe. We've had our share of would-be conquerors in our past;

476

at the time we were having our troubles, the Priest-King of Lanada attempted to conquer the other cities along the river. The Overlord allied with the Raj of Maharta to balk his ambitions. No, such men are always stopped.'

'Not always,' said Nicholas. 'My ancestors were conquerors, though now they are heroes in our history.' Glancing at Amos, he said, 'But we wrote the history.'

Amos grinned. 'Nicholas speaks only the truth. You will have to take ship and come visit someday, Vaslaw. You will find it strange, I am sure, but it *is* true.'

It was Regin who asked, 'Very well, but what possible reason would some mysterious agency have to make war across such a vast ocean – the one we call the Blue Sea – for booty and slaves, when there are wealthy prizes so close here?'

Nicholas spoke to Vaslaw. 'You said there were fourteen tribes and named them. Was there once a fifteenth?'

Vaslaw's expression turned hard. He motioned to the servants to leave. Then he said to his other guests and his daughters, 'You must leave as well.'

Tashi looked about to voice a protest over being excluded, but her father cut her off with a near shout: 'Leave!'

When the room was empty save for Nicholas and his friends and Vaslaw, his son, and son-in-law, the old man said, 'Hatonis is my last living male heir, and Regin shall be next chieftain when I die. But no other may hear further. What do you say, Nicholas?'

Nicholas dug the talisman from his pouch and handed it to Vaslaw. The old man looked hard at it and said, 'The Snakes are back.'

Hatonis said, 'Snakes, Father?' Regin also looked confused.

The old man put the talisman down. 'When I was a boy, my father who was Chieftain before me told me of the Snake Clan.' He was silent for a while, then said,

'Once we numbered a score of clans. Three died out, the Wolverine, Dragon, and Otter, and two others were destroyed in blood feud or war, the Hawk and Boar. In the memory of my grandfather's father's, the Snakes, like the rest of us, lived here in the city. There was betrayal, and a dishonor so black no man was permitted to speak of it, and the Snakes were hunted down – to the last man it was thought – and killed.' His voice lowered. 'Do you know what we mean when we say "to the last man"?' Nicholas said nothing. 'Every man, woman, and child who had Snake blood was hounded to earth and put to the sword, no matter how young or innocent. Brothers killed their own sisters who had married Snakes.' He composed his thoughts. 'You are aliens here, so there is much about the clans that you do not understand. We are one with our clan totems. Those of us who practiced magic took their form, and knew their wisdom. We spoke to them and they guided our young men on their vision quests. Something happened to the Snake Clan, which had once numbered among the mightiest. Something led them into darkness and evil ways, and they became anathema to their kin.'

Nicholas said, 'Look at this.' He produced the ring. 'This was taken from the hand of a moredhel – kin of those you know as the "long-lived" – near my uncle's home.'

Vaslaw looked at Nicholas a long time, then said, 'What are you not telling me?'

Nicholas said, 'There is one thing of which I may never speak, though it would cost my life. I've sworn an oath, as have my kin. But there is a reason we are connected, those who came with me across the sea, and you here, now. We have a common foe, and it is they who lie behind all that has transpired, I am sure.'

'Who?' asked Hatonis. 'The Overlord and Dahakon?'

'Perhaps, but even beyond such as they,' answered

478

Nicholas. 'What do you know of the Pantathian serpent priests?'

Vaslaw's reaction was instantaneous. 'Impossible! Now you spin more tales. They are creatures of legend. They live in a mysterious land, Pantathia, somewhere to the west – snakes who walk and speak like men. Such creatures do not exist save in tales told by mothers to frighten naughty children.'

Amos said, 'They are not a legend.' Vaslaw looked at the old sea captain. 'I have seen one.' He told them briefly of the siege of Armengar, when Murmandamus marched against the Kingdom.

'Again I'm tempted to call a guest in my house a liar,' said Vaslaw.

Amos grinned and there was no warmth in it. 'Resist the temptation, my friend. I've been known to spin a tale now and again, but on this you have my oath: it's true. And no man has ever called me oath breaker and lived.'

Nicholas said, 'I know nothing of your customs, as you've observed. But could it have been in the ancient days that this oneness with their totem could make the Snake Clan vulnerable to the influences of the Pantathians?'

'No one living knows what horror caused the obliteration of the Snake Clan, Nicholas. That dark secret died with those Chieftains who obliterated them.'

Nicholas said, 'But whatever that terrible deed was, it could have been something to do with the Pantathians, correct?'

The old man looked shaken. 'But if the snake people are at the root of these current problems, how do we resist? They are phantoms, and no man here has seen one. Do we ride in all directions seeking them?'

'We are not without hope,' said Amos.

'Why?' asked Regin.

'Because I've also seen a Pantathian die.'

Nicholas said, 'They are mortal creatures. I don't know yet what their plans are, and I know only that my purpose must be to find those taken from my homeland and return them. But in so doing, I believe that simple act will frustrate these snake creatures, and bring them looking for me.'

Vaslaw said, 'What would you have of the Lion Clan?'

'For the moment, peace,' said Nicholas. 'I would be happy to see you avenge yourselves upon those responsible for the death of your people. It would be in keeping with my purpose, I am sure. And I may need your help.'

'If we can, we will,' said the old man. 'Each chieftain in his turn must swear many oaths when accepting his office, but one oath is especially stressed, above all but protecting the clan to death. That oath is to hunt down any Snake. It is said as ritual, and no chieftain in four generations expected to honor it.' He fingered the snake talisman. 'Until now.'

Calis crouched low behind a hedge that shielded him from a large building. He had already explored several other buildings, locating an armory, a storage complex, a kitchen complex, and servants' quarters that were deserted. There were signs that until recently these buildings had been in use. Another kitchen complex was being utilized, and a great deal of food was being prepared, which puzzled the half-elf, as the main house was mostly dark. Only one area seemed occupied if the lights in the windows were an indication.

He had followed a pair of men dressed in black, wearing red cloths tied on their heads, who carried hot stew in buckets from that kitchen. They had entered the large building, admitted through double doors by similarly dressed guards carrying swords and bows.

Calis inspected the wall from his vantage point. The building was without windows. It looked like nothing so much as a large warehouse. He glanced around, seeking any sight of anyone else lurking nearby, then sprinted for the wall. With a prodigious leap he jumped straight to the top of the tile roof.

And almost fell down over the other side. The building was a hollow square, a covered hallway surrounding a large open court. The roof was narrow and peaked, no more than fifteen feet wide, shingled in red tiles over what was some sort of storage area.

Crouching down, he peered into the gloom, his more-than-human eyes showing him clearly what was in the courtyard. Elven-reared to hold his emotions within, he was nevertheless shaken by what he saw. His hand gripped his bow tight enough to turn his knuckles white.

More than a hundred prisoners lay shackled to heavy wooden pallets under the sky. While the season was spring, it was still cold at night. Those down below showed the ravages of being kept outside. They were haggard and gaunt and many were obviously ill. From the number of empty pallets, more than half those taken from the Far Coast had died.

But what caused Calis to feel shock and revulsion was the sight of the creatures who roamed among the prisoners. They were grotesque imitations of humans. They moved and gestured, and some moved their lips in imitation of speech, but the voices were wrong, mostly non-sense syllables. The two men carrying the stew moved through the yard, providing a bowlful for each prisoner.

Calis moved slowly along the peak of the roof, seeking to learn as much as he could about the environs and seeking sight of Margaret and Abigail. Mounting a rescue would be difficult. While those guarding the prisoners did not appear to be plentiful, there was a lot of ground to cover getting out of the estate, and most of those below looked barely fit to move, let alone run.

Calis made a complete circuit of the building, committing every detail to memory. For a moment he studied two creatures who squatted next to a pair of prisoners. One creature rubbed the hair of a prisoner, who weakly attempted to pull away. The creature's gesture was almost soothing. Then it struck Calis: the creature resembled the prisoner! He again scanned the area, and now he could see clearly that for each prisoner chained to a pallet, there was one creature who was beginning to resemble that man or woman! Calis continued around the building one last time to ensure he wasn't mistaken. When he reached the point where he had jumped up, he sprang down, hurrying to a hiding place behind the hedge. There had been no sign of the two noblewomen from Crydee.

Calis felt a small surge of doubt. Should he return to Marcus and inform him of the prisoners or continue his search?

Caution overrode any sense of urgency; his nature was not given to impatience. He headed back toward the outer wall and the path back to Marcus.

Nakor watched with fascination. He had been observing the still figure in the chair for almost half a day, and despite there being absolutely no movement from the man, Nakor was nevertheless enthralled.

Since entering the palace, Nakor had wandered completely unhindered through halls and galleries. There were no soldiers stationed inside, except for the entrance hall, and the few servants he spied had been easily avoided. Most of the rooms were unused – and uncleaned, given the layers of dust he encountered. He found it easy to slip into the palace kitchen and take what he needed, and he always had his apples, though he felt a twinge of nostalgia for his oranges. He had grown accustomed to them.

He had slept in soft beds, and even taken a bath and put on a new robe, one that had been fashioned for someone not much larger than himself. He was now resplendent in a lavender robe cropped at the knee and elbow, with a dark purple sash trimmed in golden thread. He considered the possibility of renaming himself Nakor the Purple Rider, but decided the name somehow lacked panache. When he returned to the Kingdom, he would find himself a new blue robe, if he could manage the time.

Early that morning he had spied the beautiful dark-haired Lady Clovis hurrying along, and he decided to follow her. She had moved deep into the palace, down into a lower chamber below ground level. There she had met with the Overlord and they had spoken briefly. Nakor had been too distant as he hid to either hear them or read their lips – a trick he often found useful – but when the Overlord had departed, Nakor had decided to follow the woman. Something about her was disturbingly familiar.

She had entered a long tunnel, and he had been forced to hang back so he could follow unseen. He walked for nearly a half hour before he reached the far end of the tunnel, where he found a locked door. Picking the lock caused only a short delay, and he discovered stairs leading down. Without hesitation he hurried down them, after closing the door behind him, and entered a completely dark tunnel. Nakor paused. The darkness held no fear for him, but he was not gifted with unusual sight or hearing, and he was leery of using any of his light tricks, as they would be mistaken for magic and he had no wish to be eaten by Dahakon – if indeed that was his practice. Nakor was beginning to doubt it. But it was a good story and Nakor was enough of a pragmatist to consider the unfortunate consequences of discovering it wasn't just a story. He reached into his bag and felt around for another seam he had created in it, one that went to a different place than the seam leading to the fruit bin in Ashunta. He stuck his arm in up to the shoulder and felt around on the table he had prepared before leaving to find Ghuda, almost two years before. He had moved a variety of useful items to a cave in the hills near Landreth, a short distance from Stardock, and had pushed rocks down to hide the cave from view, protecting his cache from chance discovery. Then he had carefully created the tear in what he called the stuff, at a proper height and distance from the table for him to reach anything on its surface by extending his arm through the bag.

He found the object he sought and awkwardly pulled out a lamp. Closing the seam, he paused a moment. Shutting his eyes, he extended his senses along the lines of power he detected running above him. No sudden disturbance of the fabric of stuff announced some mystic alarm. Nakor shrugged and grinned in the darkness. The magician's fabled arcane alarm must be another lie. So many lies had been uncovered in his searching the palace, and he was certain he would uncover more before this journey was through. He dug into his belt pouch and pulled out a flint and steel, and quickly had the lamp going.

Now that he could see, he stood and examined his surroundings. The tunnel sloped downward slightly and vanished into gloom. Nakor followed it until it leveled out. He examined the walls and saw green mould growing and puddles of water beneath his feet. He closed his eyes, gauged how far he had come since leaving the palace, and decided he must now be standing beneath the river. Grinning to himself, he decided he knew where the tunnel was going. The destination pleased him, so he hurried along.

After walking for nearly another half hour, he came to a ladder leading upward, iron rungs hammered into the side of the tunnel, vanishing into a well above. Being in no hurry, he blew out the lamp and climbed the rungs. When he reached the top he hit his head on a hard surface. Rubbing his bump, he cursed silently, then felt around in the dark. He discovered a latch, and pulled on it, and heard a metallic click as a release was sprung. He pushed upward and the trapdoor grudgingly moved. After the darkness, he was almost blinded by the light. He peered cautiously upward and saw that he was in a covered well near the foundation of the burned-out farm. Delighted at the discovery, he lowered the trapdoor as he returned below. He left it unlatched against the possible need of a quick exit.

Once he was back in the tunnel, he relit the lamp and continued on. He found his way to another flight of steps and took them up to another locked door. This he carefully picked, and when he had it open, he peeked through. Seeing no signs of movement, he hurried through, locking the door behind him. He blew out the lamp, for torches burned in sconces on the wall. Putting the lamp carefully back into his bag, he wandered into the basement of what he was certain was Dahakon's estate across the river from the palace. Things like secret tunnels and hidden passages appealed to Nakor, and he thought this day's exploration delightful. Besides, he was fascinated by the beautiful woman who was not who she appeared to be.

He prowled around for most of the morning, looking for her, but all he saw were silent servants wearing black tunics and trousers, and red cloths tied around their heads. At noon he smelled food and snuck into a kitchen in a building near the rear of the main house. He saw three men leave, two carrying a hot cauldron of food. Ducking into the kitchen, crouching low, he peered into the building and saw two cooks hard at work. He stole a loaf of hot bread near the door and ducked back outside. Turning a corner, he almost walked into a pair of the black-clad men, but fortunately for him, their backs were turned. He hurried the other way and hid behind a low hedge for a minute.

Chewing the bread, he decided to investigate the main house before he prowled the grounds. As he started to get to his feet, he noticed something odd in the grass. Lowering himself even closer to the grass, he saw a footprint, barely recognizable as one because the blades had almost completely recovered from being stepped on. Nakor was captivated by the way whoever had walked here had carried himself in such a way that no dirt beneath the grass had been gouged and few of the blades were crushed or broken. He grinned, for no human could have done this. Calis had been here the night before.

Nakor was pleased, for now he felt less concerned about the need to return and inform Nicholas of what he had found. Besides, he wasn't entirely sure what it was he *had* found, so he thought he had better go investigate and be certain before he returned to the hostel. And, as he counted such things, he was having a great deal of fun.

Inside the house again, he discovered a series of rooms in the center of the building. In them he found signs of the sorts of practices that were ascribed to Dahakon. The remains of several unfortunates were displayed on the wall, hanging from hooks or impaled on stakes, or upon shelves. One poor man hung from a hook through his chest, without an inch of skin upon his body. A large man-sized table was covered in brown stains that could only be blood, and the room reeked of chemicals, incense, and decay. In another, Nakor found a library, which almost made his heart leap. So many books he hadn't read! He moved to the closest shelf and examined titles. Some he knew by reputation, but most were alien to him. He could read most of the languages represented there, but a few were strange.

He began to reach for a book, when caution held that impulse in check. He screwed up his face and stared at the books through fluttering lids, almost closed, but opened just enough to admit light. He didn't know why this trick worked, but he had discovered that by doing that, he could see certain signs of tricks, or what others insisted was magic.

After a moment he detected the faint blue glow. 'Traps,' he whispered. 'Not nice.'

He turned his back on the books and crossed to another room. Opening the door, he felt his heart leap as he stared into the eyes of a man sitting in a chair. It was Dahakon!

The man did not stir. Nakor slipped through the door and closed it behind him, and saw the magician's body was motionless and his eyes were fixed on space. Nakor walked over to him and bent to stare into his eyes. There was something going on in there, he was certain, but whatever it was, he was not paying attention to Nakor.

Then Nakor saw the other Dahakon, and he grinned. He hurried over to the figure that stood motionless against the wall, and he examined it. The thing reeked of spices and fragrances purchased from a seller of colognes and perfumes. Nakor touched its hand and pulled his own away; the thing was obviously dead. Nakor looked into the eyes and considered what he had seen in the previous two rooms. Now he knew where the poor dead man's skin had gone.

Behind the real Dahakon was a study table, with scrolls and other things of interest, so Nakor sat and began to snoop.

Hours had gone by and he had investigated everything of interest in the room. In the desk he had found a crystal lens, and upon looking through it, Nakor discovered he could see the telltale energies of tricks. The blue nimbus around the books in the next room sprang out, even though he could see only some of them through the open door. And around Dahakon a ruby light shone, a thread of which rose through the ceiling. 'Pug?' Nakor whispered, and suddenly things made sense. Nakor knew with certainty what was occupying Dahakon's attention. With no apology, he put the appropriated lens in his bag.

He got up, hurried past the motionless magician, and began to retrace his steps back to the city. He decided exiting at the burned-out house would save him the irritation of sneaking out of the palace, though he would be forced to swim the river. Feeling sorry for what that would do to his fine new robe, he moved on.

Margaret tried to run, but her feet wouldn't move. She looked over her shoulder, but couldn't see what was pursuing her. Ahead she saw her father; she opened her mouth to shout for his help, but she couldn't make a sound. Panic rose up within her, and she again tried to shout. The thing behind was almost upon her. As terror enveloped her, she opened her mouth.

With a scream she awoke. The noise startled the two creatures in the room and they moved away. Margaret was dripping with perspiration. Her nightdress clung to her body as she pushed aside the bedcovers and moved to Abigail's bed. She found herself unsteady on her feet, but for the first time in days her mind was clear.

She sat on the edge of Abigail's bed and shook her. 'Abby!' she called keeping her voice low.

Abigail stirred but wouldn't awaken. 'Abby!' she repeated as she shook her.

Then a hand fell on Margaret's shoulder and she felt her heart leap. She spun to warn off the creature, but instead of an alien thing, Abby stood behind her. Margaret stood up and pressed her back against the wall, eyes wide with fear. The second Abby was nude, and perfect in every detail. Margaret had bathed with her friend enough to recognize the small birthmark above her navel, and the scar on her knee from when a brother had pushed her down as a child.

Everything about the second Abby was perfect, except

488

for the eyes. They were dead. In a distant whisper, the second Abby said, 'Go back to bed.'

Margaret glanced behind her as she moved toward her own bed and saw the second figure was sitting, slack-jawed, in the corner. Margaret's eyes widened as she saw herself, also nude, across the room. Margaret's scream tore the night.

20

Plans

Nicholas looked up.

Nakor entered the inn, still dripping from his swim across the river. The little man crossed the crowded common room and sat down at the table with Nicholas, Amos, Harry, and Anthony. Praji, Vaja, Ghuda, and Brisa sat at the next table. Grinning, he said, 'Anything hot to eat?'

Nicholas nodded and said, 'Harry, would you get Nakor some food?'

Harry got up, and Nicholas said, 'Where have you been?'

'Around. Lots of places. I've seen lots of things. Interesting things. But we shouldn't talk about them here. After I eat.'

Nicholas nodded. Harry returned with a plate of hot food and a mug of ale and the entire company sat in silence watching the little man eat. He showed no discomfort at being the object of so much silent scrutiny. When he was finished, he stood up and said, 'Nicholas, we need to talk.'

Nicholas rose and said, 'Amos?'

Amos nodded and followed them. They entered Nicholas's room and Nakor said, 'I think I know where the captives are.'

'Calis has found them,' said Nicholas. He repeated what Calis had told him.

'But not Margaret or Abigail,' said Amos.

Nakor nodded vigorously, his face split into a grin. 'I know Calis has been there. Saw his footprint. He's very good. Even a good tracker wouldn't have seen it, but I was lying hiding and my nose was an inch from it.' He chuckled.

'How did you get into that estate?' asked Nicholas.

'Found a passage from the palace that goes under the river.'

Amos and Nicholas exchanged open-mouthed expressions of amazement, and Amos said, 'And how did you get into the palace?'

Nakor told them how he had entered it, and of some of the things he saw. 'This Overlord is a strange man. He's very preoccupied with silly things: ceremonies and pretty girls.'

Amos grinned. 'Well, you're half right: ceremonies are silly.'

Nakor said, 'I think he is a tool. I think this Dahakon and his lady friend are those who are controlling things. This Overlord acts like a man whose mind has been tampered with; he serves his role. The woman with Dahakon, she's very interesting.'

Nicholas said, 'I don't care. What about Margaret and Abigail?'

Nakor shrugged. 'They must be somewhere in the big house. I didn't look. I can go back and see.'

Nicholas shook his head. 'Wait until Calis returns. I don't want you tripping over each other over there.'

Nakor grinned. 'We wouldn't. There are things about him that are very special, and I know how to hide.'

Nicholas said, 'Nevertheless, wait until tomorrow. If he's found them, there's no need for you to return.'

Nakor's expression turned serious. 'No. I will go back.'

'Why?' asked Amos.

'Because I am the only one who can face Dahakon's lady friend and live.'

'Is she a witch?' asked Nicholas.

'No,' answered Nakor. 'How are we going to get home?'

Amos rubbed his chin. 'There are two ships in the harbor, either one of which would do – they are copies of Kingdom ships.'

Nakor said, 'This is all very strange. Dahakon is making copies of people.'

'Copies?' asked Nicholas.

'Yes. He made a copy of himself. That's what I saw when the Overlord was announcing his wedding to the Ranjana. It's a very good copy to look at, if you don't get too close, but it's stupid. It can't talk, so his lady friend spoke for him. It smells very bad. I think he must make a new one soon.'

'How does he make copies?' asked Amos.

Remembering the room with the corpses, Nakor said, 'From dead people. You really don't wish to know.'

Nicholas said, 'But the prisoners aren't dead.'

Nakor nodded. 'That's the strange part. Different tricks. Dahakon's a necromancer. The tricks Calis saw are not death tricks, but' – he shrugged – 'something else. These are tricks to manipulate living creatures. These copies will not be stupid and they will not smell bad. This is not Dahakon's trick.'

Amos said, 'Well, one thing's obvious.'

Nicholas said, 'Nothing seems obvious to me. What is it?'

'They're going to take them home.'

'The prisoners?' asked Nicholas.

'No,' said Nakor. 'The copies.'

Amos stroked his chin. 'But we don't know why.'

'Spies?' asked Nicholas.

Amos said, 'A great deal of trouble for little gain. If the *Royal Gull* comes sailing into any Kingdom harbor, there'll be a lot of questions, and those copies aren't going to escape close inspection. Much easier to just slip a couple of folks into Krondor, or Crydee, or wherever, like that Quegan trader who came to Crydee before the raid. No, this is something else.'

Nakor said, 'We can find out. It will just take some time.'

Nicholas said, 'I think we're almost out of time.'

Amos said, 'Why?'

'A feeling. Calis said that many of the prisoners have already died. We don't know if it's from these copies or what, but if we're going to save any of them, we must do it soon.'

Amos shrugged. 'From what Calis said, they're not going to be in much shape for running.'

'Nakor, how far is it from the place the prisoners are being held to the tunnel?' asked Nicholas.

'Not far,' he answered. 'But it would be difficult. The prisoners would have to move into the big house, past the kitchen, and close to Dahakon's quarters.'

'How many servants and guards did you encounter?' asked the Prince.

'Not many, but there could be more close by.'

'Calis says not,' said Nicholas. 'Whatever else, the Overlord and his Adviser both seem to base their power on reputation, not on hundreds of armed men.'

'Maybe they don't want a lot of witnesses, and don't have that many men they can trust,' ventured Amos.

Nicholas said, 'As soon as Calis locates the girls, I think it's time to get out of this city. If we can get the prisoners to that burned-out house and have some boats waiting there, we can head downriver to the sea, and pick them up.'

'Which means we have to steal one of those ships,' said Amos.

'Can you do it?'

Amos looked grim. 'We don't have enough men. With thirty-five men . . . I need at least two dozen to go out and take that ship out of the harbor, and that few only if there's only a station-keeping watch aboard and the rest of the crew is out in town. If they have even a dozen men aboard, it could be a close fight, and I might not have enough crew to get her under way before others come aboard.'

'That would leave me with only eleven to get the prisoners out,' said Nicholas.

'You could get some help,' said Nakor.

'Perhaps Vaslaw would help,' said Nicholas.

Amos said, 'Those men of his are probably great fighters when it comes to riding around on horses making a great deal of noise, but we need some practiced skulkers to get in and out of that estate.'

'Maybe Brisa could speak to the thieves?' suggested Nicholas.

Amos rubbed his hand over his face in frustration. 'Perhaps, but from what she said, they sound like a pretty shy and sorry lot; nothing like our Mockers. Maybe Praji and Vaja could find us a half-dozen reliable lads who'll show some courage for the right amount of gold.'

Nakor said, 'You'll find someone. It will be good.' He turned for the door.

'Where are you going?' asked Nicholas.

'I'm going to sleep,' he answered with a grin. 'Soon it's going to be very noisy and busy, with lots of running around.'

He left, and Amos shook his head. 'He is the strangest man I have ever encountered, and I've met my share of strange men.'

Nicholas had to laugh. 'But he's been a great help.'

Amos remembered Arutha's caution about listening to Nakor and felt his own smile fade. There was something dark coming at them, and fast, and Amos knew that when he'd had that feeling before, good men had died.

Saying nothing more, they returned to the common room.

* * *

Anthony said, 'Nicholas, can I talk to you?'

Nicholas, who had been returning to his room, nodded, waving for the young magician to follow. Anthony closed the door to his own room, crossed the hall, and entered after Nicholas.

'What is it?' asked Nicholas, stifling a yawn. The tension of waiting for Calis to return was wearing him down to a nub. He sat on the bed and motioned for Anthony to sit at the single chair next to the small table provided by the hostler.

Anthony seemed to have trouble speaking, and Nicholas tried to be patient. He pulled off his boots and flexed his left leg.

'Does it hurt?' asked Anthony.

Wiggling the toes of his left foot, Nicholas said, 'No. Yes. I mean no, not really. It's . . . a little stiff, that's all. It's not a pain, just . . . I remember how it hurts, when I get overtired. It's anticipating the pain, if that makes sense, as much as any real discomfort.'

Anthony nodded. 'It makes sense. Old habits are hard to forget, and old fears are habits.'

Not in the mood to talk about his own worries, Nicholas said, 'What did you want to talk about?'

'I feel useless.'

Nicholas said, 'We've all been feeling that way, having to wait – '

'No, I mean even when there are things going on, I don't feel as if I'm much help.'

'Might I remind you that if you hadn't been able to track Margaret, we might all still be out on the sea, dead from starvation and lack of water?'

Anthony sighed. 'Since then.'

'You kept at least three men I can count from dying. Isn't that enough?'

Anthony let out a long sigh. 'Perhaps you're right.' He reached into his tunic and pulled out the talisman that

Pug had originally given to Nicholas. 'I sometimes wonder if it's time to use this. Pug said I would know.'

'If you don't know, don't use it,' answered Nicholas. 'He said it was to be used when there is no other choice, according to Nakor.'

Anthony nodded. 'That's what he said. But we still haven't found Margaret and Abigail.'

Nicholas leaned forward and put his hand on Anthony's shoulder. 'We've all been through a lot to find the prisoners, Anthony. I know how you feel about my cousin . . .'

Anthony lowered his eyes and appeared thoroughly embarrassed. 'I try to hide it.'

'Mostly you do a fair job.' Nicholas leaned back again. 'I feel something for Abigail, too, though lately it seems more like a childish affection.' He looked at Anthony and added, 'But I can see your feelings run deeper. Have you said anything to her?'

'I didn't dare,' said Anthony, almost in a whisper. 'She's the Duke's daughter.'

Nicholas smiled. 'So? We've had magicians in the family before, and Margaret's not exactly your run-of-the-mill court lady.'

Anthony said, 'I've felt terrible thinking that I might never get to say anything to her.'

Nicholas nodded. 'I understand. Still, if we can get just one of those poor wretches home again to the Far Coast, we've done right by those who look to the crown for protection.' Grimly he said, 'Even if it's too late for Abigail and Margaret.'

'You have a plan?'

Nicholas sighed. 'I've had nothing to do but sit around and plan. I think we're running out of time. I can't tell you why, but there's a . . . feeling.'

'An intuition?'

'Perhaps. I don't claim any magic powers. I just know

496

that if we don't act soon, it will be too late.'

'When do you plan to move?'

Nicholas said, 'I'm going to speak to Praji and Vaja first thing in the morning. I don't want too much time to pass between recruiting some swords and acting – less time for the Overlord's "Black Rose" to discover what we're doing. If we can get twenty reliable men, we'll go for the ship after dark tomorrow, and the prisoners before dawn. If we don't have twenty, we'll move with what we can hire the night following.'

Anthony said, 'It will be good to act.'

Nicholas nodded. Anthony rose and let himself out. Nicholas lay back in his bed, staring at the wooden ceiling and thinking. Was he really feeling some sort of intuitive leap that would get them on their way home before further disasters struck? Or would his impatience lead them into another tragedy? When he was with Amos and Ghuda, talking wth the others, he felt firm in his decisions. He knew that his training at home had been designed to give him the best tools possible for making difficiult decisions, but when he was alone, the doubts returned, and his fears with them. His foot always throbbed at night before he fell asleep, and he knew that wishing it away would not suffice. He needed to be right. Lives depended upon that. He felt like crying, but he was too tired.

Calis listened and waited. Two men walked below, speaking softly and ignorant of his hovering above them, safely hidden in the shadows of a tree. The heavy foliage and the darkness masked him from view. He waited until they had disappeared around a corner of a wall, then lowered himself, landing on the inside of the court. He waited, listening. He might be on the other side of the wall, but that didn't mean the two men might not have heard him.

His caution was excessive; no human could have heard

the faint sound of his passing; no cry of alarm was raised and no attack came. He looked around the garden. It was a small one, with a single bathing pool in the middle. Overhead a soft gauzy cloth cover had been placed to cut the harsh rays of the sun during the hottest part of the day, while keeping the garden bright. Large doors and windows opened on the small sanctuary. Calis had already investigated two other similar gardens, finding both deserted, overgrown with weeds, their ponds filled with stagnant water. This one was well tended and clean.

Calis hurried across the relatively open expanse and peered into the window. It was shuttered, but through the lattice he saw a figure on a bed. Her hair was pale yellow in the lantern light, but Calis couldn't make out her features. It was likely to be Abigail, from the description he had heard several times. Margaret he knew by sight, but this girl was unknown to him, having come to Crydee after his most recent visit prior to the raid. A less cautious being might have chanced that it was one of those he sought, but Calis knew the patience of a race that counted lives in centuries.

He left the window and examined the door. It was wood, with a single handle and no apparent lock. He listened for several minutes and heard no sound of movement.

He reached for the handle, but something made him pause. He returned to the window and looked again. He had heard a sound, though he hadn't been conscious of it. Now he saw the source. Another girl sat on the bed next to the first, and Calis's eyes widened. She was twin to the first.

Calis stepped away from the shuttered window. He had seen the horrifying vision in the large enclosed yard, and had gleaned that somehow alien creatures were being transformed by arcane, dark powers into copies of the people who had been kidnapped. Obviously it was being done to Abigail.

Then Margaret walked into view. But instantly, senses more acute than any human's recognized that this was not Duke Martin's daughter. The movement was wrong, the way she held herself was wrong, and her expression was not human.

At a loss for what to do, Calis waited. That was something that came easily to him.

Nicholas got out of bed. It was an hour before sunup, but he couldn't sleep. He went to the large room where a dozen men were sleeping, six beds against each wall, and picked his way to the pallet where Praji slept. Vaja was lying across the aisle from him. Nicholas shook Praji's shoulder gently, and the mercenary was instantly awake.

Nicholas motioned for him to follow, and Praji walked after him. He didn't bother to put on his boots or cloak, as Nicholas was also barefoot and wearing no warm outer garment. In the deserted common room, Nicholas said, 'We're going to have to make some decisions, both of us.'

Praji said, 'You're going to tell me the truth?'

Nicholas said. 'It's a long story. Sit down.'

Praji pulled out a chair while he stretched and yawned. Sitting heavily, he said, 'Make it interesting, Captain. I don't like being awakened prematurely. Most of the time it means someone needs unexpected killing.' His smile was not a pretty sight in the predawn gloom.

Nicholas told him everything, save of the Lifestone and the Oracle of Aal, that stood guard over it deep beneath the city of Sethanon. But he told of his father, and the Kingdom, and the raid on Crydee. When he had finished, dawn had broken, and Keeler had come into the common room, making ready for the day's business. Hot bread was delivered from the bakery two doors down, and fruit and cheese shortly after. Without interrupting, he brought over a meal for Nicholas and Praji, moving quickly enough to ensure he couldn't be accused of overhearing their low discussion. Keeler was experienced enough with the way of mercenary companies to know that ignorance often meant staying in business or, more important, alive.

When he was finished, Nicholas said, 'I need a dozen men – twenty would be better; they must be trustworthy, and I'll make it worth their while. They have to be willing to sail out with us and be dropped off up the coast, so they have to be tough enough to make their way back as best they can. Can you do it?'

'*Can's* not the question. *Will* is. How much is worth their while?'

'What would you judge it worthwhile to steal something very precious from the Overlord and his wizard?'

Praji grinned. 'For me, it would be a pleasure to do it for its own sake. I still have that bastard's name on my list. If I can't kill him personal-like, then I might as well irritate him. But for fellows to go against his soldiers, especially if it's them Red Slayers, well, that's real pricy.'

'How pricy?'

'A year's wages for a caravan guard, I'd think. Say a hundred golden draks – better make it a little more.'

Nicholas considered what that was in raw weight, and how much gold he had taken from Shingazi's Landing. He said, 'If you can vouch for them, I'll make it two hundred draks a man, with another hundred extra for you and Vaja to make sure they are trustworthy and follow orders. I don't want any Black Rose agents with us.'

Praji nodded. 'I know twice that number of rough fellows from my years on the road. None of them would be likely agents. It may take me all day to track them down, and I'm going to have to lie to those I don't want coming along.'

Nicholas nodded. 'Tell them we're getting ready to

transport a wealthy merchant and his family upriver, ten boats taking household and servants. Tell him the merchant is very fussy and wants your personal guarantee, so you can't hire anyone you don't know well.' Then Nicholas said, 'How'd you like to be a captain?'

'My own company?' He scratched his chin. 'Wouldn't hurt my standing any.'

'Fine, then tell anyone who asks that the merchant will give you enough to form your own company and you're taking only men you know well.'

Praji smiled and nodded. 'You're one sneaky bastard, Captain. Few men want to join a company just starting out, unless it's old friends. Now, where do you want me to muster the boys?'

'Tell them to stay close. Put them in inns nearby, in twos and threes, and have them ready to move as soon as I give the word.'

'Well, I better go wake up Vaja, and let him eat something – he's like a cranky old woman if he doesn't break his fast in the morning – makes him difficult to put up with during a siege, let me tell you.'

'Send Tuka to me as well,' said Nicholas.

Praji nodded and left. Others started drifting into the common room as the day broke, and by the time Tuka put in an appearance, sleepily scratching his head, Amos and Harry were eating at the table with Nicholas.

Nicholas said, 'I'm going to need your talents today.'

Tuka said, 'What must I do, Encosi?'

'How difficult is it to get ten riverboats for a journey northward?'

'Not difficult, Encosi.'

'How long will it take?'

'I can secure such boats for you by noon. Ensuring they are worthy for the journey will take the rest of the day.'

'Do it in half the time. By sundown I want them tied up at the docks, fully provisioned.'

Amos rested his elbow on the table, his chin in his hand. 'We're leaving?'

'Soon,' said Nicholas. 'I want you to make a list for Harry and Brisa.' To Harry he said, 'Go wake up Brisa. You two go with Tuka. Inspect the boats with him; then go shopping for stores. See that everything you can get is delivered to the docks by afternoon, and have it aboard the boats by sundown. I'll have some soldiers guarding them all night. I want to be able to move with an hour's notice.'

Harry nodded. Between his ability to scrounge and haggle, and Brisa's streetwise sense, they should be able to get what they needed quickly, without calling undue attention to themselves. The City of the Serpent River had enough foreigners with strange accents conducting business that, with a little circumspection, they would pass almost unnoticed.

Nicholas said to Amos, 'As soon as Marcus and Calis return, I want you and Marcus to go fishing.'

Amos signed and heaved himself from the table. 'I expect you'll want us to see what the catch is like near those two warships?'

'Exactly. This will all come to nothing if we can't take one of those two ships and sail to the river mouth to pick up the stores and prisoners from the boats.'

'You've got the men?'

'Praji will have another twenty for us by sundown.'

Amos said, 'That's still cutting it thin. I'll need most of the men from Crydee to take that ship. I can't count on hired swords, and few of them may have any experience in boarding a ship.'

Nicholas nodded. 'I'll keep Ghuda, Marcus, and Calis, but you take as many of the others as you need. I'm putting Harry in charge of the river boats.'

Amos glanced around as the room filled with hungry soldiers and sailors. 'Well, most of the lads will be glad to be doing something. This waiting around was beginning to get on some of their nerves. No fights yet, but some testy remarks and short tempers.'

'I think they'll have plenty to keep them busy, very soon,' said Nicholas.

Marcus and Calis entered the inn an hour later, and Calis said, 'We've found them.'

Nicholas motioned for Amos, Ghuda, and the other two to accompany him back to his room and said, 'Where are they?'

Just then the door opened, and as Nicholas had his sword half out of its scabbard, a sleepy Nakor entered. 'I heard you from the next room.' He yawned, then said, 'Where are the girls?'

Calis said, 'There is a small apartment in the southeastern corner of the estate, two rooms and a small garden. One of the rooms is empty. Margaret and Abigail are in the other.'

Nicholas said, 'Are they all right?'

'It is hard to say. I saw two Abigails.'

'They're making copies,' said Nicholas. 'Why are they not with the others?'

Calis shrugged. Nakor said, 'Maybe they need them for different reasons.'

'"Them" being the girls or the copies?' asked Marcus.

'Either.' Nakor shrugged. 'I'm guessing. But they are the only nobles among the prisoners, right?' The others all agreed. 'Then perhaps they will be subjected to closer scrutiny?'

Nicholas said, 'You're right. But how did they expect to pass off all these counterfeits?'

Amos said, 'They have two copies of Kingdom warships. It's clear to me that they intended to capture the *Royal Eagle* at Barran, take her off to somewhere near Freeport, then sink her.'

Marcus said, 'Wait. Why not sail her down here? Why go through all the trouble of making a copy?'

Amos said, 'Perhaps they didn't have enough men to sail her back here along with the black ship. They hired a lot of foreigners, including Durbin slavers and Tsurani assassins. They recruited men from Kesh and renegades from Freeport. They may not have had many men to spare for the journey, and they certainly didn't want witnesses from our part of the world coming back here with them.' He scratched his chin. 'It's been known since last winter that your father intended to establish that garrison at Barran, Marcus. And given the normal patrols I'd established, and the newer *Dragon* being the new flagship of the fleet, the *Eagle* was almost certain to be the ship sent to the Far Coast.' He shook his head. 'This has been long in planning. Nicholas, if either the *Gull* or *Eagle* came sailing into Krondor – with someone claiming to be a common sailor at the helm, claiming all the officers were dead – the people on the ship might convince your father that they had been carried down to Kesh, somehow conspired with the survivors of the raid to escape, or some other nonsense. Especially if they're all drilled in the same story. Arutha would have no reason not to believe them, and as most of those returning are from the Far Coast, who would recognize their behavior as strange?'

Nicholas said, 'But sooner or later someone from Carse or Crydee would come to see Abigail or Margaret.' He didn't mention Martin by name, for he and Marcus both knew he might be dead.

Ghuda said, 'Being hauled off by slavers would change a person, so odd behavior for a while wouldn't arouse suspicion. I've seen people who couldn't remember their own family after surviving a raid.'

'But only for a while,' Marcus pointed out. Thoughtfully he said, 'Sooner or later someone would make a mistake and give away the ruse. Which means that they don't expect the impersonations to be necessary for more than a few weeks, a few months at most.'

'So now we're back to why they're doing this in the first place.' Nicholas made a dismissive motion with his hand. 'Well, if they're undermanned, that explains why they've kept this city and region on the edge of a low boil for twenty years.'

Marcus said, 'You mean secretly causing trouble between the clans while appearing to be a mediator?'

Nicholas nodded. 'Makes sense. If this Overlord has a secret agenda, causing himself trouble such as a betrayed alliance makes sense. He looks as much like a victim of plots as the clans. If all had gone according to plan, he would have killed a lot of young clansmen, some mercenaries, and the Ranjana and her maids. He risked only a few men in battle.' Nicholas shook his head. 'And the clans would have found themselves in the position of trying to persuade him they weren't responsible!'

Amos said, 'Of course. If the clans think his plan is to take control of the city and displace them, they'd welcome any setback he suffers. But if they think someone else is trying to cause trouble, they'd try to make peace with him. And all the time he really doesn't care about consolidating his holdings.' He brightened. 'The appearance of might is just as good as real might.'

Nakor said, 'There are not many soldiers inside the palace. I saw some in the barracks outside, but inside, there were only some in the great hall, and none anywhere else. There are few living there; not many servants or guards. It is mostly empty. It is like Dahakon's estate.'

Calis said, 'That was my experience. I saw only a few men, none armed, and most of the buildings were deserted.'

Chuda said, 'If I didn't need to really fight anyone, I could keep things lively around here with as few as a hundred men, especially if I turned them out in different company uniforms from time to time, and had some dressed as Red Slayers.'

Nicholas said, 'What are they doing? Why these copies of our people?'

Amos said, 'We can speculate later, but what we need to do now is see if we can take one of those ships.'

Nicholas nodded. 'Marcus, I know you're tired, but go with Amos. Take Ghuda with you.'

They left. Nicholas said, 'Calis, rest for a while. Then you, Nakor, and I will make a plan to get into the estate and free the prisoners.'

Calis said, 'Very well.' He left as well.

Nakor said, 'I've rested. I'm going shopping.'

'What for?'

'Some things I will need. Dahakon is being kept busy by Pug. But his woman, this Lady Clovis, she will cause trouble for us.'

'Why?' asked Nicholas.

'You know what Praji said about her being a soul drinker?'

Nicholas nodded, his face showing his concern. 'Is she?'

Nakor shook his head emphatically. 'No, no. That's a story to scare people.'

Nicholas said, 'That's a relief.'

'She's something else.'

'What?'

'I don't know. I have a thought. Can't be sure until I talk to her.'

'You're going to talk to her?' Nicholas was astonished.

Nakor grinned. 'Maybe. I'd rather avoid that, but you never can tell; I may not have a choice. I do know she's very dangerous.'

'Why?'

'Because she's the one who is running things.'

'This raid?'

Nakor shook his head. 'I mean everything. She's the

506

one who controls Dahakon and the Overlord. She's the true power behind all the strange things in this city. She's the real danger here. It is likely she is the one in contact with the Pantathians.'

Nicholas said, 'Can you face her?'

Nakor laughed. 'Facing her is easy. Surviving is hard.'

Nicholas was forced to laugh. 'What do you need?'

'Oh, some things. And I'll need Anthony with me.'

'Ask him. I think he'll go.'

'Probably. He's like that,' said Nakor. 'I will be back before nightfall.'

He left the room, and Nicholas sat down to think. He began reviewing the timing of the elements of his plan in his head. The ship would have to be taken and sailed through the outer harbor to the river mouth, where it would meet the boats and load cargo and passengers aboard. The boats would have to be taken from the river docks to a beach near the burned-out farmhouse to pick up the prisoners, then move down the river to meet the ship. The prisoners would have to be freed from the estate and moved to the farm and defended until the boats got there.

He fell back on his bed and threw his arm across his eyes. His left foot began to throb. 'This will never work,' he groaned.

Ghuda stood on the roof of the hostel, atop an observation platform once used to alert those inside the small complex of approaching trouble. Praji and Nakor climbed up the small ladder from inside the building.

'What are you doing up here?' asked Praji. 'Nicholas wants us to make plans.'

Ghuda held up his hand. 'In a minute.'

Nakor said, 'Oh.'

Ghuda pointed to the sunset. 'You once said, "There are sunsets above other oceans, Ghuda. Mighty sights and great wonders to behold." Remember?'

Nakor grinned. 'To get you to come along.'

Ghuda smiled. 'I haven't taken the time to watch one. Thought this might be my last opportunity.'

Praji said, 'Grim talk.'

Ghuda shrugged. 'I'm not one given to premonitions, or fatal resignation, but in our line of work . . .'

Praji nodded, saying nothing.

The sun lowered over the city. From their vantage point at the southern end of the bazaar, a vast sea of roofs led off in all directions. The city curved back along the bay on one side, the estuary on the other, so that beyond the buildings to the west they could see the ocean, a thin strip of blue water along the horizon.

The sun sank lower, an orange ball partially masked by the evening haze, moisture coming in from the water. Low clouds presented black faces, with silver, golden, pink, and orange highlights, and the sky was streaked with reds and golds.

The orb of the sun lowered until it disappeared, and at the last instant, they saw a green flash. Ghuda smiled. 'I've never seen that before.'

Nakor said, 'Most people don't. You have to watch a lot of sunsets over water to see it. Clouds have to be right in the sky and the weather must be right, and even then you can miss it. I have seen it only once before in my life.'

Praji said, 'Worth the watching.' He laughed. 'Come along. That's the last fun we may have for a while.'

Ghuda lingered a moment, then said, 'Wonders to behold.' He turned and followed the others below.

Harry ran into the room.

Nicholas asked, 'What?'

Breathlessly he said, 'There's a detachment of the Overlord's soldiers heading this way.'

'Here?' asked Marcus, standing up and pushing back his chair.

'Maybe. I don't know. They're crossing the bazaar and heading down the street. And they don't look happy.'

Nicholas said, 'Brisa, get up on the roof and shout if they're coming this way.' He barked orders to the men of Crydee, who hurried to carry them out. It was midday, and a half-dozen strangers were in the common room. Nicholas shouted, 'Anyone here who doesn't wish to find himself in the middle of a fight better leave now!'

A couple of men ran for the door, while others moved in a more sedate fashion. Suddenly Nakor shouted, 'Nicholas! That man! Don't let him go!'

Nicholas spun around as a thin man in nondescript workman's clothing hurried toward the door. Nicholas leaped to stop him, drawing his dagger. The man pulled a dagger from his belt and lashed out. Vaja stepped up behind the man, hoisted his sword high, and slammed the bell guard down on the smaller man's head. He collapsed to the floor, the dagger falling from limp fingers. Ghuda and Praji quickly hoisted the man to his feet, bleeding slightly from a scalp wound.

'Get him out of here,' said Amos. 'Someone clean up the mess.'

Ghuda and Praji dragged the semiconscious attacker into the back room. Harry knelt and cleaned up the blood with a bar rag, then tossed it to Keeler, who hid it behind the bar.

Nicholas asked Nakor, 'What was that about?'

'I'll tell you after the soldiers have left,' answered Nakor as he hurried toward the back room.

Nicholas said, 'Marcus, you, Calis, and Harry wait in the back with Ghuda and Praji. Vaja, stay close. Everyone try to look surprised when those soldiers come in, but the moment I give the word . . .'

Marcus said, 'We'll be ready,' as they headed for the back room.

In the common room, they sat, but hands rested near sword hilts, and they inspected the room, noticing the position of tables and anticipating the best lines of attack if they had to leave their chairs quickly. Four men stood at the bar, looking into half-empty mugs, daggers hidden out of sight but ready. Keeler cocked a heavy crossbow behind the bar.

Nicholas heard a voice of female outrage and knew the Ranjana was complaining about something. He was half out of his chair to investigate when the door flew open and an officer and four guards came into the room. The officer wore a uniform similar to that worn by the twenty men Nicholas had encountered at Shingazi's Landing.

'Who commands here?' he asked loudly.

Nicholas continued coming to his feet and said, 'I do. I'm Captain Nicholas.'

The man's eyes instantly flicked to look at Nicholas's feet. The Prince felt the hair on the back of his neck stand up, but he willed himself to calmness. All the captain saw was two normal boots.

'We understand you have a girl with you,' said the captain, slowly, his voice deep, his words chosen carefully. 'If she is who we think she is, you may be eligible for a reward.'

Nicholas forced a grin. 'Girl? We don't have any girl with us.'

The captain of the guard motioned for his men to spread out. 'Search every room.'

Nicholas moved to put himself between the closest guardsman and the hallway leading to the rear. 'I have a couple of sick men back there; I don't want them disturbed. I said we don't have any girl with us.' His voice was loud and his words enunciated clearly. He let his hand rest on his belt knife.

The guardsman looked over his shoulder, awaiting instructions. The captain turned to the man closest to the door and nodded. That soldier opened the door, and another dozen men filed into the room. 'We prefer to see for ourselves,' said the captain after his men were inside.

Nicholas said, 'I prefer that you don't.'

'What's all the noise?' asked a feminine voice from behind.

Nicholas turned to see Brisa appear at the door to the back. He glanced at Amos and Anthony, both of whom stared at the girl. She was without her usual man's shirt or blouse beneath – which hung open, showing off a much fuller bosom than Nicholas had suspected, and a slender waist and flat stomach. Around her hips stretched a thin skirt, gathered up in a large knot at one hip, hanging precariously off the other, and tracing every curve of thigh and leg as she moved. Her hair was tousled and she yawned. She moved languidly across the room, swaying her hips in an exaggerated fashion. Reaching Nicholas's side, she slipped her arm through his and said, 'Why all the yelling, Nicky?'

The guard captain said. 'You lied to me!'

Nicholas responded, 'I said we had no girl with us. This is my woman.' As a guard moved toward the hallway, Nicholas said, 'I still don't want you back there.'

Brisa said, 'Oh, I don't mind,' adding, to the captain, 'Our room is a mess, so please be careful.'

Nicholas glanced at her and she nodded slightly. 'Very well,' he said.

A half-dozen soldiers moved back into the rear of the hostel, to reappear a few minutes later. 'No sign of any other women, Captain. Just some sick men lying in the common sleeping room in the back.'

The captain threw Nicholas a long look, then turned and left without comment. Nicholas nodded once to one of his own men, who glanced through the shutters on the window. 'They're leaving, Captain,' he reported.

Nicholas turned to Brisa. 'Where are they?'

'Up on the roof,' said the girl with a relieved expression. 'Nakor and Calis are up there with him.'

Nicholas grinned. 'You're brilliant.'

'This wasn't my idea,' she said, her voice turning angry as she noticed every man in the room staring at her. She pulled the tiny vest closed in front, then crossed her arms when the small garment wouldn't adequately cover her. 'Nakor heard you yelling at the captain. That litle bastard pulled me off the ladder when I started to climb to the roof like you told me. Then he pushed me into the Ranjana's room, and told Calis, Marcus, and Harry to take the girls up on the roof and pull up the ladder through the trapdoor in the ceiling. Next he grabbed my shirt and pulled it open – ripped all the buttons off and had it off me in a blink! Before I could move, he yanked my trousers down around my ankles and I was standing there starkers! Then he pushes me into this pile of clothing that witch had and said to put on something skimpy and get out and distract everyone for a few minutes.'

Amos grinned. 'Well, my pretty wench, you certain did that.'

Blushing furiously, the girl turned and headed back toward the Ranjana's quarters. 'I've never been so embarrassed in my life – parading around half-naked like a Keshian tavern dancer! I'm going to kill that little monkey!'

Nicholas watched her disappearing into the hall, and the way her hips moved under the skimpy skirt. Amos's hand fell on his shoulder and he heard Trask say, 'Harry's a lucky fellow. She is one fine-looking young woman.'

Nicholas smiled for a moment, then his expression turned serious. 'We've got to leave tonight. Did you see the way that captain looked at my foot when I told him my name?'

'Yes. They're looking for you and anyone else who might have come here from Crydee.' He rubbed his chin. 'Remember, unless they sent someone back to check, they don't know the *Raptor* has sunk. They may be expecting those they didn't kill at Crydee to be after them any day now. If Nakor's right and this Lady Clovis is behind everything, she might suspect you were on the vessel following her black ship. Her raiders probably got a description of everyone important at Crydee from that Quegan trader Vasarius. They know who wasn't killed during the raid. If Martin had been leading here . . .' He shook his head. 'Who knows what might have happened.'

Nicholas said, 'I'm glad they didn't see Marcus and Harry. Two cousins who looked like brothers and a redheaded young man of the same general age would have been too much of a coincidence. They still may come back.'

'And someone's told them the Ranjana is here,' said Amos. 'Maybe that Anward Nogosh Pata was trying to repair some of the damage done to his master's dealings with the Overlord.'

A shout caused Nicholas and Amos to hurry to the rear, where they found Brisa hitting Nakor on the head and shoulders with one hand, while trying to keep her vest closed with the other. The little man was half laughing as

513

he shouted, 'I'll sew the buttons on! I'll do it right now!'

The Ranjana's mood was no better than Brisa's. She threw a dark look at Nicholas as she said, 'That man put his hands on me!' She pointed at Calis, who smiled broadly, for the first time Nicholas could remember. 'He pushed me up the ladder, and put his hands on my *bottom*!' complained the girl with indignation. 'I will have him trampled under elephants!'

Calis shrugged. 'She wasn't moving as quickly as the maids had, and I heard the captain order the search.'

Nicholas said, 'Girl, those men would have taken you out of here, to the Overlord's palace, and I think you'd not have lived to see sundown. Now be quiet and go to your quarters and pack.'

'We're leaving?'

Nicholas nodded. 'Tomorrow, but early. So have your maids have everything ready by tonight's meal. Now, go!'

Brisa pushed Nakor away and said, 'I'll sew them on myself, but we still have a score to settle.'

She vanished into the Ranjana's room behind her and slammed the door. Nakor grinned. 'That was fun.'

Watching the door for a minute, and thinking of how attractive Brisa was when she wasn't decked out in shapeless man's clothing, Nicholas could only say, 'I imagine it was.'

'You're a strange man,' said Amos to Nakor, laughing.

'How did you know to keep that man from leaving?' Nicholas asked Nakor as Marcus and Harry came down the ladder from the roof.

'Smelled him,' said Nakor, motioning for them to follow. He led them back to the common sleeping room, where Ghuda and Praji sat on beds on either side of the unconscious man. Nakor moved over to him and opened his shirt. He pulled a small pouch on a thong from around the man's neck. 'See?'

Nicholas took the pouch and smelled a familiar pungent odor. 'Cloves?'

Nakor nodded. 'I smelled it on him before, the first time I saw him in the commons, a day or two ago. Then I smelled it again when he tried to leave.'

Amos opened the pouch and poured a pile of cloves out. 'So what's this all about?'

'Cloves. Clovis. Obvious.'

'I still don't understand,' said Amos.

'Do you know what clove is called in the Delkians dialect of Kesh?'

Amos said, 'No.'

'Black rose. Ask any spice merchant south of the Girdle of Kesh. It took me some time,' admitted Nakor. 'I couldn't understand why this man smelled like cloves. But it came to me.' He took the bag from Amos. 'If they leave a message for another agent, say, in an agreed-upon place, they put one of these cloves with it, and the other agent knows it is genuine. Simple.'

Nicholas said, 'Very.'

Amos said, 'Too simple.'

Nicholas said, 'For ruling and conquest. But remember who we're dealing with and what their motives are, and you'll see that they're effective enough.'

Amos nodded. He remembered what Nicholas had told him and what he had seen at the Battle of Sethanon. The Pantathians were not concerned with conquest and ruling. They were a death cult bent on recalling their goddess through the Lifestone. If death was the only object, one need not be that clever, thought Amos.

'What do we do with this one?' asked Ghuda, indicating the unconscious agent.

Nicholas said, 'Tie him up and keep him someplace safe. Have Keeler cut him loose after we've been gone a day. We'll be safely away or . . . it won't matter.'

The others nodded. They knew exactly what he meant by that.

Brisa pulled her trousers on, tied the waist cord securely, then sat on the floor, ignoring the black looks directed at her by the Ranjana. She refused to leave half-clothed, so she insisted on sewing the buttons back on her shirt before quitting the noblewoman's quarters. She had bullied a needle and thread from one of the maids.

'You may be used to the rough hands of common men on you,' snapped the Ranjana, 'but I am not!'

Brisa said, 'Take your black mood out on someone else, girl. I'm not inclined to put up with it.' She bit at the thread and checked the condition of the first button. Starting on the second one, she said, 'And if you're too stupid to notice, Calis is not what I would call common.'

The Ranjana lost her petulant pose long enough to say, 'He is uncommonly strong. I am not large, but I would not have guessed any man could have pushed me upward that rapidly and easily.'

'With one hand, too, if he was on the ladder.'

The maids exchanged looks of amazement, as they had all been on the roof and had seen none of this. The Ranjana said, 'He's not bad-looking, either, though there's something about him that's strange.'

'More than you'll ever know,' said Brisa with a mocking tone.

The Ranjana said, 'More than I would ever wish to know. My maids may know common men, and it's clear you're used to them, but I am to be saved for a man of rank, a man of wealth and power.'

'And you think being the fifteenth wife of this Overlord is something special?' She shook her head. 'Some people.'

The Ranjana smiled. 'Your captain is handsome, in a stern way, but I like it when he smiles.' She found Brisa staring at her in amusement, and said, 'But he's too common a man for one such as I.'

Brisa couldn't help it, and burst out laughing.

'What's so amusing?' the Ranjana demanded.

'Ah, nothing,' said Brisa, finishing the second button.

'No, what is it?' asked the Ranjana while Brisa set to work on the third button.

Brisa ignored her for a minute; she finished the third button and started on the last. 'Girl,' demanded the Ranjana. 'What was so funny?'

Brisa put down the needle and donned her man's shirt. Standing up, she said, 'Just that some people have an odd notion of what's noble and what's common. You wouldn't know a prince if you'd been standing next to him for weeks.' She left without further word.

The Ranjana stood, hands on hips, a moment, then stormed to the door and pulled it open. A guard stood outside, and as she attempted to move around him, he said, 'Sorry, my lady, but you're to stay in the room and oversee the packing of your baggage.'

'I need to talk to that girl –'

The soldier interrupted. 'Sorry, my lady. The captain was very clear you were to do nothing but pack until supper.'

The Ranjana stepped back into her room and closed her door. She turned with a thoughtful expression on her face and said, 'Prince?' After a moment of reflection, she clapped her hands together and said, 'Hurry! What are you waiting for. Everything must be packed and ready for travel by supper!'

Seeing her maids were hurrying to get her clothing and jewels packed away, the Ranjana crossed to her bed and lay down, thinking. 'A Prince?' Then a smile came to her and she began to hum a faint tune.

As the sun sank in the west, Harry stood nervously overseeing the line of carts and wagons heading for the docks. The boats were all waiting, manned by hired boatmen paid extra to be ready to leave at any time of the day or night. Tuka was at the dock to see none of them wandered off or got drunk while waiting. Praji, Vaja, and twenty-four mercenaries, posing as guards, were there to ensure the little wagon driver's orders were obeyed. Calis and Marcus would join them, and as the boats set off down the river, it would be their job to get the prisoners out of Dahakon's estate.

Harry directed the four guards to go to the head of the small caravan, while Brisa herded the Ranjana and her maids. Nicholas had decided to keep the girls with his party a while longer, before releasing them with enough money to purchase escorts back up river. Harry was worried; the Ranjana was being cooperative to the point of behaving sweetly, even to Brisa.

Brisa looked suspicious whenever the noblewoman asked a question, but she welcomed nattering over arguments. Brisa kept her eyes moving through the late afternoon shadows, looking for signs of unexpected movement, or of being watched, while she half listened to the chattering Ranjana. Most of the questions were about Nicholas, which she fended off with vague answers.

Harry was watching the last wagon leave the bazaar when he heard a shout and the sound of confusion from the north side of the giant square. A detachment of soldiers rode into view, laying about with lashes as they drove everyone out of their way. Behind came a line of wagons, each carrying what looked to be prisoners. Then Harry's eyes widened.

He turned to his wagon driver. 'A bonus if you make sure everyone in front of you gets to the docks in order. I must take a message to my master!'

As the wagon driver shouted, 'How much?' Harry raced back into the bazaar, dodging through the press of shoppers and merchants. He could see the plumes of two

518

guard officers above the heads of the crowd, which gathered to watch the spectacle, and some of the heads of the prisoners in the high wagons as well.

Harry forced his way close enough to get a good look, then turned and sprinted back through the crowd, knocking aside anyone in his way. A string of curses and oaths followed after him as he ran toward the hostel.

A few minutes later, he pushed his way into the commons, past a dozen curious soldiers and headed for Nicholas's room. Without knocking, he pushed his way in, to find Nicholas going over his plan for the night with Amos, Ghuda, Marcus, and Calis. Anthony and Nakor had already left to do some mysterious errand the little man insisted was vital.

'What?' said Nicholas. 'You're supposed to be with the wagons.'

'They're moving the prisoners!' said Harry, almost breathless.

'Where?' said Amos.

Harry sucked in a breath. 'To the southwest. It looks like they're heading for the docks!'

'Damn!' said Nicholas, pushing his way past the others, who all followed after Nicholas and Harry. In the common room, Nicholas turned and said, 'Calis, Marcus, head for the river docks. If you don't hear from us, do as we've planned. If anything changes, we'll send a runner.'

Outside the hostel, they split up, and Harry, Amos, Ghuda, and Nicholas hurried after the wagons. They dodged behind the procession and ducked around gawkers, keeping the last wagon, flanked by two mounted guards, in sight. Nicholas said, 'I recognize one of those faces – it's Edward, a page from the castle.'

He indicated a young man who sat in the rear of the last wagon, staring off into space with a vacant expression.

Amos said, 'He looks like something's wrong with him.'

Ghuda said, 'They all do.'

Nicholas moved to the side of the street and ran along to make up some of the distance, then ducked back into the road, almost knocking over a woman carrying a tray of fruit, who had been watching the wagons. She shouted at him, and one of the guards turned to see what the disturbance was.

Nicholas turned to the woman and said, 'Sorry.'

'Watch where you're going, you fool!' she shouted.

'Who're you calling a fool!' he shouted back.

Then Ghuda grabbed his arm and said, 'He's stopped watching.'

They were off, and Nicholas craned his neck to see the wagons. They followed until they were at the docks. As market traffic thinned out, they were forced to fall farther behind the wagons, lest they be noticed. When they could finally get close, by ambling down toward a line of sheds as if on some errand, they caught a good look at the proceedings. Longboats waited to carry the prisoners to a ship in the harbor.

Amos pulled Nicholas and Harry back between two sheds, and Ghuda ducked in behind them. 'What is this?' Amos said.

Nicholas said, 'I don't know. There's something wrong with our people.'

'Maybe these aren't our people,' said Harry. 'Maybe these are the copies.'

Nicholas swore. 'If that's true, we still have to go into the estate to find out.' He thought a minute, then said, 'Harry, go back to the river docks and tell Calis and Marcus to head across now. I want Calis to get in and see if our people are still there. If they are, have them bring word back to Praji and Vaja and go forward with the plan. If they're not . . . or if our people are dead, it's useless to raid for revenge. Have them hold the boats at the river docks until I tell them what to do. If our people are there, you're in charge of the river boats. Get them down to the meeting place and get our people aboard, then head for the harbor.'

Harry said, 'Got it,' and turned to leave.

'Harry!' shouted Nicholas after him.

Harry halted. 'What?'

'Stay alive.'

Harry grinned back. 'You too, Nicky,' he answered, and ran off.

The three who remained watched until the first group of boats reached the first ship, then Amos swore. 'They're taking both ships out!'

'When?' asked Nicholas.

Amos has asked around about the local tides and sailing conditions, but couldn't get too much information without arousing suspicions. He said, 'My best guess is sometime between midnight and dawn, whenever the tide turns.'

'Is there anything else there we can steal?'

Amos glanced around the bay. 'Lot of ships have come and gone. But . . .' He pointed. 'That *begala*.' He indicated a smaller sailing vessel with two masts, lateen-rigged. 'She's a coaster, but she's fast. If we get out of the harbor before those warships leave, we can intercept one up the coast. They'll have to keep close to the wind coming out of the harbor, until they turn southeast to run around that peninsula east of here. We can take whichever ship is second in line – the other can't turn to come back and help in time. But we have to close before they turn, or both ships will just run away from us.'

Ghuda said, 'Can that little ship hold everyone?'

'No,' said Amos. 'We'll have to come back, load up, then take out after the first ship.'

Nicholas said, 'We need to take one before we worry about the other. Come on. Let's get back to the hostel and send word to the river about the change.'

They set out, and suddenly Nicholas said, 'Oh, gods!'

'What?' asked Amos.

521

'Nakor.'

Ghuda said, ' "Oh, gods" is right.'

'Does anyone know what he and Anthony are doing?'

'No,' said Nicholas. 'We can only hope it doesn't stir up a hornets' nest before we're out of the city.'

They hurried back to the hostel.

As night fell, Calis vaulted over the wall of the estate. He hurried, unconcerned about being observed. He was familiar with the scant security under normal conditions, and Nicholas's message about the prisoners being moved to the ship made it even less likely anyone was about the estate.

As he turned the corner of a large hedge, part of a landscaped yard going to seed, he almost knocked over a guard. Before the man could react, Calis struck out with the flat of his hand, catching the man in the throat, crushing his windpipe. The guard fell over backward, thrashing on the ground. Calis hurried along, not waiting to watch him die.

Calis was not given to vainly cursing luck or fate, but despite the long odds of a guard left behind to patrol the estates, he still knew that time was more important than stealth. The condition of the prisoners the last time he saw them meant their captors had no concern beyond keeping them alive to make their living copies, and since it now appeared that task was complete, there would be no reason to keep them alive.

The crunch of boots on gravel announced the approach of another guard, and Calis hugged the ground behind a small gardener's shed. When the soldier walked past, Calis stood up and quickly reached out, grabbing the man by the chin and back of the head. Before the startled soldier could raise his own hands, Calis snapped his neck.

Calis ran. He reached the side of the walled court where the prisoners were kept and leaped, landing on the wall. Crouching low, he saw the prisoners still lying upon their pallets, abandoned by their keepers and the creatures that were transformed into copies.

Calis saw they were unconscious, to the last of them, but still alive. He leaped down into the compound and approached the nearest prisoner. Kneeling next to a young man, now gaunt and filthy, he attempted to rouse him. The man groaned softly, but wouldn't awaken.

Looking up, he saw that something had changed since the last time he had been to the compound. The elfling stood and trotted to the other end of the square. There was a life-sized statue there, of what at first looked to be an elf but, upon closer examination, was something else entirely. Then Calis felt his hair stand up on his neck and arms, and a rush of fear shot through him. Never in his life had he felt such dread, but never before had he encountered what stood before him. The idol was a Valheru, an icon of the long-lost masters of Midkemia. And something basic and profound in Calis's being responded. He might only be half-elven by birth, but that half cried out in fear at something no living creature had seen in this life. Only his father, Tomas, had firsthand knowledge of the Valheru, and then because he was the legatee of that heritage. For a time he had been both man and Dragon Lord, and his memories had been those of a creature dead for thousands of years.

Calis circled the statue, examining it. It was a female Valheru, wearing armor and helm. The motif was that of snakes, embossed on her helm and the shield she carried. Calis then knew that Nicholas's worst fear was well founded: the Pantathian serpent priests were behind all that had transpired so far, without a doubt. This was Alma-Lodaka, the Valheru who had created the Pantathians millennia ago, raising serpents to consciousness and intelligence, to serve in her home, amusing but trivial creatures. But in the centuries since the Valheru had quit

Midkemia, these creatures had evolved, becoming a death cult who worshipped their lost goddess, Alma-Lodaka, believing that should they conspire to bring her back to this world, all would die and enter her service, and the Pantathians would be elevated to the rank of demigods as reward for their loyalty.

Calis snapped out of his reverie and left the compound. He pushed open one of the double doors and got his first look at the interior of the square building. It was empty, save for more chains and some abandoned tools.

Calis hurried, for he needed to get word to Marcus and across the river to Harry. He knew that if he didn't get help back to the prisoners soon, they would most likely die.

Margaret fought against the restraints, tendrils of silk blowing in the breeze, which wrapped around her ankles and wrists, holding her in place. She sought to shout, to scream in anger and fear, yet her mouth filled with the soft stuff and prevented her. In the gloom a figure approached.

'Ah!' she exclaimed, sitting upright. The bed was drenched with perspiration. The room was dark. Her head throbbed with the worst headache she had known in her young life, what she imagined a hangover felt like, from things she'd overheard after the big celebrations at Castle Crydee.

From her bed, Abigail stirred, making sleepy questioning noises.

Margaret drew a deep breath and composed herself. Her heart pounded and she felt as if she had been running. She got out of bed and found herself uncoordinated, her mind spinning, only the stab of fear that she had felt a moment before giving her anything close to clarity. She put out one hand and steadied herself against the wall, while her blood rushed in her ears and her pounding heart echoed in her head with a dull throb.

She reached for the water jar kept on the table between her bed and Abigail's and found it empty. That struck her as being odd.

She moved to Abigail's bed and said, 'Abby?' Her voice sounded like a dull croak in her own ears.

She sat down and shook Abigail, who stirred, mumbling as if trying to speak in her sleep. Margaret tried to raise her voice and said, 'Abby!', shaking her friend as hard as she could.

Abigail sat up and asked, 'What – ?'

Margaret stared at her friend. Abigail looked as if she hadn't slept for a week. Her eyes were circled by dark rings, and her face was paler than usual. Her hair was unkempt and dirty, and she kept blinking, as if fighting to awaken.

Margaret said, 'You look terrible.'

Abigail blinked harder, shook her head, and said, 'You don't look like much yourself.' Her voice sounded as harsh and dry as had Margaret's.

Margaret forced herself to her feet and went to a mirror. The image that greeted her was older than the last she had seen. Her face was as drawn as Abigail's, as if she also hadn't slept for days.

Her nightshirt was damp and stank. She made a face. 'I smell as if I haven't bathed in days.'

Abigail's expression was still vague. And she asked, 'What?'

'I said . . .' Margaret glanced around the room. 'Where are they?'

'They?'

Crossing to her friend, Margaret took her by the shoulders and looked into her eyes. 'Abby?'

'What?' said Abigail irritably, pushing her away.

'Those things: where are they?'

'What things?'

525

'Don't you remember?'

Pushing past Margaret, Abby said, 'Remember what? Where's breakfast? I'm starving.'

Margaret moved back from her friend. Her nightshirt was also heavily soiled, stained below the waist, and her bed reeked. 'You're a mess.'

Abigail looked around, still as if unable to get her bearings. 'Mess?'

Margaret then noticed it was dark outside. From the way she felt, and the mess in both their beds, she knew that they hadn't merely wakened early. They had slept the clock round at least one full day, more likely two or three. Never before had they been allowed to do that. Every day a servant had come to wake them an hour after dawn, bringing them their morning meal. Margaret went to the window and looked out into the garden. It was deserted. She waited a moment and there wasn't a sound. Usually at night she could hear people moving somewhere in the grounds, and occasionally she had heard a distant voice, or what sounded like a scream.

Hurrying to the door, she tried to handle. It opened. Peering down the corridor in either direction, she saw no other signs of life. She turned to Abigail and said, 'There's no one around.'

Abigail stood quietly, her eyes fixed on a point in the air. Margaret moved to stand before her and said, 'Abby!'

The other girl blinked, but she said nothing. While Margaret watched, Abigail seemed to wilt, her body going limp as she sank back toward the bed. Her eyes closed and she was almost sitting when Margaret grabbed her shoulders. Bracing the other girl while she fought her own dizziness, Margaret shook her friend and shouted her name.

Getting no results, Margaret cursed the empty water jar. She kept her hold on Abigail and half pushed, half carried her to the door that opened onto the garden. She unlatched that door and pulled her friend through, propelling her toward the pool in the middle.

Margaret then pushed Abigail into the water. She sank a moment, then with a convulsion sat up in the shallow pool, spitting and coughing. 'What!' she said, her tone furious. 'Why did you do that?' she demanded.

Margaret stripped off her filthy nightshirt, sat in the pool next to her friend, and began washing days of sweat and waste from her. 'Because you stink as badly as I do and I couldn't seem to wake you.'

Abigail wrinkled her nose. 'Is that us?'

'It is,' answered Margaret, slipping under the water and wetting her hair. She came up and blew water from nose and mouth. 'I don't know how clean we can get, but if we're going to get out of here, I didn't want anyone finding us by our stink.'

'Get out?' said Abigail, now fully awake.

Margaret made a valiant attempt to scrub her hair with fresh water. 'The door is unguarded, and I don't hear anyone around, and those two creatures are gone.'

Abigail moved to the small sculpture of a water bearer, ducking her head under the water flowing from its jug to rinse away the dirt in her hair. 'How long?'

'Were we asleep?'

Abigail nodded.

'I don't know,' said Margaret. 'From the mess in our beds, a few days, maybe a week. I feel terrible, but I'm starving and thirsty.'

Abigail drank from the fountain and said, 'I feel rotten, too.' She stuck her head under the fountain for a moment, then said, 'I'm as clean as I'm going to be without soap.' She tried to stand up, but her wobbly knees betrayed her and she fell back into the water.

'Careful,' said Margaret, moving to drink from the fountain. 'You're a lot more shaky than I am.'

'I wonder why?' said Abigail, brushing her wet hair

527

back with both hands as she carefully stood up in the knee-high water.

Margaret finished cleaning herself and walked out of the pool. She gave her friend a hand as they returned to their room. 'I don't know. I probably fought harder against whatever they were – ' She stopped, and her mouth opened. 'They made copies of us!'

Abigail blinked. 'What are you talking about?'

'The two creatures that were in here with us.'

'The lizard things?' asked Abigail, disgust on her face.

'They changed, they grew hair, and their bodies changed – and at the end they looked and sounded like us!'

Abigail looked frightened. 'Margaret, how could anyone do that?'

'I don't know, but we've got to get out of here. Anthony and the others are out there somewhere, looking for us, and we've got to warn them that there are those things out there that look like us.'

They opened the wicker hamper used to keep their clean clothes and Margaret drew out an underskirt. She tossed it to Abigail and said, 'Dry off.' She grabbed another to use as a towel, throwing it on the bed when she was done. She selected the two least confining gowns and passed one to Abigail. 'Leave off the underskirts; we need to move as easily as possible. We may be climbing walls.'

She put on soft slippers, and when she was dressed, she looked to see how Abigail was doing. The other girl was moving sluggishly, but she was almost dressed. Margaret helped her on with her slippers.

Margaret stood up and went to the door, peeking out to make sure no one had appeared while they bathed. Seeing no one, she guided Abigail out into the hall. At the end of the hall, she opened the door to the outside and looked around. There was no one in sight. Signaling for silence, she led Abigail into the night.

'Do I really need this?' asked Anthony, indicating the pouch he carried.

'Yes,' said Nakor. 'You never know what might come in handy. This woman who calls herself Clovis is dangerous, and she uses tricks. Maybe not as powerful as Pug, but enough to kill us both with a look. We need to be ready for anything. What we have in the pouch will be totally unexpected.'

'But . . .' began Anthony, then stopped. He knew better than to argue with the occasionally cryptic little man. The content of the bag confounded him; he couldn't see what it might be good for.

They were moving through the tunnel from the palace to Dahakon's estate. Nakor had walked into the palace while the bulk of the garrison was marching to the docks. He had entered the outer courtyard carrying an empty box, while Anthony carried a sack of apples. Before the guard could challenge them, Nakor asked for directions to the kitchen, saying they were bringing part of a shipment of food that was delayed.

The guard had looked slightly confused, but nothing about the two of them looked remotely threatening, so he gave them instructions. They hurried off. Nakor went right past the kitchen entrance and around the side of the palace until he found an unguarded door. They had deposited the empty box in a side corridor, and Nakor carefully put the bag of apples into his trick rucksack before leading Anthony down into the lower levels and to the tunnel that led under the river.

Reaching the stairs up to Dahakon's estate, Nakor said, 'Do you understand what you're to do?'

'Yes, I mean no. I know what you've told me to do,

but I don't have any idea what good it will do.'

'Doesn't matter,' Nakor said with a grin. 'Just do it.'

They reached the heart of the estate without seeing another living person. It was several hours after nightfall, and Anthony knew that if all went according to plan, Calis and the rescuers would be inside the estate within the next two hours. Their job was to ensure that the magician and his soul-drinking lady didn't interfere.

They made their way through a series of dark halls, dimly illuminated by a single lamp at each intersection, and at last Nakor led Anthony into the chambers used by Dahakon. The young magician shuddered at the decaying bodies on the wall, then stood in open-mouthed amazement at the sight of the motionless magician sitting on a chair, eyes staring sightlessly into space.

Nakor went over to Dahakon and said, 'He's still busy.'

'Pug?' asked Anthony.

Nakor nodded. He fished out the lens he had taken and said, 'Look through this.' Anthony did, and Nakor said, 'They battle. I think Pug could win easily, but it might mean trouble for us. Better to keep this one out of the way.'

'So that's what's going on,' said a voice from behind them.

Anthony and Nakor both spun around to find the Lady Clovis standing at the door, her eyes narrowed as she regarded the two intruders.

Then recognition transformed her face. 'You!' she shouted.

Nakor's eyes widened, and he said, 'Jorna?' He gaped as she nodded, and he said, 'I thought it was you. You've got a new body!'

The woman moved forward and Anthony swallowed hard. Everything about her screamed at him on a level so basic he had to force himself to remember she was the evil power behind every horrible event that had occurred to those he loved. Every death, every minute of suffering, every loss of friends and loved ones was authored by her. Still, the sway of her hips, the inviting parted lips, the heave of her bosom, the deep black eyes – all called to him, and he felt his body respond.

Then Nakor said, 'Stop that silliness!' Reaching over to Anthony, he pinched him hard on the arm.

Anthony cried out and his eyes teared from pain. Instantly his desire for the woman vanished. Nakor said, 'Those smells you use to trap men stopped working on me a hundred years ago, Jorna.' Nakor then pulled an onion out of his bag and jammed his thumb into it. He stuck it under Anthony's nose and laughed. 'My friend can't get excited with his eyes watering and his nose running.'

'I'm the Lady Clovis now,' she said, looking down at Nakor. 'You haven't changed much.'

Nakor shrugged. 'You used to be a troublemaker, but nothing like this. When did you join with the snakes?'

She shrugged. 'When they gave me a way to keep my youth.' She walked away and displayed her body to good advantage, like a practiced courtesan showing herself to her master. 'I was getting old . . . What name are you using now?'

'I am Nakor.'

'Nakor?'

'Nakor the Blue Rider!' he said with pride.

'Whatever.' She shrugged, and Anthony was forced to breathe deeply the fragrance of the onion to keep his wits about him as he watched the rise of her breasts, barely hidden by the skimpy vest she wore. 'It doesn't matter. The business that brought me here is at an end; I may stay for a while and keep Valgasha on the throne, before I leave him to the none-too-tender mercies of the clans. But when my friends finish their business, I shall leave.'

'What are they offering to one of your powers?' asked

Nakor, moving slowly toward Anthony. 'You have riches, or you did when I last saw you. You have talents. You know a lot of tricks. You look young.'

'I look young, but I'm not,' she said, and almost spat the words at Nakor. 'I must kill two or three lovers a year just to age normally, five or six more to remove a year from my looks. Do you know how difficult that is when you're supposed to remain faithful to the most powerful magician in the area? Dahakon was too useful to get him angry, and he may have been stupid in some significant respects – '

'His taste in women?' volunteered Nakor.

She smiled. 'That's one example, but he was cunning; he kept me under watch most of the time. This has been a very difficult decade for me, Nakor. Fidelity was never high on my list of virtues.'

She patted the motionless magician upon the head, almost affectionately. 'Have you noticed that those who spend too much time playing with dead things seem to lose their perspective? Dahakon can do amazing things with dead people, but they tend to be such boring company, no imagination whatsoever, you know.'

'What did they offer you?'

She laughed. It was a rich sound, almost musical in tone. 'Immortality! More: eternal youth!' Her eyes were wide and Anthony thought perhaps she was also mad.

Nakor shook his head. 'You believe them?' He shook his head. 'I thought you smarter than that. They want more than you can ever give them.'

The woman said, 'Do you claim to know what their ultimate goal is, or is this some feeble attempt to get information from me?'

'I know what they're doing. You don't, or you would never have joined with the Pantathians. Pug knows what they're doing, too.'

'Pug,' she said with violence. 'The inheritor to the

mantle of Macros. The greatest magician of our time.'

Nakor shrugged. 'Some say. I know he could have ended this farce in a minute.' He pointed to Dahakon.

'Then why didn't he?'

'Because we need to find out what the Pantathians are doing, again. So we can stop them. If he kills Dahakon, you run and take the prisoners somewhere else. Or maybe he comes here himself, so you and Dahakon kill the prisoners to keep him away. We still don't know the plan.' Nakor winked. 'Instead he keeps Dahakon busy, while we come and get the prisoners, figure out the plan then defeat you.' His tone was almost apologetic. 'Nothing personal.'

She shook her head. 'I would let you live, for old times' sake, if I could, but I can't.'

'Don't make us hurt you,' warned Nakor.

She laughed. 'How?'

Nakor pointed to Anthony, who barely kept himself from trembling and stood with his eyes watering and nose running, looking at Nakor.

'He is the true inheritor of the mantle of Macros!' said Nakor dramatically. 'He is Macros's son!'

The woman looked at Anthony. 'Him?'

Nakor said dramatically, 'Anthony, we must neutralize her. Unleash the fury of your powers!'

Anthony nodded. That was the phrase Nakor had told him would mean he was to use the small pouch. Clovis began incanting a spell, and Anthony felt the hair on his arms and neck stand up at the conjuring of fey powers. He recognized the phrases, and knew she was erecting a protective barrier against a mystic attack. He also knew that he possessed nothing close to the skills or strength to breach such a protective spell.

Suddenly she stood encased in a nimbus of silver light. Anthony reached inside the bag and thumbed the small paper device Nakor had given him, then threw it hard against the floor. A column of black smoke erupted, filling the room quickly.

'What is this?' cried Clovis. She began chanting again, and Anthony knew she called on dark forces to come and destroy Nakor and himself. Praying fervently that Nakor knew what he was doing, he opened the pouch and threw it hard at Clovis.

She put up her hands as it passed through the silver barrier around her, interrupting her chanting. It struck her in the face, and she was enveloped in black powder. All three froze a moment, then she sneezed. She opened her mouth to speak, and sneezed again, her eyes tearing as she sneezed a third time. She coughed, as if choking, and sneezed violently. Anthony sneezed, too.

The woman tried to speak, to begin her spell again, but she couldn't stop sneezing. Nakor reached into his rucksack and pulled out a large cloth bag. He reached back and swung as hard as he could, striking the woman on the back of the head with it.

She collapsed into a heap.

Anthony blew his nose to clear it, and with eyes watering, he said, 'Pepper?'

Nakor sneezed. 'You can't conjure if you're sneezing. I knew if she expected some magic attack, she would neglect to protect herself from the obvious. She was always preoccupied with great things and neglected the common.' He measured the distance, then hit her hard again with the bag. 'She will be unconscious for a while.'

'What did you hit her with?'

'The bag of apples. Hurt, I bet.'

'Do we leave her?' asked Anthony.

'We couldn't kill her if we tried. If we cut off her head, it'll just irritate her more. If she thinks we ran away, she'll be upset, but she imagines her side has already won. She'll have no reason to follow us unless she finds out we've stolen one of her ships.'

He looked around the room, handed the bag of apples to Anthony, and said, 'If she stirs, hit her again.'

He ran into the other room, Dahakon's study, then returned with a brown-stained knife.

'I thought you said we couldn't kill her,' said Anthony.

'We can't. But we can inconvenience her.' He went to where Dahakon sat and slashed the magician's throat. A faint line of crimson appeared along the skin, but no blood flowed. He then used the knife to cut some cords from the curtains, which he used to bind Clovis hand and foot. Nakor threw the knife to the floor and said, 'Let's go. Calis and the others should be with the prisoners.'

They hurried from the chambers and Anthony said, 'What did you do with Dahakon?'

'If he breaks off his fight with Pug, he'll have something to keep him busy. Preventing himself from bleeding to death will keep his mind off us for a while. I can't count on his being as pragmatic about these things as Jorna – Clovis, I mean. He may come after us anyway.'

'Where do you know her from?'

'Back in Kesh, years ago.'

'You were friends?'

'She was my wife.' He grinned. 'Well, sort of. We lived together.'

Anthony flushed. 'You lived with that murderess?'

Nakor grinned. 'I was younger. She was very pretty, and very good in bed. I didn't look for the same things in a woman when I was a young man that I look for now.'

Anthony said, 'How did you recognize her?'

'Some things about people don't change. When you've gotten better at doing tricks, you'll find you can see the true person, no matter what form they put on. It's a very useful thing to know.'

'I think if we live to tell of this, you should return to Stardock and teach some of those tricks.'

'I might teach you some, then you can go back to

Stardock. I don't like that place.'

They reached the hall that led to the courtyard and found a dead servant lying on the floor. Nakor looked at him as they passed. 'She was busy before she found us.'

Anthony turned his head away. The man was nude, and his body was shrunken, as if every drop of fluid had been sucked from his flesh. The stink of black magic filled the air, and Anthony found himself deeply disturbed at the rush of desire he had felt in the woman's presence. His respect for Nakor's ability to resist it doubled.

They approached the walled court where the prisoners were being held, when Nakor stopped. 'Look,' he whispered.

Two figures huddled in the darkness, barely seen from where Anthony stood. Nakor signaled and Anthony followed.

They moved quietly and crept up behind the hiding figures, and suddenly Anthony felt a rush of heat and a tingling in his body. 'Margaret!' he gasped, and the two figures leaped to their feet.

Margaret turned and her eyes opened wide. 'Anthony?' she asked, then in two steps she flew into his arms. Sobbing with relief, she said, 'I have never been so happy to see anyone in my life.'

Abigail came to stand next to the young magician, and touched him on the arm, as if to see if he was real. 'Where are the others?'

Nakor said, 'They should be freeing the other prisoners. Come along.'

Anthony held Margaret tight, and was loath to let go of her. He forced himself to, and stepped away. 'I'm pleased to see you're safe.'

She looked at him with tears in her eyes. 'Is that all you can say?' She reached up, put her hand behind his head, and kissed him.

He stood motionless an instant, then embraced her

again. When they parted, she said, 'How could you touch me every day for months and think I'd not feel what you were feeling?' Tears ran down her face. 'I know you, Anthony. I know your heart and I love you, too.'

Nakor brushed a tear from his own eye, and said, 'We must go.'

He took Abigail by the arm and guided her toward the enclosed courtyard. The sound of hammers on metal rang out, and when they entered the court, they saw the mercenaries hard at work breaking the shackles of the captives.

Abigail saw a familiar figure and cried, 'Marcus!' With a leap over two pallets, Marcus hurled himself at the girl. He swept her up in his arms and kissed her deeply. Then he put her down.

The normally taciturn Marcus said, 'I thought I'd never see you again.' He threw his arm around Margaret and kissed her on the cheek. 'Or you.'

Nakor said, 'Save your hellos for later. We have to move quickly. How long?'

Marcus said, 'Another ten minutes. There were tools stored there' – he pointed back to the door that opened into the hall surrounding the courtyard – 'but there were only two chisels.'

'How are the prisoners?' asked Nakor.

At those words, Anthony's character as a healer asserted itself; he reluctantly disengaged himself from Margaret and moved to look at the captives. After examining a pair of them, he said, 'Get them to drink as much water as you can, but slowly. Make them sip. Then we have to get them to the boat.'

He moved among them until he came to the statue. A stange itch struck him like a force, and he called, 'Nakor?'

The little man hurried over and looked at the statue. He circled it and was about to reach out to touch it, when Anthony said, 'Don't!'

Nakor hesitated, then nodded. Turning, Anthony shouted at the prisoners, 'Did any of you touch this?'

A man nearby said, 'No. The changelings did.'

'Changelings?' asked Nakor.

'Those snake things.' The man coughed. 'They kept us chained up here with these walking snakes. They kept changing until they looked like us – those of us who didn't die,' he said bitterly. He seemed to be a young man, but his eyes were dark pits, and his face was now lined beyond his years. His hair was streaked with premature grey. 'They all came and embraced that thing and uttered some sort of vow in their obscene language. Then each of them stuck its forearm with a long needle and rubbed it on the statue.'

'Where did they take those of you who died?' shouted Anthony, showing near panic in his face.

The man pointed to a door opposite the one Calis had used to enter the square. 'Over there. They took them through there.'

Anthony hurried to the door, leaping over a pallet to reach it. He pulled on the handle, and found it locked. To Marcus he said, 'Can you force this?'

Marcus hurried over with hammer and chisel and hacked at the lock plate. In a few minutes it fell away, and Anthony shoved past the burly mercenary. Marcus stepped back and covered his mouth. 'Gods!' he shouted, then turned his head and retched.

Anthony yelled, 'Nakor, bring a light. Everyone else stay back.'

Nakor hurried, took a torch from one of the mercenaries, and joined Anthony. In the hollow of the wall, bodies lay, both human and the lizard creatures who had been their matches. The humans were grisly corpses, but it was the lizard creatures that captured Anthony's attention.

They were bloated, blackened things, with cracked skin that oozed pus and blood. Lips were split and green, while eyes were blackened raisins in their sockets. What could be made of their features showed they died in agony, and their hands were claws without nails, worn bloody trying to scrape their way through the stone wall. The effect was all the more horrifying in that some were totally alien in aspect while others showed various stages of humanity in their distorted features.

Anthony whispered, 'Do you sense it?'

Nakor said, 'I sense something. Something dark and evil.'

Anthony closed his eyes, and incanted. He waved his hands in the air, summoning magic to him, then suddenly his eyes opened, wide enough so that Nakor could see whites completely around the blue irises. 'Get out,' he whispered hoarsely.

Nakor hurried out of the hall, and Anthony came after. To Marcus and Calis he said, 'Get everyone out of here, then burn this place.' With an authority in his voice none of them had ever heard before, Anthony said, 'Burn the other buildings: the outbuildings, the stables, the kitchens; burn the main house as we go through. Burn everything!'

Marcus called, 'Get everyone out!'

The last prisoner was carried out of the square, and a torch was tossed on top of the decaying bodies. In another area of the hollow square, some lamp oil and rags were found and were tossed onto the fire. Marcus directed the mercenaries to light torches and start firing the other buildings. Within minutes they heard the loud *whoosh* as the dry hay in the abandoned stable began to burn. Then the kitchen and workers' quarters were torched and men were sent to start fires in the outer apartments of the main house.

Returning from starting a fire in the room where Margaret and Abigail were kept, Calis asked, 'What did you find in there, Anthony?'

'Bodies,' said Anthony.

Marcus said, 'Anthony, what is it?'

Anthony halted a moment, while the mercenaries carried the prisoners into the large house, following Nakor, who was leading them to the tunnel. Whsipering as tears of rage ran down his cheeks, Anthony said, 'They're sending a plague to the Kingdom, Marcus. They're sending a magic sickness to make the worst illness you've heard of seem as nothing. We've got to stop them!'

Marcus's eyes widened, and he swallowed hard, then, taking Abigail's hand, he set off toward the main house of the estate, Anthony and Margaret behind him.

22

Ambush

Harry pointed.

'What is it?' asked Brisa.

'Fire,' answered Praji. 'Big one, from the way it's lighting the sky.'

They were in the lead boat heading for the burned-out farmhouse, where, if the gods were kind, they would find the prisoners waiting to be picked up. Harry felt cold sweat break out. 'It's going to get busy around here soon.'

Praji said, 'No doubt about it. There will be soldiers coming to see what's happening up there. If they start looking around down here, we're going to have a fight.'

A boatman said something to Tuka, who said to Harry, 'Sab, we head in now.'

Harry nodded and signaled to the boat behind. While he was hard to see in the darkness, each boat had a spotter at the bow and stern specifically to relay orders. The first boat nestled into the bank with a low grinding sound and the others followed suit, until all ten boats were secure.

Harry jumped from the bow and ran to the farmhouse. The cover of the well had been pushed aside, and a man was emerging with some difficulty. Harry grabbed him by the arm and helped him climb out. 'Harry!' came a low shout from the ruins of the farmhouse, and Calis emerged, waving him over. Harry gave the weak man some assistance and, when he reached the house, let him sit on the ground.

'You just get here?' asked Harry.

'It's taking longer than we thought,' said Calis. 'Marcus and the others are down below, helping the prisoners climb, but it's slow. They're weak, and some will have to be hauled up.'

Praji came over and Harry said, 'Get some rope and rig a sling, then bring four strong men here to haul the weaker prisoners up through the well.'

Praji hurried off and Harry said, 'It's six of one or a half dozen of the other; we wait either here or out in the bay.'

Calis nodded. 'Nicholas and Amos must be bearing down on that ship about now.'

'I wish them luck.' Harry glanced at the sky, where the second of Midkemia's three moons was rising. The third would be up in another hour. 'It's going to be very bright out here soon.' Three full moons were a rare event, and the term 'three moons bright' meant almost like day. 'We're not going to have much luck sneaking around tonight. What's that fire?' asked Harry.

'Dire news, I fear,' answered the half-elf. 'Anthony says some dark plague was born there and only fire would destroy it. If we hadn't burned Dahakon's estate, he says everyone in this city would be dead within a month, two at the latest, and anyone leaving the city would carry it with them. He thinks this plague could kill half the people on this continent before it was through.'

'Gods! That's vile.' Harry shook his head in disgust. Glancing at the distant fire, he said, 'Well, we're going to have some curious soldiers here before too long.' He regarded the twenty or so sick-looking prisoners, recognizing one, a page who he had played football with. Kneeling, he asked, 'Edward, how are you?'

'Not good, Squire,' he said, trying to smile bravely, 'but I'll bounce back now that we're free.' His face was drawn, and Harry could see he was sick in spirit as well as body. He had been a captive and witnessed horrors undreamed of in his young life before the raid. Release from chains did not free him from those memories.

542

Harry said, 'I could use your assistance. Are you up to it?' The page nodded, and Harry said, 'Start helping these others to the boats. Start at the one farthest back, that's a good lad.'

The boy got to his feet and went to aid another prisoner, a young girl who stared into space with vacant eyes. The page said, 'Up, all of you; you heard the Squire. We've got to get to the boats. We're going home.' The last was said as a half-sob, but it did the trick.

The other prisoners got to their feet and began to stagger toward the waiting boats. Another figure came out of the well, and Harry ran to direct him toward the boat.

Calling down the well, Harry shouted, 'We're here with the boats! Can you hurry them?'

Marcus's voice echoed back up from the darkness below. 'We'll try, but they're weak.'

'We're rigging a sling and we'll pull up those that can't climb.'

'Good.'

Time dragged as the weakened prisoners made their way slowly up the ladder. When Praji, Vaja, and two others arrived with the rope sling, it was lowered down the well and the prisoners unable to climb were pulled up.

Harry went to the boats and told Tuka, 'When I give the word, you push off with the boats already full and get into the harbor. Move toward the mouth of the bay and wait for Nicholas.'

The little man asked, 'What about going upriver, Sab?'

'After, my friend, after.' Almost absently he said, 'We have one more stop to make.'

They both stood there silently for a while, watching the distant estate of Dahakon the magician, the Grand Adviser of the Overlord, burn in a stunning display.

* * *

'What's that?' asked Amos.

Nicholas said, 'Looks like a fire on the other side of the bay.'

Amos said, 'I hope that's not bad news for our friends.'

Nicholas said, 'Let's not worry about that. Look!'

Amos saw where Nicholas was pointing and said loudly, 'All hands! Make ready to come about!'

The begala was a pleasure boat, belonging to a merchant who used it for both business and recreation. It could comfortably carry seven or eight passengers in the three small cabins, and there was room for a reasonable cargo below. In close to the wind, it was slow, but in a following wind it raced. And Amos was turning it to move fast enough to come alongside the second ship leaving the harbor.

The first had come into view a moment earlier, the copy of the *Royal Gull*. Now the facsimile of the *Royal Eagle* hove into view, and Amos turned his boat to bring it into line. He had calculated how a knowledgeable captain would bring a ship out of that harbor, keeping tight to the wind to drive along the potentially deadly rocks of the headlands that became a long peninsula providing the eastern boundary of the sheltering harbor. While the bright moons were proving a handicap for Harry's desire for stealth, they were a boon to Amos.

The crew leaped to their jobs. They were unfamiliar with this ship, but they were all experienced sailors and had spent every moment since coming aboard familiarizing themselves with the rigging and tackle. The two guards who were taken when Nicholas and his party climbed aboard were tied up below, unhurt, but thoroughly terrified.

The begala sprang out like a predator. Ghuda stood by the bow with a rope and grappling hook ready, while three other men stood nearby. In total, a dozen of Nicholas's thirty men were ready to pull the two ships

544

together while the others swarmed aboard. Nicholas prayed that surprise would help them overcome resistance before the crew of the target ship could rally. They had no idea what the complement would be, but Amos judged no fewer than thirty seamen and whatever complement of guards and bogus prisoners they had put aboard.

A warning shout came from above as one of the lookouts cried out at the unexpected sight of the ship pulling alongside. An archer on the bow silenced him as Ghuda swung his rope and released. Instantly the others with ropes followed his example, and a half-dozen men in the rigging of the begala leaped across to the higher deck, swords and knives drawn as they looked for opponents. Nicholas climbed a ratline, then jumped across four feet of air above water to grab the rail of the other ship.

He was over and ready when a sailor came at him with a cutlass. Nicholas killed the black-clad seaman before he could strike. Around him the sound of battle rang through the darkness and faintly he could hear what sounded like an inquiring shout from the first ship.

Nicholas trusted everyone to do his job, and he rushed to the entrance to the rear cabin. If there were any Pantathians or their more powerful minions aboard, this was where they would be. He kicked in the door of the captain's cabin and heard the 'thunk' of a crossbow bolt embedding itself into the wood of the doorframe. The captain calmly laid down the crossbow and pulled out a sword. 'Surrender your ship!' commanded Nicholas, but the captain said nothing as he came around from behind his desk.

Suddenly Nicholas was defending himself as the man executed a furious attack. Nicholas backed away, then counterattacked, and the duel was engaged in earnest. Nicholas was younger and faster, but the older captain was obviously skilled and practiced. Nicholas tried to focus on his opponent, but he couldn't help but worry about how the rest of the battle was going. He knew that the plan was to cut loose the two guards below in the begala, so they could at least work to keep the ship off the rocks, while Amos and everyone else came aboard this ship. It was an all-or-nothing gamble, for if Nicholas's raiders were driven back, there was no place to go.

Nicholas slashed out and caught the captain along the arm, forcing him to drop his sword. Leveling the point of his sword at the captain, he said, 'Surrender!'

The man pulled a knife from his belt and threw himself at Nicholas, who instinctively pushed forward with his sword. The sword entered the man below the breastbone, piercing upward into the heart, and the man collapsed.

The sensation that traveled up Nicholas's arm was no different from what he had experienced when he killed Render, and it was no less disturbing, the friction of steel on bone and sinew. Nicholas pulled out his blade and turned. There were two other cabins on this level, the doors across from one another before the captain's. Nicholas chose the right-hand door. He kicked hard with his right foot, then ducked to his left, having learned his lesson. When no bolt flew through the door, he looked inside.

The cabin was empty. He repeated the procedure with the other door and a bolt flew through it, barely missing him. If he hadn't dodged aside, that one most certainly would have skewered him.

He sprang to the door, only to have a shoulder driven into his stomach as the first mate leaped through it. Nicholas heard cloth rip and felt something brush along his ribs, and he struck hard with the butt of his sword hilt at the base of the man's skull. A grunt of pain was all the response he got, and he felt another scrape along his ribs as he hammered at the man's head. Suddenly the first mate went limp and Nicholas pushed him off.

Nicholas stood up and felt a burning on his left side.

He reached down and his hand came away wet. He looked at the floor and saw the knife the first mate had tried to kill him with, blood on the blade. Nicholas examined his shirt and saw the blade had grazed him, slicing the skin, but not cutting very deep. He pulled a lungfull of air and fought off a bout of dizziness as his side began to burn and throb.

Nicholas returned to the main deck, where Ghuda and the soldiers seemed to hold the upper hand. The black-clad defenders were overwhelmed by the suddenness of the attack, and most of them lay on the deck.

Glancing to his right, he saw Amos backed into a corner by two men coming at him. Nicholas ran to his aid, but as Amos blocked one man's cut, that man engaged Amos's blade, holding it aloft, allowing the other to drive his sword into Amos's stomach.

'Amos!' Nicholas shouted as he struck out and killed the man who held Amos's blade. Then he took an attack from the second man and, with a riposte, drove his own sword's point into him.

He kicked aside the wounded men and knelt next to Amos. He was unconscious and his breathing was shallow and labored. Nicholas glanced over and saw Ghuda kill the man he was facing. There was no respite in the fighting.

Nicholas hurried from Amos's side, and fell as a hand grabbed his ankle. Nicholas rolled over and lashed out with his boot, taking the wounded sailor in the face. There was the sound of bone crunching under his heel, and the man screamed.

Nicholas leaped up and drove his sword point into the man's neck. He spun as Ghuda shouted. 'They're fantastic! They won't surrender!'

Grimly Nicholas shouted, 'No quarter!' He knew it meant killing every man on the ship. A bitter taste of acid filled his mouth and he spat, then ran to attack a black-clad sailor who, despite his wounds, was rising behind one of Nicholas's own men, to attack him once again.

The fight seemed to go on indefinitely, and twice Nicholas could swear he was killing men he had faced before. Then it was suddenly silent.

Ghuda said, 'That's all of them.'

Nicholas nodded dully. He was drenched in perspiration and blood and his knees shook with fatigue. His left foot ached dully, and his side burned. Then Nicholas remembered: 'Amos!'

He ran back to where the fallen Admiral lay, and with relief saw he was still breathing. Ghuda knelt next to Nicholas and said, 'He's in a bad way. We need Anthony and his skill.'

Nicholas said, 'Get him to the captain's cabin.'

Two sailors gently picked up Amos and carried him inside. Nicholas looked around and saw that every man was staring at him. Suddenly he realized that, with Amos stricken, he would have to sail this ship. Looking past Ghuda to one of the sailors, he said, 'Who's the oldest man here?'

The man said, 'Pickens, I think, Highness.'

'Pickens!' called Nicholas, and a voice answered from the foredeck.

'Here!' A man in his late thirties hurried down from the foredeck and said, 'Yes, Captain.'

'You're first mate, Pickens. Get these bodies overboard.'

'Aye, Captain,' said the newly promoted seaman. Turning to the crew, who were exhausted and bloody, he said, 'You heard the captain! What are you waiting for? Get those corpses over the side!'

Ghuda said, 'You all right?'

Nicholas glanced at the bloody shirt he wore and said, 'It's nothing. It's Amos I'm worried about.'

548

'He's tough,' said Ghuda, but it was clear he was also worried.

Nicholas said, 'I've learned a lot from Amos on this voyage, and I've sailed some before; I just hope I don't make too much of a hash of this.'

Lowering his voice, Ghuda said, 'Just tell your Mr Pickens what you want done, and let him fret about how to do it.'

Nicholas half smiled, half winced. 'Sound thinking.'

A sailor hurried up on deck and said, 'High – er, Captain, there's prisoners below.'

Nicholas followed after, shouting, 'Mr Pickens!'

'Aye, Captain?'

'When you're done cleaning up, turn this ship around and head back to the city!'

'Aye, Captain.'

Grimly Nicholas smiled and said to Ghuda, 'This might work.'

They hurried to the main hatchway, where he looked down. From three decks down, a dozen faces peered up at them. No one spoke.

Ghuda said, 'Are these our people or those copies?'

Nicholas said, 'I don't know.' Feeling overwhelmed, he said, 'Lock them in. We'll sort this out when we find the others.'

He stood up and felt the ship roll under him as the crew finished pushing the dead over the side and returned to the task of directing the ship. Ghuda nudged him and pointed, and Nicholas understood. Reluctantly he walked back to the companionway leading up to the quarterdeck, where he was expected to oversee the ship now that he was captain.

Climbing the ladder, he found Pickens standing before the wheel, a sailor manning the helm. The mate cried, 'Trim sails to come about!' Turning to the helmsman, he

549

said, 'Come to starboard.' Then he shouted, 'Coming about!'

Aloft, the sailors hurried to their assigned places. Pickens said, 'This ship's a wicked copy of the first, Captain. I can't tell them apart, and I sailed the *Eagle* ten years.'

'How are we doing?' asked Nicholas.

'Six wounded, three dead. Another ten minutes and we would have run aground. But we're in good enough shape.'

Nicholas softly said, 'I hope you're right.'

As Nicholas stood motionless, rolling with the deck, a warning shout from above called out there was another ship close by. Nicholas felt his pulse race, but the reassuring voice said, 'Not to worry, Captain. I won't run over the begala on our way back.' Lifting his voice, he said, 'Keep a weather eye out!'

Nicholas smiled and his newly appointed first mate said, 'Why don't you go below and have that wound looked at?'

Nicholas nodded. 'You have the helm, Mr Pickens.'

'Aye, sir!' he said, snapping a salute.

Nicholas left the quarterdeck and went to where soldiers were taking care of the wounded. One saw him and without asking helped him out of his tunic. Nicholas looked away while the man probed the wound, then held his hands up while the man wrapped a clean cloth bandage around his ribs.

He silently prayed that Harry and the others were getting through their end of the plan without problems.

Harry ducked behind the low protection of the cabin of the riverboat as arrows sped overhead. Calis rose up calmly and loosed an answering shot, then ducked back behind the cabin as a scream from the shore verified he had hit his target.

Lying on the deck, Praji said, 'That's four of them. You'd think they'd get the hint and pull back.'

Harry called past Praji's prone form to Tuka. 'How much farther?'

'I think another hundred yards, Sab.'

They were drifting down the river, being fired at by archers on horseback who had come riding to investigate the fire. A bargeman had died from the first volley of arrows, and after that everyone hugged the decks. Harry called out, 'Marcus!'

'What?' came the answer from the second boat.

'How are your people?'

There was a moment of silence, then Marcus called back, 'We've got a wounded man here, but it's not too bad.'

Calis called out, 'Marcus – there are two particularly good targets outlined against the rising moon.'

'I'll take the one on the left,' he said.

'On three,' called Calis. 'One, two,' and on 'three', he stood and fired. Harry heard an answering bowstring hum as Marcus fired, too. A pair of shouts cut the night, and no more arrows came from the shore.

Harry counted to ten, then shouted, 'Oars! Now!'

Boatmen jumped to grab the oars that had been shipped when the bowmen had begun shooting at them. They fitted them into the oarlocks and pulled hard, while the tillermen steered them back toward the center of the river. In short order, the ragged line had re-formed, and Harry shouted, 'Is everyone all right?'

The question was shouted from boat to boat and the answer came back quickly: one dead, the first man shot; two injured, neither badly. Harry moved back to the bow of the first boat, glancing down at Brisa, who still huddled behind the cabin. 'You all right?'

'Scared to death,' she snapped back. 'But other than that, I'm fine.'

He knelt next to her. 'We'll be fine soon.'

'If your friend and his merry band have managed to ambush a ship under full sail . . . I grew up around ships, remember.' She shook her head. 'I'm not holding my breath.'

He put his hand on hers. 'We'll be all right.'

She tried to smile. 'I hope so.'

They entered the bay and moved along at a good pace, the wide riverboats wallowing in the swells. Harry said, 'I'm glad we don't have to take these things out to sea.'

Praji and Vaja stood holding on to the rail that ran around the low cabin. Praji said, 'Sounds like fun to me.'

Vaja said, 'If you've not observed it before, my friend has a twisted sense of humor.'

'I get the idea,' said Harry.

A shout from the rearmost boat caused Harry to turn. It was repeated, and then he heard Marcus shout, 'There are boats coming after us.'

'Oh, damn,' said Harry, pushing past Praji to the tiller. He called to Marcus, 'How many and how far?'

Marcus relayed the question and in a moment shouted back, 'Three, a couple of hundred yards behind. They're longboats, and they're loaded with armed men.'

Harry quickly weighed his options, then said, 'We've got the most fighters on the first two boats.' He called to Marcus, 'Have your boat pull out to the right, and let the others pass. You and Calis will have to discourage those who follow.'

Praji glanced around. 'Not much room to fight. Have the girl jump to another boat as it passes.'

Harry said, 'Good idea.' Before Brisa could protest, he called out to Marcus, 'Have Margaret and Abigail get into a passing boat, and anyone else who can't fight.'

Harry ignored the rude remark that came from Margaret

about her fighting ability. He just shouted, 'You're too weak, so shut up!'

The he turned to find Brisa advancing on him. Before she could say anything, he pointed his finger. 'And you're getting off, too. I don't have time to argue!'

She stopped, blinked a minute, then threw her arms around his neck, hugging him tightly. With a deep kiss, she jumped atop the cabin and moved to where a boat was pulling alongside. 'I love you, stupid. Don't get yourself killed!' She leaped easily across the few feet of water between, landing on the deck.

'I love you, too,' Harry said.

He pulled his sword and went to the rear of the boat. He saw Abigail and Margaret on the next boat that passed, and then heard shouts from the tenth boat in line. The message was relayed and Marcus said, 'They're shooting at the last boat.'

Calis climbed up to the cabin roof and said, 'No longbows.'

Marcus climbed up on the cabin of his boat as more boats passed them, the rowers pulling furiously on the oars. The two bowmen pulled as one and let fly, and two men in the pursuing boats fell. Instantly the rowers in the longboats backed water and Harry laughed. Calis said, 'That should discourage them for a while.' He patted his quiver. 'If they don't figure out we're running low on arrows,' he added softly.

From ahead someone shouted, 'The ship!' Harry turned and felt relief flooding through him as the ship came into view. It was reefing in sails and turning into the wind, so it would slow enough for those on the boats to board. Harry said, 'We're going to have to keep those men behind us off our necks while we unload cargo.'

Tuka said, 'Sab, what about us?'

Harry said, 'We'll worry about saving your lives, then

we'll find a way to get you ashore.'

Tuka nodded, but it was clear the loss of his promised ten boats to lead on a caravan and the profits to be made was weighing heavily on the little man's mind. Harry noticed and said, 'Not to worry. We'll make it worth your while. You'll still be paid to get the Ranjana upriver to her father.'

Tuka tried to brighten at that news, but it was clear he was not convinced.

The first boat reached the side of the ship and a cargo net was lowered. The mercenaries and boatmen opened the covers of the small cabins that covered the holds, and threw them into the water. They frantically loaded the supplies they would need for the long voyage home and, when the boat was empty, climbed lines up to the ship. Harry called out, 'Some of you, wait for the second boat and give them a hand!'

A pair of boatmen who were about to climb away hung from the ropes as the first boat at the ship was pushed away by the second, then lowered themselves to the deck to help unload that boat.

The pursuing longboats hovered awhile, then one turned and retreated. 'Are they leaving?' Harry asked.

'No,' answered Calis. 'I don't think so. I think they're going for reinforcements.'

The boats moved into place, and with the additional hands on deck, the unloading went quickly. Up on the deck, Nicholas watched with concern as what had occurred was relayed to him by those coming aboard. Pickens had told him they could be under way within minutes of the order being given, but it would take them a while to get out of the harbor mouth.

Then Nicholas saw Margaret and Abigail climb aboard, helping two of the weaker prisoners get over the rail. He hurried to give them a hand, then helped the girls climb over the rail. Both gave him a warm greeting, but Abigail turned away and looked down to the boats below, asking, 'Marcus? Will he be all right?'

Nicholas felt a mixture of jealousy and relief; then both emotions were pushed aside as a voice from above called out, 'Captain! Ship weighing anchor!'

'Where away?' he called.

'Off the stern to port!'

Nicholas climbed up to the quarterdeck, hurrying to the stern. There he saw a ship unfurling sail in the moonlight. To Pickens he said, 'How long?'

'She'll be under way in ten minutes, longest. She'll be on us in twice that time.'

Nicholas shouted, 'How many boats left?'

'Two,' came the answer.

He hurried to the side of the ship where sailors and mercenaries frantically hurried to clear the cargo net, so it could be lowered to the next-to-last boat. He went to the rail and shouted, 'Harry!'

'What?' came the answer.

'Who's got the gold?'

'It's here, with me!'

'Bring it, then get off. Abandon the rest of the cargo. Get everyone aboard. We're leaving.'

A protesting voice informed Nicholas that the Ranjana was aboard and she said, 'Captain! My things are on the boat.'

Nicholas said, 'We'll buy you some new things, if we live long enough.' Looking at Margaret and Brisa, he said, 'I know I can count on you two. Margaret, this is Brisa; Brisa, Margaret. Would the two of you get the Ranjana off the deck and into the cabin to the port side of Amos's?'

They took the Ranjana and her four maids in tow, and soon Harry, Calis, and Marcus were scrambling aboard and the heavy chest of Shingazi's gold was being raised. Nakor and Anthony were among the last aboard, and

Nicholas shouted, 'Mr Pickens! Get us out of here!'

Orders were passed and Nicholas glanced around. The sailors and soldiers from Crydee who had been pressed into sea duty were running to follow Pickens's orders. The mercenaries that Praji had hired stood to one side, while the boatmen Tuka had employed huddled near the main hatch. Nicholas said, 'Just keep out of the way,' to the boatmen, then said to Praji, 'Your men may have a real fight yet.'

Some of them muttered, but Nicholas said, 'That's what you're paid to do!' He turned and hurried to the quarterdeck.

Climbing to the latter, he shouted, 'Mr Pickens, are we going to make it?'

'It's going to be close,' said the sailor. He glanced behind him, then turned with a grin. 'But we're going to leave them in our wake.'

Nicholas climbed back down to the main deck, turned to say something to the others, then collapsed in a heap.

Nicholas roused in the first mate's cabin. Sun poured in through the porthole, so he knew he had slept well past dawn. He attempted to move and found his side hot and stiff. Examining himself, Nicholas saw someone had put a fresh bandage with a poultice on his side, and put him to bed.

He pulled on his trousers and opened the sea chest at the foot of the bed. The former occupant of the cabin had only a black tunic, so he put that on, finding it a fair fit. Pulling on his boots, Nicholas moved stiffly to the door and opened it.

Before going on deck, he opened the door to the captain's cabin and crossed to the single bunk where Amos lay. His breathing was deeper but his color was still bad. Nicholas stood watching him a moment, then turned and left him alone.

Reaching the main deck, Nicholas found several knots of men standing around, while others slept upon the deck as best they could. Marcus, Anthony, Harry, and Ghuda stood near the ladder up to the quarterdeck, while Praji and Vaja stood on the other side of the main deck, talking with the other mercenaries.

Moving to Marcus's side, he asked, 'What's going on?'

Harry said, 'We've got a couple of problems.'

'Such as?' said Nicholas.

Ghuda looked around. 'Well, Calis is up on the quarterdeck behind us, just in case Praji and his friends get more emphatic about being put ashore.'

Nicholas glanced around, then took his bearings. 'When did we clear the peninsula?'

'Yesterday, a little before sundown.'

'How long have I been sleeping?' asked Nicholas.

'We left the City of the Serpent River the night before last. It's a little past noon,' replied Marcus.

Harry said, 'Your wound was worse than you thought. Anthony treated it and put you to bed. Five minutes later, the trouble started.'

'Give me the short version,' said Nicholas, watching the mercenaries.

'It was the boatmen started it,' said Ghuda. 'They wailed like fishwives about leaving their families and not being paid to cross the sea.'

'Why didn't you heave to and put them over the side after we were clear of the harbor?'

Marcus made an exasperated motion. 'I wanted to, but Anthony and Calis both insisted that Pickens keep on after that other ship.'

'Then the mercenaries began grumbling,' added Ghuda, 'claiming you're abducting them. Things got testy last night after we broke out some wine. Thought it might relax things, but instead it got everyone sore as a boil.'

Nicholas said, 'Let me see what I can do.'

557

He climbed to the quarterdeck and found Calis leaning on his bow. 'Why didn't you let the boatmen and mercenaries ashore?'

Calis said, 'I think I'd better stay here in case Praji's friends get more irritated. Anthony is down below in the crew's quarters. He can explain it better than I can, anyway.'

Nicholas asked, 'Praji?'

'He's all right. I think his friends would have been a lot more trouble if he hadn't cautioned them to be patient.' Calis smiled. 'I think he considers you a pretty decent captain and is waiting to see what you say.'

Nicholas walked down the ladder and moved to where Praji stood. 'Captain,' said the mercenary by way of greeting.

'I don't know what's going on, but I'll give you my word; those of you who want to go ashore will be put out in a boat before sundown – with a bonus for your troubles.'

Instantly the men in the circle relaxed, and Nicholas turned and motioned for Calis to join them. Looking behind the elfling, he saw a haggard first mate on the deck. 'Mr Pickens!' he called.

'Aye, sir!'

'Have you been on watch the entire day and a half?'

'Aye, sir!' came the response.

'Go below and get some sleep. Pick a man to watch our course. I'll be below for a while.'

'Aye, sir,' he said with some relief.

'Harry!' Nicholas called.

'Yes, Nicholas?'

'Get up on the quarterdeck and make sure we don't run aground. You're now second mate.'

With a rueful smile, he said, 'Aye, Captain.'

Nicholas motioned for Marcus and Ghuda to join them, and they went down the companionway to the crews' quarters. Anthony was there ministering to the prisoners, who were sleeping in the bunks, or softly talking among themselves; Abigail and Margaret were helping him.

'How is everyone?' Nicholas asked.

Anthony said, 'You're awake!'

Nicholas was about to make a quip about this obvious remark, until he saw Anthony's eyes. They were sunk in black circles, and his cheeks were hollow. 'When did you last sleep?'

Anthony shrugged. 'A day or so before we left. I don't remember. There's so much to do.'

Margaret said, 'I've told him to get some rest, but he ignores me.' Her expression was an equal mixture of irritation and admiration.

'How are the prisoners?'

'They're all fine,' said Anthony. 'The worst is over as long as they rest and eat. We got most of the provisions on board, but we will have to watch our rations.'

'How is Amos?' asked Nicholas, lowering his voice.

'Bad,' said Anthony. 'I've done all I could; the bleeding was heavy and the wound is deep. But he's strong for a man his age, and the scars on his body show this isn't the first time he's survived a near death blow. If he wakes up in the next day or two, I think he'll pull through.

'But if he does, he's going to be in no condition to captain this ship home; it's your job for at least another month, Nicholas.'

Nicholas nodded. 'What is the reason you didn't put the mercenaries and boatmen ashore?'

Anthony and Calis exchanged glances, then Anthony said, 'I don't know where to begin.' He looked at the end of his wits, so Nicholas gave him time to compose his answer. 'We can't let the other ship get too far ahead. I didn't want to risk slowing down to let down a boat.'

Something in his tone suggested grave concerns. Nicholas said, 'Go on.'

'It's worse than anything we thought, Nicholas,' said the young magician. 'Nakor has told me some things I don't think you know I know.' He glanced at Marcus who nodded. 'I don't know all of it – there's something the royal family is privy to, and that's all right – but what I do know frightens me more than anything I can imagine.

'The Pantathians have created a plague. It's worse than any illness I've seen.'

'Why?'

'There's no cure for it,' he said harshly. 'They've used magics of the blackest kind to fashion this thing. Those creatures of theirs were created to carry it to the Kingdom.'

Nicholas closed his eyes. 'It . . . makes an evil sense. They're a death cult and would gladly die to . . . further their cause.'

Anthony continued. 'I don't know how the illness works. I've seen some of their failures. It's horrible.'

'And you know it can't be cured?'

'Nakor thinks so, and he knows more about magic' – he smiled weakly – 'or tricks, than I do. Maybe Pug, or some of the more practiced priests of Dala or Kilian, or the Ishapians . . . I don't know. But I don't think we'd have time.'

'Why?'

'A . . . hunch. I think the disease progresses rapidly. From what I could see, those who died succumbed rapidly. The condition of the outer skin – what looks like human skin over their own true skin – and the other damage done by the illness don't lead me to think anyone could live for more than a few days once the sickness takes hold. I have no idea how it's spread; Nakor is with the creatures, seeing what he can learn of them.'

'Is he safe?' asked Nicholas with alarm.

'As much as anyone could be,' answered Anthony.

'Where are they?'

'In the cargo hold. We can get there through that passage,' said Anthony, pointing to a small door in the forward bulkhead.

Nicholas moved to the door and opened it, finding a short passage to another door. He moved through it and opened the second door. From the rear he heard Anthony caution the others to stay behind.

Nicholas found himself standing on the second cargo deck, with the grillwork of the main hatch above admitting light. The lowest deck in the hold had been converted to a barracks of sorts. A large open hatch looked down on it. Nicholas noticed that most of the supplies brought aboard from the riverboats had been stored on this deck. 'Where's the rest of our cargo?' he asked.

Anthony said, 'Lashed up on deck. Nakor and I wouldn't let it be put down there. Too dangerous.'

'Ah, Nicholas,' said a familiar voice from below. Nicholas glanced down and found Nakor sitting on an empty bed, looking at the people who were resting on about half the beds in sight. There was nothing unusual about any of them, and Nicholas was startled to recognize some from having seen them around the town and in the castle at Crydee.

'I . . . it's amazing,' he said softly.

'Do you begin to see?' asked Anthony. 'These creatures could return to the Kingdom and walk among us, spreading the disease until half the Western Realm was infected. Even if your father's influence could get Stardock and the temples to deal with the problem, there would be chaos throughout the Kingdom for years after these creatures set foot ashore.'

'Nakor,' Nicholas called down, 'have you learned anything useful?'

'Yes,' said the little man. 'Lower the rope.'

Nicholas looked around and saw a rope had been tied to an iron loop in the wall. He lowered it, and the little man shinnied up.

When he was standing next to Nicholas, he pulled up the rope and said, 'They are essentially harmless until the diesease begins.'

Nicholas stared down at the upturned faces. Some ventured shy smiles. A few spoke words of greeting. The Prince turned away and said, 'Looking at them unnerves me.' He returned to the crew quarters, where Marcus and Ghuda waited. The sight of the real prisoners, haggard and ill from their ordeal, seemed to put things back in perspective for Nicholas.

Anthony said, 'That's the problem.'

'What?'

'We have to kill those things.'

'What?' said Nicholas.

Nakor nodded agreement. 'They will grow ill. Not for weeks, because it would not do to have them become ill before they reach the Kingdom, yes? But they may be able to infect now. I do not know how; we only know it will spread. Some temples think it is evil spirits, while others think it is tainted air. My theory – '

Nicholas interrupted. 'Why must we kill them? Why not just stick them on an island somewhere?'

'We don't know if we're being chased,' said Marcus. 'It wouldn't do to have them dropped off on some island and have those who follow pick them up the next day. They might not be able to insinuate a false Abby or Margaret into your father's palace, but they could bring thirty plague carriers in to Krondor easily enough.'

Nicholas said, 'How do we do it?'

Nakor said, 'It is difficult. I am hard to kill – I would have to be exposed to this illness far longer than anyone else on the ship to succumb – so I should be the one to go down. I can mix something into the water to make them sleep, very deeply. If you lower a cargo net, I can pile them all into it, and you can lower them over the side.'

'Can't you mix something into their water to kill them painlessly?' asked Nicholas.

Nakor said, 'No. Too dangerous. The death of these creatures might act to release the disease to others. There is no way to know. We must be very careful. I would prefer to burn the bodies, but that is impossible here at sea.'

'It sounds cruel,' said Nicholas. 'To drown them in their sleep.'

Ghuda said, 'It is cruel, lad. But life is often cruel. If you need to steel your resolve, just remember those poor dead and injured back in Crydee.'

Nicholas sighed. 'I doubt these poor creatures knew of that. Still, your point is taken.' Looking at Nakor, he said, 'Do it.'

Nakor left. Then Nicholas said, 'We need to stop to put ashire the boatmen and the mercenaries.'

'That poses something of a problem,' said Ghuda.

'Why?'

Marcus answered, 'Because without them, we're not going to have enough men to sail this ship and board and take the other. We took this one because those who sailed it didn't expect to be hit coming out of the harbor. The fraudulent *Gull* saw us take this ship. They'll be looking for us, and they'll know we're after her. Expect a dogfight.'

Nicholas said, 'Let's go talk to them.'

Walking up on deck, Nicholas found the Ranjana and her maids taking air at the front of the ship with Brisa. She smiled broadly at Nicholas and called after him concerning his health. He made a non-committal gesture and a meaningless response as he hurried to the main deck. He signaled Tuka to gather the boatmen to him, and moved to confront the mercenaries. When they were all assembled, he said, 'My name is Nicholas. I am the son of Arutha conDoin, Prince of Krondor.'

The boatmen and mercenaries all looked blankly at him, for the names meant nothing to them. Praji said, 'We were talking about bonuses and going ashore, Prince.'

Nicholas said, 'You know we chase a ship that's twin to this. I can't spare the time to stop, but I can slow enough to lower a boat and have those of you who wish to, leave.' Some muttering began. 'I will pay every man here the bonus I spoke of.' Over his shoulder he said, 'Marcus, go find that chest of gold I had brought aboard.'

Marcus and Ghuda hurried off. Nicholas said, 'I offer much more for those of you who will stay.'

'How much more?' asked Praji.

'Watch,' said Nicholas. In a minute, Ghuda and Marcus returned carrying the chest. They set it heavily on the deck, and Nicholas opened it. The boatmen goggled and the mercenaries made low sounds in their throats at the sight of the gold and jewels. Nicholas said, 'Tuka, take from the chest what I promised your men.'

The little wagon driver hesitated, then reached into the chest. He fished around in it, finding a few small silver coins and some of the smallest gold coins. He finally stood up and held out a handful of coins for Nicholas's inspection. 'This is what is due to the rivermen, Encosi.'

Nicholas nodded. 'Praji, fish out what's due your men.'

Praji was less hesitant, but he still pulled out only a single handful of coins. Nicholas said, 'Pass them out.'

Each did so. Then Nicholas picked up a handful of gold and said, 'Pass these out as well.' Praji took the coins and spread them around to each man, who all looked surprised and pleased.

Then Nicholas said, 'Praji, hold your hands out.'

Praji did so, and Nicholas filled them with coins. Praji's eyes grew enormous, and the boatmen all stood in mute amazement. 'What I've given you is your bonus. Any man who leaves now will take that with him.' He then pointed at the gold in Praji's hands. 'But those who come with me, to my homeland, to those I will give this, and more!'

The boatmen and mercenaries spoke among themselves, and Praji said, 'Prince, where is this land of yours?'

'Across the Blue Sea, Praji. Three months' sailing, and more. The other side of the world.'

Quickly a small group split off and Tuka said, 'Encosi, these men, while overwhelmed by your generosity, have wives and children and would die to be parted from them. They would ask you to put them ashore.'

'Done.' Glancing at the others, he said, 'You'll stay?'

'To the other side of the world, Prince,' said Praji.

Orders were passed and a boat was made ready. As he went to confront the Ranjana, Nicholas turned to Praji and said, 'I didn't realize we had so many single men with us.'

'We don't,' said the mercenary. 'Just that some of them won't die to be parted from their wives and children.'

Nicholas shook his head. He found the Ranjana and her maids talking with Margaret and Abigail. Nicholas said, 'My lady, I'm putting a boat ashore. Five of the boatmen and three of the mercenaries are returning to the City of the Serpent River. They will act as your escort. I will provide funds sufficient to return you to your father.'

'No,' said the girl.

Nicholas had half turned away, then stopped. 'No?' he asked.

'I will not be put ashore so far from civilization. Besides, were I to return home, my father would have me beaten and sold to a camel driver.'

Nicholas said, 'Look, I don't know what you're playing at, but Andres Rusolavi's agent, Anward Nogosh Pata, assures me your father is a kind man who loves you, and you will in no way be punished by returning home.'

The girl's manner changed. 'You are right. I have lied. I wish to remain for another reason.'

'What?' said Nicholas, nearing the end of his patience.

Suddenly the girl was pressing against him, her arms around his neck. 'You have won my heart, my brave captain.' She kissed Nicholas passionately on the lips. As the flustered Prince attempted to disengage himself, she said, 'I will be your wife.'

Nicholas looked over the shoulder of the now firmly attached Ranjana to see Margaret and Abigail, Marcus and Ghuda fighting hard not to break out laughing.

23

Sea Chase

The lookout shouted.

'Ship ahoy!'

Nicholas disentangled himself from the Ranjana's interminable protestations of undying love, and shouted, 'Where away?'

'Dead astern.'

He put his hand urgently on the girl's chest and shoved her away with enough force that her maids had to catch her to keep her from falling. He raced to the stern and climbed to the quarterdeck, then scanned the horizon. After a moment he saw a tiny black speck.

'Mr Pickens,' he said, 'how long to put ashore the boatmen and mercenaries?'

The first mate scanned the shore and said, 'If we heave to, an hour or more, but if we slow to a crawl, and lose a jolly boat, fifteen minutes.'

Nicholas indicated all those upon the deck. 'Can we get all of those into a boat?'

'Not and have it stay afloat in the surf, Captain. Three trips, four would be better.'

Nicholas swore. 'How long before that ship's here?'

'Hard to say,' said the sailor. 'If it's the ship that tried to intercept us night before last, about an hour. If it's something else . . .' He let the thought go unfinished.

'Right.' Nicholas made a decision. 'Make ready to stand to, Mr Pickens.' To those on the lower deck he shouted, 'Get ready to put a jolly boat over the side!'

Sailors hurried to unlimber one of the large boats lashed upside down over the rear hatch cover. A boom was swung over and the boat was quickly raised, moved to just over the side, and then lowered. The boatmen and mercenaries who were the most anxious to leave scampered down a pair of rope ladders, with two sailors. When they were in the boat, they rowed furiously toward the shore, and Nicholas watched with concern as they entered the combers, then shot the breakers to the beach. Two of the boatmen helped launch the boat back into the water, and the two sailors pulled hard to get the boat through the breakers.

'This is taking too long,' said Nicholas as he glanced to where the pursuing ship was growing larger on the horizon. The boat reached the side of the *Eagle*, and the second batch of boatmen and mercenaries scampered down.

As the jolly boat reached the beach, the lookout called, 'Captain, I see her colors!'

Nicholas looked at the approaching ship and saw that she carried a black sail. 'What ensign?' he called.

'She flies a black flag with a golden serpent.'

Praji called up, 'She's the Overlord's.'

Nicholas stared hard at the approaching ship and the angle of her movement. 'Mr Pickens, I'm no deep-water veteran, but I'd say that ship is moving against the wind.'

The sailor studied her for a minute, and said, 'Yes, Captain. You're not a veteran, but she is indeed moving against the wind.'

A moment later, the lookout cried, 'Captain, she mounts a ram on her bow!'

'War galley. She can ignore the wind and row straight at us,' said Nicholas. 'I never saw one in the harbor.'

Praji shouted up from the main deck, 'The Overlord has a private pond fed by the estuary; he keeps his own fleet there.'

'Some pond,' said Ghuda.

'That's the Overlord's droman,' said Praji. 'Two banks of oars a side, and a ram and boarding bridge on the bow.

She mounts a catapult on the sterncastle and a ballista before the mast, too.'

'Make ready to sail, Mr Pickens,' ordered Nicholas. 'I'm not letting that bitch get close enough to fire on us.' He moved to the rail overlooking the main deck and shouted down, 'When the jolly boat's alongside, put the Ranjana and her maids off, and whoever else will fit, and the rest of you will have to swim. We are leaving.'

Marcus glanced around and said, 'Nicholas, the girl. She's not here.'

'Find her!' shouted Nicholas. 'We have no time for her silliness!'

Marcus hurried back toward the girls' cabin, and when the jolly boat was again next to the ship, the last of the boatmen and two mercenaries hurried down the ladder. Shouts erupted from the cabin below the quarterdeck, and Calis and Ghuda hurried to investigate. A squirming, kicking, biting, scratching Ranjana was being hauled out by Marcus, while Brisa, Abigail, and Margaret herded the maids behind her. 'Give her some gold to buy her way home, and put her over the side!' commanded Nicholas.

'I will not go home!' shrieked the girl, doing her best to claw her way out of Marcus's grip. 'The Rahajan will kill me!'

'So much for undying love,' said Brisa, glancing at Margaret with a wicked grin.

A shout from the jolly boat and splashes in the water caused a sailor to look over the side. 'Captain,' he called, 'the mercenaries have taken the jolly boat.'

Two more of Praji's mercenaries looked over the rail and shouted, then climbed up and leaped into the water after the fleeing boat. 'Should we put another boat over, Captain?' asked Pickens.

Looking at the war galley as it began to draw down on the *Eagle*, Nicholas said, 'No, there's no time.'

Marcus shouted, 'Should I pitch her over the side?'

The girl screamed, 'No! I cannot swim! I'll drown!'

Nicholas threw his hands up in resignation and said, 'No. Put her down.' Making a noise of unalloyed aggravation, he said, 'Get us out of here, Mr Pickens. Full sail!'

'Make ready on all sheets and shrouds!' cried the first mate. 'Raise anchor.'

Slowly at first, the *Eagle* moved forward, then, as her sails billowed and she caught the wind, she moved through the water like a dolphin.

Nicholas looked at the pursuing ship and asked, 'Are they close enough to fire on us?'

As if in answer, a fireball arced from the deck of the droman and landed with a hissing splash a dozen yards abaft the ship. Calmly Pickens said, 'Well, let's just hope we don't run out of wind before they run out of muscle.'

Across the water, Nicholas could hear the faint sound of the drum used to set the pace for the rowers. Turning his back on the other ship, Nicholas said, 'They can't hold attack speed very long. The slaves will begin fainting at the oars.'

Pickens nodded. 'They've still got their own sail, Captain.'

Nicholas looked back again, as the evil-looking black and gold sail billowed in the wind. 'They can't overtake us with wind.'

'No, Captain, but they could stay close enough to give us serious trouble if the wind dies.'

'Then pray for a strong wind, Mr Pickens. We've a long way to home.'

'Aye, Captain.'

Nicholas went back to the main deck and confronted the Ranjana, who stood defiantly with her fists upon her hips. 'You will not put me ashore!' she commanded.

Nicholas stopped, started to speak, stopped, then made another sound of aggravation. He turned his back and walked to his cabin.

Examining the damage the girl had done to his arm, Marcus said, 'It's a good thing he didn't order me to chuck you over the side, girl.'

The Ranjana turned and pulled a small jeweled dagger from the wide waistband of her skirt. Pointing it at Marcus, she said, 'Yes, it was a good thing!'

She flung the dagger down so it stuck quivering in the deck between Marcus's boots. She spun and with a wave of her hands instructed her maids to follow her into her cabin. Brisa laughed. 'She's full of surprises, isn't she?'

Harry said, 'I think Nicholas is going to find that out soon enough.'

Margaret and Abigail both looked on in amazement, and Margaret said, 'You said she was difficult, but nothing about being murderous.'

Abigail came to Marcus and made soothing noises, to his embarrassment, as she examined the scratches. Abigail then said, 'What did you mean, Nicholas is going to find that out, Harry?'

It was Brisa who answered. 'Let's just say that girl will find some way to get Nicholas to do what she wants. There's a lot more to her than she's letting on.'

Harry nodded. 'And Nicholas doesn't exactly have a lot of experience with women.'

Margaret said, 'And you do, Squire? This from the lad who blushed when I teased him in the garden?'

Marcus said, 'A lot has happened since we last saw you, sister.'

Harry said, 'My friend, you have a knack for understatement,' and burst out laughing. A moment later, so did Ghuda, and soon everyone in the group was laughing.

Nicholas tried to sleep; he'd kicked off his boots, but lay fully clothed on the bunk. Close to exhaustion, he still couldn't get his mind to cease racing with worry. The Overlord's ship dogged their heels. Whoever was captaining it was skilled at using wind and oars to cut the distance whenever he had the chance. Pickens had said they'd leave the droman behind once they stopped following the coast and turned to move across the sea. Nicholas had eaten alone in his cabin, after sitting for a while with Amos in his. Then he had attempted to puzzle out Amos's log, deciphering the Admiral's notes and abbreviations regarding currents and wind. Nicholas knew enough of sailing to know that they couldn't literally retrace their way home – they had to find a route close to the way down, but one that took advantage of currents and winds blowing in the opposite direction from the way they had come. Otherwise they'd be on the tack for hundreds of miles.

Nicholas finally managed to doze when a creak of the door opening brought him instantly awake. 'Huh?' he said as he drew his sword noisily frm the scabbard.

'Don't,' said a female voice. Someone sat on the bed next to him.

'Abby?' asked Nicholas, reaching for a light.

'She's with Marcus in the rope locker,' said the voice. 'They're . . . getting reacquainted, let's say.' He struck spark and brought the lantern to life, and discovered the Ranjana sitting next to him.

'What are you doing here?' he asked, irritated at the intrusion.

'We need to talk,' she said. She wore a silk gown that clung to her curves, and her hair had been done up with gold and pearl pins, accenting her dark curls.

'About what?' he asked.

'This place we're going? You're really a Prince?'

Nicholas said, 'Ranjana – what is your name?'

'Iasha.'

'Iasha, I am a Prince. My uncle is King. My brother will be King after him.'

The girl looked down as if embarrassed. 'I'm sorry to

572

have caused you so much trouble. I have been talking to the one called Margaret. I really had no idea there had been so much killing and suffering, or that you'd come so far to find the one called Abigail.'

Nicholas sighed, lying back against the bulkhead, his arm behind his head. 'When I began this journey, I would have told you how much I loved Abigail. That all seems silly now.'

'Love is never silly,' said Iasha.

'Well, I didn't mean to say it was. But thinking what I felt was love is silly.'

'Oh?'

'Was that all you came here to say, that you're sorry?'

'Yes – no.' She sighed. 'When I said I loved you, it was to keep from being sent back to Kilbar.'

'Somehow I figured that out,' said Nicholas, his irritation showing.

'But I was not lying when I said it would be my life.'

'Your father would really kill you or sell you for something the Overlord plotted?'

She sighed deeply again. 'No, it's because of something I did. Or rather, the Ranjana did.'

'What?' asked Nicholas, his face showing his confusion.

'I am not the Ranjana of Kilbar.'

'Who are you?'

'I am her maid, Iasha. The other maids are in on the ruse, as well.'

'You'd better explain this to me,' said Nicholas.

'The Ranjana had no desire to be the fifteenth wife of the Overlord of the City of the Serpent River. She has been in love with a minor prince of Hamsa since they were children together. So she bribed Andres Rusolavi, the broker, to substitute me for her and send us south, while she made her way to Hamsa to marry her prince in secret. There is almost no communication between Hamsa and the City of the Serpent River, so my lady got her

prince, I would be another pretty face for the Overlord
and would live in luxury, and the other maids would be
rewarded for their silence by me.'

Nicholas made an aggravated sound. 'So it was another
ruse?'

'I am afraid so, my Prince. Now I must throw myself
upon your mercy and beg you not to sell myself and the
others into slavery.'

Nicholas fixed her with a narrow gaze. 'Somehow I
think you've already been told by Margaret that we don't
have slavery in the Kingdom.'

There was a faint smile at the corner of the girl's lips,
but all she said was 'Oh?'

Wiping his gritty eyes with his hands, he said, 'I'd better
check on Amos.'

As he attempted to sit up, she leaned forward and her
soft lips met his. He sat motionless a moment, then, when
she pulled back, he said, 'What was that for?'

'Because while I do not love you, my brave captain, I
think you are a kind man and would treat a maid as well
as a Ranjana.'

Nicholas said, 'Fairly spoken, lady.' He stood up. 'But
somehow it's going to be a while before I take much of
what anyone from your land says at face value.'

She stood up in turn. 'Tell me of this Kingdom of yours.'

Nicholas said, 'I can show you after I check on Amos.
Come along.'

He picked up the lantern and led her into Amos's
room, where the injured Admiral lay sleeping. Nicholas
paused a moment, looking down at Amos, who was still
pale.

'Will he live?' asked the girl quietly.

'I certainly hope so,' answered Nicholas. 'He's to wed
my grandmother when we return. We – my family – love
him very much.' He stared down at Amos's still features
a long moment.

Nicholas turned to the chart locker and put down the lantern. He inspected the charts that the Pantathians had provided for the original captain. Between them and Amos's log, he hoped he could plot their way home. He selected one chart that showed the Bitter Sea and unrolled it. Pointing to Krondor, he said, 'This is where I lived.'

She squinted. 'I cannot read, Captain. What do these lines say?'

Nicholas began to speak of Krondor, and showed her how far they had sailed from the City of the Serpent River and what that looked like on the map. The girl gasped. 'So vast a land to be owned by one man.'

'Not owned,' he corrected. 'I'll have to explain it to you in detail later, but my uncle is King because it is his birthright, but he also has obligations to protect those who live here. In my country, nobility is not just a privilege but also a responsibility. We rule but we also serve.'

He explained a little of his family, and when he was done, the girl said, 'So you will not be given a city to rule?'

Nicholas shrugged. 'I don't know what my father and uncle plan for me. A state marriage, I expect, to a Princess of Roldem, or of Kesh. Or to an important Duke's daughter.' He said, 'I may be sent to Rillanon and serve in my brother's court when he becomes King.'

'Where is this Rillanon?'

He unrolled another map and laid it out next to the first, to show her the Kingdom Sea. 'This island here' – he pointed – 'is the home of my people. That is where we began and why we are called the Kingdom of the Isles.'

'You must show me this Rillanon,' said the girl, slipping her arm through his. He flushed at the feel of her breast against his arm.

'Ah, perhaps,' he said, disengaging himself and putting away the charts. 'I think, however, you'll have no trouble finding someone to show you just about anything you want to see.'

She pouted and Nicholas felt his heart skip. 'I am but a poor maid. What man of rank would look twice at me?'

Nicholas grinned. 'Any number, I dare say. You are certainly beautiful.'

She brightened. 'You really think me beautiful?'

Trying to make light of it, he said, 'When you're not trying to claw Marcus's eyes out or shrieking like a wounded cat.'

She smiled, covering her mouth with her hand. 'That is how the Ranjana acts, my captain. I sought to act as she would, to make my impersonation convincing.'

Suddenly it became silent, as Nicholas realized he didn't have any idea what to say next. The girl stood looking up at him, illuminated by the soft glow from the lantern. Their eyes met and she stepped forward and kissed him again. This time his body took over, and without thought, he pulled her tightly against him.

They stood making soft sounds for a moment, when a voice said weakly, 'Nicky, can't you and your girly find a cabin of your own?'

Nicholas turned. 'Amos!'

He took two steps toward Amos and turned to Iasha. 'Go get Anthony!' he said, and the girl hurried out to find the magician.

'Help me sit up,' Amos said.

Nicholas let Amos grip his arm while getting more comfortable, then adjusted the pillows behind him.

'Well, Ghuda owes me five golden sovereigns,' said Amos.

'Why?' asked Nicholas.

'I bet him that girl would convince one of you young lechers to bring her with us. So you're the one bedding her?'

'No, I'm not sleeping with her,' said Nicholas.

'Gods, son, what's wrong with you?' He coughed and said, 'Ah, damn me, but I hurt.'

'You're lucky to be alive,' said Nicholas.

'You're not the first to tell me that,' said Amos. 'Now, what's happened since I got stuck?'

Nicholas filled him in, and by the time he was done, Anthony appeared. The healer examined Amos and said, 'You'll do well to stay in bed awhile. I'll have someone bring you some broth. That belly wound is dangerous, so you'll have to watch what you eat for a while.'

'Would you think a little wine was in order?' asked Amos with a weak smile.

'A small glass with the broth,' said Anthony. 'It will help you sleep better.'

Anthony left and Nicholas said, 'Tomorrow, we – '

'Have to kill those things below,' said Amos. 'Yes, I was wondering why you waited.'

'It's hard, Amos. I know what Nakor and Calis have told me, and what Margaret and Abigail said, but they look like people; they look like friends from Castle Crydee.'

'But they're not,' was all Amos said. 'You're a Prince of the Blood Royal, like your father and brothers, and you have a duty. Often that means taking life to protect your own. It's not fair, or right, or even just, only necessary. That's the way of it.'

Nicholas nodded. 'I'll let you sleep. Tomorrow I'll need you to decipher those scratches in your log so we can find our way home.'

Amos said, 'Tomorrow.' Already he looked ready to go back to sleep. 'One thing.'

'What?'

'That little girl. Don't let her get too close.'

'I thought you said there was something wrong with me . . .'

Amos said, 'No, I don't mean bedding her. She could

probably teach you a thing or three. No, just remember who you are and where your destiny lies. You're free to love who you may, but the King will tell you who you're to wed.'

Nicholas nodded. 'I've been told that all my life, Amos.'

'Just remember that when she's got you by the short handle. Most men can't think well then; don't make promises.' Then he grinned and Nicholas was looking at the old Amos. 'Just because you can't allow her to take control of your life doesn't mean you can't enjoy letting her try.'

Nicholas blushed. 'Good night, Amos. I'll see you in the morning.'

He returned to his own cabin and remembered he'd left the lantern in Amos's. In the dark, he stripped off his shirt and trousers, and sat on the bed. He leaped to his feet when something moved. Iasha's voice said, 'Get under the covers. It's cold in here!'

He hesitated, then slipped in beside the girl. He felt warm skin against his own. He was motionless a moment, unsure of what to do next, when her lips found his. He responded, and then he laughed.

'What?' she asked, her tone a mix of amusement and concern. 'You think me funny?'

'No,' said Nicholas. 'Just thinking of something Amos told me.'

'What?'

'I'll tell you later,' he said, kissing her again.

Harry said, 'They're still back there, Captain.'

Nicholas had just come up on deck, to a blue sky and fresh breeze. 'How long can they keep this up? They can't be carrying provisions for a long voyage.'

'Maybe they don't care,' said Harry. 'You done with

the cabin?' With the women on board, the officers and nobles had been doubling up in quarters, so Pickens and a new bosun's mate, Gregory, shared the midshipman's bunk. Harry and Nicholas were also on opposite watches – Harry had command at night – and slept in what had been the first mate's cabin. The Ranjana, Margaret, Abigail, and the maids were supposed to be sleeping in the two small cabins for passengers or guests on Kingdom ships, but Nicholas wondered if the girls were making the same sorts of arrangements he and Harry had.

Harry said, 'You'll be a little more convincing as a commander if you wipe that stupid grin off your face.'

Nicholas said, 'Grin?'

Harry nodded. 'I know the feeling.' He smiled as he nodded toward Brisa, who was crossing the deck.

'Look, this is a funny time to say this, considering . . .'

'Considering what?'

Nicholas blushed. 'What happened last night, but we should try to be circumspect about these sleeping arrangements.'

Harry said, 'Why? I've got Brisa, you've got the Ranjana, Marcus has Abigail, Anthony is with Margaret; seems like it's worked out pretty reasonably.'

'Explain that to the other forty-nine men on this ship,' Nicholas said. Harry glanced at a knot of mercenaries sitting on a hatch cover and watching Brisa walk by. 'Our own men we can trust; they're professional soldiers and sailors of the King. But hired knives? I want a watch on how much wine and ale are dispensed at meals and an ear out for trouble. We've got three months or more of crossing the ocean ahead of us.'

Harry sighed. 'You're right. I'll say something to the others.'

'The real problem is going to be the maids,' said Nicholas. 'A little wordplay is one thing, but a knife fight over one of them, that could be disastrous.'

Harry said, 'I understand. I'll pass the word to stay alert.'

A curse from below brought Nicholas's attention to the main deck, where Amos stood waving off Anthony's solicitations. 'You may be the healer, but it's my body and I damn well know when I need some fresh air! Get away!' He slapped weakly at Anthony's offer of help and gripped the rail.

Nicholas hurried down and said, 'What are you doing out of bed?'

'I've been bedridden long enough to smell like the bottom of last night's ale mug. I need some air and some clean clothes.'

Nakor appeared from belowdecks, and said, 'Anthony, Captain.' Seeing Amos, he said, 'Admiral! Good to see you.'

'Good to see your silly grin, too,' said Amos.

To Nicholas, Nakor said, 'Those creatures have all fallen asleep. The drug should last for some time, but with inhuman things, you can't know. We must do it now.'

Nicholas closed his eyes a moment, then said, 'Do it.'

Nakor signaled to Ghuda, who led the work gang. They slid aside the cargo hatch and moved a large cargo net with small bags of lead ballast tied to it into position over the hold. Nakor nimbly jumped to the net and hung there while it was lowered. Time dragged on while they silently waited, for only Nakor would go into the lower cargo deck, to load the thirty unconscious creatures into the net. He claimed he was the least likely candidate to become infected because of some tricks he knew, and without knowing how the plague was spread, Nicholas couldn't disagree with his judgment.

Then a shout came from below, and Ghuda signaled. The men on the hoist pushed on the wooden spokes that extended from the capstan, and the cargo net rose slowly up until it cleared the deck. Nakor was hanging on the outside of the net and jumped down to the deck as it cleared the hold. It moved higher, until it was above the rail, and two men hauled on boom lines to swing it over the water. The bodies within looked peaceful, sleeping young men and women.

Then, without waiting for any order, Nakor took a knife and cut the line to the net, releasing it. With a splash it struck the water, and Nicholas watched in mute revulsion while those inside the ropy web sank out of sight without a sound as the ballast pulled them toward the bottom of the sea.

Anthony put his hand on Nicholas's shoulder and said, 'It had to be done. There was no other way. Keep in mind those creatures were created to die.'

'It doesn't make murder any easier,' Nicholas said softly.

Anthony said, 'I'm going down to the lower deck with Nakor. Between us, we can cleanse it of any possible illness left behind. Then the mercenaries will have a place to sleep besides the main deck.'

Nicholas nodded.

Amos said, 'What about that ship that's following us?'

Nicholas said, 'Praji called it a droman. It's like a Quegan bireme with a catapult and ballista; it's also got a ram and boarding ramp. Single lateen sail off a mainmast, and I think there's a spanker behind, though it never got close enough to see.'

'The captain's brave or mad. That's no deep-water ship. A storm hits, and they'll be rowing for their lives.'

'Remember who we're dealing with,' said Nicholas.

Amos nodded. 'I know better than you, boy. I've seen their butchery on a scale you can only imagine.' He glanced upward and said, 'The men seem to be taking care of their duties.'

581

'Pickens is turning out to be a good first mate, and Harry's learning as we go.' Nicholas smiled. 'So am I.'

'Sometimes it's the best way. Pickens always was a good seaman; it was his love of too much drink while in port that kept him in the forecastle.' Glancing back to where Pickens stood, Amos said, 'We get through all this and he stays sober in port, I'll make the promotion permanent.'

Amos staggered a little and had to grab the rail. Nicholas said, 'All right. That's enough. Back to bed. I'll gladly return command to you when you're ready, but that's not for a while yet.'

As Nicholas helped Amos back to his cabin, Amos said, 'Nicky, do me one favor, will you?'

'What?'

'When we get home, don't mention this business to your grandmother. No need to upset her.'

Nicholas said, 'I think she might notice that puncture wound in your stomach, Amos.'

'I'll come up with a good story by then,' he said weakly.

Nicholas helped him back into his bunk, and before he could leave the cabin, Amos was fast asleep.

Time wore on. Nicholas's fear about friction between the men with women present seemed unfounded, as long as the pursuing war galley could be seen. For hours there would be no sign of the droman, then it would reappear just before sunset, or to be back at dawn. Without sight of the *Royal Gull*, it might have been easy to grow lax and think the voyage might end without a struggle, but the black shape on the horizon behind them always reminded them a fight was close at hand.

The prisoners from Crydee were recovering their strength enough to spend some time on deck. The dozen women from Crydee and the four maids with Iasha were around to keep the single men from becoming resentful of those with Nicholas and his friends. Twice Nicholas had broken up scuffles between boatmen or mercenaries, but he judged them no worse than similar altercations between apprentices over city girls he had observed back at Krondor.

The sailors kept the ship in trim, and those boatmen who had elected to join this journey became able deckhands. Soldiers of Crydee found themselves back at tasks learned on the journey out, while Nicholas, Marcus, and Harry learned the shipmaster's craft.

Every day Nicholas conferred with Amos, who attempted to help him get some sense of navigation from the charts and his log. They were approaching the place where Amos judged them most likely to find a friendly current as they turned away from Novindus and headed across the sea. Already they had left sight of land behind, and now the water was turning a darker blue, showing a change in current. Nicholas still wasn't as confident of reading such changes as Amos was, but then, Amos had been doing it forty years longer.

Life on the ship settled into a routine, if a tense one. But few people can live constantly under a cloud; there were moments of genuine humor and no small amount of playfulness. Harry and Brisa still sparred and hurled mock threats at each other, but Nicholas noticed he rarely saw them apart.

Margaret and Anthony could often be seen on the bow, stealing what little privacy they could for themselves. They were not as demonstrative as Brisa and Harry, but few couples were.

Marcus and Abigail had settled into a quiet contentment, though Abigail could still bring a frown to his face by mentioning her desire to see Krondor and Rillanon. Nicholas was coming to judge his cousin a man unlikely to travel more than a day's ride from his home again unless it was absolutely necessary or he was out hunting.

Nicholas found his own life surprisingly satisfying. Iasha

was passionate and instructive, and he was a more than willing pupil. The duties of captaining the ship, and of overseeing the training of the men for the coming battle, the time spent with Amos – all put him into a frame of mind that could only be called happy. He knew that a fight was coming and that nothing less than disaster for his homeland hung in the balance, but he preferred to put that problem aside until necessity dictated otherwise. It was the potential of conflict that heightened his appreciation of the good things he encountered along the way. For the interim, he was satisfied to enjoy the work, the company of good friends, and the affection of a beautiful young woman.

Nicholas was too practical to think himself in love with the girl; what he felt for her was no small part affection: Iasha had revealed herself to be a shrewd and clever young woman with a keen curiosity and the same tough, street-wise savvy that Brisa displayed. What Brisa had named coldness back when they had first met turned out to be a pointed desire for survival, a trait Brisa could appreciate. Iasha's lack of formal education and her rough upbringing could not mask her intelligence, and on several occasions Nicholas had been taken to task by her for confusing ignorance with stupidity. But while Nicholas dreamed of magical love, as young men his age often did, he had known from his earliest days that he was a child of the state and that the right to chose his own life would never be his.

This interim of sailing northeast, through the hot afternoons of equatorial waters, with those he came in search of safe, was as close to freedom as the young Prince had ever known.

Late in the second month they were entering familiar waters; Amos came up on deck one night and scanned the heavens. 'The stars look like they're supposed to,' he said with a grin. 'We're heading home.' The last was said with a wistfulness Nicholas had never heard from him.

'What's wrong?' Nicholas asked.

'Nothing, really,' said Amos. He leaned against the rail of the main deck and looked out at the dark water. 'I was just thinking that this is indeed my last voyage.'

'It's not as if you're going to be walled up in the palace,' said Nicholas. 'Grandmother has her estates and loves to travel. You may wish to stay in Krondor after one season of touring the Kingdom with her – Rillanon, Bas-Tyra, down to see Aunt Carline in Salador, a visit at Darkmoor to taste the new wines, a trip up to Yabon every second year.'

Amos shook his head. 'Landed gentry. I'll never get used to that.'

Nicholas grinned. 'You will.'

Amos said, 'Just like you're going to get used to returning to your father's court?'

Nicholas lost his smile.

'I thought so.'

Changing the subject, Nicholas said, 'Do you think they're making for Krondor?'

Amos did not need to ask who 'they' were, and he knew Nicholas already knew the answer; they had discussed this several times before, but he also knew that despite his having matured greatly over the last year, Nicholas was still young in many ways, and unsure of himself.

Amos thought a moment, then said, 'It's the most logical choice.' He glanced around to ensure they were not being overheard and said, 'We know their ultimate goal: Sethanon and the Lifestone. The plague is only a means to an end; by throwing the Kingdom into chaos, they can easily send an expedition to Sethanon, to release their "goddess".'

'Very foolish creatures,' said Nakor.

They both turned suddenly, and Amos said, 'Don't do

that. Where did you come from?'

Nakor grinned. 'Where could I have come from? We're on a ship, remember?'

Nicholas said, 'How much did you hear?'

'Enough. But nothing I didn't already know.'

Nicholas chided himself that he should never underestimate the little man's knowledge, but he had been certain only a handful of people knew of the Lifestone. 'What do you think?'

'The snakes are very strange creatures. I have thought so for many years.'

'You've encountered them before?' asked Amos.

'The last time I was in Novindus.'

Amos and Nicholas said, 'You've been to Novindus before?'

'Once, a long time ago – though I didn't know it was Novindus at the time; it's a long story having to do with a trick that didn't work the way I thought it would, some temple relics I thought were abandoned, and a secret priesthood with no sense of humor. Anyway, these Pantathians are foolish creatures who would murder the planet for this false goddess of theirs; and in the end, their plans will fail.'

Amos didn't speculate on how much Nakor knew. All he said was 'Well, a man can kill you for foolish reasons just as easily as for good ones.'

'That's the thing,' said Nakor. 'You're just as dead. You can't argue with religious fanatics.'

Ghuda came wandering over and heard the last remark. 'Oh, you can argue,' he pointed out, 'but a fat lot of good it does you. A desert man I once knew called it "pounding sand down a rathole".'

They all smiled. 'How is the training going?' asked Nicholas.

'Well. Some of the prisoners have recovered enough to join us; they're very motivated to have a sword in their

586

hand when we overtake that other ship.'

Nicholas had been reluctant to allow apprentices and pages to carry weapons, fearing they would be more of a hindrance than a help. Ghuda had convinced him that they might need every sword they could muster, and the training occupied much of the passage, giving the other mercenaries something useful to do.

They passed the evening quietly; then Amos complained of growing tired and went to his cabin. Nicholas saw Harry on the quarterdeck and decided to turn in. Reaching his cabin, he found Brisa and Iasha talking. Brisa jumped to her feet when she saw Nicholas, saying, 'I was just leaving.'

Nicholas smiled at her as she walked past. As the days grew hotter, the women had taken to wearing simple shifts, and Brisa's was cut provocatively low up top and high at the hem, showing neck, arms, bosom, and legs to good advantage. Nicholas watched her leave and Iasha pointedly cleared her throat. Nicholas turned to face her with a grin.

'Come over here,' she said, 'and I'll make you forget that skinny tart.'

Nicholas doffed his sword belt and removed his boots. As he dropped them on the deck, he said, 'Skinny? Brisa?'

Iasha reached up and unfastened the top ties of her own shift, letting it fall to her waist. 'Skinny,' she repeated.

Nicholas laughed and playfully buried his face between her breasts. Then he kissed her and said, 'What were you two talking about? You've become thick as thieves.'

Removing his tunic, she said, 'She's helping me learn your barbaric tongue, if you must know. She's really not a bad sort. Once she found out I wasn't a noblewoman, she's become very civil.'

'For someone who doesn't get along with noblewomen,

she and Margaret get along famously, too.'

Iasha said, 'Your cousin is a very unusual woman. I've seen many rich and noble women, and she's unlike any other.'

Nicholas sighed as he nuzzled her neck. 'Too bad you couldn't have known her mother.' He found it difficult to picture Briana. A wistful feeling passed through him.

'What is it?' Iasha asked.

Nicholas shrugged. 'Nothing, really. People die, you mourn them, then you get on with life. That's the way it is.' More brightly he said, 'It's good you're learning the King's Tongue.'

Iasha smiled. 'If I'm to find myself a rich husband, I'll need to know it.'

Nicholas sat up. 'Husband?'

Iasha said, 'Eventually. Your wife might not wish to have your mistress nearby. And neither one of us imagines for a moment your father would allow us to wed.'

Nicholas sat up and started to protest; then he realized she was saying nothing he hadn't already considered himself. He discovered he just didn't like hearing her say it.

'Your feelings are hurt,' she said, half-mocking. She stood up. 'Let me make you feel better,' she said as she untied the belt around her shift, allowing the fabric to fall around her ankles.

Nicholas grinned as she came back to him and settled into his arms.

The pursuing galley had not been seen for a week, and Amos judged it had finally succumbed to the long passage. He came up on deck and took a deep breath of sea air. It was early spring again.

Amos went to Nicholas's side on the quarterdeck and said, 'One of these days I may ask for my command back.'

'Any time.'

Amos clapped Nicholas on the shoulder. 'You're doing a fine job.'

Nicholas said, 'I'd feel better knowing where that other ship is.'

Amos said, 'If that captain knows his craft, they're south of the Frigate Rocks, about a week south of Three Fingers Island. They'll turn there and make directly for the Straits of Darkness.'

'We're going to cut them off?'

'I don't know,' said Amos. 'This ship is almost as fast as the real *Eagle*, and the real *Gull* was only slightly slower than that. It's a difficult choice, and we didn't know the southern waters as well as their captain.' He rubbed his hand, and said, 'But no man knows the northern waters like I do, and once on the Bitter Sea, I'll use every current and eddy, every wind and comber to push us along. We'll take them, have no doubt.'

Nicholas asked, 'When is the earliest we might see them?'

'Now,' said Amos. 'We could have overtaken them anywhere along the route, depending upon where their captain starts his eastward run.'

Two hours later, the lookout called, 'Sail ahoy!'

Nicholas ordered as much canvas on as possible and every man jumped to push the ship through the water as quickly as could be done. After a while the lookout called, 'I mark her, Captain. It's the *Royal Gull*!'

Amos shouted, 'All hands to stations!'

'No,' said Nicholas.

'No?' asked Amos.

'We'll not attack her yet.'

'Why not, for the gods' sake?' asked Amos.

Ghuda came up on deck, Praji and Vaja behind him, and Nicholas addressed all of them. 'We have no idea how many men they're carrying. And we don't have surprise. I'm not going to move in on her until we've passed the Straits of Darkness and we're almost home.'

'Why?' demanded Harry, climbing up from the main deck.

Nicholas said, 'Because I'm not going to let one of those creatures reach Krondor. If I have to, I'll lash the ships together and burn them both. If we have to swim home, I'd rather have it a short distance to friendly shores.'

Amos swore. 'Well, we'll have to dog them, and I hope their captain doesn't have a lot of imagination.'

Nicholas said, 'Pass the word, we're going to run if she turns to fight.'

Amos said, 'I don't like it – '

'Those are my orders,' said Nicholas. 'We'll take her only if she turns toward the Free Cities or Kesh. Otherwise, we're going to follow her home.'

'Aye, Captain,' Amos said, saluting. His expression was a mixture of doubt and pride.

24

Battle

Nicholas watched.

The counterfeit *Royal Gull* was trimming sail, slowing in a provocative invitation for the *Eagle* to attempt to overtake it. Amos stood on the quarterdeck. He had become a fixture there for the last two weeks, but he still hadn't requested a return of command from Nicholas.

Nicholas had been open about his lack of knowledge in running a ship, but he was an apt student, and between his lifetime of small-boat experience, the time he had worked on the *Raptor*, and what he could learn from first Pickens and now Amos, he was turning into a first-rate deep-water sailor. Amos had told him that at the rate he was learning, he'd be a first-class cabin boy in a year or two. Nicholas realized the near-legendary captain had only been teasing, but his successes so far were constantly offset by a nagging doubt that his luck was about to run out.

Amos mused, 'They're really not asking for us to engage.'

Nicholas agreed, 'They know we don't want to . . . yet. But I can't fathom what they're up to.'

Amos called aloft, 'Anything to the stern?'

The lookout called back, 'Nothing, Admiral!'

They had cleared the Straits of Darkness a week before, and were now due north of Durbin. Nicholas said, 'You don't really expect to see anything back there, do you?'

'You never know,' said Amos. He spat over the rail. 'The snakes managed enough magic to create those plague carriers and had years to plan this; they probably began this plan the minute Murmandamus died at Sethanon. I

591

wouldn't put it past them to have a way to get that bitch of a bireme across the ocean.' He smiled. 'More to the point, I wouldn't put it past them to have a ship in reserve somewhere in the Bitter Sea just in case of this sort of turn of events. And their slowing down would make sense if they expect help.'

Nicholas said, 'That's a risk I can appreciate.'

Just then the lookout called, 'Sail ahoy!'

'Where away?' shouted Nicholas.

'Dead to starboard, Captain!'

Nicholas and Amos both crossed the rail and looked, and after a minute a sail could be seen. 'She's coming fast,' said Nicholas.

Amos said, 'Uh-huh. Keshian cutter. Privateer out of Durbin. Time to run out the colors.'

The imitation Kingdom warship carried a full complement of banners and ensigns, and Nicholas called, 'Run out the Kingdom banner and the royal ensign.'

Amos said, 'Put my pennant out there, too, while you're at it.'

Nicholas called out for the Admiral of the Fleet banner to be added, and soon large colorful flags flew from topmast and mizzenmast.

The Keshian cutter bore down on them, then suddenly veered to port. Amos laughed. 'That captain sees two Kingdom warships returning from patrol, one with the Admiral of the Fleet and a member of the royal household aboard. He'll give us a wide berth.'

The day wore on, and Nicholas kept his interval behind the *Royal Gull*. The pursuit took on the aspects of a tacking duel in a race, but in this race the purpose was not to overtake, or to fall behind, but to stay within striking distance.

The *Gull* put on more canvas near sundown, and Amos said, 'The bastard's going to try to run on us in the dark. Hasn't he figured out I know these waters too well? I know where he must come back to come to Krondor.'

'What if he doesn't run to Krondor?' asked Nicholas.

'He must,' answered Amos. 'He could put into Sarth, or Land's End, but why bother? Your father is almost certain to be out on the Far Coast, trying to make sense of the mess we've left in Freeport. I think that was the purpose for what we thought was a needless raid at Carse, Tulan, and Barran. With that level of destruction, your father will have pulled most of the fleet out of Krondor and sailed straight to the Far Coast as soon as the Straits cleared. Then he'll be out to Freeport.' He calculated. 'He's probably deciding to return here or go after us by now.'

Nicholas said, 'She's breaking north!'

Amos said, 'I think it's a feint. Wait a moment, run out sails, follow, and as soon as it's dark and she can't see us, turn back to this line for Krondor. I'll bet you all I've got we'll see them no farther than a mile away at dawn tomorrow.'

Nicholas said, 'I know better than to take that bet.' Putting his hand on Amos's shoulder, he asked, 'Something to eat?'

'Why not?' answered Amos.

The old Admiral was still a little unsteady on his feet by the end of the day; however, Anthony judged him fully recovered from the sword wound. His strength would return slowly, but he would be fit and well by the time they reached Krondor. Muttering as they descended the ladder to the main deck, Amos said, 'If we were sailing a straight line, we could be home in another four days. But this tacking around, like a boat race in the harbor, it's a serious waste of wind.'

Nicholas agreed. 'I'm anxious to have this over with, but I think we know that the chances of those murderous dogs accommodating our desires are slim.'

From above, the lookout shouted, 'Smoke, Captain!'

'Where away?'

'Dead astern!'

Nicholas and Amos hurried back up on deck and squinted against the setting sun. A plume of smoke rose like a tattered flag and Amos said, 'That Keshian cutter found someone.'

'Yes, but who?' asked Nicholas.

Amos's prediction had been apt. When dawn broke, the *Royal Gull* was less than a mile away, slightly to the north of them. Nicholas watched as the ship slowly grew larger, then ordered the helm ported, so their own speed fell off. The tacking duel really slowed their pace, and Amos came up on deck.

He climbed to the quarterdeck and said, 'Something new?'

'Yes,' said Nicholas. 'They're doing nothing that makes sense, except slowing down. I wonder if they're going to turn and attack?'

Amos looked at the other ship. 'If they're going to, they'll be turning about . . . now!' The other ship turned.

'All hands on deck!' shouted Nicholas. 'Mr Pickens, turn to port and see if we can be heading out on the upwind leg before they get turned around and their sails trimmed.'

Nakor came running up on deck, shouting, 'There's something! There's something!'

Nicholas said, 'What are you talking about?'

'I don't know,' said the little man, hopping back and forth from foot to foot. 'There's a trick here. I can feel it!'

Anthony came up an instant later and said, 'Nicholas, something strange is happening to us. I can sense it.'

'Do you have any idea what it is?' asked Nicholas.

Abruptly there was a sound like a giant cloth ripping, and a ringing like a chime, but loud and sustained, hanging in the air and grating on the nerves, like the shriek of broken chalk on a slate board.

Nicholas felt his skin break out in chill bumps, and his breath came short. Then Anthony pointed. 'Look!'

Through a shimmering haze on the horizon, the droman materialized. 'It's a trick!' shouted Nakor. 'They've hidden the ship from our eyes, and the other ship has slowed us down!'

Anthony said, 'A spell of masking.'

Amos said, 'Now we know who that Keshian freebooter encountered late yesterday.'

'And who won.' Nicholas judged the position of the two ships. 'Make ready for battle!' he called. 'Mr Pickens, bring her back to starboard. We're taking the *Gull*.'

Orders were passed, and Ghuda and Praji formed their mercenary companies, one in the rigging, the other on deck. Those prisoners from Crydee who were fit carried weapons, but most of them also carried ropes and grapples. Sailors above frantically reversed the set of sails they had begun trimming for a turn to port, and now were lengthening sheets they had just shortened, while others quickly pulled in those that they had just let out.

Marcus and Calis were climbing to archers' platforms in the rigging, with a half-dozen other archers. They picked their targets and began firing, their longbows able to reach farther than any other bows on either ship. Sailors on the *Gull* dived for cover, and when Calis killed the helmsman, the ship turned and wallowed.

The *Eagle* bore down on its sister ship, and Amos called ranges for Nicholas, judging the closing distance and angle with a practiced eye. At the center of the deck, Margaret, Brisa, and Iasha, with some of the townswomen and boatmen, quickly set fire pots to burning, fanning coals to life.

'Hard aport!' shouted Amos, and Pickens spun the wheel as fast as he could. The *Eagle* decended on the

Gull, and men on both decks braced themselves for a ramming collision. But as the bow of the *Eagle* seemed ready to pierce the railing of the *Gull*, the *Eagle* turned ponderously to the left. Spars on the bowsprit and braces on the fore channel shattered, sending wooden splinters flying through the air like missiles. Then the hulls struck, a glancing blow, but with enough force that one soldier was thrown from his perch in the rigging of the *Eagle*, and another was left dangling from the ropes, while his sword clattered on the deck below.

A full score of men stood ready to greet the attackers, and Nicholas shouted, 'Nakor, if you have any tricks to help, now's the time!'

Nakor reached into his black rucksack and pulled out something that looked like a ball of smoke, black churning in his hand. Then Nicholas saw it was a swarm of some kind of insects.

He threw it toward the *Gull*, and the cloud grew, and a loud angry buzzing filled the air as the two ships lurched together. The row of defenders cried out and began swatting at stinging insects.

Nakor said, 'It won't last long. Hurry.'

Nicholas gave the signal. 'Now!' shouted Harry, overseeing the men from Crydee with the grapples, and they threw the heavy three-pronged hooks. Two bounced off the rail and fell between the ships, while another bounced harmlessly off the deck when the man throwing it let go of the rope in his excitement. But the others held, and pulled, and the two ships came together with a grinding crash.

The men with the grappling ropes quickly tied them off, then drew their weapons to join in the boarding. Each wore a headband of black cloth, at Nicholas's insistence, so that should any man find himself facing an inhuman copy, he would know he faced a false human, even if the face was that of a brother or friend. Each man had been warned that to lose the headband was to chance being killed by a friend, and if the headband was lost, to fall to the deck and get out of the way.

Praji's mercenaries swarmed the deck, while those with Ghuda swung across from the rigging above. Nicholas looked to the main deck and saw that Tuka and his boatmen, and some of the women from Crydee, stood ready. They would either carry hot pitch to be thrown at the next ship, or put out fires that might erupt on the *Eagle*.

Nicholas saw that everything was as ordered as it would be, drew his own sword, and took a running leap at the rail. With one foot on the rail of the *Eagle*, he pushed off and launched himself across six feet of space high above two hulls grinding together, to land on the forecastle of the *Gull*. Nakor's stinging bugs were gone, but they'd done their job.

The ships were lashed together fore-to-aft, and their sails and rigging conspired to force the locked pair of ships to turn in a slow circle. Nicholas cursed the luck that forced him to take the *Gull* bow to stern. It would make it much more difficult to cut her loose and get away than had they overtaken her from the same direction. He hoped it would not leave them vulnerable to the approaching droman.

A black-clad officer attacked Nicholas, and the Prince parried the first blow. The man had a tendency to follow a pattern of three blows, and the third time he began the sequence, Nicholas easily took him in the chest with the point of his sword.

Nicholas glanced around and saw one of his own men being pushed over the side of the rail. Nicholas killed the man doing the pushing, and helped the man regain the deck. They saw they were alone on the foredeck, and Nicholas shouted, 'Amos, over here!'

Amos picked up a small cask, the sort used for brandy,

and threw it across to Nicholas. Nicholas's knees buckled, and he let out a *woof* of exertion as he caught it, but he held on to it.

To the soldier with him he shouted, 'Open that small hatchway, and be careful of surprises!'

The man pushed it aside with his foot, leaning away, and a crossbow bolt shot out. Nicholas didn't wait; he threw the cask down into the darkness. He heard a satisfying crash of wood and a cry of pain. 'That's one!' he shouted to Amos.

Amos tossed him another, and he quickly smashed that down after the first; then they pushed the cover closed.

Picking up his sword, Nicholas looked down at the main deck, seeing that the fighting was spread out across the deck, a no-man's-land, with no clear-cut line separating the opposing forces.

Nicholas swung down the ladder, planting his boot in the back of a man facing one of Praji's mercenaries. The black-clad sailor stumbled forward, and the mercenary quickly killed him.

Nicholas skirted the fighting until he was moving along the rail closest to his own ship. Ghuda, Praji, and Vaja were holding a clear area of deck, and Nicholas joined them, forcing their way past a small central hatchway. As soon as he was there, Nicholas turned and shouted, 'Another barrel!'

Amos and Harry carried a larger barrel and had to rest it on the moving rails of the ships while Nicholas took hold of it. Harry scrambled over and helped his friend pick up the large barrel. It was ten gallons of oil, and with the rolling deck below them, they had a difficult time getting it over the hatchway. Nicholas counted three and they dropped it.

The oil was lamp oil and wouldn't burn without a wick under normal conditions, but Nakor had insisted that if the fire around it grew hot enough, it would aid the ship in burning, melting the pitch between the planks of the hull and either burning her to the water line, or causing enough leaks to sink her.

Turning away from the hatch, Nicholas saw that the main hatchway was momentarily clear. 'Get another!' he shouted to Harry, while he raced to stand over the next hatchway.

Two sailors from the *Gull* seemed to materialize out of nowhere, and Nicholas engaged them both. He had practiced against multiple opponents in the marshalling yard as soon as he had picked up his first sword, but never before had his life been the prize. He remembered what his father and his drill instructor had told him over and over: unless the two men he was facing had practiced together, they were as likely to get in each other's way as to help each other. Wait, defend, and watch for an opening.

As if his father had staged an example for his benefit, the man on the left stepped in front of the man on the right. The second man bumped him, pushing him off balance, and he died on Nicholas's sword before he could recover it. Nicholas then pushed back the second man, and took him in the throat as Ghuda arrived, carrying a large barrel. He dumped it down the hatchway and shouted, 'That's all of them!'

'Call for the fire and get off this ship!' shouted Nicholas.

Every man on the raiding party had been told that as soon as fire had been passed to the *Gull*, the only order would be to fight back to the *Eagle*.

Tuka's boatmen stood around a small cooking pot, set over an open brazier, heating pitch. Above, men waited in the yards, while Nicholas's boarders fought a retreat.

The crew of the *Gull*, rather than press the advantage, sought to cut the *Eagle* loose, and Nicholas saw that his men were clearing the rail.

'Now!' cried Nicholas.

Above, Calis and Marcus began shooting fire arrows into the sails of the *Gull*. The other men in the yards lowered ropes and had bubbling pitch tied to them. They quickly pulled them up, for the hot pitch would cool rapidly, and the hotter the pitch, the easier to light.

Nicholas watched with trepidation: handling fire aboard any ship was risky – during a battle it was extremely dangerous. No worst disaster than fire at sea existed, for a ship was like a tinderbox. A little flame anywhere in the sail or rigging, and the entire ship could be engulfed in minutes. Most of the material used to keep water out – pitch, tar, and oil – burned furiously, and even wetting canvas during a battle was scant protection against fire arrows or hot coals.

Nicholas stood by the large brazier amidships, ready to dump the coals on his own deck and pour oil on the fire. If a blaze could not be set aboard the *Gull*, he would burn both ships, ordering his crew and passengers to abandon ship.

In the rigging, men of Crydee cautiously struck flint and steel to tinder, and brought flame to life; they shielded the flickering ember, for their own sails were as dry and vulnerable to flame as the *Gull*'s. Reaching the end of the spars where the others waited, they passed along the burning brands, which were touched to the surface of the buckets of pitch. The pitch sprang into flame, and the men quickly threw the buckets onto the rigging and yards of the neighboring ship.

Nicholas stood alone on the deck of the *Gull*, making sure his raiders were safely back, but as he started to climb back, a pair of sailors charged him and he found himself sitting on the rail, unable to move quickly. Someone hurled over the rail beside him, landing atop the two men. They all went to the deck in a heap, and Nicholas saw Ghuda get up. The big mercenary turned and started toward Nicholas, a smile on his face. 'Let's – ' he began to say, then looked surprised.

He took a step toward Nicholas, reaching behind him, as if trying to scratch his back, and said, 'Damn me!'

Nicholas, on the deck of the *Eagle*, saw Ghuda slump facedown across the rails, a knife protruding from his back. Nicholas reached over and pulled at the big mercenary, dragging him to the *Eagle* with a strength he wouldn't have thought possible.

Tuka raced forward, a burning pot of pitch dangling from one hand. He started a swinging arc, casting the pot over the rail to the *Gull*, when an arrow struck him in the chest. With a gurgling screech, he stumbled forward and over the rail, falling between the two hulls, which slid together with a sick, grinding crunch. The scream was cut off instantly.

Nicholas felt ill. Anthony hurried to his side, and Nicholas said, 'See to him,' pointing at Ghuda.

Nicholas's mercenaries hacked at the ropes that tied the ships together, while dodging sporadic arrow fire, as flames rained down on the *Gull*, perilously close to the *Eagle*. Margaret and Iasha stood ready with buckets of sand and water for any sign of flames on the deck. The men in the rigging were all carrying knives, to quickly cut loose any sail or line that might catch fire.

Nicholas saw the crew of the *Gull* was now frantically attempting to combat flames in the rigging and sails, and ordered Pickens to pull away from the enemy ship.

Pickens called back, 'We're locked up, Captain! We're into the wind and can't get loose until we turn!'

Nicholas called for the boatmen to bring oars from the jolly boats and fend off the *Gull*. A dozen oars were carried to the rail and men attempted to push away the other ship, but to no avail.

Lazily the two ships turned in the wind, locked together by circumstance. Then the two hulls began to slide along each other, with a grinding, shrieking sound as wood and metal scraped in a shuddering embrace.

Then the *Eagle* heeled around the stern of the *Gull*, and with a thunderous bump the two ships struck one last time, and the *Eagle* rolled free.

Small fires erupted in the rigging and on the deck, but these were quickly put out. Men who had been dumping flaming pitch on the enemies a few minutes before were now growing exhausted from hauling water up on those same ropes and dumping it on the sails, to keep sparks and embers from the *Gull* from drifting on the wind and firing the *Eagle*.

Nicholas hurried to the aftercastle, mounting the quarterdeck, and watched as they slid past the *Gull*. Marcus swung down from the rigging and put his hand on his cousin's shoulder. 'We did it.'

Nicholas said, 'I hope so.'

Then Nicholas felt Marcus's hand grip his shoulder hard, and he saw what Marcus was seeing. As flames began to spread through the sails of the *Gull*, figures were running up on deck. Among those coming up from belowdecks, framed by smoke and a shower of embers, stood Margaret and Abigail, shrieking in terror.

Close enough to hear them, Nicholas and Marcus stood in mute horror. Nicholas glanced down at the main deck and saw Margaret there, dressed in her short shift, while the Margaret on the *Gull* wore a Princess's gown.

Then the Margaret on the *Gull* called, 'Marcus! Help me!'

The Abigail at her side screamed, 'Nicholas! Save us!'

With a low concussion, something belowdecks in the *Gull* caught fire, and flames shot up from the hatchways. The gown worn by the Margaret on the *Gull* caught fire, and she shrieked as she beat at the flames with her hands.

An arrow sped from the rigging and caught her in the chest, knocking her back and out of sight. A second arrow caught Abigail in the chest, and she, too, fell.

Calis swung down from the rigging above, landing lightly next to Nicholas and Marcus. 'I saw no sense in prolonging that misery. They might be false, but the image was no less terrible for that.'

He nodded toward the mid-deck, where Abigail stood in mute horror, eyes wide at having witnessed her own death, while Margaret stood ashen-faced, her hands held tightly by Anthony.

Nicholas nodded, then turned to look sternward. The droman was bearing down on them, and he shouted, 'Get ready! We're not done yet! Hard to starboard, Mr Pickens.'

Amos shouted, 'Look!'

Nakor and Praji came up on deck and over to Nicholas. 'What?' asked Praji.

'Who's that in the bow?'

Nicholas felt his heart sink as Nakor said, 'It's Dahakon.'

A man in a brown robe, his arms folded in the sleeves, stood regarding the *Eagle*, and the burning *Gull*, impassively.

'He must have used his arts to bring that ship here,' said Praji.

'No,' said Nakor. 'No trick to bring it here. He followed us the entire way. He only hid it from us with his trick.'

'Impossible,' said Amos. 'That ship couldn't hold enough stores to feed the slaves and crew!'

'Look,' said Nicholas, pointing.

A figure moved to stand at Dehakon's side, Valgasha, the Overlord. His skin was pale, bloated and flyblown, his movements jerky and uncoordinated. Upon his wrist the eagle spread its wings, a rotting mockery of its former splendor.

'Necromancy,' said Nakor. 'He's an evil bastard.'

The Dehakon raised his hand, and Nicholas felt his skin

pucker with chill bumps again. 'He's incanting,' said Anthony from below.

Calis notched an arrow and let fly, but the shaft seemed to strike an invisible wall, stopping inches from the magician, falling to the deck.

Men began to gather on deck, many calling down the favor of their gods as a ship of dead men approached. Across the water, figures gathered on deck, a silent force of corpses.

Nakor closed his eyes and made a gesture, then he opened them again. 'This is very bad.'

Nicholas said, 'Really?'

'He uses very powerful tricks to keep those men moving, but, worse, they carry the plague.'

'We can't mount a second offensive against that ship,' said Amos. 'We don't have enough pitch and oil.'

'We'll ram her,' said Nicholas.

'Not in this lifetime,' said Amos. He pointed. The sails on the droman lowered, while the oars began to lift and fall. 'The rowers are rowing, dead or not.'

'Mighty arts,' said Praji, spitting over the side.

'How do you fight dead men?' asked Marcus.

'The best way you know how,' answered Nicholas, drawing his sword. He glanced toward the distant shore-line and said, 'Where are we, Amos?'

'Less than a half day's sailing from Land's End, another three days to Krondor.'

'We're going to let her close and ram us, we're going to fire the *Eagle*, then those who can will swim for shore.'

'It's more than three miles,' said Amos softly. 'Few of us are going to make it.'

Even more softly, Nicholas said, 'I know.'

Harry came racing up from the main deck. 'We're going to fight that?'

Nicholas nodded.

Nakor said, 'Anthony!'

The young magician said, 'What?'

'It's time!' Nakor said with a grin.

'Time for what?' asked Anthony, blinking in confusion.

'Use the amulet!'

Anthony's eyes narrowed, then he reached into his tunic and pulled out the talisman Pug had originally given to Nicholas. He closed his hand around it and shouted, 'Pug!' Nothing happened for a minute, then Anthony closed his eyes and shouted Pug's name again.

As he spoke the name a third time, a low thud of wind struck the ship, as if a thunderclap had sounded next to them, and the ship heeled over slightly. Men shouted and exclaimed, and pointed. Directly in front of the droman, a creature hung in the air. As large as the ship itself, its wings beat a wind with enough force to back away the bireme.

'A dragon!' said Amos.

The dragon was golden, with a silver crest. Ruby eyes the size of shields gleamed in the sunset, while talons black as ebony extended like a cat's. Dahakon gaped, and for a moment was motionless. The dragon snapped wings, held position before the droman, and opened its giant maw.

Fire erupted, white-hot and blinding, and washed over the ship. The sails and decks exploded into flames, while the dead crew ignited. The Overlord and his eagle stood like a statue, a mockery of majesty, as flames consumed them. The bird blackened and toppled from its master's arm, which shriveled moments later as the ruler of the City of the Serpent River died in truth.

For a terrible moment, the rest of the droman's crew stood motionless, their skin burning on them while they crouched for the attack. Lifeless warriors, mindless of their own destruction, they awaited the magician's com-

605

mand to swarm over the side and take the *Eagle*. Then swords fell from fingers too shriveled to hold them, and they began to topple.

The *Royal Eagle* moved listlessly, no effort being made to keep her on course as every living soul aboard was riveted by the sight of the most majestic creature in Midkemia, one told of in story and legend, hanging less than a hundred yards away, destroying the ship of the dead.

Then Anthony pointed. 'Look!'

In the midst of the conflagration, Dahakon stood motionless, surrounded by a ruby nimbus that shielded him from the dragon's fury. Nicholas said, 'Is there anything we can do?'

Calis notched another arrow and fired again, but this bounced off the ruby shield as the first had off the invisible one. Nakor said, 'I think . . .' He grabbed an arrow from Calis's quiver and broke it across his knee. Holding the broken arrow up, he said, 'His trick stops steel. Can you shoot this?'

Calis took the shaft, broken to three-quarter length, and said, 'I can try.' He notched the arrow and drew it back to its abbreviated length, then let fly. Unlike the last two, this struck the magician in the chest, and he cried out; the ruby shield instantly vanished and the dragon's flames seared him.

With a shriek that could be heard on the *Eagle*, the magician erupted into flame and spun backward, falling out of sight.

The dragon watched the burning ship, then with a snap of its wings, it moved away. It soared, gliding above the waves, toward the sunset. In a lazy, soaring circle, it rose and passed above the ship, turned toward the northwest, and sped away.

Harry whispered, 'Ryana.'

Nicholas nodded.

'Look!' said Harry.

Nicholas squinted to see what his friend pointed to, and there, upon the back of the dragon, a tiny figure could be seen riding.

'Is that Pug?' asked Harry.

Nakor grinned and said, 'I think so.' He laughed. 'Now we are done.'

Vaja called from the main deck, 'Nakor!'

They all looked and saw he was kneeling over Ghuda. Nicholas and the others followed Nakor and Anthony to Ghuda's side. The wounded mercenary lay with his head propped on a bag of sand, and blood flowed from his nose.

Anthony rolled him on his side and examined the wound, and looked at Nicholas with pain in his eyes. He shook his head no.

Nakor took Ghuda's hand. 'What is it, old friend?'

Ghuda coughed and blood ran from the corner of his mouth. 'Friend?' he said, his voice weak and liquid. 'I'm lying here drowning in my own blood because you want me to go halfway around the world with you, and you call me friend?' He squeezed Nakor's hand tightly and tears rolled down his leathery cheeks. 'Sunsets above other oceans, and mighty sights and great wonders to behold, Nakor.' He coughed violently and spat blood on Nakor and Anthony. Gasping for breath that wouldn't come, he said, 'A dragon of gold!' With his last breath, he said, 'My friend.' With a choking, strangled sound, he convulsed and thrashed a moment, then lay still.

Nicholas choked back his own pain, looking around the deck. Other wounded men lay nearby, and he said, 'Anthony.'

The young magician looked where Nicholas pointed, and hurried to lend aid and comfort to those who needed it.

Nicholas felt a hand on his shoulder and looked up to

see Iasha next to him. He rose and she said, 'Are we going to your home, now?'

Nicholas let the tears run down his cheeks as he took her in his arms. He didn't trust his voice, so he nodded then, letting the sob out, half relief, half sorrow, he said 'We're going home.'

Nicholas composed himself, and then he gently set Iasha aside. Turning toward the quarterdeck, he said, 'Mr Pickens, make for Krondor!'

Amos shouted, 'Get aloft, you dock rats!'

The *Royal Eagle* slowly turned; then, as her sails filled she moved away in stately fashion from the two burning hulks. With the sun setting behind them, Nicholas watched as first the counterfeit *Royal Gull* and then the Overlord's bireme sank into the water.

Amos came to stand next to Nicholas and put his hand on his shoulder. 'Have I told you that lately you've begun to remind me of your father?'

Nicholas turned toward Amos, and his eyes were shining with unshed tears. 'No,' he said, his voice hoarse.

Squeezing his shoulder, Amos whispered, 'Well, you do. And I'm as proud of you as if you were my own grandson.'

Nicholas drew a deep breath and said, 'Thank you, adding, with a forced grin, 'Grandfather.'

Amos gripped Nicholas by the back of the neck and shook him slightly as he said, 'Grandfather! Damn me you *are* like him. Trying to take the fun out of life!'

Nicholas smiled. Putting his hand on Amos's shoulder he said, 'No one has ever managed to rid your life of fun Amos.'

Amos threw him a sad smile and said, 'That's the truth of it, isn't it? Though days like this make you understand why the fun is important.'

Amos unexpectedly threw his arms around Nicholas

and hugged his foster grandson. 'Let's bury our dead, Nicky, hoist a drink to their memory, and go home.'

It was a subdued party on the main deck. The mood of the crew was a mixture of profound relief, stunned amazement at sight of the dragon, and sorrow at the injury and death of friends.

Ghuda and Tuka were not the only casualties. One of Tasha's maids, her friend, had been badly burned by some spilled pitch that she had smothered before it could catch fire and imperil the ship.

Five mercenaries had died, as well as three other boatmen. A dozen men of Crydee had given their lives to protect their Kingdom. Nicholas took stock and found that of those, six men who had left Crydee with him to pursue the raiders had died. Out of the sixty-five men and women on the ship, only twenty-seven had left with Amos and himself at the start of the journey.

Nicholas had ordered the brandy broken out and as they stood before him he said, 'Some of you know all we've been through, while others of you are recently in our company. But without any of you, I don't know if we could have accomplished what we have. The crown is in your debt. I've decided that whatever booty we have left in that chest below will be equally divided among all of you.' The mercenaries grinned while the sailors and soldiers of the Kingdom exchanged startled glances, but their smiles were equally appreciative. Bonuses in service to the Kingdom were rare. 'We've lost some good friends,' said Nicholas. 'Let us never forget.' He raised a glass and said, 'To Ghuda, and the others.'

They all drank and then Nicholas said, 'For you that have come across a vast ocean to a distant land, we will do all we can to make you feel at home. I don't know how we shall aid you to return home, but someday you shall. You have our word. Until then there's honest work and ample pay for all of you.'

Turning toward the sunset, made red-orange and gold by the smoke from the burning ships, he said, 'Set sail for Krondor!'

A cheer erupted from the crew and men leaped to their duties, anxious to be heading at last for home.

Three days later, near noon, they sailed into Krondor harbor. Amos ordered the royal ensign hoisted, and it was a flustered harbor pilot who raced to intercept the boat. Climbing aboard with two assistants, he greeted Amos and Nicholas with a mixture of wonder and astonishment.

Nicholas said, 'Amos, would you like to take her in for the last time?'

Amos shrugged. 'It's not really the same thing. If this were the true *Eagle*, or my *Royal Dragon*, perhaps.' The remark caused the harbor pilot to glance from Prince to Admiral in confusion. Then with an evil grin, Amos said, 'You should practice coming in under sail. Can't start any sooner.'

Nicholas returned the grin. 'Make ready to trim sail!' he shouted.

The harbor pilot said, 'Highness, I urge you; lower your sails and let us tow you in.'

Nicholas said, 'Harry!'

'What?' called his friend.

'Get into the bow and make sure that assistant pilot doesn't faint.' In an almost joyous challenge, he shouted, 'We're coming in under sail!'

Sailors scrambled as smaller boats moved out of the way. The Royal Ensign gave the *Eagle* right-of-way over any other save a smaller boat also under royal colors, and old hands in the harbor knew the Prince's Admiral's habit of sailing into the royal docks. With Trask's pennant

610

flying from the masthead, no one in their right mind was about to cross the bow of the *Royal Eagle*; the only two to ever try it now stood on the *Eagle*'s deck.

Harry shouted, 'We're on line!'

Nicholas called out, 'Reef all sails! Ready the landlines!'

The sailors above furiously pulled up the canvas. The ship moved forward, her inertia carrying her straight into the docks. Nicholas watched expectantly, waiting for the proper moment to call for the lines to be tossed to those waiting on the dockside.

The ship continued to slow and Nicholas waited, and waited, until at last Harry turned and shouted, 'We're . . . ah . . . a little short, Nicky.'

Nicholas put his head down in the crook of his arm, resting on the rail, and said, 'Master Pilot. Call for your boat, if you will.'

Amos laughed, a belly roar that rattled the sails. Slapping Nicholas on the back, he said, 'You'll get the hang of it, one of these days.'

Nicholas peeked out from the crook of his arm and said, 'Now who's taking the fun out of life?'

25

Wedding

The guests cheered.

Lyam, King of the Isles, drank the toast he had just made to the bride and groom. Amos stood grinning, looking almost unrecognizable in his formal court clothing; lace-front shirts and cutaway coats had become the fashion in the Kingdom this year. Only the desire of his beloved Alicia for him to look his best on their wedding day could get him into what he called 'those silly-looking garments'. His other choice was his Admiral's uniform, which he despised even more, so he relented on her request and dressed in current fashion.

Nicholas sat with the other guests at the head table in the banquet hall of the Prince's palace in Krondor. At his right, his sister, Elena, and her husband were speaking with Erland, one of his brothers, and Erland's wife, the Princess Genevieve. Borric, Erland's twin, spoke to his wife, Yasmine, while Alicia looked on.

Nicholas's mother had been almost overwhelmed when she saw her youngest child walk into court, without the limp that had marked him for life. Nicholas had realized that during the last battle he had been so preoccupied with making sure everything was ready in case things turned for the worse, that if the foot had hurt him, he hadn't noticed. Nakor had said that his healing was now complete.

It had taken months to plan the wedding and get everyone back to Krondor. The King had to come from his royal court in Rillanon for the wedding, and reached Arutha's court before Arutha returned. Word had finally reached the Prince of Krondor when Baron Bellamy of

Carse sent a small boat to Freeport, where Arutha and his fleet were waiting. Amos had been almost right: Arutha had decided against following after Nicholas and his companions only after a long and bitter debate with himself.

When Arutha had returned to Krondor, Nicholas and Amos told him and the King the entire story, from the raid to the destruction of the two ships north of Land's End. Lyam sent a special messenger to Sorcerer's Isle, to see if Pug could be located, and sent Nicholas and Borric to Sethanon, as only a member of the royal family could be trusted to know the mission.

Nicholas and his brother had returned two weeks later with word that all was well at Sethanon, and Nicholas had expressed his awe at meeting the Oracle of Aal. To his surprise, the Lifestone had not been in evidence, being masked by a magic time distortion that Pug had placed upon it. Still, the knowledge it was there and vulnerable despite its protection was not hard to impress on Nicholas after what he had been through the previous year.

The messenger to Sorcerer's Isle had returned with a message from Pug, via Gathis, his representative, that the magician would join them for the wedding. In time, all the guests had at last gathered and the ceremony was performed.

The celebration wore on, and Nicholas found himself relaxing for the first time in what seemed a lifetime. He glanced over at his companion for the day, and smiled. He found Iasha adapting well to the court, and her command of the King's Tongue was growing daily. She got on well with the ladies of the court. Her injured maid had recovered, and with the aid of Anthony's magic she had been spared severe scars. The other three girls were already the focus of attention of many of the younger men of the court. The story was making the rounds that they were five sisters from a distant land, daughters of a powerful Prince, and the girls showed no inclination to dispel that notion.

Marcus sat with his father and his sister, who kept a tight grip on Anthony's hand, while Marcus ignored Abigail's habit of catching the eye of the more dashing courtiers in the hall. Nicholas noticed that Abigail was now almost openly flirting with the son of the Duke of Ran's second son, Elena's brother-in-law.

Duke Martin had aged, his hair now almost all grey, and his erect carriage and vigorous step were missing. What age had not taken, sorrow had. Sadly, Nicholas judged his joy in life had died with his wife. He already spoke of retiring in Marcus's favor as Duke. Nicholas knew there would be long discussions between the King, Arutha, and Martin before that step was permitted. Still, Martin appeared profoundly relieved to have his children back. He had attempted to communicate his gratitude to Nicholas, forcing an awkward moment between them. Nicholas realized what torture convalescence must have been for Martin, while waiting for word of his children. All Nicholas could say was 'It was what you would have done in my place.'

Martin had been able only to nod, tears in his eyes; then he embraced his nephew. Nicholas knew how difficult that open display had been for him.

Abigail's laughter brought Nicholas back from his reverie. He leaned back, saying behind Iasha's back to Harry, 'How long do you think Marcus is going to put up with that?'

Harry grinned. 'Right now, I think he'd welcome someone taking Abby off his hands.'

Brisa hit Harry under the table and said, 'You two stop that.'

Iasha smiled. 'Abby's just making sure Marcus doesn't take things for granted. He was her first lover, but she doesn't wish him to think he's the only choice out there.'

She laughed. 'They'll probably end up married; she really does love him.' She studied Marcus a moment. 'He's handsome enough, in a stern way, like your father.' She glanced at Nicholas. 'Both lack your kind nature.' Then, playfully, she said, 'Besides, your cousin lacks your . . . imagination.'

Nicholas had the decency to blush. Then his face clouded over. 'How do you – '

Brisa grinned. 'Abby talks. After her first time, she had to talk to someone. You men have such a strange notion of what women talk about when you're not around.'

Nicholas put his hand to his face, covering his eyes. 'Poor Marcus.' Then his eyes widened in near terror as he looked at the Brisa and Iasha and said, 'What about you two?'

Brisa grinned and said nothing. After a moment, Nicholas couldn't help but grin back. The street girl looked stunning. Her dark red hair had grown long enough since the voyage that Anita and her maids could arrange it high on her head, setting if off with silver and pearls. She wore a specially made gown of deep green, which showed her skin and eyes to good advantage.

Iasha had chosen a gown of dark blue and was easily one of the most striking women at court. She still talked about finding herself a rich husband, but Nicholas noticed she didn't seem to be in much of a hurry to do so.

As the dinner wound down, Borric came over and put his hand on his brother's shoulder. Whispering, he said, 'Your presence, little brother, and that of your lady friend, is requested in the family's private quarters.' He glanced over at Harry and said, 'You too, Squire, and your lady as well.'

As the guests filed out, some to return to the city by carriage, others to guest quarters set aside for them while they visited Krondor, the family of the King gathered in the royal family's apartment. With every cousin, aunt, uncle, and in-law in attendance, the 'family' gathering was nearly as riotous a crowd as the entire wedding party had been.

As he entered the large room, Nicholas nodded to his aunt Carline, a still-lovely woman with silver-grey hair. Her husband, Laurie, Duke of Salador, smiled and winked at Nicholas. Nicholas knew that before the night was over, Laurie would be the center of attention, singing and playing on an old lute he took everywhere. No longer the dashing minstrel of his youth, Laurie was still a fine singer who could hold a room rapt for hours. Their daughter and two sons sat in the corner, planning to escape into the city with some of younger courtiers in the palace as soon as it was acceptable to excuse themselves. Nicholas couldn't believe he was roughly the same age as they were; he felt as if he had aged ten years in the last year.

Gunther, eldest son of the Duke of Ran, held Elena's hand as she sat next to her mother. Close to term with their first baby, she positively beamed with joy. Anita reveled in the presence of her grandchildren and would probably conspire to keep the family in Krondor days beyond anyone's scheduled plans.

Borric and his wife, the Princess Yasmine, entered, and the doors were closed behind them. Several small children were absent, and Nicholas knew that they were considered too likely to grow fussy and restless during the family's smaller celebration. The hour was growing late, and soon Borric and Yasmine's two older children would be put to bed.

Besides the family, Harry and Brisa, Iasha, and Abigail and her father, Baron Bellamy, were among the guests. Bellamy's two sons were back supervising the rebuilding of both Carse and Crydee.

A second door opened and Nakor entered, wearing a wonderfully fashioned robe of blue, with a magnificent cape trimmed in a complex design of white and silver threads. Behind him came a man dressed in black, escorting a lovely woman with golden hair.

Nicholas and Harry both stood, their mouths threatening to gape. Nicholas said, 'Pug. Ryana!' He composed himself. 'Lady Ryana, what a pleasure.'

The beautiful but alien-looking woman nodded in Nicholas's direction, and a smile passed between them. A very self-conscious-looking Prajichetas and an elegantly dressed Vajasiah entered next. Calis was the last to enter, and the door was closed again behind them.

Still powerful-looking despite his years, the King stood before a giant hearth, without a fire on this warm summer evening. His blond hair was free of all but a little grey, turning paler, almost white, over the years, and his face showed lines from the pressure of office. Lyam removed the golden circlet of his office with a sign of relief. He looked down at his wife, Queen Magda, and said, 'We live for these informal moments' – he grinned and years seemed to fall away – 'now "we" can be "I" for a little while.' Martin and Arutha went to stand next to their brother, Martin still limping from his injury.

A porter entered and held open the door as a line of servants came through, bearing flagons of wine. Lyam waited until these had been passed to everyone in the room and then said, 'Many of you know some of what transpired along the Far Coast last year. Only a few of you know all of it. But one thing I wish you all to know and that is that my nephew, Prince Nicholas, has done a remarkable thing.' He paused while all eyes turned toward Nicholas. 'In quest for his cousin and others who were taken unlawfully from this land, he sailed halfway around the world and, against any reasonable hope, back again with all he could save.

'I would have liked to propose this toast during the wedding feast, so everyone in the realm could know of this amazing feat, but as it was Amos and Alicia's moment, I thought it best to wait until we, the family and friends of Nicholas, were alone. I now propose a toast to Nicholas, who brings pride and honor to the name conDoin.'

'To Nicholas,' they said, and drank from their cups.

As the servants left the room, Nicholas could see all eyes remaining upon him. He flushed and found it difficult to swallow, and his eyes threatened to brim over with tears. He cleared his throat and said, 'Thank you all.' He squeezed Iasha's hand and said, 'But what I did, I did with the help of good men and women. Many who are not here with us today.' He raised his own flagon. 'To absent friends.'

'To absent friends,' they repeated, and drank.

The smaller gathering broke down into groups of people chatting about family and friends, inquiring into the health of elder family members or the growth of children. Nicholas was struck that except for the size of the gathering and the power of the people in attendance, it was little different from a gathering of any other family.

Pug came over and steered Nicholas to a quiet corner. 'It's our first chance to talk. You did all that anyone could have asked you to do, Nicholas, and more.'

'Thank you.'

Pug said, 'I expect you have a few questions.'

'Dahakon?' asked Nicholas.

'Truly dead,' said Pug. 'He was dangerous, and by keeping him occupied for the months you traveled, I weakened his powers. He used almost all he had left keeping that warship after you. Ryana was more than he could deal with, once Calis distracted him with that wooden shaft.'

'Nakor showed Anthony how to do it.' Nicholas smiled. 'I'm surprised you brought Ryana with you.'

Pug smiled in return. Softly he said, 'Part of her

education. Passing for human is not easy for one of her kind.'

Nicholas looked to where Vajasiah was speaking to Ryana, his every gesture and expression artfully designed to charm. 'It looks like she's getting an education right now.'

Pug smiled. 'Not as much as he will should she agree to steal away with him. There are nuances of human behavior that she just doesn't understand yet. For her age and power, in most ways she's still a child.'

'One question,' asked Nicholas.

'What?'

'When I first came to your island, how much of what was to happen did you already know?'

Pug said, 'Some.' Lowering his voice even more, he said, 'I had received a message from the Oracle of Aal, warning me of a closing pattern. There were several possible outcomes depending on what we did.

'I could have destroyed the raiders, if I had known they were coming, but then I would have known nothing about the Pantathians' part in all this, and the danger from the plague. If I had gone after the prisoners, even those few who you saved would have been lost, and the Pantathians could still seek out others to act as templates for their plague carriers.'

Nicholas said, 'One thing I don't understand: why go to all this trouble? Why not simply send some plague carriers to Krondor?'

Pug said, 'Should plague erupt in the city, every magic talent in Stardock and the Temples would work to ensure that the Prince and his highest-ranking ministers were spared. Their leadership is too important. But should the plague erupt in the palace, think of the confusion if your father and all his advisers, the ranking commanders, the most important merchants and guildsmen – if all were among the very first to die.'

Nicholas nodded. 'So that's why you let us follow and find out the real plan.'

'I thought it best to hold their most powerful magician in check, letting you undo the rest of their plan. I sensed you would be at the center of this dark confrontation, and Nakor confirmed that judgment.' Pug looked over his shoulder. 'What a fascinating mind he has. I'm trying to talk him into returning to Sorcerer's Island with me for a time.'

Nicholas sighed. 'What about that Lady Clovis?'

Pug said, 'From what Nakor told me of her, she's most likely still alive down there, plotting. We've probably not seen an end of her.'

Nicholas said, 'Or the Pantathians.'

Pug looked at the young Prince and said, 'I know that expression; I've seen it on your father enough times. Listen to me: someone will end their menace, someday, but no one said it must be you.' He smiled. 'You've done more than your lifetime's share already.' Glancing at the group of young women who spoke together, Pug asked, 'Are you going to marry that lady of yours?'

Nicholas grinned. 'Sometimes I think so, sometimes not. She talks about finding a rich husband, because she doesn't believe Father or the King would permit such a marriage.' He lowered his voice again. 'And truth to tell, sometimes I want to and sometimes I'm looking for a rich husband for her.'

Pug laughed. 'I understand the feeling. When I was very young, your aunt Carline often made me feel the same way.'

Nicholas's eyes widened. 'Does Uncle Laurie know?'

Pug said, 'Who do you think introduced them?'

The King said, 'I have an announcement to make.' All eyes turned to him and he said, 'My Lord Henry of Ludland informs me his son, Harry, is to wed.'

There were cheers and applause in the room, and

women gathered around Brisa, hugging her. Nicholas and Pug made their way to where a blushing Harry stood receiving congratulations, and Nicholas shook his hand. 'You bastard,' said Nicholas with a laugh. 'You never said a thing.'

Leaning forward so that only Nicholas could hear, he said, 'I'm the middle son of a minor earl; I had to ask her before some rich duke's boy took her away from me. When we first met her, could you believe she'd be so beautiful?'

Nicholas couldn't argue his reasons. Then Harry whispered, 'Besides, we're going to have a baby.'

Nicholas laughed and said, 'Shall I have Uncle Lyam announce that, too?'

Harry grimaced and held up his hand. 'It would put my father in his grave. We'll wait a week or two after the wedding, thank you.'

'When?'

Harry said, 'I think as soon as possible, given the circumstances.'

Nicholas agreed with a laugh.

Then Lyam said, 'My brother Arutha has something to say.'

Arutha, wearing a rare smile, said, 'My son and Harry – ' Amos pointedly cleared his throat. Arutha added, '. . . with the aid of Admiral Trask, have managed to effect the first conquest of new lands since my grandfather took the Far Coast. With a pleasant lack of bloodshed, I might add.' He raised his flagon in salute. 'As we now have need of some governance in Freeport, with my brother's permission I'm naming Harry, formerly my son's Squire, as the new Governor of Freeport and the Sunset Islands.'

Lyam said, 'And he is elevated to the rank of Baronet of the Prince's Court.'

Again they congratulated Harry, and Arutha waved

Nicholas to his side. 'What about you?' he asked his youngest son. 'Have you given any thought to what you'd like to do? I can't very well send you back to Crydee a Squire now, can I?'

Nicholas said, 'I have given it some thought, Father. I think I'd like to return to sea. I'd like a ship.'

Amos laughed. 'I said to Arutha you might be thinking of taking my job now that I'm to retire.'

Nicholas laughed, too. 'I'm not quite ready to be calling myself Admiral yet, Amos.'

Amos said, 'With the trade that's going to start coming through Freeport, Carse will also become a major trading center; it's the best port on the Far Coast. There's going to be a lot of black hearts who will try their hand at piracy, so we'll need strong men on tall ships out there.'

Arutha said, 'We're going to have to maintain a squadron in Freeport. Amos is right, with that idiotic free-trade agreement you've endorsed, we're going to have every trader, pirate, and smuggler in three nations crawling over those islands. Your Patrick of Duncastle seems a capable enough fellow when it comes to breaking heads, a fine King's High Sheriff, but we're going to need administrators, which is why I'm sending Harry. Amos said he's just the sort to deal with merchants and thieves.'

Amos said, 'It's true. If I were to go a-roving again, I'd have him aboard my ship in an instant; he's a first-rate scrounger, and has a knack for settling arguments. And Brisa certainly knows her way around that city.'

'Well then,' said Arutha to Nicholas, 'I'm sending the *Eagle* to join the two I left in Freeport. We'll give you your captaincy and put you in charge of that squadron of pirates William Swallow is organizing out there. From all I've heard, you'll be a fit match for those brigands, as you've tried your hand at the pirate's trade yourself lately.'

Nicholas grinned. 'In a manner of speaking.'

'Lyam's going to name Marcus Warden of the West when Martin retires, so you'll be answering to him.' He took on a mock-serious tone. 'I was going to elevate you to Baron of the Prince's Court, which will give you rank to see Harry doesn't go too far off course, but perhaps I should have Lyam create a special title for you – say, the King's Buccaneer?'

Nicholas laughed and said, 'Captain will be fine, Father. I'll let you know when I wish to try for Admiral.'

Arutha laughed and put his arm around his son's shoulders. 'You make me proud, Nicky.'

Anita joined them and hugged her son, saying, 'I like your lady, Nicholas. She's got a spirit that's rare.'

Nicholas said, 'She's . . . different.'

They laughed and returned to the party, and as the night wore on, memories were shared, and hopes expressed, and a family that had known joy and sorrow took profound pleasure from simply being together again.

Magician
Raymond E. Feist
New Revised Edition

Raymond E. Feist has prepared a new, revised edition, to incorporate over 15,000 words of text omitted from previous editions so that, in his own words, 'it is essentially the book I would have written had I the skills I possess today'.

At Crydee, a frontier outpost in the tranquil Kingdom of the Isles, an orphan boy, Pug is apprenticed to a master magician – and the destinies of two worlds are changed forever. Suddenly the peace of the Kingdom is destroyed as mysterious alien invaders swarm through the land. Pug is swept up into the conflict but for him and his warrior friend, Tomas, an odyssey into the unknown has only just begun. Tomas will inherit a legacy of savage power from an ancient civilisation. Pug's destiny is to lead him through a rift in the fabric of space and time to the mastery of the unimaginable powers of a strange new magic. . .

'Epic scope . . . fast-moving action . . . vivid imagination'
Washington Post

'Tons of intrigue and action'   *Publishers Weekly*

ISBN 0 586 21783 3

The Master of Whitestorm
Janny Wurts

'Janny Wurts is a gifted creator of wonder'

Raymond E. Feist

Everyone knew there was no escape from the slave galleys of the Murghai: but Korendir, a man whose past was shrouded in mystery, recognized no impossibilities in life.

After leading a desperate and successful revolt, he frees the prisoners and sets out on a series of remarkable quests; battling the sorceress Anthei to lift the curse on the blighted land of Torresdyr; challenging the elemental Cyondide to win the lost hoard of the dragon Sharkash; travelling to far Northengard to save its people from a plague of poisonous wereleopards.

Always Korendir's goal was treasure; but never for its own sake. His ultimate aim was to build a fortress at Whitestorm, impregnable against all comers, be they mortal or supernatural, to protect himself, its Master, from the dark secret of his ancestry...

'Pace and fire . . . Janny Wurts writes with astonishing energy'

Stephen R. Donaldson

'Powerful . . . epic grandeur . . . magnificent!'

Anne McCaffrey

ISBN 0 586 21068 7

**FROM THE IMAGINATION OF TWO OF
FANTASY'S BRIGHTEST STARS COMES AN
EPIC SERIES OF HEROIC FANTASY**

DAUGHTER OF THE EMPIRE
Raymond E. Feist & Janny Wurts

The mysterious world of Kelewan is encircled by magic, mystery
and murder. Here at the heart of the Tsurani empire, Mara,
Ruling Lady of the Acoma, leads her people through terror and
peril on a truly epic scale. She must contend with powerful rival
houses, strike deals with sinister rebel warriors, and forge a
treaty with the enigmatic Cho-ja – a race of alien insectoids. But
in order to restore the honour of her house, Mara must marry
the son of a deadly enemy – and carry the struggle of her people
into the heart of his stronghold . . .

ISBN 0 586 07481 3

SERVANT OF THE EMPIRE
Raymond E. Feist & Janny Wurts

Mara of Acoma is a force to be reckoned with when playing the
bloody politics of the Game of the Council and has made great
gains for her followers within the Empire.

Against advice she buys a group of Midkemian prisoners-of-war,
only to discover that one of them is a noble: Kevin, third son of
the Baron of Zun. When she interviews him, it becomes apparent that he may be of great use in the Game of the Council . . .

ISBN 0 586 20381 8

MISTRESS OF THE EMPIRE
Raymond E. Feist & Janny Wurts

Now Mara faces not only the brotherhood of assassins, and the
cunning spies of the rival ruling houses, but the awesome
Assembly of Magicians, who see her as the ultimate threat to
their ancient power.

ISBN 0 586 20379 6

'Sweeping drama unveiling a tale of love, hate and sacrifice
against the panorama of an alien yet familiar society'
Publishers Weekly